Beverly S. Martin is American by origin but has spent several years in England. She now lives in the Canary Islands and has written several novels, of which JUFFIE KANE (also available from Futura) was the first to be published in Britain.

Praise for JUFFIE KANE:

'Beverly S. Martin has a talent for creating complex characters . . . Juffie Kane is the unstereotypical heroine of this rich, amusing and sensual tale'
Publishers Weekly

'A winning, steamily sexy glitter-romance . . . A grabber – and great, good fun'
Kirkus Reviews

MOLLIE PRIDE

BEVERLY S. MARTIN

Futura

*For Bill as always, and for
my friend*

A *Futura* Book

First published in Great Britain in 1991 by
Macdonald & Co (Publishers) Ltd
London & Sydney
First published in paperback by Futura Publications 1992
This edition published by Futura Publications 1994

ISBN 0 7088 4988 1

Printed in England by Clays Ltd, St Ives plc

Futura Publications
A Division of
Macdonald & Co (Publishers)
Brettenham House Lancaster Place
London WC2E 7EN

Prologue

So there they were — adorable Mollie, gorgeous Kate, and of course, Nick. Wonderful Nick. Together again, just like the old days. But this was the first time one of them faced a sentence of death in a matter of hours.

The situation was so unreal, so removed from everything they had known and believed and been. Good and bad. Don't think about that, Mollie told herself. Don't dwell on the past. This is it, it's happening. She had to accept it. They weren't going to give her a chance to do anything else.

She stood up, carefully avoiding both Kate's eyes and Nick's, and crossed to the window. Her heels tapped a staccato rhythm on the dull brown linoleum floor the US government had deemed appropriate for this room. It went with the battered oak desk and the few scarred, hard-backed chairs.

It was July and raining. Sheets of water cascaded down the plate-glass window. How extraordinary that she could stand here and look out at sodden grass and trees and not cast surreptitious glances at the sky. No bombers lurked in the clouds ready to scatter death. This was Washington D.C., not London, and it was 1946, the war was over. Not my war, Mollie thought. My war is ending now, today. And I've lost.

There was a standing lamp behind Kate's chair. Its glow cast her reflection on to the window. Mollie caught her breath. Kate was so incredibly beautiful, even now at thirty, and even in this wavy mirror-image. The blonde hair, the enormous grey eyes, the perfect oval face were hauntingly lovely.

When you're dead, Mollie thought, you don't see anybody ever again.

Music, oh Jesus God, there ought to be music. You didn't

have to go out silent, did you? Who decreed you had to march down the corridor to oblivion in stoic quiet? Why the hell shouldn't there be music?

The tune played in her head, the song the three of them knew so well, a kind of theme to their lives. '*Charleston! Charleston! da da da-da dum dum ...*'

Spasms, born of memory and love and pain and terror, twisted themselves into patterns of dance and Mollie's body moved almost of its own volition. Her feet flew, her arms stood out at her sides, her hands made circles in the air. '*Charleston! Charleston! ...*'

Kate sucked in one long, audible breath. 'Don't,' she murmured. 'Please don't.'

Nick sprang out of his chair and reached Mollie in two strides. He grabbed her, pinning her arms to her sides, pressing her body to his. 'Mollie, stop. That's not going to help. Please stop.' For a moment she clung to him, to the beloved, familiar, warm, safe feel of his chunky muscular body beneath the dark, correct, expensive, and impeccably tailored suit. Nick would never change, thank God.

Her next thought was the same as his, unspoken but shared as always. We must not shut Kate out. They turned and opened their arms to her.

She hesitated.

'Kate,' Mollie whispered. 'Katykins, come on ...'

She stood up and moved toward them, glided almost; she was ethereal in her pale loveliness. Together Mollie and Nick drew her into the circle of their arms.

'It's still the three of us against all of them, isn't it?' Kate asked.

'Yup,' Nick said. 'The same as always.'

'The same,' Mollie repeated. 'The three of us. For always and always and always.'

Which wasn't going to be very long, considering the circumstances.

1

A lot of crazy things were happening in America in 1926. While a breathless nation watched, a couple dressed in jodhpurs and helmets tangoed from Santa Monica to Los Angeles; a high school student put forty sticks of gum into his mouth, sang *Home Sweet Home*, and drank a gallon of milk between verses; a guy called Shipwreck Kelly spent a large part of his life sitting on top of flagpoles; and from Harlem's Cotton Club to Hollywood's Brown Derby, everybody danced. For fun, for profit, for kudos — and sometimes just to stay alive.

One Saturday afternoon in May of that year, in the beachfront town of Revere a few miles north of Boston, a man in a once-dapper tweed suit and a snap-brim brown fedora was fixing a large poster to the wall beside the ticket office of the Crescent Gardens Ballroom on the corner of Ocean Avenue and the Boulevard. The poster read: ON STAGE, THE FABULOUS PRIDE FAMILY, FEATURING AMERICA'S DARLING, LITTLE MISS MAGIC MOLLIE PRIDE.

The manager of Crescent Gardens arrived as Harry Pride stepped back to admire his work. 'What the hell are you doing, bud?'

'I'm making sure tonight you get the biggest crowd you've ever had, that's what I'm doing.'

'You don't say? Well, tell you what, you're kinda short, so maybe you can't see what it says on that marquee up there. Why don't you come over here where I am and stand on your little tippy toes and get a goddamn good look?'

Harry didn't get angry. 'I know what it says.'

'Maybe, maybe not. I'll read it to you. "Marathon dancing. New contest starts tonight." That's what it says, and that's what brings in the crowds. So take your crummy poster off

1

my wall. It ain't part of the contract that you get to crap up the place.'

'It isn't hurting anyone,' Harry said quietly. 'It makes my wife and the kids feel good. What's the harm?'

The manager of the ballroom hesitated a moment, then shrugged. 'No harm,' he admitted. 'What the hell, leave it. Only you shoulda' asked first.'

'Sorry.'

'Forget it.' When he walked away he was thinking that the Fabulous Pride Family had a pretty lousy life.

The manager didn't know the half of it. They had begun by playing fairs and carnivals; most often these days they were what was known as the 'filler'. Lots of marathon sponsors hired a filler, something to amuse the public while the dancing contestants took their fifteen-minute break at the end of each hour. Harry Pride had discovered this gap in the entertainment world two years before, and promptly exploited it.

No real act would take the job. The pay was terrible and most of the audience used the dance break to go to the john or get some fresh air. The rest were avidly watching the contestants have their pulses checked and their feet massaged and the sweat wiped from their faces. Hell, one of them might drop dead before the marathon ended — that happened plenty of times, added to the interest. But for those of a less morbid turn of mind, there was the Fabulous Pride Family.

Fifteen-year-old Nick came on first. He wore tails and a top hat which he swept off when he bowed. He was still growing and the coat and trousers needed alteration every month or two. They were also shiny with wear and constant brushing, but the lighting in the ballroom usually hid these defects. 'Good evening ladies and gentlemen,' Nick would boom. Harry used to do the introduction, but the year before the kid's voice broke and left him with a terrific basso profundo which carried easily over the conversation of the crowd. 'Now,' Nick would continue, 'for your delectation and delight, the Fabulous Prides!'

He spun round, did a soft shoe routine that carried him to the piano, and played a few riffs, with his foot planted firmly on the loud pedal. Then a fanfare. 'We won't keep you waiting,' he trumpeted. 'We know what you're panting for. Here she is, America's darling, Little Miss Magic Mollie Pride!' He played what the family called Mollie's music, *Charleston! Charleston! da da da-da dum dum ...*'

She danced on to the floor. A number of people did pay attention at this point — the kid was adorable, you couldn't deny it. A month short of six years old, short brown curls and the biggest brown eyes you ever saw. Pink chubby cheeks, a sturdy little body, an enormous grin, she oozed personality. And the way they had her got up! Like a flapper. A sequined headband circling her forehead and restraining the curls, a bright red short fringed dress, a rope of beads that reached her waist, and even silk stockings secured by garters just below her dimpled knees. Adorable. And boy, could she dance. *Charleston! Charleston! da da da-da dum dum ...*

Three minutes of Mollie's solo, then Kate and Harry and Zena joined her. Harry had traded the tweed suit and the fedora for white trousers, a bright blue blazer and a straw boater. Zena, his wife, and young Kate were both dressed exactly like Mollie. A few seconds more, then Harry and Zena each took one of Mollie's hands and the three of them backed out of the spotlight. Kate stood by herself.

The few people still watching noted that this kid wasn't adorable; she was at an awkward age, eleven years and four months to be precise, and very pretty with her blonde hair and grey eyes, but gangly, too tall, too thin. Nick faded the Charleston music and went into a Gershwin tune that was already a standard. 'I'm a little lamb who is lost in the wood,' Kate sang in a wavering soprano.

'Change of pace,' Harry always said. 'Gotta give Katykins a change of pace number.'

'Don't call me that,' she usually replied. 'And I can't sing those slow songs, my voice isn't good enough.'

'Sure it is. Anyway, you just have to hold it for two verses. Then Nick brings Mollie back on with the Charleston.'

Which he did. And after her Zena and Harry. A few more bars, a few more frantic steps and arm wavings, and that was the act. Zena and the girls curtsied, Harry and Nick bowed, they went off to scattered applause while the Victrola blared

3

another fox trot and the marathon dancers came back on stage.

At Crescent Gardens the Fabulous Prides were on every hour from seven until midnight. After that the management didn't bother with a filler act.

That May night in Revere was cold, there was a stiff east wind off the ocean. Zena buttoned threadbare woollen coats over her daughters' spangled finery, preparatory to a ten minute walk to a boarding house with enough delusions of grandeur to call itself the Columbus House Hotel.

Most of the boulevard stands had not yet opened for the season, the handful which had were shut for the night. In a few weeks they would all be open into the small hours, dispensing frozen custard and fried clams and popcorn, and inviting passers-by to pitch till they won; now the five performers walked past a long line of ghosts. Six-year-old Mollie couldn't yet read the signs above the boarded-over establishments, but in the week they'd been in Revere she had identified the two that interested her, Hurley's Flying Horses where during the day she'd seen men getting the merry-go-round ready to open, and Bluebeard's Funhouse with a huge head of a giant flanked by towers and turrets painted to look like bricks. 'That's where I want to go as soon as it opens. Can I, daddy?'

'Sure, princess, sure.'

'Bet you won't come with me, Kate,' Mollie taunted. 'Bet you'll be too scared.'

Kate didn't answer, but she didn't have to. They all knew who was the brave sister and who the timid.

'We can't afford to waste money on foolishness,' Zena said. 'Kate's old enough to realize that.' It was a comment made to protect her elder daughter, but it was also the truth. The Prides could barely afford to continue breathing.

For their six performances Harry collected three and a half dollars; the only good thing about the pay was that it was handed over nightly. 'Always have jingling money in your pocket when you're in the theatre,' Harry said. It didn't jingle very long. Most of the places they stayed charged fifty cents a head for one room and two meals. For the Prides that came to two fifty; the dollar that was left went on a third meal of sorts, and transportation to what Harry called 'our next engagement'.

The Columbus House Hotel was a sprawling three-storey building clad in grey clapboards and facing the sea. The ground floor was given over to the Columbus House Cafe, the two above were carved into tiny rooms where the paint was peeling and the smell of salty damp had lodged permanently in the walls.

There was no reception desk, you gained access to the rooms on the upper floors by a narrow door around the corner on Beach Street. Since he and his brood would be returning late every night, Harry had been given a key. He opened the door and stepped aside for Zena and the children to enter. Then he followed them, pausing to lock the door again.

Mollie always hung back, waiting to hear the click as her father turned the key a final time. She had bad dreams if she didn't. In the dreams someone was always chasing her and yelling that the Pride Family weren't a family at all. Nick wasn't her brother and Kate wasn't her *whole* sister, and Harry wasn't Kate's daddy or Nick's. They didn't even all have the same last name. That was a secret. Nobody knew it except themselves, but Mollie was always terrified that someone would find out. When she heard the key turn in the lock it seemed a little less likely.

Their room on the third floor was locked too. In a few seconds Harry had it open. There were two double beds and a cot, and about six square inches of clear floor space in the middle. They had to hang their costumes over the head and footboards, and keep the rest of their clothes packed in the suitcases they kept shoved under the beds. Kate and Mollie slept in one of the doubles, Zena and Harry in the other. Nick had the cot. Some of the rooms they stayed in only had two beds. Then Harry shared one with Nick, and Zena slept with the girls. For all its crowding, the present arrangement was luxury. 'Nobody wake me up in the morning,' Harry said with a yawn. 'I'm beat. Let's all sleep late.'

'We can't sleep late or we'll miss breakfast. They stop serving at eight thirty.' Zena made the comment while she was unbuttoning Mollie's coat. She was doing it by the light

5

of the moon coming in the unshaded window because Harry was still fumbling with the old-fashioned gas jet on the wall. 'And they won't give us a refund either,' she added.

'Okay, okay. Damn, why won't this thing light?'

'Don't curse in front of the children. Nick, what do you have there?'

'A letter. It was pushed under the door. We walked right over it.'

The jet flared into light as he spoke. Nick was holding a pale blue envelope emblazoned WESTERN UNION. 'Let me have that.' Harry took the telegram and glanced at Zena. 'It's addressed to you.'

She put her hand over her heart and sank down on one of the beds. 'You open it,' she whispered.

Harry ripped open the envelope and quickly scanned the message. He held it towards his wife. She shook her head. 'No, just tell me what it says.'

Harry paused a moment, then read the words aloud.

'Joseph Driscoll died this morning stop will to be read Tuesday noon at my office Rhinebeck stop strongly recommend your presence signed Louis Thompkins Attorney at Law.'

Zena looked up, an expression of disbelief on her pale, pretty face. 'Papa is dead?'

'That's what it says, angel. I'm sorry.' The last comment was perfunctory. Zena hadn't seen her father in years and there was no affection between them. Besides, Harry was focused on the last part of the message, the stuff about the will. As far as anyone knew the old man was dead broke, so why the will, and why this summons? He felt a surge of excitement. Easy, he told himself, don't go off the deep end, no point in getting your hopes up. To Zena he said, 'Do you know this Thompkins fellow, the lawyer? How did he know where to find you?'

'I know who he is, but I've never met him, and I've no idea how he found me.' Suddenly Zena reached out her arms and pulled her daughters into them, hugging the girls close as if she feared that at any second they'd be snatched away. 'I've no idea at all,' she repeated over their heads.

Harry frowned in consternation. Nick continued to watch the scene in stoic silence.

In a sense it all began because Joe Driscoll insisted on naming his daughter Zena when she was born in 1898. His neighbours in the small upstate New York town of Red Hook weren't entirely surprised that Joe ignored all advice and chose that outlandish name for his only child, but they certainly didn't approve.

'Here's your new Katherine,' Mary Soames said as she handed the swaddled newborn to her father.

Driscoll shook his head. 'Not Katherine, there'll never be another like my Katie ...' His voice broke, but he recovered himself in seconds. 'This little girl's name is Zena.'

'Zena! What kind of a name is that?'

'Let him be, Mary.' The doctor who had just delivered the child by cutting open Katherine Driscoll's stomach seconds after her heart stopped beating was at the kitchen sink, washing the blood from his hands and arms. 'Let Joe be. Seems to me he can name the baby anything he wants.'

'Never said he couldn't,' Mary said. Bonnets were out of fashion, had been for at least a decade, but she still wore one. She tied the strings firmly under her chin and the broad brim obscured the lines of exhaustion marking her face. 'Like as not, he'll do it anyway. Just said I'd have thought he'd name the poor little thing for her dead mama, that's all.'

Joe Driscoll was forty-one years old, a big powerful man in his prime. Normally he'd have withered such impertinence with one look from his icy grey eyes, but he was grateful to the Soames woman. She'd been three days with the seventeen-year-old girl he'd married the year before and promptly made pregnant, struggling to help her survive the labour of birthing the child. 'Thanks for everything,' he murmured, ignoring her comments about the baby's name.

'Nothin' to thank me for,' the woman said. 'Leastwise, not much,' she amended, glancing at the child. Mary Soames had been unofficial midwife to Red Hook for thirty years, she considered it a personal affront when the young doctor from Rhinebeck had to be called in. That together they'd managed to lose the mother made the shame far worse. 'Just said I never heard of anybody called Zena,' she added.

'You have now.' Joe was looking into the baby's red and wrinkled face. 'You've just met Zena Driscoll, who's going to be the prettiest, nicest, most elegant little lady in all of Dutchess county.'

Because Joe said it, it had to be so.

He lived in the finest house in the town, out of the town really: a square hulk built of dark red brick with a deep porch on three sides and many big round pillars. The house sat on a hill overlooking the Hudson River. 'Exactly midway between Toronto and Manhattan,' Joe always insisted. Nobody dared question or check that assertion. He had built the place in 1896, with a small portion of the enormous profits generated by Driscoll's New Elixir of Health. The medicine was produced in a cluster of large sheds near Red Hook and Driscoll's was the only sizeable business for miles around. Joe employed twenty-six men and thirty-seven women in his enterprise, none of whom would have had paid work without him. So he could do or say pretty much what he liked.

Most people in these parts didn't name their houses, but when the builders finished Joe's new place he had a wrought iron sign made that said Hillhaven. Then he took himself to Poughkeepsie one Sunday morning. He'd heard somewhere that the best-looking women in New York lived in Poughkeepsie, so Joe got up before dawn and whipped four horses into such a frenzy of speed he nearly killed them, but they covered the seventy-some miles in less than eight hours.

He arrived at noon, when the church service was just ending, and he reined in where he could watch the congregation leave. Joe sat in his dust-covered carriage with its half-dead team of sweaty, panting horses and cast a critical eye over each young lady as she walked down the path which led from the white steepled building to the street. That's how he chose Katie Vansemple to be his bride.

That manoeuvre didn't surprise anyone: Joe did things his own way. He was what people in Red Hook called a self-made man. But not entirely. The formula for Driscoll's Elixir had been bequeathed to him by his father and his grand-father. By the time Joe was twenty-five both those gentlemen were dead, and he tinkered a bit with the ingredients and

8

renamed it Driscoll's New Elixir of Health. None of Joe's employees knew exactly what it was that was different about the Elixir. As far as they could tell the huge vats where they brewed the stuff contained the same herbs steeped in alcohol that they'd always held. But each night after everyone had gone home Joe spent a half-hour alone in the factory and added his secret ingredient.

Whatever it was, it worked. Demand for the medicine increased enormously. Joe began making it in much larger quantities. He advertised in the New York *World*, Pulitzer's remarkably popular paper, as well as the *Herald* and the *Tribune*, and he took on a staff of six salesmen to call on druggist shops and apothecaries from Maine to New Jersey. He also hired a travelling road company, like the one which had made famous Kickapoo Indian Salve, and sent them south. The show, a mixture of vaudeville and a revival meeting, moved countless numbers of green bottles of New Elixir into the homes of Georgia and Alabama and Tennessee. Not content with all this, Joe began publishing Driscoll's Almanac and distributed it free to hundreds of thousands of rural households in the mid-west and the west. Like others of its type, the Almanac was a compendium of jokes and sayings and sage advice which included an ad for the New Elixir of Health on every page, along with 'unsolicited testimonials' from satisfied users, and a mail-order coupon which brought a bottle post-free if the respondent sent fifty cents.

Still nobody really knew what was in the stuff, nor that it had actually made Driscoll more than two million dollars in fifteen years. But by the time Joe turned forty and married his Katie from Poughkeepsie everybody knew he was pretty rich, and stubborn, and not one to take advice. And that whatever he said would happen, damned well better had.

Somehow things went wrong. Zena grew up hating everything about her life. She hated the velvet and lace dresses she had to wear in the winter, and the starched cotton and lace dresses which replaced them in the summer. She hated Miss Sedgewick, the English nanny her father employed to look after her, and the series of governesses who tutored her. She hated the dark heavy furniture that filled the rooms of her

9

house, and the sombre colours painted on each and every wall. She hated the Sunday mornings when her father took her to services at the Congregational Church, almost the only times she was allowed to leave the confines of Hillhaven, because she felt that everyone was staring at her. Most of all she hated her name.

Zena dreamed of being named Mary or Susan or Patsy, or Kate like her mother had been; an ordinary name like those of the ordinary girls she watched with such envy on Sunday mornings, or whose distant laughter sometimes floated up from the banks of the river beyond Hillhaven's high stone walls. She longed to be a girl who could run and jump rope and play hopscotch, like the girls in some of her picture books, girls whose names were nothing so peculiar as Zena.

Such dreams were, she knew, impossible, but that didn't prevent her from having them. They were her only consolation apart from dancing. The dancing, at least the kind that gave her joy, was a secret. She had ballet lessons, of course. A teacher called Madame Chirault came every Wednesday afternoon — Tuesdays and Thursdays were given over to piano lessons with Professor Hyman — and taught her to arrange her feet in various stylized positions and to wave her arms in a particular way. 'Gracefully, mademoiselle, gracefully. You bend from the waist and gather the flowers ... Sweep the air, *ma chère*, sweeeep it! Good, now stretch out your hands and give the bouquet away. Lovely, lovely.'

Zena thought the ballet boring, like everything else in her life, but after she was put to bed at night and the door to her room was firmly closed she got up and danced by herself for hours. She loved the feeling of moving her bare feet over the dark red turkey carpet in time to rhythms heard only in her head.

Joe never suspected this nocturnal disobedience. When Zena was eight and it started he had little time to worry about his daughter.

Patent medicines had been big business in America for almost a hundred years. Driscoll's New Elixir of Health competed not just with Kickapoo Indian Salve but with Dr Sage's Catarrh Remedy, St Jacob's Oil for Rheumatism, Watson's Neuralgia King and Lydia E. Pinkham's Vegetable

Compound, guaranteed to cure 'female weakness', as well as such things as a toothbrush the handle of which was said to be permanently charged with a mysterious electro-magnetic current that acted on the nerve endings of the gums though it was connected to no source of electricity. Nostrums were a goldmine for a lot of people other than Joe Driscoll.

The medical profession had always railed against these home grown remedies, but the public went right on reading the advertisements and almanacs and buying the products. Then in 1905 *Collier's Magazine* published a series of articles titled 'The Great American Fraud' written by a man named Samuel H. Adams. Soon afterward President Theodore Roosevelt demanded action.

Driscoll and his fellow businessmen protested that the government was interfering with market forces and free trade, and mounted a campaign against this 'socialistic nonsense'. Their voices were drowned out by that of Upton Sinclair describing the appallingly filthy conditions in the Chicago stockyards in his novel *The Jungle*. In 1906 Congress passed the Pure Food and Drug Act.

Joe Driscoll waited for the axe to fall, but nothing much happened. Some of the cure-alls disappeared from the market, but that seemed more because they lost favour with the public than because of anything done in Washington. Driscoll raised the price of his New Elixir to sixty-five cents and redoubled his promotional efforts, and the green bottles continued to sell in great numbers. His business secure, he had time to think about Zena again. She was ten now, but it still didn't occur to him that her silence and docility were a mark of unhappiness. As far as Joe was concerned everything was going exactly as planned.

By the time Zena was fifteen she was as pretty as her mother had been. A little too short perhaps, just a shade over five feet, but nicely plump, with pink cheeks and ash blonde curls, and big blue eyes just like Katie's. Joe decided to dare a plan that had been fermenting in the back of his mind for five years. In the autumn of 1913 he booked passage on Cunard's magnificent *Lusitania*.

From Joe's point of view, the crossing was miserable. As billed, the great ship was a floating palace of incredible luxury and he had a superb cabin in first class, but the only fellow passengers who interested him — a small coterie of two Payne Whitneys, three Harrimans and one Mr Stuyvesant Fish — all cut him dead. Driscoll's money was tainted by his almanacs and travelling road shows, and the fact that it had been garnered from a public gullible enough to buy a useless concoction in a green bottle. Joe seethed and planned.

London itself was a more satisfying experience. A week before Christmas, Joe returned to Red Hook immensely pleased with himself.

January of 1914 was bitterly cold, but Joe's custom was to walk with his daughter in the gardens of Hillhaven every Sunday afternoon after lunch, and he allowed only a raging blizzard or the most unrelenting summer downpour to interfere. On this particular Sunday it wasn't snowing, the sun was shining brightly, though too far away to give any real warmth. When they paced the concrete paths laid with geometrical precision between the rose beds, Zena was swathed in a tight-waisted plum-coloured coat with a fur collar and a matching fur muff, and Joe was wrapped in a black velvet-trimmed overcoat and had a black derby on his head and a large black cigar clenched between his teeth.

'My dear,' he said, removing the cigar and flicking ash on to the snow covered garden, 'I have some rather important news.'

'What news, papa?'

'You are to be married.'

Just like that. He'd never even mentioned the word before. She had never been alone with any man other than him, or Professor Hyman her piano teacher. She had absolutely no idea what marriage meant, or why it was considered desirable. Zena stopped walking and stood very still. She opened her mouth, but she could think of nothing to say.

Joe took her arm and gently prodded her forward. 'Come along, child. It's far too cold to stand still.'

'Married.' She repeated his word. She didn't think she'd ever actually said it before. There had been no occasion to do so.

'That's what I said, yes. I've made a remarkable match for

12

you, my dear. Wonderfully suitable.'

'Married,' Zena repeated again. 'Married.'

'Yes.' A slight tone of exasperation crept into Joe's voice. There were times in the dead of night when he wondered if the girl was a bit simple, but he never allowed himself to consider that possibility in daylight. 'You're going to get married, be a wife and eventually a mother.' He spoke slowly and clearly to be sure he was understood. 'It's what every young woman does, if she can. But very few marry as well as you shall,' he added with a satisfied chuckle. 'You're going to marry an Englishman, my dear. A lord whose first wife has died. You shall go and live in England, in a palace.'

Joe made his triumphant announcement and waited for his daughter's enthusiastic gratitude. After a few silent moments he realized it wasn't to be forthcoming and he turned on his heel and marched back into the house. Simple. Had to be. But that avaricious gentleman in England probably wouldn't care, and if he did it didn't matter. He wouldn't find out until it was too late.

Consuelo Vanderbilt had done it, though she'd made the ceremony two hours late by hanging back and weeping, and Anna Gould, and Alice Thaw, and dozens of others. For nearly two decades there had been a regular export trade in the daughters of wealthy Americans bartered to European noblemen in exchange for a title. The practice was so notorious that *Life* and other magazines published cartoons lampooning it, and newspapers sermonized on sullying with greed the sanctity of wedlock.

Joe Driscoll didn't give a damn. With one grand coup he had taken himself into the midst of, if not above, the society which had ignored him. As father-in-law to the Earl of Whitby no man would dare snub him. Driscoll began dreaming of the great house he would build in Newport, but first there was Zena's wedding to be planned.

It was to be held at St Thomas's Episcopal Church on Fifth Avenue and Fifty-third Street in Manhattan, the preferred place of worship of the '400'. Joe wasn't an Episcopalian and he'd never set foot in St Thomas's. A large contribution and a discreet word to the ancient rector concerning the groom's identity solved the problem. The wedding date was set for 11 April. Miles of smilax and fern garland and thousands of white roses were ordered. Invitations went out to the Astors and the Harrimans and the Goulds and their ilk: the honour of your presence is requested by Mr. Joseph Driscoll at the marriage of his daughter Zena to the Right Hon. the Earl of Whitby.

Zena first met her husband-to-be at Hillhaven on a stormy March evening. His Lordship and entourage had arrived in the afternoon, but Miss Sedgewick decreed that etiquette would not permit an informal meeting of the engaged couple at tea. Madame Chirault agreed, the French ballet mistress had been pressed into wider service during these days of frantic preparations for the wedding, and she was proving a staunch ally of the Englishwoman.

Shortly before eight they dressed Zena in pale blue velvet with a four-foot train. 'Not too long for a dinner at home, *ce n'est pas distingué*,' Madame explained. Jewels, however, were *distingué*. Zena was draped in a heavy diamond necklace, an armload of bracelets, and a diamond tiara.

'But where did these things come from? I've never seen them before.'

'Your dear papa, mademoiselle.' Lately Miss Sedgewick too had taken to addressing Zena in French; it seemed appropriate now that she was to marry a title. 'He has been collecting these things and storing them against the moment they would be needed. Such foresight. How remarkably blessed you are, *ma chère*. How excited you must feel.'

Zena did not feel anything but terrified. She descended the stairs with a grace made automatic by her years of ballet lessons, her smile set in place by practice, but unable to reach her eyes. The gentlemen awaited her in the drawing room. The butler threw open the double doors and announced her as if she were a guest. 'Miss Zena Driscoll.' There were four men in the room and they all rose.

Joe stepped forward and took her hand. 'My dear, may I present your fiancé, His Lordship, Charles, Earl of Whitby.'

Zena kept her eyes on the carpet and curtsied. She felt a strange hand take hers. The grip was firm. Slowly, summoning all her courage, she raised her glance. Disaster.

14

She was looking at a man her father's age, with a bushy, full Victorian beard and moustache, and small brown eyes half hidden by folds of crêpy flesh. She began to tremble. 'Charmed, my dear,' his lordship said. 'I'm sure we shall be very happy.'

Joe raised his hand. The butler brought a tray of champagne. 'You may join us in a toast, my dear. Considering the occasion.' Joe smiled fondly at his daughter. Zena took a glass of champagne. They all drank to the forthcoming marriage. After that the gentlemen returned to their conversation and ignored her.

There were three visitors from England, the Earl and two younger men. Zena had a chance to observe them while they spoke. In a few moments she had figured out that the pair called Reginald and Sebastian were the Earl's sons by his first marriage. Reginald was squat and solid and ugly like his father, but Sebastian was tall and slim. He seemed only a few years older than she. He had delicate features and a shock of light brown hair which fell over his forehead, and warm grey eyes that sparkled with fun. There was a moment during the party's stately passage from the drawing to the dining room when those grey eyes met hers and held them for a moment. Zena could have sworn Sebastian was offering her sympathy and encouragement.

From the time of Joe's announcement until she met her fiancé, Zena had been paralysed by fear and surprise; after the dinner party she took to weeping and shaking and insisting that she couldn't go through with it. These protests were made only to Miss Sedgewick and Madame Chirault, she would never dare to make them to Joe himself.

At first the two women tried to bully her into the quiet compliance of earlier days. 'Nonsense,' Miss Sedgewick fumed. 'It is your duty and of course you will do it. Stop all this disgusting snivelling at once.'

'*C'est ridicule*, mademoiselle. You are acting like a spoiled child,' Madame Chirault insisted.

It didn't work. Zena stopped eating. She lost weight and became very pale, and her eyes were perpetually red-rimmed.

The English contingent had moved to Manhattan to await

the ceremony, to a suite of rooms in Louis Sherry's fashionable apartment hotel and restaurant at Fifth Avenue and Forty-fourth Street. None of them ventured back to Red Hook, so they did not see the change in the appearance of the earl's future countess. Joe was too busy and too full of his plans to notice. Only Zena's lady guardians and the dressmaker who was preparing her wedding gown and trousseau saw what was happening.

Five days before the wedding the dressmaker came for the final fitting of the gown. The white satin and lace and appliqué flowers and seed pearls had all been ordered from Paris, and were being made according to a French pattern. The seamstress, a Mrs Klein from Rhinebeck, had never had a greater challenge. Mrs Klein began muttering in German as soon as she started doing up the seventy-six tiny buttons that marched from the base of Zena's spine to the nape of her neck. By the time she reached the fiftieth button she was wailing aloud. 'Thinner she is yet! How can I make a gown which will fit when every day she is thinner! Are you crazy in this house? Do you starve her?'

Zena began to cry; it took very little to set her off at the moment. Miss Sedgewick was at the end of her patience and resources. She stood in a corner wringing her hands, seeing the handsome retirement bonus she'd been promised by Mr Driscoll melt away in her charge's tears. Only Madame Chirault kept her wits.

'Get out of here, all of you.' Madame waved her arm to indicate the German dressmaker and her three assistants. 'Out! Out! Ten minutes only.' She turned to the nanny. 'You too. Go, have a cup of tea. Control yourself. I wish to speak alone with Mademoiselle Zena.'

The French woman and the American girl were finally left to themselves in the sewing room with its walls lined with mahogany cupboards and drawers, and its big work table and long mirrors. Madame Chirault took a step toward Zena and put out her hand. 'Come over here by the window, *ma chère*. We must talk. Good, that is better. We can sit down on this little seat here.'

'I can't sit down,' Zena mumbled through her sobs. 'I'll crush the gown.'

16

'To hell with the gown. Don't look so shocked. I can curse like a man when I want to. And right now, I want to.'

'You're accent is different.' The change in the ballet mistress's intonations startled Zena enough to staunch the flow of tears.

'I came to America when I was twenty-one,' the older woman said with a wry smile. 'I've been here fifteen years. I only keep the accent because people think it's glamorous.'

Zena's mouth became a round red mark of surprise. 'Oh, I see.'

'That's not all you have to see. Listen to me, my little Zena. There are times in life when you have to face facts, and this is one of those times. Nothing in God's world is going to keep you from being marched down that aisle on Saturday morning. The only question is how you handle the situation. You can be miserable and terrified, like this. Or you can decide to beat your father and that odious old English lord at their own game.'

Zena shook her head and rubbed her red eyes with a sodden handkerchief. 'I can't.'

'Yes, you can. You can marry him, because you must, and you can make the best of it.'

'How?' The word came out in a tremulous whisper.

'What do you think marriage is? No, don't answer. You haven't the least idea, I know that. I'll tell you. For a girl like you, in circumstances like this, it is simply a legal technicality. You will be a countess in a great house, bigger and grander than anything you've ever seen, but that doesn't matter because you will have absolutely nothing to do with the running of it. There is an army of servants to take care of everything. Your role is to be purely decorative. The Earl is not particularly interested in you, that's obvious too. He cares about your father's money, nothing more.'

Madame Chirault hesitated a moment. She was pretty sure the earl had one other concern, but she had no idea how to introduce that subject. Better to skip it, she decided. There were positive aspects of Zena's future and those should be emphasized. 'Listen, all your life you have been guarded and ordered about and told what to do at every minute. Once you're married you can do pretty much what you like. Go where you like, see whom you choose. This marriage, *ma chère*, is your ticket out of prison.'

Zena began paying more attention. 'How can it be?'

'A married lady is not a child, she isn't told what to do from morning till night. Look, if you are clever you can even get some money of your own. He won't give you any, they never do, but he'll give you a bit of jewellery, and you have the things from your father. Sell some of it, find a discreet jeweller and have copies made. Then keep the money and use it to please yourself.' She leaned over and took both Zena's hands in hers. 'Don't be a fool, little girl. Your father is opening your cage. Stop crying and laugh. And fly free.'

There was silence for a moment. Finally Zena said, 'That's all I have to be, a decoration?'

Madame Chirault hesitated. 'Practically all. There is something else,' she added slowly. 'At night, a man has the right to come to his wife's bedroom. He has the right to ... do things.'

'What things?'

'I can't explain, you'll have to find out for yourself like every woman does. It's not very pleasant, but remember, we all go through it. It won't kill you,' she added firmly. 'I guarantee that. Men like it, but they get tired of the same woman after a while. For a few months your earl will make a pest of himself at night. After that he'll leave you alone, I promise.' She stood up. 'Now, you must decide, Zena. Is it to be hysteria and tears, or a smile, because in your secret heart you know you'll have your own way in the end?'

Another long pause, then Zena looked up and smiled.

True to form, Joe had chosen all the music for the ceremony and consulted no one. He decreed that he would escort Zena down the aisle to the tune of *O Perfect Love*, the same song that had ushered Consuelo Vanderbilt into marriage. Joe made the choice in imitation, with no thought of irony, but the assembled guests had to repress titters when they stood and turned to face the back of the church and heard the melody that harked back to that infamous union of nineteen years earlier.

Zena knew nothing of Consuelo and her misadventures,

18

so the meaning of the ripple of amusement was lost on her. Anyway, it soon changed to murmurs of approval. Zena looked gorgeous. Her blonde hair was piled high and diamond clips anchored a lace mantilla to her curls. It trailed to below her hips where it gracefully disappeared into the folds of the forty-foot train of her wedding dress. She was veiled, of course, so no one could see the expression of frozen terror on her face. Despite everything Madame Chirault had said, she was suffering agonies of fear. But at least she wasn't crying.

His Lordship had decreed that his son Sebastian was to be his best man. The pair stood at the altar waiting for Joe and Zena, the ugly old man and the handsome young one, each equally well served by the Savile Row tailor who had made their formal morning coats and striped trousers.

Zena and Joe reached the end of their journey and waited. The music died away. The smell of flowers in the church was overpowering. For a moment Zena thought she might faint, and tightened her grip on her father's arm. 'Dearly beloved,' the rector began. He went on for a moment or two about marriage being an honorable estate, then he looked up. 'Who giveth this woman to be wed?'

'I do.' Joe's voice swelled with pride. He'd done it, and everybody who mattered was there watching his triumph. He took a step forward, leading Zena with him, then disengaged her arm from his and turned and walked the short distance to the front pew on the right. When he turned back he gasped. Standing at the altar beside his daughter, in the groom's position, was not Lord Whitby but Sebastian.

Zena looked quickly sideways at the man who had taken his place beside her, then she looked again. Blood rushed to her face and she averted her eyes. Her heart was beating so loudly she was sure everyone in the congregation must hear it. The scent of the roses and the smilax rose in waves. She was so dizzy she swayed. A firm hand gripped her elbow. Sebastian's touch was reassuring and secure and ... kind. She shot one more quick glance at the man she was marrying. She hadn't made a mistake, it *was* Sebastian. And he was smiling, and ... yes, she was certain of it, he'd winked.

Joe half rose and leaned forward. The old earl was looking

straight at him, grinning, his eyes daring Driscoll to make a scene. For a moment they stared at each other, these two schemers so willing to use their children as pawns for their own ends. Then Joe Driscoll backed down. He couldn't do it. Not with half the '400' watching. He couldn't admit that the English bastard had made a fool of him. A total fool. He hadn't even palmed off Reginald, the heir, on Zena. Sebastian was a second son, he would inherit practically nothing, certainly not the title.

The rector was completely unaware that anything was amiss. One Englishman looked pretty much like another to him. 'Do you, Charles ...'

'It's Sebastian, not Charles,' the earl stage-whispered.

'Oh, yes, of course.' The old man looked properly chagrined and began again. 'Do you, Sebastian, take Zena ...' And after the exchange of vows, 'Repeat after me, with this ring ...' In a few moments more it was over. 'I now pronounce you man and wife. The groom may kiss the bride.'

Zena's veil was thrown back. She looked up at Sebastian. He was beautiful. There was no other word for it. He was like a fawn. And the smile he gave her was full of sunshine, and when he bent his head his lips brushed hers in a dry, undemanding kiss that was nothing so much as friendly.

The guests could barely wait to get out of the church to laugh aloud. It was glorious, the best thing anybody had seen for years. That parvenu, the social climbing country bumpkin had been completely foxed by a man of breeding. Of course he'd still managed to connect himself by marriage to a great aristocratic family, nonetheless ...

His Lordship said the same thing in a hurried interchange in the Hansom cab that drove him and Joe downtown to the wedding breakfast at Sherry's. 'Half a million dollars doesn't rate an earldom, old boy,' Lord Whitby said in his broadest Yorkshire. 'For that size settlement you get the second son.'

'We agreed, you lying cheat! You and I talked it over and ...' Joe's protests sputtered into silence. He had paid the money into his lordship's bank the day before. His rage was so total, so overwhelming, he couldn't speak.

'Calm yourself. You'll be having a stroke or a heart attack

if you don't. Very well, I bluffed you and I won. Take your loss like a gentleman. That's what you want to be, isn't it? That's what this whole charade was about. You're my relation now, nobody will dare snub you. And the two kiddies will get on famously. Make us both proud grandfathers soon enough. And your lass won't have any duties beyond her because she'll never be the countess.'

Whitby turned to Joe and offered him a cigar. 'Here, let's smoke on it. Do all the rest of 'em good if we get out of this carriage obviously friends. Well, what do you say? Is it to be a scene, or a bit of bluff people will talk about for years?'

Just as his daughter had recognized the persuasive nature of common sense as dished out by the ballet mistress a few days past, Joe Driscoll knew there was only one response which was acceptable. He took the cigar from his lordship and leaned forward while the other man lit it.

'One more thing,' the Englishman said. 'No change in the allowance you make Zena. She gets a hundred thousand a year for life or I promise you, I'll make her existence hell, and yours too.'

Joe paused in the act of inhaling. The blood started to rage in his veins once more, but he calmed it by sheer force of will. Not now. Some day he'd get even. Not now. 'I don't go back on my word,' he said between puffs of smoke. 'Whatever some folks may do.'

2

The *Mauritania* was a thirty-two-thousand-ton colossus of the sea. When Cunard launched her in 1908 they published a raft of comparisons to convey an impression of the liner's enormous size. 'Bigger than the Great Pyramid of Egypt, or the US Capitol in Washington, or St Peter's and the Vatican in Rome; carrying a crew of more than a thousand; provisioned for her five day trans-Atlantic crossing with over two thousand game birds, sixty lambs, ten calves and forty oxen, as well as countless tons of turbot, sole, salmon, haddock, herrings (both kippered and red), and an unlimited supply of oysters and caviar ...' They didn't mention the quantities of bottles in her cellars — but no one aboard the *Mauritania* would ever want for champagne or claret or whisky.

'Have another drink,' Sebastian said. 'Do you good.'

Zena sipped the last of her champagne laced with brandy and nodded. 'I think I will.'

Sebastian turned and motioned to one of the two dozen waiters on duty in the blue lounge. 'Another champagne cocktail for my wife.'

His wife. He seemed quite at home saying the words. Zena twisted the diamond-studded gold band on her ring finger. 'May I ask a question?' she murmured.

'What? Speak up, my dear. I can hardly hear you.'

'I said, may I ask a question?'

'Well yes, of course, anything you like.'

'Two questions really,' she ventured, emboldened by the wine. 'What do I call you? And what am I called?'

Sebastian was startled for a moment, then he smiled that sunny smile she was already growing to love. 'I keep forgetting how utterly innocent you are. Sleeping Beauty just

22

wakened from her long nap. But I'm no prince, I'm afraid. Haven't a title and never will have, since I'm the second son. I'm simply Sebastian Bennet-Swan.' He reached into the inside pocket of his tail coat and produced a small gold lead pencil and a bit of paper.

'It's written like this, with a hyphen. I don't think you have double surnames in America, but in England we do. You must just call me Sebastian, naturally. None of that appalling Victorian business of a wife calling her husband Mister whatever. And you're still Zena. Except formally. Then you're Mrs Sebastian Bennet-Swan. Zena Bennet-Swan.' He looked up hopefully. 'You do understand all this, don't you?'

'Yes, once you explain it I do.'

'Good. You're so quiet that sometimes I think ...'

She never got to hear what he thought because her second champagne cocktail arrived. Zena sipped it gratefully. The enormous room decorated in gilt and ivory and blue velvet was very warm. It was full of ladies and gentlemen in evening dress waiting, as were she and Sebastian, for the second seating at dinner. She fingered the stiff taffeta of her green gown. 'I do look as I should, don't I, Sebastian? I wouldn't want to embarrass you.'

'You look charming.'

There didn't seem much more to say. Sebastian drummed his fingers on the table top and drank his brandy and soda in quick gulps. Zena stared into her champagne glass. 'Look,' he began finally. 'About yesterday, I'm sorry. Really.'

She assumed that by yesterday he referred to the wedding ceremony. She had been thinking about that for thirty-six hours, up to this moment it had not been mentioned. At the reception her father and all the guests had acted as if nothing extraordinary had happened. Last night she and Sebastian had slept side by side but untouching in a big bed in the honeymoon suite at Sherry's. They had exchanged hardly a dozen words from the time he stood beside her at the altar until now. Zena had been wondering if perhaps she'd misunderstood and all along it was Sebastian to whom she'd been engaged. Apparently her first impression was the correct one. 'You and your father switched places, didn't you?' she murmured.

'Yes, of course. My God, you must know that. You were there.'

'I do know, but I wasn't sure if it was a switch. I mean ...' Zena broke off, unable to explain her confusion.

Sebastian leaned forward and took her hand. 'Look, let's get it all perfectly clear, shall we? I'm Sebastian, you're Zena. We're married. Husband and wife. You were supposed to marry my father, Lord Whitby. He set it up with your father. But at the last moment he arranged for it to be me. It wasn't really a last minute thing with him, the old sod had it in mind from the first. That's why I said I was sorry. It was cruel to do that to you. I wanted to stand up to him, but I couldn't.' Sebastian drained his drink and motioned for another. 'I never can.'

Zena thought about her own father. 'I understand,' she whispered. There was genuine sympathy in her tone.

Sebastian smiled. 'I rather think you do. Tell you what, old girl. Let's be happy in spite of them. Let's have a jolly good time and forget about our respective paters.'

For the better part of a week they had, as Sebastian proposed, a jolly good time. They drank and ate and danced and promenaded on the deck. For Zena the dancing was the best part. The *Mauritania* was a British ship, but the eighteen-piece orchestra played all the latest American dances and Zena soon learned to jerk and gyrate to the grizzly bear, the bunny hug, and the turkey trot.

The energetic dances were great fun, but best of all was being held lightly in Sebastian's arms and whirled around the floor in waltz-time. That was what Zena had been imagining all those nights by herself, barefoot on the Turkish carpet in her bedroom, though of course she hadn't really known then what it was she craved. Now she did, and she couldn't get enough of it. By the time they returned exhausted to their stateroom it was nearly always sun-up, and Zena was only too glad to let her maid undress her and tuck her into one of the two narrow beds.

Eventually, after all the lamps but one had been extinguished and the maid had left to go to her own quarters, Sebastian came in through the door that led to his dressing room where his valet had been attending him. Unfailingly he

24

went to his own narrow bed, the twin of hers. 'Goodnight, my dear,' he would murmur.

'Goodnight, Sebastian.'

Whatever Madame Chirault had meant about husbands making pests of themselves at night obviously didn't apply to Sebastian. But what she'd said about papa opening her cage and letting her fly free, that was definitely, miraculously true. Zena hugged herself in delight as she nestled among the *Mauritania*'s pure linen sheets and voluptuous silk quilts. Life had suddenly become indescribably wonderful; despite her peculiar name she had been admitted into the ranks of the happy others.

Joe had promised his daughter a palace. Whitby Hall was not that. It wasn't even in Whitby, the town at the edge of the North Sea from which in 1768 Captain Cook had set out on his expedition to explore the Pacific. The Bennet-Swan family seat was some ten miles inland. It lowered above a village called Swans Tumble and both sat on the windswept, foggy York moors in Yorkshire's North Riding.

'Bloody goddamn' awful, isn't it?' Sebastian muttered as the carriage that had collected them from the Liverpool docks hurtled on the final quarter mile of its two-day journey. 'I should have warned you I suppose, but I couldn't bear to talk about it.'

Zena just looked and said nothing. The closer the gates of the Hall loomed the colder she grew. No, she wanted to scream. No, we can't live there. We mustn't. Where has the music gone, and the starlight, and the gilt and the silk and the laughing ladies and gentlemen who dance until dawn? But as so often happened, she was too miserable to put her thoughts into words.

'You're very quiet, shocked into silence I expect.' Sebastian knew her a bit better now. 'Well, just grit your teeth and bear it, old girl. We've no bloody choice.'

The carriage came to a halt at last. The sheer facade of the Hall's east face towered above them, a stark wall of damp, moss-covered granite pierced by small leaded windows with a minimum of glass. At ground level a pair of oak doors at least a foot thick and massive enough to admit a horse and rider had been thrown open. Half a dozen people stood either side. 'Have you read *Wuthering Heights*?' Sebastian asked out of the side of his mouth.

Zena shook her head.

'Too bad. If you had I could tell you that we're fifty miles further north, and you can treble the native gloom Miss Brontë wrote about. Well, come on, we have to greet the slaves. That's the object of the exercise.'

The driver opened the door, Sebastian descended, then turned and helped Zena to follow. He took a deep breath, gave her his best conspiratorial smile, and led the way up the few steps.

For Zena the event passed in a haze, but later she sorted it out; she'd been introduced to a butler, a housekeeper, a cook, and a few assorted maids. Not quite the army Madame Chirault had predicted. There were at least as many servants at Hillhaven, and that establishment wasn't a tenth the size of this one.

That it was huge was perhaps the most positive thing to be said for Whitby Hall. It had no heat except for coal fires that barely warmed the great draughty rooms, almost no light came through the ancient windows, there was no indoor plumbing — a maid brought Zena a pitcher of lukewarm water while she was dressing for dinner — and, as far as she could see, there were no toilets. When the three cups of tea she'd drunk in order to warm herself brought her to the point of nearly bursting, she was desperate.

Zena opened every door leading from her bedroom. None of them revealed anything but cupboards. The maid stood and watched in silence. Zena crossed the worn carpet and peered into the corridor. There were at least a dozen identical doors on each side, and at the end opposite the staircase there was a bend which led to parts unknown. She turned back to the silent maid. 'Please, I must ... Where is the powder room?'

The other girl looked blank. 'Powder room, ma'am? I don't know what you mean.' She pointed to an ornate dressing table. 'You can powder your nose there if you like.'

'No, I mean the ... the water-closet,' Zena proclaimed in triumph. Thank God she'd remembered a name that was acceptable.

'Oh, I see. Course, ma'am. Right here.' The girl stepped to a red velvet drapery and drew it aside, holding it for Zena to enter. Behind the folds was a mahogany chair with a hole in the seat and a large chamber pot on the floor beneath. Zena burst into tears.

Sebastian had consumed a lot of alcohol on shipboard, but she'd never seen him drunk. By the time he appeared for dinner that first evening in Whitby Hall he was staggering. 'Wants a lot of Dutch courage to eat here.' He hiccupped and covered his mouth with his hand. 'Sorry, but you'll see what I mean.'

The meal began with a stolid lump of dough swimming in gravy that Zena was told was Yorkshire pudding, followed by overcooked tough roast beef and a heavy sickly sweet thing the butler called jam tart. The only thing bearable was the wine. 'Take that rubbish away,' Sebastian had proclaimed at the start of the dinner when the butler presented a bottle for his approval. 'Is there still some of the '82 St Julien, Wilson?'

'There is, Mr Sebastian. Three bottles. His Lordship had the rest brought to his town house.'

'I don't doubt it. Well, bring us the remaining orphans, man. Right away.'

'All three bottles, sir?'

'Absolutely. And don't look so disapproving. It's not every day a new bride comes to Whitby Hall, is it?'

'No, sir. Certainly not.'

Zena drank one of the bottles of burgundy by herself, and Sebastian finished the other two. When the meal was done they linked arms for mutual support and stumbled into what Sebastian told her was called the little red room. It was little by the standards of the place, about the size of an ordinary sitting room in America, and the flocked wallpaper, the carpet and all the furniture were red.

'My great grandmother did this room up for herself. She's supposed to have said it created at least the illusion of warmth. Too bad I never knew the old girl.'

'It is warm, at least by comparison with the rest of the house.' Zena held her hands over a blazing coal fire.

27

'Yes. I made them light that thing a couple of hours ago. Ah, here's Wilson with coffee and brandy. Good man, leave the tray there and we'll look after ourselves.' He waited for the butler to leave, then ostentatiously put his finger to his lips and winked broadly at Zena before crossing to the door and locking it and pocketing the key. 'Alone at last. My dear wife, there's something we have to walk ... I mean talk about.'

Zena giggled. 'I'm a bit too tipsy to talk, so are you.'

'Maybe. But have to nonetheless. Can't be helped. Our duty and all that. Can't forget our duty just 'cause nobody's here but us.'

For Zena the words started a sobering process. She hadn't thought about it, but there was yet another horrible truth to be dealt with at Whitby Hall: sooner or later she and Sebastian must share the residence with Lord Whitby and Reginald. 'When are they coming home?' she asked.

'Who? My father and brother? Haven't the foggiest. Not for weeks, I imagine. And God knows when we'll see them.'

'Won't we take meals together?'

'Meals? You mean here?' Sebastian clapped his hand to his forehead. He seemed to be rapidly sobering too, at any rate his words were no longer slurred. 'Good God, girl, I've let you flounder in the dark yet again. Dear old papa and dear old Reginald both have London houses, neither of them spends more than a fortnight a year at Whitby Hall. Nor do I, for that matter. We all come up for the shooting in August, that's *de rigueur*, but that's about it.'

Zena felt a surge of joy. 'You mean we aren't going to live here?'

'Bloody hell! Of course not. No civilized person could live here. We had to come because you're the new bride, have to present ourselves at the hall and in the village, spend a few days. Then we can make tracks for London. My place isn't very big, you understand. It's just a flat really, the bottom two floors of Reggie's house. But with your income maybe we can buy something more suitable eventually. Lord, I thought you understood all that.'

Zena shook her head. 'No, how could I? Nobody told me.'

Sebastian smiled at her. 'Too right. Nobody's told you

anything, have they?' He crossed the carpet and took her in his arms, humming the tune of a Strauss waltz and whirling her round for a few steps. Suddenly he stopped and looked down at her. 'You don't think it's a bit odd, do you?'

'What?'

'Me. Us. That I haven't ...'

'Haven't what, Sebastian?'

'Made love.' Her blank expression didn't change. 'Sex,' he added. 'Started a baby. Christ, you don't know a damned thing about it, do you?'

'I'll do whatever you say, Sebastian,' Zena murmured. 'Whatever you want, if you'll just tell me what it is.'

'What I want doesn't come into it,' he muttered. 'It's a matter of duty. And keeping the bloody old man from cutting off my allowance. Not to mention yours. He's scoffed the entire half a million dollar settlement, he'll get the hundred thousand a year too if we don't mind our p's and q's.'

Zena's eyes filled with tears. 'I'm sorry. I just don't know what you're talking about. I've never had anything to do with money. Or this ... what did you call it? ... sex.'

Sebastian frowned, then his grey eyes began to sparkle with pleasure. 'Who would have thought a maiden so innocent could be discovered in 1914, even in the wilds of Red Hook, New York. Zena, my love, you are a marvel. And do you know what? I find that stimulating. Believe it or not, I suddenly feel as if I can do my duty after all.'

He bent his lips to hers and the kiss was different from the brotherly sort they had shared after the ceremony and a few times since. There was a little more warmth to it, a little more urgency. 'Come over here by the fire,' he murmured, leading her to the hearth rug and gently tugging her down to it. When she was sprawled on the floor he knelt beside her and pushed up her skirt.

'Sebastian, what are you doing?'

'What husbands are supposed to do. Shut up, innocent little Zena. Don't say a word or I'm liable to be incapable yet again. Mmm, I like your bloomers. Pretty shade of peach they are. Damned corset's like iron though, got to get it off. There, over you go.'

He rolled her over and began tugging at the laces. 'Sebastian ...' Zena murmured again.

'Shut up. As I said. Please, don't spoil it. There, that's done.' Sebastian rose and swiftly unbuttoned his fly. The erection which had come on him so suddenly was still evident. 'Roll over, wench. I am about to deflower you. And it's just as much a surprise to me as to you that I really want to.'

She did as he told her. The room was lit by three gas jets on the walls and by the fire; in its red glow she saw the peculiar thing that was now free of his trousers. 'Oh my ... I never imagined ... but it does make sense of a sort.' Zena's extreme ignorance had protected her from artificial revulsion as well as knowledge. It all had a kind of obvious logic. Men went out where ladies went in, so they must be made to fit together.

He didn't have to tell her again to be quiet. Zena watched and waited in silent fascination while Sebastian lowered himself on top of her and with a shout of triumph lunged forward to do his duty.

She hadn't expected it to hurt, but it did a bit. She cried out once, then clamped her hand over her mouth. Sebastian was pumping up and down on top of her. The pain was rapidly fading. Mostly the experience seemed a little ridiculous, a silly thing to do. And the way Sebastian's face was screwed up she couldn't tell if he was experiencing pain or pleasure. A few more moments went by. He shouted again, then rolled off her. Zena felt sticky and sore, and she was completely at a loss as to what was expected of her next.

Sebastian was panting, but after some seconds he caught his breath and propped himself up on his elbow and leaned over and readjusted the skirt of her gown. 'There. It wasn't too bad, was it?'

'I don't know,' Zena confessed. Then, after a moment's speculation. 'No, it wasn't bad. Is it supposed to be?'

'Depends who you listen to,' Sebastian said with a hoot of laughter. He sprang to his feet and pulled her after him. Her bloomers and her corset lay in a heap by the fire and when she rose her silk stockings slithered down around her ankles. 'Sort yourself out, pet. Then we'll go upstairs. And thanks

30

for being such a jolly good sport. With any luck you'll get pregnant and we won't have to repeat the exercise.'

The house the two brothers shared was in Hans Crescent, Knightsbridge. Sebastian's flat occupied the ground floor and the basement. It consisted of a drawing room, dining room, and library, as well as a large bedroom and dressing room and a kitchen, behind which were two servants' rooms. 'Terribly small, but I did warn you,' he told her.

'I think it's lovely.' Zena adored the place from the first. All the walls were papered with gay prints, Sebastian told her they were William Morris designs from something called the pre-Raphaelite school, and the Edwardian furniture was simple and spare by the Victorian standards of Hillhaven. 'We have our own front door, too,' she enthused.

'Of course, Reggie and I long ago agreed to live our separate lives. We don't bother each other, remember that.' His face had grown rather dark and he was frowning, but in a few seconds the sunshine returned. 'Tell you what, let's have a party. To celebrate your first night in London.'

'You mean now, tonight?'

'Of course.' Sebastian was tugging on the bell rope with one hand and lifting the big black telephone on the desk with the other. The butler here was named Patton. Like the one called Wilson at Whitby Hall, he never smiled and he always appeared the instant he was summoned. 'Patton,' Sebastian said, 'get on to Harrods and order everything we need for a party tonight. About ten people I think. No, make that fifteen. You'll have to pop over there, I'll be using the blower for the next while. Tell cook, will you?'

Patton murmured assent and left the room, Sebastian was shouting a number at the exchange. He looked at Zena and smiled and winked and executed a fast dance step while still holding the telephone. Then he was connected and for the next forty minutes he paid no further attention to his wife. All the conversations began the same way. 'It's me, and look, you won't believe this, but I'm married. No, I'm not joking, it's true. An American girl. Jolly nice. Come over this evening and meet her ...'

It was the first of many parties. They all involved pretty

31

much the same people, mostly men about Sebastian's age or a little older, and a few girls who did not seem to Zena at all like the companions she had dreamed of having in the days when she was sequestered in Hillhaven. The girls ignored her but the men were quite friendly. They did some things she thought were odd, such as dancing with each other, but they also danced with her and asked about America and thought it hilariously funny that she'd never seen the Statue of Liberty or Times Square.

Zena usually tired before the guests left. Most nights she would excuse herself and retire soon after midnight. She never knew what time the party ended because Sebastian didn't share the bedroom with her, he always slept on a narrow cot in his dressing room. The first she saw of him in the morning was at breakfast.

'Sebastian,' Zena asked on the morning of the twenty-eighth of June when they'd been in London a little over two months, 'it's just occurred to me that we're the only married couple we know. I mean none of your friends are married, are they?'

He didn't look at her. 'No, they're not.'

'Isn't that a bit strange.'

'I don't think so.' He rose and left the room so there could be no further discussion.

There was another party that night, with the same people, but for once there was something different to talk about. That day the Austrian Crown Prince, Franz Ferdinand, had been assassinated by a Serbian nationalist at Sarajevo.

The life of the Bennet-Swans changed little when England went to war in August 1914. The battles were taking place far across the channel in Belgium and France, and the British army was made up of career officers and volunteer troops. Sebastian and his friends were neither. What was more important to the rhythm of the days and nights at Hans Crescent was the fact that Zena was pregnant.

She had not at first realized what it was that was making her miss her monthlies and be sick in the morning and start gaining weight. It was when she hesitantly mentioned to Sebastian that she didn't feel well enough to attend one more

32

of the parties that he realized what was happening. He explained things to her quite gently and with much patience. He even produced a medical book for her to read.

The book raised more questions than it answered. She sorted out the business of pregnancy and birth easily enough, there were diagrams and lengthy explanations that made it all quite clear. What she couldn't quite figure out were the references to 'normal relations between man and wife ...' The more she read the more Zena became convinced that something was definitely not normal between herself and Sebastian.

Apparently other couples did that in and out business all the time, and had to be cautioned to give it up while the woman was expecting. There was a clear implication that men wanted to do it frequently, which tied in with what Madame Cherault had told her back in Red Hook. But Sebastian had never approached her again after that single event on the hearth rug in the red room at Whitby Hall. Zena remembered his exact words. 'There, with any luck you'll get pregnant and we won't have to repeat the exercise.'

The conclusion seemed obvious: there was something terribly wrong with her which made her totally undesirable to her husband. Worse, she had no idea how to change things. As usual, Zena could only suffer in silence.

'Father's coming to tea,' Sebastian announced gloomily across the breakfast table on a September morning.

'Here?'

'Of course here? Why the bloody hell would I mention it if he weren't coming here?'

Zena shrivelled at his anger. 'I'm sorry,' she whispered. 'I just didn't realize. He's never done it before.'

'And please God never will again. He just wants to see for himself that I'm not lying and you really are, as they say, with child. Oh, stop snivelling, Zena. I'm sorry I snapped at you. It's not your fault.'

The few kind words loosed the flood of tears more effectively than his anger. For a moment Sebastian tried to comfort her, then he gave up and left the house. He did that with great frequency lately. Sometimes he was gone for days

33

at a time. Once or twice she'd ventured to ask him where he'd been and the answer was always the same: 'With Nigel.'

Nigel Turner was Sebastian's closest friend. Zena had tried hard to like him, but she couldn't. Nigel made her uncomfortable. To begin with his hair was too long for a man, and he was far too pretty. And he lisped. And at the parties everyone but her seemed to think everything Nigel said was outrageously funny. So he confirmed her terrible sense of failure and inadequacy, and she was not altogether sorry that Sebastian had taken to seeing him at places other than their flat.

However, her husband was home by four o'clock that afternoon, and at five Lord Whitby appeared and tea was served in the drawing room. His first words to Zena were, 'Stand up, lass. Let me get a good look at you. Yes, yes. Good.' Then he turned to his son. 'When?'

'Some time in January we think, sir.'

'Good,' his lordship repeated. 'I knew you'd manage all right once you put your mind to it. Don't keep standing there like a ninny, Zena. Sit down and pour the tea.'

For the rest of the hour the two men discussed the war and ignored her.

At the beginning of November Zena broached the subject of a nursery. 'Sebastian, have you thought about where we're to put the baby when it comes?'

He looked quite startled. 'No, I can't say I have. But you're right, of course. We have to make some plans.' He glanced around as if expecting the flat might contain an extra room he hadn't noticed before, but finally he shook his head. 'Nothing for it, we have to move. It might be rather fun at that, doing up a new house. Tell you what, old girl, you ring up Harrods' estate agent. Have a look at a few houses. When you find something you like I'll go see it.'

Zena opened her mouth, then closed it again. She could not find the words to deal with the enormity of such a request. How could she look for a house to buy? She had absolutely no idea of what was involved.

Sebastian chuckled. He had become quite adept at reading her face those many times when Zena could not express her thoughts. 'Nothing to be terrified about,' he assured her.

'Harrods will look after you. Say we want a place suitable for a young couple with a child and the ordinary amount of staff. They'll do the rest.' He leaned over and kissed her forehead. 'That's my girl. You'll handle it with no bother. Do you good to get out and about.'

Two days later Zena announced at breakfast that she had an appointment with Harrods' estate agent that afternoon. 'I'm to see him at two. I used the telephone and made the appointment myself,' she added proudly.

Sebastian feigned an expression of astonishment. 'Well done. Just imagine it, you used the telephone all by yourself.'

'I'm sorry,' Zena murmured. The tears were very close to starting again.

'For heaven's sake, don't cry. There, it's me who should be sorry. None of it's your fault. You've done exactly the right thing, Zena. I mean it. I'm proud of you. Make sure the chap actually takes you out and shows you a house or two. Got to get stuck in right away if you're going to do the job. I won't expect you back until early evening. I'll tell Patton you won't be home for tea.'

Zena dressed carefully for her appointment. She had a dark blue two piece maternity dress, the skirt had an elasticized waist and the loose top came down to her knees. When she put her ankle-length grey coat over the dress she didn't look pregnant, just a bit plump. The coat was closely woven gabardine and had a big fox collar and fox cuffs and a deep border of fox around the hem. Before leaving, Zena surveyed herself in the hall mirror, gave a final tug of adjustment to her navy felt hat, pulled on her kid gloves, and stepped into the street with something very close to confidence.

She hadn't far to go: the world's greatest department store had a rear entrance in Hans Crescent, some ten yards from Zena's front door. The store had been there first. It was opened in 1848 as a country grocer's shop on rural Brompton Road. The smart red brick houses in the surrounding streets were built somewhat later, but being so convenient to Harrods was always considered an advantage.

At the beginning of the century the store had been granted the telegraph address, 'Everything, London'. It wasn't an exaggeration. Harrods not only sold every conceivable type of merchandise, it ran its own bank, booked anything from theatre tickets to a fully equipped African safari, catered for weddings and christenings, insured the belongings of its clientele, and when they had the misfortune to die, Harrods' admirable mortuary service arranged a funeral in the best possible taste. Finding a new residence for one young couple was hardly a challenge.

'Please sit down, Mrs Bennet-Swan. I do hope his lordship is well. And Mr Reginald, and your husband.' The estate agent always made it his business to check on the connections of people who made appointments, and then to speak as if he were an old family retainer. It was the sort of thing expected from the employees of Harrods.

'Very well, thank you,' Zena managed to say. She felt quite faint. The store was so enormous it had taken her half an hour to find this office on the third floor, and it was very warm. But she had to go through with it, she'd promised Sebastian. 'I want a house. That is, my husband ... I mean we need a ...'

'Yes, of course. I understand perfectly. Somewhere central, I imagine. There's nothing in Knightsbridge at the moment, but we've some choice properties in Mayfair and one or two in Belgravia. About twelve rooms, wouldn't you say? Plus the usual below stairs offices.'

Zena nodded.

'Indeed. I thought so. I've taken the liberty of looking out a few places to show you. Quite suitable houses I think. There is the matter of price, of course. Those I'm suggesting are each asking in the vicinity of fifty thousand pounds. Is that acceptable, Mrs Bennet-Swan?'

Zena stared at him. She had no notion of what a house was supposed to cost. She'd forgotten to ask Sebastian about the money. Perhaps she was supposed to pay for it right now. Today. Perhaps Sebastian had neglected to give her the money. Or maybe she was supposed to have it. But she never had any money. He knew that. She staggered to her feet, clinging to the edge of the desk for support.

'Mrs Bennet-Swan, are you ill? Here, let me help you ...'

'No, no. It's all right. I'm sorry. I must go.' Summoning all her strength Zena fled Harrods and ran across the road to her flat.

'You weren't expected home until later, madam,' Patton said. 'Here, let me take your coat and bring you some tea in the drawing room. I'll tell Mr Sebastian you've returned.'

Zena pushed past him and ran toward her bedroom. She needed to lie down. She needed to talk to Sebastian, to explain why she had made such a mess of everything. He wouldn't be angry with her if she could only manage to explain how it had happened. 'Sebastian ... Sebastian, where are you?'

'Madam, please. Don't go in there. You mustn't.' Patton was bounding down the hall after her, but Zena was propelled by her great need and she was faster.

She reached the door to her bedroom and flung it open. 'Sebastian, thank God you're ...'

She stopped speaking. Her husband was lying in the big bed in which she usually slept alone. But he was not alone. He was on top of Nigel. Doing the in and out thing. With Nigel. But Nigel was a man. Sebastian was a man. So the craziest thing of all was that they were each wearing one of her silk and lace nightdresses. And when they rolled apart and stood either side of the bed and stared at her she saw that both had rouged their cheeks and their lips.

'Oh Christ,' Nigel murmured. Sebastian said nothing.

'I'm sorry, sir,' Patton said, coming up behind Zena and surveying the scene. 'I tried to stop her bursting in.'

Sebastian ignored his lover and his devoted butler. He looked long and hard at Zena and finally stretched out his hand to her in a gesture of supplication. 'I'm ever so sorry, old girl,' he said softly. 'But I can't help it, it's the way I'm made. You had to know sooner or later.'

Zena fainted.

3

Zena's daughter was born on 8 January 1915, a few months before Zena herself turned seventeen. Sebastian had told her that Lord Whitby insisted that if they had a son he must be named Percival. 'He didn't say anything about a daughter, he doesn't think girls are important,' said Sebastian, looking ruefully at the infant cradled in Zena's arms in the nursing home in Portland Square.

'I want to call her Kate,' Zena said.

'Kate's a nickname. You mean Katherine. That's rather common, don't you think?'

'It was my mother's name.' At the best of times she could not have explained to him why it was so important that this child have one of the names she had dreamed about in her room in Red Hook. Today, when she was still exhausted from the labour and delivery, it was impossible.

'I see.' Sebastian nodded. 'Very well, Kate it will be. Seems the least I can do under the circumstances.'

He was still marvelling at the fact that when Zena discovered the truth about him she didn't walk out or make a scene or summon his father and his brother and denounce him. She went to bed for a few days after the terrible event, then she got up and went on as if nothing had happened. When he tried again to apologize and explain, she had silenced him with a wave of her hand. 'Please, Sebastian, I don't want to talk about it. We don't have to, do we?'

'No, I suppose we don't.'

'We'll just go on as we were. Nothing will change. Promise me that.'

Sebastian had promised. They didn't mention the subject again. Zena was quite relieved. She had figured out what her options were: ignore Sebastian's peculiarities, which she only vaguely understood, and go on living with him as his wife, or go back to her father in Red Hook. She had no doubt which option was preferable when she compared the virtual prison of Hillhaven to life with her husband, however strange some of his habits might be.

Gratitude made Sebastian more than usually patient, and he took on all the responsibility for making the arrangements for her confinement and locating a new home for them to live in after the baby was born. He'd bought a place on Duke Street in the heart of Mayfair and had it entirely redecorated in time to bring Zena and the baby there when she was released from the nursing home after three weeks.

'It's lovely,' Zena said admiringly that first day. Miss Dalgleish, the Scottish baby nurse Sebastian had hired, immediately disappeared with the infant in the direction of the nursery. Zena had nothing to do but walk around and admire Sebastian's efforts. He'd chosen all the vivid colors he knew she liked. 'It's perfect,' she said when they'd completed their tour and returned to the drawing room where tea was waiting.

'I'm glad you like it. You're a jolly good sport, Zena. I won't forget it. And there'll never be any ... any nonsense here in the house. I promise. I'll protect both you and little Kate from any scandal. You have my word on it.'

Zena didn't answer, but he knew she had heard and that they had reached a new stage in their silent agreement.

Everything went according to plan for almost a year. There was peace until Joe Driscoll announced he was coming to London to see his new granddaughter and help celebrate her first Christmas.

German U-boats were the scourge of the Atlantic, but America wasn't in the war; besides, since the sinking of the *Lusitania* the previous May, the Germans had agreed not to harm passenger ships. Joe sailed on the White Star Line's *Olympic*, sister ship of the *Titanic* which had gone down three years earlier. He arrived on 3 December of that year of 1915; by the tenth he had strong suspicions about his son-in-law. Joe took to following the young man when he left the house in the morning. Sebastian was not by nature furtive or mistrustful, he had no idea he was being watched. He simply continued his ordinary routine.

Sebastian's daily round did not openly betray his secret life. He usually went first to a coffee house in Curzon Street or perhaps to Boodle's, the club to which, like his father and his brother, he belonged. If the weather was fine he might stroll in Green Park or St James's. Around lunchtime he would disappear into some house or flat and not emerge until shortly after four when he'd return to Duke Street for tea. These mid-day venues were varied, but Joe noted that Sebastian most frequently visited a small house in Ennismore Mews.

The more Driscoll observed Sebastian the more convinced he became that his daughter's husband was a nancy-boy, a pederast. He'd fathered a child on Zena, but his true tastes lay elsewhere. Sure though he was of the fact, Joe knew that to be absolutely certain he must get inside the mews house. He did so one early afternoon by the simple expedient of ringing the bell half an hour after Sebastian had entered. A short slim manservant opened the door. Joe pushed his large self past the man without a word.

He stood in the hall for a brief moment. Mews houses were tiny affairs of two or three rooms on the ground floor and the same or fewer above. He could see nothing extraordinary in the drawing or dining room, the doors of which both stood open, but he heard music and laughter from above. Joe took the narrow stairs two at a time, the servant following him, wringing his hands and protesting loudly. Not loudly enough, however, to warn Sebastian and Nigel where they cavorted upstairs.

When Joe burst into the bedroom he found both young men wearing petticoats and wigs, their faces made up like Soho tarts, dancing a polka. Joe stood there watching them and grinning. At last he would get even with Lord Whitby.

Boodle's was a bastion of red leather and mahogany and polished brass. Members so totally respected each other's discretion that the most personal conversations were held in murmured tones in full view of anyone who happened to be present, but on this occasion his lordship took Joe and Sebastian into a small room off the main hall and locked the

40

door. He turned to Driscoll. 'Well, say what you have to say and get it over with.'

'I will,' Joe said. 'Soon as I light up. Cigar, your lordship? No? Pity, they're Havanas. Very fine. What about you, lad? No, not to your taste. I thought not.' Driscoll held a match a quarter inch from the tip of his cigar and drew inward, sucking the flame to the tobacco. When it was lit he exhaled luxuriously and sat back in his seat. 'Well, now.'

'Yes, well now what?' Whitby asked.

'Well, now I know your stinking little offspring is a nancy-boy. Your precious Sebastian buggers men. Has done for years, I expect. I'm also pretty damned sure you've always known about it.'

The earl stared straight ahead and said nothing. He'd guessed what this meeting was about as soon as Driscoll demanded it, he'd surmised as much from what the American said. And when he confronted Sebastian privately, the whole sorry mess had been confessed. So there was nothing for him to say until he learned what Zena's father proposed to do about the matter.

It was Sebastian who summoned the courage to speak in his own defence. 'I've not hurt Zena. She's perfectly happy. It's a private business. Mine.'

Driscoll answered him in a calm tone that belied the venom of his remarks. 'Do you imagine, you disgusting little pederast, that I will permit my daughter and my grand-daughter to live with a degenerate, immoral creature such as yourself?'

'Get on with it, man.' Whitby spat out the words through clenched teeth. 'What do you want?'

Joe flicked the ash from his cigar into the large brass ashtray on the table beside his chair. 'He goes to the front.'

'For Christ's sake! What will that prove?'

'Make a man of him maybe. Get him away from Zena and the child at any rate.'

Sebastian had gone quite white. 'I can't,' he whispered. 'I couldn't possibly kill anyone.'

Joe shrugged. 'Then maybe you'll be killed yourself. It's all the same to me. If you're not in the army by the end of the week I shall file for divorce in Zena's name and see to it that

41

The Times has the whole story.'

The earl leaned forward, peering closely at his adversary's face. 'She's your daughter. The child's your granddaughter. You wouldn't pillory them just to get back at me.' Driscoll did not reply. After a few seconds Lord Whitby sighed. 'Yes, I see you would.' He turned to Sebastian. 'You've no choice. I'll arrange a commission for you right away. And don't look at me like that, you pitiful young sod. I gave you your chance and you muffed it; you've no one but yourself to blame.'

Joe returned to Duke Street quite pleased with himself, but before he could explain to Zena how he had saved her and little Kate from a terrible fate, Patton handed him a cable. 'This came while you were out, sir. If there's a reply I can send someone to the telegraphic office immediately.'

Driscoll ripped open the envelope and read the message, then he grew very red in the face. 'Get me passage on the first ship to New York and have someone pack my bags.'

In March 1916 the case of Timothy MacDonald vs Driscoll's New Elixir of Health was decided in favour of the plaintiff. Mr MacDonald had sued Driscoll's for alienation of affections. He claimed that his wife Sheila became so enamoured of the Elixir that she spent every penny he gave her on buying it and neglected him and their seven children. During the trial Mrs MacDonald suddenly dropped dead. The attorney for the plaintiff asked for a meeting with the judge in chambers.

'Your honour,' the young man who had requested the meeting said solemnly, 'I realize this is highly irregular, but my associates and I can prove that our client's wife died of an overdose of Driscoll's Elixir.'

The judge peered at the lawyer. 'And how might you prove that, counsellor? And what has it to do with this case?'

'We can prove it, your honour, because the local druggist has signed a statement to the effect that Mrs MacDonald purchased four bottles of the stuff the afternoon of the day she died. And all four bottles were found empty beside the corpse.'

'Hmm ... And is there a link to prove cause and effect?'

'As you know, sir, we have plans to introduce three noted

42

chemists as witnesses over the next few days. All three are going to tell the court and the jury that Driscoll's Elixir is loaded with laudanum. Tincture of opium, sir. No bottle tested has had less than twenty-five per cent of the stuff, some a good deal more.'

'Opium is illegal in this country, is it not?'

'Yes, your honour. Since the passage of the Pure Food and Drug Act in 1906 a doctor's prescription has been required to purchase the drug in any form.'

The judge turned to Louis Thompkins, the defendant's attorney. 'And what will your client have to say to all this?'

'Mr Driscoll maintains that he has no way of knowing how the laudanum got into the Elixir, your honor.'

The judge made a loud sound rather like a snort and stood up. 'As the plaintiff's attorney is well aware, the case before us is one of alienation of affections. Any other evidence of a crime must be turned over to the Dutchess Country District Attorney. Naturally I will not allow it to be raised before this jury. Now, let us return to the courtroom, gentlemen.'

Five days later the trial ended. The judge directed the jury to return a verdict of guilty, but he needn't have bothered, they'd have done so anyway. Damages were set at seventy-five thousand dollars, high enough for the case to make headlines across the nation. The following week the DA obtained an injunction and the police closed Driscoll's factory and impounded every drop of New Elixir they could find.

In return for disclosing his source of the illegal tincture of opium, a small backroom laboratory in the Bronx, Joe Driscoll escaped prosecution, but he had to pay fines amounting to more than a million dollars. He sold the newly completed house in Newport to raise the cash, but just when he thought he'd stopped the bloodletting, a storm of new suits descended on his head. Nearly everybody who had ever taken the Elixir was claiming damages. Thompkins's advice was to settle each of them out of court and Joe knew he had no choice. By July 1916 he was a virtual pauper and a pariah in the community and he retired behind Hillhaven's stone walls. One of his final instructions to the attorney was to write to Lord Whitby and to Zena to say that he could no longer make his daughter an allowance.

It was also in July 1916 that Lieutenant Sebastian Bennet-Swan of the Border Regiment was killed in the Battle of the Somme. Patton, the butler who had gone to war as his batman, held the dying young soldier in his arms and accompanied his corpse back to England, along with the letter Sebastian had written before the battle.

Ten months later, on 6 April 1917, America declared war on Germany. Among those who volunteered to fight was a young man lately of New York City, but originally from Zanesville, Ohio, by the name of Harry Pride.

The patriotic impulse that propelled Harry Pride into the recruiting office was born of six neat bourbons and a bet in a Third Avenue bar. By August he was in London, and quite tickled at how nimbly he'd landed on his feet. He was not, thank God, an infantryman, a doughboy as they were called. The army made him a clerk and stationed him in an office in the American Consulate in Grosvenor Square. He thought London 'a gas', and he settled down to enjoy the war. Harry did not yet know that the most important thing about his posting was that, as it happened, Grosvenor Square was just around the corner from Duke Street.

Zena was spending quite a lot of time in the consulate that summer of 1917. She was trying to obtain an American passport for Kate. It seemed to her to be a simple matter; she was an American so surely her child must be. But the staff had a lot of other things to worry about at that moment, and someone had raised the question of whether a child born in London of an English father could have American citizenship.

Corporal Pride first noticed the little blonde when she was sitting on a bench at the end of the corridor which led to his office. A looker, just the sort he liked, petite and fair. Harry was short and dark, with a well-knit muscular body and brown eyes that almost twinkled with fun. 'Morning, ma'am,' he said as he walked by Zena. He touched his forehead as if to tip a non-existent hat.

'Good morning, soldier.'

He spent much of the next few hours thinking of her brief

44

greeting and trying to figure out if the three words betrayed an American or a British accent.

The next day she was there again and they exchanged pleasantries a second time. American, he decided. Definitely American. After that he made it his business to go out to the corridor at the same time every day; often she was there and they would each smile and say a few words. It got to be a regular routine.

'Good morning, ma'am.'

'Good morning, soldier.'

'Nice day, isn't it?'

'Yes, very nice.'

In London August was sunny that year. It was pouring cats and dogs in France and Belgium and mud and slime were making the trench warfare yet more gruesome, but neither Zena Bennet-Swan nor Harry Pride felt it necessary to comment on the slaughter taking place on the continent. Nonetheless, the war could not be entirely forgotten. Harry noticed that the blonde wore a wedding ring; he figured she must be trying to find out about a husband at the front, a guy listed as missing in action most likely. The morning he saw her pressing a handkerchief to her eyes and suppressing sobs he was sure she'd had news, and that it was bad.

He started to walk by her in respectful silence, then stopped and turned back. There was no one around and impulsively he sat down beside her. 'Don't mean to be forward, ma'am, but I'm sorry. Really. Don't suppose there's anything I can do, is there?'

Zena sniffled one last time and put her handkerchief away. 'Thank you, you're very kind. But I don't imagine the army has anything to do with issuing passports.'

'A passport, ma'am? Is that what you're after?'

'Yes.'

'You're an American, aren't you? I mean, your accent sounds as if you are.'

'Of course I'm an American, I was born in Red Hook, N.Y., so my daughter must be an American too. That's what I keep telling those fools in there.' She nodded her head at the closed door of the office across the hall and the perky green feather in her straw hat bobbed up and down. 'But they say it's not so simple.'

'Oh, I see. You're trying to get a passport for your daughter. I thought ... I mean I just assumed your husband must be at the front and ...'

'He was,' Zena said quietly. 'He was killed over a year ago, at the Somme.'

Harry made appropriately sympathetic noises while his brain raced ahead. 'Look,' he said finally. 'Lots of times you can get things done if you just manage to talk to the right people. About the passport, maybe I can help.'

Zena's blue eyes opened very wide. 'Do you think you could?'

'I can't say for sure. But I can try. Of course I'd have to know the facts.' He looked around. The corridor was still miraculously empty, but it couldn't be expected to stay that way for long.

Zena understood. 'We can't really talk here, can we?' She pursed her lips in hesitation, then made up her mind. 'Is there any chance you could come to tea at my home this afternoon? It's just around the corner and you wouldn't have to be gone long.'

'Every chance, ma'am,' Harry said with a grin. 'You can bet on it.'

Five days after Harry heard Zena's story the words 'And Kate Bennet, child of the above,' were added to Zena's passport, which was still in her maiden name. Somehow the Swan had been omitted. 'I don't think that matters,' Harry said.

'No, I'm sure it doesn't. Anyway, it's much more sensible for her to have just one last name if she's an American.'

'Sure it is.' Harry looked around the charming drawing room. He hadn't before commented on what he took to be Zena's wealth. All their conversations had been about the passport. 'Can't say I understand why you want to take her away from all this, though,' he said now.

'All this is going in any case.' Zena had been force-fed the realities of life during the past year. She was quite matter-of-fact about the whole thing. 'My father lost all his money last year and he's cut off my allowance. I've been selling my jewellery to support us.'

46

'But what about your husband's family?' Harry blurted out.

'My father-in-law isn't very fond of either me or Kate. It was his suggestion that I go back to the States.' What Lord Whitby had said was, 'It's your bloody fault that my son is dead, why don't you take your snivelling brat back where you came from,' but she didn't feel it necessary to repeat the words verbatim.

'Hard luck,' Harry said. 'How's the jewellery holding out?'

'It's all gone. Miss Dalgleish, that's Kate's nurse, has been handling everything for me. She sold the last diamond bracelet and ring a month ago. I'd have thought diamonds would bring more than a few pounds, but apparently they don't.'

Harry realized instantly that the servant must have been skimming, but he didn't say so. No point in making her grieve over spilt milk. He eyed the lavish furnishings of the room. 'Well, you'll get a bundle if you sell all this. Enough to take you and the little tyke home in style.'

Zena shook her head. 'The auctioneer's been and given me an estimate. It will just about cover my bills here and passage. There'll be a bit left over, but not much. I'm hoping we can live more cheaply in America.'

'You can live cheaper than this a lot of places, ma'am.'

'Please, won't you call me Zena? I'm so grateful to you, Corporal.'

'I'd be pleased to do that. But you'll have to call me Harry, won't you?'

Zena smiled. 'I guess I will.'

'When's the sale?' he asked. 'When are you planning to go home?'

'I'm told it isn't safe to travel until the war is over. I'll have to try and hold on until then. Will it be much longer now, do you think?'

'Hard to say, Zena.' He didn't think it prudent to tell her that in Ypres the British had just fought a bloody battle in which they gained two miles at the expense of thirty-two thousand men. His gaze fastened on the tea things on the table between them. 'Are those things real silver?'

'Yes, of course.' She stretched out a hand to the tea pot

and milk jug and sugar bowl. 'Those three pieces are early Georgian. Almost two hundred years old.'

Harry bit his lip. 'I don't like to say, but since you've been so frank ... Well, I think I could get a good price for them from one of the officers. Would you like me to try?'

'Oh, I would, Harry. That's enormously kind of you.'

By the end of the war there wasn't much left of value in the house on Duke Street, but Zena and Kate had managed to live in relative comfort. The only servants now were a cook-general and one parlour maid. Miss Dalgleish had vanished soon after Harry entered the picture, and Zena had decided that she quite liked looking after Kate herself. In fact she enjoyed the freedom from formality which her new household arrangements allowed. The best times of all were when Harry came and they put records on the gramophone and danced.

He'd always been a perfect gentleman, and Zena felt no guilt at all about the hours she spent with him. She suspected the neighbours probably talked about the fact that she enter-tained an American soldier so frequently, but she didn't care. They'd never been friendly to her anyway, and she and Kate were leaving London as soon as they could.

On Armistice Day, 11 November 1918, that was the thought uppermost in her mind. Thank God, soon we can go home. She hadn't yet figured out exactly what she meant by that. Certainly she didn't plan to take Kate to Red Hook; she had written to her father after the lawyer's letter came, but he never answered. In any case, she wouldn't allow her daughter to be incarcerated at Hillhaven the way she had been. There had to be something better for Kate, but Zena wasn't at all sure what it must be. Until now she'd been able to put the question aside, a decision she would make when the time came. Well, the time had come, and she still had no idea what to do.

Harry came that night. He brought a bottle of champagne and a chocolate bar for Kate. 'Here, little lady, see if mommy will let you eat the whole thing. We're celebrating this evening.'

Kate was a few months short of four years old. She had Sebastian's wide grey eyes and delicate features and Zena's blonde hair, and she was already taller than most children her age. She also had an inbred reserve and an almost royal bearing. Zena said she favoured her English half. The little girl took the present with her customary grave expression and curtsied. 'Thank you, Uncle Harry. I think I'd rather save it until tomorrow.' Kate put the chocolate in the pocket of her starched white pinafore.

Zena saw the fleeting look of disappointment in Harry's eyes and she went to the gramophone. 'We're having a party, Kate darling. The bad old war is over and we can go home soon.' She gave the handle of the machine a few vigorous twists and the overture of the hit musical *Watch Your Step* filled the drawing room. Harry had brought Zena the record, and taught her to dance in the style of Irene and Vernon Castle, whose grace had weaned America from the bunny hug and the turkey trot.

Harry turned to the little girl. 'Right, it's a party, Katy-kins.' He stretched out his arms. 'You remember the steps to the Castle Walk that I showed you last week.' Harry had a plan and he suspected it might not work unless he won over little Kate Bennet; he'd been trying hard, but so far she'd proved an unbeatable challenge. Now she consented to do a few steps with him, but after a moment or two she pulled away. 'That's all, Uncle Harry. You dance with mummy, I'll watch.'

He loved taking Zena in his arms, but having the kid looking on with those big eyes of hers made him nervous. He was glad when Zena said it was her bedtime and led her away.

'I think she's a bit worried about going to America,' Zena said when she returned. 'Probably I shouldn't have talked about it so much.'

'Sure you should. She'll get excited soon as she realizes it's really going to happen. Best thing for a kid is to have something to look forward to. Didn't you love that when you were her age?'

'I never had anything to look forward to. Everything was always the same in Red Hook, at least at Hillhaven. Not like you, Harry.'

She'd told him a lot about her childhood, and he'd told

49

her about his. She knew he'd grown up in a small town in Ohio, the son of a blacksmith, but that he'd decided to become a song writer and performer like George M. Cohan, so he went to New York in 1914 when he was eighteen years old. 'I was working with a music publisher when I enlisted,' he'd explained. 'Right down on Fourteenth Street in the heart of tin-pan alley.' He hadn't bothered to tell her that he wasn't writing songs, he'd been a file clerk. 'Had to do my duty once the war came, but soon as it's over I'll take up where I left off. Maybe get to show some of my stuff to Mr Cohan himself, then I'm on my way.'

Zena had complete faith in everything Harry said, he'd not let her down once since she met him. So when he told her now that Kate would be happy and excited as soon as they were actually on their way to America, she wanted to believe him. 'I hope you're right about Kate, but she never seems to get excited about anything.'

Harry decided to take his shot. 'She needs a daddy, Zena. Every kid does.'

Zena looked away. 'Perhaps you're right,' she murmured.

'Sure I am.' He moved to where she was standing and laid his hand lightly on her shoulder. 'How about me?' he whispered. 'Do you think I might be good enough to be a daddy to Kate?'

'Oh, Harry, of course you're good enough.'

'Does that mean you'll marry me?'

She hesitated only a second. Then she whispered, 'Yes, if you want me.'

'I do, honey. I've never wanted anything or anyone so much in my life.'

Harry kissed her then. It was not at all like Sebastian's rare kisses had been. Zena realized instantly that she still had a lot to learn about men and women and marriage, and the in and out business of which she'd had such a fleeting experience.

They were married in New York on 8 January 1919. It was Kate's fourth birthday and she went with them to City Hall. Harry had bought her an orchid corsage as well as one for Zena. A few weeks earlier Kate had accepted the fact that she was now to call Uncle Harry daddy. She had not, they presumed, any memory of her own father.

'I can adopt her legally,' Harry had said, but Zena had shook her head.

'Please, don't be hurt, but I don't think we should do that. I think she should continue to be Kate Bennet.'

'Mind telling me why?'

'I can't explain it,' Zena whispered. 'I just think that's the way it should be.' She could never explain most things about Sebastian, certainly not why she felt it wrong to deny his claim on the child he'd fathered.

'Okay,' Harry had agreed. 'If that's how you want it, that's how it will be. Maybe when Kate's old enough to understand we can ask her what she wants to do.'

'Yes,' Zena said, glad to be so easily out of an awkward situation. 'Maybe we can do that.'

It was the closest they'd ever come to a disagreement. Everything between Harry and Zena was love and laughter in those early days. She finally knew what the medical book had meant about 'normal relations between husband and wife'. It wasn't at all like that swift performance on the hearth rug at Whitby Hall. With Harry it was giggles and tickles and lots of kisses before the serious part began. And afterwards he held her and cuddled her and told her how terrific she was and how much he loved her.

The first fifteen months of their married life they lived in a furnished four room apartment in New York on Twenty-second Street. It was what Harry called 'a swell place,' — a sublet from an elderly couple who were going to try out Arizona and see if it improved the wife's health. The rent was forty-six dollars a month, but they could afford it because thanks to Harry the final sale of the Duke Street house and what was left of the furnishings netted a bit more than the original estimate. He'd found an auctioneer willing to take a smaller cut.

'We'll be on easy street as soon as some of my songs sell,' Harry promised, and he used thirty dollars of their money to buy an almost new spinet piano and install it in the living room on Twenty-second Street. He spent a lot of time at the piano, and at least twice a week he made the rounds of the music publishers in the Brill Building on Broadway, but nothing happened.

Once he wrote something he was absolutely sure was perfect for a George M. Cohan show and he sent it to the great man by registered mail, return receipt requested. The receipt came back signed, so they were sure Mr Cohan got the song, but they never heard anything more about it.

That was in April 1920. Zena was expecting a baby in June and money was becoming a problem. 'Maybe you could get some other kind of work, Harry,' she ventured. 'Just until you sell your songs.'

'Sure, honey, sure. Don't worry, everything's going to be fine.'

Zena wasn't so confident. But her spirits rose one day in May when there was a knock at the door and she opened it to find a little boy dressed in short trousers, a heavy sweater and a peaked cap. 'Does Mr Harry Pride live here?' the child asked.

'Yes, he does. He's not in right now, but I'm Mrs Pride, can I help you?' She was sure he was a messenger from one of the music publishers, perhaps even from George M. Cohan himself.

'Thank you, ma'am, but I'm supposed to see Mr Pride. I'll wait out here if you don't mind.'

The boy had straight dark hair and big, sad dark eyes. 'There's no need for that,' Zena said. 'Come in.' Zena was alone with the boy, for Kate was at the nearby kindergarten where they'd enrolled her the previous September. The Bide-a-Wee Nursery School only cost a dollar a week, and Zena hoped that being with other children would take Kate out of herself a bit, maybe even do something about her accent. Kate still spoke with a combination of English broad 'a's and the Scots' lilt she'd picked up from Miss Dalgleish. 'What's your name?' she asked the lad when he followed her inside.

'Nicholas Frane, ma'am.' He pulled the cap off his head and held it behind him. 'Mostly I'm called Nick.'

'I see. And how old are you, Nick?'

'I'm nine, ma'am. Be ten on Christmas, that's my birthday, same as God's.'

The assertion struck Zena as extraordinary. Everything

52

about this child seemed remarkable. He stared at her with unwavering eyes so dark they were almost black, and he seemed to read her thoughts. There was something absolutely unmovable about this Nicholas Frane, as if he could withstand any blow. It was unnerving. 'Would you like some milk and cookies?' Asking that made her feel more like the grown-up she was supposed to be, reminded her that Nick was a child.

'Thank you, I'd appreciate that if it's no trouble.'

She went into the kitchen and came back with a glass of milk and two Fig Newtons. The cookies came from a packet. Zena had learned the rudiments of cooking and cleaning since she married Harry — servants were out of the question until they got to that 'easy street' he was always promising — but she'd never tried to bake. It didn't matter, the boy wolfed the snack eagerly and she realized he'd been hungry. 'Here, I'll get you some more,' she said, taking the tray with the empty glass and plate.

'Don't mean to be any bother, ma'am. Ma said I shouldn't be.'

Zena stopped in mid-step. The comment didn't exactly make sense if he'd been sent by someone in the music business. 'Your mother is obviously bringing you up well. Do you live near here?'

'Don't live anywhere at the moment,' Nick admitted. 'Used to live in Zanesville. That's in Ohio. Then ma died and I came here.'

'Zanesville ... Are you a relative of my husband's, Nick?'

'I guess so. He's my uncle, least that's what ma said. She gave me a letter with this address on it just 'fore she died. Said I was to bring it to him.'

'And you've come all this way by yourself?'

'Yes ma'am.'

She had no time to respond to that extraordinary admission because Harry came in just then. 'Hello, who's this?'

'Your nephew, apparently. His name is Nicholas Frane and he's come all the way from Ohio by himself. He has a letter for you.'

The boy had stood up as soon as Harry arrived, now he stared at the man with the first hint of uncertainty Zena had seen him display. Harry sensed it too, and was quick to respond. 'You don't say? You're really Nick, my sister Phoebe's kid? Hey, that's terrific.' Nick was promptly wrapped in a bear hug.

Zena knew it was silly to be angry with the child because he wasn't who she'd thought he was. Besides, she saw the way Nick clung to her husband. She swallowed a lump in her throat, but she was scared too. Some instinct told her this visit boded no good. They were already teetering close to the edge of real trouble, and her baby was going to be born in about six weeks.

'Nick says his mother is dead,' she told Harry. It was a harsh way to announce the fact, but as far as she knew he'd never even written to his sister. They couldn't have been close.

'That's awful,' Harry said, thrusting the boy away from him and looking into his face. 'I sent your ma a letter soon as I got stateside, but she never answered. Where's your daddy, son?'

'He's dead too, Uncle Harry. It's all right if I call you that, isn't it?'

'Of course it is. That's what I am, your uncle. Only relative you've got from the sound of it. When did your dad die, how did it happen?'

'Couple of years ago, sir. He got a job working on the railroad in Columbus and there was an accident.'

'And your ma?'

'It was her chest, Uncle Harry. Consumption, the doctor called it. But before she died ma gave me this,' he held out the letter, 'and a ticket to New York, and said I was to come here when she went. So I did,' he added simply.

Harry took the letter and ripped it open. He read it quickly then passed it to Zena. It was a straightforward enough request. Phoebe Frane wrote that she'd always trusted her older brother and she was sure his wife was a lovely lady and he was making good in New York, just the way he'd written her last year. She didn't know anybody in her late husband's family: he'd come to Ohio from Arkansas and lost touch. So she was writing this letter for Nick to bring to Harry when she died, which the doctors told her would be fairly soon.

'You was gone by the time I got married so I suppose I better tell you I didn't actually birth Nick. He was my husband's boy, but I brung him up since he was a tiny baby and always thought of him as my own son and as far as he knows, I'm his ma ... I've a bit left from the insurance the railroad paid after the accident. I'm sending that with Nick too. I know it's not much, but it's all I have. Take care of him, Harry, please. You're the only chance Nick has of staying out of an orphanage.'

There were four ten-dollar bills in the envelope.

Zena finished reading and looked up at her husband. He was looking at her. Nick was watching them both. Harry's eyes asked wordless questions. She hesitated. According to the letter the boy wasn't even a blood relation. But Harry's eyes told her that didn't have anything to do with it, and after a few seconds she nodded. Harry grinned and turned to the boy and gave him another bear hug.

'Welcome to the Pride family, Nick Frane. We're glad to have you.'

Zena and Harry's daughter was born at one a.m. on 10 June 1920, in St Vincent's Hospital on West Eleventh Street. The forty dollars Nick had contributed to the family coffers paid for Zena's confinement. Almost all the rest of their money went on the expense of moving to a five-room cold water walk-up on Bleeker Street in Greenwich Village. 'Got to have a bigger place now, honey,' Harry had said.

'And a cheaper one,' Zena agreed.

'Just until I connect and we can move to Park Avenue,' Harry promised with a grin. 'And meanwhile I've got a job in the billing department at Macy's. So you stop worrying.'

The job at Macy's paid twenty-three dollars a week, the place on Bleeker Street cost thirty a month. If they were very careful they would get by. Zena was a lot more relaxed about her life when the time came for her child to be born.

Things seemed to be looking up for them, she decided. Maybe Nick's unexpected arrival hadn't been a blow at all, maybe it heralded a change in their luck. The birth confirmed that notion. It was an easy labour, perhaps because Zena was just twenty-two years old and perfectly healthy. When they wheeled her out of the delivery room and she saw Harry standing there grinning, she knew a moment of the purest happiness.

Harry returned the following morning with his arms full of flowers and kissed Zena fervently. 'You're terrific, sweetheart. So's the kid.'

'Have you told Kate?'

'That she has a new sister? Sure I did. First thing this morning.'

Kate had accepted the arrival of Nicholas with her customary lady-like reserve. Zena didn't know what the little girl really thought of this cousin who had suddenly joined the family, nor how she would react to a new baby. 'How did she take it?'

'Like Kate,' Harry said. 'She said, "That's very nice. Tell Mummy I hope she comes home soon." Five years old going on fifty.'

Zena smiled. 'Just like Kate,' she agreed. Then, 'Have you seen your new daughter yet?'

'They held a bundle up to the nursery window and told me it was mine. I hope they got the right one, the kid they showed me was gorgeous.'

Zena laughed. 'She's not, she's all wrinkled, like a little old lady. Kate was too. They don't get gorgeous until later.'

'Nope,' Harry shook his head solemnly. 'This one's gorgeous right now. Time to make up our minds, sweetheart. What are we going to call her?'

Since he'd learned of his sister's death he'd been agitating for Phoebe if it was a girl. A boy was going to be Harry Junior.

'I just don't like Phoebe,' Zena said now. 'Let's try and find a compromise. What was your mother's name, Harry? You've never told me that.'

'Mollie. She spelled it with an ie at the end, not a y.'

'Mollie! That's perfect. Let's call her Mollie.'

Harry nodded. 'I like it. Mollie. Little Miss Magic Mollie Pride.'

4

They never understood Kate. Neither her stepfather nor her mother correctly analysed the little girl's character. Harry didn't think deeply about much of anything, and Zena's life had made her too introspective to allow her to put herself in her daughter's place and figure out what she was thinking or why. They didn't understand that from Kate's point of view everything in life was transient. Things kept changing and people were prone to disappear.

Men were the worst offenders: both her grandfathers had made brief appearances in her world, then gone. One of her earliest memories was of another man who held and cuddled her and called himself Daddy, then he was gone too. When the man she had been taught to call Uncle Harry became Daddy, Kate expected the change of name to herald a disappearance. Women were only slightly more reliable: Miss Dalgleish had always been there, until suddenly she wasn't. Mummy was a constant, but Mummy was always so vague and preoccupied. Kate would not have been in the least surprised if one morning Zena evaporated in front of her eyes.

So it was with a great deal of hesitance that she accepted the fact that the boy called Nick had come to live with them. All that meant to the five-year-old was that he was there for a time. Which was a pity because within two days she loved him, though she was far too reserved to show it.

From the first Nick really paid attention to her — not the way grown-ups did, always watching for something you might do wrong — but as if he were interested. 'What's the bear's name?' he'd asked the afternoon he arrived, when Zena and Harry were talking in the kitchen and he followed Kate into her bedroom.

'Cornelius.' Kate didn't look at him. She picked up the bear and hugged it and stared out the window, waiting for Nick to say something about her accent. The other children at the Bide-a-Wee Nursery School always teased her about talking funny.

Instead Nick said, 'I like the way you talk, it sounds nice, but Cornelius is a long name for a bear. Can I call him Corny?'

'If you like.'

Nick looked around the small bedroom. 'Boy, you sure have a lot of toys.'

'I had a lot more until we went on the boat.'

'What boat?'

'The one that brought us to America.'

Nick had drawn his eyebrows together and the dark eyes grew darker still. 'My ma told me Uncle Harry was in the war over in Europe for a while. I didn't know any kids were in the war.'

'What's a war?' Kate asked.

Nick grinned. 'How come you don't know that? A war's when lots of guys get dressed up in uniform and helmets and shoot guns at each other.'

Kate sat down on the side of her bed. 'Why do they do it?'

'Don't know.' Nick folded himself into an Indian squat on the rug at her feet. 'Because there's good guys and bad guys, I suppose. So if you weren't in the war how come you had to take a boat to America?'

'Because first we lived in London, now we live in New York.'

Nick nodded. 'Like I used to live in Zanesville, now I live here.'

'Here in this house, with us?'

'Yup. Your ma told you so, I heard her.'

'You mean my mummy?'

'Ma and mummy, it's the same thing. Sort of a way of saying mother.'

It was Kate's turn to nod in understanding. She thought for a moment, then held out the bear. 'You can hold Cornelius if you want.' It was a small thank-you for the first genuine conversation she'd ever had.

Soon after that they moved to Bleeker Street and Kate watched warily to be sure Nick was really coming with them. The first night she slept in her new bedroom she kept waking and running across the hall and looking into the room where Nick was sleeping, just to be certain he was still there.

As the days passed and Nick remained, Kate relaxed a little. Since it was May it had been decided not to enroll Nick in school until the autumn, and Kate didn't go to nursery school anymore. They'd told her Bide-a-Wee was too far from her new house, and that anyway after the summer she would be in the first grade in a real school which was right around the corner. Mummy wasn't feeling very well, she was awfully fat, and tired all the time, and she complained that her back hurt; so in the mornings Nick would take Kate for a walk around the new neighborhood.

'Don't go too far,' Zena always admonished the children when they left. 'Nick, do you have our address pinned inside your shirt pocket?'

'I do, ma'am.' He had yet to call Zena anything but ma'am.

'Very well, you may go then. But take good care of Kate, don't let go of her hand. And be sure and come back before lunch.'

So off they would go, Nick and Kate, hand in hand; he in his shorts and sweater and peaked cap, she in one of her flowered cotton dresses, the hems of which had been let down repeatedly, with a pink or blue cardigan for warmth and the sturdy brown lace-up shoes which had been bought for her just before they moved. Kate didn't have to struggle to keep up with the boy four years her senior, for although the top of her head came to his shoulder, her legs were almost as long as his, and Nick didn't race along. He set a slow pace so they could observe everything and discuss what they saw.

For the little girl who barely remembered London and the boy from a semi-rural part of Ohio, all of Greenwich Village was worth a second look. Twenty-second Street had been rows of prim and proper brownstones with tightly shut doors, behind which whatever happened was unknowable; on Bleeker and Carmine and Macdougall Streets life was lived in the open and at full cry.

Italians who were just beginning to spill over from Little Italy further downtown hawked fish and fruit and used clothes from barrows they trundled in every direction. Here and there an artist had set up an easel and was painting, as oblivious to onlookers as if they didn't exist. Women dressed entirely in black mingled with ladies dressed in less and less as the spring days warmed to early summer. 'Never saw anything like that in Zanesville,' Nick would murmur as one after another remarkable sight presented itself. Kate would nod in solemn agreement.

On the morning when it was Harry who gave the children breakfast, and made the announcement that Kate had a new baby sister and Nick a new little girl cousin, the boy's instructions were explicit.

'Nick, I'm going to the hospital to see Auntie Zena and the baby. You have to take care of Katykins. Can you light the stove?' Harry pointed to the gas burners set in a huge black cast iron contraption with a chimney that disappeared through the ceiling.

'Yes, sir. I do it lots of times.' Zena was afraid of the stove, which inevitably made a loud bang when you put a match to it, so Nick usually did it for her.

'Good. I left some tomato soup in that pot there. All you have to do for lunch is heat it up. And there's bread in the breadbox. There's no milk, but you can go down to Agnelli's and get a bottle. Tell Mrs Agnelli to put it on the bill. Get some cookies too, if you want. I have to go to work after the hospital, but I'll be home by six and we'll have supper then. Okay?'

'Okay, Uncle Harry.'

During the fourteen days that Zena was kept at St Vincent's Nick did all the shopping and most of the cooking, but he and Kate managed to explore further than ever. They went all the way to Christopher Street and came back along Sixth Avenue. Nick never lost his way, and no matter where they went Kate held his hand with perfect confidence. But at night, when she was alone in the room she would soon share with her little sister, she reminded herself that probably it would be the same as always. Some day

60

she'd wake up and Nick would be gone.

Which was why she fell so instantly, utterly, irrevocably in love with Mollie when Zena and the baby came home. Mollie couldn't walk. She couldn't talk. She couldn't even feed herself. Kate had never before seen a baby up close, she'd never realized that everything had to be done for them. Here was salvation. Clearly Mollie couldn't get away, so it was absolutely safe to adore her.

In August 1922 Harry lost his job in Macy's billing department. 'The bastards are letting the guys go and hiring more and more women,' he told Zena as he slammed his hat on the kitchen table. 'Pay 'em half as much as a man, so why wouldn't they?'

Zena's heart sank. She was too overwhelmed even to reproach his bad language. Harry had invaded their meagre savings of seventeen dollars and forty cents the week before. He'd taken the whole family to Coney Island on Sunday and spent nearly five dollars on the subway fares and buying lunch and supper out. All she said was, 'Don't worry, honey, you'll get something else soon.'

Harry didn't answer. Instead he went into the living room and sat down at the piano and began playing. It had been ages since he'd spent more than a few minutes at the piano or written a song. Working from eight to six at Macy's six days a week left very little time for composing. His lined music sheets were still propped up on the spinet, however, and he flicked through them until he came to one that was blank, then played a few bars and stopped and made some notations on the paper. Ten minutes later he called to his wife, 'Hey, listen to this.'

Zena stopped in the act of mashing the potatoes for supper and listened. 'It's very nice, dear.'

'It's better than that, it's terrific. I think Mr Cohan will love this one.' He played a few bars more. 'It's a natural, sweetheart. Soon as the right people hear it we're on easy street.'

Moving to easy street proved to be as difficult as it had been before. Harry was determined to pursue his dream. 'It's now or never,' he insisted. He didn't look for another full-time job, instead he eked out his two weeks' severance pay and their few dollars savings by picking up odd jobs in the garment district.

Harry had discovered that he could go over to Seventh Avenue and stand around with a lot of other men and fairly often get hired to help load and unload the bales of fabric which were endlessly shuttled around the factories and workrooms of the area. Pushing the racks of finished clothing was easier, but that job went to the regulars who worked every day. Harry only appeared two or three days a week, and he put in just enough hours to earn a dollar or two. The pay was handed over in cash as soon as a job was done, and the minute he had it Harry went home and resumed his place at the piano.

One late November afternoon he came in a little after four, and stopped in the long dark hall in the act of removing his fedora. Someone was playing the piano. The notes of *Alexander's Ragtime Band* echoed through the apartment. Harry walked to the door of the living room.

'Hey, kid,' he said softly. 'I didn't know you could tickle the ivories.'

Nick stopped in mid-bar. 'Hello, Uncle Harry. I didn't think you'd be home yet. Auntie Zena said it was okay if I fooled around.' He got up hastily from the stool and spun it rapidly back to the height that suited his uncle.

'Sure she did. Why wouldn't it be okay?'

'It's your piano.' Nick didn't meet Harry's eyes.

'That's okay, kid.' Harry said quietly. 'It takes a hell of a lot of use to wear out a piano.' He noticed the girls sitting on the sofa on the other side of the room. 'I see you got an audience.' Neither seven-year-old Kate nor two-year-old Mollie ever sat and listened when Harry was at the piano.

Nick came up with an inspired answer. 'That's because I'm just fooling around. When you're in here you're working.'

Harry brightened. 'You got it right, Nick my boy. Tell you what, why don't I sit down too, and you show me what else you know.'

He crossed to the sofa. Mollie was on Kate's lap, Harry lifted her off and put her on his, then he slung an arm around Kate's shoulders. 'By the way, where's your mother?'

'Gone shopping,' Kate supplied.

'Okay, well since we're all here — Maestro, let the entertainment begin.'

Nick hesitated. He had taught himself to play, picking out melodies after school. His aunt knew, of course, but they never talked about it, and he'd always had a sneaking feeling that his uncle wouldn't like it. Now he decided he had no choice but to perform for Harry, and since he had to do it he'd show off good and proper.

Nick played four songs in a row, without a break between them: *Oh How I Hate To Get Up In The Morning*, *When The Midnight Choo Choo Leaves for Alabam'*, *A Pretty Girl Is Like a Melody*, and *Araby*. He didn't get a note wróng and what he lacked in technique he made up for with enthusiasm.

Despite his mixed feelings, and the eleven-year-old boy had not misjudged the way his uncle would react to this secret talent, Harry was soon tapping his feet. When Nick got to *Midnight Choo Choo* Kate began clapping her hands in time with the music, and when he played the final number of the medley Mollie began to sing the words.

Harry had been surprised to hear his nephew play; he was positively stunned when his daughter began lisping, 'I'm the Sheik of Araby, your love belongs to me ...' He knew the kid could talk, they always joked that Mollie had been born talking, but here she was belting out '... at night when you're asleep, into your tent I'll creeeeeep.' She hit a high note — flat, but high nonetheless — and held it. Then Kate joined in. 'So rule this land with me, I'm the Sheik of Araby.'

'Jesus,' Harry murmured. 'Jesus Christ.'

'Don't use language like that in front of the children.' Zena had come in without any of them hearing her. Now she was standing in the doorway to the living room looking at them.

'Hi, honey. Sorry about the swearing. I'm just so darned astonished.' He jumped off the sofa, unceremoniously depositing Mollie beside her sister, and crossed to where his wife was leaning against the doorframe. 'Have you heard this triple act? Why didn't you tell me?'

'I've heard them. But there didn't seem anything to tell

63

you about. They were just amusing themselves.'

'But they're terrific, real pros, we can ... Honey, what's the matter?' He'd finally noticed the expression on Zena's face.

'Mrs Agnelli refused me any more credit. She put all the things I ordered on the counter and added them up and said it came to two dollars and ten cents, and when I told her to put it on my bill she refused. She says you haven't paid the bill in six months. That's since before you got fired from Macy's.'

'Aw gee, honey, I'm sorry. I've been meaning to go in and pay it. I just forgot. C'mon, don't cry. What's Mrs Agnelli know? Does she have three kids who can put on a slam bang show like these three?'

'There's nothing for supper,' Zena said as if she hadn't heard him. 'There's absolutely nothing to eat in the house.'

Harry put one arm around her and held out the other to the children. 'It doesn't matter, I made a couple of bucks today. C'mon you troupers, come over here and get in the cuddle-huddle. We're gonna' have supper out. We're all going down to the Blue Spot Cafe and celebrate, because very soon now, the Pride Family is going to be on easy street.'

Zena might have refused, she had developed a will of her own since she had the children to look after, except that by the summer of 1923 they owed everybody in the neighbourhood and were six months behind in the rent. At least three eviction notices had arrived and the final one said that in two days the sheriff was coming to put them out. The thought of what that would do to Nick and Kate and Mollie made her sick to her stomach. So she agreed that they'd just quietly leave the night before the sheriff was due.

'There's nothing here we need, anyway,' Harry said. 'Except maybe the piano. But never mind, all the theatres have pianos of their own. Better ones.'

'What theatres, Harry?' Zena asked wearily.

'The ones we're going to play, naturally. Small ones in small towns at first, then it'll be two a day at the Palace, our name up in lights. The Fabulous Pride Family.'

'Will we have somewhere to sleep tomorrow night?' Zena could not manage to think beyond the next twenty-four hours.

'Absolutely,' Harry assured her, and this time he was as good as his word. He'd already got them their first booking. The Fabulous Pride Family were scheduled to appear at the Topsfield County Fair in Topsfield, Massachusetts. The organizers had suggested that Harry and his wife and kids could stay at a boarding house in the town. 'All we have to do is get ourselves up there and we're on our way,' Harry promised.

'How far is it?'

'Not very far, a couple of hundred miles.'

Zena's blue eyes opened wide. 'Are we going to walk all that distance?'

'Don't be silly, of course we're not. There's a bus. I've got the tickets.'

Zena puzzled about where he'd found the money for bus tickets, but she decided against asking. Neither did she ask what was in the extra cardboard suitcase Harry collected from a locker in the bus station on Tenth Avenue. She had packed the two suitcases which contained the children's clothing and their own, but apparently her husband had been making quite a few arrangements she knew nothing about.

They were in Boston by mid-morning and Harry bought them all breakfast at the counter in the drugstore across from the station. Then they took another bus to Topsfield. Fortunately it stopped right near the fair grounds and the boarding house was only two blocks away. 'That's lucky,' Harry confided. 'I spent my last dime on breakfast; we couldn't have taken a taxi.'

'I thought you spent your last dime a week ago,' Zena said, more in puzzlement than complaint.

'I know you did, sweetheart, but I've been holding back a bit. Had to get things ready for our debut. You gotta' make your own breaks in this life, don't you forget it. And don't worry, we get paid right after we finish tonight. One good thing, now that we're in show business we'll always have jingling money in our pockets.'

When they got to the boarding house Harry said the

children could nap for an hour or two, then they'd all have to rehearse.

'You've been rehearsing us for months,' Zena reminded him. Harry had been trying out various combinations of music and songs and dances in the living room on Bleeker Street since the day he discovered that Nick could play the piano.

'This is different,' he told her. 'This is a dress rehearsal.' With a flourish Harry opened the mysterious suitcase and displayed its contents. He had purchased five costumes from a theatrical outfitter in Manhattan. 'You and Kate and Mollie have these gowns, see they're all pink and ruffled, just alike. Nick and me, we both wear toppers and tails.'

They were all sick with nervousness that first night in Topsfield, but the audience quite liked them, thought the kids were cute as hell, and by the end of their week's engagement they were seasoned performers, even little Mollie.

'We're playing the Pittsfield Fair next, then on to the Catskills,' Harry said.

'Until it's two a day at the Palace,' Mollie piped up. She was the quickest among them, could mimic just about anything anybody said or did.

'You bet, princess,' Harry said, picking her up and swinging her around. 'Just you wait and daddy's going to make you a star.'

The summer was fun. Even Zena enjoyed it. They weren't in any one place long enough to run up any bills, so there were no bill collectors to hound them. And they always had three meals a day, and it was even fun dancing on stage with Harry and the children. It didn't get hard until after Labor Day when the weather started to change and Zena began worrying about where the kids would go to school.

'The hell with that,' Harry told her. 'For this year anyway. Won't kill 'em to miss school one year. Mollie's too young in any case, and you can give Nick and Kate some lessons. You never went to school, you told me so yourself.'

'But I had a governess, Harry. And real teachers who came to the house.'

'Sweetheart, trust me. As soon as we're in the big time the kids'll go to a special school for people who are on the stage.

The kind that makes allowances for their rehearsal and performing time. But right now we have to improvise.'

'All right, I guess missing a few months of school won't kill them. But where are we going to live, Harry? How are we going to survive? There aren't any fairs in the winter.'

'Not here in the north there aren't. That's why we're going south.'

They got all the way to Texas that first year. Then they worked their way back east and played a lot of the same fairs and carnivals they'd appeared in the previous summer, as well as a few new ones. Life was a long series of bus rides; sometimes whizzing along black ribbon highways, at others jouncing on dirt roads with washboard hills and valleys that, as Harry said, 'shook your back teeth'. The only constants were dust and little cafes and roadside diners, and the intervals of being on stage and making the crowd clap. Until the spring of 1925 when the bookings dried up.

'Folks like to see something new, Mr Pride. They've seen you and your wife and the kids for two years running. Have to give 'em something new if we're going to keep 'em happy.'

It was Nick who solved the problem, at least indirectly. The boy had always had an insatiable curiosity about the world around him. His dark eyes constantly observed and he seldom forgot what he saw. Now that he was fourteen he'd also taken to reading the newspapers left lying around in the various boarding houses where they stayed. Harry Pride never bought a paper, and if he happened to glance at one he turned immediately to the entertainment pages. If it weren't for Nick, Harry would have missed the long, thoughtful article about the craze for marathon dancing.

'It says here it's sweeping the country. Packing in the crowds,' Nick said without lifting his eyes from the *Atlanta Journal.*

They were at breakfast in a boarding house which looked like a hundred others they'd been in. Harry poured himself another cup of coffee. It was cold and he made a face, but kept drinking it. 'So what else is new; that's been going on for a couple of years now. Bound to die out pretty soon.'

'No, Uncle Harry, it's bigger than ever. Honest, this guy says so. He says it's got so they have to provide entertain-

67

ment for the times when the marathon dancers are resting. Otherwise the crowds will riot or something.'

'You don't say? Here, let me see that.' Harry had only to read a few lines to see that salvation had arrived. The Fabulous Pride Family couldn't compete in the marathons, the contests were far too strenuous, but they sure as hell could qualify as a filler act. That morning their new career was born, and as part of his grand strategy Harry switched Mollie from singing to dancing.

Mollie was going on five now and it was no longer such a wonder that she could open her mouth and belt out a number. Particularly since she couldn't carry a tune. Mollie had rhythm and stage presence and as much personality as it was possible to cram into one small body, but she really couldn't sing. What had been forgivable in a baby, false notes and flats, wasn't acceptable in a little girl. So they taught Mollie to do the Charleston. And she was terrific. Even better than she'd been as a precocious singer.

Harry got four new costumes. Zena and the two girls would be flappers and he'd wear a blazer and a straw hat, but he kept Nick in top hat and tails. 'Nick's the maestro, it's up to him to give the act a little class.'

The truth of the matter was that for all his song-writing and the fact that he'd long ago taught himself to read music, Harry couldn't play half as well as Nick. And once the kid's voice broke he was a better announcer as well. Harry was smart enough to know that their survival depended upon using every possible asset. Not even he really believed any longer in two a day at the Palace or easy street. Not until May of 1926 when the telegram from the lawyer came to say that Joe Driscoll was dead and his will was to be read in Rhinebeck the following Tuesday.

Thompkins's office was in a red brick building on the main street, above a place called Slater's Dry Goods Store. The store had a display of ladies' nightgowns in its window. They were all in thin cotton batiste and had lace trimming and satin ribbons at the neck. Kate and Mollie pressed their noses to the glass and looked. 'Come along, children,' Zena said.

'After we're rich can we come here and each get one of

these?' Mollie was thinking of the flannel nightgown she wore every night. It had turned grey with countless washings and it had neither lace nor ribbon trim.

'Yeah,' Nick chimed in, 'and look at those silk ties, Uncle Harry. That blue one's swell.'

Zena wanted to shout at them that they weren't going to be rich, that Harry had been filling their heads with useless tales since the telegram came. Everyone knew her father had lost all his money years before. But she couldn't bear to squelch their enthusiasm. 'We'll see,' she murmured.

Harry didn't say anything. For once he was the most nervous member of the group. He kept buttoning and unbuttoning the jacket of his tweed suit, and wishing the trousers weren't so shiny. Now he buttoned it one last time and squared his shoulders and led his family to the door beside which was a brass plaque that said LOUIS THOMPKINS, ATTORNEY AT LAW. SECOND FLOOR.

A secretary sat at a desk in the front office. 'Good afternoon, may I help you?'

'I'm Harry Pride, this is my wife Zena. Zena Driscoll Pride.'

'Oh yes, Mr Thompkins is expecting you. Please sit down and I'll tell him you've arrived.'

Harry and Zena and the children sat on the straight-backed wooden chairs provided. There were only four of them so Nick took Mollie on his lap. In a moment the secretary returned. 'Mr Thompkins will see you now, Mrs Pride.'

Zena and Harry stood up.

'I'm afraid only Mrs Pride is a beneficiary, sir. Mr Thompkins wishes to see your wife alone.'

Harry opened his mouth to protest, but his tongue was too thick and dry to allow the words to form. He sat down again after giving Zena one encouraging pat on the arm. She stood quite still for a moment, then followed the secretary into the inner office.

'How do you do, Mrs Pride.' The man who rose behind the desk and held out his hand was quite elderly, not surprising since he'd been papa's attorney for years. 'Permit me to offer my condolences on the death of your father.'

69

Zena shook his hand. 'Thank you,' she murmured as she took the seat he indicated. There was a moment's silence while the lawyer shuffled some papers on his desk. 'Mr Thompkins,' she blurted out. 'How on earth did you find me? I hadn't been in touch with papa for years.'

'Yes, I know.' Thompkins was entirely bald except for a fringe of white hair that circled his head like a halo. He wore thick glasses that kept slipping down his long, pointed nose. Now he pushed them up and gazed at her. 'As you'll see, your father had made himself aware of your fortunes and whereabouts since you returned to America and married Mr Pride. This was among his papers.' He passed a manilla envelope across the desk.

The envelope contained clippings from a variety of small town newspapers announcing the appearance of the Fabulous Pride Family at one or another fair or carnival. Zena thumbed through them. 'There's nothing here about the marathons, we're almost never written up as the filler act at the marathons.'

'No, I know that. Mr Driscoll was quite agitated when the clipping bureau he employed to check all the newspapers had no further news of you. He asked me to engage a private detective.'

Zena's blue eyes opened very wide. 'A detective? Papa hired a detective to spy on us?'

Thompkins cleared his throat. 'It wasn't exactly spying, was it? He simply wanted to know where you were.'

'But why? And how could papa afford all this ... this surveillance? I understood he was penniless.'

'Yes, it seemed best if everyone believed that. The litigants were quite merciless in their demands those first few years.'

'Are you telling me that my father had some money left after all?'

'No point in denying it now,' the lawyer said. 'The will makes a number of things clear. Mr Driscoll did manage to secure some assets against the onslaught. It wasn't easy, he had to be most circumspect, but ...' He let the sentence trail away and shrugged.

Zena's heart began to beat wildly. Harry had been right after all! They were going to be rich. She would live again the way she hadn't lived since Sebastian was killed, the children could have the best of everything, just the way she had. No, better than she'd ever had. They could go to the best schools and have parties and friends.

Mr Thompkins must have read her thoughts in her face. 'I think I'd best get on with reading you the will, Mrs Pride. Mr Driscoll has it all spelled out.' He didn't meet her eyes.

'Yes, of course. Please do.'

A few more clearings of the throat and shuffling of papers, then he began. 'I, Joseph Driscoll, being of sound mind and of my own volition ...' The legalities droned on for a while, then he got to the important part. 'My daughter Zena has always been a great disappointment to me, moreover she has seen fit to align herself with a ne'er-do-well of no social standing whatever, and has lumbered herself with two little girls and a boy who is blood relative neither to her nor her husband. Despite all this I am inclined to remember her in this my last will and testament for the sake of her dear departed mother, whom I truly loved regardless of the brief time of our union. I therefore instruct that my daughter, Zena Driscoll Bennet-Swan Pride, is to live in Hillhaven, my home in Red Hook, with her family, and endeavour to give the three children for whom she is responsible some sort of a decent upbringing. It is absolutely against my wishes that she sell Hillhaven, as I know that if she does the worthless man to whom she is married will squander the capital generated thereby. I therefore place the ownership of the house in a trust, with the understanding that it is to be used by my daughter for the duration of her life.'

Mr Thompkins stopped reading and looked up. 'Do you understand, madam?'

'The house is mine but I can't sell it.'

'That's correct, and strictly speaking it isn't yours. It is an asset of the trust your father has created. After your death the trustees may sell it.'

Zena nodded. She wasn't sure of all the ramifications, but she had the broad outlines of the legacy fairly clear. She also understood the extent of her father's venom: it came through the words of the dry document quite clearly. But she still had left a small particle of the hope which had been born a few minutes before. 'Is that all, Mr Thompkins?'

'As concerns you, yes, it is. Everything else goes to charity. As will the proceeds from the sale of Hillhaven after your ... Whenever it's sold.' He dropped his eyes.

'What charity?' Zena asked.

'A fund for the care of old horses.' Thompkins mumbled the words.

'I see.' Zena began drawing on her gloves. 'May I ask one more question? Just how much did papa leave to the old horses?'

'Well, not counting the house, the estate is worth some half a million dollars.'

Zena had risen, now she had to drop back into the chair. She felt as if someone had punched her in the belly. Papa had salvaged half a million dollars from the wreckage he'd made of his life and hers. And he'd kept himself aware of what she was doing, how she was doing. So he'd always known how close to the bone things were, how much they needed ...

'Are you all right, Mrs Pride?'

The old lawyer knew she was not all right and he knew why. They were just polite words. Zena summoned all her strength and what she could muster of dignity. 'Yes, thank you, I'm fine.' She rose and walked out of the office, thinking about how she would explain things to Harry and the children.

Zena and Harry stood in the middle of the drawing room at Hillhaven. They could hear the voices of Kate and Nick and Mollie as they explored upstairs, but the light laughter of the girls and even Nick's resonant tones were muffled by the thick velvet draperies, the tapestry hangings, the oriental carpets, and the plethora of overstuffed furniture which crowded every corner.

'Jesus,' Harry murmured. He ran his hands over the back of a brocaded sofa, then picked up a heavy crystal vase and a silver ashtray. He held the objects, one in each hand, testing their weight and nodded. 'Unpack one of the suitcases, honey. Right away.'

Zena wasn't following his train of thought. 'Harry, how

72

much money do we have?' She knew he'd borrowed fifteen dollars from the manager of the Crescent Gardens Ballroom so they'd be able to make the journey to Rhinebeck, but not how much the bus fares had been. Mr Thompkins had driven them here, so at least there had been no need for a taxi to drain their resources further.

'A couple of bucks,' he answered offhandedly. 'Don't worry, it'll be enough.'

'Enough for what?' she demanded. 'In God's name, Harry, how are we going to get back to civilization and survive until we find another job?'

'We're not going any place. At least you and the kids aren't.' He put down the vase and the ashtray and went to Zena and put his hands on her shoulders. 'Honey, it's going to be fine, great in fact. I'm going down to New York and get us enough money to live for as long as we need.'

She still didn't understand. 'How?'

'I'm going to hock as much of this junk as I can stuff into a suitcase, that's how. We'll have the last word on your old man yet, sweetheart. Trust me. We're going to be on ...'

'Don't say it,' Zena interrupted. 'I can't bear to hear you talk about easy street one more time.'

Mollie came in just then. 'This place is super,' she announced. 'You have to show us which was your room, mummy. Me and Kate are going to sleep there.'

Zena stared at her daughter's innocent face. Mollie of the big brown eyes and the turned-up nose and the pudgy cheeks, little Mollie the bundle of dynamite, wanted to put herself in the prison that had held her mother for sixteen years. 'Third door on the left upstairs, that was my room,' Zena whispered. 'But you don't have to sleep there, darling,' she added anxiously. 'You and Kate can sleep wherever you want. Just for tonight, until we leave.'

'Leave?' Mollie was incredulous. 'But why are we going to leave. 'Isn't this easy street?'

'Here they are! Right on time.' Harry threw open the double doors at the side of the house where deliveries had always been made. 'Come this way, fellas. The piano is going in the front parlour.'

Three men manoeuvred the baby grand through the house into the drawing room and uncrated it. 'Sign here,' one of them said. Harry signed and added the date, 12 August 1926. He had affixed his name to a large number of such slips since they'd arrived in Red Hook in May. Harry had discovered the magic of instalment purchases.

He had brought back nearly a hundred dollars from his first foray into Manhattan with as many of the gew-gaws of Hillhaven as he could fit into a suitcase. 'Hocked every damned one of 'em,' he'd told Zena proudly. 'And when this is gone I'll do it again. Can't imagine when we'll come to the end of the stuff in this place.'

'Won't the trustees find out?' The trust was administered by the local bank, and Zena imagined that the old men who were the trustees kept a constant baleful eye on her.

'Don't see how they can. And if they do, what difference does it make? What are they going to do, throw us out of this mausoleum? Who cares?'

Zena had no answers to those questions, so she stood by and let Harry arrange everything. She understood his frequent trips to New York City, but not exactly what he was doing when he went to Rhinebeck and Poughkeepsie. Until a series of delivery vans arrived bringing a gramophone, one of the new electric refrigerators, a vacuum cleaner, a washing machine with a wringer on the top, new clothes for all of them, and finally this enormous piano. 'Little easy payments,' Harry explained. 'Soon as I tell 'em where we live they let me have anything I want and we only gotta pay a fiver or so a month.'

'On each purchase,' Zena said, rapidly doing sums in her head. 'We have to pay five dollars a month on each of the things you've brought. That will come to ... I don't know, but it's a lot.'

'Doesn't matter, sweetheart. I'll just go see Mr Rothman the pawnbroker and get more whenever we need it.' Harry turned away from her and looked out to where Nick and the girls were sitting under a poplar tree on the front lawn. He crossed to the window and opened it. 'Nick, hey come in here a minute, fella.'

Nick got up and came toward the house. A moment later

he joined his aunt and uncle in the drawing room. 'You want me, Uncle Harry?'

'Yeah. I changed my mind about where the piano is going. I think it should be on that wall over there. But we'll have to rearrange the rest of the furniture to make room.' Harry was rolling up the sleeves of his new white shirt as he spoke. Nick took off the linen blazer he was wearing and began rolling up his sleeves as well. A few days before Harry had bought the boy his first pair of long pants, not counting his stage costume. Three pairs actually. And a couple of jackets, and six shirts made of imported English broadcloth which cost a dollar forty-nine each.

'You look great, kid,' Harry commented as they prepared themselves to move furniture. 'Doesn't he look great, honey?'

'Yes,' Zena agreed. 'He does. You're very handsome, Nick.' It was true. And she felt a certain pride when she looked at him. Whatever her initial reluctance to take on the responsibility of Nicholas Frane, Zena now thought of him as her own son. 'Maybe you both ought to wait until after lunch to do this job. And change into your old clothes.'

'No need,' Harry said. 'Nothing to it, it'll only take a few minutes.'

Actually it took seven. Seven minutes of that hot and humid summer morning went by while Harry and Nick tugged and pulled the heavy sofas and chairs over the carpeted floor. Then they got to the piano itself. The very first effort they made to heave that across the room resulted in Harry Pride screaming once in pain, convulsively clutching his chest, and dropping dead of a heart attack.

There was a period of some twenty-four hours after they buried Harry Pride in the churchyard on the hill at the top of Red Hook's main street when the three children had to fend entirely for themselves. Zena disappeared into the big bedroom she had shared with her husband.

As usual it was Nick who took over. He made pancakes for their supper on the evening of the day after the funeral. Kate set the pine table in the kitchen where once Joe Driscoll's servants had eaten and where his grandchildren were accustomed to taking all their meals, while Mollie sat on a tall stool in the corner and watched the preparations. 'Get the milk,' Kate told her finally. 'The blue pitcher in the refrigerator.'

For Mollie it wasn't so much sadness as silence, it was as if there had been a constant hum in her life which had suddenly stopped. She went to the big white enamel appliance with its circular topknot housing the fan coils and took out the pitcher of milk. 'Do you think it's extra quiet?' she asked.

'What? The refrigerator?' Kate had a literal turn of mind. Things had to be exactly what they seemed, ideas too.

Mollie shook her head. 'No, not the refrigerator.' She didn't know how to explain what she meant because she couldn't quite understand it.

'I know,' Nick said softly. 'You mean it's quiet since Uncle Harry's gone.'

'Yeah.'

'Oh, I see,' Kate murmured, taking her place at the table and staring into space, examining the idea Mollie had introduced. 'He was sort of noisy I guess,' she pronounced finally.

'That's not what Mollie means. Here, sit down, little pest.' He often called her that, but it was okay, Mollie knew he didn't really think she was a pest. Nick patted the chair beside him and Mollie took it. 'I think I know what she does mean,' he said finally. 'She means that Uncle Harry was like a song in our lives and now the music has stopped and it's sort of as if you can still hear it, but you know you can't.'

Mollie nodded solemnly. 'That's it,' she whispered. 'You're just hearing it inside your head, not really.'

'But it never was real music that you heard outside your head,' Kate insisted. 'You said "sort of like a song in our lives", Nick. That's not real, anyway.'

Nick and Mollie looked at each other. There were many times when it seemed as if they understood each other far better than Kate could understand either of them. 'It's okay, Katykins,' Nick said finally. 'Forget it, eat your pancakes before they get cold.'

'Is there enough for me?' Zena emerged from the shadows of the hall into the warm yellow light of the kitchen.

Nick jumped up. 'Sure there is, Auntie Zena. There's

plenty of batter left. Take mine, I'll make some more.'

'Thank you, Nick.' Zena accepted the gracious offer and sat down between her daughters, but she didn't lift her fork. Instead she took hold of the girls' hands. 'Listen, my darlings, I'm sorry I just sort of collapsed on you. I needed to have my cry,' she added frankly. 'And get used to the idea that daddy's gone.'

'Mollie says it's like a song that has stopped.' Kate volunteered that not so much in admiration of her sister's poetic gift as in hopes that Zena might explain it.

'Did she? That's a lovely way to put it, Mollie darling. But we're going to go on singing even without daddy. The four of us.' She looked up to where Nick was flipping pancakes on the cast-iron griddle of Hillhaven's enormous stove. 'You're the man of the family now, Nick. And I know you're going to do splendidly.'

'Yes ma'am,' he murmured. He hadn't called her ma'am in years. It wasn't a retreat to the old shyness, just an acknowledgement of the title she had given him.

Zena nodded. 'Yes. I had a good long cry and I thought it over and I realized that nothing is going to bring daddy back, so we have to roll up our sleeves and learn to manage without him. And as long as we have each other we're going to do just fine.'

The best thing that ever happened to Zena Driscoll was marrying those two unsuitable husbands. Each gave her a daughter, and Harry gave her Nick as well; the children provided her with a reason for living. And since neither man was cut out to make her happy ever after, it was just as well that both conveniently died. She'd figured it out upstairs. Now she was hoping she could find the name and address of the pawnbroker among Harry's yet-to-be-sorted personal effects.

5

Mollie skipped along beside Zena, holding her hand. She had no memory of living in New York, they had left to take their act on the road when she was barely three, and Manhattan's noisy crowded streets delighted her. 'I bet Nick and Kate are going to be jealous when I tell them what *I* saw.'

The older children had been deposited at the Roxy Theater on this bitterly cold January day. They were going to see Douglas Fairbanks in *The Thief of Baghdad.* It was rare for Zena to spend money on such a treat, but she didn't want to take Nick and Kate to the pawnbrokers. Six-year-old Mollie she deemed too young to be damaged by the degrading ordeal, and she needed at least one of them along to encourage Mr Rothman to be generous. He'd never done as well for her as he did for Harry, and when she'd come just before Christmas, he had given her only seventeen dollars for an entire suitcase full of things.

Today Zena wasn't carrying a suitcase; she had a painting wrapped in brown paper under her arm. When they arrived at the store on Eighth Avenue she paused a moment, looked at the huge cluster of gold balls hanging over the door, read the sign which said BROKE – CALL ON UNCLE, and took a deep breath; then she shepherded Mollie inside.

Mr Rothman was in the back, talking to another man. Zena pulled the paper off her painting, set it on the counter, and waited her turn. Mollie waited beside her, examining the variety of silver candlesticks and gold cigarette cases in the glass showcase. 'You got a lot of stuff in here, mister,' she commented when Mr Rothman appeared.

'I suppose I have. Good afternoon, Mrs Pride. Is this your little girl?'

'Yes, my youngest. Say how do you do to the gentleman, Mollie.'

The child knew her cue, the years doing the act had trained her well. She bobbed a curtsey and gave the pawnbroker her widest grin. 'How do you do, thir.' Her two front teeth were missing, which might have accounted for the lisp, but in reality Mollie put it on because she knew grown-ups found it adorable.

'I do fine, and I hope you're likewise.' Mr Rothman smiled at the child. 'She's pretty as a little picture, Mrs Pride. You must be very proud of her.'

'I am, Mr Rothman. And speaking of pictures, what can you give me for this?'

The man had been aware of the painting on the counter while they spoke, he'd merely waited for the customer to mention it. Now he picked it up and held it to the light and made sounds under his breath. 'Hmm, hah, hmm ...' The picture was a hunting scene, four men on horseback in front of a stable with a pack of dogs at their feet. It was in a heavy gilt frame. 'For the frame,' the pawnbroker said finally, 'nine dollars.'

'Nine dollars, is that all? But what about the picture?'

'The picture I'll roll up and you can take it home. It's worthless, Mrs Pride. A copy only. I'm sorry.'

'But nine dollars ...' Her bills at the various stores in Poughkeepsie and Rhinebeck came to a little over forty dollars a month. And that was before she'd bought food or replaced the shoes the children were always outgrowing. Worse, there was a telephone at Hillhaven. It wasn't only another bill to pay, it meant that people could hound her for money without even coming to the door. Zena looked at her daughter. 'Mollie, go over there and look at that wooden Indian. I wish to speak privately with Mr Rothman.'

Mollie wandered over to a life-sized carved figure standing near the back of the store. The Indian was painted in vivid reds and greens and menaced her with a tomahawk, but the colours were flaking off and the thing was so obviously fake she didn't find it scary. She pretended to be examining it, but she was listening to her mother and Mr Rothman.

'I simply must have more than nine dollars,' Zena was

saying, her voice tinged with panic. 'Please, Mr Rothman. If you can just see your way clear to giving me a little more today, I'll bring a lot more vases and trays and things next week. A whole suitcase full.'

'Vases I ain't interested in. Already I got a packed show-case from your husband. Trays maybe, if they're silver. Precious metals, Mrs Pride. That's what I can make substantial loans on, precious metals. Ain't you got any silverware in that big house of yours?'

Zena shook her head. The first week they moved in Harry had turned the place upside down looking for silver and gold. But the elaborate things Zena remembered from her girlhood were nowhere to be found. She and Harry had decided that Joe must have sold them years before, as part of the effort to consolidate what was left of his fortune. So he could leave half a million dollars to a charity for old horses and finally tell his daughter what he really thought of her.

'There's nothing like that, I'm sorry.' For some reason Zena felt as if she owed Mr Rothman an apology. 'There are three very pretty trays, however,' she added brightly. 'They're tin with flowers painted on them.'

'Tolewear ain't popular nowadays. Look, I don't like refusing you, but I got a business to run. Kids of my own, and grandchildren too. What do you say, Mrs Pride, you want the nine dollars for the frame?'

Zena nodded miserably.

Before they left, Mr Rothman gave Mollie a sea shell with a picture of Coney Island painted inside.

Zena hurried Mollie out of the store, but she paused before heading uptown toward the Roxy. A large placard stood on the sidewalk in front of an imposing-looking granite faced building. CHILDREN WANTED TO AUDITION FOR NEW RADIO SHOW, it announced. Zena read it carefully, then took another of the long deep breaths which heralded so many of her decisions in these difficult days.

'Come along, Mollie, we have to meet Kate and Nick.'

'What's the little one do?' The man conducting the audition ignored Kate and Nick and fixed his gaze on Mollie. Panic rose in Zena's throat. Kate had already sung *Someone to*

80

Watch Over Me and Nick had played a spirited medley of ragtime. The man who had introduced himself as Ben Porter had shown little enthusiasm for either performance. 'She dances,' Zena whispered.

Porter shrugged. 'That's not going to do us much good. This is radio, lady. Nobody can see her dance.'

Mollie jumped out of the chair. 'I can sing too.'

Kate and Nick both suppressed groans. Zena closed her eyes. Mollie was aware of her family's reactions, but she ignored them, and she didn't wait for an invitation. 'You cannot make your shimmy shake on tea ...' She belted forth the lyric of the song Irving Berlin had written the year before prohibition became law, while wriggling her meaty little body, and she threw in a few Charleston steps for good measure.

Porter leaned on his desk and put his chin in his hand and watched her. He let her get all the way through the number, then he said. 'You got it wrong, kid. You can't sing.'

Mollie put her hands on her hips. 'I can too. I started singing on the stage when I was three years old.'

'Mollie,' Zena whispered. 'Please, darling ...'

'Well, it's true, isn't it?' The little girl turned to her mother, brown eyes blazing. 'Didn't I sing on the stage until daddy decided I should dance?'

'Yes, but ...'

'She's a terrific dancer,' Nick piped up. 'Maybe somebody could sort of explain what she was doing while she did it. Since it's radio, I mean.'

'I could sing while Mollie just kind of moved her mouth.' That was Kate's contribution, though it was hard to see what her suggestion was going to achieve.

Porter listened to the four of them talking at once for a moment. Then he bellowed, 'Shut up! Pipe down all of you.' He turned to the little girl with the bouncy brown curls and the blazing temper. 'Tell me again, what's your name, kid?'

'Mollie Pride. I'm billed as Little Miss Magic Mollie Pride. Nick introduces me.'

'Oh, he does, does he. And how old did you say you were, Little Miss Magic whatever?'

'Ten,' Mollie lied instantly.

'She'll be seven in June,' Zena said at the same moment.

Porter had come out from behind his desk by this time. Now he grabbed Mollie by the collar of her blue and white sailor dress. 'Don't you ever lie to me, you smart-mouthed brat. You do and I'll put you over my knee and spank you good and proper. Anybody ever do that before?'

'Nobody better try,' Mollie hurled back.

'Oh yeah? Well I will, I promise you.'

Zena knew she had to do something. The audition was going disastrously wrong. It was becoming a test of wills between this Mr Porter and Mollie, and Zena knew that her youngest daughter absolutely never backed down. 'Mr Porter, please. Mollie has a most unladylike temper. I'm sorry, it's the way we raised her, I'm afraid. Entirely my fault and my late husband's. But if you could just listen to Nicholas and Kate one more time, I'm sure . . .'

'I don't have to hear any of 'em again,' Porter said, quite calm now. 'The only one we can use is this little stick of dynamite here.'

'Mollie? But she can't . . .'

'She can't sing,' Porter supplied. 'Don't worry, I got ears. But with that personality and that trumpet voice she doesn't have to. I'll write a skit for me and her to do together. A funny bit. We'll call her Baby Brat. The audience is gonna' love her. Take my word for it.'

As recently as 1919, listeners to radio had been a handful of fanatics in earphones who struggled to hear something on their crystal sets. They thought of themselves as pioneers, but those avid hobbyists were already well behind the times. In 1906 a man named Lee De Forest had invented the triode, a vacuum tube containing three electrodes. The triode was a signal amplifier — De Forest had made it possible for the airwaves to carry clear sound of every type.

Nobody paid a great deal of attention until 1920, when station KDKA in Pittsburgh announced the returns of the Harding-Cox presidential election. This modest triumph led KDKA into transmitting regularly scheduled broadcasts of news, church services, and music. By the time Ben Porter auditioned Mollie Pride there were over five hundred stations on the air, many of them broadcasting coast to coast. The most popular show using children was WCBS's *Capitol Family Hour,* a programme hosted by a man known as Major Bowes. That winter of 1927 *Grandpa Ben's Family* was the riposte planned by station WATL.

'What'd you do today, Little Brat? Were you a good girl like you promised last time?' Porter would intone in a honeyed voice of grandfatherly benevolence.

'I really was, grandpa. I thought about pouring a bottle of ink in ma's new washing machine, but I didn't do it.'

'You didn't? That's wonderful! You keep up that way and we're gonna have to start calling you Miss Mollie, not Little Brat.'

'Oh goody! I want everyone to call me Miss Mollie. That's why today I only tied the cat's tail in one knot, not three like last time.'

'Come here, you little brat,' Porter shouted into the microphone. Behind him a man stepped up and delivered a series of open-handed slaps to a pillow.

'Waaa ...' Mollie wailed convincingly. 'Waaa, waaa, waaa! I'll be good, I promise! Don't spank me anymore, Grandpa Ben.'

Audiences loved the skits. Mollie even got fan mail from mischievously-minded listeners suggesting new pranks for her to play. More to the point, she earned six dollars a week.

The show was broadcast on Saturday evenings from seven to seven-thirty. Mollie had to be at the studio by five. That's when Porter would give her the script he'd written during the week. She had until six to learn her lines, then they rehearsed for about half an hour. After that she just hung around until they went on the air. Nick hung around with her.

Zena wouldn't have dreamed of allowing Mollie to make the weekly trip from Red Hook to New York alone. During the first month of broadcasts she accompanied her daughter on the three-hour bus journey to the city, waited at the studio until the programme was over, then took Mollie home on the last bus which left the station at nine. It meant they didn't get back until the early hours of Sunday morning. It was exhausting and it cost two dollars and twenty-five cents. It would have been more but for the fact that Mollie could travel on the half-price ticket available to children under fourteen.

Nick had turned sixteen the previous Christmas Day, but he was on the short side and he still had a boyish face and no trace of a beard. Only his deeply resonant voice made him sound older. If he kept his mouth shut he could easily pass for fourteen. So he could travel for seventy-five cents, not the dollar and a half Zena had to pay. 'Just let Mollie do all the talking,' she admonished the boy the last Saturday in February when she sent him to New York with her daughter.

'Nothing new about that,' he said sullenly. 'She does anyway.' Nick knew the money was important and he'd never have refused to go, but he hated having to put on short trousers and a sweater and a cap like a kid. 'What if somebody from school sees me?' he demanded. He was a sophomore at the local high school; Zena had enrolled all three children in schools as soon as they moved to Hillhaven.

'Why should anybody from your school be going to New York on a Saturday afternoon? Nobody will see you.'

'Don't worry, Nick,' Mollie chimed in. 'You can close your eyes. Tell you what, you can be my blind, deaf and dumb brother. Nobody's gonna' guess nothing.'

'Anything,' he corrected. 'You can't use a double negative in a sentence. Besides, what's that going to solve? If I'm blind it only means I can't see other folks, not that they can't see me.'

Mollie pursed her lips and thought about that for a while. 'What's a double negative?' she asked. Safer ground.

'Two "no" words, they make a yes.'

'No, no means yes? I don't get it.'

Nick had become very conscious of Mollie's ignorance. This was the first time in her life she'd attended a real school, and though she was six she'd had to go into the first grade with mostly five-year-olds. She was learning to read fast enough, but she still used the bad grammar she had picked up from the carny folks and dance hall people she'd been around all her life. 'Look,' he said, controlling his exasperation, 'I'm going to read to you on these bus trips. Books that will improve your mind.'

Mollie thought for a moment, 'Yeah, I guess you could be

fourteen and do that. But you'd better not be blind, some-body might figure something was fishy.'

The Saturday trips to New York were more fun once spring came and the days lengthened. They got to the city while the sun still shone, and even after Mollie finished learning her lines and rehearsing with Ben Porter there was some daylight left. Often Nick took her out for a walk to pass the time until the show went on.

She was looking forward to that break on the first Saturday in June. On the bus Nick read to her from a book called *Tales from Shakespeare*. It was supposed to be for kids, but she thought it was silly. All that guy Hamlet had to do was make up his mind and there wouldn't have been any trouble. She forgot about it when they got to Thirtieth and Broadway. There was a man on the street demonstrating little toy wind-up dogs that barked and danced. She wanted to stay and watch, but Nick said they couldn't. 'We'll come down again later and see if he's still here,' he promised.

They were getting ready to go after Mollie finished rehearsing, but Porter reappeared. He was with another man whom they'd never met. 'There they are,' Porter said. 'That's the kid I told you about.'

Mollie waited to see what this new man would demand of her, but it was Nick he addressed. 'I'm Jack Ellis, general manager of the station. Ben here tells me you can play the piano, son.'

'Yeah, I can,' Nick said warily. He had a thrilling vision of getting a job and being able to bring Auntie Zena a little extra money, but he didn't want to get his hopes up. Life with Harry Pride had taught him a lot about letting your dreams carry you away. 'I play pretty good,' he added.

'So I hear. Can you read music?'

Nick's heart sank. 'No, I can't. I play by ear.'

Mr Ellis frowned. 'Hard to see how that's going to help any.'

'Try me.' Nick's voice betrayed his eagerness. 'I know just about everything that's ever been written.'

Ellis smiled. 'Maybe. But what we need isn't a regular song. The pianist who normally does the theme music for the shows this evening just got run over by a car. We need someone who can play our themes. We've got the sheet music, but if you can't read it ...'

Nick looked around for a piano. There wasn't one out here in the hall, but there was a spinet in the studio where Mollie usually rehearsed. He'd seen it plenty of times. 'I know the music for *Grandpa Ben's Family*. Let's go in there and I'll show you.'

The two men led Nick into the rehearsal room, Mollie trailed along behind. Nick sat down and ran his fingers over the keys for a moment, then played the music which introduced Porter's show.

'That's great,' Ellis said. 'But we've also got the *Nabisco Half Hour* and *Tales from Other Lands* tonight. You don't know those by any chance?'

Nick shook his head. He was on the bus with Mollie while the remainder of the station's Saturday night schedule was broadcast, he'd never heard the programmes. 'Can you hum the tunes?' he asked.

'Well, yeah, I guess so.' Ellis hummed a few bars. Nick moved his fingers over the keys, made two false starts, then got it. 'Hey, you're pretty fast at that,' Ellis said. 'Maybe you really can help us out.'

They began rehearsing in earnest.

Mollie listened for a while, then she got bored. It was the same thing over and over, they wanted to be sure Nick would remember the melodies. She wandered out the door and no one paid her the least attention.

She intended to go downstairs and see if the man with the wind-up dancing dogs was still in the street, and she reclaimed the sweater she'd left in the hall and began pulling it on. A woman and a young boy were sitting there now, they must have arrived while she and Nick were in the rehearsal studio. They seemed a little odd to Mollie, she'd never seen anyone who looked quite the way they did. She carefully avoided meeting their eyes while she buttoned her sweater. Then she started for the door.

'Little girl,' the woman said softly, 'are you going out all by yourself? Where's your mother?'

'Home,' Mollie mumbled, still not looking at the woman.

'She doesn't come to the show.'

'Are you all alone then?'

'No, I'm with my brother Nick. He's in there rehearsing.' Mollie jerked her head toward the studio.

'Don't you think you'd better wait until he's finished before you go?' the woman said gently.

Mollie shrugged. 'It's okay, I go out plenty of times by myself.'

'Not in New York City you don't.' Nick's voice broke in, he'd realized she'd left the studio and come looking for her. 'You just sit down there and wait until it's time to go on. Come on, Mollie, behave. I have to rehearse these numbers. I can't do it if I'm worried about you.'

Mollie gave him the full benefit of her sunniest smile, 'Okay, okay. Keep your powder dry, Nick. I'll park the petutie right here and not budge. Promise.' Referring to her rear end as a petutie to be parked was something she'd learned on the carnival circuit. She demonstrated by sitting down and folding her hands in saintly calm.

Nick shook his head, smiled apologetically at the woman and the boy, and disappeared back into the studio.

The woman was staring at Mollie in a mixture of fascination and disbelief. The boy was less reserved. 'What's a petutie?'

'Your rear end. Your hindquarters.' Mollie watched him, he still looked blank. 'Your bum.' No reaction. 'Your ass, for God's sake! Don't you speak English?'

The woman gasped, but the boy just grinned. 'Sure I do, but not like you I guess.' He put out his hand. 'My name's Lee Mitsuno. What's yours?'

'Mollie Pride. I'm Little Brat on the *Grandpa Ben* show.'

'Oh, I see,' the woman murmured softly.

'Are you his mother?' Mollie said turning to her.

'Yes. Lee is going to play tonight. He's a guest on the *Nabisco Half Hour.*'

'Hey, that's terrific. What do you play, Lee?'

The boy lifted a long black case Mollie had yet to notice. 'The flute. I'm eleven. I'm a child prodigy.'

'Terrific,' she said again. 'So am I.'

Nick appeared just then. 'Ten minutes to air time,' he told Mollie. 'Meanwhile I have to find a telephone. If I don't call

87

home and say we can't make the nine o'clock bus your mother's going to worry herself sick.'

He returned in a few minutes looking glum. 'We've got a big problem. Auntie Zena says there's no bus after nine p.m. Not until tomorrow morning.'

'Does that mean you're not going to play for the other shows?'

'I don't know.' Nick was trying desperately to think of a solution. 'I have to do it, Mollie,' he murmured. 'They're going to pay me ten dollars for the night. Besides, if I let them down now maybe they'll get mad and fire you from *Grandpa Ben*.'

Mrs Mitsuno cleared her throat. 'Excuse me, but your sister said ...' she hesitated. 'She is your sister, isn't she?'

'Yeah, I am,' Mollie said.

'Shut up,' Nick told her. 'Just shut up for once, will you? We're cousins. But we live together.'

'Oh, I see. My name is Grace Mitsuno, this is my son, Lee. Is your problem simply a place for the two of you to sleep tonight?'

Nick nodded. 'Yes, ma'am. We live up in Red Hook, near Rhinebeck.'

Grace Mitsuno smiled. 'Well, we live here in the city. Our apartment is small, but you and Mollie could sleep in the living room. If your aunt would approve, of course. I could speak to her if you like.'

Nick's smile lit his whole face. 'Gee, that's really kind. It would be wonderful. That is if you're sure we wouldn't be any trouble.'

'No trouble at all.'

It was not until they were on the bus the next morning that Mollie got a chance to ask about Mrs Mitsuno and her son Lee, and the strange neighbourhood they'd found themselves in when they woke up that morning. 'They're chinks,' Nick explained. 'Chinese. They live in Chinatown. I never knew Chinese people could be so nice,' he added. 'Even if they do eat rice for breakfast.'

'But how can they be Chinese? They talk the same as we do, like Americans.'

'They are Americans. They're from San Francisco in

California. Mrs Mitsuno told me. She said her grandfather came to America seventy-five years ago, to work on the railroad.'

Mollie nodded, content with the explanation. 'Good, if they're American I can invite them to our house for my birthday next week.'

Grace Mitsuno and her son couldn't come to Red Hook for Mollie's birthday, but Zena asked them for the Fourth of July and they agreed to come then.

'We'll have a party,' Zena promised the children. 'A real party with cake and ice cream. And afterwards we can walk down to the village and see the fireworks.'

Lately Zena was feeling very expansive, even happy. She would never actually say aloud that Harry's death was a relief, but she knew it was. She had loved him in her way, but Harry Pride created chaos just by breathing, and Zena was made for calm and placid days without challenges — not to mention bill collectors.

Things were much better financially now. The washing machine and the vacuum cleaner and the refrigerator had been repossessed, so she didn't have to keep paying on them. Zena was glad to be rid of them. She could manage five dollars a month for the piano, and that was the one thing they all truly enjoyed. Better still, Nick was working steadily as well as Mollie. The radio station had hired another piano player, but they gave him Saturday nights off and Nick filled in for him. The two children were bringing in sixteen dollars a week, so she could afford a party. It was the least she could do as a thank-you to Mrs Mitsuno and Lee, considering that Mollie and Nick slept at their house every Saturday night.

'I've never actually met any Chinese people before,' Zena admitted to Grace while the two of them sat in the overgrown gardens of Hillhaven eating ice cream on the Fourth of July.

'And how do you find us?' Grace asked with a tolerant smile.

'Just like everybody else,' Zena admitted.

The Chinese woman stopped smiling. 'Yes, I suppose I am. But not my son.'

'Lee seems a perfectly charming young man to me,' Zena said quickly.

'I hope he is, and he's very talented. It's not that. My husband was Japanese, you see. Lee is half Chinese and half Japanese.'

Zena couldn't see what that had to do with anything. Surely there was little difference between one kind of Oriental and another. But the question of Lee's father puzzled her. 'The children have never mentioned Mr Mitsuno,' she murmured. 'Is he ...'

'Dead? No, at least I don't think so. He couldn't stand the shame of having a Chinese wife,' she said softly. 'It meant that he wasn't accepted by his people or mine. He left soon after Lee was born.'

Zena nodded sympathetically. Struggling to bring up a child alone was something she understood very well. 'Do you have family in New York to help you?'

'No, both my husband and I are from San Francisco. I hardly know a soul in New York.'

'But how do you manage?'

'I've been lucky. I was able to get a job in a restaurant. And sometimes I give Mah Jong lessons. And of course now that Lee is playing on the radio, things are much easier.'

'Mah Jong!' Zena said enthusiastically. 'I've always wanted to learn how to play.'

The ancient Chinese tile game had swept the country in the past few years. Like marathon dancing it was a veritable craze, and Grace was not surprised by Zena's reaction. 'Perhaps some day I can teach you.' She turned and smiled at her hostess. 'Considering the way our children get along, I think we'll be seeing more of each other.'

Zena followed her guest's glance. The youngsters were sitting by the cracked ruins of a stone fountain which long ago Joe Driscoll had brought over from Italy. They were all laughing, Nick Frane and Kate Bennet and Mollie Pride and Lee Mitsuno — laughing and laughing and obviously having a wonderful time.

6

It would be Mollie's sixteenth birthday on 10 June 1936. 'Sweet sixteen,' Zena said the week before. 'We must have a party.'

Mollie did not want a party, at least not the sort her mother envisioned. Zena imagined that both her daughters had somehow sloughed off the oddities of their upbringing and become typical American young ladies. She had only a vague idea of what a typical American young lady should be; but whatever the phrase meant, it was what she wanted for her girls.

'You can invite all your friends from high school,' she said on the afternoon she began planning Mollie's party. 'And I'll make some nice little sandwiches. You know, the ones without crusts. I can use cream cheese and colour it pink with beet juice. I read about that in *Ladies' Home Journal.* And we can have fresh strawberries and I'll order a pink cake from the bakery. With your name written on it.' No echo remained in her mind of Sebastian's parties, or the kind of blow-outs they'd sometimes seen among the carny folk. She'd been determined to forget all that and she had. Genteel, normal — Zena was determined to be both these things for the sake of her girls.

'Mom, I don't want a party.'

'But why not? You're young, Mollie. You should have a good time. I never did. When I was your age I was married to Kate's father.'

'No party,' Mollie said again. 'I think cream cheese with beet juice sounds vile, and I don't have any friends to invite.'

'Of course you do, dear. All the girls you go to school with.'

'The girls I go to school with are silly fools. And they think

91

'I'm stuck-up because I'm on the radio.'

Mollie hadn't played Little Brat since she was ten, but she'd never stopped working. These days she was the voice on a variety of commercials that told ladies to Lux their undies every night, or how Rinso would get their clothes whiter than white, or that Borden's cheese was made from contented cows. The transition from performer to huckster had come about easily, because she'd developed an excellent delivery as she grew older. She had a unique voice, a combination of velvety softness and crystal clarity which came over the airwaves as nothing short of fabulous. Besides, Nick was assistant general manager for WATL, as well as reading the news at weekends. His connections ensured that Mollie was never out of work.

Zena felt somewhat guilty about her daughter's radio career. It certainly made her different from the other girls in Red Hook, but without it they'd not have survived. Not even after 1933, when twenty-two-year-old Nick landed his really good job and moved to New York, and began sending Zena fifteen dollars a week. That was a lot in these depression days, but Mollie's contribution remained vital. Besides, not being on radio hadn't helped Kate in the least.

Kate was the one who really worried Zena. She was twenty-one years old and achingly lovely. That had happened almost overnight, around five years ago when Kate was the same age Mollie was now. It seemed as if they'd gone to bed one evening and Kate had been the slightly gawky, pale and pretty girl she'd always been — and woke to find that she'd turned into a beauty. She was five foot eight inches tall with long shapely legs and a handspan waist. Every part of her was perfectly proportioned, her hips, her bust, even her graceful tapering hands. And as if that were not enough, Kate had the face of a madonna painted by some Renaissance genius, a perfect oval with slightly slanted grey eyes and lashes so long they shadowed her cheeks. Her nose was short and straight and her mouth a vivid rose-pink flower. Atop all these glories was a tumble of ash-blonde hair that nearly reached her waist when she brushed it out, though most days she wore it twisted into braids wound round her head.

Kate had a job too, which was very fortunate in 1936 when so many were out of work. She was a clerk in Slater's Dry Goods Store, the very place where she and Mollie had pressed their noses to the window and admired the night-gowns on the day they first came here.

Kate rose each morning at six and took the seven-fifteen bus to Rhinebeck. She didn't get home until seven-thirty, and she did this six days out of seven and was paid twelve dollars and fifty cents a week. It seemed to Zena like not much of a life. She didn't see how Kate was going to meet some nice young man and get married. Almost the only customers who came into Slater's were women. And Kate was painfully timid, she never asserted herself.

'A party would be nice for Kate, too,' Zena told Mollie now. 'Your birthday's on a Sunday this year. It's perfect.'

Mollie softened. 'Okay, tell you what. We'll have a party, but just for the family. I don't want anybody from school.'

'But some new faces would be so good for you, darling.' She'd been hoping that a school chum of Mollie's might have an older brother for Kate.

'They're not new faces. As you've just said, I go to school with them every day.' They were sitting on the screened porch and the lilacs were in bloom and filled the air with scent. Mollie reached up and picked one, burying her face in it, then looked up at her mother.

Zena knew that, unlike Kate, Mollie was not a great beauty, but looking at her youngest daughter gave her just as much pleasure as marvelling at the perfection of her eldest. Mollie was the same height as Zena herself, five foot three, and she had her mother's figure, small but meaty, with lots of curves. She had Harry's dark eyes, brown with little flecks of gold, and now, in the sunlight, there were golden highlights in her brown curls as well.

Mollie saw her mother studying her, she knew from the expression of indulgent love on Zena's face that she'd already won the argument. 'We'll do it my way, okay? Since it's Sunday Nick can come up from the city.'

'You're sure that's the way you want it?'

'I'm sure.'

'Very well. It's your birthday, darling, I want you to have

93

exactly what you want. And I imagine you mean me to invite Grace and Lee as well.'

'Of course, I said the family.'

'Yes, so you did.'

Zena quite liked Grace Mitsuno and her half-Chinese-half-Japanese son. And, like Mollie, after ten years of friendship she thought of them as family. But Lee was certainly not a prospect for either Kate or Mollie. Lately she was more and more concerned about finding eligible young men for her daughters; what was there for a young woman to look forward to if not marriage?

'Hello there, birthday girl, you're looking great.' Nick strode across the lawn toward Zena and Mollie and Kate who were sitting on the grass with Grace Mitsuno.

Soon after his seventeenth birthday Nick had put on a burst of late growth. At twenty-five he was no longer short and slight, he was five foot ten and had the kind of broad, square build people called husky. The man with him was entirely different, tall and slim. Nick moved with purpose and direction, as if he always knew where he was going. The stranger following him sort of ambled along with the air of a guy who might have lost his way, but was nonetheless enjoying the trip.

'This is Steve Rogers, and it's his fault we're late. We drove up in his Olds and had a flat tyre.' Nick leaned over and kissed his aunt's cheek, then he kissed Grace and Kate in a similar fashion. But when he got to Mollie he held out his arms. 'Come on, birthday girl. A big hug in honour of the occasion. Sweet sixteen and never been kissed.'

Mollie moved into his embrace, but it was a slightly mechanical greeting. She was looking over Nick's shoulder at the red-headed man still standing on the fringe of the little group. 'Aren't you going to introduce your friend?'

'I thought I did. His name's Steve Rogers, he's a canuck from Montreal.'

The redhead grinned. 'Watch it, fella. Them's fighting words.' It was obvious he wasn't really offended.

'It's okay,' Nick said. 'He's gone straight, left the frozen northland and become an engineer at the station.' He turned from Mollie to his friend. 'Steve, this is my Aunt Zena, and Grace Mitsuno who's honorary family, except the honour is ours. And that gorgeous creature is Kate, and this not so gorgeous one is Mollie. She can't help it, she was born ugly.'

The man from Montreal shook everyone's hand.

'Where's Lee?' Nick asked.

'Gone inside to get more lemonade,' Zena answered, but she wasn't paying attention to Nick, she was watching Steve Rogers stare at Kate. It was quite obvious that he was stunned by her. And Kate was smiling at him. Zena did not turn her head away from that satisfying vignette, so she didn't see Mollie's reaction.

It wasn't that he was at least six feet tall, nor that he had curly red hair and electric blue eyes that crinkled at the corners. It wasn't even his dark tan, so striking against the white summer shirt he wore tieless and open at the neck. It was his smile. What knocked Mollie out, committed her irrevocably in those first five minutes, was that when Steve Rogers smiled he filled the world, at least her world. Mollie heard a hum, a dimly remembered buzz. Like before daddy died, she realized at once. As if life were magic and you never could be sure what was going to happen next. She'd stood up to greet Nick, now she had to sink back to the blanket spread on the grass, because if she didn't she might fall down.

Lee arrived carrying a large pitcher of lemonade. 'Hello, who's this?'

Nick took the lemonade from Lee while he introduced the Canadian. 'We're roommates as of last Wednesday,' he added. 'Steve found a terrific furnished apartment on West Sixtieth Street. It's a sublet, but the rent's more than either of us could swing on our own, so we decided to take it together and split the costs.'

Lee shook Steve's hand and nodded. He wasn't really interested in Nick's living arrangements. He was studying Mollie and Kate as they reacted to the newcomer.

'Nick tells me you're a musician with the New York Philharmonic,' Steve said.

Lee finally looked at the man next to him. 'Gave you

plenty of warning about the peculiar Orientals you were going to meet, did he?'

Mollie was watching the interchange. Steve's eyes narrowed. She saw them turn cold and hard. 'Not exactly,' Steve said softly. 'He was explaining about his family and his friends. Perfectly natural.'

Lee shrugged and turned away.

'Lemonade for everybody,' Nick said loudly. 'And in honour of the occasion we've brought something to juice it up a bit.' He produced a bottle of champagne and opened it with a flourish and a loud bang and poured a little into everyone's glass. 'I propose a toast,' he said finally. 'To the birthday girl. To Mollie.'

'And to happy times, to all of us here together,' Zena added. 'Welcome to Hillhaven, Mr Rogers. I hope you'll come again.'

'I will, ma'am, you can be sure of it. Thanks for asking me.'

They drank. Zena produced sandwiches. Mollie had made her give up the notion of pink cream cheese, so she'd settled for ham. There was coleslaw as well, and potato salad, and birthday cake and ice cream. They ate and talked and laughed and the sun shone, and looking at them from afar it would have been hard to find a flaw in this small manifestation of the American dream.

Eventually Mollie manoeuvred herself into a private conversation with Steve. 'How come I've never met you at the station?'

'I've only been there a couple of months, and so far I guess we've always been in different studios. But don't worry, I always wash my clothes in Rinso and I only eat Borden's cheese. Haven't tried Luxing my undies yet.'

She flushed. 'They're pretty silly commercials.'

'Don't apologize, it's what pays the bills. We wouldn't have jobs in the fastest growing business in America if it weren't for the sponsors.' He smiled at her, that incredible earth-shaking smile, and turned to Kate, drawing her toward them with his voice. 'What do you do, Kate? Nick says you're not on the radio.'

'No, I'm a clerk in a store in Rhinebeck.' She said it

simply, as if it didn't occur to her that selling dry goods was less glamorous than advertising soap and cheese on the radio.

'Lucky store, lucky customers,' Steve said.

Don't look at her like that, look at me, Mollie wanted to shout. She didn't, of course. But she made up her mind then and there that she wasn't giving up without a fight.

Steve took Zena at her word. All that summer he kept turning up at Hillhaven without warning. He worked erratic hours, something common in radio, and since he had an automobile he wasn't dependent on the buses or trains. Steve could drive to Red Hook whenever his schedule allowed, but the journey took over three hours by car, so usually he arrived in the early evening and spent the night. Many times he'd drive Kate to work the following morning, then continue on to Manhattan.

'Can I hitch a ride into New York with you tomorrow?' Mollie asked on a Thursday evening in late September.

'Sure, if you like. But what about school? I have to leave first thing in the morning, got to be at work by noon. I can drop Kate in Rhinebeck, but I'll need to go straight into the city.'

'That's okay. I'm skipping school tomorrow.'

Steve cocked his head. 'That doesn't sound like such a good idea. Does your mother know?'

'Of course. Stop trying to sound like my grandfather. I'm sixteen, you're twenty-two. That doesn't make you the guardian of my morals.'

'What morals? Nick's told me all about you, little brat.' He picked up a small pillow and tossed it at her. Mollie tossed it back.

'Nick's got a big mouth. But ...' She broke off and smiled.

'But what?'

'Nothing. You'll see.'

Whatever her secret may have been, Steve immediately lost interest in it because Kate came into the room.

In the morning Zena gave them all breakfast and made a special point of kissing Mollie goodbye just before they left. 'You're sure this is the right thing to do, darling?'

'Very sure,' Mollie told her. She picked up the small suitcase waiting by the door. 'Stop worrying, we talked it over, remember?'

Zena nodded.

'What's in that suitcase and what are you doing that's worrying mother?' Kate asked in the car.

'Mind your own business, and I'm not worrying mom. She knows exactly what I'm doing.'

'Which is?'

Mollie shook her head. 'You'll see.' It was what she'd said the night before.

Kate was in the front seat, beside Steve, and he obviously didn't want a discussion of Mollie's plans to occupy all their time together. He distracted her with jokes. Kate laughed appreciatively, her head bent close to his. Mollie didn't mind a great deal. They'd be in Rhinebeck in a short time, then she'd move up front and have Steve to herself for the rest of the wonderfully long drive. Right now, while he was pre-occupied with Kate, she could think about Nick. If her plan worked it was Nick who would be the biggest problem. She could convince Zena of anything, Nicholas Frane was a much tougher nut to crack.

They got to Slater's and Steve parked, jumped out, and ran around to the passenger side and opened the door. Kate stepped on to the running board and descended gracefully into the street. She didn't walk, she floated. Like a damned queen, Mollie thought. Oh well, Kate didn't mean anything by it, she just naturally moved with regal bearing. Something to do with being the granddaughter of an English lord, even though she'd never heard a word from him in all these years.

Mollie watched Kate give Steve her hand and wondered if she expected him to kiss it. He kissed her cheek instead, a light, brotherly peck, but Mollie could tell from Kate's re-action that it wasn't the first one. Neither of them were paying any attention to her. Mollie let herself out of the car and took the seat her sister had vacated.

Steve walked to the door of the store with Kate and they shared a moment's animated conversation which Mollie couldn't hear, then Kate waved to her and went inside. Steve was frowning when he got behind the wheel. 'I'm not sure I understand your sister.'

'What's to understand? Kate's exactly what she seems. Beautiful, but not a lot going on between the ears.'

Steve cocked an eyebrow and looked at her. 'Aren't we catty this morning. I thought you two got along perfectly. That's what Nick says.'

'Nick doesn't know everything, he just thinks he does.'

Steve concentrated on moving the car from the kerb into the street. They drove for nearly twenty minutes in silence. 'You going to tell me what's behind your mysterious trip into the big bad city?' he asked finally.

'No, because you'll tell Nick.'

'Aha, the plot thickens, as they say.'

'If that's what they say, they're pretty corny.' She bit her lip. That sounded as if she were criticizing him. God knows she didn't intend to, how could she when he was perfect? 'I didn't mean that the way it sounded. I'd love to talk to you about it, but you'll have to swear not to mention it to Nick. I want to tell him myself.'

'Your mother knows what you're doing, right?'

'That's right, she does.'

'And the suitcase doesn't mean you're running away from home?'

'Don't be silly, of course I'm not.'

'Okay, then I guess I can promise not to tell whatever it is to Nick before you do.'

'I'm reading for a part.'

'Another commercial?'

'No, a real part.'

'I'm not sure I understand. What show? What about school?'

She just didn't dare go further. It was as if she'd be jinxing her whole plan. 'You'll see, that's all I'm going to say for now.'

Steve had called radio the fastest growing business in the country. Whether or not he was statistically orrect, it was certainly the most popular. The nation was addicted to the entertainment which flooded the airwaves.

In the earliest days of the medium stations were independent, but soon Capitol Radio evolved into CBS and National into NBC. Within a decade the two networks had become powerful forces; it no longer mattered if it was Hoboken, New Jersey or Anaheim, California, the same programmes issued from the big wooden box. It occupied a place of honour in most American living rooms, and offered a chance to escape hard times. Factory closures and crop failures and dust storms and soup kitchens, the whole sorry mess could be forgotten when you laughed and cried with larger-than-life heroes apparently oblivious to the Depression.

Many of the most popular shows were weekly events. Sunday nights between seven and nine meant Jack Benny and Phil Harris and the ventriloquist Edgar Bergen with his dummy, Charlie McCarthy. For those who wanted to stay up late, *Phil Spitalny's All-Girl Orchestra* came on at ten.

On Wednesday nights at eight CBS aired a variety show called *Cavalcade of America*, and at nine NBC presented *Town Hall Tonight* with Fred Allen, whose comic feud with Benny was legendary. On Thursday evenings NBC had *Mr Keen, Tracer of Lost Persons* followed by the crooner Rudy Vallee, but CBS captured the biggest audience with the lady billed as America's favourite songbird. The orchestra played her theme song, *When the Moon Comes Over the Mountain*, and some sixteen million fans waited breathlessly for Kate Smith's cheery, 'Hello everybody!'

But for sheer audience loyalty no weekly show could compare with a comic duo who broadcast nightly at seven on NBC. Amos and Andy were played by two white actors who wrote and presented their own material in an exaggerated 'black' voice. The word racist was in the vocabulary of only a tiny minority. Every evening from seven to seven-fifteen the nation's telephone use dropped fifty per cent, huge numbers of cars were stolen because the streets were empty, and movie theatres shut down their projectors and piped in the programme. Even President Roosevelt was said to be a devoted fan.

The airways were almost never silent. From morning until late afternoon, serial dramas — called soap operas because most were sponsored by soap companies and, like opera, had plots which stumbled from crisis to crisis — followed each other in rapid succession. *Our Gal Sunday, Portia Faces*

Life, and *The Romance of Helen Trent* were every house-wife's best friend. Nor were the kids neglected. In the late afternoon Ovaltine brought them *Little Orphan Annie,* and Wheaties introduced them to *Jack Armstrong, the All American Boy.* Another fifteen-minute slot was filled by Tom Mix, the cowboy who made his reputation in the movies and now broadcast daily at quarter past five.

'Reach for the sky! Lawbreakers always lose, Straight Shooters always win! It pays to shoot straight!' Mix leaned into the mike and delivered the lines that thrilled his young listeners. Mollie sat cross-legged in the studio and watched.

In tonight's episode the cowboy had been shot and knifed, but he'd survived. Now he was bringing the bad guys to justice. 'Here they are, sheriff, signed, sealed and delivered.' The show's engineer produced the sounds of neighing horses and hooves galloping off into the distance.

Mix moved away from the mike and looked at Mollie. She'd heard he had an eye for the ladies, and the way he was studying her legs convinced her it was true. Mollie uncrossed them and tugged down her skirt. The star grinned. 'Don't forget, kids,' the announcer was saying. 'Just send in a nickel and two Ralston box-tops and we'll send you your very own Decoder Badge, just like the one Tom Mix wears ...'

A few seconds more while poverty-stricken America was milked for the few cents it might be able to spare, then the red light which meant they were on the air turned green. Mix came over to where Mollie was sitting. 'What's your name, sunshine?'

'Mollie Pride.'

'And what are you doing here, pretty Mollie Pride? You related to one of these bozos?' It wasn't unusual for a member of the cast or crew to allow a relative to witness a broadcast first hand.

Mollie shook her head. She'd left the house that morning in a white blouse and button-front blue wool skirt and brown and white saddle shoes, now she was wearing a red gabardine dress with white collar and cuffs and high-heeled black pumps with a strap across the instep. Courtesy of the suitcase she'd carried with her. 'I'm hoping to be Ginger, Mr Mix.'

'Ginger? I don't get it.'

The show's producer had joined them. 'You remember, Tom, we talked about putting a girl in the show. Ginger who owns the local café.'

'Kids aren't interested in romance.'

'Not a girlfriend, just a girl.'

Mix grinned. 'Is there a difference?' He was married to his third wife and was working on squandering what remained of four million dollars; in private the Straight Shooter was not what his legion of hero-worshippers believed him to be.

'Sure there's a difference,' the producer insisted. 'This little lady is great, she'll be a terrific foil for you. Come on down the hall and listen to her read.'

Mollie's heart was thudding, not because of Tom Mix — she was too seasoned a performer for any try-out to make her nervous — but because if this worked she'd see Steve every day. If she got the part she was going to quit school and move to New York. Naturally Zena would allow her to live nowhere but with Nick. Who just happened to live with Steve. Mix had asked her a question, which Mollie hadn't heard because she'd been day-dreaming. 'Excuse me, I didn't get that.'

'I said how old are you, Mollie Pride.'

'I've been working since I was three,' she said instead of answering. 'I started in radio when I was six. With Ben Porter on WATL. I was Little Brat on *Grandpa Ben's Family*.'

The radio cowboy cocked his head. 'That was on about ten years ago. So if you were six then, you're sixteen now.'

She'd blown it. The producer knew her age because he'd seen her professional résumé, but he'd told her it would be best if the star thought she was a bit older. She'd been so anxious to impress she'd said the wrong thing. Now she could do nothing but nod.

'Jail bait,' Mix said decisively. 'No thanks.'

He walked out of the studio and left Mollie and the producer staring after him. 'Sorry, kid. I told you it wouldn't work if he knew your age.'

'I'm sorry. It was my fault.' She'd ruined everything. Mollie felt tears sting behind her eyes, but she blinked them away.

'Can you get home okay?'

'Yes. I'll be fine. I'm spending the night with my cousin Nick.'

'Okay, tell Frane I'm sorry you didn't get the part, but Mix has the final word about everything on the show. He's the star.'

'He's a lecherous old fraud,' Nick said when he heard the story. 'What the hell got into you, Mollie? How come you did dumb thing like that without discussing it with me?'

It was the first time she'd been to the apartment on West Sixtieth Street. Before this Nick had lived in a grubby furnished room in the twenties. This place boasted a book-lined living room, pictures on the wall, and furniture in elegant blond wood with pale blue upholstery. Classy surroundings, but there was a lot of junk strewn about. She didn't recognize any of it so it must be Steve's. He wasn't home.

Nick hadn't planned to be home either. He'd had a date with a blonde secretary from the station, but he'd cancelled it when Mollie telephone and asked if she could spend the night. She hadn't actually made the arrangement beforehand as she'd told the producer, but she'd known right along it was what she would do. It was a simple matter to telephone Nick at his office and her mother at home and set everything up. She'd expected to be here celebrating a triumph with Steve. Instead it was just she and Nick and she was bemoaning a disaster.

'I was good as Ginger, I really was.' Mollie pressed a handkerchief to her eyes and blew her nose.

'I don't doubt that. But you're a kid, you don't know what men are like. You've got to finish school, Mollie, get a diploma. Maybe even go to college.'

'Don't be stupid,' she said through her sobs. 'I'm not going to college. I'm a performer. What's college going to teach me about that? Or high school, for that matter.'

Nick reached over and took her hand. 'Listen, some day you're going to be a much better wife and mother if you have an education.'

It was on the tip of her tongue to tell him that she had already fallen in love. Confiding in Nick came naturally

103

because she'd been doing it all her life. 'Listen,' she began. Then the door opened.

'Hello, what have we here? You didn't tell me you were coming to our place, Mollie.'

Just the sight of him made her feel weak. 'I wanted to surprise you.' She had to whisper the words, her throat had suddenly gone dry and her tongue became thick. Usually she could hide her feelings when Steve was around, but tonight she was already riding an emotional roller coaster.

Nick glanced from his cousin to his friend, then back again. His dark eyes became darker still. He was trying to think of something to say when the telephone rang.

It was Zena. She'd called because she couldn't wait to tell them the news. Kate was engaged to be married.

His name was Armando de Cuentas and he was tall and slim and dark and handsome and came from South America, though he spoke with only a trace of an accent.

'But why didn't you tell us you were seeing him?' Zena asked plaintively after Armando paid his first visit to Hill-haven.

'I didn't know he was gong to ask me to marry him.' To Kate that seemed like an adequate explanation.

'Where did you meet him?' Nick had come up from New York to meet Kate's fiancé, now he was part of the attempt to understand what was happening.

'At the drugstore across from Slater's. I left my lunch on the bus, you see. So I went across to the drugstore and had a grilled cheese sandwich.'

Mollie shook her head. 'And Armando, what was he eating, peanut butter and jelly?' It was hard to imagine the suave gentlemen they'd just met choosing anything other than caviare or lobster. He'd only toyed with the creamed chicken on mashed potatoes which Zena had given him for Sunday lunch.

Kate drew her eyebrows together. 'I'm not sure I remember. I don't think he was eating anything.'

'Katykins,' Nick said gently. 'When did all this happen? How long ago?'

'During the summer, right after the Fourth of July. And

he's come back two or three times a week since then. To Rhinebeck I mean. He waits for my lunch hour and we go sit on the common and I eat my sandwich and we talk and feed the pigeons.'

'Jesus,' Mollie muttered.

'Bad language won't help, Mollie,' Zena said stiffly.

Mollie rose and stalked to the ice box and poured herself a glass of milk. 'I'm not sure anything will help, but do we want it to? Kate, do you want to marry this guy?'

'Oh yes, of course. That's why I got engaged to him.' Kate twisted the very large diamond ring she was wearing.

Mollie stared at it a moment, then turned away. 'Okay, then why are we all giving her such a bad time?'

Nick looked at Mollie and his dark eyes smouldered. 'That stinks. You're just saying it because it suits you if she's out of the running with Steve.'

'That's a rotten thing to say! Really rotten. Just because I think Kate's got a right to make up her own mind about who she marries, you make a remark like that.'

Zena shook her head in puzzlement. 'I don't understand. What does Nick mean? Steve's a friend, and Mollie is too young ...'

'Forget it,' Nick interrupted. 'I was out of line. And Mollie has a point. If Kate wants to marry this guy we should probably all butt out.' He turned to Kate. 'Just tell me one thing, honey. What does he do? I listened to everything he said here this afternoon, but I still don't understand how your Armando gets along.'

'He's in café society,' Kate said.

Nick sighed. 'That's just a name for a bunch of silly people who show up in the hot spots. A stupid name made up by the newspaper gossip columnists. You don't earn a living by boozing with the debs and swingers, Kate. That's what I want to know, how does he make his living?'

Kate was not entirely unaware of the puzzle. 'I think he has investments,' she said slowly. 'I don't really understand it, but he comes from a very wealthy family in Caracas. That's the capital of Venezuela.'

Nick still couldn't figure out what Armando de Cuentas had been doing in Michaelson's Pharmacy in Rhinebeck, but he looked at Kate's enormous diamond and her glowing, happy, gorgeous face, and decided there was little point in asking.

'Who giveth this woman to be wed?'

Kate's left arm rested lightly in Nick's. The sleeve of her lace gown came to a point on the back of her exquisite hand and her diamond ring winked in the morning sunlight streaming through the drawing room windows of Hillhaven. 'I do,' Nick said, releasing her.

Armando's face broke into a smile of pure pleasure as Kate took her place beside him. She turned to Mollie and handed her sister the bouquet of waxy white stephanotis and pale cream roses she carried, then Kate gave her groom one adoring glance before looking expectantly at the minister from the congregational church in Red Hook. He was the same one who had buried Harry ten years earlier and none of them had been near his church since then, but apparently they were still considered members of the flock. The minister had been quite gracious about coming today and performing the ceremony.

Mollie was Kate's only attendant. She wore a yellow taffeta gown with a low square neckline and what Zena called leg-of-mutton sleeves. The skirt was enormously full, it made swishing noises each time she moved, so she tried to stand very still. But she couldn't concentrate on the minister's words. She kept thinking that this whole thing was impossible. It was barely six weeks since Kate astonished them with her engagement to a stranger, then all of a sudden she was getting married.

There were only a small numbers of guests watching it happen. Grace Mitsuno was here, but Lee had said he couldn't come because the Philharmonic was rehearsing. Too bad about that, it didn't seem right for something this important to be happening and someone to be missing from the tiny group they considered family. But Mr and Mrs Slater from the dry goods store had come, so had a teacher Kate had known and liked in high school. And Steve, of course. Mollie thought she could feel his eyes boring into her back, but that was silly. He'd be watching Kate today, no one else.

'Do you, Armando, take Katherine to be your lawfully wedded wife?'

'I do.'

'Will you honour and cherish her and cleave only unto her until death you do part?'

'I will.' Armando's voice was quite firm, he didn't seem a bit nervous.

He'd damn well better remember about the cherishing part, Mollie thought. For the past month she'd been trying to form a definite idea of the man who was to be Kate's husband, her brother-in-law, but it wouldn't take shape. He was handsome, charming and apparently rich — he had to be judging from the expensive gifts he lavished on all of them. There'd been a diamond watch for Zena, a gold bracelet and earrings for her, an endless succession of jewellery and perfume and flowers for Kate, and even a pair of solid gold cufflinks for Nick.

It was where the money came from that still wasn't clear. It had to be Armando's family, because he obviously didn't have a job. But how had they made their money? Who were they? If they were so rich how come none of them had come to the wedding? The only representative of the de Cuentas clan, apart from Armando, was his best man, a guy called Miguel whom he'd introduced as a cousin. Which almost didn't count, because Miguel hadn't journeyed from Caracas to be here today, he'd been here right along. He was always with Armando. Kate said he'd been in the drugstore the day the pair met. Miguel drove Armando's new Packard and lit his cigarettes and ran errands for him. 'More like a flunkey than a cousin or a friend,' Mollie had said to Nick.

'My idea too,' he'd admitted when they talked about it the week before. 'And a damned ugly one, it's hard to imagine that Miguel and Armando are related.'

The cousin was a squat, powerfully built man with dark hair that grew low on his forehead, a protruding jaw and hands like two hams. 'Do you think they really are cousins?' Mollie had asked.

Nick had nodded. 'Near as I can find out, they are. Listen, kid, I think I better tell you, I've done some checking.'

'On Armando? What kind of checking?'

'Well I know he doesn't have a police record. And neither he nor Miguel are illegal immigrants, they've both got visas. And there's no previous wife lurking in Armando's past, at least none I can discover.'

'Boy, you really did the cops and robbers routine on him.'

'As far as I could. I figured I had to since Kate's so ...'

'So dumb,' Mollie supplied when Nick searched for a word.

'No, I don't think she is really. She just doesn't have a lot of imagination. I think that's why she always takes everything literally, sort of at face value. But as far as I can find out there's no reason she shouldn't marry de Cuentas if she wants to.'

'She wants to,' Mollie said. 'Boy, does she want to. Kate's head over heels about him.'

'Yeah, so we'd better just smile and be happy for her. She deserves all the support we can give.'

Nick's support had been demonstrated by paying for Kate's trousseau and her gown and Mollie's, and supplying a case of champagne for the reception. 'You can't afford all this,' Mollie had admonished him.

'No problem,' Nick assured her. 'I took a little loan from the bank. Just like your dad would have done if he were here.'

'Yeah, but you'll pay it back.'

Nick had grinned ruefully. 'Steady work and paying the bills weren't Uncle Harry's long suit.'

'Let's just hope they're Armando's. Katykins will fall apart if she has to go through what my mom went through.'

Oh God, she prayed now, let it be okay. Please, God. I know you don't know me very well, but you can't say I've been a pest, can you? So since I'm asking only this once, let it be okay.

Mollie came out of her reverie just as the minister pronounced them man and wife and it was time to help Kate throw her veil back from her radiantly beautiful face.

With so few guests at the wedding the case of champagne should have lasted longer than it did. It was still early in the unseasonably mild afternoon when Steve found Mollie on

108

the screened porch and held up what he said was the last bottle. 'You want another jolt of this before it's all gone?'

Mollie looked at him. Jesus, he was gorgeous. Even drunk. His red bow tie was undone and the jacket of his dark-blue pinstripe suit was unbuttoned, but he looked wonderful. She held out her empty glass. 'Who's been drinking it all, you?'

'Though I remain disgustingly sober, I did my share,' Steve admitted. 'But I had help.'

'Nick?'

'Hell no, he's like a zombie today, something about being up all last night. It's Armando's sidekick Miguel who seems to have a wooden leg.'

'Oh no! That's awful, Miguel is driving them to Niagara Falls. He can't be drunk.'

'Don't worry. Grace has him cornered in the kitchen and she's administering an old Chinese remedy. I think it's based on pouring black coffee down his gullet. Not that I'd care if Miguel and the Caracas cowboy finished up in a deep ditch somewhere.'

'Kate will be in the car too,' Mollie reminded him. 'She's upstairs changing right now.'

'Yeah, I know. That's the hard part.' He finished his drink and poured another. 'I'm trying to be a good loser, but I'm not sure I'm doing so hot.'

'You're doing fine.' She put down her glass. 'Steve, kiss me.'

He cocked his head and looked at her. 'And just how much champagne have you had, little brat?'

'Not that much.' About six glasses, which was five more than she'd ever had before, but there was no need to tell him so. 'Listen, remember the day we met?'

'Your birthday?'

'Yes. Nick said I was sweet sixteen and never been kissed. It's true. And I don't want it to be. So kiss me.'

'Well now,' he said softly, 'I never was one to refuse a favour to a lady. But if we're going to do it, let's do it right.'

Steve set his glass on a nearby table and took hers from her hand. Then he put his arms around her. That was enough to make Mollie's heart start thudding in that crazy way it did only when he was around. When his lips actually fastened on hers Mollie waited for the trumpets and the sirens and the bells. They didn't happen.

Steve tipped her head back and put a hand under her chin, raising her face to his. 'Relax. You're stiff as a board.' He traced her lips with one finger. 'Relax and let me really kiss you.'

It was something she'd wondered about for years, were you supposed to kiss with your mouth open or closed? Open apparently, she'd kept her lips tightly shut the first time and that hadn't pleased him. Now she parted them slightly. Oh God, he was flicking his tongue over them, doing the same thing with it that he'd just done with his finger. Oh God ...

He broke it off again. 'Give me your tongue, too,' he whispered. She wasn't sure she could do it, but she did. Because he told her to. Trumpets, Bells. Sirens. The whole thing. The way she'd dreamed it would be since the first moment she set eyes on him.

'Mollie, where are you, darling?' Zena's voice floated out to the porch.

They ended the embrace instantly but Steve looked at her for a long moment. It was a strange look, his eyes had gone smokey and she couldn't read the expression on his face. 'Better answer your mama,' he said finally.

'Coming.' She meant to call it out, but the first time Mollie only managed a whisper. 'Coming,' she repeated more forcefully and went back in the house.

'There you are, Mollie. Kate's coming downstairs now. I knew you'd want to be here to say goodbye. Take some rice. We're going to throw it when they go out to the car.'

The minister and the high school teacher had left earlier. The remaining guests congregated at the foot of the wide staircase. In a moment Kate appeared in a slate-blue wool suit and a tiny hat made entirely of grey feathers. The hat had a little veil which brushed the tip of her perfect nose, and she was carrying a silver fox jacket. The fur was Armando's wedding gift. Mollie had seen it that morning for the first time.

There were murmurs of appreciation as Kate descended the stairs. Mollie stole a quick look at Armando. He was grinning from ear to ear and his eyes glistened with pride. Be good to her, Mollie thought, be good to her or I'll personally slit your silly throat.

'Mollie.'

She looked up when her sister called her name. Kate had stopped half-way down the stairs. As soon as their eyes met Kate tossed her bouquet. Almost involuntarily Mollie reached up and caught it, and everyone laughed and applauded. She was suddenly intensely aware of Steve standing just behind her. As if his body radiated some secret heat that only she could feel.

They all went out to the big circular drive in front of the house. Miguel looked okay, the coffee had apparently worked. The newlyweds climbed into the back seat of the shiny black Packard. Someone had tied streamers and a 'Just Married' sign to the rear fender. 'Goodbye, good luck,' everyone cried. And they threw the handful of rice that Zena had distributed in little pleated paper cups.

The party broke up quickly once Kate and Armando had gone. Mr and Mrs Slater shook Zena's hand and congratulated her and left. She turned to Nick as soon as they were out of the door. 'You look terrible. Go on upstairs and get a few hours' sleep.'

'I think I will, but wake me by six. I have to be in the city tomorrow, so I'd better go back tonight.' He disappeared in the direction of his old room.

Mollie watched him go, wondering exactly what had kept him working all Friday night and required his presence o Sunday. When she turned to Steve to ask if he knew, he was gone. She saw him helping Grace into his car. Leaving, just like that. Without a word. After he'd kissed her the way he had. She felt like crying, the tears were actually about to start.

'Don't cry, darling,' Zena said softly, putting her arm around her youngest daughter. 'Just because she's married Kate isn't gone forever. You'll be married too some day. And before I know it you'll both be bringing my grandchildren here to visit. Nick too, I expect.'

'Yeah, sure.' Mollie wiped her eyes. 'C'mon, I'll help you clean up this mess.'

It was four o'clock before they finished and Zena went

upstairs and Mollie wandered out to the garden in the waning late autumn sunlight. It had turned chilly. She got as far as the old cracked fountain, then decided to go back and get a sweater. Might as well get out of her yellow gown, too. The ball was ended and she was going to turn back into scruffy old Cinderella any minute.

'Hi, I've been waiting for you.'

'Steve! What are you doing here?'

'I just said, waiting for you.'

'But you left, I saw you. With Grace. I figured you were driving her back to the city.'

He shook his head. 'Nope, only to the train station. Told her since tomorrow was Sunday I'd decided to finish the weekend up here in rural heaven.'

'Oh, I didn't realize.' She couldn't think of anything else to say.

'You look cold.'

She thought he meant to give her his jacket. It was still unbuttoned and now his tie had disappeared and the neck of his shirt was open. 'No, no, I'm fine,' she protested.

'You're not, you're shivering. Here, try some of this, guaranteed to warm you up.' He held out a bottle of Seagram's Rye Whiskey.

'Where did you get that?'

'Package store in Rhinebeck. Thank God for the twenty-first amendment and the end of prohibition. I bought this little taste of paradise right near the drugstore where beautiful Kate met her handsome Armando.'

'It's half empty. You've been drinking it.'

'That's usually what folks buy whiskey for, to drink. Here, have some. Haven't got a glass I'm afraid. But we're through being formal for today, aren't we?'

She nodded and took the bottle and held it to her lips. It was her first taste of whiskey. The only thing she'd drunk up to now was champagne, three times. Last Christmas at the station, on her birthday, and today. She took a bigger swallow of the rye than she meant to, because she'd never drunk from a bottle before. The whiskey burned her mouth and her throat and made her eyes water. Steve saw her reaction and chuckled.

112

'You're adorable, you know that? Nick told me what they used to call you, Little Miss Magic Mollie Pride. Said you could Charleston like nobody's business, almost before you could walk.'

Mollie wiped her eyes with the back of her hand. 'He's told you a lot, the big mouth.'

'Not enough.' He got up stood beside her and took the bottle from her hand, the way he'd taken away her glass a while ago on the porch. 'Not how good you taste, for instance.'

Then he was kissing her again. Quite a few times. And their bodies were pressed together and she wasn't cold any more. She was on fire. 'Listen,' Steve said when they came up for air after about fifteen minutes. 'I want to ask you something.'

'What?'

'Will you marry me?'

'I ... Do you mean it?;'

'Yes, I wouldn't say it otherwise.'

'But ... But you don't love me, you love Kate.'

'No, I thought I did. That was before I kissed you today. Marry me, Mollie.'

She hesitated for only the briefest second. 'Yes. Oh yes, of course I'll marry you, Steve darling. I love you so much.'

'I know you do.'

She put her head against his chest, feeling the reality of him, reminding herself this wasn't a dream. 'Mom and Nick aren't going to believe it,' she murmured. 'That you love me, I mean.'

'They will after we're married.'

'When's that going to be? We could have a Christmas wedding, what would you think of that?'

'I can't wait until Christmas. I want you now, Mollie. Today. Tonight.'

She tipped back her head and looked at him. His features were fading in the rapidly falling dusk, but she knew each line of his face by heart. 'I don't understand what you want me to do.'

'Just what I said, marry me. I want us to go out to my car right now and drive away and get married.'

'Elope?' She didn't actually say the word, she breathed it. Then breathed it forth a second time. 'Elope?'

'Yes, we can go up to New Hampshire and find a Justice of the Peace. Fourteen is legal marrying age in New Hampshire, and they give you a licence right away.'

She paused just long enough to write a note for her mother and Nick to find when they came downstairs. She said that she and Steve had decided to go away and get married and they'd be in touch in a short while. She didn't really think either Zena or Nick would have serious objections, they both liked Steve. All the same she was prudent enough not to mention New Hampshire.

7

The Monadnock Inn was slightly west of the little town of Jaffrey, barely over the state line in the southern part of New Hampshire, but fairly deep into New England.

They checked into the inn only because it was close by, but it had turned out to be a wonderful choice. The lady who ran the place, a Mrs O'Donald, was delighted to have two obvious honeymooners. 'Bet you just ran off and got married without a word to anyone,' she said, looking at Mollie's rumpled yellow taffeta gown.

When Mollie and Steve admitted that was just what they'd done she laughed and showed them to their room at once. 'Now you two don't pay any mind to anything. When you want something to eat I'll be downstairs.'

There was a moment after the door to the little room was closed behind them when Mollie was numb with terror. 'You don't have any more of that rye, do you?'

Steve shook his head. 'No, but anyway you don't need it, I'm not going to hurt you. There's nothing to be frightened of, my sweet Mollie. The whole thing's natural as hell.' He smiled and held out his arms. 'Come here.'

She went to him, and he sat down on the bed, pulled her on to his lap and kissed her quite a few times. And waited until she was as breathless and excited as she'd been in the garden at Hillhaven before he began unbuttoning the back of her gown. 'I have to tell you something,' she murmured agianst his cheek. 'I haven't the faintest idea what happens next. What I'm supposed to do, I mean.'

'Relax. As long as one of us knows what to do we'll manage fine.'

They did.

'The first time hurts a bit they tell me,' he whispered at an advanced stage of the proceedings, 'but I don't think it hurts bad.' And a few minutes later. 'Are you okay? Was it very painful?'

'No, not at all. Just sort of ... I guess peculiar is the word.'

He hooted with laughter and smacked her rump. 'Peculiar, eh? I'll give you peculiar.'

There was a bit of tickling after that, and nuzzling, and cuddling. Then he did again the thing he'd done earlier, and this time it wasn't peculiar at all. It was wonderful. And each time thereafter, three separate occasions by Mollie's count, it got better.

On Monday morning Steve went downstairs and asked if he could bring some toast and coffee to their bedroom on a tray.

'I'd a mind to do that myself,' Mrs O'Donald said. 'Got it all ready in the kitchen. You can take it up yourself, since you're here. And I looked out a few things of my daughter's. She's married now, lives up in Keene. But she's about your wife's size. I thought this skirt and sweater might tide Mrs Rogers over.'

Mollie tried on the outfit as soon as they'd eaten everything on the breakfast tray. 'Well, it looks a little strange with my yellow satin pumps, but it beats wearing a gown around all day.'

'I know something that looks better.'

'What?'

'You in the buff,' Steve said. 'Please, take the clothes off.' His voice was hoarse with passion. 'I want to see you over here by the window with the sunlight coming in. Just you, the way God made you.'

She wasn't embarrassed. Nothing they did together seemed anything but right and natural and as it should be. She removed the borrowed clothes and went naked into his arms and rejoiced in the obvious delight he took in her — and she in him. They skipped lunch and supper that day too.

'We should have started back a couple of hours ago,' Steve said when it was long past midnight and they had slept and woken and slept again. 'But since we didn't, let's get a little more sleep and push off at dawn.'

They woke when they heard the grandfather clock in Mrs

O'Donald's front hall chime five o'clock. Then they looked out of the window and saw it was snowing heavily and had been for hours.

Steve called the station in New York. 'The road's impassible. Yes, I know tomorrow's election day, but I just got married. Yes, that's what I said, married. To Nick Frane's cousin.'

Mollie took a step closer to the telephone that was hanging on the wall. It was the old-fashioned sort with a flared trumpet fixed in position. You had to shout into it while you held the stubby black receiver pressed to your ear. She had decided not to telephone her mother until they returned to New York, but she suddenly had an overwhelming desire to talk to Nick. 'Is Nick there?' she whispered. 'See if we can speak to him.'

Steve nodded. 'Let me talk with Frane,' he said as soon as whoever was on the other end had stopped shouting at him. 'Oh, okay, I see. Yes, I promise. I'll get underway the minute they have the streets ploughed.'

He looked puzzled when he hung up. 'That's funny.'

'What is? Why didn't you talk to Nick?'

'Because he's not there. That's what's funny. They say he quit. Walked out Monday morning without giving notice. The day before election day, no less.'

Mollie frowned. 'That's completely unlike Nick. He's so responsible it hurts. Steve, there has to be something wrong.'

'Maybe not. Anyway, we can't find out about it until we get back to civilization. And we can't do that until this damned snow stops.'

The snow didn't let up until Wednesday, but they knew what had happened to Nick before then. Late on Tuesday night they turned on the big wooden radio in Mrs O'Donald's front parlour so they could hear the election returns.

'We're not going to get WATL up here,' Steve muttered as he fiddled with the dial. 'But we're bound to get an NBC or CBS station. Hang on, I've got something.'

'This is WNAC in Boston, 820 on your dial,' a voice was saying. 'Tonight we're proud to tell our listeners that we've become part of the brand new Mutual Broadcasting System.

117

It's a union of independent stations, just as America is a union of independent states, so we're calling ourselves the Yankee Network, and right now, election night 1936, the Yankee Network News Service is on the air. Here's your commentator, Nicholas Frane. Over to you, Nick.'

'Good evening, ladies and gentlemen, welcome to what we hope is going to be the best news broadcasting in America. Now we're going to bring you up to date with what's happening during this critical moment in our nation's history.

'As you know, Alf Landon, the Republican candidate, and his running mate, Frank Knox of Illinois, have been bitterly critical of President Roosevelt's New Deal. F.D.R. and Garner have been telling the Democrats and the rest of the nation that they were running on their record. So this is pretty much a case of the country taking its temperature and deciding if it approves of what's been going on in Washington these past four years. Well, judging from the early returns we have in, it looks as if we Americans think things are going the way we want them to. Or at least as well as we think they can go ...'

'That's why he was so exhausted at Kate's wedding,' Mollie said. 'It's why he was up all Friday night and had to be in New York on Sunday. He must have been having meetings about this new network.'

'Looks that way.'

She grinned. 'You know what I think? I think it's terrific. They never really appreciated him at ATL. This is Nick's big chance. He's going to be wonderful, Steve. Don't you think he sounds wonderful?'

'Sure. The boy wonder is doing great.'

Mollie didn't hear the note of sarcasm. She had her ear pressed to the radio's speaker and was concentrating on every word Nick said.

During the long intervals when there was nothing new to report and when the well-known broadcaster Gabriel Heater wasn't talking to the various political experts who had been hired for the night, Nick described the scene at the studio itself. 'We've got a big board on the wall with the names of all the states and a large number of their individual precincts. About a dozen pageboys are constantly relaying information from the telephones outside our broadcast studio and marking it up on the chart ...'

Soon after midnight Mrs O'Donald appeared in the door to the sitting room. 'You folks listening to the election returns? How's Mr Lemke doing?'

Steve flashed his wide grin. 'Pretty bad from the sound of things so far. Might not carry a single state.'

The old woman looked at him. Her hair was tied in rag curlers and she was wrapped in a shapeless old chenille robe. She drew the robe closer to her body and stared at her paying guests. 'Guess you're not churchgoers or you wouldn't have eloped. So I suppose that means you're not supporters of dear Father Coughlin either. Well I don't mind telling you, I am.' With that she turned and left the room.

'What was that all about?' Mollie's puzzlement was total. 'Is there some Catholic priest running for president? How come she's mad at us all of a sudden?'

'The priest isn't on the ticket, but he's been the moving force behind Lemke and his Union party. Coughlin goes on NBC once a week and tells everybody who will listen that F.D.R.'s a commie, and Jews and reds are running the nation. I guess sweet old Mrs O'Donald listens.' He rumpled Mollie's tangle of curls. 'You really haven't a political idea in that pretty head, have you?'

She looked chagrined. 'No. Nick's always bawling me out for being such an imbecile.'

'The hell with Nick, I like you the way you are. Hold on, speaking of Nicky-boy, he sounds as if he's got something to tell us.'

They both pressed closer to the radio once more. In heightened tones of excitement Nick announced that Maine had now been conceded to Landon and the Republicans. 'Apparently the manager of President Roosevelt's campaign up in the pine tree state has thrown in the towel and gone home to bed. But for those of you who can keep awake, the night still has a long way to go.'

Mollie and Steve stayed with it. Mollie dozed a few times, her head in Steve's lap, but he kept listening until Nick announced that every state except Maine and Vermont had decided to give Roosevelt a second term. And that not one

119

had gone for Lemke and the Union Party.

She was sleeping again when the new network signed off the air. She woke when she felt Steve kissing her cheek. 'Time to get up, sweetheart.'

'Is it morning? Did Roosevelt win?'

He assured her the New Deal was safe. 'Time to get our stuff together and get ready to leave.'

'Yup. Nothing out there but birdsong and sunshine.'

The freak storm had blown itself out. The snowploughs had been working much of the night and the roads were clear. It was time to head back to New York.

'A new life,' Mollie murmured as they drove along a highway which passed between farms and fields blanketed in white and shimmering in golden sunlight. 'We're starting a whole new life, darling.'

Steve nodded and kept his eyes on the road.

'Oh, Mollie,' Nick said when they walked into the apartment on West Sixtieth Street at noon. He was sprawled in an armchair, a welter of newspapers scattered at his feet. He stood up and looked at her and repeated the words. 'Oh, Mollie.'

She studied his face, trying to come to grips with an almost overwhelming emotion which she hadn't expected and couldn't identify. 'Nick,' she whispered finally. 'Nick, it's okay, isn't it? You still love me?'

'Always have and always will, kid,' he muttered hoarsely, still not moving, still staring at her.

'Well, what do you say, old buddy? Aren't you going to congratulate me?' Steve's response to the charged atmosphere was to cross to the other man and take his hand and pump it heartily, as if Nick had been the one to get married.

Mollie knew instantly that whatever Nick felt towards her, he was furious with Steve. She saw his anger in the set of his square shoulders, the angle of his jaw. But then, she knew him as well as she knew herself. Steve did not. Her brand new husband was acting as if he did not recognize the rage just below the surface of Nick's calm. 'Well, come on,' he persisted. 'Say it. You're supposed to say, "Good luck, fella. You're a lucky guy." Something like that.'

'Am I?' Nick looked once more at Mollie. She was holding her breath, pleading silently with her eyes. He turned back to Steve. 'Okay,' he said softly. 'Congratulations.'

Mollie exhaled in a shivering sigh of relief.

Steve smiled and dropped Nick's hand. He took a step closer to Mollie. All at once she realized that he had know what was happening. The way he put his arm around her waist was a declaration of ownership. She felt a little like a prize that had been won, something special that two little boys wanted and only one could have — somehow it wasn't a nice feeling. 'One potato, two potato, three potato four,' she murmured. Steve glanced at her with a quizzical lift to his eyebrows, but Nick gave her a wry smile.

They held the pose for a moment, then Steve broke the tension. 'Have to get changed and out of here pronto. The station's doing somersaults because I got waylaid up in the wilds.' He took a step toward the door of his bedroom, then paused. 'By the way, we heard about your flight to greener pastures. I'm looking forward to the details as soon as we have a chance to talk. Meanwhile, keep an eye on the bride, will you?'

Nick waited until Steve disappeared into the bedroom, then turned to Mollie. 'You'd better call your mother right away. She's pretty upset. Telephone's over there on the desk.'

She nodded, not trusting herself to say anything and walked over and picked up the receiver. She waited a moment for the operator to come on, then she asked for long distance, gave the number and waited again for the connection to be made.

'Mom,' she said when at last Zena was on the line. 'Mom, it's me. We're back, that is we're in New York.'

She had to listen to Zena's tearful voice for a full minute before she got a chance to say anything else. Then she could only insist, 'It's okay, mom, really it is. I'm fine, we're very happy. Everything's going to be wonderful.'

There were more tears, more regrets and more assurances. At last she could hang up. Nick was still watching her. Mollie said the first thing that came into her head. 'She's going to pack my clothes in cartons and send them down by parcel post.'

121

'That's good.'

'Jesus! Stop staring at me, making me feel like a criminal. You heard me promise we'd go to Red Hook the minute Steve has a day off.'

'It was a terrific shock for her, Mollie.'

'But why? Kate got married to some clown we all hardly know, and that didn't throw her.'

'Kate's twenty-one.'

She waved her hand to dismiss the matter of age.

'Anyway it's done. I couldn't ask mom because she was too busy crying, but has anybody heard from Kate?'

'Not me. I don't know if she's been in touch with your mother. I doubt it, they're not due back from Niagara until the middle of next week.'

'Well, I think ...'

Steve came back into the living room. 'Don't think. I like my wives to be sweet and pretty and not think too much.'

'Hah! And how many have you had? Six? A dozen?'

She went to him and put her arms around his neck, and Steve hugged her and kissed her mouth with a loud smacking sound. 'Only one, but I know exactly what I want her to be.'

Mollie stayed in his arms a bit longer than was necessary for a casual goodbye. A small voice in her head said she was doing it because Nick was watching, because she wanted to demonstrate that she was an adult, a wife, that Steve loved her. The small voice added that it was a stupid way to behave, but she ignored it. It was her husband who finally broke the clinch, murmuring that he had to go.

Then they were alone again, Nick and Mollie. And all that unresolved emotion was still charging around in the atmosphere. At last Nick exploded. 'You crazy, unpredictable kid! Little Miss Magic ... Damn you, Mollie Pride, why the hell didn't you tell me what you were going to do before you did it?'

She was standing in the middle of the room, wearing the borrowed skirt and sweater and the ridiculously inappropriate yellow satin high heels, brown eyes smudged with tiredness, short curls in disarray, arms akimbo. All the defiance was gone, her only thought was to make things right with Nick.

'I didn't know he was going to ask me. Honest to God, Nick, I didn't have the least idea until he did it. Then I just thought about how much I loved him and how wonderful it was going to be to marry him. You know I wouldn't have done it without telling you first, if it had happened any other way.'

'Yes, I know.' He took a step towards her, then stopped. The intensity dissipated itself, burned out by its own power, and his realization that what she'd said earlier was the truth, the deed was done and nothing was going to change it. 'You look exhausted. I'll run a hot bath for you.'

'Okay, but I imagine you're pretty tired yourself. We heard your twelve-hour marathon last night.'

'Did you like it?'

'Oh yeah, I thought it was swell. Roosevelt getting a second term, I mean. He's been a good president.'

'Not that, you little devil. Me. My new job. What do you think?'

Mollie grinned. 'Got a rise out of you, didn't I? Always can.' She ducked, half expecting him to throw something, but he didn't. Instead he was staring at her again, his eyes as dark and full of hurt as they'd been when she walked in. 'Nick, don't look like that. I was only kidding. You were wonderful. I think your new job is marvellous. I want to hear all about it.'

'Okay, but have your bath first.'

She soaked for a long time in the soothing hot water. Trust Nick to suggest something so exactly right; like when she was little, and exhausted by some endless bus trip to wherever they were playing. A lot of the memories of those early years were hazy, but not that one. When at last they got to a boarding house her father used to find the bathroom right away — it was always at the end of some smelly, dark hall — and run a bath for her. 'C'mon, Mollie,' Harry would say, 'you'll feel better when you're warm and clean. You'll be my little sunshine again.'

Finally the water grew tepid and not so nice any more, and she got out and dressed in a pair of Nick's old pyjamas and a flannel bathrobe he said was Steve's. When she returned to the living room he'd made peanut butter sandwiches and poured big glasses of milk. 'Have some lunch.'

'Great, I'm starved.' She took a large bite of one of the sandwiches. 'Who does most of the cooking around here, you or Steve?'

'We don't have a lot of meals at home. Mostly we're working. Mollie, where are you and Steve going to live?'

She was startled. 'I never thought about it. Steve didn't say anything. Here, I guess. I mean I just always figured we'd stay here.' She looked around. 'Four rooms, that should be big enough for three of us, shouldn't it?'

'Yeah, plenty big enough I suppose,' he murmured.

Kate Bennet had fantasized that marriage would be wonderful, even though she'd observed something less than wonderful while she grew up. But as Nick had said, the thing about Kate was that she had no imagination.

'Is this your house?' Kate stood in the foyer of the five-storey grey stucco townhouse at 53 East Eight-second Street and stared.

'Our house,' Armando amended. 'There is an expression in Spanish, "*mi casa es tu casa*". My house is your house. You're supposed to say it to guests to welcome them.' He put his arm around her. 'I'm saying it to my beautiful wife, *mi casa es tu casa.*'

She turned to him with one of those brilliant heart-stopping smiles, the effect of which she never realized. 'Thank you, it's a lovely house.'

Armando chuckled. 'How do you know? You've only seen the front hall.'

Miguel came in just then, carrying the luggage. They'd been ten days in Niagara Falls on what Kate thought of as a blissful honeymoon. She had adored being the centre of Armando's attention. It was wonderful to be petted and pampered and treated like a queen by her handsome romantic husband. And she had loved being addressed as Mrs de Cuentas by the white-gloved staff of the fancy hotel. So what difference did it make that Miguel was always around? She'd quickly become accustomed to Armando's cousin doing countless little errands for them; like her husband, she'd come to expect them. 'Oh, do be careful of that hatbox, Miguel. The cord is fraying.'

'*Sí, Doña Katarina.*' He always called her that. Armando had explained that, roughly translated, it meant Lady Katherine, that it was a mark of respect, that even though Miguel was a cousin-in-law he felt more comfortable using the formal title. His voice was grave, sincere, self-effacing. 'Tomorrow I will take the hatbox to be repaired.'

'Put the suitcases in the white bedroom,' Armando said. 'We'll use that one. I think. Now, *querida*, I'll show you your house.' He gestured to the door at the end of the spacious hall in which they stood. 'The kitchen and the servants' rooms are through there. The butler and one maid live in, the others are dailies, but you don't have to concern yourself with any of that.'

Kate started for the stairs, but Miguel pulled open a door, then slid back an accordion-style metal gate. Kate clapped her hands in delight. 'An elevator! Armando, I didn't know there could be an elevator in a private house.'

'There is in this one.' Armando waited for her to enter, then followed her. There wasn't room for Miguel and the luggage, so he closed the hall door and stayed behind. Armando switched on an overhead light and pressed a button. The gate closed by itself and the elevator rose with stately slowness to the hallway above. 'The drawing room and the dining room are here on the second floor,' he explained.

Both rooms were exquisitely decorated in rich, dark-coloured brocades and velvets, with countless paintings, gilt mirrors and furniture that seemed far too exquisite to use. The table in the dining room was huge, Kate was sure that at least twenty people could sit around it. Nothing in the faded and fusty Victorian apartments of Hillhaven had prepared her for this.

'But where will we eat? Surely not in here. I mean, it's so big ...'

'But we will have many guests, *querida*. And there is a breakfast room.'

There was, and it was small and cheerfully painted in blue and white. It made her feel a bit less intimidated. So did the white bedroom on the fourth floor when she finally saw it.

Armando's study and an all-chintz sitting room on the third floor had been as overwhelming in their way as the drawing and dining rooms, but this bedroom was totally different. It had white wall-to-wall carpet and white and gold furniture, and the bed was a huge expanse of quilted white velvet. The only colour in the room came from the tumble of pastel satin pillows on the bed and the dark suitcases standing in the corner. Miguel had brought these up while they were exploring.

Kate ignored the luggage and crossed to the bed. 'How lovely. Armando, it's beautiful.' She drew her hand across the sumptuous bedspread. 'It's as soft as a kitten.'

'That's good, isn't it?' He'd come up behind her and slipped his arms around her waist. 'You will be my kitten, and I will be your tiger.' He nuzzled the back of her neck.

She knew now what he meant and what would happen next; the ten days of her honeymoon had taught her. Kate stood placid and acquiescent in his embrace, waited for him to turn her round and begin unbuttoning the jacket of the slate-blue wool suit. When she'd worn this outfit the day of her wedding she'd had a rayon blouse; since then, Armando had bought her one of silk in a shop in the lobby of the Hotel Niagara. It had a bow at the neck and he untied it.

'These are as perfect as the rest of you,' he murmured when at last he'd exposed her breasts and cupped them in his hands. 'You are even more beautiful than my house, *mi amor*. I knew that the first day I saw you.'

Kate was happy when he kissed her and petted her and murmured endearments. The rest she found quite tolerable, even if a bit boring.

'Wow! Kate, do you actually live here? In a house with an elevator and all this gorgeous stuff that looks as if it belongs in a movie?'

'Yes, it's Armando's house.'

'Yours too, since you're married. Wow,' Mollie said again.

Kate sat on the flowered chintz sofa of the sitting room, the folds of her blue satin hostess coat surrounding her with a pool of shimmering light. 'I don't want to talk about the house, I want to know why you eloped.'

It was 17 November, they'd both been married a bit over two weeks and this was the first time they'd been together since Kate returned from her honeymoon and heard the extraordinary news. 'The same reason you did,' Mollie said.

'I didn't elope. I got married.'

'So did I. Because I love Steve and he asked me.'

'But you're only sixteen. You haven't even finished high school.'

'Not very original.' Mollie took a sip of the coffee Maria, Kate's maid, had served in delicate white porcelain cups with a gold rim. 'That's what mom and Nick said too. You guys ought to get together and think up some new lines.'

'Don't be flip, Mollie. It's crazy, you can't be married when you're only sixteen.'

'You're crazy. Mom was married when she was sixteen. And so am I. I'm Mrs Steven Rogers. But I'm going to use Mollie Pride for the show.'

'What show?'

'*One Man's Family*. Mornings on NBC. I'm playing a new character, Sheila Raymond, she's Claudia Barbour's friend. Mother and Father Barbour don't like Sheila much, they think she's a scatterbrain.'

'I think you're a scatterbrain. Since when are you an actress?'

'Since I auditioned for the part and got it,' Mollie said. 'I'll be earning enough money of my own to help mom out. Besides, the commercials don't keep me busy enough, and it's boring just sitting around the apartment while Nick and Steve are at work. You know about Nick's new job, don't you?'

'Yes, mother told me.' Kate stretched luxuriously. 'Isn't it amazing how all our lives have changed so dramatically in such a short time?'

'Mmm, I suppose it is. But Nick's life isn't changed that much, he's just doing more of the same thing and getting paid better for it. He's making a fortune, ninety-five dollars a week. Though I suppose Armando makes a lot more than that.'

Kate didn't respond. The house spoke for itself, of course, but she hadn't shown her sister the new clothes rapidly filling her closets upstairs. Mollie wasn't usually the jealous type, but Kate didn't feel comfortable about her sudden affluence. Particularly since she still really had no idea where her husband's money came from, and he hadn't said a word about contributing to the support of Kate's mother.

'As long as Nick's happy, that's what matters,' Kate said. 'And you. That's what I want, Mollie. For us all to be happy.'

Mollie didn't feel like going home when she left Kate. The thought of rattling around by herself in the apartment was depressing. Impulsively she stayed on the Madison Avenue bus until it arrived at Fortieth Street, then she walked three blocks west to Broadway. She hadn't seen Nick's new office yet and this seemed like a good time.

The directory next to the elevator told her that Nicholas Frane could be found on the twenty-second floor. When she got there she discovered a secretary placed like a guard dog in front of a glass door with Nick's name on it.

'Hi, I'm Mollie Pr ... Mollie Rogers, Nick's cousin. Is he in?'

The secretary eyed her from top to toe, apparently not prepared to trust anyone who wasn't sure of her own last name. Finally she leaned over and pressed a button and spoke into the intercom on her desk. After a moment she said, 'Mr Frane will see you. You can go right in.'

For the second time that day Mollie was impressed by physical surroundings. Nick's office was huge. Opposite the door was a window facing east which framed a chunk of the Manhattan skyline. The Empire State Building looked like a picture hung there to enhance the decor.

'This is really something, Nick. Ten people could sit at this desk.'

'Yup, but it's all for me. I'm an important executive, not just a newscaster — Director of Current Affairs. I'm entitled to some respect.'

'Okay, I respect you.' Mollie plopped into a leather armchair that had a swivel seat and a steel frame on wheels. She spun herself round and examined the office in more detail. There were shelves crammed with books and the walls were covered in maps and charts. 'I don't know any announcers at ATL who have a set-up like this.'

'I'm not an announcer, I'm an executive, as I said. And a news commentator. ATL doesn't have a real news department, that's the main reason I left. In the old days they didn't do anything but hand some guy a bunch of wire service reports to read over the air. Do you know the only reason they stopped that?'

Mollie had no idea. She shook her head.

'Because in 1930 the newspapers made a stink, and the wire services shut out radio. That's when my wonderful ex-boss hired one girl to clip stories from the dailies. Listeners heard the same thing they'd heard before, but a day later. That's not a news department. Especially not when you think about what's happening right now.'

'You mean the alphabet soup?'

Roosevelt had persuaded congress to set up a plethora of agencies to attack the economic malaise of the nation; they were known by their initials, so nicknamed the alphabet soup.

Nick had always been the only member of the family interested in politics, and in the last few years he'd become passionate about them. 'Not the New Deal; it can't be stopped now. What's happening in Europe. Do you know who Adolf Hitler is?'

She stood up and wandered toward the window, intent on the spectacular view. 'Of course I do, I'm not a complete dummy. He's the President of Germany.'

'You are a dummy. He's not the President, he's the Chancellor, head of the Nazi party and the German parliament. Except there isn't any parliament. He made them vote themselves a vacation until next year. Meanwhile old buddy Hitler is calling all the shots. A few months ago he swallowed a place called the Rhineland, just marched in and took it over. The rest of the world said, "Hey, that's not nice," then forgot about it. You can bet the Nazis didn't forget. They think he's marvellous, they call him the Führer, it means leader. The little jerk thinks he's a Roman emperor. Everybody's supposed to salute him. Like this.'

Nick did a few goose steps across the carpeted floor, in imitation of the German Army. Then he stood at attention, clicked his heels, put a finger under his nose to represent a moustache and stuck out his right arm. '*Heil Hitler!*' He dropped the pose. 'It means hail, as in hail Caesar.'

Mollie was laughing so hard she had to bend over and grab her stomach.

'What are you laughing about? Damn it, Mollie, the whole thing's serious as hell.'

'I know,' she managed to gasp. 'At least if you say so it must be. But I can't help it, you looked so funny.'

Nick sat down heavily behind his impressive desk. 'Believe me, there is nothing funny about our little friend with the slicked-down hair and the moustache. Nor about Franco and his fascist Falange murdering half of Spain in a civil war either. And the Ethiopians aren't killing themselves laughing at Mussolini and the Italian blackshirts who have invaded their country.'

He'd been reciting the litany of horrors as much to himself as to her, now he glanced up. Mollie looked thoroughly perplexed. 'You don't understand a word I'm saying, do you?'

She shook her head. 'No, I'm sorry, I really don't. She hated to disappoint him, always had. 'Maybe you better start reading to me again, Nick.' Her voice was a whisper, made hoarse by the lump which memory suddenly raised in her throat. 'You know, we could take a long bus ride and you could improve my mind.'

His eyes held hers for a moment, then he shook his head. It was a gentle gesture this time, his voice was gentle too. 'Afraid not, kid. You bought a ticket on another bus and I can't go along.'

She had to turn away, the look on his face was painful. She knew what he meant, she'd quit school and got married and now she would never go to college and become as smart as he wanted her to be.

She heard him blow his nose hard. By the time she turned around he was returning a spotless white handkerchief to his pocket, and she'd thought of a good way to change the subject. 'You should have seen the thing Kate was wearing this morning. A blue satin gown, just to sit around the house and have coffee with me.'

'I think it's called a hostess coat. That's what all the ladies in her new crowd wear, until they get dressed up to go out and get their pictures taken for the gossip columns. Café society, like she told us the day we met Armando.'

Mollie perched on the edge of his desk and picked up a paperweight. 'Well, she's learning fast, you have to give old Katykins that much credit.'

'Armando must be a good teacher.'

'Looks like it.' She was still toying with the paperweight. It was some kind of rough stone and a beautiful shade of purple, pale and rich at the same time. 'This is nice. Where did you get it?'

'It's what they call raw amethyst, an uncut gemstone. I bought it a few days ago. When I got my bonus for the election night coverage.'

'Really? Why?' It struck her as a funny thing to choose for a splurge.

'Because it's beautiful. Not all that expensive, but not something I could have afforded until now. Beautiful things give me pleasure.'

'Then you ought to go and see Kate in her new house. It's straight out of Hollywood.'

'So I hear. And I am going. I've been invited there tomorrow night.'

'Does that mean you won't be home for supper?' She had taken to cooking meals for the three of them. Steve had simply presumed she would. Mollie didn't mind; that's what ladies — wives — did, and even now that she'd landed a job with a regular show, most days she would be the first one back in the apartment.

'No, I won't be. Not tonight either.'

'Where are you going tonight?'

'I'm having dinner with Gabe Heater. Even you must know he's a top dog in the news business.'

'I do know. I'll wait up and you can tell me all about it when you come home.'

'No, I'm going to come back here and do some work afterwards. I'll probably just flop on the sofa over there.'

Mollie looked at the leather couch in the office. 'That doesn't look as comfortable as your own bed.'

'It's fine. And listen, Mollie, I've been thinking of looking for a little place of my own. I can afford it now, and since I work a lot of strange hours ... I think it will be better. Besides, you and Steve are newlyweds, you ought to be by yourselves.'

She hesitated only a moment. 'Okay, if that's what you want.'

'It will be better,' he said again.

She didn't contradict him, but the thought flashed into her mind that when he did it she was going to feel the way she'd felt when he first moved to New York and left the rest of them behind in Red Hook. Terrible. As if part of her had been cut away. But it had been silly then and it was sillier now. She was a grown-up married lady and she wasn't supposed to need her big strong cousin around to take care of her.

'You're the boss,' she said lightly. 'Have to go. I bought a Betty Crocker cookbook and I'm going home to try and make macaroni and cheese with buttered bread crumb topping. So just think about what you're missing when you tuck into your juicy steak with Mr Bigshot Heater.'

'Yeah, I will.'

No, he wouldn't. He'd think about the fact that he wouldn't hear the springs creaking in the next room when they'd gone to bed and Mollie and Steve were making love.

Dinner on East Eighty-second Street the following evening had nothing to do with macaroni and cheese, and not much connection with a thick steak. It began with cocktails served by a butler in the sitting room on the third floor, then progressed to turtle soup and oysters Rockefeller, and a marvellous sauce on a meat Nick couldn't identify, and ice cream parfaits — all served with much pomp in a dining room lit by candles and sparkling chandeliers, and full of the tinkling sound of vintage champagne being poured into thin crystal goblets.

'We'll have coffee in the drawing room,' Armando announced as he rose from his place at the head of the long table and nodded to his wife at its foot. Kate had been watching for his signal. She stood up instantly, breaking off in mid-sentence what she'd been saying to the man on her left, and led the eighteen guests forward to the next splendour.

Nick manoeuvred himself next to his cousin while the liqueurs were being passed. Kate turned to him with a smile of genuine pleasure. 'I feel so much better because you're here,' she confided. 'All these important people ... But you look just like them, and you're still my Nick.' Her long fingers hovered for a moment near the lapel of his black tuxedo. 'You knew what Armando meant by black tie, didn't you?'

'Yeah, I had to learn that when I first came to the city. New York hostesses are kind to radio people, invite them everywhere. But they always want them to dress up like penguins.'

'You make a handsome penguin. I keep wondering if I look all right.'

He knew her well enough to know she wasn't fishing for compliments. Kate still had no idea of the combined effect of the golden hair piled on top of her head and her pale loveliness set off by diamond earrings and what had to be a designer original gown. 'You look gorgeous, Katykins. You put every woman in the room in the shade.'

She flushed with pleasure. 'Do you really think so? I keep worrying that these things behind me are going to trip somebody.' The things she referred to were two floating chiffon panels which descended from the shoulders of the skin-tight sheath of seafoam green silk that covered her from neck to ankles.

'I really think so,' Nick said. 'You'd be beautiful in a burlap sack, but what you're wearing is a lot nicer.'

She thought of telling him about buying the gown at Bergdorf Goodman on Fifth Avenue. How the day after they'd returned from Niagara Falls Armando had taken her to the store and they'd sat down and watched models parade a host of different dresses until Armando chose half a dozen for her and waited while she was fitted. But Nick probably wasn't interested in the details of her transition from buying markdowns at Slater's Dry Goods Store to selecting a wardrobe at Bergdorf Goodman.

'Have you met everybody?' she asked instead. 'I'm sorry I didn't take you around and introduce you when you arrived, but Armando told me to be specially nice to Mr Carter from the museum. I couldn't get away from him.'

'It's okay, Miguel did the honours. Your Armando has gathered quite a group. A mixed bag, but except for me they're all lions of one kind or another.'

'You're a lion too,' Kate protested loyally. 'Especially now that you have a wonderful new job.'

Nick chuckled. 'I'm small potatoes in this company, but I'm glad to be here. It's fun watching the sharks feed.'

Mr Carter from the museum was George Carter, curator of American Art at the Metropolitan. The tall grey-haired man with the woman who reminded Nick of a buzzard was a very rich stockbroker, and the Texan with the loud voice was, of course, in oil. Nor was Nick the only representative of broadcasting. Hans Kaltenborn was standing in a corner talking animatedly to a woman in chic black and pearls. She was hanging on to every word. Kaltenborn had become a hero a few months ago when at his own expense he went to Spain to cover the civil war, sending broadcasts back from the actual scenes of battles, using a mobile transmitter and a French engineer.

The newsman was a known quantity, Nick was more interested in Ed Murrow, who'd recently joined CBS. He'd been hearing that the tall handsome newcomer was exerting a lot of influence at the network. For a few seconds he watched Murrow talking to Walter Winchell, the columnist who also did a programme on NBC, then Nick flicked his eyes over the rest of the assembly. There were at least four newspaper reporters, as well as a guy who wrote regularly for Colliers and Redbook and had recently authored a piece in the *New Yorker*.

Kate was still by his side. 'Your guest list is heavy on communication types,' Nick murmured.

'What?'

'I've just realized that the majority of the people here are in the business of telling folks things, one way or another. Opinion makers.'

'Oh, are they? I don't know who most of them are.

Armando arranged everything for the party.' She wasn't half as interested in talking about her new life as her old. 'Mother's still very upset about Mollie, I spoke with her today.'

'Yes, I know she is. She'll get over it. We'll all have to get over it. It's done.'

'Nick, she's going to be all right, isn't she? Steve's going to be a good husband and Mollie's going to be happy, and it will work out for the best, won't it?'

Typical Kate, just wait for somebody to say everything's okay, then relax. He took her hand. 'Sure she's going to be all right. Mollie always lands on her feet. But ...'

Whatever reservation he was going to express was never spoken. 'My friends,' Armando said loudly from the centre of the room, 'I must confess to bringing you here under false pretences. Kate and I haven't told you, but tonight's little gathering is a celebration of sorts.' He looked for his wife over the heads of the crowd and caught her eye. 'Are you ready, darling?'

'All ready, Armando.' She detached herself from Nick's side and went to stand beside her husband. Then the butler appeared, carrying something large wrapped in white paper. A painting, Nick thought at once. The size and shape of the parcel could easily make it a painting.

He looked immediately at George Carter, the single representative of the art world. Carter was trying to suppress what Nick thought of as a shit-eating grin, though he wasn't doing a very good job of it. And, Nick noted, he was not the only newsman in the group to have guessed what was about to happen. The writer and the reporters and Winchell and Murrow and Kaltenborn, every one of them had turned to stare at the curator.

'George, this is for you,' Armando said. 'I mean it is for the Metropolitan Museum and the American people. My way of celebrating my marriage to the most beautiful woman in the world.'

There was laughter and a smattering of applause, then gasps as Kate tore away the paper and revealed the painting Armando held. Even if you knew nothing about art, this was impressive; the colouring was rich and vivid, the thing seemed almost alive.

135

Carter had obviously known beforehand about the 'surprise'. His words were assured and sounded practised. 'I'm sure you all know that Winslow Homer's *The Fox Hunt* is a masterpiece.' He pronounced the name of the artist and the work slowly and clearly, for the benefit of the philistines among them. 'Buying this picture from its private owner and giving it to the museum was a mark of our host's outstanding generosity, not to mention his superb taste. Now it will hang where it belongs, in the finest collection in the country's greatest city. Armando, on behalf of myself, the Metropolitan, and the American people, my heartfelt thanks.'

Armando flashed his handsome smile and drew Kate closer to his side. 'There's a special meaning for us in this small offering. I told you the gift was in my wife's honour. You may be interested to know that *The Fox Hunt* is particularly appropriate for that purpose. Though she's been brought up here in America, Kate is the daughter of an English Lord.'

'Granddaughter,' Kate murmured.

Armando ignored her correction, anxious to make his own point. 'Even in Venezuela we know that fox hunting is the English national sport.' He shrugged and laughed and nearly everybody laughed with him.

Nick managed only a faint smile. He was looking at the painting, now in Carter's hands. It was of a fox ploughing through deep snow. A bird of prey hovered overhead. You could practically see the animal's black tipped ears and tail quiver in response to danger. For the past couple of years Nick had been spending much of what free time he had in museums and galleries. He knew the Homer was a wonderful example of artistic realism. He knew too that the scene had nothing whatever to do with fox hunting for sport in the English countryside. No more than Kate had anything to do with the titled family who had rejected her long ago.

Forget it, he told himself. So Armando got a little confused, he never claimed to be a genius. The picture's terrific, it's a fabulous gift. Must have cost a fortune. Genuine, of course, that was obvious from the look on George Carter's face. The painting was unique and expensive, and it went with Kate's gown and her jewels, the house, and the broad smiles of the rich and famous people gathered in the room. Okay, most of them had been invited to ensure that Armando's gift to the Met would be reported in the press and over the airwaves. Nothing wrong with that. The problem was that Nick couldn't shake off a nagging feeling that the one false note in the scene was Armando de Cuentas.

One Man's Family went on the air at eight in the morning, the breakfast-time slot, but it was rehearsed in the afternoon. Mollie was thinking of her lines as she waited at one-thirty on a Tuesday in early December for the elevator in the lobby of the building that housed the NBC studios. The shiny brass doors slid open and Lee Mitsuno brushed past her. He was carrying his black leather flute case and his head was bent in thought. 'Lee! Lee, it's me. Wait a minute ...'

They hadn't seen each other since she got married, and now he looked as if he didn't recognize her. That lasted only a second or two, until he came back from whatever dream-world he'd been inhabiting, then he smiled. 'Mollie, how nice to see you. You look wonderful.'

'So do you.' Lee was wearing a dark overcoat and a maroon scarf. He looked very grown-up and successful. But then, her navy plaid suit and matching coat with a red flannel lining made her look a lot older too. That's why she'd bought the outfit with half her paycheque of the week before. Lee's coat might well have cost more, it had a collar of Persian lamb. 'You look like a star,' she told him.

Lee laughed. 'Hardly that. Just a musician.'

Mollie had half an hour free. She'd planned to spend it going over her lines. But it wasn't really imperative, she knew them. 'Got time for a cup of coffee?' she asked.

Lee nodded. 'I always have time for you. Let's go.'

There was a Rexall Drugstore next door. They went in and took stools at the corner and ordered, then Lee cocked his head and studied her. 'You look wonderful,' he said again. 'I was amazed when I heard you'd got married, but it must agree with you.'

'Yes, I guess it does. What have you been doing? How's your mother?'

'She's fine. And I'm doing all the usual things. At least usual for now. Did you know I'd left the Philharmonic?'

'No. Why?'

'Too time-consuming. I'm playing with a few of the radio orchestras these days. It's less demanding and the schedule is more flexible.'

Mollie put three heaped teaspoons of sugar in her cup and stirred vigorously. The pause gave her a chance to think of something to say. Lee's promise, that precocious talent which had made him a child prodigy, had never quite materialized. Once he got into his teens he was just another flautist. Mollie knew that part of the story, but it sounded as if the next chapter had been that he wasn't good enough to hold a job with a major symphony orchestra. 'That sounds nice,' she said brightly. 'What are you doing with all the extra time?'

'Lots of things.' Lee had ordered tea and he drank it quickly, replacing the empty cup in the saucer and fidgeting with it rather than looking at her. 'I ... I've been seeing my father.'

Her eyes opened wide. In all the years she'd known Grace and Lee, the absent Mr Mitsuno had neither appeared nor been discussed. 'No kidding? That's great.' Lee didn't reply. 'It is, isn't it?' Mollie asked softly.

He still didn't look at her. 'Yes and no. It was wonderful meeting him again after all these years, but a little strange too. I hadn't seen him since I was five.'

'What about your mother? Does she know? Are she and your father ...'

'She knows, but it's nothing like that. He just came backstage to see me one night after a concert. I didn't recognize him. Isn't that crazy? My own father, and I didn't recognize him.'

'How could you?' Mollie put her hand on his arm and Lee covered it with his for a moment, then quickly withdrew. They never talked about it, but both of them knew that people stared when they saw them together. An Oriental male and a white girl, it always raised a few eyebrows. 'What's he like?' she asked.

Lee thought for a moment. 'Different.'

'From what?'

'From what I thought he would be like. I had such mixed feelings, Mollie. I was so mad at him because he'd gone off and left us, but I always remembered that I'd love him too. Now I've had to think the whole thing through again.'

'And what have you decided?'

'That people do what they have to do, what their honour tells them they must do. There's no point in getting mad about it, it's just the way it is.'

'That sound like your Chinese fatalism to me.'

'I'm Japanese.'

'Only half, don't kid me. I knew you when ...' Her tone was light and bantering, but when he answered, his was not.

'I'm Japanese,' he repeated stiffly.

'Okay, if you say so.' His father's reappearance must have changed a lot of things for Lee, but she didn't know how to respond to them. Better to talk about something else. 'Have you seen Kate's name in the gossip columns?'

'I don't read the gossip columns. Haven't got time.'

If he'd been stiff before, he sounded genuinely angry now. Mollie didn't know what to do except plunge ahead. 'She's always in them. Our Katykins has become a real social butterfly. I suppose it had to happen since she's so gorgeous and Armando's so rich.'

Lee took a quarter from his pocket and put it on the counter. 'Have to go, Mollie. Great seeing you. Give Nick my best. And Steve, of course.'

'Of course. So long, give my love to your mother.' She said her goodbyes to his departing back.

Nick still hadn't found a place of his own and officially moved out, but Mollie and Steve saw very little of him in early December. A major international news story was breaking and Nick was on the fringes of it, trying desperately to be more involved.

The cat poked its nose over the top of the bag when a small item appeared in the *Chicago Daily News*. In the town of Ipswich in Suffolk, England, a Mrs E.A. Simpson had filed for divorce. What someone would later call the Wally and David show was about to begin.

The affair had been going on for nearly two years, but this

139

was the first time the general public were being let in on it, and in England they were still dependent on nothing but whispered gossip. The man his friends and family called David was better know as Edward VIII, King of England, and Mrs Simpson was not only married, she'd been divorced once before. The idea of an American lady of questionable morals as England's queen was outrageous, and the inner circle of politicians and advisers were desperate for the King to come to his senses and break it off. If he did not the country would face a constitutional crisis, but in deference to the royal prerogatives the story was blacked out in the British press and on radio.

Not so elsewhere. It made front pages all over the world — especially in the US — but here was a case where radio could do it better. There wasn't a lot of detail to report, you didn't need the length and clarity of a newspaper column to say that Mrs Simpson had been seen here or there, or that this or that piece of information had come out at the divorce hearings. What the public longed for was a sense of the immediacy of the thing, an awareness of the tight-rope being walked, the crisis about to come. Which was what broadcasting could give them, and why there were bulletins coming over the air from early morning until late at night. *The New York Times* called it a steady tattoo between London and New York.

'We're virtually out of it at Mutual,' Nick said glumly when on 11 December he and Mollie had lunch at the Longchamps on Forty-third and Fifth. 'We haven't got the chips, so we can't play.'

Mollie took a large bite of her ham and cheese on rye. 'Who cares? The whole thing's silly. I read in the *Tribune* that Parliament won't let him go on being king if he marries her, so he'll never do it.'

He cocked his head and grinned at her. 'I'm happy to hear you're reading anything, but if it's so silly how come you're following all the details?'

'I am,' she admitted. 'But not just about the King and Wally, I read at least two newspapers every day, and I listen to you give the news every night while I'm making supper.'

'How about books?'

'Damn it, Nick, there's no pleasing you. I haven't got time

to read books.' Neither of them said anything else until she finished smearing bright yellow mustard on the second half of her sandwich. 'What kind of books?' she asked before she bit into it.

'All kinds, especially history. Biography maybe. I'll send you a few good ones. Listen, if you're going to eat nothing but sandwiches we should go to a deli next time.' He cut into his sautéed kidneys on toast while he spoke.

Mollie made a face. 'How can you eat that stuff? Will he do it, do you think?'

'This "stuff" is delicious. Will who do what?'

'The King, will he marry Mrs Simpson?'

'I thought it was silly and you didn't care.'

'Nick!'

'Okay, the answer is I don't know. And I should. Part of my job is, or should be, getting background information and analysing the news. You can't do that if you're in New York and the story is happening thousands of miles away in England.'

'But there are lots of stories happening right here.'

'Not the important ones at the moment. I thought you said you'd been reading the papers.'

Mollie frowned. 'I have. I just wish they'd print some good things once in a while. Nick, I read a column by a man who said he thinks there's going to be another war. Do you think so?'

'Yes, I'm afraid I do. Will you have another root beer or do you want to taste this wine?'

She said she'd try the wine and he motioned to the waiter to bring her a glass, then poured her some of the chilled white burgundy. 'Like it?' he asked when she'd taken a sip.

'Yes, it's got a nice fruity taste that stays on your tongue after you swallow it.'

Nick laughed. 'That's exactly what the wine experts try to say in their fancy language. Good for you.'

'You're becoming an expert in everything. And you're even getting to be kind of handsome in your old age. Nick, how come you don't have a girlfriend?'

'How do you know I haven't?'

'Come on, I'd know if you did. I always know everything

about you. You haven't answered the question.'

'I don't have time for a girlfriend. I've got to figure out how I can deal myself in to what I think is pretty soon going to be the only game in town.'

'Reporting on Europe?'

'Reporting from Europe. That's what makes the CBS and NBC coverage so good. Mutual is setting up chains of stringers to keep us informed, and we're supposed to get information from a dozen different sources, but then other networks have their own people on the scene. They can relay live broadcasts. As things stand now, there's no way we can touch that.'

Mollie had a sudden understanding of what he might mean, but she wouldn't let herself think about it. The idea that Nick could go so far away was intolerable. She certainly didn't want to talk about that. 'I ran into Lee Mitsuno last week, did I tell you?'

He said she hadn't, so she repeated the things Lee had told her. 'Isn't it amazing? His father showing up after all these years?'

'Yes. Mollie, are you sure Lee said he was Japanese?'

'Very sure. I made a crack about his Chinese half, and he got cold as ice and said he was Japanese. Like he was announcing that the sun comes up in the east, something any jerk should know.'

'The sun's been rising in the east in more ways than one,' Nick said thoughtfully.

'What do you mean?'

'Read your papers more carefully. Japan has been sabre rattling like crazy for years. They marched into Manchuria in 1931.'

'Where's Manchuria?'

'In Asia, on the Russian border, the northeaster part of China. At least it was. Now it's a place called Manchukuo, supposedly independent, but that's a myth. The Japanese are calling all the shots. Korea's nervous as hell and the Chinese aren't too comfortable. They're both in Asia too, in case you're not sure.'

Mollie looked glum. 'You're full of cheerful things today. Lets have apple pie and ice cream for dessert.'

He had arranged this lunch to make sure she was all right. He shouldn't have to worry about that now that she was married, but he still did. She seemed fine, and Nick started feeling guilty about his professional responsibilities. 'No time for dessert. I shouldn't have left the studio for this long.'

He called for the bill and paid it and they left, but by the time Nick got back to the office it was too late. CBS had scooped everybody. A few minutes earlier they'd aired a live news flash direct from their correspondent in the House of Commons in London. The Prime Minister was about to tell the members of parliament that the King had abdicated. A few hours later Nick was among the many millions around the world who heard Edward VIII say, 'I cannot go on without the help and support of the woman I love ...'

The entire episode had not only shaken the mighty British Empire; it had given Nicholas Frane a lot to think about.

'Steve, should we have a baby?'

'No.'

It was nearly midnight on 7 July, and stinking hot. They were lying in bed, Mollie with her head on his chest, Steve with one arm around her, the other holding a copy of *Time*. He didn't take his eye from the page when he answered her, just went on reading a long piece about President Roosevelt's enemies.

Mollie waited for a further comment, there was none.

'Why not?' She sat up, pushing the hem of the thin cotton batiste nightie to the top of her thighs in an attempt to feel a little cooler. 'Don't you like kids?'

'Sure I like kids. Only not yet.'

'Kate's pregnant. I saw her today and she told me. Four months, the baby's due in early January.' He didn't say anything, just sort of stiffened. She saw his reaction because she was watching for it. The muscles in his arms rippled and got tense. 'Steve, did you hear me?'

'I heard you.'

'Well, aren't you going to say anything? It's big news, Kate having a baby. I'd think you would say something.'

'Yeah, well it's bound to be the event of the social season. Armando will see to it. Listen, Kate's five years older than you. You're just seventeen, Mollie. You're too young to have a baby. Besides, we can't afford it.'

She got off the bed and walked to the open window, hoping for a breeze. There was none, Sixtieth Street lay dark and silent under a blanket of humidity and heat. 'My mother had Kate when she was seventeen.'

'And look how wonderful that was. From the stories I've heard your mother didn't have any bed of roses in England.'

'But she had Kate. Kate's wonderful. Don't you think so?' She didn't turn around, she tossed the question into the quiet room and let it hang there. And when he didn't reply. 'Well, don't you?'

Steve put down the magazine. 'Mollie, would you care to tell me what this conversation is about?'

'You know what it's about. I think we should have a baby.'

'Well I don't. It's a crazy idea. The world's about to blow up, we couldn't live, much less help your mother, without your salary, and you suddenly decide you want to saddle yourself with a kid while you're still a kid yourself. Why?'

'I don't know. I guess because it seems such a nice idea. A baby is all your own, something to love that belongs to you.'

'I thought you loved me. We're married, I belong to you, don't I?'

Mollie turned to him, the reading lamp beside the bed shone on his body but not his face. She could see the red hair curling on his bare chest, the tie that held his striped pyjama bottoms, everything but his eyes. 'Do you?' she whispered. 'Do you belong to me?'

'What's that supposed to mean?'

'I ... Nothing. It doesn't mean a thing. It was a stupid question.' She crossed to the bed and hurled herself back into his arms. It took a few seconds, but eventually he put them around her. 'Hang on to me. I get crazy, Steve. Sometimes I think you really love Kate, not me. That you're sorry you married me.' And sometimes she thought that he worked too many hours to tally with the size of his paycheque, too many late nights which should bring in overtime but somehow never did. 'Say you love me,' she pleaded.

'Of course I love you.' He put his hand on her breast,

fingering the nipple through the sheer garment. 'Guess I'll have to prove it.'

Her kisses were hungry, demanding, she wished she could swallow him, make him part of her so she would stop having the terrible doubts which plagued her nights. As always, her passion triggered his. Steve made love to her deftly, swiftly with practised ease. When he paused a moment to ensure that there would be no consequences of this coupling, Mollie did not again say she wanted a baby.

Afterwards she was drowsy, but Steve picked up the magazine and went back to reading.

'What you said before,' Mollie asked, 'about the world blowing up, do you think it will?'

'Yeah, I'm afraid I do.'

'So do I,' she admitted. 'I keep hoping it won't happen, but everything I read says it's bound to. I don't think we'll get into it, though. I think it's all going to be in Europe and this time we'll stay out.'

He rumpled her hair with a slightly preoccupied gesture. 'Been reading a lot lately, haven't you?'

'Nick says I have to. He says I can't go on being an idiot all my life. He gave me Hitler's book, *Mein Kampf*. A short version in English, he found it in a second-hand store. It's pretty scary stuff. After I read it I knew the little jerk really wanted a war.'

'My wife the sage,' Steve said softly. 'This family of yours makes no end of trouble for me. Between your sister and your cousin, I never know what you're going to spring next.' His tone was light and bantering but there was an undertone she preferred to ignore.

'Speaking of family, are we going to go to Canada next month?'

She knew a little about his background, he'd told her the story in instalments, a brief chapter each time she pressed him for details about his childhood. His father was a pork butcher and not a real *Québécois*, he'd gone to Montreal from some little town in Saskatchewan and married Steve's mother. She died when Steve was seven, but her name had been Marie Dampierre and he remembered that she was beautiful and gentle, and that French was her native tongue and she never spoke anything else to him. His father still lived in Montreal and he had a married sister there. Mollie had never met them.

They had talked about driving north for a visit when Steve got his vacation in August. 'I don't think so,' he said now. 'I've about made up my mind to hang around here and work some overtime while I'm on vacation.'

She raised her head and looked at him. 'But why? I spoke with the producer, they can write Sheila out of the show for a couple of weeks. He said it's no problem.'

'Vacations are expensive, I don't think we can afford it.'

She started wondering again about their finances, but it didn't seem like the right time to ask any more questions.

On a Wednesday afternoon in August, when she and Steve should have been going on vacation to Canada but weren't, Mollie was at the studio rehearsing an episode of *One Man's Family*. They finished a little before four. She gathered her things and started for the door. A man was leaning against it, blocking her way. 'Hi, got a minute?'

'Sure.' She waited for him to explain. He was no one she'd ever met, a short skinny guy, about forty-five probably. With thinning light brown hair and a face that looked like those maps of Europe that were always in the papers these days, lots of white space criss-crossed with lines.

'Okay, c'mon up to my office, I want to talk to you.'

'Don't you have a name?'

'Yup.' That was all he said, he didn't volunteer it while he led the way to the elevator.

His office was a small square room stuffed with papers and books and a variety of other paraphernalia — including at least four ashtrays that looked as if they hadn't been emptied in a month. 'Sit here.' He swept a pile of glossy black and white photographs off a hard-backed chair.

There was something about his manner that set her teeth on edge, and the office smelled foul. All those cigarette butts. She sat down, cocking her head and looking at him, and waiting.

He pushed a pile of scripts from a corner of the desk and perched on it, then put out his hand. 'Phil Rosenberg.'

'Mollie Pride.' She shook his hand.

'I know. I even know it's actually Mollie Rogers. But you were right to keep Pride professionally. Mollie Pride's a great name.'

'You seem to know a lot of things, Mr Rosenberg.'

'Phil. And I do. I know just about everything.'

'Terrific. I've always wanted to meet somebody who knows everything. Now tell me what I'm doing here.'

'That's easy. You're going to save my ass.'

'Oh, how am I going to do that? And why should I?'

'The answer to both those questions is that I'm going to make you a star.'

Mollie exploded with laughter. 'Say, mister, you mean it? Like in the movies? A real star with my name in lights?'

He shook a Camel from a pack and held it between his teeth and lit the match one-handed. 'You've got a smart mouth, but that's part of your charm.'

'So some people say. Okay, Phil, enough with the games. What do you want?'

'A morning show. A talk slot. Charming sassy lady interviews celebrities.'

In spite of herself she was intrigued, a little buzz of excitement started in the back of her head. 'Yeah? And what charming sassy lady did you have in mind?'

'Betty Chandler.'

Shit. The buzz died away and left the sour taste of disappointment. Betty Chandler was a famous actress. She'd been in lots of plays on Broadway and in at least half a dozen movies. 'That's nice.' It was the only thing she could think of to say.

'No, actually it ain't.' Rosenberg took his second long drag of the cigarette, exhaled through his nose, then stubbed it out. 'It's a pain in the *tochis*.' He paused and grinned at her. 'Do you know what that means?'

Mollie shook her head.

'*Tochis* is a Jewish word. Yiddish. It means ass, behind. But it's better.'

'Okay, so tell me why your show is a pain in the *tochis*.'

She pronounced it with a hard k sound and he laughed, then grew serious. 'Betty Chandler had a heart attack

147

yesterday afternoon. She's going to be out of commission for a long time. Sad for her, since she's only thirty-something, but for me, a pain in the behind.'

Mollie grinned. It wasn't just that she saw where he was going, she'd decided she liked him. Lately radio was mostly uptight types in suits and ties. It had become very big business and very respectable. Phil Rosenberg was a throwback to her early days with brash Ben Porter, or even further, to the carny people. 'What kind of celebrities?' Mollie asked. There was no need to pussyfoot around, now they both knew what she was doing in his office. 'What airtime? Live?'

'Theatre types. Broadway. Nine-fifteen to nine forty-five Monday to Friday. Of course live. You haven't asked me how much.'

She frowned. 'It's not going to matter a whole lot. I've never been in a Broadway theatre in my life. I couldn't talk to them.'

'Baloney. They talk, you only ask a few questions. They've all got egos a mile high. Love to talk about themselves. And you have a great delivery. I used to listen to you as Little Brat with that horse's ass Ben Porter, and who can forget "Rinso white, Rinso white, happy little washday song ..." You'll do fine.'

Mollie cocked her head and narrowed her eyes. 'I only do the talk part, never sing the jingle. I can't carry a tune. See, you don't know everything. And there's something else.'

'How much?'

'No, not that. You conceived the show with a well-known actress. How come if she can't do it you just didn't go to the next well-known actress on your list?'

Rosenberg's grin nearly split his face. 'Because of a question like that. I never wanted to use Miss Chandler. She's a nice lady, very talented. But that's not what makes a good interviewer. Smart questions, good radio delivery and timing. Those are different skills. The management types upstairs shoved Betty Chandler down my throat. Now they've got their jockstraps in a twist because we're scheduled to start the series this Monday and she's flat on her back. So I figured I could make a quick move and be a hero, and put a better show on the air at the same time.' He lit another cigarette with the same one-handed trick he'd displayed earlier. 'Any further questions?'

'Yeah, how much?'

'Sixty a week.'

Jesus. That's what Steve made, sixty a week. Mollie stuck out her hand. 'It's a deal.'

'Of course it's a deal. I knew that before I brought you up here. Otherwise why would I be wasting my time with a little *shixsa* who can't even pronounce *tochis*?'

She made a mental note to ask him the meaning of *shixsa*, but not now, later. Now she had to tell Steve the big news, and Nick. God, she couldn't wait to tell Nick.

8

By March 1939, *Mornings with Mollie* had been on NBC for nineteen months. It was the most popular show in its time slot on any station. Phil Rosenberg had kept his promise: he'd made Mollie a star of sorts, or perhaps more accurately, a celebrity.

Phil was not a celebrity. He was a bachelor who lived in a big old house just across the Brooklyn Bridge, alone since his mother died a few years before. Mollie knew him well enough to know that he wasn't a pansy, and probably hadn't been a mama's boy. He was simply married to his job. Invariably he was waiting for her when she arrived at seven forty-five to prepare the morning broadcast. He usually greeted her the same way. 'Hiya, sunshine. How's tricks?'

Mollie's response was just as standardized. 'How can you be so cheerful at this hour?'

'I'm cheerful because I'm seeing you, and because we've got a hell of a show this morning. Have some coffee.'

No more cream and sugar, she'd taken to drinking her coffee black, and so strong a spoon would stand up in it. 'Thanks,' she murmured, taking a sip. 'What do we have?'

'Good stuff. We don't need the poopsie with the big boobs.'

The poopsie was a bit player from the hit show *DuBarry Was a Lady* playing at the 46th Street Theater. Her charms were not of the intellectual sort, they'd been unsure if she'd be able to answer Mollie's questions in coherent English. It sounded as if they weren't going to have to worry about it.

They'd tried for one or the other of the show's leads, and only booked the bit player when they failed to induce Ethel Merman or Bert Lahr to come on the programme. But the show had a lot of clout, and perhaps the queen of Broadway had reconsidered.

'You got Merman?' Mollie slung her crocodile shoulder bag on the desk. She carried her life in that bag — all her make-up, a flashlight for emergencies, a change of accessories in case she stayed out for an entire day — it landed with a thump. Phil shook his head. Not Ethel. 'Lahr?' she prompted.

'Nope.' Phil looked smug.

Mollie shrugged off her sheared beaver coat. It came from Macy's and cost five hundred dollars. She'd bought it this winter, forty down and twenty a month. It would take her two years to pay it off, but God, she loved that coat. 'So tell me why you look so pleased with yourself.'

'I got you a real live genuine Nazi from the Fatherland, who just happens to speak English as well as you or I.'

'Her eyes lit up. 'Fabulous! That's terrific, Phil.'

They had been trying to find such a guest for weeks. *Mornings with Mollie* had veered from the original concept. Mollie frequently interviewed theatre people, but nowadays she spent at least fifteen minutes of her half-hour on what they called current affairs, and sometimes devoted the entire programme to a subject of pressing national concern. What made the show such a knock-down, drag-out giant killer in terms of audience loyalty was that she did it her way.

People loved the simple direct manner in which Mollie interpreted and explained world events. Her listeners were mostly housewives fed a daily diet of soap operas and music, and the occasional bit of homemaking advice. The news programmes were aimed at their husbands, they came on when the women were busy cooking supper. But Mollie Pride talked to them about the major happenings of the day in terms they understood.

The technique came naturally to her, because like most of her listeners she had no formal training in politics, only a lively curiosity.

There was a memorable week in early 1938 when she interviewed the only woman in F.D.R's cabinet, the Secretary of Labour, Frances Perkins, on three consecutive mornings. When that mini-marathon ended Mollie's listeners understood that if they'd liked Social Security, which had become the law of the land in 1935, they were going to love a national Minimum Wage — if the administration could get congress to pass the law. They also had Mrs Perkins's recipe for meat loaf and her opinion on whether a woman should dye her hair. 'It's a bit silly, isn't it? You have to be careful of the roots all the time, it's one more thing to worry about.'

Whatever the subject, Mollie asked the questions ordinary American women wanted to ask, and if an answer wasn't clear to her she knew it wouldn't be clear to them. So she asked it again, and again if necessary, until the facts were spelled out in terms comprehensible to wives and mothers in Bangor and Topeka and Dallas and Seattle. That was important too. *Mornings with Mollie* wasn't a local show any longer, it was heard live on eastern and central time, and rebroadcast a couple of hours later over NBC stations in the mountain and Pacific time zones. Ninety-five per cent of the local affiliates took the programme.

Lately Mollie's focus had shifted. The New Deal was mature and had borne fruit, more people were employed, the economy was alive and, if not exactly kicking, at least breathing. These days she talked about the possibility of war at least twice a week. Nothing was more contentious than the question of war in Europe, and whether if it happened American boys should once more be sent to fight and die far from home. Sponsors didn't like controversy. 'Screw 'em,' was Phil's comment. 'You're a star, babe. If one guy doesn't want to pay to put you on the air there'll be another ready to take his place. Meanwhile we do what we goddamn please.'

What pleased Mollie was to examine the issues which were the subjects of Nick's nightly newscasts. 'Which Nazi?' she asked now, slipping into the chair beside Phil's. 'Give me everything you've got.'

He opened a file and handed her the sheet of paper on top. 'Name's Heinrich Kalman. Born in Stuttgart in 1909. Father was a grocer, so Kalman's got credentials as a man of the people. But he was a smart kid and managed to get himself an education and became a journalist. He's based in Berlin now, writes a popular column for a paper called *Deutsche Allgemeine*. Part of the popularity comes from the fact that Kalman seems to think the Führer is God. He even farts *Heil Hitler*.'

Mollie ran her eyes over the list of the German's curriculum vitae, then reached for the next paper in Phil's pile. 'These are excerpts from his columns?'

'Yes. I woke up a girl I know at three a.m. to get them translated for you. Didn't get Kalman's agreement to do the show until ten last night. I tried to call you, by the way; no answer.'

Mollie didn't look up. 'We were out. Nick got tickets for *Straw Hat Review* at the Ambassador.'

'Good?'

'Wonderful. There's a guy called Danny Kaye who ... Jesus, have you read this stuff?'

'I read it.'

Mollie was scanning the excerpts from Heinrich Kalman's articles. She flipped through them quickly, then went back and studied them more closely. 'Talk about spouting the party line, if Hitler had a brother he couldn't be more devoted than little old Heinrich here. What do I say to somebody who claims to believe all this garbage?'

Phil put his hand over the page she was reading. 'Mollie, if you don't want to do this we can get out of it. I'll tell him the sponsor objected, or you objected, anything. You can just chat about whatever you want and play some records.'

She stood up, tapping the sheets of paper into a neat pile on the corner of the desk. 'Forget that, we're not turning into *Milkman's Matinee*. I'll handle this ... What's that Yiddish word you taught me last week?'

'*Momzer*, it means bastard.'

'Yeah, that's the one I was thinking of. Only it's not strong enough. Haven't you got something better I can call him?'

Rosenberg thought for a moment. '*Shmuck*. Yeah, I definitely think our esteemed guest is a *shmuck*.'

Mollie didn't wait to ask what it meant. She looked at the clock and yelped. It was two minutes past nine. She was on air in thirteen minutes and she still hadn't worked out her lead questions. 'Get out of here! Out! Now! I have to get ready.'

'Here are a few suggestions to prime the pump.' Phil tossed her a list of possible queries and headed for the door.

*

'Allow me to quote from your article of 5 January, Mr Kalman. "President Roosevelt's speech to Congress was designed to make war happen. The man is a liar and once more he has misled the American people. Germany bears the United States no ill will, the Fatherland doesn't threaten America in any way, but the Jew-lover Roosevelt wants Congress to repeal the Neutrality Act and give weapons to Germany's enemies." You did write those words, didn't you?'

'Yes, I did. They're the truth.'

Kalman was short, fair and paunchy, and wore gold rimmed glasses and a tweed suit; he looked like a benign professor and he bent toward the mike with an air of serious attention, as if he were anxious that the listening audience should hear clearly every word he said.

'But it's not the truth, Mr Kalman,' Mollie said sweetly. 'You have written absolute nonsense.'

In his seat in the control booth Phil Rosenberg grinned. She always used that specially mild and reasonable tone just before she came in for the kill. He winked at the engineer and the engineer winked back. Kalman was protesting but they ignored him and waited for Mollie's next words.

'Nobody in America wants a war,' she interrupted. 'Least of all F.D.R. It is Germany who has been the aggressor in Austria and the Rhineland and Sudetenland. Is that not so, Mr Kalman?'

'Austria has joined us of her own free will, the German people wish to be one nation. We are of one pure race. The same is true of the people of the Rhineland and the Sudeten-land.'

'But the Sudetenland is part of Czechoslovakia. Nazi troops invaded a sovereign nation without provocation. That's not war-mongering, Mr Kalman. That's making war.'

The German grew red in the face. 'You don't understand. It is always the same. Decent American people are being lied to by Jews and Jew-lovers like Roosevelt and the kikes around him.'

The engineer looked at Phil, his fingers on the dial that would kill the live mikes and segue into a commercial. Phil held up a hand to forestall him.

'Listen, Mr Kalman,' Mollie was saying. 'We don't use

language like that in America. Frankly, we think it's pretty disgusting. You're entitled to have any opinion you want, but you're not entitled to call some Americans names because you don't approve of their religion. I think you owe my listeners an apology.'

Kalman pulled back his shoulders and looked solemn, as if he thought he could be seen by the audience. 'I will never apologize for calling vermin by their proper name. The Jews are like the rats that carried the plague in the Middle Ages. They infect everyone they touch. In Germany we know that, the Führer knows it. We will rid ourselves of them.'

Phil tensed, any second now he knew he'd have to make the slashing motion across his throat which would cause the engineer to cut them off the air. Kalman lifted his arm, thrust it stiffly in front of him and shouted '*Heil Hitler!*' into the mike. Phil started to raise his hand. Mollie spoke before he completed the motion.

'I'll tell you what you are, Mr. Kalman. In the expressive word of the people you're maligning, you're a *shmuck*.'

Phil gestured wildly, the engineer spun the dial. 'Ladies,' a voice said, 'nothing works harder to whiten your clothes than Twenty Mule Team Borax in the black and red box ...'

'What did she call him?' Armando asked.

Kate twisted the knob which shut off the radio. 'I'm not sure, a jerk I think. Isn't it amazing that Mollie can be so fresh on the air and get away with it?'

'Perhaps she will not get away with it for very much longer.'

Kate looked at her husband. Armando was frowning, as if he was the one Mollie had insulted. 'Her programme is very popular, darling. You know it is.'

'Yes. Some fools will listen to anything.'

She thought she ought to defend her sister, but when Armando's dark eyes narrowed like that she didn't dare contradict him. 'Where's Beatriz, with Ricardo?' Asking about her fifteen-month-old son and his nurse was safer than talking about Mollie.

Armando glanced at his watch. 'She will be here in a few seconds.'

They were in Armando's study, where they spent the hours between nine and ten every weekday morning. Kate sat beside his desk and listened while her husband told her what she was to do that day, carefully noting down each instruction in a red leather diary that had its own gold pen attached by a fine gold chain. If the list wasn't too long they would sometimes switch on Mollie's show. Then, promptly at nine forty-five, the nurse brought her charge to his parents.

There was a light tap on the door. '*Adelante*,' Armando said. Señorita Beatriz entered with the blond blue-eyed child in her arms. He stretched out his arms to his mother as soon as he saw her and Kate took him, hugging him close with a sigh of pleasure.

'Armando,' she said over the baby's shoulder, 'couldn't I skip the hairdresser and the gallery luncheon today and just stay home with Ricky? It's such a nice morning. We could go for a walk in the park.'

Armando had been speaking in Spanish with the nurse, now he broke off and smiled indulgently at his wife. 'Darling, you know how important this luncheon is. I'm arranging for a private showing of a Gauguin to a client who happens to be the richest man in Columbia. He relies on my judgement for all his investments in art. And when he sees you he will know that my taste is impeccable. So you can't skip the luncheon. And you certainly can't show up without a perfect hairdo. Don't worry, Beatriz will take my son to the park. We were just talking about it.'

Beatriz understood English, but she received all her instructions from the man she called Don Armando. Every servant in the house was Spanish-speaking. Kate had almost nothing to do with any of them. Between them, Armando and Miguel handled everything.

Kate spent fifteen minutes cuddling the child and cooing to him and trying to get him to say 'horsie', then reluctantly returned him to the nurse and started upstairs to dress for her day. 'The grey wool, *querida*,' Armando called after her departing back. 'And your pearls. And take the new grey hat with you so Joselito can style your hair to suit it.'

The hat was made of crushed grey silk and trimmed with full-blown silk roses in the very palest pink, and the label inside said Lily Daché. All Kate's clothes had impressive labels. The grey dress, for example, was designed by Balenciaga, and the sable coat came from the fur salon at Bonwit Teller. It was all fearsomely expensive. When she got out of the elevator in the front hall of the house it occurred to Kate that she was worth some ten thousand dollars, on the hoof so to speak.

Gradually the mystery about Armando's source of funds had evaporated. She understood now that his income came from the huge sums put into his hands by Latins who didn't speak English or understand the art market as he did, and that it was her husband's job to come up with wonderful things the South Americans could buy. She understood too that she was part of Armando's success, or at least his image. So she repressed her distaste when Miguel glanced impatiently at his watch and opened the door. 'We are late, Doña Katarina. We should have left five minutes ago.'

'Then you'll just have to drive a bit faster, won't you?' she said tartly.

Miguel pursed his lips as if he were annoyed, but he didn't say anything. He never said anything that could be construed as offensive, his mild reproach of a moment ago was as strong as any he ever made. Nonetheless, he offended Kate.

She had gone from enjoying the constant attendance danced upon her by her husband's ugly cousin to resenting the fact that Miguel was always present, seemed almost to be keeping an eye on her. She sat in the rear seat of the big Packard and stared at the back of his neck, imagining what he'd say if she suddenly raked her long fingernails over the soft flesh. It wasn't Miguel's fault that she had so little time to spend with her son, but it was easier to blame him than Armando, and Kate did. Miguel seemed entirely unaware of how she felt about him.

Mollie and Steve had been forced to give up the sublet on West Sixtieth Street six months before, when the original tenants returned. They'd found another apartment in the same building, a one-bedroom with a large living room looking out on Columbus Circle and Central Park.

Mollie heard voices when she got to the door. Steve must

be home. That was unusual, he was seldom home at noon. She had her key in the lock, so she didn't bother to ring the bell, just let herself in.

The apartment was unfurnished when they got it, and it still looked as if they hadn't quite finished moving in. Steve and Nick occupied the only seating in the room, a couch upholstered in what had once been a green nubby fabric. The nap had worn off years before, and the colour had faded past recognition. Mollie had carted it down from Red Hook, also the two tables and the small bookcase which completed the room's furnishing. Steve had his stockinged feet on one of the tables and his tie had been pulled askew. Nick, as always, was impeccably groomed. Both men held glasses of beer.

'Hi, I didn't expect to find you two here.' Mollie took off her coat and hung it in the closet. She was as careful of her clothes as she was careless of her home.

'We've got a few things to discuss.' Steve didn't look at her. No surprise. He seldom looked at her. 'Needed to be someplace where the walls don't have ears.'

'Oh, why is that?' She kicked off her red high heels and sat down on the worn beige carpet the previous tenants had left behind.

'I heard you pulled a duzie on the air today,' Nick said.

It was a pretty obvious change of subject. Mollie looked at him, but she answered without comment.

'Apparently, though I didn't know it at the time. Phil told me the word *shmuck*, but not what it meant. Anyway, that jerk Kalman made me so mad I'd probably have said it even if I knew what it meant.'

'Just what I've always wanted,' Steve said, tipping his head back and looking at the ceiling. 'A wife who calls a guy a prick on national radio.'

She wouldn't let on how much his words and his tone stung her. She never did. 'Doesn't matter,' she said easily. 'We cleaned it up for the west coast, and we figure most listeners think I said jerk. I hung around for an hour to see if there was going to be trouble, but there wasn't a peep out of the sponsors or the gods of management on the twenty-fifth floor. What is it you guys need to talk about in secret?'

The two men looked at each other; neither said anything.

158

'C'mon,' Mollie protested. 'I'm not a spy for whoever the other side is. What's going on?'

'Business,' Steve said shortly. 'Is there anything in the kitchen that could masquerade as lunch?'

Mollie's eyes went from her husband's face to Nick's. Steve wouldn't meet them. Nick did for a moment, then looked away. The silence lengthened until it was perceptible. 'I'll see,' she said finally, standing up.

Apart from beer the refrigerator contained one egg and some sliced ham that was slimy and smelled awful. They almost never ate at home. Both she and Steve had what passed for breakfast at their offices, and Mollie usually had lunch alone in a coffee shop on Fifty-ninth Street. Dinner, too, most nights. Steve worked late much of the time. If he didn't they went to a restaurant. Sometimes, more and more rarely, they'd bring in hamburgers from the White Tower on Columbus Avenue and listen to the radio or read while they ate.

Mollie opened the cupboard and found a box of Wheaties. She poured the cereal into three bowls, put them on a tray and added a bottle of milk. She could hear the low hum of voices in the next room, but the building was old and solidly built and sounds didn't carry well. So why did she have prickles of apprehension racing up and down her spine? She didn't have any data, knew nothing which should be worrying her. Except the fact that they were here in the middle of the day and talking about something, and they didn't want her to know what it was.

'Lunch,' she said, returning to the living room. 'I'm sorry, there's nothing else.'

Steve leaned forward and poured milk into his bowl. 'What else is new?'

'Not much,' Mollie said quietly. 'At least not with me. I never said I was the Betty Crocker homemaker of the year. But stupid I'm not. What are you guys cooking up? And why don't you want to tell me about it?'

'You might as well know,' Steve said. 'Nick's going across the pond.'

She didn't get it at first. 'What pond?' There was a pond near Hillhaven. They'd sometimes ice-skated on it when they

159

were kids. She couldn't make the connection. 'Are you going to Red Hook?'

Nick smiled at her. 'A little farther than that. To London.'

'On assignment,' she said brightly. 'A special assignment in London. That's great, Nick, how long will you be gone?' She knew it wasn't that. She wasn't kidding anybody but herself. Not Nick certainly. He was looking at her in that rueful way which meant he knew she was fibbing, or at least saying one thing and thinking another.

Steve leaned forward and put his empty cereal bowl on the floor. 'For the duration. Old Nick's going to be a hero, help the folks back home hear the screams and smell the stink. Here it is, America, war right in your living room. Brought to you by Milky Way, the nation's favourite candy bar. Send in two wrappers, kids, and we'll send you a spent cartridge of your very own.'

'No,' she whispered. 'No. You can't, Nick. You're an executive, not just a commentator. The brass will forget you while you're gone, you'll be passed over for promotion, you'll be just one more voice on the air ...'

'Ladybug, ladybug fly away home,' Steve said softly. 'Your house is on fire and your children are burned. Any other magic charms you want to use, Mollie?'

She ignored him, kept looking at Nick. 'There may not even be a war. Chamberlain's still trying to head it off. Maybe he'll do it.'

'Neville Chamberlain's the British Prime Minister,' Nick said, 'not Jesus Christ. He's not in the miracle business, even if he thinks he is. Appeasement isn't going to work, you know that as well as I do. Maybe he's buying time, or maybe being a damned fool and letting Hitler get further entrenched. I'm not sure. But war is going to come, I'm sure of that.'

She nodded. She was sure too, that's what made it so terrible. 'All the same, you don't have to go.'

'It's not a question of have to, I *want* to. I decided some time ago that news was my business. This is going to be the central event of the decade, maybe the century. I have to cover it.'

'God, Nick, I'll miss you so much. What about me?'

Steve sucked in his breath, it was a sound as expressive as

words. 'Aye, there's the rub,' he quoted softly. 'What about little Mollie who can't function without her security blanket?'

She looked at him, brown eyes blazing, a dozen retorts on her lips. They all died, she could not bear to take the lid off that particular can of worms. Things were so bad between them, had been bad for so long. They weren't even happy in bed any more, Steve hadn't made love to her for months. She felt as if she walked at the edge of a precipice, that if she gave Steve half a chance he'd tell her he didn't love her any more, maybe had never loved her. That he wanted a divorce. Then she'd tumble over. And now she was losing Nick.

She turned back to him, clawing for a handhold on life. 'I thought Mutual wasn't prepared to support overseas correspondents. Just stringers.'

'That's still their position. I've quit, I'm going overseas as an independent. Going to set up my own unit, file stories with whoever will give me airtime. If the coverage is good enough there'll be buyers.'

She'd been around radio long enough so it didn't have to be spelled out. 'That's what you're talking to Steve about, isn't it? That's what you didn't want to chance anybody from ATL overhearing. You need an engineer. You want him to go with you.'

'It crossed my mind,' Nick admitted. 'Among other things the fact that he speaks fluent French could be very useful.'

'They speak English in London,' she protested, and knew what a dumb remark it was before the words were out of her mouth.

'Yeah,' Nick agreed. 'But I might cross over to France to do some stories.'

'Steve's an American citizen now, he hasn't spoken French in years. Tell him you're an American citizen.' She turned pleading eyes to her husband.

'He knows that,' Steve said. 'But dry your eyes, sweetheart, no need to weep bitter tears for your dearly beloved. I told Nick I'm not hero material. Besides, how can we both go off and leave little Mollie? Who's going to look after her if the big boys go play somewhere else?'

Zena was no longer pretty. She was only forty-one, she could have been, but she'd put on a lot of weight and her blonde hair was streaked with grey and she didn't take much care of it these days. In the restaurant of the Waldorf Astoria no one would notice her among all the fashionable women having lunch. Her daughters, however, were bound to attract attention.

Zena noted with satisfaction that although Mollie had grown up so dramatically in the past two years, beneath her purple hat with the curled black ostrich feather she still wore her short mop of curls and her pixie grin. Her suit was nice, too. A dark heather-coloured tweed with a fitted waist-length jacket and a full skirt. Mollie remained adorable, but Kate, well, Kate was nothing short of exquisite.

'Your table is ready, Señora de Cuentas,' the head waiter had said, bending low over Kate's hand. And he'd led them to the most coveted table on the upper tier that circled the room. Behind Kate was a potted palm. The green fronds of the tree formed a backdrop for the black silk turban which covered all but a tiny bit of her pale blonde hair, they etched a frame for her slim body draped in a black silk faille dress decorated with a single spray of diamond and ruby flowers. Slung over the back of her chair was a sumptuous black Persian lamb jacket trimmed in mink. Kate was breathtaking. Every eye in the room was drawn to her.

A small smile played over Zena's lips. She couldn't help thinking of what Lord Whitby would say if he could see his granddaughter now.

'I don't know what you're smiling about, mom,' Mollie said. 'I think it's awful. Nick's going to be risking his life.'

Zena had come to New York for the day and Kate had arranged this lunch so the three women could talk about Nick's plans. 'I wasn't thinking of Nick,' Zena said now.

'Well I am,' Mollie insisted. 'I'm thinking of him every minute. God, don't either of you realize what it's going to be like? There's going to be a ...' She searched for a word. War wasn't strong enough. They'd all been bandying it about for months. The word 'war' had numbed their ears, died of overuse. 'A holocaust,' she said. 'A firestorm. I promise you this is going to make any war that's gone before look like a tea party.'

'The First World War wasn't a tea party,' Zena said softly.

Mollie reached out and covered her hand. 'I know that, mom, I'm sorry. I forgot for a moment about Kate's father ... But that was then, we can't do anything about it. This is now.'

'We can't do anything about this either,' Kate said. 'I've spoken with Nick. He's made up his mind and booked his passage.' She turned to her sister. 'He told me he asked Steve to go with him.'

Zena's eyes opened wide. 'But that's terrible. What about Mollie?'

Mollie waved the objection aside. 'It doesn't matter. Steve said no, he doesn't want to be a hero.' She didn't add that if Nick were not well aware of what neither her mother nor her sister knew, that she and Steve were something less than a happy couple, he'd not have made the suggestion in the first place. They hadn't talked about it, but Mollie understood why Nick had asked Steve to accompany him. He hoped it would take some of the pressure off the marriage, that maybe when Steve returned things would be better. She was sure that had influenced him more than the fact that Steve was an excellent engineer.

'All the same,' Zena murmured.

Kate started to say something, but was interrupted by one waiter removing their pink grapefruit cocktails while another brought lobster in cream sauce for Zena, and chicken and walnut salads for Kate and Mollie.

Zena ate enthusiastically, but she noticed her daughters toying with their food. 'Cheer up, darlings,' she said brightly. 'Nick is far too clever to let any German get the better of him. Don't forget he was nine years old when he came all the way from Ohio to New York by himself, with nothing but forty dollars and the address of an uncle he'd never met.'

They'd heard the story before countless times, but they listened again. Because the very familiarity was comforting, and because it made Zena happy to tell it. Midway through the account of Nick stuffing milk and cookies into his mouth because he hadn't eaten in two days the head waiter approached. 'Señora de Cuentas,' he said softly, 'your driver asked me to tell you he's waiting.'

Kate glanced at her watch. It was quarter to two. She had to meet Armando in a gallery on Madison Avenue in fifteen minutes. 'I'm afraid I have to run, don't you two rush. Have dessert. The bill's all taken care of.'

Zena and Mollie accepted the kisses she bestowed and watched her leave — that is, they watched everyone else in the restaurant watching her leave. 'She's too damned beautiful to be real,' Mollie murmured.

'Yes,' her mother agreed. 'And isn't her marriage perfect? I mean I was worried at first, but who could be a more ideal husband for Kate than a man as rich and handsome as Armando?'

'Yeah,' Mollie said softly. 'Perfect. That's why she has that haunted look in her eyes and why she doesn't get to blow her nose unless that damned Miguel is holding the handkerchief.'

'I don't understand.' Zena's blue eyes clouded with worry.

'It's nothing, mom. I'm just talking. I'm probably jealous because she has half a dozen fur coats, each more stunning than the next, and I'm stuck with one.' She ran her hand over the sleeve of the sheared beaver draped across the back of the chair. 'Oh well, I'd look silly in sable or Persian lamb. Little Mollie trying to be as gorgeous as her big sister. What about dessert? Last time Kate brought me here I had the brownie with ice cream and fudge sauce. Terrific.'

Zena's frown disappeared.

'Dinner,' Nick said on the telephone. 'Thursday night. Just you and me. To say so long for a while.'

'You sound like a goddamn song.' Mollie gripped the receiver. Tears were choking her voice so she practically growled the words. 'When do you sail?'

'Friday morning. I don't want anyone to come to the pier. That's why I want us to have dinner. How about Sung Ho's on Pell Street?'

She had to smile. They had developed a taste for Chinese food in those long-ago days when they slept at Grace Mitsuno's apartment on Mulberry Street every Saturday night. Grace always gave them boiled rice and hot milk for Sunday breakfast, but neither of them liked it. So after they left they would stop at a Chinese bakery near the subway station and treat themselves to soft doughy buns filled with roast pork in some strange but delicious sauce. Two for a nickel, that's what the fat rounds redolent with lard and spices had cost. They'd both felt guilty about the indulgence until they confessed to Zena and she gave them formal permission to spend the money.

'Okay,' Mollie said. 'But I think dinner's going to set you back more than five cents. I'm not so easy to please these days.'

'I'll go to the bank before I come,' Nick promised.

He was waiting for her outside the restaurant. 'Brought you a present,' he said, kissing her cheek and putting his arm around her.

'I just realized we should have gone to a corned beef and cabbage joint, it's St Patrick's day. What's my present?'

'Open it.'

She untwisted the paper bag he'd handed her and peered inside. Two round buns were nestled in a napkin already stained with grease. 'Oh Nick. Damn you, you're going to make me cry. I promised myself I wouldn't cry. My mascara will run.'

'Don't bother, I'm crying enough for both of us. These things cost a dime apiece now. Come inside.'

This wasn't a Chinese restaurant for the barbarians who thought chop suey an authentic dish. There were no red tassels or gilt pagodas, just hard chairs and bare wooden tables. Sung Ho's was run by Chinese for Chinese, it was spotlessly clean and it smelled wonderful.

Nick had eaten here before, but the waiter who approached their table didn't recognize him. He looked skeptical, convinced they'd wandered in by mistake, until Nick ordered cold eel with ginger and lotus root to accompany their drinks, a gin rickey for her, a manhattan for him. After that the waiter just looked puzzled. When he brought the dish and saw them each pick up chopsticks he smiled broadly.

'I think he's the same guy who used to live next door to Lee and Grace,' Mollie said when the waiter left. 'He's missing the same front tooth.'

'A mysterious oriental ritual, they yank one out when you

165

join the secret society.'

'Maybe more truth than fiction in that. Phil had a line on a story about Triads operating here in Chinatown, but we decided not to do it. Too local. As Phil said, "What do they know from Triads in Kansas?" By the way, have you spoken with Grace?'

'Sure. I saw her Sunday night after I got back from Red Hook. To say goodbye. She's pretty worried about Lee.'

'Why?'

'Remember his telling you that he was seeing his father?'

'A couple of years ago, sure I remember. I haven't seen him since then. I keep meaning to call him, but something always comes up.'

'Yeah, I know how it is. I've lost touch too. But Grace says Lee doesn't see many people from the old days any more. He's wrapped up in some project of his dad's.'

Mollie took a long swallow of her drink. 'What project?'

'I don't know. If Grace did, she didn't say. But it worries me, Mollie. As nations go, Japan's become a man-eating shark. They're spreading further inland in China, bombed civilian populations recently, and they definitely want French Indo-China.'

'You'd think that would make Lee hate them. On the other hand, it's got nothing to do with him, Lee's an American.'

'I know that and you do, I wonder if he does.'

The waiter returned to take their dinner order and they didn't talk more about Lee. There were so many other things to discuss, all the things she wanted to say. Take care of yourself, don't be crazy, don't be a hero, be cautious so you're sure to come back in one piece . . .

She didn't actually speak any of those words. Instead they talked about the old days, about the carnivals and the fairs and the dance marathons and Miss Magic Mollie Pride, and Nick doing the soft shoe over to the piano and playing her intro number. And Kate singing her solo in a wispy, winsome voice that quivered on the high notes. 'I guess after all she's got what she always wanted,' Nick said finally. 'Someone to watch over her.'

'Yeah, Armando does that all right. At least Miguel does

it on his behalf. Do you know she only gets to spend about an hour a day with Ricky? And that only in shifts. Fifteen minute slots, it's like programming.'

'I know. We had a farewell drink yesterday at her place. Do you think she's happy, Mollie?'

She hesitated. 'What's happy?' she asked finally.

He reached out and took her hand, pushing aside the chopsticks and the little handleless cup of tea so he could make contact. 'I'm not sure, but it's what I want you to be.'

'I'm doing fine. I haven't told anyone yet, but there's talk about giving me a Sunday morning show in addition to my weekly slot. Nothing definite yet, just talk.'

'You're still knocking 'em dead, kid. That's nice, but it's not what I meant.'

'I know what you meant. Nick, let's not talk about it, okay? Not until you come back.'

'Okay.' He stared at her a moment, then he started to hum. '*Charleston, Charleston, da da da-da dum dum ...*'

'Don't. I can't stand it.' She had to pull her hand from his and rummage in her bag for a hankie. 'Listen, I want to tell you something. If you don't come back from this lark in good shape, just the way you're leaving, I'll ... Well, I'll kill you.'

It was after eleven when he put her in a taxi and told the driver Sixtieth and Eighth Avenue. Mollie stopped the cabbie before he got there. It was unseasonably mild, the first warm Saint Patrick's day she ever remembered, usually it snowed. 'Let me out here, will you,' she said when they reached Fifty-fifth Street. 'I'll walk the rest of the way.'

She strolled slowly uptown on Eighth Avenue, past the windows filled with spangled leotards and blonde wigs because the block had a concentration of theatrical costumers. The feathers and furbelows looked weird tonight. Everything was so quiet, not a lot of cars and just one half-empty bus. When she got to Fifty-seventh Street she noted that most of the crosstown traffic was headed east. Of course, it was still early enough to join the Irish revels in the shadow of the Third Avenue church. That's where the crowds had gone. Suddenly she felt very alone and vulnerable. On impulse she turned west on Fifty-eighth, deciding to approach her apartment building from Columbus Avenue rather than walk through Columbus Circle.

It was a block mostly of old brownstones. Many had been private mansions until about fifty years ago when they were cut up into apartments. She was the only person in the street until up ahead a man let himself out of one of the brownstones. He stood on the stoop a moment, talking to someone she couldn't see. Mollie stopped walking. The man she was watching was her husband.

Instinctively she stepped into the shadow beyond the street light. Steve leaned forward. The angle of his back and his shoulders told her he was kissing someone goodnight. A few seconds later he straightened and lifted his hand in a farewell salute and ran down the steps to the street. He moved with a jauntiness she hadn't seen him exhibit in years. Since before they were married, she realized suddenly. She hadn't thought about it until seeing him now. Steve wasn't the same as he'd been when she first met him. He had changed. Well, so had she. No, she'd grown up, what had happened to him was something different.

He's cheating on me. The thought didn't surface until a few more seconds passed and she watched him stride to the end of the block and disappear around the corner. He's cheating on me. Steve has a girlfriend. She stood very still. She couldn't move if she had wanted to. Her feet were rooted to the sidewalk. She'd heard the phrase about legs turning to jelly. It was wrong. Hers had become steel poles, she could neither bend nor lift them. She couldn't walk. But she had to, she couldn't stay here all night. Steve expected her ...

The thought struck her as absurdly funny and she began to giggle, then to tremble. Well good, at least she could move. Mollie forced herself to take a few steps forward, and when she drew level with the door Steve had closed behind him she paused and examined it, noting the number, and that the only apartment with a light behind the windows was on the second floor. Then she walked on. By the time she got to their apartment he'd had at least a ten-minute headstart.

Her hand was shaking when she put the key in the lock. I don't know what to say, she told herself. I don't know how to deal with this. She opened her mouth to frame some words she couldn't yet imagine, but he wasn't sitting in the living room. It was dark. The whole apartment was dark. There wasn't even a sliver of light from beneath the bedroom door. Maybe he hadn't come home. But where would he go at this hour? A bar somewhere, perhaps.

Mollie turned on a lamp and went to the bedroom and looked inside. Steve was in the bed, covers pulled up above his head, pretending to be asleep. So she'd think he'd been in all evening, or at least since whenever he came home from work.

She closed the door and walked to the bathroom and stripped off her clothes and turned the shower on full force and stood beneath it, and at last allowed herself the tears she'd been suppressing all evening. After a while she realized she didn't know if she was crying for herself or for Nick or for Steve. Maybe for all of them. And for Lee Mitsuno and Kate if it came to that. Where had they gone, all the hopes and dreams of childhood? She didn't know. All she could hear was Nick's voice, humming, as he had earlier. '*Charleston, Charleston, da da da-da dum dum . . .*'

She took to standing on West Fifty-eighth street across from the brownstone, staring at the second floor, but only when she knew for sure that Steve was working and wouldn't be there.

It was impossible to see anything in the apartment, even when the shades were up. The windows were full of plants. Mollie felt fairly safe while she kept vigil, all that greenery must make it impossible to see out as well as in. Still, the girl might know what Mollie looked like, so she took care to hide herself in a doorway. At first she worried that a cop would come along and ask why she was loitering, but nobody paid her any attention. Hell, this wasn't Red Hook. You could do almost anything on a New York street and get away with it.

The girl's name was Lois Lane. It was crazy, but that's what it said on her mailbox. Mollie had watched her leave one afternoon, and dashed into the foyer of the building and checked. Lois Lane. Like Superman's girlfriend. So who did Steve think he was, the guy in the red and blue tights or

169

Clark Kent? Oh shit, she knew who he thought he was. Mr Average American Guy. Because Lois Lane was Miss Girl Next Door.

She was tall and slim and had blonde hair and light eyes. Probably blue, though Mollie never got close enough to be sure. She looked a little like Kate, though she certainly wasn't gorgeous. Pretty though, definitely pretty. And maybe not a bad figure. It was hard to be sure about that either, she always wore a navy beret and a navy plaid scarf with her tailored camel's hair reefer coat. Gloves too, of course. Lois Lane never went out without navy blue woollen gloves. Her excursions usually took place in the early afternoon. Mollie knew where she went, she'd followed her.

Steve's girlfriend apparently didn't work, in fact she only seemed to do one thing, go shopping. Not for clothes or anything foolish like that, she went to the A & P on Columbus Avenue, or sometimes the First National on Seventh Avenue. There was a Gristedes on Broadway, but Lois was obviously the frugal type. She shopped at the economy stores and before she went in she spent a long time studying the lists of specials posted in the window. Half a hour later she'd emerge carrying two or three big brown bags. The markets charged extra for delivery.

While she stood across the street staring at the second floor on those late March days Mollie imagined what was happening inside. The bitch was cooking, she was sure of that. What else would she be doing with all those groceries? She was making beef stew and dumplings for Steve. Or maybe salmon wiggle, or chicken fricassee. And corn bread probably. Maybe biscuits.

Once she actually saw Steve come down the street and go into the building. It was a terrific shock. She was standing there on 29 March, a Tuesday afternoon. Steve was the engineer for a programme called Smarty Smarts, brainy kids who answered questions about everything under the sun. ATL aired the show live on Tuesday afternoons and Steve was always the engineer. So what was he doing bounding up the stairs to Lois Lane's apartment? She must have telephoned to say she was making something special and he couldn't resist.

Mollie waited until he was safely inside, then ran all the way home. She'd bought a cookbook two and a half years ago when they were first married. She'd only made one thing from it, macaroni and cheese which had come out a cross between glue and lead. Now she fished the book down from the shelf and thumbed through the pages, choking back sobs while she did so. Creamed chicken on toast. That was perfect. She ran back into the street and went to the small mom and pop grocery on the corner. It was a lot more expensive than the A & P or First National. Well screw you, Lois Lane, I'm making seventy-five bucks a week these days.

Steve arrived home a little after seven. He stood in the living room and sniffed the unfamiliar cooking smells. 'What the hell did you burn?'

'The toast. But it's okay, I scraped it. We're having creamed chicken on toast.'

'Oh. What got into you, a sudden urge to domesticity?'

'I just thought it would be nice. We haven't had a home-cooked meal for a long time.' Not true, he had lots of home-cooked meals. But not with her.

'I'm not hungry. Going to take a shower and go out. Some of the guys from the station have organized a poker game.'

'But I made supper for you. Look, the table's all set.'

She'd found a clean sheet and spread it over the coffee table and even discovered a candle and a candle holder in the back of one of the almost empty kitchen cupboards. Steve looked at the arrangement and shrugged. Then he walked into the bathroom without saying another word.

Fifteen minutes later he was gone, still without speaking to her. Mollie stood at the stove and watched her creamed chicken turning gelatinous in the chipped enamel sauce-pan. Eventually she scraped it into the toilet and pulled the chain.

The next day she was back at her post on West Fifty-eighth Street. She went there as soon as she left the studio and was in position by eleven-thirty. Lois Lane didn't appear. She must have decided she didn't need anything today, or maybe she'd gone out earlier in the morning. A little after two Mollie made up her mind. She took a deep breath and crossed the road and walked into the brownstone and climbed the stairs to the second floor and knocked on the door.

'Yes, can I help you?'

She wasn't as pretty close up. Her skin wasn't great, and her teeth were crooked. And she was wearing an apron. Jesus, an apron with a ruffle. 'I'm Mollie Pride.' For a moment there was no flicker of understanding in the girl's eyes. They were blue, Mollie noticed. Light blue. 'Mollie Rogers,' she added. 'Steve's wife.'

'Oh, I see.'

Mollie craned her neck to look over Lois Lane's shoulder into the apartment. 'Do you? What do you see?'

'I mean I know why you're here. It's kind of silly to pretend I don't, isn't it?'

'Yeah, kind of silly.'

'Maybe you'd better come in.'

The living room had a rag rug on the floor and a matching three piece suite upholstered in wine-coloured boucle. The couch and the chairs had lace doilies on the arms. There were lots of framed pictures of dogs and flowers hanging on the walls. And plants. A goddamn' forest of plants; the ones in the window were only the tip of the iceberg. Scattered around the room were red geraniums, and trailing ivy, and at least three spiky snake plants.

'Jesus,' Mollie said.

'I beg your pardon.

'I said Jesus. You probably don't swear, sorry if I'm shocking you. But you don't draw the line at adultery, do you? I mean that's okay in this little corner of domestic heaven, is it?'

'Steve and I love each other. He isn't happy with you, hasn't been for a long time.'

Rage began to race through her, there were a dozen retorts on her lips. She started to say something, then stopped because all the breath was suddenly knocked out of her. Her fury was smothered by what she had suddenly noticed.

There was a large easy chair in one corner of the room. On the floor beside it was a pair of men's slippers which could only be Steve's. And Mollie knew that the sweater neatly draped over the back of the chair was his, she'd bought it for him last Christmas. She looked at the scene and at Lois Lane, then she turned and fled.

That night Steve didn't come home until after ten. Mollie was sitting in the living room waiting for him.

'Still up? I figured you would be. Lois called me at the station.'

'Then you went over there, because I upset her so much, right?'

'Right.'

She waited a moment. He took off his coat but didn't say anything else. 'Aren't you going to apologize?' she asked. 'Maybe explain?'

'No. There's not much point, is there? You've seen her, seen the way she lives. I don't think there's much to explain. Not much to apologize for either. You created this situation, Mollie, not me. You had to go on being Mollie Pride, girl wonder. It wasn't enough to be Mrs Steve Rogers. I wasn't enough. Because I'm not like Nick. I suppose. He's the one you measure everything against. Lois just loves me for what I am.'

'That's not fair! God, it's so unfair. I'm the one who wanted to quit work and have a baby when we were first married. I did, Steve, you must remember.'

'Yeah, sure. But it was crazy then, you were too young. And I haven't noticed you suggesting it lately. Not since you became Miss Expert on Everything Important.'

She was still sitting on the couch, hugging herself, rocking back and forth as if the motion might make her feel less miserable. 'How long?' she whispered. 'How long have you been playing Superman for Lois Lane.'

'Not Superman, just an ordinary guy. I don't remember exactly, a long time. Over two years I think.'

'Oh Jesus.' He hadn't made love to her in what, six months? But before that their sex life had been what she thought of as normal. So for a long time there'd been an overlap. Screwing Lois Lane on Fifty-eighth Street, then coming home to Sixtieth and screwing her. 'Oh Jesus,' she said again. The pain inside her eddied in sickening waves.

173

She tried to fight it off to retain control, but it was closing over her head, sucking her into a pit of misery.

'Mollie . . .' She made herself look up. He was still standing near the door. But his hands were outstretched, reaching out to her.

'Tell me something.' Her words came out as a moan, she didn't recognize her own voice. 'Tell me one thing. Why didn't you simply say you wanted a divorce?'

'Because I didn't.'

She stared, opened her mouth, closed it again. She was choking on pain and despair.

'I didn't and I don't,' Steve said quietly. 'That's the hell of it, sweetheart. I loved you. I still do.'

She stretched out her arms to him, wanting to grab him, swallow him, beg him to say it again — to mean it. 'Steve,' she said. It was all she could manage. 'Steve.'

He crossed to her and pulled her close, they clung to each other for a long moment. Then she was lying on the couch and he was on top of her, pushing up her skirt, fumbling with the buttons of his fly. She waited for him to enter her, arched toward him. Nothing happened. 'Steve . . .' A whisper, a plea, a question. 'Steve . . .'

'Shit!' The exclamation burst from him as he pulled away from her. 'Shit!' he said again.

'It's okay, listen, it's okay. We're both so upset. We'll try again, darling. This time we'll do better. I don't mean sex.' 'I mean our lives.'

'Yeah, sure.' He walked to where he'd dropped his coat, then he left, pulling the door softly shut behind him.

The next morning was 31 March. However she felt, Mollie was a trouper, had been trained to be one since almost before she could walk. She was at the studio exactly on schedule, seven forty-five. Phil didn't greet her in the usual way. 'You look like hell,' he said instead.

'Yeah, well I feel like it too. Is Birney all set?' She was scheduled to talk about the big band sound with Ben Birney who'd made famous the phrase. 'Yowza, yowza, yowza.'

'No, I called him off.'

'For Christ's sake, why? I'm not in the mood for any

174

games, Phil. If something's going on tell me about it in words of one syllable, okay?'

'I don't know how many syllables, but it's simple enough.' He waved a piece of paper from from the teletype machine. 'The end of the world as we know it. Chamberlain's told Parliament that if Poland is threatened Britain and France will come to her aid. For aid read bang, bang you're dead.'

Wheels started turning in Mollie's head. She'd been so steeped in all this manoeuvring for so long that the pieces fell into place automatically, their import immediately clear and superceding her personal misery. 'He's going after Danzig and the Polish Corridor. As far as our friend Adolf is concerned they're his by divine right. That's been in the cards for months, everybody knows it.'

'Yup. So it's the end of appeasement. Good ole' boy Neville has drawn the line and said I dare you.'

She put her hands to her head and sat down hard. 'How are we going to handle it? I mean this morning's show.'

'I've lined up La Guardia.'

'The mayor! What kind of a crazy idea is that? What's he going to say, that New York City will decide whether American kids should go get shot in Europe? We're talking foreign policy, Phil. What does it have to do with Fiorello?'

'Not a lot,' he admitted. 'But he's smart. So he'll give you somebody to bounce ideas around with. In terms of knowing what's happening you could go on and commentate this yourself, Mollie. But the format says you need somebody to talk to. So I've got you somebody. Now you can explain to all the ladies in America what's happened and what it means.'

She narrowed her eyes. 'How come the little flower agreed to play straight man for my act?'

'Because I didn't put it to him exactly like that. And because he's Italian and Italy is Germany's ally, and he's desperate for as many chances as he can get to prove that he's as loyal as any American named Smith or Jones. He's squeezing in a half-hour with us because your show is one of the best forums he could possibly find.'

Mollie nodded, then she sat down at her desk and began scribbling a list of the points she wanted to cover.

She didn't get home until after nine in the evening, she'd hung around the station listening to the relay broadcasts from Europe and watching the teletype. So did everybody else, the place had been like Grand Central Station at rush hour. They finally got Chamberlain's exact words. He'd made his statement almost casually, in Parliament, in response to a question from another member. '... in the event of any action which clearly threatened Polish independence, and which the Polish Government considered it right to resist with their national forces, His Majesty's Government would feel themselves bound at once to lend the Polish Government all the support in their power ...'

'Well, that should be clear enough for the bastards,' Mollie said when she read the despatch.

Some of the newsmen disagreed. 'Not necessarily,' Fulton Lewis said. He was top dog in the NBC news department, the star. 'If the Brits want to wriggle out of it, they will,' he muttered.'

'Would you mind explaining that, Mr Lewis?' Mollie asked.

Lewis leaned forward and snatched something he'd been reading off the teleprinter. 'Here's the editorial of the London *Times*, it makes my point.'

Because of the time difference the article was datelined 1 April. The writer had taken full advantage of his paper's legendary role as the old thunderer, the voice of Britain, empowered to interpret government for the public, and sometimes for government itself. For months now *The Times* had been squarely in the camp of appeasement. It did not mean to shift its position just because the Prime Minister had gone off half cocked in the House of Commons.

Mollie read the editorial with a growing sense of disbelief: '*The importance of the government's declaration is that it commits them to stand for free and fair negotiation.*'

'But they've been negotiating since the mess began!' Mollie exclaimed. 'That's what appeasement really is, negotiating without getting anything in return.'

176

Phil was looking over her shoulder. He read the next lines aloud. '*The new obligation does not bind the government to defend every inch of the present frontiers of Poland. The key word is not "integrity" but "independence ..."* What a crock of horse manure.'

'British horse manure,' Fulton Lewis said. 'Carefully shovelled into nice neat piles. So they can walk around it without getting their shoes dirty.'

Her head was still ringing with the arguments and speculation when she finally walked into her apartment. Then she stood in the doorway and all the sordid details of her personal drama slammed her in the face, as if the pain and the ugliness had been lying in wait for her here.

The living room was dark. She'd telephoned four times. Each time there had been no answer, but she'd been sure Steve would be home by now.

Steve,' she called. 'Are you here?'

There was no reply.

'Steve?' Softly this time, because she knew she was summoning a ghost, that he wasn't home. He was two blocks away playing house with Lois Lane.

Mollie switched on the light and saw the letter. She couldn't miss it, he'd pinned it to the back of the couch.

'This is to say goodbye, sweetheart, or maybe only see you later, I'm not exactly sure. But I'm sure I can't hang around and keep living a double life. Besides, it looks like Nick was right. Heard your show this a.m., so I know you know what's happened. I've managed to get a seat on the Pan American clipper ship to London. If the plane doesn't sink into the sea at takeoff, or fall out of the sky en route, I'll hook up with Nick. Can't let him have all the glory, can I? Besides, there's probably not an engineer in England who can keep up with him. Take care of yourself.'

She read the note three times. Then she sat down on the couch and waited to cry. No tears came, only a dull, dry, aching pain, the same anguish of loss she'd felt when her father died. Once more there was no buzz in Mollie's universe.

Mollie felt as if the NBC teletype was her only link to reality.

Suddenly half her life, the half that really mattered, had transferred itself three thousand miles across the ocean, and the teletype was her only connection with it. During that first week of April, Holy Week as it happened, the news kept coming; jungle drums beating out a tattoo of bravado with a counter-point of dread.

The Commons debated Chamberlain's statement about defending Poland. Endlessly, it seemed to Mollie. The Prime Minister insisted that he'd meant what he said, *The Times* notwithstanding. Winston Churchill, Chamberlain's most bitter opponent, congratulated him on this transformation of policy. A man she'd never heard of called Cripps said that it was just talk, that the government was in sympathy with totalitarian views and would do nothing whatever happened. Lloyd George, who had guided Britain through the First World War, pointed out that the country was so ill-prepared to fight that its declaration of support for Poland meant nothing.

Mollie devoured as many foreign and domestic newspapers as she could find at the newstand in Grand Central Station. She read endless column inches of reporting and analysis, then she distilled what she'd learned and passed it on to her listeners. 'England must make a pact with Russia so the Red Army is firmly on the side of democracy,' she told them. 'Until they do, they can promise anything they want, but it's not going to mean much because they can't back up the words with deeds. What's more, if Stalin and the communists decide to play on Hitler's team they will represent a force so enormous it's hard to see who could stop them from simply taking whatever they want.'

But her own problems couldn't be clarified or explained by any newspaper. All that week she raced back to Sixtieth Street as soon as she was off the air and flung open her mailbox; it was invariably empty. It's too soon, she told herself. Nick's only been there a couple of weeks, Steve's just arrived, they haven't had time to write to me ...

'What's with you?' Phil asked on Thursday. 'You look half dead. Mollie, is something wrong at home?'

She fumbled in her bag and found a compact and a lipstick. 'Steve's gone to England.' She studied herself in the mirror and avoided Phil's eyes.

'I take it you mean for an extended stay, not a vacation.'

'That's right. He's going to work with Nick. You know about Nick, don't you?' she added, hoping to deflect him.

'Sure, but I didn't know Steve was involved. I ran into Frane before he left, he didn't say anything about taking Steve with him.'

'It was a last-minute decision.' She shut the compact with a snap. The sound was a period signalling that the subject was closed.

Phil hesitated a moment, then went back to discussing the morning's show, an interview with Danny Kaye, the young comic she'd enjoyed so much the previous month. 'I hear he's got a really funny line of double talk, fast patter. See if you can get him to do a bit of it.'

Mollie had walked to the window, she was staring out at the Manhattan skyline, at the people who looked like scurrying ants on the street below. 'It seems a little silly to be talking to a comedian at the moment, doesn't it?'

'No, I don't think so, Mollie. In fact I think we'd better lighten up.'

'What the hell's that supposed to mean? It's not our fault the world's going down the tube. We're not going to change anything whether we play it light or heavy.'

'Yeah,' Phil said softly, 'we'll change a few things. Make the sponsors happier, for instance. They think we're rather over-emphasizing the doom and gloom.'

'Screw the sponsors, isn't that what you always tell me? Plenty more where they came from.'

'That's what I used to tell you,' he amended. 'And as long as the listeners love you it's true.'

She turned to face him. 'But? C'mon, Phil, there's a but in that sentence. I want to hear the rest of it.'

'Not now,' he said quickly. 'You're on the air in less than half an hour. We'll talk later if you want.'

'I want to talk now. Are you telling me my audience is switching me off?'

He had his foot up on the desk, tying a shoelace with slow, deliberate movements. As if it were the most important task in the universe. 'We've had a few indications.'

'Indications of what? Jesus! Will you give it to me straight and stop all this pussy-footing around!'

'Okay. The calls have been coming in fairly heavy for the last couple of weeks. Letters too. They're running sixty–forty against you.'

'Against me? But it's not my fault that things are such a mess. I'm only telling it like it is.'

'I know that, Mollie. Thing is, your average American housewife is sick of being reminded of how it is. At the moment they don't want to think about it. They want to think about baseball games and Hollywood and the World's Fair that's going to open in a couple of weeks. Sweetness and light and it's gonna be a lovely day tomorrow.'

'Yeah, we're all going to have our own private aeroplanes, you'll press a button in the kitchen and a meal will magically appear on the table and all stories end "happily ever after". Am I the only person in the United States who doesn't believe in fairy tales?'

'Not exactly, the rest of them only believe in American fairy tales. You know how isolationist most of the country feels. What's ours is ours and the rest of the world can go to hell. Mollie, the great thing about you has always been that you gave them the facts of life in a nice sugar-coated pill they could swallow. A little here, a little there, just enough so they felt informed without getting indigestion.'

'And now?'

'Now they think ... Well, one lady said if you were so obsessed with Europe maybe you should move there.'

She sat down hard behind the desk. He didn't have to spell it out. In her business you were allowed very few mistakes. The slightest sign that the audience had lost interest, and the sponsors withdrew. The second that occurred, the show was cancelled. 'Oh shit,' she said quietly.

'My sentiments exactly.' Phil leaned forward and tugged on the bow at the neck of her red silk blouse. 'C'mon, sunshine, smile. I was going to tell you later rather than now, but it doesn't matter. I've got a nice bunch of celebrities for you to talk to over the next couple of weeks. You'll turn the whole thing around before the end of the month.'

She was terrific with Danny Kaye. He really was very

funny and his double talk even broke up Phil and the engineer. 'Nobody switched you off this time,' Phil said after the show. 'I guarantee it.'

Mollie didn't answer, just gathered her things together prior to leaving. 'Hold on a second,' Phil said. 'I read in this morning's *Trib* that some guy from Mexico bought a Gauguin painting for a king's ransom. Right here in New York. The story mentioned your brother-in-law, de Cuentas. It suddenly hit me that your sister would make a great guest. She's always in the gossip columns and the society pages, what do you think?'

'I think it's a lousy idea. You don't know Kate, her long suit is not clever talk. Besides, she's got a goddamn bodyguard who has to be wherever she is. I'm not thrilled by the thought of having Miguel hovering in the background while I'm on the air.'

Phil shrugged. 'Okay, it was just a thought. Go on, get out of here. Do something that makes you happy for the rest of the day, then get a good night's sleep and come in here in the morning ready to give 'em hell. It's Brenda Frazier tomorrow.'

'How exciting,' Mollie murmured. 'Debutante of the year. Is it true that you can dance until five every morning, Brenda, and still put in a strenuous day shopping?'

'Mollie ...'

'I know, I know. We have to lighten up. Okay. I'll ask her if it's true that Douglas Fairbanks Jr is crazy about her, and whether he's a good kisser. That's bound to thrill the ladies in Oshkosh.'

9

Mollie had taken to getting off the subway one stop early, so she could walk home via Fifty-eighth Street. She knew it was crazy: what did she want to do, ask Lois Lane to lunch? That was over, Steve had walked out on them both. Crazy. But she did it anyway, almost automatically this time, because she was still thinking about her conversation with Phil, and about interviewing Brenda Frazier tomorrow.

But she wasn't so preoccupied that she forgot to look at Lois Lane's building. The brownstone looked the same, even to the plants in the second-floor window. Mollie paused, stared at it a moment, then walked on.

When she let herself into her apartment the telephone was ringing and she lunged for it. There had been no mail yet again, maybe this was a long distance call from England.

It wasn't, the call came only from as far away as Chinatown. 'Mollie, it's Grace, how are you?'

'I'm fine. Nice to hear from you, Grace.' She shrugged out of her coat while she spoke. 'How are things?'

'Well ...' There was a long pause on the line.

'Grace, is something the matter?'

'I'm not sure. Mollie, can I see you?'

'Of course. When? Where?'

Grace wanted the meeting to be immediate. She suggested Central Park on Fifth and Fifty-ninth. The urgency in her voice couldn't be denied or put off. Mollie agreed.

She arrived first and took a seat by General Sherman's statue. A lovely day, warm sunshine, a few crocuses flowering beneath the leafless trees, grass that was already bright green, a couple of kids playing nearby, watched by uniformed nurses. Why did kids make her think of Steve? Don't think about it, she told herself.

Still, she couldn't take her eyes off the children. One of them might be hers. Or Kate's. That was another dead-end thought. If one of the laughing little boys happened to be her nephew she probably wouldn't recognize him. She hardly knew young Ricardo de Cuentas, and he didn't know her. Nor his grandmother either. Not really.

Zena had imagined them all spending holidays at Hill-haven, but that wasn't Armando's style. He'd arranged to take his family to Acapulco last Christmas, and to Havana the Christmas before. As far as she knew they were in New York for Easter, but it was a safe bet they wouldn't be going to Red Hook. She should go. She'd call her mother as soon as she got back to the apartment. She had to tell Zena about Steve sooner or later, maybe she'd also report on whatever it was that Grace wanted to talk to her about. As if summoned by her thoughts, at that moment Grace walked towards her.

At first it was just greetings and idle chatter, then a cold wind sprang up and they went looking for a coffee shop where they could be warm while they talked. They found one on Fifty-seventh Street with a long, almost empty counter and two stools at the far end which provided maximum privacy. A bored waitress took their order for tea.

'Now,' Grace said, 'tell me why you have those horrible bags under your eyes.'

'I thought we came here to talk about something that's bothering you.'

'At the moment you're bothering me. Why do you look so terrible?'

'It's Steve,' Mollie admitted. 'He's gone to England to work with Nick.'

'Does that mean he's left you?'

'I thought Chinese people were supposed to be subtle and indirect.'

'Right now it suits me to be very American and direct.' Grace reached for Mollie's hand. 'I've been wondering about you and Steve for some time. Is there trouble? Come on, Mollie, you have to talk to someone.'

'You might call it trouble, he has a girlfriend. Had. He's left her too.'

The tea came while she explained about Lois Lane. Grace

listened and nodded and made sympathetic noises, because there was nothing else she could say. 'Have you told your mother?' she asked finally.

'Not yet. And I'll probably only tell her that he's gone to work with Nick. Not all the other stuff. Mom's got a wonderful heart, but I don't think she understands about things like this. At least, she doesn't want to understand.'

'She's the product of her background, Mollie. We all are.' She added the last words very softly, with a pensive air.

'Grace, we've been talking about nothing but my troubles. Tell me why you wanted to see me.'

'Because Lee's gone too.'

'Lee! To England?' The thought just popped into her head, because of Steve and Nick.

'No. I'm not sure where, but certainly not to England. Mollie, you're so well-informed these days, I listen to you every morning and I always learn something new, but you only talk about America and Europe. What do you know about the way things are in Japan?'

'Not a lot,' Mollie admitted. 'Nick spoke a couple of times about them wanting to take over Asia and how militaristic they've become, but it's the other side of the world, Grace. Not something my listeners are very much affected by.'

Their cups were empty, so Grace signalled to the waitress to bring them each a refill. 'No, I know they're not. Besides, one Oriental looks pretty much like another to Caucasians. Japanese, Chinese, we're all the same, little yellow people with slanty eyes.'

'Grace, I didn't mean ...'

'Don't be ridiculous. I know what you meant and didn't mean. I'm just commenting on the general state of the world. I was in Ohrbachs the other day and the salesgirl talked to me as if I were a foreigner, you know, slowly and very clearly. I think she was Irish, but I didn't bother to tell her that my family have probably been in America longer than hers.'

'You live with it all the time, don't you? The misunderstanding and the prejudice.'

'All the time,' Grace agreed. 'I don't let it bother me. Lee was always different.'

'You still haven't told me where he is.'

'I told you, I don't know where he is. He bade me a formal goodbye, like a well-brought up Oriental son, and said he was going somewhere with his father for a while. I think maybe Japan, but I'm not sure. You probably don't know this, but my husband went back to Japan after he left us. He didn't return to America until 1936. That's when he got in touch with Lee.'

'Was he born in Japan?'

'Lee's father? Yes. That makes him Issei. Issei can never become American citizens, there's a law against it. My husband's parents brought him to California when he was two. That's where we met. I'm from San Francisco. We came east because with a mixed marriage like ours, living near our families was impossible. But you know all that.'

'A little bit about your history. Not much about Japan today.'

'It's complicated. The military have a lot of constitutional power. They're split up into groups, factions really. The Koda-ha, that means Imperial Way, are extremists. They were behind the taking of Manchuria and the war in China.' She stopped. 'Mollie, that's not a surprise is it? You know the Japanese have occupied large parts of China?'

'Since 1937, yes, that much even I know. Are these Koda-ha top dogs in Japan now?'

'Just the opposite. They tried to take over Tokyo a couple of years ago and failed. Their rivals, the Control Faction, became much stronger as a result. Saito, that's my husband, was involved with the Koda-ha. I think he only came back here when they got into trouble.'

'And Lee?' Mollie prompted gently. 'What does all this have to do with him? Lee's an American citizen, isn't he? I always assumed he was.'

'Oh yes, of course. He was born here, that makes him Nisei, second generation on his father's side, that's different. But he's spent so much time with Saito these past few years. I think he's started imagining that he's really Japanese. Not American, and certainly not Chinese. After Kate got married, well, he was particularly vulnerable.'

'Kate! Grace, I'm sorry, you've lost me. What does Kate

have to do with any of this?'

The older woman smiled. 'You're one of the least prejudiced people I know, but even you never saw it because you considered it simply unthinkable. Like Zena. Lee's been in love with Kate since the moment he laid eyes on her.'

'Everyone's knocked out when they first see Kate. They can't help it. But that's not the same as being in love with her. Aren't you maybe exaggerating a bit?'

'Not at all,' Grace said simply. 'Lee worships her. At least he did. When she married Armando he changed. Don't you remember that he didn't come to the wedding?'

'Now that you mention it, yes I do. What do you mean he changed. How?'

'Love is very close to hate,' Grace said softly. 'Rejection, real or imagined, does funny things to people.'

Mollie put her head in her hands. 'Oh God, what a mess we all seem to have made of our lives. Grace, is there something I can do? About Lee, I mean. You wouldn't have wanted to see me today if you didn't think there was.'

'It's probably a foolish idea. I thought maybe you could find something out. Because of your sources. Because you're so close to the news.'

'I'll try,' Mollie promised. She didn't really think she would find out anything about Lee Mitsuno, but it was impossible to say that to a dear old friend who at this moment was a mother worried about her only child.

'Did you work out any wonderful questions for me to ask Brenda Frazier?' Mollie hung up her coat and sat down across from Phil. 'Besides how Fairbanks kisses.'

'Here's a list.' He handed her a sheet of paper. 'I concentrated on her charity work. She was on fifteen different committees last year. Maybe you can find a brain beneath all that fluff and feathers. Otherwise you can get her talking about café society and show her up for the bubble-head I think she is.'

'Okay.' Mollie took the list but didn't look at it. The Brenda Fraziers of this world she could handle with one hand tied behind her back. 'Phil, do you know anything about Tokyo, and the Koda-ha or the Control Faction?'

'Only that they're rival Japanese groups struggling to get power. Mollie listen, you can't do anything with that, not right now. The sponsors won't stand for it.'

'I'm not planning a broadcast about them. I'm asking for myself. I think a half-Japanese friend is somehow involved with them and I ...'

She was interrupted by a clerk from the teletype room.

'Hi, I thought you guys might like to see this, just came over the wire.'

Phil took the proffered paper. Mollie watched him read it. 'What is it?' she demanded when he didn't say anything.

'Albania. It's fallen. Mussolini and his blackshirts are in total control. Zog, the Albanian king, has left for parts unknown.'

It wasn't a surprise. It had been recognized for some time that Mussolini wanted to secure the Adriatic coast across from the heel of the boot of Italy. Still, it was one more step on the road to total war. 'That sound you just heard,' Mollie whispered, 'it was the rifles being cocked. Any minute now somebody's going to yell "Fire!"'

'Mollie, we can't ...'

'I know.' She stood up. 'Don't say it because I know. If I want to keep my show I'd better get out to that studio and talk to the debutante of the year. Who have we got for Monday, Mickey Mouse?'

What happened below stairs didn't concern Kate. The house on East Eighty-second Street ran like clockwork, but it was Armando who did the winding. So she was amazed when she rang the bell beside her bed on a May evening and nobody came to see what she wanted.

A second time Kate pressed the ivory button within its brass surround. Two minutes passed, then three, then five. Nothing happened. She tossed back the linen sheets and the satin quilt and got out of the bed. A silk peignoir lay on a nearby chair. Kate slipped it over her bare shoulders and put her feet into feather-trimmed satin mules. She dressed as carefully to go to sleep as she did to face the world. Armando expected it.

He never came to the bedroom until long after she retired,

but many nights when he did he would reach for her, and they would make love while she was still half asleep. In the morning he would inevitably wake when she did, and watch her get out of bed, his dark eyes missing nothing. 'How lovely you are, *querida*,' he'd say. 'You were made for French lingerie ...'

The hall was dim, lit only by a shaded lamp at the far end. Kate rang for the elevator, tapping her foot impatiently. She listened for the whirring sound of the motor. Silence. She rang again. Still no result. A door must have been left open somewhere in the house. She started for the stairs.

On the third floor Armando's study and the sitting room were empty, so were the dining and drawing rooms on the second. It all looked like a stage set, everything perfectly appointed and arranged, and nobody in sight. Maybe she should go up to the nursery at the top of the house, check on Ricky ... No, that was silly. Beatriz slept in the same room with the baby, she would never leave him alone for an instant. Kate continued descending the stairs.

The front door was locked and bolted. She stood in the foyer looking around, trying to make up her mind. Finally she tried the door to the back hall. It was unlocked. The two live-in servants slept here, the door to Maria's bedroom and to Tonio's stood open and each was empty. Ahead of her was a narrow set of steps leading down to the basement kitchen. When she got to the top of them she finally heard some sounds. Thank God, at least she wasn't alone in the house. She couldn't imagine why her husband and everybody else should be in the kitchen, but they must be.

Kate's thin slippers made no sound as she hurried down the stairs. It wouldn't have been heard anyway, there was a lot of thumping below, the sounds of tugging and hauling. She recognized Armando's voice, obviously issuing some sort of instruction, but he spoke in Spanish and she didn't know what he'd said.

For a moment she was blinded when she got to the foot of the steps. They led directly into the vast kitchen and it was ablaze with light. The room housed three enormous stoves and an entire wall of refrigerators. She'd been down here once before and it had astounded her to see that the kitchen was equipped as if it served a large restaurant, but that was how her husband did everything, lavishly. Except that right now he wasn't being lavish, he was being insane.

When her vision cleared Kate saw that Armando, Miguel and Tonio were shoving big boxes into one of the ovens. The doors to three of the refrigerators also stood open. There was no food in them, just more of the boxes. The men were engaged in unloading the dumb waiter and the elevator, both propped open here in the kitchen, and transferring dozens of unmarked cardboard cartons.

No one noticed her, Armando and the other two were intent on what they were doing. Kate had never before seen her husband engaged in any physical work. He was sweating and had his jacket off, and the sleeves of his shirt were rolled up above the elbows.

'*Hai!* Who is this?'

The voice came from a far corner of the kitchen. Kate swung round to see who had spoken. An Oriental man sat on a tall stool; apparently he'd been watching the proceedings, now he was staring at her. '*Hai!*' he shouted a second time.

Armando, Miguel and Tonio stopped what they were doing and followed the man's pointing finger. They stared at her, astonished. Armando recovered first. 'Kate! What are you doing here?'

'I ...' Why was she suddenly so nervous? Why was her throat closing? 'I couldn't sleep,' she stammered finally. 'I rang but no one came, so I ...'

'Yes, *querida*, yes, I understand.' He came to her and put his arm around her shoulders. 'We have some work to do down here. I'm sorry you were disturbed, I should have told you we'd be busy. Miguel, take my wife to her room. See that she has whatever she needs.'

Miguel joined them and Armando passed her to him as if she were a child. Kate hated Miguel to touch her, she shook off his arm. He acted as if he hadn't noticed. 'Come, Doña Katarina. I will bring you upstairs. The elevator is engaged, we will have to walk.'

She took a last look at the remarkable scene, saw Armando cross to the stranger and heard him say, 'Nothing to worry about, it's just my wife. In the confusion we didn't

189

hear her ring.' Then she followed Miguel up the stairs.

'What did you want?' he asked when they got to the floor above.

'Just some warm milk, I couldn't sleep. Miguel, what are you doing down there? Who was that man?'

'A business associate. We are storing some valuables for him. Only for a few days.'

'Is he Chinese?'

'No, Japanese.' They had arrived at her bedroom and Miguel pushed open the door she'd left ajar and waited for her to enter. 'I will bring you some warm milk *en seguida*, Doña Katarina. Right away.' He touched her again, put his hand on her arm and urged her forward. This time Kate didn't pull away, but she resisted the pressure and glanced upwards in the direction of the nursery. 'Ricardo is fine,' Miguel assured her, reading her thoughts. 'Señorita Beatriz is with him as always.'

After a few seconds Kate nodded and went into her room.

Miguel returned in less than five minutes, bringing warm milk in a crystal goblet set on a silver tray. 'I have put some herbs in it, Doña Katarina. Special herbs from Venezuela. They will help you to sleep. I will bring you the drink every night from now on.'

Kate merely nodded and waited for him to leave. She didn't taste the milk until he'd gone. It was very pleasant and it certainly calmed her. She stopped puzzling over the remarkable scene in the kitchen. And she didn't feel nervous any more, she felt wonderful. When she slept it was as deeply as a child, with no dreams and no fears. At one point she was vaguely aware of Armando beside her, and then on top of her. She put her arms around him, rather as if he were a pillow, and held him close. It seemed to her that the love-making went on a long time, was particularly energetic, but it was merely a hazy impression on the edge of her perfect calm.

In the morning she was astounded to see that she had black and blue marks on both thighs and that the lovely nightgown was torn. Kate decided that the wisest course was to say nothing about either. For once Armando hadn't awoken when she did. He was sleeping peacefully and she crept away to the bath, thinking that she felt particularly refreshed and only half remembering the boxes and the little man pointing at her and shouting *hai!*

'Hey, Mollie, hold on a minute.' An engineer named Jim Hawkes hailed her when she arrived at the studio on a brilliantly sunny May morning. 'I seem to remember that Nick Frane's your brother, right?'

'My cousin. What about it?' She didn't try to disguise the eagerness in her voice. 'He's in England ...'

'Nope,' the man interrupted. 'He's in Germany, at least he was. Got an interview with the Führer, no less. We're going to run portions of it on tonight's news. Maybe the whole thing tomorrow afternoon.'

'Can I hear it?'

'Sure, come on up after your show and I'll set it up for you.'

She was scheduled to interview Orson Welles that morning. Last year on Hallowe'en the twenty-four-year-old Welles had produced and narrated a show that terrified the entire country, a simulated news broadcast purporting to document an invasion from Mars. It had been so realistic that police stations were flooded with calls from terrified citizens. In New Jersey, where the aliens were supposed to be landing, the roads were clogged with whole families trying to escape, wet cloths tied over their faces to protect them from poison gas. Since that bit of creative mischief Welles had done nothing special, but Mollie figured he'd still be an interesting guest.

In fact he was more than that, he gave her a scoop. 'I'm going to Hollywood to make a movie. That's where the future is, radio's going to die pretty soon. Did you know that in England they've invented a way of showing the news in pictures?'

Mollie was familiar with newsreels shown in theatres, everybody was. 'What's remarkable about Movietone News?' she asked. 'I'm sure all our listeners have seen it.'

'A newsreel is a film, a kind of short movie. What they've done in England is to project live pictures onto a receiver that can be miles away. Last month they showed a prizefight

191

while it was actually happening, relayed it to dozens of movie screens in London.'

'Are you telling us that in New York we'll be going to the movies to see things while they're happening in California? It sounds fabulous.'

'It's better than that, Mollie. Someday we're going to have receivers in our living rooms, sort of radio with pictures.'

'This isn't another one of your pranks, is it, Orson?'

'Definitely not, it's the real thing.'

'Well, I'll have to find out more about it so my listeners will be the first to know. And from now on I'd better make sure my hair's combed and my lipstick isn't smudged when I come into the studio.'

Chuckle, chuckle. Phil gave her a thumbs-up signal from the control booth. Mollie turned back to her guest. 'Tell us what kind of a movie you're going to make in Hollywood. Something scary?'

'Not exactly. I'm thinking about something based on the life of a famous newspaper tycoon. Not anybody real, of course. The character is tentatively named Kane.'

It was a good show. Phil gave her a big kiss when they went off the air. 'You were great. And I've just had word that the mail's all for you again. Mrs America loves Mollie Pride, so she'll be sure of add 20 Mule Team Borax to her wash, even if she doesn't listen to *Death Valley Days*.'

'Fine. Listen, if there isn't anything special you want to talk to me about I'm going upstairs.'

'Nothing that can't wait. What's upstairs?'

'Nick.' Phil did a double take. 'Not in the flesh,' she explained. 'They've got a broadcast by him from Germany.'

Mollie had known Jim Hawkes for years, he'd been the engineer on *One Man's Family*. He was a guy in his forties who'd always been fatherly toward her, and an old hand who had grown up in the business, like Phil and a few others.

'The technique's amazing,' Hawkes assured her while he arranged things in the control room of an empty studio they'd commandeered. 'This was relayed from Germany to a transmitter in Geneva, then beamed to London. From there it was jumped across the Atlantic to the RCA shortwave receiving station out on Long Island. Frane must have been pretty busy, he had to lay all that on, sell the piece to us, and negotiate Hitler into granting him an interview. All at the same time.'

No wonder she'd had no letters. 'Pretty busy,' she agreed. 'I take it you disced it, is it clear?'

'Judge for yourself.' He had the playback ready now. He slipped earphones over Mollie's head and his own, then put the big acetate record on the turntable and adjusted the playing arm.

'This is Nicholas Frane reporting from Berchtesgaden on the German side of the border with Austria. As many of you probably know, Berchtesgaden is the country retreat of the German Chancellor, Herr Adolf Hitler. It's a beautiful spot. Right now I'm half-way up a mountain, looking out at the first signs of spring in a magnificent pine forest. Herr Hitler is with me, as well as a translator. First of all, Chancellor, thank you for agreeing to speak with the American people this afternoon. That's Austria we're looking at, isn't it?'

Mollie heard a sparkling, resonant voice, one she instantly recognized as a natural for radio. It came over with lilt and enthusiasm and clarity, although she couldn't understand a word; it was Adolf Hitler speaking in German. Then the flat, expressionless tones of the translator. 'The Führer says he is delighted to have an opportunity to convey his best wishes and his friendship to the people of America. He especially wishes them to know that all this talk of war is foolishness. Germany has no desire to make war on anyone, least of all the great and peaceful United States.'

Jim Hawkes tapped his earphones and looked at Mollie and grinned. 'Just a down-home friendly type.'

'Shh!' Nick was speaking again, she didn't want to miss a word.

'Führer, can you tell us if you chose this location for your vacation home because it's close to Austria where you were born?' Through the translator Hitler admitted that was one of the region's charms, though of course Austria and Germany were one nation since the Anschluss of the previous year. 'And can you tell us if you have any further territorial demands? Do you feel that the German people now have sufficient *lebensraum*, living space, for their needs?'

Again that rich, vibrant voice speaking in German, followed by the slightly British-accented English of the translator.

'We are only interested in restoring the integrity of our Germanic lands and peoples. We are an ancient race with a noble and distinguished past, our destiny is to carry that heritage into the future. Germany is ordained to lead Europe into a new era of peace and prosperity. Naturally, to fulfil that great design we must have everything which is historically and geographically ours.'

'Does that include Danzig and the Polish Corridor, Herr Hitler?'

Go to it, Nick! Ask him flat out. She was so excited she wriggled in her seat. God, he sounded wonderful. So clear, and somehow authoritative and friendly at the same time. He was even better than he'd been on his regular newscast. Nick seemed to have grown to suit the historic occasion he'd created.

'We must have what is ours by birthright,' Hitler replied. Mollie looked at Hawkes. He was as mesmerized as she by the German voice ringing in their ears. 'To be separated from East Prussia as a result of the unjust treaty signed at Versailles in 1919, that is not a natural or comfortable state of affairs ...'

The entire broadcast was on six records and lasted for just under an hour. It was a coup of heroic proportions. 'If the coverage is good enough there'll be takers,' Nick had said before he left. With one brilliant first stroke he'd proved that the coverage he could provide was extraordinary.

'Terrific stuff, isn't it?' Hawkes asked as he closed down the borrowed control room.

'Fabulous,' Mollie agreed. 'And I suppose that's why the powers that be have agreed to break the live rule.'

'You got it. No recorded news. Except that this isn't just news, it's history.'

She grinned, remembering Nick telling her that you couldn't understand what was happening unless you knew what had preceded it, and giving her history books to read.

Hawkes didn't ask what she was smiling about, he was thinking thoughts of his own. 'Hitler doesn't sound so fright-

194

ening. I mean what he wants isn't really unreasonable, is it?'

She didn't have the emotional energy to lecture him on the evils of Nazism she'd discovered when she was sixteen and read *Mein Kampf*, and began to realize that the world was a dangerous place and she'd better try to understand it. 'Maybe,' she said wearily. 'I hope you're right. Listen, Jim, you don't happen to know who Nick's engineer was for this caper, do you?'

'Nope, sorry, but I don't. The commentators get the glory, while we engineers do most of the work.'

She wondered if Steve would agree. Yes, probably. All the rest of the day she had mental pictures of him sitting in some German version of a cross between a hunting lodge and a palace, red hair doubtless tousled as usual, tie askew, giving hand cues to the Führer of the all-powerful German Reich.

The following week she received three letters from Nick; they'd been written at different times, but all mailed together. 'Sorry,' he'd scrawled on the back of one envelope. 'I forgot to get the other two off earlier.'

Each letter was only a single sheet written hurriedly; the first while he was on the high seas, funny stories about his fellow passengers and how he felt a growing sense of both excitement and dread as they approached Europe. He'd written the second on stationery headed Brown's Hotel, Dover Street. 'Can't afford this place for long, three pounds a night — that's over twelve dollars, but I think I'd better put on the front of a successful man while I try to worm my way into the places that matter ...'

The third was even shorter than the other two. 'I'm in a terrific rush, kid, leaving for Germany in an hour. But Steve arrived yesterday, and while he isn't saying much it's pretty obvious you two had some kind of blow-up. I hope this separation is a good thing, give you both a chance to cool down and think things over. Anyway, it's great for me to have an engineer I can absolutely rely on. As I said above, we're on our way to Germany. I think you'll know fairly soon what we're doing there. Maybe before this letter reaches you. I've got two others in my pocket that I forgot to mail and I'm going to send all three of them this afternoon before we leave London. Keep your chin up, Mollie my girl. I love you, and

I'm sure Steve does too ...'

At last she sat down and had a good cry, but it was as much relief at finally hearing from Nick as grief over Steve. And it did give her a lot of comfort to think of the two of them together.

She didn't really expect a letter from Steve, so she wasn't surprised when spring slipped into summer and none came, not even on 10 June, her nineteenth birthday. Nick sent her a birthday card, and wrote brief, hurried notes fairly frequently. He still seemed to think time would heal things between her and Steve. Mollie was less sure, but when she wrote to him she didn't mention her marriage or her husband. Instead she composed long letters about what she was doing, who she had on her show, whatever news she had of Zena and Kate, and of course her reactions and those of the country to the latest happenings in Europe, and the frequent broadcasts about them which Nick was sending home.

At the end of June it turned fiercely hot and throughout July the temperature never dipped below the high eighties. The heat was stultifying, it turned life into a somnolent slow-paced thing.

Mollie saw Kate only twice that summer; the first time was at Hillhaven on the Fourth of July. Miguel drove Kate and her son and his nurse upstate to pay a rare visit to her mother. Zena provided fresh salmon, new potatoes and peas and ice cream, and the town of Red Hook supplied a spectacular firework display on the village green. Nevertheless the day wasn't a huge success, Ricky was fretful and cried — Señorita Beatriz said he never ate fish — and he screamed in terror at the fireworks.

The sisters met for a second time a couple of weeks later, just before Kate and Armando and their entourage left for a vacation in Buenos Aires.

'I envy you,' Mollie said when she and Kate were seated at their table in the Old South Tea Room on Madison Avenue. 'It will be winter. At least you'll be cool.'

'Winter?' Kate asked. 'How funny, I didn't know it was winter in Argentina.'

'Of course it is. It's in the southern hemisphere. How can

you know what to pack if you don't know what the weather's going to be like?'

Kate waved her hand. 'Oh, Armando takes care of all that.' She looked around her vaguely, and it seemed to Mollie that Kate's eyes weren't focusing. 'Didn't we tell them to bring us coffee?' she asked.

'Not yet,' Mollie said gently. 'We haven't had our lunch yet. Katykins, are you okay?'

'Yes, of course. I'm fine.'

'You don't look fine. You're too thin. And your eyes are funny. Maybe you should see a doctor.'

'I'm fine,' Kate repeated. 'It's just that I haven't been sleeping too well. Or at least I don't think I am. I fall asleep right away, as soon as I drink my hot milk, but I don't feel rested in the morning.'

'That's not normal,' Mollie insisted. 'Listen, I'll ask at the station. Somebody must know a good doctor. I'll make the appointment and go with you. How about it?'

'No, don't bother, Mollie. I'm okay, really I am. I just need this vacation, to get away from the heat. I'm so glad you told me it's going to be winter in Argentina. I'm sure that's going to make me feel better.'

Mollie decided to ignore her sister's protests and did get the name of a doctor for Kate. But it was the end of the week before she managed to arrange an appointment, and when she telephoned to tell Kate about it a servant said that Señor de Cuentas and his family had decided to leave a few days early for their vacation.

Mollie was concerned and disturbed. She sat down that evening and wrote a long letter to Nick about the whole peculiar business, but after she finished she realized that there was nothing he could do from so far away except worry, so she tore it up.

And the heat continued. And J. Edgar Hoover told the nation that the FBI would never become a threat to the liberties of American citizens, that his enemies had 'mental halitosis' and that the campaign to malign him was a Red Plot. And a riot broke out at Brooklyn Stadium when the Dodgers blew a three-run lead in the ninth innings and lost to the Giants, their arch rivals from the Bronx. And Tom

Dewey, the ambitious New York District Attorney, came on Mollie's show and said he was offering a $25,000 reward for the capture of Lepke Buchalter, the Manhattan racket czar and boss of Murder, Inc. And on 25 July Mollie learned that her fan mail was the heaviest it had ever been. No daytime show approached her popularity, and among the evening programmes, apart from the music and comedy specials, the only one that even came close was *Mr Keen, Tracer of Lost Persons*.

On the strength of that she and Phil slipped in a fifteen-minute segment with an expert on Russian history from Columbia University. In response to Mollie's probing, the professor said that he was fairly certain Russia would align herself with the west against Hitler and Mussolini.

'Mr Stalin has no philosophical basis to cause him to join up with the fascists,' he assured them.

The entrance to Mollie's building wasn't very grand, it had nothing in common with the sumptuous lobbies of the magnificent Art Deco apartment houses recently constructed on nearby Central Park West. There was no doorman, just a door that usually stood open, a small foyer whose only claim to elegance was a marble floor, and a wall of mailboxes. She didn't notice anything unusual when she came home on 2 August and as usual stopped first at her mailbox.

'Miss Pride?' A man stepped out of the shadows near the elevator and approached her.

'Yes, can I help you?'

'I rather hope so. My name is Nigel Turner, I'm from London.'

Her heart shot to her toes, then bounced back. Suddenly she was drenched in sweat that had nothing to do with the temperature. 'Nick,' she whispered. 'Steve. What is it? What's happened?'

The man looked puzzled. 'Sorry, I'm afraid I don't know what you mean.'

'My husband and my cousin ...' She broke off. 'No, you don't know what I'm talking about, do you? So it can't be anything about them. What can I do for you, Mr Turner?'

He glanced around. 'Is there somewhere we can talk privately?'

She sized him up quickly, the way she'd learned to size up guests on her show. Tall, thin, almost willowy. In fact the word that fitted him best was effeminate. Something about the way he carried himself, the way his blond hair shot with grey was cut a trifle too long, the slight lisp at the edges of his words. Fifty-odd she judged, but an air of eternal youthfulness. Definitely not a threat. 'We can go up to my place if you'll wait until I check my mail.'

The mailbox yielded nothing but a few bills and an envelope addressed in her mother's careful hand. Nothing from England, nor from Argentina. She shook off her disappointment and turned to the man who was patiently waiting. 'Okay, the elevator's this way.'

When she led him into the apartment she was suddenly conscious of how bleak and unattractive it looked, as if she were seeing it through the eyes of her mysterious visitor. 'Sorry the place is such a shambles, I'm not home much.'

He murmured something polite and meaningless and allowed her to take his black overcoat and soft black hat. Beneath the coat he wore a three-piece suit in dark blue, with the vest buttoned high on the chest below a polka dot bow tie in maroon and white. 'Please sit down, Mr Turner. And tell me what this is about.'

'I'm here on behalf of Mrs Clementine Churchill,' he began.

Mollie's eyes opened wide. 'Hold it a minute, do you mean Winston Churchill's wife?'

'Yes, I do. Mrs Churchill is aware of your programme, and the interest you've taken in international affairs, especially British affairs. She's asked me to convey her compliments.'

'Well I'll be damned. Excuse me, I mean thank you very much. But how ...'

'I think we'd best leave aside the matter of how Mrs Churchill came to know these things. For the moment may I just say that we're grateful for your support.'

'Who is grateful for what support?'

'Mrs Churchill and her associates. They appreciate the job you're doing in building understanding and friendship among American women for their counterparts in our country.'

'Oh, is that what I've been doing?'

'We think so, yes.'

'Okay, if you see it that way, that's fine. Mr Turner, I'm slightly in shock at all this. I'd like some coffee, would you?'

He said he would and Mollie went into the tiny kitchen and put the percolator on, grateful to find a can of Chase and Sanborn in the cupboard which was as usual nearly empty. Her mind raced while her hands performed the ordinary tasks. Clementine Churchill. Wow. Never in her wildest dreams had it occurred to her that somebody like the wife of one of the most prominent men in England knew who she was.

'Listen,' she said when she went back to the living room, 'you said Mrs Churchill and her friends. What friends? And what's your part in this?'

Nigel Turner smiled. 'May I begin at the beginning, or at least a little earlier than the present moment?'

When Mollie nodded he went on. 'As I believe you know, Mr Churchill is a private citizen at present. But he is very well known in our country and he has held high government offices in the past. These last few years, while it's been so apparent that Nazi Germany was bent on war ...' He broke off. 'Do you agree with that assessment, Miss Pride?'

Somehow it was astonishing to be asked her opinion by a man with an English accent. All Mollie managed to do was nod again.

'Good,' he said. 'I'm glad we see eye to eye on the basics, it makes the rest so much simpler. As I was saying, though he's not now in government, Mr Churchill is deeply concerned about the future of the nation. He has tried repeatedly to sound a warning. A number of like-minded people have coalesced around him. They often meet at the Churchills' flat in London, or their country home, Chartwell in Kent. By the same token Mrs Churchill has gathered around her some ladies who support the same ideas. And that rather brings me to the present. Er ...the coffee, if I might suggest ...'

'Oh God! Of course.' She'd been hypnotized by his voice, oblivious to the frantic sounds of perking coming from the kitchen, or the hiss of steam as the brew boiled over. Mollie dashed to the stove and salvaged two small cups of thick black sludge. 'I hope you don't take cream, Mr Turner. There isn't any.'

'No, black coffee suits me perfectly.' He reached for the cup she offered. 'Thank you, that's very kind.' He took a spoonful of sugar from the chipped bowl she'd carried to the living room. Mollie noted that there was a crust of sticky crystals around the edge of the cover. God alone knew the last time she'd emptied or washed it.

'I'm not very domestic, I'm afraid.' Then without waiting for another of his polite disclaimers, 'Mr Turner, I still don't know what your role is in all this, or what you want from me.'

His smile was slightly sheepish and his lisp became a trifle more pronounced. 'My role is simple' (it came out 'thimple'). 'I'm private secretary to one of the gentlemen in Mr Churchill's circle. As to what is wanted of you, Mrs Churchill and her associates have dared to hope that you might come to London and prepare a broadcast for American ladies here. Tell them how British women are determined to resist tyranny, and how they require help and support from all their friends.'

'It's a load of crap,' Phil said. 'Number one, everything I've heard indicates that Clementine Churchill isn't particularly political. She supports her husband, but she doesn't instigate things on her own. Number two, the average British house-wife doesn't want war any more than women here.'

'Nobody wants war,' Mollie protested. 'But being willing to fight if you have to is different from wanting it. And how do you know what kind of a person Clementine Churchill is? You've never even been to England.'

'I read things.'

'So do I. And if what this guy Turner told me isn't the truth, what is? He really did show up at my place and say all those things. I'm not making it up.'

'I didn't think you were. And I don't doubt there are some people anxious to have you lend your name and prestige to a campaign to get America firmly on Britain's side.'

Mollie had been pacing the small office while they spoke. Now she flopped into the chair behind the desk. 'My name and prestige. Jesus, I could get delusions of grandeur out of all this. What name? What prestige? I put one foot wrong and that lovable team of twenty mules are ready to pull me over a cliff faster than you can say Mollie Pride.'

'Yup. The network too. Don't ever forget it. But as long as you put both feet right then you've got what we're talking about. Name and prestige.'

She veered off on another tack. 'If not Clementine Churchill, who is behind it?'

Phil chewed on an unlit cigar. He'd started smoking stogies instead of cigarettes, but Mollie objected to the smell so he hadn't lit this one. 'I'm not sure. Could it be Nick, do you think? Maybe even your husband?'

She shook her head. 'Turner says he's never met them, though he heard the Berchtesgaden interview. Apparently the BBC ran it too. Anyway, Nick and Steve wouldn't be so subtle. If either of them wanted me to come over they'd just telephone or send a cable and say so.' And Steve didn't seem to remember she existed, and Nick had never mentioned the possibility of her joining them even for a vacation. She didn't say any of that to Phil.

'Yeah, I suppose so,' he agreed. 'Okay, then it's gotta be Winston himself. Much more his kind of tactic, he's a regular Machiavelli when it comes to machinations behind the scenes. Remember Bernard Baruch?'

'The financier who's part of the brains trust? Sure I remember him. We tried to get him on the show a year or so ago but he wouldn't play.'

'The very same. Well, I heard through the producers' secret grapevine that Baruch is thick as thieves with Churchill. Winston's counting on him to whisper the right advice in the President's ear when the time comes.'

'You mean when the war comes.'

'Yup. Given that the British are about as prepared to fight as a bunch of kids in kindergarten, they're going to need all the help they can get. Where's it going to come from if not here?'

'And that's what they want me to get involved in? I'm supposed to become part of the softening-up process, so the country will back Britain and not Hitler?'

'You got it.'

'Okay, I'm all for it. You know what I think of the Nazis and the Fascists. Why shouldn't I do it?'

'Three little words, or rather letters. NBC.'

'Meaning?'

'Meaning that they'll never agree to your making a broadcast for the BBC.'

'But that's not the plan. Mr Turner says they want me to do a series on Britain as part of my regular programming. The BBC has simply offered to help.'

Phil sighed. 'Mollie, we've been over this ground a dozen times. The station will let you get a little political around the edges once in a while, but they do not want you to start sounding like Hans Kaltenborn in a skirt, or Nick Frane for that matter.'

'Jesus! What do they think women are? Dodos? Whose husbands and sons and lovers and friends go off and get themselves killed? What are we supposed to do, just tend to our knitting and not even think about the meaning of any of it?'

'This country is not at war.' He stood up and waved the dead cigar to emphasize his point. 'It's not planning to go to war. And as far as a lot of people are concerned, including a good many ladies, if we did it might be a damned good thing if we went in on Hitler's side.'

'Then they're idiots, and somebody'd better tell them so.'

'Not you,' Phil said. 'Not if you want those twenty mules to keep pulling in your direction.'

That afternoon she called Nigel Turner at his room at the Biltmore and told him she needed time to think about his proposal.

'How much time, Miss Pride?'

'I'm not sure, a few days. Maybe a week.'

'But can I assume you are giving it serious consideration?' he pressed.

'Oh, yes,' Mollie assured him. 'Very serious.'

Three days later, on Sunday, there was a series of violent thunder storms. They lasted all afternoon, even knocked the NBC transmitter off the air for a couple of hours. When at last the front blew across Staten Island and out to sea the heat had broken.

In the gathering dusk Mollie left her apartment and walked in Central Park, relishing air you could actually breathe without searing your lungs. A number of New Yorkers obviously felt the same, the broad paths beneath the trees were crowded with people of all ages. A group of young women caught her eye; they wore cotton dirndl skirts and bobby-sox and they were talking and laughing. To Mollie they seemed like the most carefree people in the world.

She sat down on a bench, crossing her legs and staring at the crease in her navy linen slacks and at her feet. She had on white wedgies with an ankle strap, and no bobby-sox. She didn't even own any bobby-sox, she'd thrown the last pair away two years ago. Nineteen years old, probably the same age as those laughing kids, but she was a woman, not a girl. A career woman. And married. And separated. Maybe about to be divorced. She had responsibilities. An apartment with a year left to run on its lease, charge accounts, a sister who couldn't focus her eyes or remember whether it was the beginning or the end of a meal, a mother who lived in a dreamworld where everything had to be all right all the time, whether it was or it wasn't, and ... And what? Not a lot besides.

She'd never made friends apart from her work. Not when she was a kid and not now. She and Steve had never gone out with other couples. The hours she spent away from the studio were occupied with reading, because books and magazines and newspapers were her window on the wider world, the antidote to having grown up as a performer, then quitting school at sixteen. She wondered if Clementine Churchill knew that the lady she claimed to admire so much didn't even have a high school diploma. Probably not. Don't worry about it, Nick had told her when she'd once admitted that she was embarrassed by the decision she'd made, so impulsively. Education is what you do with your brain, he'd said, not whether you go to school.

Nick. God, how she wished he was here now. Nick could advise her on what to do about Nigel Turner's offer. Or Steve. That was a guilty afterthought. If her husband was with her she'd have somebody to talk to about how to convince her network and her sponsors that she should go to England and make a series of broadcasts which maybe nobody would want to hear. Right? Wrong. Even if this had happened before they both left, she'd have gone running to Nick, not Steve.

It was a little before eight, getting dark, and the breezes which had been so welcome had become a chilling wind. Mollie got up and started to walk back to Sixtieth Street. Once she turned and looked for the girls in the bobby-sox, but they were gone.

If she hurried she'd be in time to hear Ted Granik on the *WOR Forum of the Air*. They might even have a dispatch from Nick.

By Tuesday she still hadn't made up her mind what, if anything, to do. Mr Turner had called her once more, but she'd stalled him. That morning she interviewed Chester Gould, the artist who'd created Dick Tracy. Gould hadn't only invented the hero of practically every kid in the country, he'd changed the nature of comics. During the inaugural week of his strip he'd claimed the distinction of being the first cartoonist to have somebody gunned to death on the funny pages. 'The way I figured it,' he told Mollie, 'big gangsters were running wild, but going to court and getting off scot free. So I thought, why not have a guy who doesn't take the gangsters to court but shoots 'em?'

'Doesn't that seem to you to be pretty strong stuff for kids?' Mollie asked.

'The kids don't think so. My strip runs in hundreds of papers from Maine to California, and of course there's the Dick Tracy radio programme ...'

When the show ended Mollie felt she hadn't handled it well. There was a story behind the violence in Gould's work. He was glorifying a kind of vigilante justice, downplaying the rule of law. String 'em up from the nearest tree, like the old west. The world wasn't like that anymore, but she hadn't thought enough about it before the programme, so she hadn't got to the meat of it on the air. In fact almost the only things she was thinking about were her personal problems, and that she had to tell Turner yes or no.

'Don't forget to listen to Churchill tonight,' Phil said when she went into the office to collect her things.

'What do you mean? Is Churchill in America?'

'No, he's broadcasting from London over the usual short-wave relay. It'll be carried coast to coast, six p.m. our time.'

He wasn't looking at her, not meeting her eyes. 'So all of a sudden you're a big Churchill fan,' she said. 'What happened to Machiavelli?'

'Nothing. I still think that's what he is. But maybe the way things are right now, it's what we need.'

At six Mollie sat beside the radio in her living room. She heard a British accent, clipped and unfamiliar but clear, and a voice which was sonorous, magnificent. It was a superb answer to the ringing tones she'd heard speaking German from Berchtesgaden. 'If Herr Hitler does not make war there will be no war. No one else is going to make war. Britain and France are determined to shed no blood except in self-defence or in defence of their Allies ...'

The world was on the edge of something unthinkable, enormous, earth-shaking, and she was talking about the funnies. Mollie made up her mind.

'Listen, Mr Douglas, the broadcast by Winston Churchill the other night, the whole country listened. The response was tremendous.'

The man from 20 Mule Team Borax looked at Mollie and nodded his head in solemn agreement. 'Of course, Mr Churchill is a very well respected man.' He emphasized the last word.

'Yes, he is,' Mollie said. 'And that's just the point, isn't it? The reason your company originally sponsored my show was because you wanted to reach the women's market, widen the appeal of your product. 20 Mule Team Borax isn't only for the men who listen to *Death Valley Days*, it's not just for use in their workshops and factories, housewives will find it invaluable in the home. Right?' He nodded again.

Mollie didn't let up. 'So if we scoop everybody, if we do a few programmes about how English women are living right now, how they're coping with the threat of war that's hanging over them, we're going to do wonders for the product. It's a hard-working serious cleaner, and the company that makes it knows that women are intelligent. That they make choices based on information.'

She ran out of breath and shot a quick glance at Phil. Her producer, her reluctant accomplice in this foray into the lion's den, didn't have a thing to add. He was sitting with one leg angled over the other, doodling on a clipboard he held in his lap.

'Miss Pride, what makes you think you can get the co-operation necessary to do this? If we were to agree, that would only be the start of it. You'll need facilities abroad, studios, engineers, the whole enormous system that makes broadcasting possible. It would cost a fortune.'

'NBC has an excellent team in place in London,' Mollie said.

'A news team,' Douglas added. 'You and Mr Rosenberg aren't part of the news department, are you?'

'Well, no, we're not. But of course we'd get help just because we work for the network. And I've been promised assistance from English sources.'

Douglas raised his eyebrows. 'Oh, have you? Isn't that pretty unusual?'

Phil uncrossed his legs, stopped scribbling and shoved the pencil behind his ear. 'It's all laid on,' he said quietly.

The other man looked at him. 'Can you explain a little more about that?'

'Nope. It's a very private kind of help. But take my word for it, it'll be there when we need it.'

They'd agreed on this tactic beforehand; now, seeing the look on Douglas's face, Mollie wondered if it had been a wise decision. Maybe they should have knocked him out by throwing the names Clementine and Winston Churchill at him. But it had seemed a breach of confidence that could backfire. She had to stick to that reading now that Phil had finally opened his mouth to support her. She knew better than to change the game play when you had the ball on the five-yard line. She watched the two men and waited.

'I'll have to think about it and talk with my superiors,' Douglas said after a moment. 'We'll let you know what we think.'

'At least he didn't say no and throw us out,' Mollie said brightly when they left the office.

'He didn't say yes either,' Phil said glumly. 'And when they find out on the twenty-fifth floor that we went over their heads and brought a programming idea directly to a sponsor, all hell's going to break loose.'

'All hell's going to break loose whatever we do,' Mollie said firmly. 'At least this way we have a chance to cut ourselves into a piece of the action.'

Another week went by. Mollie had told Nigel Turner that she'd decided to do what he wanted, if she could persuade her bosses it was a good idea. That had pacified him for a while, but he was pressuring her again, saying he couldn't stay in New York much longer and she'd have to tell him very soon whether the plan was on or off. 'I'm doing the best I can, Mr Turner. The only thing to do now is wait.'

She spent a good bit of time thinking about what she'd do if the mules wouldn't pull in the direction she wanted to go. The options were limited. She could forget the whole idea and go on as she was. She could try and sell the concept to Mutual or CBS and leave it to them to find a sponsor. Or she could go to England on her own and make the programmes and hope she could persuade somebody in America to air them. The only choice that carried any security was the first. If she did anything else the bottom line was that she'd be out of a job.

The better part of a second week passed. She was sure the answer was no; if there had been any enthusiasm for the idea she'd have heard before this. Then she found a most unlikely ally. On 23 August Joseph Stalin concluded a mutual non-agression pact with Hitler. Russia and its powerful Red Army had aligned themselves with the Nazis. The world went into shock and everyone over the age of ten knew that war was now a virtual certainty.

On the twenty-fourth, 20 Mule Team Borax informed Mollie and the NBC executives that they would be delighted to sponsor a series of broadcasts from England dealing with the subject of housewives and the war effort. 'Lots of human interest, that's what they want,' the brass told Mollie.

'Lots of *schmaltz*,' Phil promised. 'A sob in every sentence. Don't worry, we'll deliver.'

The network heads were pleased to have had this plum fall into their laps, so they didn't comment on the unorthodox way in which it had been shaken loose from the tree. 'You do that,' they told Mollie. 'You go over there and give listeners a soap opera better than *Helen Trent*. Only this one's for real. Yeah, they're going to love it.'

On 1 September, the day before Mollie and Phil were scheduled to leave for England, German troops marched into Poland and on the twenty-fifth floor they congratulated themselves on their foresight and courageous programming. Who else would send a young woman into the eye of a hurricane to report on how her counterparts were weathering the storm?

'Mollie, did you pack a warm scarf? It will be quite chilly in England this time of year.' Zena looked at the two suitcases standing by the door of the apartment as if she intended to open them and make sure her daughter had included the right clothes.

'Mom, I packed two scarves, maybe three. I don't remember.'

'But if you don't remember maybe you didn't pack any.'

'I did,' Mollie assured her. 'I swear I've taken all your advice about the English climate deep into my heart.'

It was so damned typical. For all intents and purposes she was walking into a war zone, but her mother was worried about whether she was taking a warm scarf. Mollie crossed to Zena and put her arm around her. 'You're going to be okay here on your own, aren't you? You won't miss Hillhaven too much?'

Zena made a face. 'I would never miss Hillhaven.'

'Yes, so you've said.' Mollie spoke thoughtfully; she'd been amazed when her mother suggested that she stay in Mollie's apartment during the month her daughter was to spend in England. Zena had said she'd enjoy some time in the city, and that Kate was due back from Argentina any day and it would be lovely to be closer to her and Ricky for a while, and that she and Grace were going to go to the movies and do things together. It all sounded quite sensible, but it had astounded Mollie nonetheless.

'You're meeting Grace for lunch, right?' she asked now.

'Yes. At Schraffts.' Zena's face clouded. 'Poor Grace, she's so worried about Lee. You did try to find out something for her, didn't you?'

'Every way I knew how. But I couldn't get any information. I'm sorry, mom. It's really not my line, I'm not Brenda Star, Girl Reporter, I only pretend.'

'It's such a shame Nick isn't here, he could probably find out where Lee is.'

'Maybe,' Mollie agreed. The very mention of Nick's name made her want to laugh aloud with pleasure. She'd be seeing him in a short while. The Pan American Clipper flight took sixteen hours from the time it lifted out of the sea in Port Washington Bay, stopping to refuel at Newfoundland and the Azores, to the time it arrived at Southampton in southern England. So, allowing for the five-hour time difference, she might even have lunch with Nick tomorrow. Or with Steve. She'd cabled them last week as soon as her plans were definite — that is she'd cabled Nick, she didn't have an address for Steve. But he'd know. So perhaps one or the other of them might meet the plane.

'That's everything, is it?' Zena interrupted her thoughts. 'That's all the luggage?'

Mollie nodded at the cases. 'That's what's going in the baggage compartment. I'll carry this with me.' She reached for a leather hatbox with a zipper and her initials. Phil had given it to her as a *bon voyage* present. 'But you're coming with me,' she protested.

'What's that got to do with it?'

She hadn't known, but it seemed funny. Still, it was nice to have somebody make a fuss about her big adventure. The only person who would accompany her to the seaplane was Nigel Turner. He was returning to England by ship, but he'd arranged to pick Mollie up and take her in a taxi to Port Washington.

The bell rang. She manoeuvred her way around the suitcases and threw open the door. 'Right on time, Mr Turner. I hope everyone in your country is as reliable and efficient ... What's the matter?'

He wasn't listening to her, he was staring over her shoulder as if he'd seen a ghost. 'Zena? I'm not mistaken, am I? It is you?'

'It's me, Nigel. What are you doing here?'

Mollie turned to look at her mother. Zena's hands were clenched by her side. She looked like a big cat prepared to attack.

'I'm accompanying Miss Pride to the airship,' the Englishman said, his lisp suddenly very apparent. 'I didn't know she knew you.'

'Yes, she knows me. I'm her mother.'

Nigel gasped in astonishment. 'But she's too young, and Sebastian's daughter was called Kate ...'

'My second daughter,' Zena said quietly. 'I married again after Sebastian was killed.'

Mollie was looking from one to the other, trying to follow their conversation. 'Would somebody tell me what's going on? Mom, do you know Mr Turner from the time when you were married to Kate's father?'

'Yes, I know him.' Her words dripped venom.

'It wasn't my fault,' Nigel whispered. He ignored Mollie, all his attention was focused on Zena. 'I didn't know about your father. I never dreamed he — '

Zena interrupted him. 'That's all in the past, it doesn't matter now. But what have you got to do with Mollie?'

'He's the one who brought me the request from Mrs Churchill. I told you about that, mom. That it was Mrs Churchill who asked that I do a series of programmes about women in England.'

'You didn't mention that she'd sent Nigel Turner as her messenger.'

'It never occurred to me that you'd know him.'

She was growing anxious. She'd had such a light heart until a few moments ago, been so happy that she'd managed to achieve this trip, so sure it was going to be wonderful and exciting. But the look on her mother's face alarmed her. It was the same look she'd worn when Harry Pride talked about easy street, or two a day at the Palace. As if she didn't believe a word, and she was going to fight to the death before she let anything bad happen to her children.

211

'Mom, it's okay. Don't be so upset.'

Zena was still concentrating on Nigel. 'How do you know Mrs Churchill? What does she have to do with someone like you?'

'I don't actually know her,' he admitted. He seemed to be shrinking while Mollie watched. Zena had utterly unnerved him. It was as if he felt some enormous burden of guilt and only she could relieve him of it. 'I work for Reggie,' he said pleadingly. 'His father died, Reggie is Lord Whitby now. He's a friend of Churchill's, and I'm his private secretary. He hired me after Sebastian was killed.'

'To keep you quiet, I suppose. Once I'd left England you were the only person who knew the details of the whole sordid business and could talk about them.'

'I'd never have done that. I loved Sebastian. I tried to persuade him to run away with me, you know. Before he had to take up that commission. He wouldn't do it. Said it would be terrible for you and the little girl.'

'Sebastian never wanted to hurt us,' Zena said.

'That's what he said. Neither did I.' Nigel's words came out in a harsh whisper. 'I never meant to hurt you, Zena.'

Zena waited a moment, staring at him. It was as if she were judging him, making up her mind on what sentence to pass. 'If you cause Mollie any harm I'll tell the whole story to the papers in London,' she said finally. 'It's not too late, they'll still be interested. And I can be as wicked as my father was if I have to be.'

'I'm not going to harm Miss Pride. How could I? Why would I want to?'

Mollie exploded before her mother could answer. 'Look, the only one who's going to harm me is Phil. He'll murder me if I'm late and we miss the flight, there's not another one for a week. So you two are going to have to settle your old scores some other time.'

She moved decisively toward the suitcases. The Englishman dashed ahead of her and picked them both up. He looked back at Zena for a moment, but didn't say anything. He just shook his head and went through the door that Mollie held open.

She watched him until he reached the elevator, then

turned to her mother. 'Don't worry about me. I don't understand your feud with Mr Turner, but it's got nothing to do with me. I'm going to be fine, mom. Don't forget, Nick will be there. And Steve, of course,' she added hastily. Zena still didn't know that the separation between Mollie and her husband was more than a matter of physical distance.

'I know, but be careful, darling. You think you know all about the world, that I'm the innocent one. I could tell you things ...'

'Miss Pride,' Nigel called softly. 'The elevator is here.'

She kissed her mother quickly and they parted.

Mollie and Phil arrived in London on 3 September at six a.m. British time. A car and chauffeur had been sent to meet them at Southampton. Mollie wondered who'd laid it on. It could have been the BBC, or Mrs Churchill, or maybe even Nick. She'd been disappointed that he wasn't at the Clipper port, but he had a job to do, he could be anywhere, interviewing anybody, maybe the Prime Minister, or even the King.

She'd have loved to ask the driver who had sent him, but she was too intimidated by his air of English correctness, and too disorientated by the unfamiliar sights and sounds on the narrow roads winding their way through verdant countryside. Besides, she was scared that if she said anything the haughty gentleman behind the wheel would realize that she'd never before in her life been in a Rolls Royce with a chauffeur. She was supposed to be a professional, she reminded herself, not a tourist, so she mustn't ask any dumb questions, and she'd better stop hanging out of the window and gawking.

Phil seemed equally awed. They din't say much on the long journey to London. They arrived at the Hotel Russell in Russell Square at ten past eleven. The lobby was crammed with people, but nobody paid any attention to them. The young bellboy who carried their luggage from the car dropped it by the reception desk and disappeared, just melted into the mêlée of guests and staff who were crowded around a radio. It stood on a table in the middle of the carpeted floor, obviously a temporary addition to the decor.

Mollie and Phil looked at each other, then sidled up to the throng, listening as intently and silently as everyone else.

Within seconds they heard Neville Chamberlain's voice. He sounded much the same as he had when after the 1938 conference at Munich, the world's airwaves broadcast his promise of peace with honour. But his message was different today.

'This morning the British ambassador in Berlin handed the German government a final note, stating that unless we heard from them by eleven o'clock that they were prepared to withdraw their troops from Poland a state of war would exist between us. I have to tell you now that no such undertaking has been received, and that consequently this country is at war with Germany.'

10

The voice of the Prime Minister faded away. No one in the lobby of the Russell Square Hotel said anything. Except for a woman crying quietly into a lace-edged handkerchief, there was only shocked silence. Mollie swallowed hard and turned to Phil, but whatever she was going to say was stillborn. Once more the radio compelled all attention. This time they heard the classic broadcasting voice — neutral, uninflected — delivering a few short official announcements.

'Closing of places of entertainment,' the voice said. 'All cinemas, theatres, and places of other entertainment are to be closed immediately until further notice. The blowing of whistles and blaring of horns is forbidden as they may be misconstrued as an air-raid warning. Now, an announcement about food ...'

The voice suddenly died away. There was the sound of shuffling papers, much magnified by the microphone. Phil winced and put his lips close to Mollie's ear. 'Don't the silly bastards in the control room have enough brains to shut off his mike?'

'Doesn't sound like it,' she whispered back. 'We'll have to show them how ...'

There was another burst of sound from the brown wooden box on the table. Only when a number of people around her straightened their stance and looked solemn did Mollie remember that what she thought of as *My Country 'Tis of Thee* was *God Save the King*, the British national anthem. Like everything else that had happened in the past half-hour, it too was interrupted. For the first time Mollie heard that sound which was to become so terrifyingly familiar, the long shrill tone of the siren which dropped slightly at the end of a burst, only to pick up again and repeat the sequence. It was a moment before she realized the noise was coming from the street, not the radio.

And still they stood there, all those ordinary people in the lobby of the Hotel Russell. British visitors to the capital, and foreign tourists, and business people; they were all paralysed by events which, however long they'd been expected, burst into their everyday world with the shock of an exploding cannon.

'Jesus,' Mollie murmured under her breath. 'Oh, Jesus ...' She half-turned. She wanted to run out into the street. She wanted to search for Nick and for Steve. Phil seemed to sense her irrational need. He put his hand on her arm, but he didn't have any more idea than she of what else to do.

It was a youngster in hotel livery who galvanized them, the same boy who half an hour earlier had unloaded Mollie's bags from the Rolls Royce.

'It's an air raid,' he announced matter-of-factly. 'Everybody's supposed to go down to the cellar.'

The boy's coolness set the tone for the rest of them. Workers and guests filed down the stairs in orderly fashion and waited for fifteen minutes, until the long, single high-pitched note of the sirens signalled all clear. It had not been the first German attack of the war, only the first false alarm.

Later Mollie could never remember with clarity her initial twenty-four hours in London, it all became a kaleidoscope of impressions. There was her room at the slightly shabby but enormously comfortable old hotel — big, square, with a fireplace and tall windows looking onto a back garden filled with flowers, and a four-poster bed with chintz hangings.

Two vases full of flowers, each accompanied by a note, waited for her in that lovely room. The pink and purple asters and the handwritten letter on thick cream stationery came from Clementine Churchill, welcoming her to London and saying that in the present crisis it had been possible only to send a car to Southampton to collect her and that hopefully they would meet in a few days. 'In the meantime,' Mrs Churchill added, 'Miss Cecilia Reeves of the BBC Foreign Department in Broadcasting House expects you ...'

The second bouquet was of dark crimson roses, a dozen of them, and a typed note from Nick dated 29 August. 'Leaving this and instructions with a florist, kid, because when you get here Steve and I will be in Poland. We're leaving this afternoon. I'm pretty sure that's where the next blow's going to fall ...'

He'd been right, of course. Within twenty-four hours of his writing that note, the Nazis had invaded. That was another of Mollie's strongest memories of the first day, evening and night she spent in the London she would come to know so well — the newspaper headlines tracking the fighting in Poland. Edition after edition appeared on the streets, each with a new set of headlines. *Poland Stands Firm* was the first, then *Poles Move Capital to Lublin*, and finally *Cracow in German Hands*.

And there was Broadcasting House; a large white building adorned with flagpoles and metal towers which sailed like some futuristic battleship above elegant houses in Portland Place, a ten-minute walk from the hotel. They'd gone there after lunch. Mollie was never to forget the big bronze doors, or the men who were installing a second set behind them. These were steel, with rubber flanges all around. 'Gas-tight,' someone explained. Memories of the last war and the devastation worked in the trenches by mustard gas were very much alive. People remembered the bombs as well. Mollie saw sandbags everywhere she looked.

There was a warm welcome despite all that, and the promise of '... all the help you need. No, of course it's no trouble.' And everybody acting quite normally, as if they hadn't declared war a few hours earlier.

There was one other thing she always recalled with absolute clarity: the moment when the lady whom Clementine Churchill had told them to see introduced them to Sandra Marks.

'She'll be your liaison,' Miss Reeves said. 'And don't worry, we're accustomed to the time difference. You'll want facilities here after midnight if you're to be on the air in the States in the early evening.'

'Not a problem for us,' Phil said immediately. 'We do a morning show, nine-fifteen eastern time, so it'll be mid-afternoon here.'

Sandra Marks nodded agreement. She was dark and slim,

regal looking, the sophisticated type who immediately intimidated Mollie unless she had them on the other side of a microphone. But she smiled at Phil, and the smile lit her face and softened her sharp features. 'How delightful,' she said in a low, throaty voice. 'No night work.'

'Maybe, maybe not,' Phil answered.

The Englishwoman was much taller than he and Phil had to look up at her, but his eyes never left her face. Mollie didn't forget that, nor her first sight of R.T. Clark, the news editor.

Miss Marks was giving them the requisite tour of the building. They walked through studios that looked much like the studios Mollie knew at home, and finished up in a lounge crowded with newsmen. A man came in just then. Apparently the others had been waiting for him. 'That's R. T. Clark,' the Englishwoman whispered. 'Our senior news editor.'

Mollie saw a wiry, greying figure in shirtsleeves and slippers. He climbed on to a chair and clapped his hands and waited until he had everyone's attention. 'Well, brothers,' he began. 'Now that war's come your job is to tell the truth. And if you aren't sure it's the truth, don't use it.' End of special instructions. Clark climbed down from his perch and disappeared.

The rest of it was a blur, a jumble — a sense of disbelief when she was handed a rubber gas mask shaped like a pig's snout and told to carry it with her at all times, a terrible worrying dread when she thought of Nick and Steve in Poland, a repeated experience of delight when she walked through London streets and, despite the piles of sandbags on every corner, recognized the smell and the feel of the scenes in the stories by Dickens and Shakespeare which Nick had read to her long ago; and a pounding excitement when she realized that she was facing the greatest professional challenge of her life.

Because Phil had arranged a number of pre-recorded broadcasts to be aired in the States during the transition period, they had a few days to acclimatize themselves and decide on the shape of their shows from England. Mollie was nervous about it, she still imagined the BBC as different, more important, than the radio she knew at home. It was partly the accents, British English sounded so ... so formal. And the way they dressed: she'd actually seen a guy read the news in a tuxedo.

It didn't help her self-confidence when — on their second evening in London — they were invited to dinner with Fred Bate, the head of NBC Europe, at his elegant home in Gordon Square. Bate was a handsome, urbane man who dripped charm and was said to be on intimate terms with royalty. Compared to anything she'd ever seen his house was a palace, it even made Kate and Armando's place look showy and overblown. When she'd dressed for the evening Mollie had thought she looked good in the lilac coloured silk dress that hugged her bodice and swung free over her hips. Once she was sitting in Fred Bate's dining room all she could think of was that her clip-on 'pearl' earings came from Woolworths. She felt completely outclassed and hardly opened her mouth during the meal.

Bate tried to explain the local scene, but he never finished a sentence because the butler was always appearing and summoning him to the telephone. It wasn't surprising since this was the second day of war, but what Mollie did consider remarkable was that he'd found time to see them in the first place.

'You don't know how important you are,' Phil said when they returned to the Russell Square Hotel. 'He had to see you. You've got a devoted audience, sunshine, and a satisfied sponsor. That means you've got clout.'

'I don't feel as if I have anything except the jitters.'

'You look a little pale around the gills. Tell you what, we'll have a nightcap before we go to bed.'

Phil led her towards the hotel bar. The door was locked. An elderly man appeared at Phil's elbow. 'Sorry, sir, public places of entertainment have to be shut. Since yesterday. The war you know. But I can get you something if you like, you can have it right here in the lobby. Nice and quiet it is.'

The lobby was deserted. They might have been the only guests in the place, perhaps the only people who hadn't fled London the minute war was declared.

'That will be fine,' Phil said. 'Beer for me. And how about

a cider for the lady?' He turned to Mollie. 'According to my guidebook, that's what English people drink, beer and cider. C'mon sit down over here and I'll finish the story his highness King Fred started but never finished.'

'Yeah, tell me how come there are no sponsors and no commercials on the BBC. How do they put on programmes for free?' Mollie sank gratefully into a big leather chair that was drawn up beside a coal fire.

'They're not free, but they're supported by public money. They get a grant from the government.'

'Nobody in Washington would be that generous,' Mollie said.

'It's not generosity. Over here when you get a radio you have to have a licence to turn it on, you know like a driver's licence. You pay for the licence, and that money goes to support the programmes. Not us, by the way. Bate tells me we're going to have an NBC engineer, but nobody puts one word over the airwaves in this country that doesn't go through the BBC.'

'How do you know all this?' she demanded. 'What did you do, take an instant expert pill?'

'I took Sandra Marks to lunch.'

'Okay, but what about censorship? If the government owns the BBC then it must decide what goes on the air.'

'Not exactly. The BBC's a corporation, has its own board of directors. The theory is it's only answerable to the board. In practice ...' Phil shrugged. The old man brought their drinks on a silver tray, then withdrew a discreet distance.

'Hell,' Phil said. 'Everybody's got somebody breathing down their necks. With us it's the sponsors, with them I suppose it's some government flunkey. The interesting thing is that they started out privately owned, just the way we are. Did you know that when Marconi invented telegraphy he demonstrated it in England, and set up a company to market his brainchild?'

Mollie said she hadn't known.

'Yeah,' Phil went on. 'It was the Marconi Company that began commercial broadcasting here, same time as Westinghouse was doing it back home.'

'Then what happened?' She took a sip of the cider. She'd

expected apple juice, but this had a kick, and bubbles that got up her nose.

Phil watched her and chuckled. 'Stick with me, sunshine. I got all the native customs down pat. As I said, at first they had privately owned radio stations, then in the early twenties, while local stations were springing up in the US like dandelions, these folks decided that something as powerful as the airwaves had to be centralized and controlled. So the government established the British Broadcasting Corporation.'

For the first time she saw the obvious connection that had eluded her. 'That's where the initials BBC come from.'

Phil leaned over and pinched her cheek. '*Mameleh*, you gotta get some sleep. Your brain's working at half time.'

'I can't sleep. I'm too excited. And what does that mean?'

'*Mameleh*? Little mother, only you say it to little girls.'

'Yiddish is illogical.'

'Maybe,' he agreed, reaching for his beer. 'Warm beer, that's illogical too.'

Mollie took another swallow of the cider and felt the punch in her stomach. 'I still can't get over that guy we saw reading the news yesterday.' The cider on top of the wine at dinner was thickening her speech slightly, it came out 'yethterday'.

Phil chuckled. 'Yeah, that was amazing. Who'd believe they wore a tux to read the news? Sandra told me they decided years ago that was the right way to do it. Because announcers were "going into people's homes at the dinner hour". Jesus.'

'Who's Sandra?'

'Miss Marks. Our guardian angel with the la-de-da accent. The one I took to lunch.'

'Oh. She's Sandra now, is she?'

'That's what she told me to call her.' Phil shrugged. 'She's okay. She just sounds hoity-toity. We're going to do fine with her.'

Phil summoned the old man with a wave of his hand, but when he wanted to pay he was told the drinks would appear on their bill. 'Bedtime, Mollie my girl,' he said, standing up. 'I've left six o'clock calls for both of us. Tomorrow we go to work.'

Mollie wondered if the funny feeling in her stomach was a result of the time difference, or the rich food and the alcohol, or just knowing what lay ahead, working with people who wore evening clothes to do a broadcast. 'Knock 'em dead, kid,' that's how Nick's letter of welcome had ended. She wasn't sure she could do it. But she was here. Hell, she'd moved heaven and earth to get here. She had to try.

The outskirts of Mexico City were a tangle of dirt roads so narrow they were alleys rather than streets. The big Packard had to move slowly, its sides almost touching the squat white adobe hovels and nearly knocking over the flimsy tarpaper shacks which were crammed into the interstices between them.

'Where are we going, Armando?' Kate asked plaintively. 'You said we were going home, but this isn't New York.'

'No, *querdia*, it's Mexico City. We will go home later. Remember, I told you I had to see someone, and that afterwards we would meet Beatriz and the *niño* at the ship. Then we will all go to New York.'

Kate nodded as if she understood and sat back and fanned herself with her handkerchief. It had been bitterly cold in Buenos Aires, it was blisteringly hot in ... Where was it Armando said they were? Oh yes, Mexico. All these changes, she was very confused. 'Will it be summer or winter when we go back to New York?' she asked.

'Autumn, *querida*. It is September.' He took the handkerchief from her hand and wiped the perspiration from her forehead. 'You will be more comfortable as soon as we're aboard the ship,' he promised softly. Then he leaned forward. '*Debes parar los druges*,' he said almost in Miguel's ear. 'You have to stop the drugs, she is getting crazy.'

Miguel didn't turn around, he continued to concentrate on his driving and stare straight ahead. '*No puedo*. I can't stop them now, she will miss them too much.'

'I never said you could make my wife a hop-head! You told me you were only helping her to sleep! The herbs in the milk, *bueno*, okay, but the stuff you are injecting into her veins ... *Parar los druges*!' Armando banged his fist on the top of the seat back. The blows fell inches from Miguel's ear, but none of them touched him.

'*Callete*! Shut up, you'll cause an accident.'

Armando sat back and took hold of Kate's hand and swallowed the lump of anger and frustration in his throat.

She didn't know what Armando and Miguel were shouting about. They shouted at each other a lot, but she never knew the cause. When they were first married she'd thought of learning Spanish. Why hadn't she done it? Kate couldn't remember. She watched the half-naked children who were running alongside the car. The children were yelling in Spanish too. Every once in a while Armando opened the window a crack and threw some coins into the street. Then the children would fight to get them and for a few minutes they were left in peace.

The Packard made its way through the shantytown and came out on a slightly wider street. The children followed. Miguel opened his window and yelled something at them and they stopped running alongside, but they stayed where they were, watching. '*Estamos aqui*,' he said to Armando. 'We're here. You wait, I'll go inside.'

'No.' Armando spoke with more than his usual forcefulness. 'I'm going with you.'

Miguel shrugged. 'Suit yourself. But if you leave her alone those little monsters will tear her apart.' He jerked his head back towards the cluster of watching children.

'I'm not leaving her here. We're both going with you.'

'I don't give a shit what you do with her. She doesn't know her ass from a hole in the ground. But what about the car? They'll strip it the second we're gone.'

Armando thought for a moment. 'You stay with the car.'

Miguel grinned. 'Going to go do the whole thing by yourself, are you? Listen, you stupid sonofabitch, this isn't one of your rich old farts with pesos where his brains should be. You won't charm *el gallo* with your soft talk and your perfect manners and your pretty face.'

'I'm not letting you make this deal.' Armando's voice had become a growl. 'If you fuck this up with your strong-arm tactics we're down the tube. The Jap will eat us for breakfast.'

Miguel stretched and yawned, as if none of it were very important. 'Go ahead, take your hophead wife in there and make the deal. I'll stay here, and if you haven't come out in half an hour I'll drive away. They can put what's left of the two of you out with the garbage in the morning.'

Armando opened the door of the car. 'Come, *querida*, I am going to talk to a man and you are coming with me.'

Miguel watched in amazement. It hadn't occurred to him that Armando would really go in there alone. When he saw the other man actually knock on the low green door facing the street he shrugged again. 'Fuck both of you,' he murmured. 'Especially Kate.'

That made him chuckle. Fucking Kate that one time while Armando was busy with the Jap had been okay, even with her brains turned to jelly she was some piece. Of course if Armando ever found out ... No, he never would. Kate had been too far gone to know what was happening, let alone tell Armando. In a crazy kind of way that added to the enjoyment. But some day ... Yeah, some day he'd stick it to her when she knew it was him. The thought gave him a hard-on right there in the street. That distracted him and the next time he looked at the green door it was closed as tightly as it had been before, but Armando and his wife were nowhere to be seen.

'Señor de Cuentas,' the man known as *el gallo*, said. 'And this must be your beautiful señora.' He took Kate's hand and bent over it, brushing the air with his lips. Armando finally understood why the Mexican was called the rooster. His hair was dark brownish-red and it stood up from his scalp in a stiff brush that was like a cockscomb.

El gallo straightened and smiled. 'I am surprised that you bring this lovely lady to our business meeting.' He looked at her for a moment, narrowing his eyes and staring into hers. 'But it doesn't matter, does it? She hasn't any idea where she is. What a pity, señor, I did not know the lady was over-fond of such wicked pleasures.'

Armando ignored the reference to Kate's addiction. 'She speaks no Spanish, not a word. You can say whatever you like.'

'Very well. But not here. Please, follow me.' He led them across the patio then through a narrow corridor to a flight of steep stairs. They descended in darkness lit only by the oil lamp he carried. There was another corridor, and another. The passages wound below the street like a maze.

Armando felt cold sweat breaking out on his back. If *el gallo* did not lead them out of here they would never again see daylight. There was no hope that he could find his own way and run if necessary. Particularly not with Kate. He bitterly regretted leaving Miguel in the car. Stupid to make an issue out of this meeting. What he was really angry about had nothing to do with it. His fury over Kate had made him forget how useful Miguel was, why he couldn't survive without his cousin.

They came at last to a room lit by unshaded bulbs strung on thin wires. Two other men were waiting for them. '*Mi dependentes,* my assistants,' *el gallo* said, but he didn't introduce them by name. 'Now, you have the money?'

'Twenty thousand dollars, as agreed. The rest you get when you bring me the picture in New York.'

El gallo nodded and held out his hand. Armando didn't move. 'Not until I see the painting.'

The Mexican shrugged. 'As you wish.' He turned to one of the pair standing behind him and murmured something. The man stepped out a door Armando had not previously noticed and returned in seconds, carrying a three foot by seven canvas shrouded in a piece of cloth. 'Put it here,' *el gallo* commanded. The painting was placed on a waiting easel and the Mexican uncovered it with careful reverent movements. He didn't say a word, just held up the lantern so the picture was bathed in light, and waited.

'*Caramba...*' Armando's reaction came out in a long sigh of pleasure. 'It is magnificent.'

'*The Annunciation to the Virgin* by Fra Filippo Lippi. Painted in Florence circa 1460, and only now discovered in the private collection of an Argentinian of Italian descent. One of my better efforts, isn't it?'

Armando bent towards the picture and studied it for long minutes before he spoke. 'I have seen nothing else of your work,' he said finally. 'But this, yes, it is remarkable. No one would know... You're very sure of the provenance? You've left no holes?'

'None,' the Mexican said softly. 'The provenance is

correct to the last detail. I make no mistakes, Señor de Cuentas. I trust that you can say the same thing.'

'We wouldn't be here if you didn't already know that,' Armando said.

'True. I laid an interesting trail for you to follow from Buenos Aires to Mexico City, did I not?'

'It was very inconvenient. You don't have to go to such lengths. My reputation is well known among men like yourself. You could simply have approached me in New York.'

El gallo chuckled. 'There are no men like myself. The rest are all amateurs. Besides, I don't like the company you keep, señor. I am not fond of little people with slanted eyes who want to rule the world. Now, enough talk. The money.'

He'd had no idea that *el gallo* knew about the Jap, but Armando did not allow his shock to show. His hands were steady when he paid over the twenty thousand American dollars and made arrangements to take delivery of the painting. Not here, but in New York. Smuggling it into the States was the Mexican's problem.

Ten minutes later he led Kate back to the car, and she got in and settled in the seat without a word about where they'd been or what had happened. She had, in fact, already forgotten the entire episode. 'Miguel,' she murmured. 'Isn't it time for my medicine?'

Miguel patted the little black box containing the hypodermic and the syringe, and the tiny quantity of white powder which was beside him on the front seat. 'Soon,' he promised. 'Soon, Doña Katarina.'

Armando looked pained, but he said nothing.

'Good morning ladies,' Mollie said into the handheld microphone. 'Today I'm speaking to you from Waterloo Station. It's a large train terminal near the River Thames in London, one of some half-dozen such places in this city of four hundred square miles and eight million people, at the moment a very tense city. As you know, Britain and Germany are now at war, and as we can understand so well, British mothers and fathers are frightened for the safety of their children. Today the government has arranged for thousands of them to be moved to the country, where it's

226

hoped they'll be safe from the bombing raids expected to begin at any time.'

The NBC engineer walking ahead of her, with a wheeled case full of equipment and long electrical lines he was careful not to tangle, jostled a weeping woman in a brown hat. The engineer didn't take the time to apologize, he just waved Mollie forward. She pushed past another pair of curious onlookers and deftly avoided tripping over the cord of her mike.

'It's nearly half past two in the afternoon here on Monday, 4 September, a bright sunny day. Everywhere I look I see children in school uniforms, a sea of youngsters, and not one of them making a fuss. They may be scared, I'm sure they must be bewildered, but no one is crying. The teachers are leading them to the trains that have been assigned by grades. They too are keeping the famous stiff upper lip we've all heard about. Some of the parents are a bit emotional though.'

The woman with the brown hat was still sniffling and still nearby. Impulsively Mollie thrust the microphone toward her. 'Excuse me, madam, I'm Mollie Pride and I'm on the air to America. Would you tell us how many of your children are being sent out of London today?'

'Cor!' Her sniffles stopped instantly and her close-set rheumy eyes glowed with pleasure. 'D'ya mean if I talk into that there thing in yer 'and they can 'ear me in America?'

Mollie felt a moment of pure panic. The woman had a thick Cockney accent, probably unintelligible to listeners in the States. Nothing for it, she'd started so she had to finish. 'Yes, madam, all America can hear you. Please tell us which of these children is your son or daughter.'

'None of 'em's mine,' the woman said smartly. 'Miss Jermin, I am. Ain't never been married.'

The engineer grinned wickedly at Mollie. Behind him she saw Phil grab his head. Mollie took a tighter hold on the mike. 'But you were crying, Miss Jermin. So I thought ...'

'Oh I ain't cryin' for myself. Why would I? It's jus' all these little ones lookin' so brave and all. Make anybody with a 'eart cry, they would. Course that's what's wrong with that there 'itler feller, ain't it? Ain't got no 'eart.'

227

'It doesn't seem so. Thank you for speaking to us.' Mollie moved off before the woman had a chance to air more of her opinions over the intricate relay system that was carrying this edition of *Mornings with Mollie*.

She couldn't move very fast. They had in effect set up a broadcasting studio in the terminal; it was a technical marvel, but the large quantity of clumsy equipment allowed them only a few feet of manoeuvring room. Across the vast cavern of Waterloo Station Mollie could see a similar BBC set-up, but it seemed she was the only American in the place. There were no newsmen from NBC or CBS or Mutual. This wasn't hard news, it was a human interest story. Just her meat, and as far as US networks went, she had the field to herself.

'The boys are all in short pants,' Mollie told her distant audience, 'with knee socks, and most of them have caps on their heads. The girls wear berets. Their clothes make them look different from American school children, until you study their faces. Then they look just like youngsters you might see in a playground in Boston or Detroit or Dallas or Spokane. They could be our children, ladies. Except that we're the lucky ones at the moment. Nobody is threatening to drop bombs on our kids.'

Phil gave her a thumbs-up sign and Mollie went on. She described the pathetic amount of baggage the children were allowed to take with them. 'A toothbrush and a comb and enough food for the day, that's what the mothers were told to pack. And, of course, a gas mask. This morning when they sent their youngsters off to school the ladies of London put those few pitiful necessities in a paper bag or a tin lunchbox and kissed little Janey or Jimmy goodbye. Those mothers don't know if they're going to see their sons or daughters again,' she added, her voice becoming lower and emotional. 'It takes a lot of courage to send your child away when you know a bomb may get you before it's safe for that child to come home ...'

Phil gave her the wind-up sign that meant her time was almost gone. Mollie looked around her quickly. 'On my left,' she said slowly and clearly. 'I can see one little girl with blonde braids beneath her navy beret. She's waiting patiently for her turn to board the train and she has her gas mask and her tin lunchbox, like all the rest. About six I think, maybe seven, certainly no older. She's carrying one item of baggage that isn't regulation. A teddy bear. It's pretty battered and worn out, no doubt from a lot of hugging and kissing. Let us hope and pray that this child and her teddy bear can be kept safe from Nazi bombs.'

Phil gave the engineer the cut signal. They were off the air.

Mollie bought a newspaper before they left the station. *'British Expeditionary Force Lands in France'* was the headline. The first British soldiers had been sent to the continent, two hundred thousand of them. The French had mobilized an army of six million and were said to be grumbling that their allies weren't taking the war seriously enough. They were being cheerful about it, though. The same song blared out everywhere: *Wish me luck as you wave me goodbye, cheerio, here I go on my way ...*

Mollie found herself humming it along with everybody else.

Eight days later, on the nineteenth, the papers were calling it rape. Russian and German troops had met at Brest-Litovsk and Poland was being partitioned between them. Only Warsaw still held out. There was music for that, too, not the cheery *Wish Me Luck* ditty all England had been singing. Warsaw radio constantly played the Polish national anthem, but it was a voice crying in the wilderness. Poland as such had ceased to exist. The promises of French and British support had come far too late, and the 'aid' had been nothing more than words.

The anguish was made most real for Mollie when she heard the BBC broadcast to Warsaw a little after nine p.m. on the twentieth. She was in the Foreign Department making arrangements for her own show the following day, a story on farm wives, and she saw a crowd outside one small studio.

'What's happening?' she asked when she joined them.

'They're sending a message to Warsaw on the Polish service,' a man answered.

He had an accent, was probably a Pole himself, Mollie realized. That judgement was confirmed when he quietly translated for her the words another man was speaking into the mike. 'All the world is admiring your courage ... We,

229

your allies, intend to continue to struggle for the restoration of your liberty. If you can, please reply to this message on SPZ 7170 kilocycles during the night.'

Mollie never found out if there was an answer from Warsaw. She lay sleepless in her bed in the Russell Square Hotel, thinking of the Polish people and of what it must feel like to see hostile soldiers marching down your street and hear them banging on your door. She thought of Steve and Nick. As neutral Americans they might be free to stay in Poland, but logic said they'd return to London, please God, before her month in England ended. The story wasn't in Poland any longer; she knew that, so they must. The epicentre of the storm had moved west. What mattered now was what happened in Britain and in France.

'Well, well,' Steve said softly. 'Who'd o' thunk it? Little Mollie summoned to the crisis by no less a luminary than Winston Churchill himself.'

'I don't know that for certain.' Mollie pushed her plate away and glanced around the crowded pub. A week ago the government had rescinded the regulation closing all places of public entertainment. Somebody had decided that general morale was worth the risk of hundreds of people being in one place when a bomb struck.

That and the fact that as yet there still had been no bombs had cheered up the Londoners. This pub was jammed, and the noise level was terrific. Except at their table. She and Steve seemed to be sitting in an island of strained silence broken only by sour comments. Mollie's nervous fingers made precise piles of crumbs from a piece of bread lying on the bare wooden table. She kept waiting for his smile, that smile which still made the sun shine in her world.

'I was told it was Mrs Churchill who wanted me to come, but Phil said it must have been Winston.'

No grin. None of the old magic. He wouldn't turn it on for her. Steve shrugged and lifted his glass of beer. 'Not much difference, is there? You're in the big league, babe, playing on the team of the ... the what of the Admiralty? I can't remember the title Churchill has now.'

'First Lord of the Admiralty,' Mollie supplied eagerly, as if

230

she were giving him a gift. 'It's like being a Cabinet Secretary at home. See, what happened was that Chamberlain brought him into the government the day war was declared, and ...'

'Thanks, I knew you could explain it so I'd understand.'

'Oh God, I didn't mean ...'

He waved her words away. 'Forget it, sweetheart, I know what you meant. And you'll do a good job, no doubt about it. You'll push all the right buttons and tug every heartstring in America. I hear you're sending back great stuff.'

'It's okay. I take the opportunities I find. Or that Phil finds.'

'Yeah. Producers are like engineers, you know that? They work their balls off and all the credit goes to the voice on the air.'

'Steve, listen, I found out you were in Berchtesgaden with Nick. That was a remarkable achievement. And the broadcasts from Warsaw were fabulous. I'm so proud of both of you.'

'That's good, Mollie. That makes me happy, that you're proud of me and dear old Nick.'

She took a deep breath. 'I can't say anything right, can I?'

'Maybe not,' he admitted. 'It's my fault, probably. I haven't had time to get used to the fact that you're here. Until last night when I got back from Poland I didn't really believe that this afternoon I'd be sitting in the Cobblers' Arms with my loving wife.'

'I am, you know,' she whispered.

'Here? Don't worry, I know that. I don't think you're a figment of my imagination.'

'That's not what I meant. I was referring to the loving part.'

Steve still didn't smile, but he stared at her for a moment, then took a long swallow of his beer and gestured to her half-eaten plate of sliced ham and limp lettuce. 'Do you want to finish that?'

'Not particularly.'

'Okay, then let's get out of here.'

They stood up and got their raincoats and stepped into High Holborn. A hazy grey mist obscured the view of the shops and office buildings, and made the scene look like something out of an old, slightly out-of-focus movie. 'They tell me that a few centuries back this was the heart of London's shoemaking district,' Steve said. 'Isn't that romantic? Merry Old England.' He pulled up the collar of his coat and turned left, setting a brisk pace.

Mollie had to trot to keep up with him. 'Where are we going?'

He didn't answer until they'd gone about fifty yards, then he stopped beside a white door in a red brick facade. The top of the door was a window curtained in starched white lace. 'I've got a room in here.'

Mollie glanced up at a sign that said The Cobblers' Guild Hotel. In the window was a hand-lettered notice, 'Bed and breakfast 2/6 per night.' Bed. That's where they were going, forget about the breakfast part. 'Two shillings and sixpence,' she said brightly. 'That's fifty cents isn't it?'

'I guess so.' Steve pushed open the door and waited for her to enter. 'I haven't spent enough time in London to figure out their crazy money.'

'You and Nick have been everywhere, haven't you? Rome, Berlin, Belgrade, Danzig, everywhere ...' She realized she was chattering to cover her nerves and she stopped. It was awful, stupid. He was her husband, damn it. They'd been married over three years. It was ridiculous to start acting like a shy virgin.

The Cobblers' Guild wasn't a real hotel. There was no lobby and no reception desk, just a narrow hall with a table, and beside it a board with hooks containing numbered keys. Steve took the one marked 24. 'There's no elevator, we'll have to walk.'

'Okay.' She followed him to the stairs, but stopped when a woman suddenly appeared from the back of the hall.

'Afternoon, Mr Rogers,' The woman looked at Steve, then at Mollie, then back to Steve.

'Good afternoon, Mrs Kelly. This is Mollie, my wife.'

'Oh, your wife is she? Sure, didn't you say your wife was in America?'

'I was,' Mollie explained. 'I came over a few weeks ago, on the third.'

Her obviously American accent seemed to allay some of

the woman's suspicions. 'Did you now? Mollie, that's an Irish name. Are you Irish?' Obviously Mrs Kelly was, she had a brogue you could cut with a knife.

'No,' Mollie admitted. 'At least I don't think I am.'

'Ach, sure you can't help that, lass. Good day to you.'

'We seem to have a talent for appealing to the romantic notions of Irish landladies,' Steve murmured after Mrs Kelly had beamed on them, then disappeared in the direction from which she'd come.

'Like on our honeymoon,' Mollie said. 'Mrs O'Donald in the Monadnock Inn. I haven't thought of her in years.'

'I have. I think about her often.' There was something very bitter in his tone. Mollie didn't know how to respond to it so she climbed the stairs in silence.

'Here we are,' he said, putting the key in the lock of a door marked 24. 'It's not much. Just a place to leave my stuff while we're out of the country.'

What passed for decor was faded beige wallpaper, a worn rug in dull red with garish mustard-coloured flowers, and a narrow bed with a dark green spread. Mollie stood in the middle of the floor and looked around. She shivered.

'Hold on a minute.' Steve shrugged out of his coat and tossed it on the only chair in the room. 'There's some kind of excuse for heat, but you have to feed it with money to make it come on.' He fished some change from his pocket and selected three shilling coins — they looked a bit like nickels. He dropped them one at a time in the slot of the strange-looking apparatus that filled what had once been a fireplace opening and they landed with a dull clinking sound which echoed in the silent room. 'Now I have to light the damned thing. Do you have a match?'

Mollie shook her head.

'I forgot you don't smoke,' he said.

That made her feel a lot colder. They'd been separated only a few months and already he'd forgotten that she didn't smoke. And until this moment she had not realized that he wasn't smoking either. 'Have you stopped?' she asked.

'Yes.' He offered no explanation, just kept pawing through the drawer of the table beside the bed. Finally he found a box of matches and returned to the fireplace opening and knelt beside the heater. 'Now that I've given this gizmo its dinner of shillings the gas will come on.' He struck a match and held it to the grid while turning a knob. There was a loud bang that made her jump, then a steady hiss and a red glow.

Mollie moved closer and felt the sudden intense warmth. Steve was still kneeling on the floor. He stretched out his hand and ran it up the calf of her leg, stopping a moment at her knee, then letting his fingers march along the soft flesh of her inner thigh.

Mollie said nothing, but she began unbuttoning her coat. A moment later she slipped it off and let it fall to the floor. Steve pushed up the skirt of her tweed wool dress and the taffeta slip she wore beneath it. 'Still don't wear a girdle, I see.' His voice was husky. 'Just a garter belt and panties, like a kid. I like your belly, Mollie, always have.' He tugged the pants down over her hips. 'It's a nice flat belly, but soft.'

He pressed his lips to her skin and Mollie moaned. He was kissing her everywhere, letting his tongue roam over her flesh. God, he hadn't done that in months, maybe years. Not since their lovemaking had become a perfunctory performance in the dark. This room wasn't dark. It was filled with the grey light of the rainy afternoon and the hot red light of the gas fire. Steve pushed her back toward the bed and she went gladly, eagerly, falling on it and opening her arms to him.

His mouth came down on hers, his body writhed on top of her — then, like the previous time in New York, the last time she'd seen him — he cursed softly and pulled away.

'Steve, what's the matter?'

'I'm the matter. I can't do anything.'

'What do you mean? I don't understand ...'

'Don't you? Well I'll spell it out, kid. I'm impotent with you. I can't get it up. I want to, but nothing happens. Is that clear enough for you?'

She heard the phrase 'with you', understood the implication, but chose not to comment on it. 'It doesn't matter,' she whispered.

'That's what you said last time we went through this charade, but you're wrong. It matters like hell.' He'd got off the bed now and he crossed the room and picked up her

234

coat, scooping her underpants off the floor as a kind of after-thought. 'Go on, get out of here. Sorry not to be gentleman enough to take you back to your hotel, but I expect you'll manage.'

'Steve, listen ...'

'Just get out,' he said gruffly. Then, more gently. 'Please, Mollie, go. It's better if you do.'

She stood up and slipped into the coat he was holding for her. Steve buttoned it, as if she were a child, pulling the collar up close to her chin. 'There, that will keep you warm until you get home. Goodbye, Mollie.' He shoved her pants into the coat pocket.

She didn't move, just stood where she was. 'Steve,' she whispered finally. 'Are you going to divorce me?'

'I haven't had time to think about it. Anyway, I don't have any grounds and I'm not that much of a shit. You can divorce me whenever you want. Adultery, that's what I think it's called. You can throw in desertion for good measure.'

Mollie shook her head. 'No, I don't think I will.'

'Suit yourself,' he said. 'But get out of here. Please.'

She walked to the door and opened it, stood there a moment, then left, pulling it closed behind her. Downstairs Mrs Kelly was in the hall. She was fiddling with some letters lying on the table, but Mollie had the feeling the landlady had been waiting for her. It wouldn't surprise her if the woman had been listening outside Steve's door and knew exactly what had happened.

'Oh, going out are you?' Mrs Kelly asked. 'Is your husband upstairs? I was wanting to tell him that I can move the two of you to a double room later today if you like.'

'No,' Mollie said. 'That's all right. I won't be staying.'

She had to walk home; she didn't see a tube station, couldn't find a taxi, and didn't know which number bus to take. All the way she kept her hand in her pocket, clinging to her crumpled underpants, and her tears mingled with the soft never-ending rain.

'You'll find the pub with no trouble,' Nick promised on the telephone. 'Corner of Grafton Way and Tottenham Court Road; you can't miss it.'

Mollie walked there with confidence. It wasn't quite five, still light. Besides, after a little over three weeks in London she felt like a native. Well, maybe not that exactly; it was an enormous city, full of twists and turns and strange little alleys — the complete opposite to New York with its planned grid of streets and avenues — but she didn't marvel at the quaint names any more, or think it strange that social life revolved around one or another pub. The one where she was to meet Nick was called The Spiteful Wench, and she spotted the swinging sign, a buxom female holding a tankard of foaming ale, and crossed the road.

It was crowded, but she expected that. Six o'clock on a chilly, late September Monday evening, it was bound to be. She stood just inside the front door and peered at the throng. She'd almost decided he hadn't yet arrived when she heard his laugh. She knew it was him, that deep joyful guffaw couldn't belong to anyone else.

'Nick ... Where are you?' Silly, he couldn't hear her over all this. She pushed forward through the mêlée at the bar murmuring, 'Excuse me.' Finally she spotted him at a tiny table in the rear. 'Nick!'

His back was to her but he heard her voice and turned. For a moment their eyes met and held, it was an instant frozen in time. Mollie felt something very peculiar, a flush of warmth that spread from her toes to her scalp. A galvanizing energy propelled her forward into his arms. And when he hugged her, holding her close for a long few seconds, she felt something then too. It was not what she expected to feel, not a rising of that deep river of affection which had flowed between them almost from the moment she'd been born. This was different, a new current that threatened to carry her away. He was a man, and she was a woman and she was suddenly aware of being totally enfolded in his maleness and wanting ... wanting ... Mollie closed off her feelings with an act of will, and promptly told herself they didn't exist. She was not a pervert. This was the man who was her surrogate brother and father rolled into one, her first cousin. 'Nick,' she squealed with an almost deliberately childish enthusiasm. 'God, I'm glad to see you.'

'Me too.' He let her go, holding her at arm's length for a

moment, studying her face. 'You look terrific. Here, sit down.'

There were two men with him and they'd stood when he did, now they all sat down, pulling an empty chair for her into a space they created between Nick and someone he introduced as a fellow American, Henry Carson of Reuters' News Service. 'And this other oaf is also one of our countrymen, Dan Fleming. He's with CBS, though I promised you wouldn't hold that against him. Gentlemen, may I present the one, the only, the inimitable little Miss Magic Mollie Pride.'

The men shook her hand and made polite comments about her broadcasts. 'The word is there's not a dry eye left in the entire USA,' Carson said. 'I hear Kleenex wants to sponsor you.'

'They'll have to fight the twenty mules,' Fleming said. 'What did you call her, Nick, Miss Magic? It fits.'

'Little Miss Magic,' he repeated softly, looking not at Fleming but at Mollie. 'It's a hangover from years ago, but I agree, it fits.'

She was embarrassed by all the attention. 'I just do the light stuff. The stories from Warsaw were incredible, Nick. Listening to them felt like being there.'

His face grew dark. 'No, I don't think so. Not exactly.'

Mollie didn't know what he meant, but the other two men seemed to. There was a weighty silence that quickly became awkward. Fleming stood up and Carson followed him. 'Have to be going,' the first man said. 'See you around, Frane.'

Then they were alone, the two of them in the midst of a sea of strangers it was easy to ignore. 'What was that all about?' Mollie asked.

'Forget it, I don't feel like going through the whole argument again.' He'd ordered a sherry for her and another beer for himself and the drinks appeared just then, making a welcome diversion. 'You look terrific,' he said again. 'London agrees with you.'

'I'm enjoying it. But you don't look so terrific.' There were bags beneath his eyes and deep lines between his nose and mouth. 'Nick, was Warsaw terrible?' Softly, because she only had to look at him to know she was probing a wound.

'That's one word for it.' He took a long drink of beer. 'Have you talked to Steve?'

'Yes. We had lunch together yesterday.' And then we went back to his room and he told me that I turn him off and he can't make love to me, and he threw me out. No, she wouldn't say any of that.

She didn't have to. He could read her face as well as she could read his. 'I guess you two didn't have time to talk about Warsaw,' Nick said.

'No, we didn't.'

'No happy ending? The prince and the princess back together again?'

'Not yet,' Mollie admitted.

He took her hand. 'Sorry, kid. I hoped the separation would fix things.'

She shrugged. 'I don't want to talk about Steve. If you won't tell me what was poisoning the atmosphere between you and those other two guys, or what happened in Warsaw, what will you tell me?'

He hesitated a moment. 'Oh shit, the whole story I guess. If not you, who? They won't let me put it on the air. The worst thing about Warsaw wasn't the battles and the soldiers and hopelessness of the Polish situation, or the fact that the British and the French made pious noises and did nothing. It was a little thing the Nazis have imported straight from hell, they call it the SS. That stands for *Schutz Staffeln*, storm troopers. Adolf's buddy Himmler is in charge of them.'

'And?' Mollie asked. 'Come on, tell me the rest of it.'

'We saw them in Cracow and in Lublin. The SS don't goosestep down the street with the ordinary bastards. These are elite conquering heroes, the flower of Aryan manhood. They arrive in open cars driven by lesser mortals. Then the suicide rate suddenly leaps up.'

'I'm sorry, Mollie said. 'I still don't understand.'

'It was the same in the Rhineland and Czechoslovakia and now Poland. As soon as the SS arrives dozens of Jews kill themselves. The ones with imagination, I guess. The ones who know what's coming.'

She started to feel a little sick to her stomach. 'I've heard stories, everybody has. But other people say they're exagger-

238

ated. There was an argument in Parliament about taking more Jewish refugees into England or Palestine. The Prime Minister opposed the bill and it didn't pass.'

'The last night we were in Warsaw,' Nick said softly. 'I was standing in a bar, not very different from this one, and a Jewish-looking guy next to me suddenly took out a razor and slit his throat.'

She saw his hands start to tremble and she waited while he finished what was left of his beer. 'They round them up,' he continued finally, 'all the Jews. Wherever they march in, the SS gets them all together and pens them in.'

'Then what?'

'God knows,' Nick said softly. 'I've heard stories, the same ones you've heard, that there are special camps in Germany full of Jews who've been stripped of everything they own, that Hitler's going to ship them all out of the country. I don't know how true any of it is. Besides, where's he going to ship them to? Nobody wants the poor bastards.'

'At home the senate passed a special resolution saying we'd take in twenty thousand Jewish refugee children,' Mollie said eagerly. She wanted to give him something, anything to make him look less despairing. 'Everybody's not heartless.' She decided not to mention the fact that the American Legion had opposed the measure, saying the country had needy children of its own.

'Yeah, sure. I know about the senate resolution. Twenty thousand. Mollie, there are millions of Jews in Europe, and at the moment they're being hunted with fixed bayonets. What's going to happen to all of them?'

'I don't know,' she admitted softly. 'You said they wouldn't let you talk about it on the air; who wouldn't?'

'The whole stinking lot of them. I made a programme and tried to sell it. No takers. Too grim and gruesome they said. You don't like the news, kill the messenger.'

'Is that what you were arguing about with those other two guys?'

'Sort of, though it was more like how can we sit with our collective finger up our ass and let this happen? Like most good Americans, Fleming and Carson think we can and we should. C'mon, let's get out of here.'

It was a clear night, bright with moonlight despite the total absence of any artificial light. They walked east, vaguely in the direction of her hotel. 'The blackout's lethal,' Mollie said. 'I don't know how many people have already been killed in accidents.'

'Yeah, so they tell me.' Nick looked up. The silhouettes of the barrage balloons, huge inflated dirigibles with long metal tails which were supposed to interfere with aircraft, were clearly outlined in the luminous night sky. 'They also say that when the *Luftwaffe* pays London a visit it will be on a night with a full moon, exactly like this.'

'When, not if?' Mollie asked softly.

'I think so, yeah. I don't see what's going to stop them.' They were passing a pub, yet couldn't see any lights, but they could hear the raucous crowd behind the door singing about the fortification Hitler had erected on Germany's western border: '*We're going to hang out the washing on the Siegfried Line, if the Siegfried Line's still there ...*'

'I think so, yeah. I don't see what's going to stop them.'

'What about the Maginot Line? Ed Murrow did a great broadcast about it. He said the French had miles of underground tunnels equipped to withstand anything, that the Maginot Line seemed impenetrable.'

'I don't know, but I'm pretty sure we're going to find out.' Nick took her hand, making an obvious effort to lighten the mood. 'Like most things in life, Mollie darling, it's usually not as bad as you think it's going to be, if you just manage to hang on.'

'Sure, all you have to do is hang on,' Mollie said softly. 'Then pretty soon it's easy street and two a day at the Palace.'

Clementine Churchill was attractive rather than pretty. Her hair was somewhere between blonde and brown shot with grey, and she wore it in a pageboy held back with combs. Lovely light eyes, but her nose was a shade too long and thin. It was the chin that said most, however, a sharp determined chin which Mollie suspected was permanently in the 'up' position. 'Please sit down, Miss Pride. I'm so pleased to meet you at last.'

'Thank you for seeing me, Mrs Churchill, I know how busy these days are for you.'

'But, my dear, to have brought you all this way by personal request, then ignore you ...' Mrs Churchill waved a graceful hand, dismissing the circumstances they both understood. 'Tell me,' she said with a wide smile, her eyes meeting Mollie's over the teacups, 'how do you find us?'

Mollie hesitated only a moment. 'Charming, and different, and very brave.'

'Yes, well we'll need to be. Winston says ...' A butler interrupted that confidence. He murmured something in the older woman's ear and she stood up and excused herself. 'Please forgive me, this will only take a moment, but it can't wait.'

Mollie didn't mind being left alone. It gave her a chance to study the room. She was on the third floor of a grand mansion near the river, tucked between the broad street called Whitehall and an open concrete paved yard known as Horse Guards Parade. This was Admiralty House; if she threw a stone in any direction she could hit Buckingham Palace, or the Houses of Parliament, or Westminster Abbey. And here, in this ancient seat of power, the curtains of the room she was sitting in were printed with red and green sea horses.

'A little silly for a drawing room, aren't they?' Mrs Churchill had come back, and noticed Mollie staring at the windows. 'This was the nursery, you see. The way things are, well, we're only using the two top floors of the house.'

Mollie found that small truth a revelation. Here was a grand lady, dressed in clothes Mollie herself could never afford, married to one of the most well-known men in the world. And she was sleeping in the attic and having tea in what had been a bedroom for kids. 'I think the curtains are great, terrific.' The words burst from Mollie. Her enthusiasm was without plan or forethought. 'Mrs Churchill, can I tell my listeners about them?'

Clementine hesitated only a moment. 'Well, yes, I suppose you can. I guess it's a good thing if people in America know exactly how things are over here. And radio is so powerful.' She paused, then asked, 'have you heard that awful William

Joyce, the one they're calling Lord Haw Haw?'

Mollie nodded. 'I've heard him. He turns my stomach. How can an Englishman broadcast from Nazi Germany and tell you all how you're going to be invaded?'

The older woman held up her hand. 'Don't. But, do you know, I'm not so sure he's English. His accent's so exaggerated. That's why they're calling him Lord Haw Haw, of course.'

Mollie wondered if Mrs Churchill knew about the other major propaganda effort, a whole station on the air from Germany for hours at a time, programmes in English but with a Nazi twist. They called themselves the New BBC. She decided not to mention it. 'Two more London broadcasts,' she said instead. 'Then I go back to New York.'

'Do I detect a slightly wistful note in your voice?'

Mollie grinned. 'Does it show? Well yes, it's going to be hard to leave all the excitement behind.'

'And what is your opinion, my dear; will America insist on remaining neutral?'

'At least until after the election next year.' Mollie set down her cup. 'I wish I could say we're going to throw ourselves into the fight and support you all the way. But I'd be lying. I don't expect it to happen.'

Mrs Churchill must have known those facts as well as Mollie did, but she seemed taken aback by her visitor's frankness. 'I suppose you're right,' she said finally. Then, brightly, 'Ah, here's Reggie.'

The door had opened and the butler was showing in another guest. Mollie half turned in her chair. The man who'd arrived was of medium height, swarthy, thickset, in his fifties she decided. And, Jesus, it was hard to believe, but he was wearing a monocle. He looked like a caricature of an Englishman.

'Miss Pride, may I present Lord Whitby? He specially asked to meet you.'

She stood up and put out her hand. How did you address a lord? She hadn't met any before. And he wasn't going to shake her hand, he kissed it instead. At least the air above it. The only other man she knew who did anything so asinine was Armando de Cuentas.

'Charmed, Miss Pride. Nigel has told me a great deal about you.'

She had to think for a moment before she knew what he was talking about. Then she realized that Nigel was the effeminate Mr Turner who'd got her into all this. And that during the crazy scene between him and her mother the day she left New York something had been said about a Lord Whitby. She didn't have to decide whether to mention any of that, the man with the monocle did it for her.

'I knew your mother years ago, she was married to my brother Sebastian. He was killed in the last war,' he added in an aside to Mrs Churchill, then he turned back to Mollie. 'I hope we'll have a chance to talk sometime. I'd love to hear how Zena is these days, and of course my niece Kate.'

Suddenly it was over. The last few days flew by and on Friday 29 September Mollie did her final London show. In a live broadcast from outside the wrought-iron gates of Buckingham Palace, she described the changing of the guard and talked to people in the street — preselected and interviewed this time, there would be no repeat of the fiasco with the unintelligible cockney woman at Waterloo Station.

'As I stand here watching these folks,' she finished up, 'these ordinary London people who are determined to stand firm against the evils of Hitler and Nazism, I can't help but wonder how we're going to live with ourselves if we stay out of it. Whose responsibility is it to keep the German storm troopers and secret police out of New York and Chicago and St Louis and Denver and Los Angeles? Is it theirs or is it ours?'

Phil was staring at her, a look both sad and astonished on his face. The engineer glanced at him, waited for the wind-up signal that didn't come, then cut Mollie off the air on his own authority. Mollie held the microphone to her mouth a moment longer, as if she didn't know it was dead. Then she slowly lowered her hand and let the useless instrument dangle by her side.

'Well, that'll finish it,' Phil murmured softly. 'Or you.'

'I'm sorry. I didn't really know I was going to come on so strong until I did. It seemed as if I had to.'

'Yeah. I understand.'

'I wasn't thinking about you,' Mollie added. 'I should have, it's your show as much as mine.' The engineer took the microphone from her and replaced it in his box, not saying a word.

'It's okay,' Phil said. 'It doesn't make any difference to me. Besides, I agree with you.'

'Why doesn't it make any difference?' She knew something momentous was coming just from his tone and the look on his face. 'Phil, what's happening?'

He took her arm. 'C'mon, I'll buy you a cup of coffee and we'll talk.'

They went to a café on Victoria Street, a dingy place frequented by the porters who worked at the nearby train station. The coffee was terrible. 'We should have had tea,' Phil said. 'When in Rome and all that.'

'Stop stalling. There's something on your mind, tell me about it.'

He smiled at her. 'Don't ever stop doing that, Mollie, going for the jugular. It's what makes you such a great interviewer.'

'Phil . . .'

'Okay. Here it is, short and sweet. I'm not going back with you. I won't be on the clipper tomorrow morning. When the networks and the sponsors want to dump you I'm not going to be there to tell 'em to shove it up their ass.'

'Why?'

'Because of what you said on the air just now. Forgive me for being more than usually crude, but the twenty mules must be shitting bricks.'

'I don't mean that. I know what the reactions will be. Screw them. I want to know why you're not coming home. Phil, this is the last flight Pan American's scheduled. For the duration, they said. Whatever that means.'

'I know,' he said. 'But it doesn't matter. Sandra and I are getting married.'

'Sandra Marks! The proper English lady?' She was so astonished she said the first thing that came into her mind. 'Jesus, Phil, she's a head taller than you.'

He chuckled. 'Yeah, and she talks like she's got a hot potato in her mouth.'

244

'I wasn't implying ... I didn't mean ...'

'You, the big mouth, at a loss for words. Listen, *mameleh*, I'm almost fifty years old and until now I never wanted to marry anybody. But I want to marry Sandra. And, miracle of miracles, she wants to marry me. And at my age there isn't any time to footsie around.'

Mollie took a deep breath. 'That's great.' She paused. 'Phil, is she by any chance Jewish?'

This time it wasn't a chuckle but a belly laugh. 'You sound like my mother, may she rest in peace. Yeah, Mollie, she's Jewish. But frankly I wouldn't care if she was a Hindu.'

'It's better if she's Jewish,' Mollie said firmly. 'You'll have more in common. And when you come to New York she'll fit in better. You are coming to New York after you're married, aren't you?'

'Eventually, maybe.'

'What the hell does that mean?'

'It means there's a war on. Maybe everybody in America can kid themselves, but I can't and neither can Sandra. Things are pretty quiet so far, but I'll give you any odds you want that they're not going to stay that way. Sandra says this is no time to desert, and I agree with her. The BBC thinks it can maybe use me, if not, I'll get something with one of the networks. Thirty-plus years of experience should make me useful for something.'

So there it was. Before she came over here she'd mourned the half of her life that had transferred itself to London, Steve and Nick. Now, with Phil staying behind, it was more like two-thirds. And there were so many things she hadn't seen and people she hadn't met. She'd not even had an opportunity to talk to Lord Whitby; she wanted to do that so she could report back to Zena and Kate, but there hadn't been time. A little corner of her mind suggested that she stay too, but Mollie ignored it. She couldn't walk out on her mother and her sister, not to mention her job.

She said goodbye to Steve on the telephone — he refused to see her again, saying there was no point — and Nick came to Southampton to see her off. Mollie hugged him hard and boarded the seaplane with a heavy heart.

The following Monday morning she was at the studio. A

245

man from the twenty-fifth floor was waiting for her. Not one of the very top brass, a young underling with his eye on the boardroom.

'Good morning,' Mollie said when she walked into her office at seven-fifteen and found him there. 'I have to tell you about Phil, but it had better wait until after the show. No problem about this morning, we arranged everything before we left. I've got a dress designer from Seventh Avenue coming in.'

'No you haven't.'

'What do you mean? Don't tell me the rat let me down!'

'No, I called him off.'

'Jesus! Why?'

The answer was two words. 'You're fired.'

11

Who killed Cock Robin? I, said the sparrow, with my bow and arrow ...

Why was she thinking of nursery rhymes, struggling through days and nights and weeks of disappointment, frustration and worry with the silly verse repeating itself in her head? Because she'd made up a parody.

Who killed Mollie Pride? I, said the guy who flied.

Stupid to blame Lindbergh; he was a hero, the first man to fly solo non-stop across the Atlantic, and a bereaved victim whose child had been kidnapped and murdered. He was also the guy who made speeches across the nation saying that Nazi Germany was really an okay place, and anyway the US should remain neutral.

They'd really creamed her, those isolationists by principle and the Irish and German Americans with their own axes to grind, that whole hard nut of lobbyists determined to keep America out of this war. They'd mounted a two-pronged attack, pressuring the brass at NBC as well as the drivers of the twenty mules, and *Mornings With Mollie* had tumbled off the wall and shattered into so many pieces that not all the king's horses and all the king's men ... Damn! She had to stop thinking she was Mother Goose and start making a plan of survival.

First of all, Mollie reminded herself, long-range career goals were not the issue, the issue was eating. She'd never saved a penny in her life and no one would buy her groceries and pay her rent — not to mention Zena's — if she didn't. Okay, face it, the name 'Mollie Pride' was splattered with mud, it had a stench about it. 'Can't touch you with a barge pole, kid,' the guy at Mutual had told her, and he was echoing the sentiments of all three networks. 'Wouldn't dare.

Sorry, but Nick's an old friend and I know you're his cousin, so I'm giving it to you straight. You're poison.'

'Okay,' Mollie said, taking one long breath while she choked down her pride. 'My name maybe, but what about my voice?'

'I'm not sure I get you.'

'Commercials,' she explained. 'I used to do them and I'm still damned good at it. Nobody knows or cares whose voice is telling them to Lux their undies.'

'Yeah,' the guy said thoughtfully. 'You're right. And you've got great delivery, Mollie. No doubt about that.' And he was, as he'd said, an old friend of Nick's. So she was back in business as a freelance, unnamed radio voice, plugging the virtues of soap and cereal and coffee on the daytime shows which didn't have regular announcers. Only for Mutual at first, then for NBC and CBS, because the jobs were so run-of-the-mill and minor that the network bosses never saw her, and hadn't the least idea she was working in their studios.

It wasn't really a living, the work was neither frequent enough nor regular enough to be that. Still, it helped keep Mollie and her mother alive. 'I'll stay in New York with you until Steve comes home.' Zena had said that first week in October when Mollie was frantically trying to find her feet in a universe suddenly swaying. 'If I close up Hillhaven it doesn't have to be heated and that will save quite a bit.'

It did. Besides, having her mother around to look after her was really quite pleasant, especially in her present bruised and battered state. 'Yes, do stay,' Mollie agreed.

'Maybe I can see more of Kate and Ricky, as well,' Zena had said wistfully. 'She hasn't had much time to be sociable since she came home from Argentina, but that might change.'

Ah yes. Mollie bit her lip and made no reply.

Her voice was low and warm and full of promise. 'Remember, ladies, she's lovely, she's engaged, she uses Ponds.' Music up, then down ... fade out, cut.

'Good job, Mollie. Thanks.' The producer of the commercial gave her a brief wave of the hand, then turned back to more important concerns. Mollie slung her bag over her shoulder and picked up her coat and left the studio. She had to stop on the seventh floor of the building on Madison Avenue to get her cheque. She kept careful records, and knew she'd earned 119 dollars from CBS in November, but she only collected 111.

'What happened to the other eight bucks?' Mollie demanded, examining the cheque.

'New deductions,' the payroll clerk explained. 'See, it says right there,' she gestured with her pencil to the slip of paper that had been included with Mollie's pay. 'Three dollars for social security ...'

'I understand about that,' Mollie interrupted.

'Yeah, but now we gotta take out five for income tax withholding as well.'

'Terrific. The feds get it before I do,' Mollie muttered as she shoved the cheque into her bag. Actually she approved of withholding tax, in principle. But in practice, right now, she was going to miss that five dollars.

She left the building by the Fifty-first Street exit and headed west, walking past the imposing grey stone facade of St Patrick's in the thin sunshine of the early December afternoon. There was beginning to be a Christmas feel to the city. When she got to Fifth Avenue she saw half a dozen people dressed in the uniform of the Salvation Army, ringing a bell and singing about joy to the world. What about the Finns who'd just been invaded by Russia? How much joy were they going to have this Christmas? Stop it, she told herself. You're not in the current affairs business, Mollie my girl, not any more. The Finns have to look after themselves, tend to your knitting.

She knew the huge tree in Rockefeller Center had been lit a few days before, but she turned uptown so she wouldn't have to see it, and she averted her eyes from the rubies and emeralds in Tiffany's window. It was harder not to pause and look at Bonwit's display of holiday evening dresses. In her palmiest days she'd never been able to afford jewels, but the clothes ... Oh, what the hell, the way her life was now, where would she wear an evening dress if she had the money to buy one?

These days she walked all over town to save bus fare, but

God, it was cold today. Mollie huddled deeper into her raincoat and mourned her sheared beaver. She'd pawned it a few weeks before, carried it to Rothman's and stood beneath the three gold balls, pausing a moment to look at the sign that still said BROKE - CALL ON UNCLE and remember coming here so many years ago with her mother, on the trip that was the start of her radio career. Her terrific radio career which was now in such a shambles.

Mollie had allowed herself one sigh of regret before she mustered her courage and walked into the store. The man who waited on her wasn't the elderly gentleman she remembered, he was probably long dead. This Mr Rothman was his son, or maybe his grandson. When he offered her twenty-five dollars for the fur coat Mollie didn't argue. He had a hard look in his eyes and she knew there wasn't any point.

Hocking the coat had made her sad, but she'd not really missed it until today. This was real winter cold, the first of the season. It hurt to breathe, and she was chilled to the bone by the time she reached Fifty-seventh Street. Mollie cursed softly and fished a dime out of her pocket and boarded the cross-town bus.

She still couldn't get over the shock of opening her door and seeing her apartment as it was now. Zena had wrought changes while Mollie was in London. Like her mother, they were still there; ruffled gingham curtains with eyelet edgings, a flowered bedspread thrown over the shabby couch, lots of cushions. 'It's homely, darling,' Zena had said.

'Not like any home we ever lived in,' Mollie had commented through clenched teeth. Zena had become more and more domestic in recent years, all part of that quest for normality she'd been engaged in since Harry Pride died. Mollie understood, more or less. What got to her were not the 'decorations on a budget' Zena had lifted straight out of *McCalls* or *Ladies Home Journal*, what set her teeth on edge the first time she saw Zena's additions were the four potted plants in the window. Ivy plants, just like the ones at Lois Lane's. 'I'm allergic to green leaves,' she'd said instantly.

'Oh, I'm sorry, I didn't know,' Zena murmured. 'I'll throw them out.'

'No, don't do that.' Mollie immediately felt guilty. 'Put

them in the bedroom. That will be your room while you're here.' Which was the way it had worked out. The room Mollie once shared with Steve was occupied by Zena and the potted ivy. Mollie slept on the sofa. She didn't mind that, but her jaw got tight whenever she walked into the house. To her it still looked like Lois Lane's.

That was silly and illogical, like thinking Lindbergh was out to get her. Besides, she was pretty sure Lois Lane didn't live on Fifty-eighth Street any longer. She had walked by the building recently and noted that the windows on the second floor were bare of plants and had different curtains. Lois Lane must have moved away when she realized Steve had deserted her as well as his wife. So it was crazy to think about her: she was shopping for bargains in some other neighbourhood these days, probably looking after some other man. Anyway, cheating was a symptom of the disaster which Mollie called her marriage, not its cause.

She pushed away thoughts of Steve and Lois Lane when she arrived home that December afternoon. 'Hi,' she called, her voice as cheery as the Salvation Army's bell. 'Mom, are you home?'

There was no reply. Mollie took off her coat and dropped it on the couch. The *Times* of that morning lay on the coffee table. It was open to the art page. '*Venezuelan Millionaire Discovers Italian Renaissance Painting*' screamed the headline. There was a picture of Armando. Smiling. Mollie scanned the column. No wonder Armando looked so happy: according to the *Times* the painting he'd found was by a very famous artist named Filippo Lippi, and it was probably worth half a million dollars. 'Perhaps more,' the article speculated, 'if Señor de Cuentas decides to sell it on the open market.'

She heard the key in the lock.

'Hello, darling,' Zena said. 'What do you think?'

'Hi mom. I take it you mean what do I think about Armando's painting. Fabulous, naturally.' There was an edge to her voice. 'Money goes to money, just like the old wives tell us.'

In the past it hadn't bothered Mollie that Kate left the matter of supporting their mother to her and Nick. Kate was married to a foreigner, maybe that's how they did things in

251

his country. But now, well, a little help would be welcome. Only she still hadn't managed to see Kate alone and ask her about it. That damned Miguel was always there. And Kate was so vague. 'Fabulous,' she repeated, getting up and heading for the kitchen. 'Just what Armando needs, another old master to hang on his walls.'

'Or another half million dollars,' Zena said curtly. 'I had lunch with Kate. At her house.'

Mollie lit the gas under the percolator. 'How did you manage that? I called a few days ago but she said she was tied up all this week.'

'Yes, that's what she told me too. So today I didn't call first, I just went over there and rang the bell.'

Mollie returned to the living room and watched her mother picking up her coat from the couch and hanging it neatly in the closet. 'And?' Mollie prompted.

'And they had to let me in, naturally. Miguel answered the door and said she was busy, but I said in that case I'd just spend a little time with my grandson. And I stood there.'

'Jesus,' Mollie murmured under her breath. Then, before Zena could reprove her for her bad language. 'Mom, sometimes you amaze me. You're such an innocent, but every once in a while ...'

'I was an innocent, then my two husbands taught me the facts of life. And I'm not talking about the bedroom.'

Mollie's brown eyes opened until they were as wide as saucers. It was the very first allusion to sex she'd ever heard pass her mother's lips. 'Don't look so shocked,' Zena said smartly. 'You're a married woman.' Then her bravado seemed to ooze away. She took a handkerchief from her pocket and wiped her eyes.

Mollie crossed to her and put an arm around her shoulders. It was so like Zena, the mix of timidity with sudden unexpected courage. For her children she'd risk anything, even that miserable Miguel. 'Mom,' she said gently, 'you'd better tell me the rest of it. What happened after you got in?'

'Miguel put me in a room and left me there for about fifteen minutes. I suppose he expected I'd go, but I didn't. And eventually they produced lunch, and after that they

252

produced Kate, then Ricky and his nurse. He's fine, a perfectly adorable child, but Kate ... She's so peculiar, Mollie. She doesn't seem to remember anything. I spoke with Armando before I left. He finally appeared to show me out. He said Kate has had a bad cold and the doctor is giving her something for it, and that's what's making her so forgetful.'

Mollie bit her lip. 'But you don't believe it?'

'I suppose I should, but I don't.' Zena went into the kitchen and returned with two cups of coffee. 'I think something is very wrong in that house, Mollie. And I don't know what to do about it.'

'I'll call her tomorrow,' Mollie promised. 'Make a date to see her. This time I'll insist, just like you did. Don't worry so much about it.'

'Yes, darling, you do that.' Zena was staring into her coffee cup. 'If only Nick were here,' she murmured. 'You don't think there's a chance he'll come back soon, do you?'

Mollie shook her head. 'No, to be honest I don't.' She didn't want to talk about Nick, because if she did she'd have to talk about Steve and it was becoming more and more difficult to keep up the fiction that they were separated only because of his work. Particularly since there had been no letters from him and only one brief note from Nick. She kept telling her mother the reason was the vagaries of mail from a war zone. But the excuse was wearing thin.

A change of subject was required. Mollie flicked through the newspaper. 'Did you see this article about the new arms policy? The hitch is precisely what this guy says. What's the point of telling Britain and France we'll sell them whatever they need as long as they pay cash? They'll soon be stony broke.'

Zena shook her head. 'I'm sorry, darling. All the international news confuses me. I think it was so silly of them to cancel your show. I'm sure thousands of women like me only understood the news when you explained it.'

Ah yes. All the while Congress debated amending the Neutrality Act she'd fantasized about the programmes she'd have done if *Mornings With Mollie* were still on the air. There'd be one with the prominent senator from Idaho, naturally. Oh yes, he'd be the first guy she'd want to confront. *Senator Borah, this statement of yours that if we send them arms can we then refuse to send our boys, does that mean you propose we give up any moral responsibility for anything that happens beyond our borders?* ... Fat chance. 'They don't want to understand,' Mollie said, finding it hard to keep the bitterness from her voice.

She felt Zena's eyes on her. There was no point in making her mother worry about her as well as Kate. Have to keep morale up around here, Mollie reminded herself. She continued turning the pages of the paper, feigning a degree of indifference. Then another headline caught her eye and she couldn't stifle her reaction. 'Look at this! God, I don't believe it. According to the latest Roper poll, more than sixty-seven per cent of the country wants America to remain neutral.'

'Well,' Zena said, paying only slight attention. 'You can't blame people for not wanting a war.'

WOR News carried a great story by Nick that night. His stuff was coming over Mutual Network stations more and more, Mollie noted. 'We've a report from Nicholas Frane who's in Finland tonight,' the announcer said. 'Nick, can you hear us? Come in Nicholas Frane in Finland.'

Naturally, Mollie thought. Where would he be except at the heart of the action? Zena came in from the kitchen and stood beside Mollie, her hand on her daughter's shoulder. The familiar voice filled the living room.

'This is Nick Frane and I'm speaking to you from a small town in the Finnish countryside. That noise you hear in the background is Russian shells. They've been bombarding this village of five hundred people for nearly three hours. But for the moment they haven't been able to get close enough to find the range or do any real damage. It's bitterly cold here, nine below zero, and I'm standing on about six feet of hard-packed snow.

'This country's best defence is its harsh climate and difficult terrain. The Russian troops are no match for the Finnish soldiers. The Finns dress entirely in white, which is perfect camouflage in these snow-covered mountains, and they operate on skis, outflanking the enemy over and over again. Still, this is a very small nation trying to defend itself against

254

one that's enormous. And they're doing it alone ...'

It was pretty terrible news, but the sound of his voice comforted Mollie. She could picture him, and Steve of course, Steve must be with him.

'I'm sure he knows we're listening,' Zena said. 'I feel as if Nick's speaking directly to you and me. And Steve is thinking of you,' she added, smiling fondly at her daughter. 'He's sending you smiles through the radio.'

A nice romantic notion, just the kind of thing her mother would think of. Mollie knew better.

She had to do it, she'd promised her mother. Besides, in those moments when she could find time to think about something besides her own screwed up life, Mollie really was worried about Kate. She waited until the next morning when Zena had gone to the A & P, then she picked up the telephone and called her sister.

'Doña Katarina is resting,' Miguel said. 'I will ask her to call you when she wakes up.'

'No, wake her up now. C'mon, Miguel. I have to talk to her. She won't mind since it's me.'

There was a pause on the line, and Mollie had the impression that Miguel was whispering to someone else. Armando perhaps. Finally he said he'd try to get Kate and she should wait. A minute passed, then two. Nearly five had gone by before she heard Kate's tentative, 'Mollie, is that you?'

'Yes, of course it's me. What's wrong, honey? Why are you whispering?'

'I have a sore throat.'

'Mom said you're seeing a doctor.'

'Yes, that's right.'

'Katykins, I want to see you. We're worried, both mom and I. Can you come here?' Maybe Kate would be more normal if she could get her away from that house.

'No, no, I can't do that.'

'Okay, I'll come to your place then. This afternoon.'

'No. Mollie ...' Another long pause, then that thin, strange voice whispering her name over and over. 'Mollie, Mollie, Mollie ...'

Jesus! The whole thing was weird, there was something very much the matter. It was far worse than it had been last summer, worse than even a few weeks ago.

'Kate, listen to me.' Mollie spoke very slowly, as clearly as she could, almost in her radio voice. 'I'm going to come to your house. I'll be there in fifteen minutes. Try and be near the door so you open it yourself. Do you understand me, Katykins? I'm going to come and if you open the door I'll do all the rest.'

'Yes. Goodbye.'

She didn't know if that soft yes had been a sign of understanding and agreement or merely an automatic response, but Mollie had to act on the hope that it was the former. She pulled on two sweaters and her raincoat and wrapped her head in a kerchief and ran out of the house. It was a dull grey morning, cold and damp. By the time she got to the street it had started to snow. She dashed for Columbus Circle and ran down into the subway, cursing the fact that she didn't have enough money for a cab.

Her heart sank when Maria, the maid, opened the door of the house at 53 East Eighty-second. Kate hadn't understood after all. 'I want to see my sister,' Mollie said. She shoved her foot across the threshold, the way salesmen did in the movies, and wished fervently that it was a bigger foot, that she was a tough man who could push his way in.

'Please wait,' Maria said. 'I'll see if the señora is receiving.'

It was a civil enough response, at least in a place like this, but it didn't satisfy Mollie. 'I know she wants to see me, I just talked to her on the telephone.' She began to move forward, to elbow her way past the other woman. The maid, seeing her intention, started to close the door. 'Hey, hold on a minute,' Mollie shouted.

'It's all right, Maria. I'm here.'

That same whispered voice which had become Kate's, that same tone which sounded as if it were composed of half-terror and half-dream. Over Maria's shoulder, Mollie saw her sister appear in the spacious foyer. She made another effort to get in and this time she succeeded, because the maid had turned in the direction of her mistress's voice, and that left the door unguarded just long enough for Mollie to slip through it. 'Kate,' she said, stretching out her hand.

'Señora,' Maria's voice took on a tone of urgency, 'Don Armando said you were to rest.'

'It's all right,' Kate repeated.

She was making a tremendous effort, Mollie could see that in Kate's face, in her stance. She shoved past the maid and put her arm around her sister. God, Kate was so thin. She was wearing a silk negligee and beneath it she felt like skin and bones. 'Do you have a coat handy, Katykins? We can go for a walk.'

The maid stared wide-eyed at Mollie. 'The Señora cannot go out. It's forbidden.'

'By whom?' Mollie demanded, tugging Kate towards the door. The hell with a coat, they had to get out of here. There was something malevolent in this house, something evil. Mollie kept glancing over her shoulder at the elevator, terrified that at any moment it would open and Miguel would appear.

'Forbidden by her doctor.' Armando's voice. He hadn't used the elevator, he came tripping down the stairs, moving with his customary grace, looking as elegant as always. 'Hello, Mollie, how nice to see you. Kate's had a bad cold which has turned into grippe. The doctor wants her to rest.' He came up beside them and kissed his wife's cheek. 'You're a very naughty girl to be out of bed. Now why don't you and Mollie go upstairs and she can sit with you and the two of you can have a nice long chat. Maria will bring you some tea.'

He sounded so normal, so much the loving husband. And he wasn't making any effort to keep them apart. Mollie breathed more normally, the adrenalin which had flooded her system began to ebb.

'Come along.' Armando opened the door to the elevator. 'The two of you, up to the bedroom.'

He got in with them and pushed the buttons and asked Mollie if it was very cold out, and the little panelled box lifted them through the heart of the house and deposited them on the fourth floor. 'Here we are,' he said heartily. 'Now you get into bed, *querida*. Once you're there I can stop worrying and go back to work, and you and Mollie can have a nice visit.'

257

Then they were alone. No Armando and no Miguel. God, she'd been acting like such an idiot, imagining all kinds of things. But none of them were true. It was only Kate being more like herself than usual. Without imagination, as Nick used to say. Kate had always been a little peculiar, it was simply getting worse as she got older. Living in a protected cocoon like this, with a doting husband, probably it was to be expected.

Mollie reached out her hand and stroked Kate's forehead. She felt feverish. Grippe, just as Armando had said. And she'd been ready to drag her sister into the freezing street in nothing but a silk negligee. Probably give her pneumonia. 'Someone to watch over you,' Mollie murmured softly. 'It's what you used to sing about, and it's what you got, isn't it?'

Kate's response was not at all what Mollie expected. The grey eyes grew very large and they filled with tears. 'Mollie, oh Mollie, help me ...'

'Oh Jesus ...' Mollie felt again all the anger and the terror of a few minutes ago. She dropped to her knees beside the bed and gripped Kate's hands in hers. 'Sweetie, what's the matter? What are they doing to you? What can I do?'

'Mollie.' That was all Kate could say. She just kept repeating her sister's name. 'Mollie. Mollie.' Then, 'I always loved you so much. From the minute you were born, when you were starting to walk and talk like my Ricky is now ... I loved you so much.'

'I know you did, sweetie. And I loved you. I still love you. And I'll do whatever you want. Only tell me what it is.'

'I want ...'

Kate had no opportunity to finish the sentence. There was a tap on the door. It opened immediately and the maid came in, carrying a tray with tea things. 'Shall I put it here by the bed, señora?'

Kate nodded and Maria deposited the tray and poured the tea, then she paused and looked at her mistress. She turned to Mollie, and their eyes met. The silent tableau held for a few seconds. It occurred to Mollie that this Maria could be an ally, she wanted to help. Then, before she could say anything, the woman turned and left.

'Kate,' Mollie said again. 'Tell me.'

'Tell you what?'

The moment of need and lucidity seemed to have passed. Kate was staring at her as if she weren't quite sure who she was. 'Mollie?' she said again, but this time it was a question.

'Yes, sweetie, it's me. You asked me to help you. I want to, but I don't know how. Shall I get the police, Katykins?' She whispered the words very close to Kate's ear, so if Miguel or Armando were listening at the door they wouldn't hear. Suddenly it seemed entirely possible that someone was listening at the door. In this place anything seemed possible. 'Do you want me to leave and come back with the police?'

Kate looked astonished. 'The police, but why? What for?'

'Shh ... Darling, listen to me. You're ill. Something's not right.' The hell with the police, she wasn't leaving this place without her sister. 'I'm going to take you away and we'll go to a proper doctor and get you whatever you need.'

There was another lucid moment, half a moment really, just long enough for Kate to say, 'I can't go anywhere without Ricky. I have to take my baby with me.'

Mollie couldn't worry about the child just now. She had to deal with Kate's problems first, they were all she could manage, perhaps more than she could manage. Later there would be time to see about Kate's son. After she'd found out what was wrong with her sister. Then they'd get the police if necessary, and maybe a lawyer. She stood up and went quickly to the closet and opened it.

'Ah, isn't that just like two ladies,' Armando said heartily as he came into the room. 'Leave them alone for half an hour and they're talking about clothes. Was Kate going to show you her new Balenciaga gown, Mollie? It's this one here.'

He came up beside Mollie and reached into the depths of the enormous closet and pulled out a velvet hanger from which was suspended a shimmering vision of silver lamé with intricate beading and embroidery across the bodice. 'You can't imagine how exquisite she looks in it,' Armando said. 'It's one of my Christmas presents. A little early so she can wear it to the party at Mrs Guggenheim's next week. If she will be a good girl and take her medicine and get better,' he added sternly, replacing the gown in the closet and closing the door.

'Now, *querida*, you have to rest or the doctor will be very angry with both of us. I'll take Mollie downstairs, you just stay there and get some sleep.'

Mollie looked at her sister. Kate was closing her eyes, as if the mere suggestion from Armando had been enough to put her to sleep. She looked at the handsome man standing and smiling at her. 'Armando ...'

'Yes, Mollie? What is it?'

'Look, I'm worried about Kate ...' she began lamely.

'And that's perfectly understandable. She's been very peculiar, hasn't she? I was worried myself.' He took Mollie's arm while he spoke, ushering her out of the door and toward the elevator. 'I thought she was getting so vague, and then she started imagining all kinds of strange things. It turned out she was having a reaction to some medicine the doctor put her on months ago. After Ricardo was born he gave her a tonic to build her up. It seems she was allergic to it and none of us realized. She was much better when he took her off it, then she got this bad cold and the grippe and she got a little funny again. But he says it's temporary. She reacts very strongly to whatever he gives her, but once the grippe is over and she isn't taking the medicine she'll be fine.'

It was all so sensible, so straightforward. And when in the elevator he punched the button numbered two and said, 'Have you a moment to stop by my study and see the new painting, Mollie?' it was hard to think of Armando as anything but a loving husband and perfectly pleasant brother-in-law.

The painting was glorious. It was standing on an easel beside Armando's desk. Mollie had no training in art, very little understanding of what made a painting great, but she knew that this was a beautiful picture. 'It's lovely,' she murmured finally. 'Where are you going to hang it, Armando?'

'Nowhere, I'm afraid,' he said ruefully. 'A painting like this is too valuable for a minor private collector like myself. I bought it to sell.' He grinned at her, gorgeous white teeth gleaming against tanned skin. Trust Armando to somehow maintain a tan in New York in December. 'But I can enjoy it for a few weeks anyway. Until after Christmas, then it goes

260

on the block. Which reminds me, Mollie, can you and Zena have Christmas dinner with us? Steve too, of course, and Nick, if they're back from Europe. Things are pretty quiet over there aren't they? Maybe the whole war thing's going to blow over.'

He kept up the idle chatter until they were back in the green and gold foyer, and then he kissed her cheek in a brotherly fashion and waved before he closed the door behind her.

Mollie was half-way back to Sixtieth Street before it dawned on her that in the brief glimpse into Kate's vast closet she hadn't spotted one warm coat or jacket, and no sign of the famous furs. It's a way of keeping her in the house, she thought first. Then she remembered Armando and how friendly and matter-of-fact he'd been and she decided her sister must have yet another closet for coats.

'Mom, I don't believe it! How did you manage this?'

It was Christmas Eve and Mollie had just opened Zena's present. It was a beautiful wine-coloured wool coat with a warm flannel interlining and collar and cuffs of curly black Persian lamb. When she pulled it out of the box she saw the matching hat, a high Russian toque, also of Persian lamb. The coat was marvellous, she tried it on over her slacks and twin sweater set and danced around the small tree hung with ornaments from the five and ten.

'How did you do this?' Mollie asked again. Suddenly she stopped. 'Mom, don't tell me ... It wasn't a dollar down and a dollar when they catch you, was it?'

Zena chuckled. 'Shades of your father. No, I went to see my old friend, Mr Rothman. He's not there any more, but his son took care of me.'

'Oh, mom, no. You shouldn't have done that. What did you pawn?'

'My wedding ring. The one Sebastian gave me was sold years ago, but I still had Harry's. And the little earrings with the diamonds that Kate and Armando gave me for Christmas last year.'

'Oh no,' Mollie said again. 'But why? I didn't want you to do anything like that.'

'Of course you didn't. I wanted to do it.' Zena patted her daughter's cheek. 'Don't be silly, darling. I don't go anywhere I can wear diamond earrings, and Harry's been dead for years. You're alive and here, and I was determined to get this for you.'

'It's marvellous,' Mollie said in wonder. 'Spectacular. But I still feel terrible that you ...'

'Hush,' Zena interrupted. 'It's Christmas. You're not supposed to feel terrible about anything.'

Mollie reached beneath the tree and claimed a present wrapped in green paper printed with red Santas and gold bells. 'I don't have anything very grand for you, I'm afraid.'

Zena removed the wrappings and revealed warm fleecy slippers in bright blue wool. 'They're lovely, darling, exactly what I needed.'

Mollie ran her hand over the sleek wool coat. 'This is what I needed,' she whispered. 'And not just to keep warm. I suppose it's foolish, but no matter how rotten you feel, it's a lot easier to face the world when you're wearing something great, isn't it?'

Zena smiled. 'I think every woman since Eve has known that.'

'Yeah, maybe some fig leaves were better looking than others.' Mollie glanced back under the tree and saw the two boxes remaining, and her mood changed abruptly. These presents were beautifully wrapped in gold paper with professionally-tied bows made of gold ribbon. 'I suppose we should open the stuff Armando sent over.' She couldn't work up any enthusiasm for the prospect.

What she had been looking forward to was Christmas dinner at her sister's house. She'd consoled herself with that promise for three weeks, every time she mentally replayed the extraordinary scene with Kate. On each occasion she first told herself she'd been crazy to let Armando dupe her into believing everything was all right, then she remembered his perfectly plausible explanation for Kate's behaviour, and the picture of her sister that had appeared on the *Tribune's* society page a few days later. 'Señor and Señora de Cuentas at Mrs Guggenheim's ball,' the caption read.

In the newspaper photo Kate was on her husband's arm,

gazing adoringly at him and looking gorgeous in the Balenciaga gown. How could anything be wrong with the couple smiling so lovingly at each other in the newspaper? Mollie didn't know but a small part of her brain still wasn't satisfied. On Christmas Day, she'd promised herself, I'll really be alert on Christmas Day. I'll watch her for a few hours, and if there's even a hint that she's still frightened I won't leave the house without her.

But there would be no such opportunity. She and Zena wouldn't be going to 53 East Eighty-second Street for the big family dinner Mollie had imagined. It was Kate herself who had called two days ago and cancelled the invitation. 'I'm so sorry, Mollie,' she'd said. 'It's just that I still have a touch of the grippe and the doctor thinks I should get some sunshine. So Armando's made arrangements for us to go to Miami for the holiday.'

'Kate, listen, are you sure you want to go to Miami?'

'Armando's made arrangements,' Kate repeated. As if she were programmed. Only she didn't sound programmed. She sounded a little hoarse, but apart from that quite normal, at least normal for Kate. 'I'm so sorry,' she said again.

'Yes,' Mollie had agreed, 'so am I.' She couldn't think of anything else to say. 'Do you want to talk to mom?'

'No, Armando's made arrangements.'

'Damn it, Kate, you already told me that. I thought you might want to wish mom a merry Christmas.' She knew she had to be patient, you always had to be patient with Kate, but it was so difficult. And getting angry was a way to cover her own feelings of guilt for not doing enough. Mollie sighed and tried again. 'She's right here, Katykins, I'll put her on.'

But before she had a chance to hand the receiver to Zena, Armando came on the line. 'I wanted to add my apologies,' he said. 'We were really looking forward to having you and your mother come for Christmas. But really, Kate needs some sun and warmth. I wanted to take her to Havana, but I didn't think a boat trip was such a good idea. The newspapers say the German ships are everywhere. What do you think, Mollie? You're the best informed member of this family.'

It was hard not to be flattered by Armando, seduced by

263

his charm. Mollie had given her assessment of the situation on the high seas — yes, pocket battleships and U-boats were known to be in southern waters, but the Nazis were unlikely to attack any ship flying the US flag because the last thing they wanted was to give America a reason to go to war, though it was probably better to be safe than sorry — and hung up before she realized that Kate never had spoken with Zena. Now she looked at the beautifully wrapped presents with a mixture of guilt and irritation and worry. It was the same discomforting blend of feelings she had whenever she thought about her sister.

Zena didn't share her reactions. She was far less worried about her eldest daughter since Mollie had reported Armando's explanation. At least she acted as if she were less worried. Now she untied the gold ribbon with a smile of anticipation apparently unmarred by any other emotion. 'Go on, darling,' she urged. 'Open yours too.'

Both boxes were small, and both revealed the same beautiful and thoughtful present, charm bracelets. The heavy gold chain Mollie extracted from the tissue paper was hung with four charms, a radio, a tiny figure dressed like a twenties flapper, and two flags, one the stars and stripes, the other the British Union Jack. Zena's bracelet was composed of intricate links from which were suspended four round discs. Each gold circle was carefully engraved with the names of Kate, Mollie, Nicholas, and Ricardo. The dates of birth of each of them were marked below their names. 'My jewels,' Zena said softly. 'They're remarkably thoughtful presents, Mollie. Don't you think so?'

'Yes, I do. I'd never have imagined Kate would dream up something like this.' Mollie's voice was low, filled with emotion. Okay, maybe it had been Armando's idea. So much the better. He couldn't be a villain if he encouraged his wife to do something this nice for her sister and her mother. She put down her bracelet and reached for Zena's. Her eye went quickly to the disc marked Nicholas. 'You do really think of Nick as your son, don't you?'

'Yes, I always have. Well, maybe not always, but for many years now. It's got nothing to do with blood you know, Mollie.'

'No, I never thought it had.' Mollie eyed her mother a moment; Zena had a remarkable facility for closing out any topic she didn't want to discuss. Over the years she'd told selected stories of her girlhood to her daughters, but Mollie always knew they were highly edited versions of extraordinary events. And no amount of probing could get more out of her. Like the business with Nigel Turner. As soon as she returned from England she'd told Zena about meeting Lord Whitby. 'Oh yes, it's Reggie who's lord of the manor now, isn't it?' Zena had said mildly.

'I guess so. That's what Mrs Churchill called Lord Whitby, Reggie. He looked like he'd stepped out of the funny papers. A little moustache and a monocle.'

'I can't imagine Reggie with a moustache. But I suppose he's changed a lot. Why shouldn't he? It's been more than twenty years.'

'Mom, what happened with you and Kate's father? What were you and Nigel Turner shouting at each other about that day I left for London?'

Zena had shrugged. 'It doesn't matter. Nothing bad happened to you in England, so there's no reason to go into all that.'

Mollie had tried to get her to say more, but to no avail. And she knew her mother wouldn't now explain her early feelings towards Nick. She picked up the chain with the four engraved discs. 'Let me put it on.' She fastened the bracelet around her mother's wrist. 'There, it looks lovely.'

Zena held out her arm and admired the glint of the gold against her pale skin. 'The only thing that's missing is a disc for Steve,' she said. 'And Armando, of course. I think both my sons-in-law should be represented too.'

'Yeah, sure.' Mollie didn't look at her mother, she was busy fastening the catch of her own bracelet, watching the little flapper twist and turn. 'Maybe for your birthday,' she murmured.

Christmas was on a Monday that year. Mollie had no work lined up for the rest of the week so they accepted Grace Mitsuno's invitation for lunch on Wednesday. The apartment in Chinatown looked the same as always, but Grace didn't.

265

Mollie hadn't seen her since she returned from England and she was shocked. Their old friend was painfully thin, very drawn. Her dark hair had turned almost entirely white, and she looked like an old woman. Lee, of course. According to Zena, Grace hadn't heard from her son in almost seven months.

There were pictures of Lee all over the apartment, many from the time when he'd been a child prodigy. On one table was a posed studio portrait of a little boy in a miniature tail-coat and stiff white bow tie, clutching his flute and looking solemn, next to it was a shot of Lee standing next to Leopold Stokowski, with the Philadelphia Symphony Orchestra in the background. There were less formal pictures as well; one was of the three of them, Mollie and Nick and Lee. It had been taken on a summer Sunday morning right downstairs on Mulberry street. A man with a tired old horse and a big black camera had come around and offered to take pictures of kids for a quarter. Grace herself had posed the three of them, Mollie in the saddle and Lee and Nick standing beside her.

'Do you remember this?' Grace picked up the photograph and handed it to Mollie for closer inspection.

'Yes, vividly. I'd never been on a horse before. Not been on one since, come to think of it.' She studied the faces of the three of them. So young, so full of hope and promise. 'Grace,' she asked softly, 'have you had any news?'

'Not a word.' She turned away. 'Come sit down, lunch is ready.'

They didn't talk about Lee again. Grace fed them a delicious concoction she called chow mein, chicken and chestnuts over pan-fried noodles, and crisp wonderfully seasoned vegetables which didn't taste a bit like the ordinary carrots and cabbage Zena cooked. Mollie remembered her last Chinese meal, the time she'd come down here with Nick just before he went to Europe, and her throat closed up and she almost couldn't swallow.

After lunch they sat in Grace's living room and she gave Zena a Mah Jong lesson. Zena had been trying for years to learn the game, but she'd never quite mastered it. 'Is this a wind or a west wind?' she asked, holding out the yellowed ivory tile blazoned with the dark blue Chinese character.

'You're hopeless,' Grace said. 'West, of course, that's why it has a W in the corner.'

Zena stared at the little token. 'Oh I keep forgetting the letters are English. I expect them to be Chinese so I don't even try to understand.'

'This is an American set, made especially for barbarians,' Grace said, laughing and sweeping the tiles into a pile in the middle of the table. 'But you're worse than a barbarian, you don't have a gambler's instincts, Zena. Every Chinese does, you know. We're born wanting to gamble.'

Mollie thought about China, at the moment being systematically raped by Japan, and wondered how many people in Shanghai and Peking and Canton were laughing over Mah Jong tiles now. She didn't voice the thought, but it was as if her gloom was broadcast. The mood in the living room changed and Mollie and her mother left a short time later. 'Poor Grace,' Zena murmured. 'She's heartbroken about Lee.'

Mollie choked back her anger and made no reply.

'Oh, Johnny! Oh, Johnny, how you can love ...' That was the hit song in the nation when the bells and the whistles and the hooters ushered in the year 1940. A few weeks earlier, *Gone With the Wind* had opened in a gala premiere in Atlanta, and now crowds were lining up at movie theatres across the nation, waiting to have their hearts beat faster when Clark Gable told Vivien Leigh, 'Frankly, my dear, I don't give a damn ...' and on New Year's day a number of radio stations pre-empted their regular programming to bring listeners the Rose Bowl battle between Tennessee and Southern California.

Late that night, after Zena had gone to bed and presumably was sleeping, Mollie fiddled with the dials on the short-wave band of the big Philco radio that stood in the living room. Sometimes ... Yes! She was lucky tonight, there was a lot of static, but she could hear an English voice saying, 'This is the BBC Empire Service.' Then the chimes of Big Ben. Mollie counted five. Of course, midnight here, five a.m. over there. Over there. It didn't mean to her what it had meant to doughboys singing their way into war the last time. It meant not all Europe but one place only, it meant England. She didn't have to close her eyes to see the great clock looming over Parliament Square.

'Here is the news from London,' the voice said, calling her back from reverie. 'Yesterday the RAF flew another successful mission over Germany. Leaflets wishing Germans a Happy New Year and reminding them how terrible war is for all of us were dropped over Berlin and ...' Suddenly there was nothing but static and silence. Mollie twisted the dial with a vengeance, but it was pointless.

Shortwave was notoriously unreliable. Years ago Steve had explained it to her. Reception was dependent not only on the size of the transmitter and the quality of the receiver, but on esoterica like sunspots and phases of the moon. Wrong phase tonight, apparently. No amount of tuning would reclaim the signal. England was as far away and as silent as ever.

Leaflets, she thought, as she tossed and turned on the narrow lumpy couch. Leaflets. Appeasement in another form. Chamberlain and his government hadn't learned a damned thing.

Two days later Mollie's bell rang about four in the afternoon. She was home alone and she went to the door half expecting that Zena had forgotten her key. But there was a man standing in the hall. Tall, good looking, with his hat pushed back on his head and a big smile on his face.

'Hi, remember me? Henry Carson. Nick Frane introduced us in London.'

As soon as he spoke she recalled that evening in the crowded pub called The Spiteful Wench. 'Reuters,' she said. 'I do remember. Come on in. When did you get back?'

'Middle of December. I've been on the west coast. Sorry I didn't get here sooner.' It was a bit of a non sequitur and Mollie looked blank. 'With this, I mean.' He opened a large briefcase and produced a bulky brown paper envelope. 'Nick sent this stuff for you. Figured it would get here faster with me, mail from England's a bit of a crap shoot these days. I expected to give it to you before I went to LA, but plans changed and I only had an hour in New York. Then I thought I'd be coming any day, so I didn't mail it from California . . .' He shrugged. 'Like I said, I'm sorry.'

'Forget it, I'm tickled to have it now.'

She offered him a beer and he accepted, sitting cross-legged on her sofa and regaling her with talk of London — 'You have to hand it to them, they stay cheerful whatever happens' — and a wonderful BBC story she hadn't heard before. 'Turns out they went on what they call a war footing two days before old Neville told them they weren't going to play patty-cake with the Germans anymore. Weeks before that a lot of BBC people were given sealed envelopes and told not to open them until they got the word.'

'You're kidding me, it sounds like something out of a book.'

'Honest injun,' Carson said, grinning. He had a nice grin, Mollie noted, and his crew cut somehow suited his blond hair and blue eyes. An all-American boy, and built a little like Steve. She pulled her mind back to his story.

'The best part is everybody swears there wasn't any peeking. So on the Friday before what I think we call "that fateful day" of the Prime Minister's announcement, all these guys got some secret signal and started ripping open their sealed instructions.'

'Instructions to do what?'

'Move. Get out of the big bad city and take up stations in the countryside. You probably didn't realize it, because you'd just got there, but up until that weekend the BBC broadcast over eight stations, eight programmes as they put it, on two wavelengths. The signal was strong enough to maybe give enemy aircraft a boost in finding them. Besides, if London had been bombed off the map, like they expected, they wanted to be able to stay on the air. So they spotted engineers all around the country and put the whole domestic transmission into that hybrid they call the Home Service.'

Mollie leaned forward and refilled Henry's glass of beer from the quart bottle she'd opened and left on the coffee table. 'Unbelievable.'

'Yeah, isn't it?'

'I take it the engineers are still living like Tom Sawyer in the country.'

'Yup. No bombs though, not a one. The whole thing's the proverbial tempest in a teapot. Probably blow over by spring.'

Mollie cocked her head and looked at him. 'Do you really think that? In spite of all the news you've been reporting from Europe?'

'I do. Look, old buddy Adolf's got what he wanted. Half of Poland and all of Czechoslovakia, so his precious master race has plenty of room to spread out. Russia's got the other half of Poland and pretty soon they're going to have Finland. Now everybody can pick up their toys and go home.'

'I see, that's how it's going to be, is it?'

'Sure thing. Unless the warmongers here at home get their way and we stir the pot and make it all worse. Then God knows what will happen.'

Mollie took a deep breath and ran her fingers through her short curls, tangled as they so often were. 'I see,' she repeated, very softly this time. She kept tugging at her hair, using the tingling pain in her scalp to keep her from telling this jerk what she thought of him. Zena still hadn't returned from her attack on the A & P, but she might come in any minute. Mollie didn't want her to return to a shouting match.

Carson was eyeing his empty glass, waiting for her to offer him a third beer. Instead Mollie stood up. 'Thanks for bringing me the stuff from Nick.'

He took the hint and stood up too, and took his coat and hat when she held them out to him. But he stopped by the door before he left. 'Say, Mollie, I'm not going back to London for a few more days. Maybe you and I could have dinner some night.'

'When are you leaving?'

'Friday morning.'

'Oh, what a shame,' she said. 'I'm tied up all week, I was going to suggest Saturday night. So long, Henry. Have a nice trip.'

She spent the next hour digesting the material Nick had sent. There was a cheque for five hundred dollars drawn on a New York bank. That was an incredible sum, she couldn't believe it. He'd clipped a brief note to the cheque. 'Hope this helps out. Mutual owed me quite a bit that was piling up, so I told them to deposit it to my stateside account.'

She understood better when she opened his main letter. The first page was devoted to commiserations for losing her show. Nick said he'd just heard about it. She glanced again at the date scrawled on the top of the page: 10 December. Their personal world had slowed down to some kind of parody of normal life, it was like an exaggerated mime in which action and reaction took place at half-speed.

The rest of the letter was general news. He spoke of his travels and mentioned that all Europe was having the worst winter for forty-five years. '... In England they had to get the troops to dig out the railroad tracks so the trains could run, and there's a coal shortage. Which means it's freezing inside as well as out ...'

Nick also had a BBC story, but it wasn't funny. 'They're getting tight as hell, nothing like as relaxed as they used to be. There are censors looking over everybody's shoulder and Americans are less and less popular. Can't blame them under the circumstances, but it's making it pretty tough to operate as a freelance. I may have to become a card-carrying member of some network again. Mutual's been making noises like they want me back, as a foreign correspondent this time, so we'll see ...'

There was more in the same vein, and love for Kate and Zena, and not a word about Steve. She kept reading the letter over, to see if she'd missed some reference to her husband, but it wasn't there. Finally, when she knew by heart every word Nick had written, she looked at the other thing he'd sent, the enclosure which had made the envelope so big and bulky. It was a bound copy of what was called a White Paper, an official government report. This one had 1 October as its date of publication, and it contained details of conditions in the concentration camps, based on information received throughout the year from British officials in Germany.

On the front page the government explained that it had withheld the facts so as not to exacerbate a delicate situation, and for as long as there seemed a chance of peace. 'Does this strike you as strange reasoning?' Nick had scrawled in the margin.

Mollie read on, feeling sicker and more upset by the minute. Zena came in when she was half-way through the document, and found her sobbing. 'Mollie! What's the matter, darling?'

'Nick sent me this.' She waved the thick report. 'It's awful. They're making people work all day without even a glass of water in these camps at Dachau and Buchenwald where they send all the Jews. And if they complain they hang them from a tree by their wrists and whip them. They made one man crawl naked on a gravel path ...'

Zena was frozen in the doorway, the door still open behind her. 'Mollie,' she interrupted. 'Mollie!'

'What?' Still sobbing, still hanging on to the gruesome report.

'Is Nick all right?'

'Yes, he's fine. But this stuff is all true, they've got proof. It's not just war propaganda ...'

'Is Steve all right?' Zena demanded, interrupting a second time.

'I guess so. Yes, of course he's all right, Nick would have said otherwise.'

Zena took a deep breath and came in and closed the door. 'Thank God. The way you were crying, I thought something terrible had happened.'

'But it has. This is barbarism, mom. It's like something out of the middle ages.'

Zena studied her daughter, pressed her lips together once, then decided to speak. 'Listen to me, Mollie. I feel very sorry for anyone who is suffering like that, of course I do. But it's not the same as if something awful happens to your own family. And it's hypocritical to pretend that it is. Do you know what I think,' she added when her daughter stared at her in disbelief. 'I'm sure partly you're crying because you feel bad about what's in there,' she gestured to the White Paper. 'But it's more because you're out of it. You're sitting on the sidelines right now, and you don't like that. I guess that's perfectly normal, Mollie. But you shouldn't fool yourself into thinking it's something else.'

Mollie had a job lined up for 12 January, a bright but freezing cold Friday. A little before noon she was at NBC. 'Just the lady I wanted to see,' Jim Hawkes said, loping towards her along the corridor outside the studio. 'I called your house and your mother said you were here.'

'Well, don't tell anybody upstairs I'm here. I'm still persona very non grata, in case you don't know.'

'I know. Don't let the brass get you down, Mollie. Most of 'em look under the bed for bogey-men each night.'

'Then they're looking in the wrong place. They'd better open their eyes and read the papers. What did you want to see me about?'

Hawkes spoke in an exaggerated whisper. 'Not here. The walls have ears. How long are you going to be?' He jerked his head toward the studio.

'Fifteen minutes. Beginning and end of the Gal Sunday slot.'

'Great, then we can have lunch.' Hawkes glanced at his watch. 'Say one o'clock at the Algonquin.'

Mollie raised her eyebrows. 'Very nice. Are you buying?'

'Yeah, I'm buying.'

'Okay, see you at one.'

She got into the studio minutes before the red light came on over the door and signalled that they were on the air. Somebody shoved a script in her hands and pushed her into position in front of a hanging mike. She just had time to slip out of her coat before the engineer manipulated his dials and flipped his switches and brought up the music. Mollie sang it in her mind, a way of giving herself the rhythm of the show. *Remember the Red River Valley, and the cowboy who loved you so true* ... Fade. Cut to the guy at her side who leaned into the mike.

'Once again,' he intoned, 'we bring you *Our Gal Sunday*. Can a girl from a small mining town in the west find happiness married to England's richest Lord, Henry Brimthorpe? In just a moment today's thrilling episode, but first a word from our sponsor.'

Her cue. 'Angelus Lipstick,' Mollie read. 'The most beautiful crimson in the world, and the most natural because it matches the rich, vibrant color of human blood. And in these cold winter days creamy Angelus Lipstick protects

273

against chapping too. Angelus Lipstick, at your favorite drugstore.' Another few bars of Red River Valley, then the man beside her began detailing the latest apparently hopeless dilemma in Sunday's life.

It was a little past twelve-thirty when she left the building and made her way to the Algonquin on Forty-fourth and Sixth. She was early, but Jim was waiting for her. 'Well, give it to me straight. Can Sunday find happiness after all?'

'Maybe, if it turns out that her sister-in-law doesn't have tuberculosis, her favorite horse wasn't poisoned by the gardener, and her husband isn't playing footsie with Lady Marjorie.'

'A tame episode I see. How about in here?' He led her into a small dim bar off the side of the lobby.

'I thought we were having lunch,' Mollie said. 'This looks like a home for alcoholics who don't want the night to end.'

'The dining room's too public,' Jim said. 'This is better.'

The Algonquin's cocktail lounge was making a real effort to help chronic night owls feel at home. There wasn't a hint of daylight in the room. A guy at a piano in the corner was playing Gershwin. 'S'wonderful, s'marvelous that you should care for me,' he sang softly.

'S'awful nice, s'paradise,' Jim Hawkes chimed in.

'Listen,' Mollie said. 'Is this a pass? Am I supposed to feel romantic?'

He stared at her a moment, then shook his head. 'For one thing I'm old enough to be your father. For another, if that's what I had in mind you would just have killed it. Very effectively. Has anybody ever told you you'd scare the pants off any red-blooded American man, Mollie Pride?'

Mollie sighed. 'Yes, as a matter of fact they have. I'm sorry.'

'It's okay. This isn't about romance. Do you want a drink?'

She said she'd have a Lime Rickey and he ordered it and rye and ginger for himself, and a couple of cornbeef sandwiches on rye. 'Pretty cold in New York right now, isn't it?' Jim said when the waitress left.

'Yes. Is that what it's about, the weather?'

'Not exactly. Mollie, where did you grow up?'

274

'Curiouser and curiouser,' she said softly. He looked blank but she didn't explain that it was a quote from *Alice in Wonderland*, or that she knew it because a long time ago Nick Frane had read her the story. 'Upstate,' she said. 'A little town called Red Hook.'

'Anybody you knew back then ever become real famous, real important? Say in the government?'

'No, I can't say they did. Red Hook wasn't exactly a cradle for world leaders. Jim, do we have to keep talking in riddles?'

He didn't give her a direct answer. 'Me, I grew up in a small town too. In Iowa. And it just so happens that somebody I knew back then is pretty important now.'

'I see. Are you going to tell me who? And what it has to do with me?'

The waitress brought their order. Jim took a swallow of his whiskey. 'The cornbeef's great here, try it,' he said.

She took a bite of the sandwich. 'Great,' she agreed. 'Now, what about your friend from Iowa?'

He reached into the inside pocket of his jacket and pulled out a folded sheet of paper. 'This is the address of a place in Queens. You ever been in Queens?'

'No. And I'm not sure I want to go.'

'Go,' he urged. 'Tomorrow afternoon. Be at this address at three p.m.'

Mollie took the paper but she didn't look at it. 'Listen, what the hell is all this bullshit? Do I knock three times and say Joe sent me?'

'Nothing like that. Just go, Mollie. You'll be glad you did.'

'How do you know what will make me glad?'

'In this case, I know. Anybody who's heard you on the air for the past couple of years would know.'

She remembered his mentioning government. 'This is something political? Is that what you're trying to tell me?'

'I'm trying not to tell you anything. Because that's what I was asked to do. But I wouldn't be playing patsy in this thing if I didn't know it was okay, Mollie. Really. Go to Queens, whatever happens I guarantee you won't regret it.'

'*Mornings With Mollie* is dead, buried,' she said. 'Nothing can resurrect it, you realize that?'

'I realize. Go to Queens, Mollie.'

She went. Because she was curious. Because after all these years she had no reason not to trust Jim Hawkes. Because her life was a mess and anything that offered the faintest hope of getting her moving was irresistible. And because the truth of what her mother had said the other night, that she was upset about the war mostly because she was playing no part in it, still rankled. But when she came up out of the subway on the corner of Jackson and Vernon Boulevards it was hard to imagine there was anything here that would improve things.

This was the Jackson Heights part of Queens and it looked like most industrialized American cities, it was completely divorced from the glamour of Manhattan right across the river. In fact it was precisely the kind of place where sixty-seven per cent of the people were in complete opposition to the cause Mollie Pride had espoused. On this sunny Saturday afternoon, mothers shopped for bargains, pushing baby carriages along narrow strips of sidewalk cleared of snow. Fathers and sons looked in store windows at train sets and footballs marked down in post-holiday sales.

Mollie stopped a grandmotherly-type lady and asked where she could find the address on her little piece of paper. The woman looked a bit surprised, but explained with much arm waving and finger pointing exactly how to get to 35 Fifty-fourth Avenue. 'It's about four blocks. You can walk it easy. But are you sure you've got the right address?' she added with some hesitation.

'Oh yes, I'm sure. Thank you.'

Mollie hadn't walked more than half the distance when she understood what had been troubling the grandmother. She'd crossed some kind of invisible border and left workaday, family-oriented Queens behind. Now she was in a seedy area of factories and warehouses. She was the only woman in sight, and her new coat with the fur trim and the matching fur hat made her feel like a clown who had wandered into a wake.

Number 35 Fifty-fourth Avenue turned out to be a bar huddled under the perpetual shade created by the Pulaski

276

Bridge. No sun ever penetrated here and the snow and ice looked as if it would stay for ever. Someone had shovelled a path to the bar's door, but she hesitated before she went in. What the hell, she decided finally. She'd come this far. Onward and upward. Push on and get the story.

Inside, the bar was blacker than the one where she'd had lunch with Jim Hawkes yesterday. And this place smelled of stale beer and cigarettes and a lot of things less pleasant. It took a moment for her eyes to adjust to the gloom. When they did she saw that there was a guy behind the bar staring at her. A cigarette dangled from his lips and he'd been wiping the counter with a rag, but stopped when she appeared. 'Get you something, miss?' he asked.

Mollie had to swallow hard before she could find her voice. 'I don't know. That is, I'm not sure. I'm supposed to meet someone here, but ...'

'Miss Pride,' a man said as he approached from the shadows in the rear of the establishment. 'Mollie Pride?'

He was in his late forties, neither short nor tall, skinny, with thinning hair. There was nothing particularly noteworthy about his appearance and he was a man whose face might not be known to the bartender; but it was one which someone like her, someone who had steeped themselves in news and politics for over three years could not fail to recognize.

'Jesus,' Mollie said in stunned surprise. 'I don't believe it.'

12

'Jesus Christ I'm not,' Harry Hopkins said with a lopsided grin.

'I'm sorry,' Mollie stammered. 'But I was so stunned.' She looked around her. 'I mean, finding you in a place like this ...'

Hopkins took her arm. 'Sorry it's such a dive, can't be helped. What will you have to drink?'

'A Coke, thanks.' Mollie was still reeling, she needed a clear head. The things Jim Hawkes had said, about somebody high in government, should have prepared her. But they hadn't. In her wildest dreams she hadn't expected to meet Harry Hopkins in the shadow of the Pulaski Bridge in Queens.

He was ignoring her confusion, taking her arm. 'Bartender,' he called, 'a Coke for the lady, another bourbon for me.' Then, to Mollie, 'C'mon, I got a booth in the rear. Sorry to bring you to a dive like this,' he repeated when they sat down in the dim hinterland of the long, narrow room. 'I told Hawkes it had to be somewhere where nobody was going to recognize either of us and he suggested this joint.'

'Of course, you're from Iowa. I knew that but I didn't think of it.'

'I'm not sure I follow.'

'Jim Hawkes told me he was the go-between because he'd just happened to grow up with somebody who was important now, somebody in government. He also said he was from Iowa. But I didn't put two and two together.'

Hawkins was busy lighting a Chesterfield. When he'd done it he exhaled through his nose and studied her through the smoke. 'No reason you should. But they tell me you're a smart girl. A very savvy lady, that's how it was put.'

'Put by whom?' Mollie asked.

'Frannie.'

'Francis Perkins,' Mollie said. Ordinarily she'd not have connected the Secretary of Labour with the name Frannie, but one of the many jobs Hopkins had held was Secretary of Commerce, and it must come naturally to him to call a fellow cabinet member Frannie.

Hopkins nodded. 'You've got it.' The bartender brought their drinks and Hopkins took a long swallow of his neat bourbon before saying anything else, then he scrubbed out his cigarette and lit another, and stared at her some more.

The silent scrutiny began to get under Mollie's skin. 'What did you want to see me about, Mr Hopkins?'

'Nazis. And isolationists.'

'I don't like either.'

'Yeah, that's what they tell me. You sure you don't want anything stronger than a Coke? It's pretty cold out.'

'I'm warm enough.' In fact the bar was overheated. She unbuttoned her coat. 'What about the Nazis and isolationists?'

'They're a pain in the butt,' Hopkins said. 'They're giving the boss a bad time.'

She knew who his boss was. Harry Hopkins had been close to Roosevelt since F.D.R. was governor of New York; in some circles he was as well known as the President, and aroused feelings equally as strong. Hopkins was unique, an original. He had surfaced as someone to be reckoned with in 1932 when he'd been named Federal Relief Administrator and within two days gave away more than five million dollars in emergency funding — on the telephone, with few formalities. Nobody had ever been so lavish with government money. The old guard puritans did not approve.

The recipients of the aid approved mightily, and so did Mollie when she read about it years later. Hopkins was one of her heroes, and she knew Nick idolized him. But Nick wasn't here and she was, and she still didn't know why. Unless ... No, Harry Hopkins couldn't know what had happened to her. But if he didn't, then what was she doing here? Mollie hesitated, then spoke. 'The boss, as you call him, isn't the only one the isolationists are hurting.'

'Nah, I guess not.' Once more he took a deep drag of his cigarette, then narrowed his eyes and studied her through the veil of blue smoke. 'How old are you?' he demanded.

'What does that have to do with anything?'

'Look, I set this up. I get to ask the questions. How old are you?'

'Twenty.' It was a lie, she wouldn't be twenty until June.

'A baby. Frannie didn't tell me you were only a baby.'

'Mr Hopkins, I presume your interest in me is somehow professional ...'

'It is,' he interrupted.

'Okay. I've been doing what I do, or rather what I did until NBC fired me, for a long time. So if I have to prove anything, well, I think I already have.'

'Yeah, I guess you're right.' He took an envelope from the jacket of his frayed suit. That was another thing the Washington bigwigs had against him, he always looked as if he bought his clothes from the Goodwill store. Yet another was that he was master of the brief but killing comment. All the stories were running through Mollie's head in double time. Like the one about the senator who complained that in the long run the New Deal would be the death of America. 'People don't eat in the long run, Senator,' Hopkins had told him. 'They eat every day.'

Mollie's heart was thudding. If for some political reason of his own the President of the United States wanted her on the air there was no way NBC could refuse to reinstate her show. She didn't take her eyes from Harry Hopkins's face. He smiled at her and she was convinced they were both thinking the same thing. 'If I were broadcasting *Mornings With Mollie*,' she said softly, 'your boss would have a supporter he could depend on.'

Hopkins shrugged. 'Yeah, but don't sweat it. We can use you in other ways.' He passed her the envelope. 'Don't open this until you're out of here and alone. Then go to the address written in there.'

It took her about twenty seconds to understand that she'd misread the situation, then she exploded. 'Now wait a minute! That's the second time in twenty-four hours somebody has told me to go some place and see somebody else,

280

and explained nothing. I happen to be a fan of yours, Mr Hopkins. And of your boss. But I am not going anywhere until I know why and who and what.'

Hopkins grinned. 'You'll do fine, Mollie Pride,' he said. 'You'll do just fine. Frannie got it dead right.'

'Terrific. I'm glad you approve of me. But that's not an answer to any of my questions, and I'm not playing along until I get some answers.'

'Have a drink,' he said, looking at her empty glass. 'Keep me company, and I'll tell you as much as I can.' He leaned out of the booth and waved his hand at the bartender, who came. 'Another bourbon for me. And for the lady ...?' He looked questioningly at Mollie.

'Could I have a lime rickey?'

The bartender looked at her, then at the man with her. 'Is she kidding?'

'Bring her another Coke,' Hopkins said. And when the bartender had shuffled away. 'Some day you'll come see me in Washington and I'll take you somewhere decent and buy you champagne.'

'I see you're figuring on being in Washington a while longer.' Mollie was still bristling and her tone was brusque. 'Like maybe another four years?'

'That's what I think.'

In spite of her anger she was intrigued, and couldn't pass up the opportunity to get information from as close to the horse's mouth as she was ever going to get. 'But he hasn't said he's going to run for a third term.'

'He will,' Hopkins assured her. 'The convention will insist. It'll be a "spontaneous" draft,' he added, grinning. Then, without the smile, 'We need him, now more than ever.'

'Now. You mean because of the war in Europe?'

Hopkins shrugged. The drinks came.

Mollie took a sip of hers before she spoke. 'The way things are these days, the only chance of getting elected in this country is to pander to the isolationists. Nearly everybody agrees with them.'

'I know. Have you heard what Joe Kennedy said in Boston last month?' She shook her head. Hopkins stared at the ceiling. 'It went something like this, "If you love America,

281

don't let any country in the world get us into this war. There's no place in this fight for us." That may not be word perfect, but it's damned close. And that SOB's our ambassador to what they call the Court of St James, which means Britain.'

'But what are you going to do about it? More to the point, what do you want me to do about it?'

Hopkins didn't answer directly. 'Look, there are two possibilities. Either this damned war will finish itself without our having to lift a finger — Hitler might drop dead or something wonderful like that — or we'll have to get into it. Don't quote me, because we'll say whatever we have to say to get re-elected, but if the war doesn't end quick we're going to be involved. And if we are, I almost want to say when we are, we're going to have to know a lot of stuff pretty fast.'

'Okay, I see that. But what does it have to do with me?' Mollie was thoroughly confused now. Still angry, but intrigued at the same time, and thrilled. Harry Hopkins was talking to her as if she were an equal. And they weren't even on the air.

'It's simple. We happen to know that your husband's based in Europe, in England. And that your cousin is Nick Frane, the newsman. So what could be more natural than for you to go live over there? And you could easily keep your eyes open and send back reports.' Mollie stared at him in astonishment. Hopkins tapped the envelope still lying on the table between them and leaned forward. 'You make reports,' he repeated. 'To the guy whose name is in here. Very much on the q.t.'

She took a deep breath, then stood up. 'You seem to know a hell of a lot about my personal life, Mr Hopkins. But not enough. For one thing I'm in the radio business, I'm not some kind of a spy. For another, I've never in my whole life managed to keep my mouth shut about anything. So I wouldn't be any good at doing things on the q.t., as you put it.' She began buttoning her coat.

'Who said anything about spies? We need information, ordinary stuff a smart girl like you will notice simply by being on the spot. Look, don't make up your mind right away. Sleep on it.'

282

'Mollie pulled on her gloves. 'Your data is incomplete, Mr Hopkins. I can't move to England. I have a widowed mother to take care of. I'm her only source of support.' That wasn't entirely true, there was Nick, but it was true enough. 'Sorry you wasted your time,' she said. 'And mine.'

Hopkins rose and picked up the envelope and held it out to her. 'Mollie, take this with you. In case you change your mind.'

She shook her head. 'I won't change my mind.' Then, the instant before she left, she reached out and snatched the envelope from his hand.

'The most amazing thing happened this morning,' Zena said a few days later when Mollie came home from doing a commercial for Carter's Little Liver Pills. 'Madame Chirault called me. She's right here in New York.'

'Who's Madame Chirault?' Mollie wasn't really listening. She was tired, she'd been sleeping badly since that crazy meeting in Queens. No, earlier than that. The insomnia dated from when her mother had blasted her with the accusation that she was power hungry. Those hadn't been Zena's words, but that's what she'd meant. 'Is she French?' Mollie added, taking off her coat and trying to summon her disappearing attention span because Zena looked so excited.

'Yes, she is. She taught me ballet when I was a little girl.' Zena stretched out her arms and demonstrated. 'Take the bouquet, mademoiselle. Give it to the lady. Sweep the air. Only she said it sweeeep.'

Mollie giggled. 'I never knew you studied ballet.'

'Of course, it was the correct thing for young ladies. At least the kind of young lady I was meant to be.'

'And what did this ballet mistress want? Are you going on the stage at this late date?'

'No, of course not.' Zena sat down on the couch and patted the seat beside her. 'Come sit down, darling, and I'll tell you all about it.' Mollie sat and Zena took her hand. 'Madame isn't teaching any more.'

'I should think not,' Mollie said. 'She must be ninety.'

'I thought that, too. But she doesn't look it. In fact I was astounded to see that she didn't look like an old woman. She only seemed like that to me because when I knew her I was so young. Don't you find that, darling? When you meet someone you knew as a child it's always such a surprise to discover how wrong your impressions were.'

'Mom, you're jumping around too much. Back up and explain. Are you telling me you saw this lady? You said she telephoned you.'

'Yes, she did. And it turns out she's living right around the corner. So naturally I went to see her. She'd just moved in, as it happened, and the place was full of boxes and suitcases and nothing had been unpacked yet, but she looked very well, and not particularly old, as I said. In her mid-sixties I imagine.'

'But how did she find you? What did she want?'

'I don't know how she found me. I meant to ask, but we got caught up talking and I forgot. That's not important. What matters, Mollie, is that she's offered me a job!' Zena sat back and waited for her triumph to be applauded.

'A job! That's crazy. You haven't worked in years. What are you going to do, for Christ's sake? Teach little kids to sweeeep the air?'

'There's no need to use bad language, Mollie. And I'm not such a fool as to think I could teach ballet.'

'I'm sorry, darling, I didn't mean to explode like that.' Mollie saw the hurt in her mother's eyes and she hugged her and kissed her cheek. 'Say you're not mad at me and tell me what kind of job.'

'Of course I'm not mad at you. You have the Driscoll temper, Mollie, I've always known that. I never did, but you're like your grandfather in some ways. Anyway, the thing is, Madame Chirault is opening a book store on Broadway and Fifty-seventh Street. Isn't that marvellous? It's only a few blocks away, and she wants me to work there mornings, and she'll pay me thirty dollars a week.'

Mollie let a few seconds pass while she disgested this, and tried to figure out how she was going to reply. 'Mom,' she said finally. 'Doesn't it seem a bit ... well, a bit too convenient? You haven't seen this woman for thirty years and all of a sudden she appears out of the blue and calls you up and moves in around the corner and offers you a job?'

Zena was genuinely puzzled. 'But it's a coincidence, Mollie. Coincidences happen all the time. In the short story in *Redbook* last month there was this woman who ...'

'That was a story, this is life.' Mollie didn't wait for the synopsis of the plot or the details of the coincidence.

'You're being difficult.' Zena got up and started for her room. 'I had a lovely surprise to tell you about and you've spoilt it. Besides, I have reason to trust Madame Chirault. She once gave me some excellent advice.'

'What advice?'

'Never mind. You wouldn't understand that either.'

The door to the bedroom closed. Mollie sat where she was for a few moments, then she got up and opened the drawer of the bureau she'd moved in here when Zena came to live with her. She found the envelope beneath her bras and underpants. It was still sealed. For a few seconds she held it in her hand. Then she opened it. It contained a business card. William Donovan, it said, Attorney at Law, 2 Wall Street.

'Sit down, Miss Pride,' the big man extended his hand. 'I'm very glad you decided to come and see me.'

Mollie took the seat he indicated. The windows of his office had a wonderful view of lower Manhattan and Battery Park, but she hadn't come here to admire the scenery. 'I was persuaded to come and see you,' Mollie said.

Donovan smiled. 'Harry can charm the birds out of the trees when he wants to.'

'Not this bird. I didn't fly down here because of anything Harry Hopkins said, I came because of my mother.'

'I'm not sure I understand.'

'I think you do. I'm young, Mr Donovan, but I've had a fairly extensive political education. That's why you guys were interested in me in the first place. And I learned a long time ago that the most amazing things can happen when the big boys in Washington decide they want them to. Truly amazing, like a woman my mother hasn't seen in years appearing out of the blue and offering her a job.'

Donovan wore a three-piece suit and he had carefully-combed sandy hair and the florid complexion she always associated with people of Irish descent. Taken all together he

285

looked rather the way Mollie expected lawyers to look, as if he could deal with anything, but his diffident, slightly casual air surprised her. He pushed his chair back on its rear legs and picked up a gold-topped letter-opener and toyed with it. 'They told me you were pretty smart,' he said mildly. 'I see they were right.'

'I suppose "they" is Harry Hopkins and whoever's in this with him. Well I'm smart enough for one thing, Mr Donovan, to know it's despicable to involve somebody like my mother in your business. You got her hopes up and ...'

'There's no reason to dash her hopes,' Donovan interrupted. 'There really will be a bookstore and she really will have a job. We merely ... well, let's say we expedited a few things.'

'And this French lady, this Madame Chirault, is she one of whoever you mean when you say "they"?'

'Not exactly. It was a matter of looking and finding. There was an old governess too, but as it happened we found the ballet teacher first.'

'At least you're frank.' Mollie sat back in her chair. 'You've gone to a lot of trouble, Mr Donovan. Or somebody has. And spent a lot of money. So what's it all for?'

'I understood that Harry told you all that.'

'About the spying, yes he did. But why me? And why go to such lengths?'

Donovan did not tell her it wasn't spying, the way Harry Hopkins had. She had to admire him for that. 'You are an ideal candidate for the job,' he said simply. 'Tailor-made for it. For the past few days I've been reading transcripts of your old broadcasts. They've convinced me you'd love the work we want you to do. People who can do something difficult, even risky, and are likely to enjoy doing it, they don't come along every day. When you find one you make the most of it.'

'Difficult in what way? According to Hopkins I was only supposed to keep my eyes open and write you chatty letters about whatever I noticed.'

'Look, let me clear something up. Hopkins doesn't work for me, he's sometimes my liaison with ... shall we say higher authorities, that's all. But basically what he told you is correct, you observe and inform me of your observations. That's all there is to it right now. But later ...' He shrugged. 'We're in a very delicate situation, it's impossible to know how it will turn out, what may be required.'

'Okay, what about the risky part? It doesn't sound risky.'

'At the moment it's not. But if things heat up, if ...' He paused and looked at her. Mollie could see him make up his mind to go ahead. 'If England is invaded, say. If the Nazis were to occupy the British Isles as they have Poland, well, then it would be very risky indeed.'

Mollie swallowed hard. 'You think that might happen?'

'I have to look at the possibility. It's what usually happens in wartime. One side or the other invades. Germany and Britain are at war, and Germany is much better prepared to fight.'

'There's something else,' she said. 'Us. The USA. We're supposed to be neutral. God, we're so busy protecting our neutrality we almost don't have time for anything else. So what are we doing playing Mata Hari games? Who's behind it?'

Donovan let his chair drop forward and fixed her with a hard stare. 'Nobody is behind it. There are no spies. None. The president knows nothing about any of this. Do you understand me, Miss Pride?'

'Yes.' She didn't flinch or turn away. 'I understand you, Mr Donovan. You have just explained what I think is called the "public posture", and I know that if I chose to blow the whistle I couldn't prove a thing. But I sure could raise a lot of dust with some pretty important people. Senator Borah say, or Charles Lindbergh, or Joe Kennedy.'

'The isolationists might get pretty excited, I agree.'

'So what's to stop me from taking this whole story to them? Or to the newspapers?' She expected a threat, braced herself for it. That's what had provoked her words. Mollie wanted to know exactly what she was up against.

'Nothing but your conscience.' Donovan said. 'Everything you've said on the air — especially that last remark from London, the one that got you fired, about who was responsible for protecting us from Nazism — I believe you meant it.'

For almost a minute Mollie sat absolutely still. 'Yes, I

meant it,' she said finally. She looked hard at him. 'Mr Donovan, are you Irish?'

'That's my background, Irish and Catholic.'

'I thought so. A lot of Irish people, most of them I imagine, think it doesn't matter if England sinks into the sea. They've got scores of their own to settle and they're desparately anxious for America to stay out of this. Maybe even back the Germans.'

'I understand their feelings, but I believe they're mistaken, or perhaps misinformed. In the end they'll support us, you know. They're loyal Americans and when they understand who our real enemy is, how evil a thing Nazism is, then ...' His voice trailed off and he sat back and waited.

It wasn't his words that convinced her, it was the look on his face when he said evil. Mollie stared at her hands for a moment, she thought of *Mein Kampf*, and of the White Paper that reported on the concentration camps. Finally she raised her eyes and when she spoke her voice was firm. 'What do I do, Mr Donovan? How do we arrange things?'

Mollie had told Bill Donovan how things were between her and Steve, she'd felt she had to, but he'd already known. That had astonished her, but she was quickly becoming accustomed to being astonished by the big man. 'Okay, there are some problems between you, that makes it the most natural thing in the world,' he'd told her. 'You're going over there to try and save your marriage. Wouldn't surprise anybody.'

It was less of a problem than he realized, since almost nobody else knew the marriage required saving. Mollie told Zena she was going to England to do a series of radio programmes. 'It's a project that may or may not come off,' she explained, not looking at her mother. 'This guy I know wants to do some shows about English life, and since there's nothing exciting happening for me here right now ...'

'Yes, of course, darling,' Zena said. 'But they're still at war with Germany, aren't they?'

'Sort of.' Mollie waved her hand in dismissal. 'But nothing's happening. It's what Senator Borah called it, a phony war.'

Zena narrowed her eyes and studied her daughter. 'You told me Senator Borah was a fool.'

'Did I? I guess I must have, sometime or other. But he does seem to be right this time. Nothing's happened.'

'Not yet.' Zena hesitated a moment longer, then she nodded. 'All the same, I think you should go.'

'You do? Why?'

'Because Steve's there. This separation has gone on far too long, Mollie. If you want to hang on to your husband I think you have to go to England.'

Bingo. Score one for Bill Donovan, he'd read the situation perfectly. That gave Mollie confidence. Anybody who could guess what Zena Driscoll Pride would think had to be remarkable.

So that was that. The only other person who might require an explanation was Kate — if she was in any condition to understand one. Mollie was determined not to leave without seeing Kate. Her sister had returned to New York a week ago in mid-January, but so far there hadn't been a convenient time for her to have lunch with Mollie, or invite her to the Eighty-second Street house.

'I'm going to London for a while, Katykins,' Mollie said on the telephone the Monday following her meeting with Bill Donovan. 'The clippers aren't flying and there aren't too many ships, but I was lucky enough to get a berth for Saturday. So we have to get together this week.'

'Yes,' Kate said. 'This week. See you then, Mollie.'

'Wait a minute! Don't hang up. See me when? We haven't arranged anything definite.'

There was a pause. Mollie heard some murmurings on the line but they were muffled, as if somebody had covered the mouthpiece with a hand. Then she heard Kate's voice again. 'Come Wednesday afternoon, about three.' The line went dead.

Jesus! It was an order not an invitation. What if she couldn't make it on Wednesday at three? Then she wouldn't see her sister. Period, end of story. She thought of the same word that had occurred to her last month when the plans for Christmas were cancelled. Kate sounded programmed. Well, there was no point in worrying about it until she saw her.

Mollie made herself forget about Kate and go on with preparations for the journey.

Packing for London was straightforward enough; she'd simply take every warm thing she owned. And a few summer clothes, she decided, because it was entirely possible that she'd still be there next summer. That was the real worry, the long time Zena might be left on her own. Her mother didn't seem in the least bothered by the prospect.

'I start work Thursday, darling. Isn't that exciting? Madame Chirault's done everything so quickly. The store is almost entirely stocked. We're concentrating on art books, did I tell you that?'

'No, you forgot to mention it. Mom, what do you know about art?'

'Not much,' Zena admitted laughing. 'But Madame is going to teach me. Like the old days, she says. And she says I was always a good pupil.'

'Yeah, I know. Sweeeep the air. Look, are you sure this is going to work? Are you going to be happy?'

Zena had just finished ironing a blouse of Mollie's. She contemplated the neatly pressed collar for a moment. 'Funny, I never thought of it exactly like that. Happy. I don't usually expect to feel happy. What I want is for everything to be quiet and peaceful.'

Mollie took the blouse from her hand and began folding it. 'That's a kind of happiness, isn't it?'

'I suppose it is.'

'And will you feel that way about your life after I'm gone? Will you be peaceful working in the bookstore mornings and living here alone the rest of the time?'

'I'll miss you,' Zena admitted. 'But I'm used to that. I was alone for a long time after you and Kate got married. And that was at Hillhaven, which I've always hated. Now I'm here in this nice little apartment. Yes, I think I'll feel quite peaceful. Besides, as I told you, I think you have to go.'

'Because of Steve.'

'That's right. Mollie, you do want to hang on to him, don't you? To stay married to him, I mean.'

'Yes. Very much.' Mollie whispered the words and didn't look at her mother.

'Then there's no point in talking about it anymore. You have to go to London and I have to stay here.'

Zena reached for the next item in the pile of ironing. Mollie continued putting neatly folded slips and nightgowns and blouses into one of the four suitcases she was taking with her. They didn't discuss it further. Mollie's move had acquired the patina of rightness and inevitability.

'Mollie, I'm so pleased you could come.' Armando himself opened the door. He swung it wide and waited for her to enter. 'Everybody's upstairs in the drawing room.'

'Everybody? Armando, I only came to say goodbye to Kate. I'm leaving for London on Saturday.'

'Yes, so Kate said. But I suggested it would be fun for you to come to our tea party.'

'Tea party? Kate didn't tell me it was any kind of party.'

Mollie glanced down at herself. Armando had taken her coat, not the new red one but a heavy loden cloth jacket she'd had since she was fifteen. Beneath it she wore an equally old pair of brown wool slacks and a sweater Zena had knitted for her years ago. The sweater was a complex Argyll pattern in yellow and brown and white and Mollie wore it seldom because Zena hadn't got it quite right and the shoulders didn't sit properly. She'd put on this outfit today because she wasn't taking any of these things with her and it didn't matter if they got dirty. 'I'm not dressed for a party,' she told her brother-in-law.

'Too bad Kate didn't explain. But it doesn't matter, Mollie, come along upstairs.'

She had to go because she knew if she didn't she wouldn't see Kate, but Mollie fumed all the while the elevator made its slow ascent. She didn't know whether to be angry at her sister or her sister's husband. Who was to blame for putting her in this spot, not to mention lousing up what she'd hoped would be a long private talk during which she could assess Kate's situation?

Armando, she decided as soon as she walked into the splendid drawing room. Armando had to have planned this event and picked out all the guests. There were about a dozen people in the room. The men wore well-tailored business suits and the women little silk dresses, the kind of thing the fashion magazines told you were perfect under furs. And pearls, of course. An ocean full of oysters had been plundered to decorate these ladies. Mollie felt so out of place and conspicuous she had to fight down the urge to turn and run.

'What can I get you, Mollie?' Armando asked. 'Tea or coffee or hot chocolate? And there's sherry and champagne as well.'

'Coffee,' she murmured through clenched teeth. 'Where's my sister?'

'Be along in a moment. She went up to the nursery to see Ricky. He's had a cold since we came back from Florida.'

'Everybody in this family seems to get colds. How's Kate's?'

'Completely better.' He smiled at her, that perfect smile which looked like an ad for toothpaste. 'She's fine, you'll see. Florida did her a lot of good.' He'd taken her arm and by this time he'd steered her through the guests to a long table draped in white linen with a glittering display of elaborate silver tea and coffee pots. The maid Maria was standing behind the table. '*Café para mi cuñada*, Maria. Cream and sugar, Mollie?'

She nodded, letting her eye roam over the throng. No one seemed to be staring at her, they were all far too well-mannered. Society types, moneyed people who travelled in a world about which she knew nothing. Only one man looked vaguely familiar, and he wasn't anybody she knew, just someone whose picture she thought she remembered seeing in a newspaper or a magazine.

Armando handed her the cup of coffee. 'The presentation will be in about ten minutes. We're waiting for George Carter.'

'What presentation?'

Armando clapped a hand to his forehead. 'Of course, I forgot Kate didn't tell you any of this. The painting, the Filippo Lippi I showed you last time you were here. It's been bought by the Metropolitan. Carter's got nothing to do with the Lippi, old masters aren't his department, but he was my original contact with the museum, so I think I'd better wait until he gets here.'

Little confidences, the kind you only share with someone who's family or a close friend. Mollie started to say something but stopped when a woman approached.

Mollie put the woman's age somewhere around sixty. Her pale blue dress matched her blue rinsed hair. 'Armando, I was telling my husband that — Sorry, am I interrupting something?'

'No, Rose, of course not. May I present my sister-in-law, Mollie Rogers. You might know her better as Mollie Pride. She's on the radio.'

The woman looked at Mollie, sized up her inappropriate clothes and dismissed her as someone entirely unimportant. 'Yes, of course. How do you do. What I wanted to say, Armando, is that the museum should mount a major Renaissance show next year. With the Lippi as the centrepiece. It will be expensive but perhaps we can ...'

Mollie turned away and moved a few steps closer to the door, so she could grab Kate the second she came in. Maybe they could slip away and go somewhere else to talk. She swallowed the remains of her coffee and set the cup on a small gilt table that held a bunch of lush red roses. The colour of the flowers exactly matched that of the velvet-upholstered furniture. The butler appeared at her elbow with a tray of tiny sandwiches. 'No thanks,' Mollie said. Then she remembered that she'd met the butler before and dragged his name up out of her subconscious. 'Tonio, do you know where my sister is?'

'She is coming now, señora.' He nodded his head in a direction over Mollie's shoulder and she turned in time to see Kate enter the room. Miguel was at her heels, but few people were likely to notice him, Kate was stunning, a vision. Her spun gold hair was drawn severely back in a chignon which emphasized the classic perfection of her features. She wore large gold earrings and a heavy necklace of gold over a black silk dress with a fitted, high-necked, long-sleeved bodice and yards of swirling skirt. It was a daytime dress and the skirt was short, but Kate looked like a queen. She completely outshone the ladies in pastel prints.

Mollie took a step toward her. 'Kate ...'

Her sister turned with a look of pleased surprise. 'Mollie.

I'm so glad. I didn't know you were coming.'

'But you did. You told me to come on Wednesday at three. Remember?'

'Armando is waiting for you,' Miguel said before Kate could reply. 'To make the presentation.'

'No,' Mollie said quickly. 'He's waiting for some guy named George before he does that. Katykins, let's go somewhere and talk. We can come back when this presentation business happens.'

'Oh yes, I'd like that, Mollie.' Kate linked her arm through her sister's, but she turned to Miguel. 'It's okay, isn't it? I haven't seen Mollie in such a long time.'

'These people are your guests, Doña Katarina.'

'What ...' Kate looked around, as if seeing the others in the room for the first time. 'Yes, I understand.' She withdrew her arm from Mollie's.

'Kate,' Mollie pleaded.

'Maybe later,' Miguel said, manoeuvring himself into a position between the two women with more grace than Mollie would have expected from a guy who looked so oafish.

She didn't have a chance to protest further. Another man entered the room and Armando went to him immediately, saying loudly. 'Look everybody, George is here. We can begin.'

Mollie had no opportunity to get Kate alone during the next half-hour. The painting was brought in and admired and the man Mollie thought she recognized turned out to be a curator from the Metropolitan Museum. He took charge of the picture and gave them a brief lecture on the rarity of a Filippo Lippi done on canvas and not as a wall fresco. He said everyone was in Armando's debt because he'd discovered it. 'But perhaps I might exclude the museum from the list of debtors, Armando. Considering this.' He passed over an envelope which Mollie guessed contained a cheque. There was laughter and low murmurs of approval. Through it all Kate stood at Armando's side and kept smiling.

That was the hell of it. When you looked at her it seemed crazy to imagine that Kate was anything but the luckiest woman in America. She was so gorgeous. She looked so happy. Armando was so attentive. The house was so beautiful. The cheque was doubtless so big and they were so rich. What was she supposed to make of the whole thing?

Shortly after four, people started leaving. It was Armando who came up to Mollie and suggested she stay behind. 'Give us a few minutes to say a proper goodbye, Mollie. Since you're going so far away.'

He was always doing that, disarming her, making her think her suspicions were insane because he acted so normally and so friendly. So maybe she was nuts and Kate was simply being herself, as she was now that she'd become Señora de Cuentas. Maybe not having a worry in the world had made Kate a little crazy. Her entire life before she married Armando had been a struggle, a fight to survive. It had been like that for all of them. But now that Kate's struggle was ended maybe a wire had snapped. The tension which held her earthbound was broken and she'd floated higher into that dreamworld she'd always half-inhabited.

As soon as the last guest was gone Armando took both their arms, Kate's and Mollie's, the way he had when she'd come here before Christmas, and guided them towards the elevator. 'Let's go up to my study so the servants can clean up in here. Miguel, tell Beatriz to bring my son so he can see his auntie Mollie.'

It was all so natural. They sat in the comfortable warm study with a fire burning in the grate and the curtains drawn because it had grown dark outside, and Armando opened a bottle of wine and asked Mollie a million questions about London and what she was going to do there. She was so concerned with answering him, lying to him because she couldn't tell him she was going to England to spy for a guy named Bill Donovan, that she couldn't concentrate on observing Kate. What she did notice seemed okay.

Kate smiled at Mollie a lot, and when her son was brought into the room she held him on her lap and spoke softly into his ear and pretty much ignored her sister and her husband. Ricky was two, he'd had a birthday the week before, and he looked like a cherub, as blond as his mother, and chubby and adorable, and he chattered in a funny mixture of Spanish and English. About the only thing Mollie could fasten on as a false note was that her nephew didn't seem to have a cold. Armando had said he did, but the little boy didn't sneeze once. Big deal.

After half an hour his nurse reclaimed him and somehow Armando negotiated Mollie downstairs to the front door. Kate came with them and kissed Mollie goodbye and hugged her. 'Come back and see me next week, Mollie.'

'I can't, Kate. I've told you, I'm going to London.'

'Oh yes, I forgot. Well, have a lovely time.'

'Good luck, Mollie,' Armando said, kissing her cheek. 'Take care of yourself. We'll be listening for your shows.'

Then she was on the street, being shown into a taxi by Miguel, who'd been sent by Armando to get one for her.

Mollie watched the door of 53 East Eighty-second Street through the rear window until the cab made a turn on Fifth Avenue. For as long as she could see them, her sister and brother-in-law remained at the top of the stairs waving goodbye.

Crazy to think Armando had set it all up, the party at which she'd feel uncomfortable because she wasn't dressed properly, and which supplied an excuse for her not to see Kate alone, the family scene in his study with Kate pre-occupied with her son ... The misunderstanding about the party happened because Kate was always so vague. Hell, Zena was like that too, and nobody was victimizing Zena. As for the rest of it, she was going away for an extended period, it was natural for them to all say goodbye to her together. That's what families did.

'How was Kate?' Zena asked as soon as Mollie got home, a trace of the old concern in her voice.

'She seems fine,' Mollie said. She had no real reason to say anything else, and the last thing she wanted was for her mother to have a lot of needless anguish. 'More gorgeous than ever. And Armando sold his painting to the Metro-politan. I think they paid a small fortune for it.'

'That's good. I won't worry about her then. And I'm not going to worry about you, either. I just heard a man on the radio say it was practically a sure thing that England would make peace with Mr Hitler before the summer.'

*

Bill Donovan had made all the arrangements for Mollie's crossing. The luxury liners were out of service for the duration, and she sailed on a freighter called the *Stockholm* which flew the flag of neutral Sweden. The uneventful passage took six days and the only excitement was once when they spotted a German battleship on the horizon. But the big guns didn't turn in their direction, the ship didn't approach and the *Stockholm* sailed on unmolested.

There were only six other passengers, and like Mollie they seemed content to keep to themselves. On 1 February when they steamed up Southampton Water Mollie felt as if she'd had a rest cure: there'd been little to do but sleep and eat the simple but plentiful food. When she walked down the gangplank Mollie told herself she was ready to face anything.

She had no reason to expect a chauffeured Rolls Royce this time and she didn't look for one, merely waited until her luggage had been cleared through customs, then began searching for a porter to help her get a taxi to the train station.

'Hi,' a familiar voice said. 'I had a chance to borrow a car, so I came down to meet you.'

Mollie turned and saw her husband. 'Steve ... I didn't expect you.' Her heart gave a lurch of pure pleasure.

'Yeah, I know you didn't. But Nick told me you were coming and like I said, I had a chance of a car. So here I am.'

They shifted her suitcases to the automobile. The trunk wouldn't take all four of them, one had to be stowed on the back seat. 'Looks like you're planning to stay a while,' Steve said as he turned the key in the ignition.

'Yes.'

'Mind telling me what you're going to do here?'

Her cable to Nick had contained no explanation, only the fact she was coming. But Bill Donovan had told her what to say. He'd worked out what he called a cover story for her. 'I had no reason to remain in New York. I'm a pariah as far as the networks are concerned. I thought maybe I could get a job with the BBC, through Phil Rosenberg perhaps. If not, well, possibly I can try writing some articles about London in war time and sell them to magazines back home.'

'London's pretty much the same as always. There's a war on, but not so you'd notice.' Steve negotiated the turns which took him through the city of Southampton on to the London road. 'That your only reason for coming?'

Mollie didn't look at him. 'You're here. That was another reason.' Donovan hadn't told her to say that, it was entirely her own idea.

Steve nodded, but made no comment. They drove in silence for a time, then he began telling her stories of how he and Nick worked, and the places they'd been. 'Getting back and forth across the Channel's become pretty difficult, but we have an arrangement with a French fisherman.'

'Your French has come back,' Mollie said.

'Never really left, I guess. It was my first language, took it in with mother's milk. Though I've had to smooth out the *Québécois* accent to be understood.'

'But you are?'

'Understood? Yeah, no problem. We've got this French car, started life as a Renault taxi. A big baby. We leave it at Guinés, a little town not far from Calais. I've fitted the Renault out with all our gear, we can do a live broadcast if we've got a relay station to tie into, or record if we haven't. The recording's a bitch, the damned equipment weighs over five hundred pounds, I had to reinforce the floor of the cab. And once we cut a disc we have to find somebody to bring it to London, unless we're coming right back ourselves, which usually we're not. You try to make them understand about being careful, but ...' He shrugged.

'It hasn't seemed to matter, you've done some great stuff, and it was all remarkably clear, a technical marvel.'

He didn't bridle at her praise this time, not the way he had a few months ago. Now he looked pleased and launched into a story about how they'd gone out to the Maginot line and seen what the French soldiers saw, German troops a few yards away, kicking a football around, acting like school-boys on a holiday. 'Nick asked why the French weren't shooting at them,' Steve said. 'The officer giving us our tour said why should they? The Germans weren't shooting at them.'

'But they're at war,' Mollie said.

'I know. Only the word is that everybody who matters is still hoping things will quieten down and peace will break out. The French generals are left-overs from the last war, they think this one's going to be the same. Guys facing each other across clearly defined battle lines. So the French won't shoot until the Germans do.'

'And do you think it's going to be like that?'

'Nope. I think it's going to be a nightmare, like nothing we've ever seen.' His voice was very low, full of feeling, but that wasn't the thing that struck Mollie most forcefully. What she realized with a sense of wonder as they went on driving through the wintry countryside was that he was talking to her, they were having a real conversation, an exchange of ideas. Maybe for the very first time.

At about three she looked at her watch, and at the sky. 'The light seems odd.'

'Yeah, it would to you. We're still on daylight saving time. They decided not to turn the clocks back in October. Because of the blackout.'

So the weak winter sun lingered and the afternoon went on and on. It was still bright shortly after five when they were leaving a tiny village in Surrey and had to stop the car and wait for a herd of cows to cross the road. The animals' breath raised a cloud of steam in the frosty air and by the time the last one passed the windshield was streaming, as if with rain. They both got out and wiped it, and for some reason that struck them as funny and they laughed a lot.

'I've missed you, Mollie,' Steve said when they'd climbed back into the car and were underway. 'I've missed you a lot.'

'I've missed you too,' she murmured. It was truer than she'd known. How much she'd missed him was only now becoming apparent.

The last hour of the long trip was a race through the sprawling districts of outer London. 'Have to beat the sunset,' Steve explained. 'After all those people died in the blackout they okayed masked headlights for night driving, but it's still dangerous as hell.' It was well past six-thirty when they crossed Vauxhall Bridge. The last of the rose glow had disappeared and the sky was flushed grey and rapidly darkening. 'Have you got somewhere to stay?' he asked.

Was she imagining it, or did the casualness sound phoney? She hesitated, but he didn't say anything more, just waited for her answer. Mollie reached into her bag for an address book and held it close to the window and read it in the fading light. Arrangements had been made, as with the passage. 'Twenty-nine Berry Street, Islington,' Mollie said.

'Damn, that's clear across town. It's too risky.' Steve looked around. 'What do you say we try that place over there, the Victoria Hotel? Just for tonight.'

'Sure, why not?'

She thought he meant to leave her alone at the hotel, but he asked for a double room. When the bellman took them up Mollie noted that it had twin beds. 'This okay?' Steve asked, turning to her.

'Fine.'

She watched the bellman pull down heavy black shades and draw the curtains. For a moment they were in utter darkness, then the man flipped a switch and a small lamp came on and made a pale yellow circle in the darkness. 'You'll be wanting this as well,' he said, plugging in an electric heater which began to glow almost immediately. 'Can't run the boiler now, not with the coal shortage.'

'At least we don't have to keep feeding this heater money,' Mollie said when the bellman left. Then she bit her lip, sorry to have brought up the last, disastrous time they'd been together.

Steve must have been thinking of the same thing. 'Mollie, let's not talk about the past. None of it.'

'Suits me fine,' she said brightly. 'What about dinner? I'm starving.'

He glanced at his watch. 'They said the dining room would open at seven. It's almost that now. Tell you what, I'll go down and get us a table, give you a chance to freshen up or change if you like.'

As if he were not her husband, as if she couldn't change with him in the room. Mollie waited for him to go before she pulled off her hat and found her hair brush and make-up bag and began to repair the damages of the long drive.

When she went down to the lobby Steve was nowhere in sight, but the man behind a desk marked Hall Porter directed her to the dining room. It seemed abnormally small until she realized they'd divided the space with screens. 'The hotel's apparently three-quarters empty,' Steve said as he stood to greet her. 'I suppose it's not surprising.'

There were gas heaters here, one was right behind Mollie's chair and she found the warmth welcome. 'I didn't realize the city had become so bleak.'

'Does it seem like that? I hadn't noticed.'

'Because you've been here all along. I just left the land of plenty.'

'Plenty of stars in their eyes,' Steve said. 'And cotton where their brains should be.'

She wanted to ask him more about that, how he perceived the situation at home from here, but the waiter came and they were distracted by ordering. There wasn't a lot of choice. Consommé or eggs to start, grilled sole or roast beef as a main course. They both decided on the soup and the beef; the only thing to drink was beer. Mollie remembered the lavish meals she'd had in London a few months before. 'That was before they lost nearly a million tons of merchant shipping,' Steve said. 'The Nazi U-boats are very efficient, and this country's been importing more than half her food from her empire for years. Now that's getting hard to do.'

Dessert was some kind of solid steamed pudding which Mollie found awful. She pushed it around on her plate and thought about the fact that in this whole long day, all the hours they'd spent together, they hadn't talked about Nick. In the first ten minutes, while they were loading the car at Southampton, Steve mentioned that Nick was fine, after that nothing. And she was reluctant to ask for details. Why? There was a truth here, some kind of insight, but she couldn't bring it to the surface of her mind. 'Tell me more about Phil,' she said. Phil Rosenberg did not seem to be a forbidden topic.

'As I said, he's doing great. He and Sandra live in Maida Vale, not far from the centre of town. Phil's working for the BBC. Most Americans couldn't get a job, but since he's married to an Englishwoman all the red tape got swept under the table.'

'Is he producing shows?'

'Not exactly. Some kind of liaison with the American networks. By the way, do you know that Nick and I are both on Mutual's regular payroll now?'

'No. Nick wrote me that it was a possibility, but I didn't know it had happened.'

'Yeah, a couple of weeks ago. It was impossible to keep on as freelances, the way things are.'

He'd mentioned Nick, not her, that made her feel she could ask for more information. 'Where's Nick living these days?'

'When we're in London, on Wimpole Street. That's a pretty fancy address, in case you didn't know. Nick's got a taste for the high life.'

'That's something new.'

Steve shrugged. 'Maybe.' They were drinking coffee by this time. 'Tired?' he asked.

'A little. It's been a long day.'

'Yeah. You'd better go up.'

So he was leaving her. Mollie started to say something, then thought better of it. 'Yes, I guess I should.'

He walked with her to the elevator. 'I'm going to have another beer down here in the bar,' he said.

What did that mean? Was he coming up to the room after his beer, or going out into the blacked-out streets to make his way to some place she knew nothing about, to some life he'd fashioned for himself in the ten months since he'd walked out on her in New York? She'd already asked him about the Cobblers' Arms Hotel and he'd said he moved out of there months ago because the landlady got on his nerves. But he hadn't said where he'd moved to. 'Okay,' Mollie said now, as she got into the elevator.

Steve smiled at her, that smile which still lit her world. 'See you later.'

When? At breakfast? Next week? All the while Mollie undressed, shivering in front of the electric heater which didn't seem to do much to dispel the damp cold of the room, she cursed herself for a fool. He was her husband, damn it, and she hadn't had the guts to ask him what he planned to do. Because it would have meant opening up a discussion of the whole sorry mess that was their marriage, and she couldn't face that.

She crawled into one of the narrow beds, still shivering,

and was delighted to find that a maid had put a hot water bottle between the sheets. Mollie pressed her icy feet to the warmth and felt slightly comforted. A minute or two later a key turned in the lock and she sat bolt upright, terrified. The room was dark and there was only a dim light in the corridor. The figure in the door was backlit and she couldn't be sure who it was. 'Steve?'

'Yeah. Sorry, I didn't mean to scare you. Were you sleeping?'

'No. I just got into bed. You startled me, that's all.'

He closed the door behind him and locked it carefully, then stumbled towards her in the pitch dark. 'Put the light on,' Mollie said.

'No, that's okay.'

She felt his weight as he sat down on the side of the bed, then she felt his hand take hers. 'Mollie, listen. I don't know if things can ever be, well, normal, but can I stay? In the other bed I mean.'

'If you want to.'

'I do. What I'm trying to find out is if you want me to.'

'Yes.'

'You're sure?'

She nodded, then remembered he couldn't see her. 'I'm sure,' she whispered.

He didn't say anything but she felt his lips brush her forehead briefly, and then she heard him undressing in the dark, and finally the sound of creaking springs as he got into the bed on the opposite side of the room. 'Have you got a hot water bottle?' Mollie asked.

'Yeah.'

'Nice, isn't it?'

'Great. Goodnight, Mollie.'

'Goodnight, Steve.'

Then a moment or two later. 'Mollie, I'm so damned glad you came.'

'So am I,' she whispered. 'Awfully damned glad.'

The time change meant that dawn came late, and the blackout curtains prevented them seeing it when it arrived. It was past ten when they went down to breakfast. The morning was a feast of brilliant sunshine, even the gloomy dining room had become cheerful. By eleven Steve was driving her to the boarding house in Islington through busy London streets which seemed exactly as she remembered them, until she noticed the gaping wounds in the earth.

'What are all those holes? God, I didn't know there'd been any bombs.'

'No bombs,' Steve said. 'They're trenches, home defence.'

He said it easily, but she remembered Bill Donovan talking about the Nazis invading England and shuddered.

They found 29 Berry Street easily enough; it was an ordinary house in a quiet block, but in a neighbourhood which Mollie called 'Not all that great.'

'That's sort of an understatement.' Steve pulled the car over to the kerb, but he made no move to get out. 'Mollie, listen, are you sure you want to stay here?'

'I don't know, I haven't seen the place yet.'

'It will be like every other furnished room in London, bedsits they call them. A combination bed and couch and a hotplate in one corner, bathroom down the hall. I've got one too. Mine's pretty big though, and it has a real stove and its own bathroom.'

'Sounds like paradise.' She kept her voice neutral because she couldn't face it if he rejected her again.

'Not exactly, but it's okay. And it's on Foley Street. That's near the BBC.'

'Convenient for you.'

'Could be convenient for you, too.'

'Yes, I suppose it could.'

He slammed his gloved hand on the steering wheel.

'Jesus, Mollie, what I'm trying to say, at least to suggest, is that you move in with me.'

'Does that mean you don't want to divorce me?' she asked in a very small voice.

He turned to her, putting a hand on her cheek. 'I never wanted to. I said it was okay if you divorced me.'

'I didn't.'

'I know. How about it, Mollie?'

'It sounds great,' she whispered.

They knocked on the door of the Berry Street house. A

304

woman with a broom in her hand and a bandanna tied round her head listened to Mollie explain who she was, and that she was expected but had changed her plans. Then they drove back more or less in the direction from which they'd come and Steve carried her four suitcases up a short flight of stairs to his flat on Foley Street.

It was one room, just as he'd said, but very spacious. 'This was a private house until recently,' he explained. 'I've got what was the living room; drawing room they'd call it.'

The room contained two couches, both could obviously be used as beds, and two large wooden wardrobes, as well as an assortment of tables and chairs. 'You can put your stuff in there,' he said, indicating the larger of the two wardrobes. 'Take half the other one too if you want. I don't need a lot of closet space these days.'

He left her to unpack and went down to get some groceries. The two cupboards behind the screen which hid what passed for a kitchen were practically bare, Mollie noticed. Apparently he ate all his meals out. And he wasn't kidding about not needing much space for his clothes. All but one drawer was empty and she saw only one suit and one sports coat hanging in the second wardrobe. All the same, she left a suitcase packed with summer clothes and shoved it under one of the couches. She had finished the job when Steve returned, his arms loaded with bundles.

'I think I got all the basics.' He began unloading things on to the tiny table beside the stove. 'Butter, eggs, milk, tea ... A few things are rationed, by the way, bacon and cheese and butter for a start. Only two ounces of butter per person per week. We'll get you a ration book. This passes for coffee,' he added, holding up a bottle of dark brown liquid. 'You put a spoonful in hot water. It's all I could get, coffee's scarcer than hens' teeth.'

'Steve, listen, I still can't cook. I haven't turned into a domestic marvel in the past year.'

He smiled at her again. 'I didn't think you had. It's all right, we'll make out fine. We always did.'

Yes, until Lois Lane. She turned away so he wouldn't read the accusation in her eyes. 'Listen, I'd better call Nick. He'll be expecting me to.'

'Yeah, sure. His number's on that pad by the telephone. That's another good thing about this place, by the way. You wouldn't believe the number of private homes in London that don't have telephones. Luckily there was one here when I moved in.'

She'd actually picked up the receiver when he said, 'Mollie, listen, don't be surprised if a woman answers. Nick has a lady friend.'

Years ago she'd asked him why he didn't have a girlfriend. Now he did and Mollie hated Fiona Winslow the minute she set eyes on her. They went to Nick's that same evening; her second night in London, and minutes after he'd swung her off her feet in a massive bear hug a petite blonde appeared from somewhere in the rear and was introduced.

They were about the same size, Mollie noted, but the resemblance ended there. Fiona was older and her hair was long and worn in a sleek pageboy that made Mollie very conscious of her eternally tangled curls. The other girl's clothes were also a good deal more expensive than anything Mollie owned. Fiona had on a black dress and pearls. She looked like the ladies who went to parties at Kate's. Mollie instantly felt outclassed, though she'd worn her best plaid suit tonight.

Nick's apartment — he called it a flat the way Fiona did — was definitely not what Steve had described as a typical bedsit. It was three large rooms, beautifully furnished in what Mollie guessed were antiques. 'We were lucky,' Nick explained. 'This place belongs to a friend of Fiona's. She's gone back to live with her family in the Cotswolds for the duration. Scared to death of bombs.'

Mollie didn't give a damn about the girl who had fled to the country. She'd noted his use of the word 'we' and nothing else seemed important.

Dinner was wine and oysters and tiny roast birds Mollie thought were some kind of miniature chickens, until Fiona said they were quail, and Stilton cheese and port for dessert. Whatever shortages might be afflicting England didn't seem to apply to Nick's kitchen. It was all Fiona's doing, Mollie figured out as the evening progressed. Fiona was the daughter of somebody with a title, she had connections. She also had a cook whom she'd lent Nick for the evening. Course after course appeared and was cleared away without any of the four of them having to lift a finger. So there was plenty of time for conversation, and they talked about the war and the fact that there remained a million and a half unemployed men in Britain because Chamberlain had still not, in Nick's opinion, put the country on a real war footing. 'He thinks the Nazis are going to go away,' Nick said bitterly.

'Don't get yourself all upset, darling.' Fiona patted his hand. 'We'll muddle through, we always do.'

Mollie wanted to scratch her eyes out. Who the hell was she to call Nick darling? His lady friend, as Steve had put it. And his lover, Mollie was pretty sure. Their intimacy showed in a thousand small ways of which she was suddenly painfully aware. But she didn't let on. She was damned if she was going to let this blonde bitch know she was jealous.

Instead Mollie showed her she was smart. She paraded everything she knew about the war and the situation in America. Except for Harry Hopkins and Bill Donovan, and she couldn't tell them about that because she'd sworn to tell absolutely no one. And she couldn't talk about Kate or Zena except in the most general terms. She'd wanted to, had planned to detail everything for Nick and see what he thought, but in the circumstances it didn't seem possible. So she said they were fine and left it at that, and she was desperately glad to leave at ten and walk through the dark streets back to the single room on Foley Street.

'Nick's fallen into a featherbed,' Steve said when they got back to his place. 'To put it crudely, he's happy as a pig in shit.'

'Yes. Lucky Nick.' She didn't want to talk about it, and she was glad Steve was sleeping in a separate bed, so he wouldn't know how rigid with tension she was, or how long it took her to fall asleep.

'Kid, you are the answer to a prayer,' Phil said the minute she walked into his cubbyhole of an office at the BBC. 'I am losing my mind and I just got permission to hire an assistant. You'll do fine.'

Mollie looked at the chaos. Books and papers covered his

desk and the shelves behind them, the debris spilled on to every available surface including the window sill. In fact, this office looked exactly like the one he'd had at NBC.

'I don't know,' she said tentatively.

'What do you mean you don't know? You told me on the phone you were looking for a job.'

'I am. But you need somebody to organize you and stay nicely in the background. That's not my style, Phil. It never has been and I'd be lying if I said it would be now.'

'So who knows that better than me?' he demanded. 'You think maybe I've forgotten who Mollie Pride is? Sit down, listen to me.' He swept a pile of papers off a chair and made a place for himself on the corner of the desk. It was practically a replay of the scene of their first meeting years ago in New York. 'Listen,' he said again, 'what I'm doing is trying to make sense out of the biggest cock-up you ever saw. I need somebody with a brain and you're it.'

'I'm a broadcaster, Phil. Not a secretary.'

'I know that too. But it will get you in, Mollie, on the spot. Then we'll see.'

'What will we see?'

'Who knows? Gotta play this one by ear, sunshine. At the moment it's a pretty iffy situation. Getting permission for Americans to do any live broadcasting around here is becoming harder than finding a virgin in Times Square. You know what they tell me?' He did a broad caricature of an English accent. 'Sorry, old boy, we're not running a box-office war for the benefit of the Americans.'

'A box office war,' Mollie repeated. 'That's one way to put it.'

'Yeah. But I think the script stinks. And they're writing it, not us. There's this guy Wood, he's Secretary for Air, an old-fashioned gentleman. Somebody suggested maybe instead of dropping little notes telling the Nazis war's not nice, they should drop fire bombs on German forests. Burn up the trees they need for fuel and building, minimum loss of life, not a bad idea. So what does Wood say?' Again the broad parody of an English voice. 'Are you aware those forests are private property? Good heavens, what will you think of next, bombing Essen?'

'They haven't exactly figured out what's happening, have

they?' Mollie said with a sigh. 'They still think they can play by the rules.'

'Whose rules? Not Adolf's, I can promise you that.' Phil began pawing through the papers on his desk. 'I got something here you have to see. Wait a minute, here it is.' He pulled a single sheet from the bottom of a mountainous pile. 'Look at this.'

'Mollie looked. As far as she could see the paper was covered with lines and arrows and meant nothing. 'What is this? What am I supposed to be looking at?'

'It's a map of Europe, sort of. Just the borders of France, Germany, Holland and Belgium. R.T. Clark did it, the BBC senior news editor. Do you remember him?'

'The guy we saw the day war was declared, the one who told the newsmen all they had to do was tell the truth. Yes, I remember.'

'*Mameleh*, take it from me, that is one smart sonofabitch. We were having a drink one night and he pulled this out of his pocket. Told me it was Adolf's plan of attack.'

Mollie looked at the paper again. 'His attack on Britain? But Britain isn't on this map.'

'His attack on France,' Phil explained. 'Forget the Maginot Line and the Siegfried Line and all those stupid bastards staring down each other's throats. They're going to do it like they tried in the last war, up through Holland and Belgium and down into France.'

Mollie studied the scrawled outlines again and pointed to what she took to be the northern border of France. 'What's this part of the country like?'

'Woods. Heavy forest. The Ardennes.'

'And that's what the French are counting on to protect them, a few trees?'

'Yup. According to them the tanks can't get through the forest. Did Nick or Steve tell you about the German tanks?' Mollie shook her head. 'Well, ask 'em sometime,' Phil said. 'Nick told me all about it, he'll tell anybody who will listen. He saw them in operation in Poland. *Panzers* they're called. Ask Nick.'

'I will. Phil, if everybody knows this, what's being done about it?'

'Near as I can figure out, not a fucking thing.' He stood up and walked to the window, running his fingers through his thinning hair as he looked out over London. 'I'm sorry, Sandra says I've got a mouth like a sewer. But Jesus, the whole thing makes me so mad. The Brits are sitting here, Mollie, and the French are sitting over there, and we're sitting back home, and nobody's doing a goddamn thing to get rid of this bastard. Meanwhile he's building up planes and weapons and arms like nothing you've ever seen. Pretty soon he'll be invincible. What are we going to do then?'

'There have been some sea battles,' Mollie reminded him. 'The English navy's sunk a couple of their ships.'

'Yeah. And that and a nickel and you can make a phone call. Only over here it costs two cents. Two pennies, big ones. They make nice coins. I've been collecting them. Something to remember this place by when it's been wiped off the map.'

She felt his despair, intense and personal, and she knew what was behind it. Phil must have read the White Paper, he knew about Dachau and Buchenwald. Phil and Sandra were Jews. Mollie looked around her once more, sizing up the mess. She thought about Bill Donovan and the 'newsy' letters she was supposed to write. 'Okay,' she said finally. 'When do I start?'

13

Looking back she remembered the first few months of 1940 as peaceful, but unreal — like those scenes locked inside a glass ball which makes snow when you turn it over. The only remarkable event occurred one day soon after she arrived in London, in the middle of February. A man appeared at her side when she left Broadcasting House.

'Miss Pride? Or is it Mrs Rogers?'

Mollie kept walking, she'd learned years before that it was the best technique for discouraging a masher. 'Either one will do. Have we met?'

'Not exactly.' The man fell into step beside her. 'I'm Jack.'

'Jack who?'

'Jack from 29 Berry Street.'

She had to think a moment. 'Oh, the place I was supposed to stay.' Mollie stopped walking. It was pretty unusual for a landlord to chase a potential tenant this hard; besides, how did he know where to find her? 'I changed my plans.' It was the only thing she could think of to say.

'Yes, I understand. Not to worry. It's just that I'm the postman.'

At that point they were standing outside a swanky little shop on Regent Street. The window had a display of spring hats trimmed with lots of flowers, except for one very smart black straw trimmed with a small cluster of bright red cherries and a red bow. 'I'm afraid I don't know what you're talking about.' Mollie kept her eyes fixed on the black hat, somehow that seemed safer than looking at the guy who called himself Jack.

'You know, the postman. For your letters to America.'

'Oh.' And then again, 'Oh.' Because suddenly she understood that he had something to do with Bill Donovan, and that startled her, scared her in a way. It made the whole

311

spying thing so real and so ... not nice.

'That's right,' the man said cheerfully. 'You remember now, don't you? Not to worry,' he repeated. 'Would have been easier if you were living at my place, but it doesn't really matter. I'll meet you after work, like today. Every Friday, say. You can give me the letters.'

'I thought I was supposed to mail them,' Mollie said weakly.

'Nah, love, better like this.' He spoke in the nasal accent of a man of the London streets, but he seemed entirely sure of himself, very much in charge. 'Fridays at half past five. You just toddle out of the BBC and I'll be waiting, take whatever you've got off your hands. You haven't anything to go right now, have you?'

'No.' She felt she had to explain, apologize. 'I've been here less than two weeks, I'm still sort of finding my way.'

'Right, no bother. Next Friday will do. See you then. Cheerio.'

And he was gone, leaving her feeling very peculiar. But she'd promised so she had no choice.

That same night Mollie began a regular one-way correspondence with Bill Donovan. She didn't have anything startling to tell him, but he'd told her simply to keep her eyes open and report what she saw, so she wrote about the BBC. The work with Phil was frustrating, she explained. You had to get used to being told 'no' almost every time you tried to get permission for live American broadcasting, but it was interesting. At least she found it so, and she hoped Donovan agreed.

Then, before she folded the two handwritten sheets and tucked them in an envelope, she paused, thought for a moment, and turned the second page of the letter over so she could add a third.

'This may not mean much, it's just gossip, but you said to keep my eyes open, so I'll tell you. Most of the BBC staff are fabulous people, but there's one guy who's always making anti-Semitic comments. I overheard him refer to Phil as the American Jew-boy, and when he couldn't find any sugar for his tea he said, "I guess the Jews have been pinching it again ..."'

312

She stopped, chewed a moment more on the end of her pen, and finally signed her name with a flourish. There wasn't anything else to write to him about. Certainly she wasn't going to detail her private life.

Not that she'd know how to explain her life with Steve if she wanted to. It was ... Well, it was ... Mollie couldn't think of a word for it, even in her mind.

Nothing that happened over the next few weeks clarified it for her. When Steve was at Foley Street he was sweet, attentive, fun to be with, though he certainly didn't act like a husband. More like a buddy, a roommate, a brother maybe, more like Nick. At least the way Nick used to be, before Fiona. Fiona was the one black spot, the one thing in this new life she couldn't handle. Mollie hated her. She hated her laugh and her smile and the proprietary way she acted with Nick. It was stupid, irrational, she knew that, but knowing it didn't change how she felt, so Mollie avoided seeing her. And the way things were, that meant she saw very little of Nick.

Not that she had a lot of opportunities to see either her cousin or her husband in the first three months she was in England. The arrangement Nick had with Mutual gave him a lot of freedom; he wasn't tied down to regular broadcasting. His job was to find stories, preferably stories the other networks weren't covering. 'No point in trying to get them here,' Steve explained. 'Since you and Phil have a line of guys waiting to get permission to do any story that comes down the pike, we have to take our turn. The action's all across the Channel anyway.'

Nick and Steve spent a lot of time in France, driving around the country in their converted taxi covering the bitter political in-fighting. The French were waging a more violent war with each other than anything they directed at the Nazis; Reynaud, the Prime Minister, seemed sure to be ousted.

In London spring happened around late March — at least to the extent that the snow disappeared and the trees began to leaf out, and daffodils bloomed in the parks and on the small green quadrangles of grass in the many squares — but it remained cold and windy. It was dry, however, and that was a blessing.

Mollie was thinking about that on the last day of the month when she let herself into the Foley Street flat. Somehow rain in London was more uncomfortable than rain in New York ... She was flipping through the pile of letters she'd picked up in the foyer downstairs, most of which were bills. But almost as if thinking about New York had summoned word from the distant city, she came to one addressed in her mother's hand.

The note itself was cheerful and pleasant. Zena was enjoying her job at the bookstore, the weather was surprisingly mild for late winter, the landlord had painted the hall and the corridors of the building, she'd finally managed to see *Gone With the Wind.* Then, 'I'm enclosing a clipping from the *Tribune* about Armando. Such a shame if he has to give gack all that money. But I suppose he has enough so it doesn't matter. I spoke with Kate and she said there was nothing to worry about. She seems fine, no more colds ...'

Mollie unfolded the bit of newspaper Zena had carefully cut out for her and read it quickly, then more slowly a second time.

... Professor Giuseppe Tocci, an art expert from Italy, has questioned the authenticity of a recent acquisition by the Metropolitan Museum. The painting, said to be by the fifteenth century artist Filippo Lippi, may be a fake according to Mr Tocci, an expert in such matters ... The Lippi was sold to the museum by Venezuelan millionaire Armando de Cuentas. Mr de Cuentas, who represents numerous wealthy South Americans dealing in art in this country, said he believed the Lippi was too rare and remarkable to be in private hands, so he approached the museum. De Cuentas told the *Tribune* that he still believes the painting is genuine, as do the museum's own experts who examined it originally. More tests are to be undertaken ...

'Mollie, come on, hurry! Sandra can't get away from here, but she wangled us a couple of passes.'

'For the debate?' Mollie grabbed her coat without waiting for an answer.

'No, to see the King. What the hell could it be except the

debate? For Christ's sake, don't bother about your hat. There isn't time, as soon as the Visitors' Gallery is full they'll seal it off and the passes won't mean a damn thing.'

Mollie yanked her bag from the desk of the small office which adjoined Phil's, and pulled her coat on as she ran behind him. 'No time to look for a taxi,' he said when they came down the stairs of Broadcasting House and turned right into Regent Street. He strode forward, shouting to her over his shoulder as Mollie struggled to keep up. 'We can take the tube at Oxford Circus. I've got ten bucks says Chamberlain goes.'

'You mean ten pounds,' Mollie tossed back. The sharp May wind caught her words and took her breath away. 'Slow down, damn you. I can't keep up.'

'Dames,' Phil said as if it were a curse, but he slowed down. 'How come you can't walk any faster? Sandra can walk fast.'

'Sandra's legs are twice as long as mine. I'm sorry God made me short. When I kill you and you meet him you can complain.'

They were at Oxford Circus by this time and Phil led the way across the road and down into the tube station. Mollie paused at the top of the steps and looked back at the thoroughfare where normally cars raced in four directions at once. There was almost no traffic. 'It's like a tomb,' she whispered. 'What's going on?'

'A government's about to fall, that's what's going on. Let's go.'

When they came up at Westminster the wind was even colder because it was blowing across the river. Still, there were tulips in flower; they bent their red heads in the stiff breeze. Nothing, not even the recent military disaster in Norway, could stop the flowers blooming in England. 'At least now we know where everybody is,' Mollie whispered.

They were in a crowd of bodies, a thick clot of humanity which moved as one when it had to, but mostly stood still and turned a collective eye on the Houses of Parliament. Ninety-nine per cent of these people had no hope of getting inside and hearing the debate about the fiasco in Norway, that futile attack which followed the early April invasion of

Denmark and Norway by the Nazis. The British and their French allies had been creamed, because they had no proper supplies and were wholly untrained to operate in the deep snows and freezing cold of northern Europe. 'How long do you think they'll stand here?' Mollie asked, more in wonder than curiosity.

'As long as it takes,' Phil said. 'That's what people do when their fate is in the hands of idiots. Stand around and wait, and hope for something to change.'

They pushed their way through the crowd, murmuring apologies, and the always polite British parted and let them pass. Inside there were people scurrying in every direction, but Phil knew where to go. Thanks to Sandra he was practically a Londoner, she'd taught him the ins and outs with remarkable speed. 'This way,' he said, tugging Mollie up the broad marble stairs.

There was a guard on duty outside the Visitors' Gallery, but Phil produced his two passes and the door was opened and they were allowed in. There were no seats, they'd have to stand, perhaps for hours, but it didn't matter. The sense of history in this place was palpable, and today the excitement was like the infamous London fog, so thick you could practically part it with your hands.

A member was on his feet, speaking, shouting rather; there was nothing tame about debates in Parliament. 'That's Amery,' Phil whispered, 'he's in Chamberlain's party, a Conservative, but look at our boy Neville.' Mollie looked. The Prime Minister was white with rage. She thought she could see him trembling in his fury.

'You've been here long enough for all the good you can do.' Amery hurled the words at the leader of his country and his party. 'Now for God's sake, go.'

'Cromwell's words,' Mollie heard someone whisper behind her. 'Three hundred years later they still make sense.'

They must have made sense to the members of parliament as well. A shouted chorus rose from both sides of the house. 'Go, go, go.' Chamberlain's fellow Conservatives as well as the Liberals and Labourites sitting across from him hurled the same taut. 'Go! Resign! Go!'

The Prime Minister rose, the House held its collective

breath, but Chamberlain turned and walked out without saying a word.

The issue was not resolved even some hours later. 'You owe me ten pounds,' Mollie said when she and Phil left the gallery. 'You said he was going to resign and he didn't.'

'Not yet, but he will. Besides, I said ten bucks, not ten pounds, it's a lot less. And anyway, you never said you were taking the bet.'

'Crook,' Mollie said. 'Welsher.' She put her arm through his.

'Yeah. Don't trust anybody, not even your dearest friends. Let's call Sandra and go somewhere and get something to eat.'

The following day was 8 May. The Commons were scheduled to continue the debate, but despite Sandra's fabulous connections she couldn't get another set of passes. Instead she poked her head into Phil's office during the afternoon. Her husband was there and so was Mollie. 'I just heard a fascinating bit of gossip.' Her listeners looked up expectantly. 'A little bird told me the ladies are going to force the issue.'

'What ladies?' Phil asked.

'What issue?' Mollie said at the same moment.

'Chamberlain's resignation, you foreign idiots.' She wedged her way into the tiny space, dropping a brief kiss on her husband's forehead and finding a bare edge of the window sill to lean against. 'See,' she said to Mollie, 'he's making me as disgustingly demonstrative as a Yank.'

'What ladies?' Phil demanded a second time.

'The women members of the house. They have an all-party common room of their own. Very cosy too, you know, a place where you can put your feet up and have a cup of tea and chat about the smashing new hairdresser you've found, and how to get a Prime Minister to resign.'

'How?' Mollie and Phil asked together.

'Simple, you force the issue. They've told Labour that if the loyal opposition doesn't demand a division, they will.'

Mollie had been here long enough to know a division meant a vote, and that if the house voted 'no confidence' in a Prime Minister he had no choice but resignation. 'Will they get a majority?' she demanded.

'Hard to say. My informant wasn't offering any odds. But we're the natives who are restless in the jungle tonight, and the drums are making a terrific racket.' She started for the door. 'Have to get back to work. Oh, there's one other thing. Some of the news people are reporting a bit of activity across the water.'

Mollie's muscles tensed. As usual, Steve and Nick were both on the continent. 'What kind of activity? Where?'

'Too soon to say. Nothing but more jungle drums at this point. I'll let you know if anything is decoded.'

'That is one super lady,' Phil said when she was gone. 'Tell me I'm not the luckiest guy alive.'

Mollie smiled fondly. 'Maybe you are. The luckiest guy I know, anyway.'

He looked at her for a moment. '*Mameleh*, you want me to mind my own business, or is it okay if I ask you how things are now that you and Steve are back together?'

'It's okay,' Mollie said, not meeting his eyes. 'We're doing fine. Of course he's away a lot.'

'Yeah. Listen, what Sandra said, don't get nervous. There have been a hundred rumours about activity across the water, nothing ever happens. Give you another bet,' he added, 'something else to think about. I got a *finif* says Winston ain't gonna make it. They'll go with Halifax after they dump Neville.'

'This time you're going to pay when you lose,' Mollie said sternly. 'And is that five dollars or five pounds?'

'Five pounds. I'm the last of the big spenders when it comes to sure things. The good old boys in Whitehall are scared to death of Churchill. He's an adventurer. Hell, the whole Norway caper was his idea in the first place. Nope, they're gonna play safe and choose Halifax as the next Prime Minister.'

'Wrong,' Mollie said. 'And you're on. So it's official, right? We've got a bet.'

'We've got a bet.'

There was a division that night in the house, but it was inconclusive. A large number of Conservatives voted with the Opposition, but the Government still had a majority.

Chamberlain was still in place, at least theoretically. 'They'll make a deal,' Phil said. 'It'll be Halifax.'

'Churchill,' Mollie insisted. 'You'll see, it will be Churchill.'

She slept badly that night, got up four or five times and fiddled with the radio, mostly tuning across the high numbers where the continental stations could be found, because the Home Service didn't broadcast at this hour. Once she heard Lord Haw Haw's voice, telling his former countrymen how wonderful the new order would be as soon as they were conquered. 'Bastard,' she murmured, giving the dial a vicious twist.

That was it. Except for one French voice speaking calmly in English about the music of Claude Debussy, she raised nothing but static. Whatever Sandra had heard about activity across the channel was only another false alarm. When it was nearly three a.m. Mollie finally fell asleep, and then, strangely, she dreamed not of Steve or Nick but of her sister.

Kate heard the noises at first as if they were part of a dream. The shouting voices echoed through the house and came into her bedroom and into her head, and mixed with the fantasies of her drugged slumber. At first she thought it was Nick yelling at the audience while she and her stepfather and Zena and Mollie were dancing on a stage. Gradually the dream faded.

Kate tried to hold on to it — she loved the escape to childhood which came each night — but she couldn't. The noise got louder and louder and she woke up.

Her window was open and the breezes of the May night ruffled the sheer curtains. Kate stumbled out of bed and went and peered into the tiny backyard and the rear of the buildings on Eighty-third Street. No, she realized after a few moments, the shouting wasn't going on out there, it was here in the house. She heard something else then, a baby crying. Ricky! Kate ran out into the hall without pausing to put on a robe or slippers.

She hesitated a moment looking at the ceiling, listening for any sound from the nursery upstairs. Oh God, she was so confused. Why couldn't she think clearly? She had to think clearly because there was all this shouting and screaming going on and her baby was crying and she had to get to him. But he wasn't crying now. She listened and listened, for what seemed an age, and there wasn't another sound from Ricky's room. But maybe she was wrong. Maybe the nursery wasn't upstairs but down. It had been such a long time since she'd been there. Months and months. Perhaps years. Maybe Ricky was sleeping downstairs now, the noise was downstairs ...

Kate started to descend, clinging to the banister, shivering, afraid she would stumble and fall because her head was spinning. Ricky. She thought she'd shouted the word, but maybe she hadn't, maybe she hadn't made a sound. Sometimes when she thought she was talking, and saying a lot of things, nobody answered her. Then she realized the conversation had taken place entirely in her mind. I'm going crazy, she told herself. She thought that a lot these days. I'm going crazy and if anybody finds out they'll put me in a lunatic asylum and I'll never see my son again, and everybody will say poor little Ricky de Cuentas, his mother is crazy ...

She was at the landing of the third floor now. The screaming was louder. It was coming from behind the closed door to Armando's study. The shouting voices weren't saying anything she could understand, they were screaming in gibberish. No, Spanish. She knew what that sounded like. But something else too. Something entirely unlike anything she'd ever heard.

Maybe there were no voices, and nobody was shouting. Maybe it was all happening in her head. That's why it made no sense, nothing in her head made sense. It was as if horses were pounding up and down in her brain. Kate sank down to the step, still clinging to the banister, and laid her flushed face against her arms and began to cry.

The door to the study opened. She realized it had, not because the voices got louder, but because yellow light suddenly spilled into the hall. Slowly she lifted her head and peeked through the railings. She could see them all. Armando and Miguel and the funny little man who was ... Yes, she remembered! He was Japanese. That was a triumph, remembering that. She usually couldn't remember anything. She was so pleased. Even more pleased than she was by proof that the screaming had really been going on and that it wasn't her imagination. Kate savoured that for a moment, examined the wonder of it.

She watched them, face pressed against the carved wooden uprights which supported the banister railing, her half-clad body crouched in the dark. The Japanese man was waving his arms and wagging his finger under Armando's nose and yelling at him.

'Speak English,' her husband shouted. 'English, you idiot, you know I don't understand Japanese.'

'Yes, I tell you in English, Mr de Cuentas, you are a greedy fool and we are not pleased. The museum is making tests ...'

'The museum won't discover a goddamn thing. The forgery is perfect.'

'They are making tests,' the other man continued, standing very close to Armando and shouting into his face. 'They will be suspicious of everything you sell them for the next two years. Everyone who buy something from you will be suspicious. They look more closely at things that come from us.'

'What the hell difference does it make? You've got your money. By now you've taken it all back to Japan.'

'Money is not in Japan. Money is here in New York. We buy things here in America, what good is foreign currency in Japan?'

'What about us?' Now it was Miguel who was shouting at Armando, but in English for once, so Kate knew what he was saying, though she couldn't understand what any of it meant. 'What will we do if the police come here?'

'Police will come.' It was the Japanese again. 'Police will arrest you and you will talk. That is not allowed to happen Mr de Cuentas. You come with me now. Not be here when the police come.'

'I'm not going anywhere. My wife's here, my son. Get out of my house you little yellow bastard! You too,' he turned on Miguel, lunged for him. 'Get out! I'll deal with the police. Just go!'

Kate heard a tremendously loud noise. She gasped and

321

jumped and had to cling to the banister to keep from falling.

Suddenly all the shouting stopped. There was complete silence. Miguel and the Japanese stared at each other. Kate smelled something very strange, an acrid burning smell. Then she saw the body of her husband sink slowly to the ground, and she saw the widening pool of red that was seeping into the carpet near his head. She screamed.

The two men still standing whirled in the direction of her voice. 'Is the woman!' the Japanese yelled.

'*Cuño*,' Miguel cursed in Spanish. 'She saw.'

Kate stood, started to run up the stairs towards her bedroom. 'Get her.' It was the Japanese man again, but he wasn't shouting now, simply issuing orders. 'Get her. We must go, we take her with us.'

She tried to move faster but she couldn't. Miguel overtook her and pulled her down the stairs. Then she was just a few feet away from the man with the yellow skin and the black eyes, and she saw that he was holding a gun. 'We go,' he said to Miguel. 'Out back door, bring her.'

'No!' Kate screamed. 'No! I can't leave my baby.'

Miguel slapped her twice in the face. 'Shut up. Be quiet or I'll knock you out.' He picked her up and threw her over his shoulder and hurried to keep up with the Japanese who was racing through the rear hall and down the steps to the kitchen.

They'd reached the side door that led to the alley and then to the street when there was another interruption. 'Señora ...' a voice screamed. 'Stop, where are you taking her?' It was Maria the maid. She and the butler were hiding down here, sheltering from the storm which had been taking place upstairs this past half-hour. 'Señora,' Maria shouted again. 'Tonio, for God's sake, do something.'

The butler lunged forward, tried to wrestle Kate from Miguel's grasp. The Oriental turned, saw what was happening and lifted the gun again. There was another of those horrific bangs, then Tonio reeled back and fell.

Kate screamed once more, and this time she kept on screaming. Miguel let her slide off his shoulder and held her up. He delivered one solid punch to her chin, and after that she didn't know anything.

On 9 May the only noteworthy event was a change in the weather; it turned hot. Neville Chamberlain remained Prime Minister, but London was suddenly plunged into advanced summer. The sun blazed down on the capital, and ladies in cotton dresses and white gloves appeared as if they'd been waiting in the wings for a cue.

The two tiny offices that made up the domain of Mollie and Phil were airless and they sent someone searching for a fan, but without any luck. No luck in the more important issues either. They were trying desperately to get permission for American broadcasters to have a microphone installed somewhere in the Houses of Parliament. Not in the chamber, they knew that was out of the question. But if they could have some little unused room somewhere, then they could relay the fast-breaking news as it happened.

In the afternoon word came from the Speaker's office. The answer was no, because he couldn't do it for the Americans and not other foreign broadcasters. 'It's not the other foreigners who are saving their asses with guns and planes and ships,' Phil said bitterly.

'Who's going to tell Murrow, you or me?'

Phil said he would, and went off to find the top man for CBS.

When she went home that night Mollie slashed a big black mark through 9 May on the calendar. It had been a washout as far as she was concerned. An anti-climax. Her head was splitting, the flat was hot and the tiny refrigerator didn't make ice, so she couldn't have a proper cold drink. She took a couple of aspirin, went to bed and tried to read. About midnight she fell asleep, and against all the odds had a much more peaceful night than the previous one.

When she woke she felt a lot better. She made toast and tea for breakfast, it had to be tea, she couldn't face the liquid coffee substitute first thing in the morning. The sun was shining, it would be another warm day. Mollie switched on the radio.

The eight o'clock news had the story, but in those first few moments no one realized that they were reporting the advent of Armageddon. The announcer's voice was calm and neutral. 'This morning at dawn German tanks invaded Holland and Belgium ...'

By noon the reports were coming so fast no one could keep up with them. Nazi paratroops had captured key bridges and airfields near Rotterdam and were in control of The Hague. The rest of the German army was on the march and would soon link up with them. A few minutes before one, Sandra flew into Mollie's office. 'Come on, quick, Nick Frane's coming on the air from Breda.'

'Where the hell is Breda?' Mollie demanded as she ran down the hall after the Englishwoman.

'Haven't a clue, but I expect he'll tell us.'

Then, through the earphones picking up the remote, Nick's voice; so cool, so assured, but not masking the urgency or the importance of his report. 'Good morning, America ...' It was early morning at home, he was broadcasting to his countrymen while they ate breakfast. '... here in a town in the northwest of Holland. It's a fair size city as these things go in Europe, and I'm on the roof of the city hall because that was the best vantage point I could find. When I look west, over nests that the storks have suddenly deserted, I can see the first of the French troops who have come to reinforce the valiant Dutch soldiers. Until a few hours ago the Dutch were neutrals, now they're fighting for their lives, and the survival of their country ...'

That evening, as if it were an afterthought, the news came that Chamberlain had offered his resignation to the King, and that His Majesty had graciously accepted, sent for Winston Churchill and asked him to form a government.

At midnight they were all still at Broadcasting House, waiting for any scrap of news that would tell them how things were going across the Channel. Mollie turned to Phil. 'I just remembered. You owe me five pounds.'

He took a note from his billfold and handed it to her. 'Tell you something, this is one bet I'm glad to lose. What are you going to buy with your ill-gotten gains?'

Mollie thought for a moment. 'A new hat,' she said. 'A while ago I saw a black straw trimmed with red cherries in a shop in Regent Street. If it's still there, I'm going to buy it.'

Phil smiled at her. 'Good idea. You'll look gorgeous when your husband comes back.' He took her hand. 'Don't worry, kid, they're pros, both Steve and Nick. They'll stay one step ahead of the bastards.'

'I know they will.' She did know it, so why were her eyes full of tears? Mollie fished out a handkerchief and blew her nose hard.

Voices assailed her. For the next few days they made a storm of information and of terror, but it all came so fast that reaction was impossible. In the end Mollie was numb, she was only able to nod head dumbly as horror followed horror.

The French had fallen back to Antwerp. Queen Wilhemina and the Dutch government had fled to England. There was gallant resistance by the Belgians and the British Expeditionary Force, the BEF. Mollie remembered the headlines when they'd gone abroad last September, she remembered Gracie Fields singing *Wish me luck as you wave me goodbye* ...

'Something new to tell you, brothers.' Soft-spoken R.T. Clark, who always called his colleagues brothers, in his shirtsleeves and slippers as usual, poking his head through the door. 'The German tanks have broken through the Ardennes.'

'I don't think he takes much comfort from being proved right,' Phil said softly after Clark pulled his head back and closed the door. 'So the bastards are in France now. Anybody want to drink to the Maginot Line?'

It remained a war on all fronts. Soon afterwards they heard that the Belgian city of Liège was occupied. Bernie Stubbs was an English newsman Mollie liked a lot. She'd been in a pub with him only last month, having a beer and joking about the differences between English and American women. Now she heard him report on lines of refugees fleeing the Nazi advance, and the *Luftwaffe* deliberately strafing them, and then, in what seemed the most senseless atrocity of all, systematically shooting all the cattle in the fields.

Voices, voices. But nothing from Nick. Not a word since Breda. She pictured them in the Renault, broken down by

325

the side of some road, Steve using all his skill and a piece of string to repair the old car, to get their equipment working, to get them on the air. Do it, she kept thinking, willing the message to get to them. Do it! Do it! Do it!

Voices, voices. On the afternoon of the thirteenth it was Winston Churchill, now head of an all-party government. 'I have nothing to offer but blood, toil, tears and sweat. You ask what is our policy? ... to wage war by sea, land, and air ... What is our aim? Victory — victory at all costs ... in spite of terror ... however long and hard the road may be.'

'That's what a lot of us were afraid of,' somebody said. 'No appeasement and no making terms. Winston wants to beat their asses.'

Then, the next day — thank God, thank God — Nick. From Rotterdam. Speaking of dogged resistance, of grim courage, of people racked by fear and agony, of screaming hysteria.

'It's impossible to be in this country only as an observer,' he said at the end. 'We, my engineer and myself, have been ferrying children from the front lines here to comparative safety in Rotterdam. Little kids are usually frightened of strangers, but these come with us without protests. The noise of the guns and the shells, the screams and the stench, it's numbed them. They're past being scared. When you pick them up and run with them to the car they're limp in your arms, and when you turn them over to the nurses in the emergency centres they still don't make a sound.'

Mollie ran to the Mutual office. She'd practically worn a path to the door. 'Where are they now? What time did they say they'd come on next?'

The exhausted guy behind the desk shook his head. 'Sorry, Mollie, it wasn't like that. They recorded the segment yesterday, got the disc out to us with a diplomat accompanying the Dutch officials. Hey, don't look like that. Nick Frane's a born survivor and your husband's the best engineer on two continents. I'll let you know the minute we hear anything else, promise.'

When she returned to the studio where Phil and Sandra were waiting, the news about Rotterdam was coming through. The city had fallen, the *Luftwaffe* had levelled it.

326

Nothing left but rubble. 'They say it's a warning, so everybody will know that resistance is futile.'

Phil reached for her hand, but Mollie pulled away. she wrapped her arms around herself, leaned against the wall, shut her eyes tight and prayed. Please, God, please. I'll never do anything bad again if they just get out. Please.

It was an erudite gentleman from the German division of the Foreign Department that put a name to it for them. '*Blitzkrieg,* that's what they call it. Lightning war. Advance on all fronts with the tanks, the *panzer* units, and the paratroops, let the rest of the army catch up later. It's what Hitler's planned all along. One of his generals wrote a book about the strategy. Nobody on our side paid any attention.'

Later that evening there was a brief announcement on the Home Service. Mollie and Phil heard it over the radio in Phil's office. 'Here is a message from the Admiralty. Will the owners of self-propelled pleasure craft between thirty and one hundred feet in length send all particulars to the Admiralty, if their boats have not already been offered or requisitioned.'

'I suppose that's Winston moving fast,' Phil said quietly. 'They're sure as hell going to need some kind of a coast guard.'

'Shh,' Mollie was still bent towards the radio. There was another announcement; this one asked all men between the ages of fifteen and sixty who were not in the armed forces to come forward and join a new organization to be called the Local Defence Volunteers. People who could fight in their streets and backyards were needed to form a home guard.

Voices, voices. And the prayer, the constant prayer which went on day and night, a chorus in the back of her head, please, God, please. Let them be all right, let them get out. Until finally, on the sixteenth, a live broadcast.

'This is Nicholas Frane reporting from Belgium. We're with the British forces here in Antwerp. Every effort is being made to hold this city and the connection into France, but —'

Suddenly nothing.

'For God's sake, what happened?'

Mollie realized she'd screamed. She took a deep breath and made herself be calm. 'What do you think's happened?'

She addressed the question to the little group of people with her listening to the broadcast being relayed to the states. 'Probably the transmitter,' Mollie added, answering her own question. That's all it was, a break in transmission, a technical fault. It happened more frequently than any of them liked to admit. That's why nobody answered.

Moments later another Englishman came into the room. 'It's all right. It was the censor who cut him off. Sailed a little too close to the wind did your Nick.'

Bad luck, they'd be furious. But so unimportant. They were alive. Right now, this minute, Nick and Steve were alive and in Belgium.

'Is there somebody named Mollie Pride in here?' A pageboy stood in the doorway.

Mollie stood up. 'That's me.'

'Telephone for you, Miss. Emergency. Switchboard say they'll put it through to your office if you'll please go back there.'

She ran down the corridor, her head still full of Steve and of Nick. How could they manage to get a line to her so quickly? Why? They had been on the air until two or three minutes ago.

'Mollie, thank God I got through. They kept telling me there were no long distance lines available unless it was an emergency. But I said ...'

'Mom? Is it you, mom?'

'Yes, darling, it's me. Can you speak a little louder, I can't hear you very well.'

Mollie shouted into the telephone. 'What's wrong, are you all right?'

'I'm fine. Don't shout, dear, it makes it worse. I'm okay. But Armando is dead. He was shot. The police found his body the day before yesterday.'

'Oh my God ... Who shot him? Why?'

'I don't know. Nobody knows. A robber maybe, somebody who broke in. But, darling, listen ...' Zena's voice broke, then she continued. 'It's Kate.'

'Kate? Oh no! Mom, did they ... is she ...'

'I don't know, darling. Nobody knows where Kate is. She's disappeared.'

*

She wanted to go home, felt she must go home. Mollie went to every travel agency and steamship company in London. 'No berths for private citizens,' they told her. 'Sorry, miss. Try again in a few weeks. Maybe the regulations will ease a bit.'

But she wasn't a private citizen, damn it. She'd come here because her government asked her to. Except that nobody knew that, and she was sworn not to reveal it. The promise didn't seem very important, not compared to Kate, but Mollie decided there was no point in making Donovan and Hopkins mad at her, not now when she needed them. She waited until Friday afternoon, the twenty-fourth, when she met Jack, the guy who called himself the postman.

'I have to get back to New York. Right away.'

He was always breezy and cheerful, and his manner didn't change now. 'Oh, why's that, love?' He had a bag of peanuts and he was cracking them in his teeth and feeding the kernels to the pigeons who clustered around the tiny garden in the middle of Cavendish Square. 'Have one,' he said, offering her the bag.

'My brother-in-law's been killed.'

'Bad luck. But then,' he added softly, 'a lot of folks are being killed these days.'

'No, you don't understand. It's not because of the war. He was shot in his house in New York. Probably a robber. And his wife, that's my sister, she's disappeared.'

'Cor, just like in the films. Think your sister did him in then?'

'Of course not. Kate couldn't kill anybody. But my mother's beside herself with worry. So am I. We have to find her. My mother can't do that on her own. She needs me.'

'Finding folks, that's the coppers' job, ain't it? Even in America. Same as here.'

'Yes, of course it is. But they're not doing much. And it's impossible to stay in touch from London. The telephone lines are restricted and it takes days to place a call. I have to go home,' she repeated. She handed him an envelope. 'I've explained it all in this week's letter.' She'd done her job first, written to Donovan about a few people she'd overheard making anti-Churchill remarks, negative comments about refusing to do a deal with the Nazis, but she'd finished up by explaining about Armando and Kate, and why she had to get home immediately.

Jack tucked the letter in his pocket before he answered. 'Tell you what,' he said finally. 'I'll pass the word along. Anything that can be done, I'll let you know next Friday.'

'That's not soon enough,' Mollie exploded. 'I can't wait another whole week. I need to go now.'

Jack grinned. 'Seems like there'd be enough excitement here to keep you happy for a week at least.' He cracked another peanut while he stared up at the sky. 'Cor, pretty soon they'll be dropping down right here in Cavendish Square. Nazi paratroopers. Let 'em come, I say,' he added. 'I'm ready for 'em.'

She tried again. 'Look, Jack, I've never asked for details, but obviously you're in touch with Mr ...'

'No names,' he interrupted sternly. 'I keep telling you, no names. Bloody amateurs,' he added under his breath.

'With the man in New York,' she went on, ignoring his disdain. 'Please, won't you tell him I'm desperate? I'm sure if he understands he'll do something.'

'We'll see, love.' And he tipped his hat, the funny beat-up cap he always wore, and sauntered off.

She only went back to Foley Street once during the next few days, to bathe and change; the rest of the time she spent at Broadcasting House. There wasn't a lot of work for her to do, the situation was chaotic beyond the possibility of shepherding requests through official channels, but like the rest of the staff she felt somehow more in touch with what was happening if she was at the studio.

Saturday and Sunday provided little to satisfy their hunger for facts, there were only vague bulletins about fierce fighting and gallant allies. And reports from the east coast of England. People standing on the Dover cliffs could see the smoke and the flames, and hear the guns booming some twenty miles across the channel in Calais. Calais. What was it Steve had told her? *We keep the Renault in a little village near Calais ...*

Monday was equally unsatisfactory. Moreover, Mollie's attempts to place a long-distance call to her mother were frustrated at every turn. On Tuesday things started happening again, or at least they were made aware of what was happening. Belgium collapsed. King Leopold surrendered his country to the Nazis.

'What about our guys?' Mollie demanded when she heard the news. The British soldiers had become 'our guys' now; it had happened without her even being aware of it.

'Pulled back to here,' someone pointed to a map that had been tacked on the wall when war was declared eight months earlier. 'Word is that they've retreated to the area around the beaches of Dunkirk.'

'Trapped,' someone else murmured, 'like rats in a hole. How the hell are they supposed to get out of there, swim?'

Mollie went back to Foley Street that night, sick with weariness and worry about Steve and Nick and Kate, and anguish over the surrounded BEF. The telephone was ringing when she opened the door. 'Mrs Rogers? Hold on please, there's a call coming through from New York.'

She expected Zena's voice, but she heard a man, vaguely familiar though she couldn't immediately connect a face or a name with the voice. 'Mollie, glad we got you. Rang the BBC first, they told us to try your home. How are you doing?'

'I'm fine. Look, who is this?'

There was a soft chuckle on the other end of the line. 'Your pen pal.'

Oh God, it was Bill Donovan. 'Why are you calling me? No, don't answer, I know. I told Jack I have to leave London. Did he explain? Do you understand?'

'About your sister, yes, I understand. Listen, Mollie, I'm with your mother right now. I told her I was a friend of yours and she very graciously let me come to her apartment. We've talked it over, and Zena agrees you're better off where you are.'

'What? That's ridiculous, she can't find Kate on her own.' It was incredible, his nerve was incredible, as well as the fact that he'd already put himself on first-name terms with her mother. 'I want ...'

Donovan didn't let her finish. 'Zena wants to speak with you, but I think I'd better tell you what's been happening here first. There's been a note from your sister.'

'From Kate? Is she all right?'

He didn't answer directly. 'I'll read it to you. Mollie, can you hear me okay?'

"Yes, I can hear you. Tell me what Kate said.'

'Dear Mother,' Donovan read. 'Don't worry about me. I am fine. I had to leave New York after I shot Armando.'

Mollie waited, but he didn't say anything else. 'Is that it?' she demanded.

'That's it.'

'Well it's a crock of horse manure. I don't know what's going on, but Kate didn't write that, not of her own free will. It doesn't even sound like her. Kate couldn't shoot anybody. For a start, she wouldn't have the vaguest idea how. Look, I can't prove anything, but I think Armando was terrorizing her somehow, maybe drugging her.'

'Then perhaps she had a motive.'

'No! That's not what I meant, only that she's not in charge of herself. Please, I want to talk to my mother.'

Zena came on the line. She sounded controlled, even calm, but Mollie could hear the suppressed tears in her voice. 'Mom, it's going to be okay. Kate didn't kill Armando, I don't care what that note says.'

'I know she didn't. I said that right away. But it is her handwriting, Mollie.'

'Then somebody forced her to write it. What about Miguel?' Mollie asked. 'Why don't the police find that goddamn Miguel? And where's Ricky?'

They're all gone. Miguel and Ricky and the servants. The police broke into the house when the milk bottles kept piling up on the doorstep. That's how they found Armando.'

It was too much to take in during the brief time of a long-distance telephone call. 'Listen, I'm going to come home. As soon as I can get on a ship.'

'No, don't do that, darling. I've been talking with your friend. It would be very dangerous for you to sail now. The Nazi U-boats ... Stay in London, Mollie. Don't try and get home until things calm down.'

'But what about you? What about Kate?'

'There's nothing we can do until she comes out of hiding or is found. Your friend's a lawyer, he promised me he'll handle everything as soon as they find Kate. And I'm managing quite well. Madam Chirault and I are very busy at the store.'

So that was that, for the time being at least. Once she stopped struggling to find passage out of London, she could return her attention to worrying about the Nazis, and about Steve and Nick.

Blitzkrieg was swallowing Europe. In the northwestern corner of france the Nazis had reached the Channel coast. The heart of the country still resisted, but the roads west were solid with refugees fleeing Paris. Then, in the waning days of May, amid black and terrifying news, they heard something else, something extraordinary. Like sunrise it began as a distant brightness, a rim of light on the horizon; then it was a glory which focused all eyes, outshone every other event. In Belgium, on the beaches of Dunkirk, a miracle was taking place.

'Everything that can float,' Phil said softly while he and his wife sat with Mollie in a pub called The Crown across the street from her flat and drank warm English ale, and marvelled at the folly and the wonder of it. 'Everything. Not just the Navy, they're taking the men off the beaches in tugs and fishing boats, even the little paddle steamers from the summer vacation places like Brighton and the Isle of Wight.'

'I've been thinking about that announcement we heard a couple of weeks ago,' Mollie said thoughtfully. 'The one telling people to register private boats with the Admiralty. This must be what they wanted them for.'

'A few weeks ago,' Sandra said bitterly. 'Were they planning to lose as early as that?'

'Contingency planning.' Phil patted her head. 'It's what the best generals do. Don't think about that. Think about the raw guts of it.'

Raw guts. They went back again and again, the little ships. Meanwhile the artillery boomed and the *Luftwaffe* strafed and bombed, and the RAF desperately held them off. But

God, as they all knew, was an Englishman. The weather held. The Channel — that vicious stretch of water so often the womb of hellish storms — was like a mill pond. For some reason Hitler didn't order his *panzers* to attack; though the Nazis bombed ambulances with impunity, and no one was fool enough to think the tanks were holding off out of charity.

And they brought them home. For over a week the little unarmed ships manned by ordinary private citizens went backwards and forwards through the twenty-mile inferno, and salvaged over three hundred thousand fighting men, and disgorged them on England's east coast.

It was a terrible defeat, even Churchill admitted it. '... we have lost nearly a thousand guns, all our transport, all the armoured vehicles.' Half the strength of the RAF's Bomber Command had plunged into the seas around Dunkirk. But. But.

'We have been told that Herr Hitler has plans for invading the British Isles,' the Prime Minister continued. 'This has been thought of before ... We shall prove ourselves once again able to defend our island home ... if necessary for years, if necessary alone. We shall go on to the end, whatever the cost may be ... we shall fight on the landing grounds, we shall fight in the fields and in the streets, we shall fight in the hills; we shall never surrender.'

Brave words, and when Churchill spoke them Mollie believed them, everyone believed them. Dunkirk was the most marvellous of defeats, the kind that was a magnificent victory. But ... But ...

Nick Frane and Steve Rogers had disappeared into the smoking cavern of the Nazi advance, there had been no word of them since they'd tried to broadcast from Antwerp almost two weeks ago. No one spoke the official phrase, but still it kept playing in Mollie's head. Missing, feared dead.

On Tuesday, 4 June, the last of the ships arrived home from Dunkirk. Mollie spent the night with Phil and Sandra at their place in Maida Vale. She shouldn't be alone, they said, no point in staring at the four walls and worrying herself to death. In the morning they suggested she stay with them that night as well, but Mollie resisted. 'No. Thank you, but I'd rather go home.'

She worked late at the office that day, and walked home to Foley Street in the dark, along a route now so familiar that the blackout held no terrors. Mollie knew all the rules; she unlocked the door, and went to the windows and pulled the shades and curtains before she switched on a lamp.

Steve was sitting on a hard chair beside the table. He didn't look at her, he kept staring at his hands, clasped loosely between his knees.

'Oh my God ...' A whisper at first, because she thought maybe he was a mirage, a ghost, and that if she spoke too loudly the magic spell would be broken and he'd disappear. 'Oh my God.'

'Hello, Mollie.' Still not looking at her.

She shrieked then, and threw herself at him and wrapped her arms around him and hung on. 'Are you all right? Oh Jesus, Steve, are you all right?'

'Yeah. Fine. Nick's fine too.'

That's when she started to sob, great heaving gasps of swallowed air that made her sick to her stomach, but made her feel wonderful at the same time. Steve put his arms around her and he was crying too. Holding her and crying and rocking back and forth. He was filthy, unshaven, soaked with sweat. She didn't care, to Mollie he was beautiful. 'Darling,' she murmured over and over. 'Darling, darling, darling.'

Then somehow they were on the floor, writhing together on the thin beige carpet, and he was on top of her and then inside her. It wasn't really lovemaking. It was a swift, explosive copulation, a reflex, the exercise of something primitive and instinctual. 'I'm alive,' he whispered when it was over. 'I'm alive.'

And she clung to him and kissed him. 'Alive,' she agreed. 'You're alive.'

Later, after he'd had a hot bath and she'd used up a week's rations to make him scrambled eggs and bacon and toast, she put him to bed and sat beside him, holding his hand.

'Mollie, listen, about before. I was like some kind of animal. After all this time, I didn't mean it to be like that. I'm sorry.'

'There's nothing to be sorry for. It was perfectly natural, I understand. Steve, do you want to tell me what happened?'

'I suppose you mean how we got out. Simple enough, we got on the last ship to leave Dunkirk, the *Shikari*, an old Navy destroyer. After midnight on the morning of the third.'

'And you'd been on the beaches all that time?'

'Yes. Shortly before Antwerp fell, I think it was the eighteenth, we had to decide whether to stay with the BEF or try to get to Paris. We chose the BEF. The poor bastards. And in the end, it wasn't worth much. Our staying, I mean. A shell blew up the Renault. One shell and there went all our equipment and all the discs we'd cut. The last few days we were nothing but two more useless mouths. We figured we wouldn't go until every one of the soldiers had gotten off that goddamned beach.'

'That was heroic,' Mollie said softly.

'Yeah, that's us, me and Nick, a couple of fucking heroes.' He turned over and seconds later he was snoring, in the deep sleep of total exhaustion.

Mollie kept hold of his hand for a long while, but finally she disengaged herself and got undressed and crept quietly into the other bed. She took a couple of deep breaths and let herself really feel the exquisite relief. She thought of Nick, doubtless sleeping a short distance away in Wimpole Street. Doubtless in Fiona Winslow's arms. She thought of her sister. Kate, oh Katykins, where the hell are you? What's happening to you? Why? Don't, she told herself, don't dwell on it. Not tonight. Steve and Nick have come back. Kate will come back too.

The room was bare, it wasn't even a room, not like anything she was used to. The walls were paper screens and the only bed was a straw mat on the floor. Kate lay on the mat for hours, for days and weeks perhaps. She had no idea, no sense of the passage of time. There was only now, two or three different nows.

In one of the nows she was alone, sometimes sleeping, sometimes staring at the bamboo ceiling or the paper walls. Another was when Miguel came and forced things down her throat, some hot liquid, tea or soup, maybe a few spoonsful of rice. Or gave her the 'medicine' he'd been giving her for such a long time, the stuff he shot into her arms and legs with a needle.

The medicine made her float off the mat and rise in the air, it made her fly like a bird. It was much nicer than the other now, the one when he did things to her. The things Armando used to do. Except that he wasn't her husband. Her husband was dead. Kate didn't let herself think of that, or of Ricky, or of her mother or her sister or Nick, or anything else that belonged to the real world. Because whatever it might seem to anyone not inside her head, Kate was fighting. She wanted to survive, had to survive. So she stopped thinking. It was the only way.

When the others came, when she heard Miguel speaking to the Japanese man who had killed Armando, or to strangers who sometimes appeared in the doorway and looked at her before disappearing back into the shadows, she didn't allow their words to penetrate her unknowing. Nothing must disperse the fog which protected her. Nothing. Not until she was home again. Someday she would go back to New York. She would hold her son in her arms, see Zena and Mollie and Nick. They would talk and laugh. Then she would think.

'How long have you been here? How long have you kept her like that? When did you leave the States?' Once she thought she heard someone shouting in the next room. A familiar voice. No, it couldn't be. She was crazy. Crazy Kate. They're going to put you in an insane asylum. You can't get out of an insane asylum. They lock you up and you stay there for ever. So don't listen and don't hear. And don't give in to foolish dreams like a familiar voice. But it was so loud. Until now everyone had whispered, this man was screaming.

'Answer me, you pig, or I'll slit your throat.'

'Don't! Put the knife away. I'm gonna tell you. Why shouldn't I tell you? It's not my fault, they made me do everything. Armando and the Japanese guy. We've been here a little over three weeks. Before that we were a couple of weeks hiding and then on the ship.'

'Why did you come? Why did you bring her with you?'

337

'The other guy, Haito, your boss. I just did what he told me.'

'Haito's not my boss. He told you to bring Kate to Japan?'

Kate tried to concentrate. Maybe she wasn't imagining the familiar voice, the one she knew though she wouldn't let herself think his name. The voice had used hers. Kate, it had said. As if she were a real person. Not merely a doll, something lying here on this mat for Miguel to do whatever he wanted with. Concentrate. Listen. But don't hope.

'Yes.' That was Miguel. She was sure of his voice. 'They don't give me a choice or ask what I think. I'm like a servant. Bring her, Haito said. He had a gun.'

'Why did he want her? Did he tell you that?'

'No. He tells me nothing. Only that I have to do what he says. Jesus, why don't you put the knife away? I'm telling you everything. So why don't you put the knife away?'

Miguel did not sound powerful and strong. Not the way he did when he spoke to her. He sounded frightened. Kate liked his fear. She let herself listen to it more closely. And to the other voice which belonged to ... No! She mustn't think his name.

'It's not a knife. It's a ceremonial dagger. A Samurai dagger. It has been in my father's family for generations. And it's the sharpest dagger in the world. See?'

'Ahhh! You crazy fool. You cut me, I'm bleeding.'

'Yeah, I noticed. Why did Haito want you to bring Kate to Tokyo?'

'I already told you. I don't know. He said maybe she'd be useful. Listen, I need to go over there and get something to stop the blood.'

There was silence then, the voices stopped for a few seconds. Kate could hear the sound of someone stumbling around, she could hear Miguel groaning as if he were in pain. But when he spoke again he didn't sound as frightened as before.

'Haito said she might be useful. So you'd better watch your step. He's not going to like it that you come here and cut me, and maybe mess up his plans.'

'Haito's dead.'

Silence again. And finally Miguel, more scared than ever

338

this time. 'What are you going to do with us? No, no, don't
... Ahhh ...' A dull thud, as of something heavy falling to
the floor, then a low whistle followed by voices whispering in
Japanese. Kate listened, but she could understand nothing.

The screen which made a door was pushed aside. 'Kate.
Kate, are you in here? Can you hear me? Kate, it's me. It's
Lee.'

'Lee.' She managed only that one word through swollen,
parched lips. She had not spoken aloud for such a long, long
time.

'Yes, Lee Mitsuno. You remember me, Kate.' He was
kneeling beside her by then, staring at her in the shaft of light
which entered from the other room. And he was crying, tears
were rolling down his cheeks. Kate wanted to tell him not to
cry. That he didn't have to. That it was going to be okay, that
some day they'd all be kids again and have a picnic by the
old fountain at Hillhaven, the broken one that hadn't ever
worked. But she couldn't say any of those things. She could
only think them. But no, she mustn't think.

'Kate, oh my God, what have they done to you?' He
reached for the small lacquer jug on the low table near the
screen wall and poured some clear liquid into the little
lacquer cup beside it. He started to hold it to her lips, then at
the last moment he smelled it, and he gasped out a curse in
Japanese and threw the thing against the wall. 'Drugs.
They've kept you so doped up they didn't even have to tie
you. Oh Kate ...'

He picked her up then, murmuring something about how
skinny she was, how she didn't weigh anything, and carried
her past the bamboo curtain into the next room.

Kate was completely relaxed in Lee's arms. She could
afford to be relaxed because this was only a dream. Lee was
in America and she was imagining that he was here. She
must be imagining that Miguel was gone, too. Or that he was
dead. Like Armando was dead. Only that was real. Armando
must be dead or she wouldn't be here. He would not let this
happen to her, let Miguel do those things to her. But Miguel?
No, Miguel must be dead only in her dream.

'Listen,' Lee's voice, close to her ear. 'Listen to me, Kate,
don't make any noise. Just trust me. I've got to get you out of

339

here to somewhere safe. Somewhere Haito's friends can't find you.'

She could not have made a sound even if she'd wanted to, but she didn't. She only wanted to close her eyes and pretend this was real, that she had found Lee again and they were both children and happy.

When Mollie woke on Thursday morning Steve was gone. His bed was empty, but there was a note for her on the table. 'Didn't want to disturb you, you looked so peaceful. I need a few days on my own, sweetheart, some time to think. Don't worry about me. See you soon.'

She was startled at first, terribly disappointed, but when she thought about it she decided it made a kind of sense. He'd been through such an awful time, a terror she couldn't imagine. Okay, she'd be patient and understanding. The way wives were told to be in the magazines her mother read. At least she was a real wife again, she reminded herself. Steve had had no difficulty proving that last night.

She was still thinking about it when the telephone rang. 'Mollie, it's me. How are you? How's Steve?'

'Nick. God, it's so good to hear your voice. I was so scared.'

'Yeah, frankly I was pretty scared too. So was Steve. Is he there?'

'No, not right this minute.'

There was a long silence on the other end of the line. Then, 'Mollie, did he come home last night? We got out of Dover on separate trains, but he said he was going to Foley Street.'

'Of course he came home, but he's not here. He went for a walk,' she lied. Why? Because somehow it made her feel devalued that her husband needed to get away from her in order to think. Nick didn't need to get away from Fiona. She could hear music in the background and she knew he was in the apartment on Wimpole Street. The phonograph was playing, or maybe the radio. They'd be having breakfast. Fiona and Nick lived like normal people. Suddenly she was in a great hurry to get off the telephone. 'I have to go into the office,' she said. 'I'm already late. Talk to you later, okay?'

'Sure. Listen, why don't we all have dinner together tonight? You and Steve can come here.'

'No, not tonight,' she said quickly. 'Nick, I'm so damned glad you're all right ... But not tonight.'

He sounded disappointed, but he let her hang up. I have to tell him about Kate, Mollie thought. About Armando being dead. I have to tell him about Zena. But how could she tell him any of those things without telling him about Bill Donovan? It was too much. The whole last few days had been too much. Mollie dressed and went into the office; at least she could make Phil happy by telling him Steve and Nick were safe. Phil wouldn't ask any awkward questions.

Two days later, Saturday afternoon, Nick wouldn't take no for an answer. He insisted she meet him for lunch in that pub he liked on the Tottenham Court Road. He was waiting for her when Mollie walked into The Spiteful Wench at noon.

They kissed and she clung to him for long seconds. Mollie didn't want to let him go — ever. She knew an instant of sharp pure joy, of protective tenderness and fierce delight. Nick was alive, he was here with his arms around her ... He was Nick, hers but not hers, not in this way. He never could be and she must not feel these feelings. She moved away. Nick did not try to hold her longer. They sat down at a booth in the rear and he disappeared for a few moments, then returned with two glasses of beer and a plate of sandwiches. At least what the English called sandwiches, thin slices of white bread enclosing a barely visible layer of ham. 'It's not cornbeef on rye,' Mollie said brightly. 'But I guess it will do.'

'Yeah. Mollie, cut the crap.'

'What are you talking about?'

'You, the runaround you've been giving me since Thursday. This is me, remember? What the hell's going on? Why didn't you want to see me?'

She didn't look at him. 'It's not like that. We've been awfully busy at the station. Every American for miles around wants broadcasting facilities.'

'Bullshit.'

'It's not bullshit, it's true.'

'That's not what I meant and you know it. What's going

341

on?' he repeated. 'Where's Steve?'

Mollie waited a minute, took a sip of her beer, then bit her lip.

'When you start chewing on your mouth that way, it means you've got something to say and you're scared to say it. You've done it since you were a little kid.'

She looked up at him. 'I'm not a little kid any more.'

'I know. Please, Mollie. Let me help, I want to.'

'Steve's gone. I don't know where he is.'

Nick sighed. He sounded regretful rather than surprised. 'Since when?'

'Since you called me on Thursday morning. I told you he'd gone for a walk, but he hadn't. At least I don't know if he had. What he did was leave me a note that said he needed to be alone for a while.'

'Shit.' He said only that, then picked up one of the sandwiches and took a single bite before he set it down in disgust.

'I have to tell you something else,' she said. The words tumbled over themselves, because she needed so desperately to say them, to share this horror with the one other person in the world who would feel it as she did. 'Kate's disappeared, and Armando's dead. He was shot. The police think it was a robber. At least they thought so until Kate's letter came. The letter said she'd done it, but that's a crock, it has to be because ...'

Nick was staring at her, disbelief writ large in his dark eyes, his square jaw rigid. After a few seconds he held up his hand. 'Wait a minute. I'm not getting any of this. Begin at the beginning. Go slow.'

She told the story again, this time using her brain as well as her emotions. Organizing the facts for him, presenting them in clear sequence, all the way back to her suspicions that her sister was being manipulated in some sinister way, and how Armando had managed to dispel her fears each time she got close to doing something. She gave him all the details except one, Bill Donovan and his role in her life and in this drama.

'Jesus,' Nick said softly when she'd finished. 'Jesus, Mollie, how the hell could you keep all this from me? Why didn't you tell me before? When maybe I could have done something?'

342

'I've explained. Last winter, when I first started suspecting something, there wasn't anything concrete to tell you. Everytime I thought it through I figured I was imagining the whole thing.' She began rummaging in her bag. 'Look, I'll give you an example.' Mollie withdrew the charm bracelet and laid it on the table between them.

Nick picked it up. 'What's this?'

'My Christmas present from Kate last year.'

'A flapper, a couple of flags, and a microphone. Cute, but I don't see the connection.'

'It's thoughtful, tender,' Mollie said. 'And it wasn't Kate who did it. The card had her name on it, but she wasn't in any condition to think of it, not the way she was last December. It had to come from Armando. He sent mom one too.' She described Zena's bracelet with the discs containing her children's names and birth dates. 'Do you see what I mean?'

'No.' He was staring at her.

'Nick, don't be so obtuse. I'm trying to make you realize how plausible Armando was. Why every time I decided he was the villain in the piece he calmed me down.'

'I guess I see that. Barely. So what?'

'So that's why I didn't write you about any of this. What was I going to do, drag you back to New York on a wild goose chase based on nothing but suspicions I was sure were crazy?'

'Okay, okay, leave that for the moment. This telephone call from your mother, the first one? Where was I then?'

'It was May. You were in Holland, broadcasting from Breda. I couldn't exactly pick up the telephone and tell the Nazis I had to talk to you about something private.'

Nick ran his hands through his thick straight hair. He inished his beer, got up and went to the bar, and returned with a refill. 'Tell me again what Zena said about your staying here. Why we shouldn't do anything about Kate.'

'There's nothing to do. Besides, we can't get out of here. No passage for private citizens. There's something else, mom's talked to a lawyer.' That was as close as she'd come to explaining Donovan's part in the tale.

'That's hard to imagine,' he said quietly, 'Zena acting so

cool and collected, going to see a lawyer.'

'She's always been cool when she had to be,' Mollie reminded him. 'When she had to go to the pawnbroker's, or take us to an audition, or when it was important for one of us kids. Besides, she has this friend now, Madame Chirault. I told you about her. I think mom leans on her a lot.'

'Yeah, the old ballet teacher. Mollie, I don't know ...'

'Neither do I,' she admitted. 'But what the hell can we do? If I couldn't get passage home four weeks ago, you can be damned sure there won't be any chance of getting it now.'

'No,' he agreed, 'probably not.' The preparations for invasion had already begun, the whole country was on a war footing. Men were digging trenches down Oxford Street and in Piccadilly Circus. Tourism was not on the agenda. 'Maybe there'll be some special arrangements though, some effort on the part of Washington to get American nationals out.'

'Yes, maybe. Nick, do you want to go?'

He shook his head. 'Not really. But if Kate needs us ...'

'If she needs us there's no choice.' Mollie said. 'But what does she need us for? Nothing's happening. What are we going to do if we get home?'

He thought for a moment. 'Tell you what,' he said finally. 'I'm going to try and get a call through to Grace Mitsuno. She's reliable, Grace always has both feet on the ground. I'll find out how much she knows, tell her what I have to. Then I'll ask her to go see Zena and report back on how she sizes up the situation. How does that sound?'

'Good,' Mollie said. 'It sounds really sensible. I should have thought of it.'

He took her hand and grinned. 'See, old Nick's still good for something, even if you are a big girl now.'

Mollie smiled at him. They'd both forgotten about Steve, or at least they both pretended they'd forgotten.

14

On 10 June Italy declared war on France and Britain, so she could share in the spoils. On the fourteenth the Nazis marched unopposed into Paris. The French asked Hitler for an armistice. It was signed in the railway car in the forest of Compiègne, the same site where such bitter terms had been extracted from the Germans in 1918. Afterwards Hitler ordered the car to be taken to Berlin.

One more humiliation remained for France. The Nazis paraded, they goosestepped their way beneath the Arc de Triomphe and along the Champs-Elysées, following the route of the French victory parade twenty-two years earlier. There were trumpeters on horseback with silver horns, and the sun shone, and the world heard it all because German-controlled French radio carried everything; the tramping of the soldiers' feet, the music, the voices shouting, '*Heil Hitler*!' Everything.

In five weeks *blitzkrieg* had conquered all of western Europe. The continent was now a Nazi fortress.

'The battle of France is over,' Churchill said. 'The battle of Britain is about to begin. Let us so conduct ourselves that ... for a thousand years men will say, this was their finest hour.'

'I finally got the call through,' Nick told Mollie the next day, 'but I couldn't raise Grace. No answer at her place. So I called your mother.'

Mollie was gathering papers from her desk, putting them in carefully labelled boxes. Nick was lounging in the doorway, his back to the Broadcasting House corridor which was strangely empty. 'And?' she asked.

'And Zena told me Grace has gone out to the west coast, she thinks she's got a line on Lee. That's what this war feels like to me,' he added softly. 'People keep disappearing.'

Mollie was still thinking about her mother. 'How did she seem to you?'

'Zena? You were right. She's upset about Kate, naturally. And worried. But underneath that she seems pretty cool, she's got all the confidence in the world in this lawyer who's helping her. She's worried about us, too, by the way. Wanted to know if we were coming home.'

'What did you tell her?'

'I said not yet. I told her we were perfectly safe, that everything was fine.'

'Yeah, we're terrific,' Mollie said. She turned to a shelf of maps and books behind her desk and began stacking them in an orange crate. 'This must be pre-war,' she said, pointing to the flimsy wooden box. 'When do you think was the last time there were fresh oranges in London?'

'I don't remember. Mollie, listen, I talked with somebody from the American Embassy. Off the record. There are no plans to evacuate us, we're civilians. Expendable. But there are still a few ships, they're taking English kids to the US for the duration. I could get you on one of those.'

'Don't be a jerk.'

'Who says you have to be a heroine?' he demanded. 'What the hell are you doing that's so important? Paperwork, that's all. If you went home you could go on the air, tell people what's going on over here.'

'There are plenty of people telling them what's going on over here. Besides, according to the papers the isolationsists are still having it all their own way. There's some kind of new committee, "America First".' She stopped what she was doing and looked at him. 'Nick, Steve came home last night. I think we're going to be okay.'

'You sure?'

'No,' she admitted. 'But I think so.' She wouldn't tell him that Steve had said nothing about where he'd been or why. That he'd just come in and acted as if nothing were changed, and that when bedtime came he went to his bed and she to hers. 'I think we're going to be fine,' she said brightly. 'So I have to stay.'

'Okay. You want a hand with all this junk? Where are you taking it, anyway?'

'Downstairs to the sub-basement. Here, you can carry the orange crate. Maybe you'll take in some Vitamin C by osmosis.'

The entire operation of the BBC had moved to the two levels below ground. Upstairs, volunteer guards paraded with loaded rifles, beneath the earth they carved out broadcasting studios and newsrooms, overlooked by a balcony with a machine gun emplacement so they'd be able to stay on the air until the last possible minute. There was also a makeshift dormitory, for the last survivors who would need a place to sleep. Iron bunk beds had been squeezed in between the boilers, electrical lines and drainpipes. Somebody said that when the Nazis came the last person out of Broadcasting House would cut the drains and flood the place with sewage. It wasn't the most outlandish of the contingency plans.

There was one brief interview which Mollie happened to hear, and which symbolized for her everything that was happening. Ed Murrow talked to a young boy on a strip of beach somewhere on the east coast of England, the censor wouldn't let him say where. The kid was commanding two ancient naval guns and twenty-seven rounds of ammunition. He calmly told the American how he planned to use them when the Nazis hit the beach. 'Don't worry, guv,' he said. 'I got it all figured out. I'll get quite a few of 'em before they get me.'

Others had no weapons at all. The civilian Local Defence Volunteers trained with broomsticks because there weren't enough rifles to go around. The beaches were shrouded in barbed wire, the off-shore shallows mined, obstructions were readied to be placed down the centre of streets and act as anti-tank defences. Those who had seen the efficient Nazi slaughter machine in action on the continent, Nick and Steve for instance, watched and said nothing. What made it all the more surreal, this David and Goliath campaign, was the weather. In this land where summer was a sometime thing, June, July and early August were brilliantly sunny and hot.

They armed themselves and prepared and waited, and nothing happened. The lull before the storm, the pessimists said, and they were right. The *Luftwaffe* arrived on 13 August.

At first it was the airfields which were pounded, a ring of seven of them around the capital. Hitler's strategy wasn't any mystery: to invade the British Isles he first had to achieve total air superiority.

By day and by night the German bombers and fighter planes came in a steady stream. Time after time the RAF turned them back. Death and destruction poured out of the sky and a handful of men, some fourteen hundred of them, braved anything and faced anything and fought back. It was Churchill, once more, who praised the valiant and encouraged the faltering. 'We have rearmed and rebuilt our armies ... We have ferried across the Atlantic, in the month of July, thanks to our friends over there, an immense mass of munitions of all kinds ... all safely landed without the loss of a gun or a round.' And of the RAF, 'Never in the field of human conflict was so much owed by so many to so few ...'

And in the midst of it all, like news from another planet, reports that the Democratic convention had 'drafted' Roosevelt to run for a third term, and the Republicans had nominated Wendell Willkie; and both platforms and candidates were pledged to absolutely no participation in any foreign war.

Suddenly the Americans were back on the top priority list. At last the government had decided that the more publicity Britain's plight received the better. News flooded the airwaves; NBC, CBS and Mutual broadcasters could go almost anywhere, and live relays were always made available during the night hours which were prime time in America.

In the subterranean depths of Broadcasting House they also monitored German radio, and the Nazis knew it and sent them messages. 'People in Britain keep asking when Hitler is coming. Be calm, he's coming, he's coming.'

'Thanks, love, that'll do nicely.' Jack took the letter Mollie handed him and kept walking. 'Missed you these past couple of Fridays. Him over there, he missed you too.'

'I've been a little busy,' she said tartly. 'Maybe you haven't noticed there's a war on. You'd better tell him about it.'

'Don't get mad at me, love, I ain't no bleeding Hun. Hey, hold on a minute, don't go. Got a message for you.'

She'd started to walk away, now she turned back. 'What message? From who? Is it about my sister?'

'Can't rightly say. Only you're supposed to go to Millwall on the seventh. That's Saturday, tomorrow.'

'Millwall?' It was the heart of dockland, an area of congested slums she'd never been in. 'What am I going to do in Millwall? I don't even know how to get there.'

'Number eight bus,' Jack said calmly. 'Be at 42 Chapel Ho Street 'bout five o'clock. Plenty of light then, you won't have no trouble. Do you good, love,' he added with a chuckle. 'See how the other half lives.'

She had to go, because whoever wanted to see her might have news about Kate. Steve was away, he and Nick had gone up to Liverpool to do a broadcast about the bomb damage in the north. Mollie left the house at two, wearing slacks and an old striped shirt of Steve's, with her bag and her gas mask slung over her shoulder. It was so warm she didn't need to take a sweater.

The bus was a double decker and she found a seat on the top and watched as the London she knew, only the centre of the city really, change to a warren of crowded streets filled with tenements and barrows and open-air market stalls. The lovely weather had brought London outdoors; housewives haggled over cabbages, children played and shouted, men stood on corners and in doorways, talking and laughing.

She'd asked the conductor to let her know when she should get off. After some twenty minutes he came up and motioned to her. 'Next stop's yours, miss.' Mollie nodded her thanks and made her way down the narrow twisting stairs while the big bus lurched to a halt on West Ferry Road. It was clogged with traffic and bodies. 'Chapel Ho's the second turning, right up that street.' The conductor pointed across the way.

Mollie began walking, then stopped in surprise. A radio truck marked NBC was parked on the corner and an engineer she vaguely knew was busy setting up his equipment. 'What are you doing down here?' Mollie asked.

'Just what I was going to ask you,' he answered, grinning. 'Have they sent somebody from home base to check up on us?'

'No, nothing like that. I'm a private citizen today. I have to meet somebody.'

The engineer's name was Bob Pulansky. He looked around him, grimacing in distaste. 'Funny kind of social life you have.'

'A girl has to do the best she can,' she said breezily. Then to deflect his curiosity, 'You haven't told me what you're doing.'

'Story about the way London life goes on no matter what for the one o'clock news. It was somebody's idea in New York.'

'That figures, they're just full of great ideas. Who's broadcasting?'

'Our own little Tommie Clifford, and before you ask I'll tell you that I don't know where he is, he disappeared into a bar in the next block fifteen minutes ago.' Pulansky glanced at his watch. 'We're on the air in half an hour. I hope to Christ he's not too sozzled to talk.'

Mollie nodded. Tom Clifford was an old-timer, a guy who'd been on the air for years. Everybody in the business knew he drank like a fish, but that it never stopped him. 'Don't worry. He always manages somehow.'

'Yup. If I'm lucky today won't be any excep ...'

His words were cut off by the wail of a siren. 'Oh shit,' Pulansky cursed. 'Why now, for Christ's sake?' It was a rhetorical question aimed at the skies; he didn't wait for an answer, simply grabbed Mollie's arm. 'C'mon. We can't just stand here.'

If there was an officially designated shelter in this district they didn't know where it was. They dashed into the nearest doorway. It was a grocer's shop full of people. 'Down in the cellar,' Someone called out cheerfully, as if it were a sort of game. 'Everybody down in the cellar.'

Mollie and Bob Pulansky followed a dozen Londoners down a few rickety steps to a damp hole with a minimum of head room and the pervasive stink of rotting cabbage. Seconds later they felt the earth shudder as the first bombs hit. Then a great cacophony of sound penetrated the flimsy walls of the grocery and the dirt banking which was all that really surrounded them; airplane motors, anti-aircraft fire.

350

the chatter of machine guns, all wailing and pounding in concert.

Mollie wanted to put her hands over her ears, but no one else had done so. 'Well 'ere they come, I guess,' a woman shouted. 'Adolf's droppin' in for tea.'

'What I think ...' another woman began. Then she stopped speaking. Because they felt a great wrenching pull, heard a shattering, whistling, whooshing sound, and the wall the woman was leaning against simply crumbled away and she dropped from sight into a gaping hole which appeared as if by some deathly magic.

Nobody screamed, they were too stunned to scream. They felt the building above them shake and shiver, then settle back with what seemed a sigh of relief. But around them the three dirt walls still standing began to seep. A few flakes of earth trickled to the damp floor, then more; within seconds showers of pebbles and clods were cascading toward their ankles.

'Jesus Christ.' Bob Pulansky didn't shout, he breathed the words into Mollie's ear. 'Jesus H. Christ. That was a direct hit, right behind us, in the next street. It's undermined the foundations.' He raised his voice. 'Listen everybody, this place is going to collapse, we've got to get out.'

You could smell the panic starting, feel it. It was like heat, radiating from the bodies of the people with them in the cellar. 'There's nothing to worry about,' Mollie said loudly. 'We can climb out of that hole there.'

A man turned and looked more closely at the place where the fourth wall had given way. 'I can't climb over all that rubble,' he moaned. 'Me old legs, they won't make it.'

Pulansky had started to squirm through the tightly packed people to get to the opening, now he changed his mind and moved back to the stairs they'd come down. By this time the falling dirt was practically up to his knees and it seemed to be coming faster. Pulansky tested the steps first with his hands, pounding on them with closed fists, then with a tentative foot. 'It's still okay,' he pronounced. 'C'mon, grandma, out you go.' He hoisted the old woman nearest him up the stairs.

Mollie saw at once what the engineer was doing and what needed to be done. 'Okay,' she said, grabbing the arm of the woman on her right. 'You're next. Everybody start crawling this way. Be careful, don't move fast or we might shake something loose. Come on. That's it.'

Mollie and the engineer worked in tandem, ushering the occupants of the disintegrating cellar across the floor and up the stairs, and all the while the smell of smoke and burning became more pronounced. The dust began to choke them and the noise grew louder and louder, waves of it eddied in through the hole left by the missing wall.

Luck of the draw, Mollie kept thinking. Steve had said that about the war he'd seen across the Channel. It's all the luck of the draw. You're standing in one spot and two yards away somebody gets killed. If you'd happened to move a little to the left or the right ... That's what this was, luck of the draw. So thank God the cellar was small, thank God there were fewer than fifteen people down here in the first place, thank God the building above didn't crash down on their heads and bury them alive. Thank God they all got out.

At last she struggled up into the street, Bob Pulansky right behind her. It was chaos, utterly disorienting. Noise, so goddamn much noise. She looked up, tried to get her bearings by finding the sky. Mollie expected to see parachutists dropping, but there were none. Only the planes, barely discernible in the smoke-filled air, like silver birds shining dully through the sudden gloom. She dropped her eyes to street level and understood why it was so unbearably hot. The city was on fire. By some miracle the street they stood in was untouched, but they were surrounded by the undulating glare of the flames and the roaring, crackling sound of them.

'Holy shit, look at that.' Pulansky pointed to his truck and his equipment. It sat there exactly as he'd left it. Untouched and waiting. Mollie followed his glance and shared his wonder. It took a few seconds for either of them to realize that they had a possible escape from the holocaust. 'We can drive out of here,' he shouted. 'Let's go.'

They ran to the truck, Pulansky wrenched open the door. At that precise instant a voice cackled into life, the American accent unmistakable. 'Calling London, calling London. Come in Tom Clifford in London. Can you guys hear me? Pulansky, where the hell are you?' The engineer looked at

Mollie. 'Come in London,' the disembodied voice demanded again.

'It's the cue line.' He reached into the back and managed to grab the headset which put him in direct contact with the producer in New York.

Mollie couldn't really understand what was being said, there was too much other noise and Bob had to cup his hand around the receiver to make himself heard in the States, but after a few seconds he clutched the instrument to his chest and spoke directly to her. 'The relay's open,' he murmured in awe. 'They've kept the relay open in all of this. They can transmit. I told them I think Clifford's probably dead, but that you were with me. They want to know if you'll broadcast.'

Mollie looked around her once more, fought down the need to run, and took a deep breath. Somebody had to tell America what was happening here. She felt like the last person in the universe, with a responsibility to record the end of the world. She hesitated a second more while another bomb screamed somewhere overhead and fell to earth nearby. Then she backed out of the passenger seat and ran around to the rear of the truck and grabbed the microphone. The engineer shouted a few words into the cue line receiver, then followed her.

Mollie glanced at him and nodded. Pulansky twisted a couple of dials, flicked a switch. She was on the air. Live.

There wasn't time to figure out what she was going to say, only to summon her broadcasting voice, that vibrant, silken, absolutely clear delivery which had been second nature to her for so long. 'Hello America, this is Mollie Pride. And right now, as I'm speaking to you, London has been turned into an inferno. This city is burning...'

Kate moaned and twisted and lay in a pool of sweat on another mat on another floor. Not in somnambulant peace any longer; she was ill, desperately ill. And Lee wouldn't give her any medicine. Now she knew it really was Lee Mitsuno; he wasn't a creature of her happy imagination because he was one of her tormenters. So he must be real, and he was kneeling beside her.

'Give me my medicine,' she moaned through cracked and

parched lips and clawed at his arm with bloody fingers. She'd bitten them bloody during this endless time of agony. 'Please,' she whispered. 'I'll do anything, you can do anything you want, only give me my medicine.'

'No. Kate, look at me. You have to listen. Can you hear what I'm saying?'

For answer she only repeated. 'Please, give me my medicine.' Then she screamed it. 'Give it to me! Give it to me! Why are you tormenting me like this? Ahh ...' She fell back, her body racked with dry heaves as she tried to vomit. But there was nothing in her empty stomach, she'd spewed up even the last of the bitter bile hours before.

'Oh sweet Jesus,' Lee murmured. He reached out, tried to hold her shoulders, ease her torment. She yanked away from him, sobbing and gasping and cursing all at once.

He rose and stood over her, trembling almost as much as she was. 'It's not medicine, damn it!' he shouted. 'That's what I'm trying to tell you. It's drugs. That's what they were giving you all that time, Kate, drugs. Heroin I think, that's what they injected into your veins. And something else you drank, some South American stuff. I don't know what it's called. They made you an addict. But you can get over it. You have to. I'll help you, I promise.'

She tried to grab him, she actually got to her knees and reached up and tried to grab the neck of the funny thing he was wearing that looked like a bathrobe. That's what some of the men who used to come and stare at her in the other room wore too. Here in hell all the men wore bathrobes. Her hands were too weak to grasp the cloth. 'Miguel,' she whispered. 'Where's Miguel? He'll give me my medicine and I'll get better.'

'Miguel's gone. He can't hurt you any more. I'm going to take care of you, Kate. They were evil, Miguel and your husband, they did this to you.'

'Armando loved me,' she murmured. 'Armando loved me. He wanted me to be happy.'

'No! He used you, damn it, why can't you see? He used you, they all did. Even Haito, the Japanese. He was selling phoney artworks through Armando, using the proceeds to buy arms for Japan. Haito's dead too. But there are others

354

from the same faction. They planned to use you too. It won't matter if you kick the drug habit. If you get well, we can outwit all of them ...' He saw her eyes — staring, blank — and knew it was useless and broke off.

Behind him on the other side of the shoji screens he heard the soft sound of feet walking on straw mats, then felt the movement of air as the screen was pushed back.

'Your friends are here, Lee-sama. They are waiting for you. I will stay with the lady.'

He turned to the nurse, and nodded. 'Yes, Yoko-san, you stay with her. I must go back to the city.' His Japanese was perfect now, fluent and effortless. The taint of his birth in America, his Chinese mother, neither showed. 'I'll return in a few days, as soon as I can get away from Tokyo. In the meantime, take care of her.'

The woman bowed, and Lee looked once more at Kate before he left the little room. 'My medicine,' he heard her moan, as he walked through the bamboo curtain. 'For God's sake, give me my medicine.' Lee shuddered, feeling her words like darts that landed between his shoulders, then he closed his ears to her.

The tallest of the two men waiting for him bowed. 'Good afternoon, Lee-sama. She is no better?' He inclined his head toward the room where Kate lay.

'Not yet, Soju-sama, but she will get better soon.'

The third man, short and heavy set, with thick ugly features, bowed, but the gesture was stiff and without true respect. 'She is better dead. The drugs have made her useless, even as a whore.'

'No, Buntamo-sama,' Lee insisted. 'She will get better, she didn't make herself an addict. They did it to her, Haito and his lackeys. She will get better and then she will be very useful. I promise you.'

The heavy man grunted, stared at Lee a moment, then turned and walked out. After a few seconds Soju and Lee followed. Lee was half-way down the path through the pine trees before he stopped hearing Kate's pleading screams. He could only keep from crying when he remembered the other screams, Miguel's. They had crucified him and he'd taken two days to die.

*

'Hello, America, this is Mollie Pride ...'

On that infamous September Saturday which began the battle for London, Mollie stayed on the air live for an hour and a half, as long as Bob Pulansky could manoeuvre the sound truck into relatively safe corners, and as long as Broadcasting House managed to keep the relay open. NBC made an instant decision to pre-empt its regular programme and transmit her historic broadcast. By sheer luck the team of Pride and Pulansky had given NBC a programme that would live for ever in radio legend.

Within hours there were vast numbers of newsmen telling Americans about the day's devastating raids, but the memory of Mollie's scoop lingered, it left a sweet aftertaste in the mouths of the NBC brass back home. So they gave her a show again. Within thirty-six hours the network managed to slot into the morning schedule a fifteen-minute programme called *The Mollie Pride Report*.

'Who's the sponsor?' Mollie asked, gripping the telephone that linked her with New York and trying to be sensible despite the excitement that was making her blood pound.

'The hell with that,' the guy on the other end of the line said. 'We'll find a sponsor as soon as we have time. You work with Pulansky, give us the human side, Mollie. Tell us what it feels like and looks like, the ... What's that word they're using?'

'The Blitz,' Mollie supplied. 'That's what they're calling it. It's short for *blitzkrieg*, lightning war.'

'Yeah, that's it. Tell us what the Blitz feels like to ordinary people. You know, a little of the old Mollie Pride magic.'

The bastard. Where was he when they'd canned her the last time? She didn't say that. It didn't matter. She had her own show again, and carte blanche to report the kind of stories she'd been wanting to tell for years.

'Just do it, Mollie,' the man in New York said as he hung up. 'Just do it.'

And do it now. Because maybe there isn't going to be any London in a couple of weeks, maybe it will have burnt to cinders, or be part of the Fatherland.

356

London was going the way of Rotterdam, it was being bombed to rubble, and there was nothing anyone could do to stop it. From his impenetrable fortress on the continent of Europe Hitler was unleashing a torrent of terror on the city which had stood beside the Thames for more than two thousand years. The anti-aircraft guns boomed back each time the planes filled the sky, but it was only a gesture, only something to give the Londoners courage. The shells lobbed from the ground hadn't a hope of hitting anything. The RAF went up again and again, but the summer's desperate struggle to save the airfields had cost them dear, and what resources they could muster to fight this new menace were inadequate.

Just do it, the man had said.

Mollie did it, she told them what Londoners felt, and how they were coping. Her first programme, was about the tube stations, the subways. They'd been taken over as air-raid shelters. That had been made illegal a year ago, but the ordinary people decided to ignore the law. So ... 'Hello, America, this is Mollie Pride. I want to tell you about ladies who set their hair in curlers every night while they're sitting on a subway platform and the bombs are falling overhead ...'

The next day she explained about a new kind of bomb. 'Hello, America, this is Mollie Pride. What do you think of when I say breadbasket? Hot baking-powder biscuits wrapped in a gingham napkin, I bet. Well that's not the image that would come to mind if you were here in London. Yesterday we were treated to a new horror, a demolition cluster that scatters fire bombs as it explodes in mid-air. And this morning people started calling them breadbaskets ...'

She didn't know Bill Donovan was in England until she saw it reported in the morning newspapers on Friday, 13 September. Was that some kind of evil omen? Mollie wasn't sure. All *The Times* said was that President Roosevelt's personal emissary was conferring with Churchill.

'Our friend's sorry he missed you last week,' Jack said as they strolled along Regent Street late that afternoon.

Mollie was still thinking of the broadcast she'd completed half an hour ago. 'What friend?'

'Him from over there. Only he's over here. Don't you read the papers?'

'Oh, him.' Her brown eyes widened. 'Is that who I was going to meet in Millwall?'

'Yup.'

'Then he was right in the thick of it, he could have been killed.'

'Right. So could you, if it comes to that. But you're both still breathing. And he still wants to see you. Different place this time, maybe luckier. My place on Berry Street.' He glanced at his watch. 'In about half an hour. You'll make it fine if you nip onto a bus right now.'

The rage she felt was intense, blinding, completely out of proportion to the occasion, but she couldn't suppress it. 'Listen, I am not some kind of puppet you can jerk around. How do you know what I have planned? It might not be convenient for me to nip on to a bus right now, as you put it.'

Jack looked at her with tired eyes. 'Save it, love. I haven't got time for ladies with hysterics. Number fourteen bus, lets you off right on the corner. Take it or not, whatever suits you.' He peeled off abruptly and left her standing in Oxford Circus.

Mollie remained where she was, staring after him. Then, out of the corner of her eye she saw one of the enormous red buses lumber to a stop a few feet away. It was a number fourteen. Karma, or whatever it was called. She grabbed hold of the pole in the rear and swung herself up to the open boarding platform.

'Thank you for coming,' Bill Donovan said when they were seated in the tiny front parlour of the Islington House. 'Will I pour or will you?'

The lady who'd shown her in, the same one she'd seen here before with a bandanna tied round her head and a broom in her hand, had brought them a tea tray.

'I'll do it.' Mollie busied herself preparing cups of tea, then, as soon as they both had one, 'Mr Donovan, I know you've got an agenda of your own, but I want to talk about my sister before we discuss anything else.'

She'd thought of that while she was on the bus. Not going

to see Bill Donovan would have been cutting off her nose to spite her face, because in a way he was her link to Kate. Now she was prepared to do whatever she had to do in order to get him to focus on her concerns rather than his own.

'Of course,' Donovan said mildly. 'That's what I wanted to see you about, your sister.'

The fight went out of her in a great sigh, like the air leaving a balloon. He was F.D.R.'s emissary to Churchill, but he'd twice tried to contact her to talk about Kate. 'Where is she?' Mollie whispered. 'How is she? Do you know anything?'

He sat back in his chair, stirring his tea but not drinking it. 'Not a great deal, not as much as I'd like to know, but I'll tell you what I can. It may help if I back up a bit. Your brother-in-law was dealing in phoney art, apparently for a long time. The FBI's put together quite a dossier on him. He was buying from the world's best forgers and dumping the stuff on wealthy Latin Americans through New York dealers.'

Mollie bit her lip. 'I should have known. We all suspected Armando, right from the start. But we didn't have any proof and he was always so charming ...'

'A very plausible man, apparently.' Donovan put his still untouched tea on the table. 'But that's not all. The money behind a lot of his deals was Japanese.'

'Japanese?' She repeated the word in tones of amazement.

'Yes. Japan's been at war for some time on the Chinese mainland, now they've signed an alliance with the axis powers, with Italy and Germany —'

'I know all that,' Mollie interrupted. 'What does it have to do with Armando?'

'Only convenience. The Japanese have been buying arms in the west for some time, and for that US dollars are the most practical currency. They needed a form of foreign exchange which wouldn't come under close scrutiny. Armando de Cuentas provided it.'

'But Kate wouldn't have known anything about that.' She leaned forward, desperately anxious that Donovan should believe her. 'You've never met Kate, but take my word for it. There is no way on earth she would understand a scenario such as you're describing.'

'I don't doubt that, Mollie. Neither do the police. They think your sister murdered her husband for entirely different reasons. Personal reasons.'

'She didn't murder him! She couldn't.'

Donovan was silent for a moment. 'Perhaps you're right. Frankly, I think you are. There's a lot more to the story than …' He broke off. 'None of that's important right now. What I wanted to tell you is that I believe your sister is in Japan.'

She was too stunned to speak. He watched her for a few moments, then said gently. 'I'm working on getting her out. I'll do the best I can.'

'But how did she get to Japan?' Mollie managed to stammer. 'I wouldn't have expected Kate to even know where Japan is.'

'She was taken there.'

'By whom? The people Armando was working with?'

Donovan nodded. 'Quite probably.'

'But why? How? Is Ricky with her?'

'The child's not in Japan, no. But Miguel de Cuentas is.'

'Miguel.' She spat out the word. 'I'd give you odds that he's the one who murdered Armando.'

'Perhaps.' Donovan stood up. 'Mollie, I'm sorry, I haven't any more time. I wanted you to know as much as I can tell you, and that I'm on top of it. You're doing wonderful work here, you know. I owe you.'

'Work for you?' She stood up too, fixing him with her large brown eyes. 'Wonderful work for you? My gossipy little letters? The ones that make me feel dirty as soon as I've written them? I can't believe they're worth a damn thing.'

Donovan hesitated. 'Do you know what a Fifth Column is?'

'The enemy within? Of course I know.'

'Yes. Well that's what you're alerting us to. The possibility at least.'

'That's a lot of rubbish,' Mollie said calmly, eyeing him. 'If England's got a Fifth Column that's their worry, not ours.'

'Not if we're allies,' Donovan said softly.

Mollie pulled her fingers through her curls. 'You mean official allies?'

'Very official. As in fellow combatants.'

'I see.'

'I hope so, because that's why your letters are invaluable. They're first class. I told Jack to tell you so.'

'Maybe he did, I don't remember.'

The big Irishman smiled. 'Do I take it from your tone that you're not a fan of Jack's?'

'That's one way of putting it. Another might be that I loathe him.'

'Try to tolerate him,' Donovan said chuckling. 'He's okay. Very useful.'

They were in the front hall by this time, then out on the street. 'I've a car waiting round the corner,' Donovan said. 'I'd offer to drop you, but it's not prudent. Better if we're not seen together.'

'That's okay. I can take a bus.' She looked up at the sky. It was bright blue and empty of enemy aircraft. 'Might even get back before the *Luftwaffe* comes calling.'

He hesitated, put out a hand to stop her walking away. 'Mollie, one last thing ... So you'll know it's all worth while. This isn't for publication, of course, but we believe the invasion of Britain was scheduled for this weekend, and that it's been postponed.'

It didn't even occur to her to ask how he knew. Bill Donovan was a man who knew things, a man deep inside the mechanism of wheels within wheels that was turning this war. 'I suppose you mean Hitler's not coming.'

'Apparently not right away. That's thanks to the courage of the Londoners and the RAF, and people like you and Jack.' He grinned at her. 'Ever read Sherlock Holmes?'

'One or two of the stories, when I was a kid.'

'The Baker Street Irregulars, that's what Jack and his crowd are called, after the urchin kids who helped the great detective. That's what you are too, Mollie, a Baker Street Irregular.'

Two days later, on the fifteenth, the Nazis launched a massive air attack. More than the East End was hit this time; the *Luftwaffe* extended its range to include many of the most fashionable suburbs. Everything in the Nazi arsenal fell on them — ordinary bombs, the incendiary breadbaskets, even land mines that floated down by parachute and went off a few minutes later. Almost the whole of the historic old City of London burned, but despite being in the middle of it the landmark church of St Paul's escaped destruction. The RAF put every available plane in the air and won a stunning victory, and people took heart. Movietone News even made a short called *London Can Take It* which was distributed on both sides of the Atlantic.

'He ain't comin',' Jack told Mollie the following week. 'Not this year, anyway. Tried to bomb us into crying "uncle", but it didn't work. Too late for an invasion now, maybe in the spring.'

It was a consolation of sorts, even though the raids and the terror didn't stop, and she had nightmares about Kate dressed like a Japanese geisha girl and bowing and scraping to Miguel.

After the cataclysm of the fifteenth the bombs only fell by night, the RAF had made daylight raids too expensive for the *Luftwaffe*, but still they were devastating. *The Mollie Pride Report* didn't stress that. Mollie's brief, at least the one in her head, was to convince the American public that the bravery of the British had earned US support.

She talked about the heroic efforts to house those made homeless by the bombs, and about the mobile kitchens which appeared almost the instant the all-clear sounded. She did a show about the shops that stayed open despite how damaged they were. 'I walked along a main shopping street yesterday,' she told her distant listeners. 'It was a ruin, blackened craters and buildings half destroyed, but every store had a sign in the window saying "open", or "business as usual". The display windows of one department store were entirely blown away. They put up a sign that said "more open than usual".'

It was powerful, emotive broadcasting; even Fred Bate, the debonair NBC chief who had so intimidated her a couple of years before, dropped by her office to tell her in person how great her stuff was, but Mollie didn't want to do an exclusively studio programme. 'We've got to get out on the streets,' she told Bob Pulansky in early October.

'Hold your horses, lady, I'm working on it. There's the small problem of gas, you know.' Petrol, as the English called it, had been put on strict rationing.

Like all good radio engineers, Pulansky was resourceful. By the middle of the month he'd commandeered one of the small vans used as a sound truck, enough gas to run it for a few miles, and the necessary relays. Mollie decided they'd go back to the East End, where it had all began, for London and for them.

It happened that this first non-studio broadcast coincided with another innovation. *The Mollie Pride Report* had adopted a signature tune. They cued in the music in London, using an old record Mollie had found in the BBC library. *Charleston, Charleston, da da da-da dum dum ...*

'Hello, America, this is Mollie Pride. I'm speaking to you from an outdoor market near the London docks. Before we talk to the man who's here with me I want to mention my new theme song. I hope you like it, and that you don't think it's entirely inappropriate. I know it seems a bit frivolous for this desperately serious situation, but it really sums up the attitudes of people here, the courage and good cheer they manage to muster, despite anything the Nazis can do.'

She turned to the man waiting beside her. 'A fellow called Frankie the Fish is with me this afternoon. He's what they refer to here as a fishmonger, which explains his nickname. What do you say, Frankie? Is the Charleston out of place to introduce our show?'

'Nah, it's perfect, ducky. I 'opes 'itler can 'ear it. It's bleedin' awful, the blitz. But you gotta keep dancing and smiling no matter what, don't you?'

'No matter what, Frankie. And that's the way people here feel ...'

And she was off on another fifteen-minute segment carried live to the US. In New York they said that when Mollie was on the air you could practically smell the fires burning in London.

'Great stuff, kid,' Nick told her. 'You're getting the truth to them in a way none of us hard news guys can.' Even Steve had words of praise for her. This time he didn't seem to resent the time and effort she put into her show. In fact it was Steve who had suggested the Charleston music as a theme.

She'd been musing on what to use, the brass in New York

had said she needed something, that the show should be introduced by some kind of ordinary music to separate it further from the news broadcasts. 'What about the dance number you told me about?' Steve had said. 'The one you used to do when you were a kid.'

'The Charleston?'

'Yeah, why not?'

Why not, indeed. She suggested it to the network and they agreed. By November, along about the same time that F.D.R. was elected to his third term, it was a fixture, a familiar sound on the airwaves, as well-known as Walter Winchell's, 'Good evening, Mr and Mrs America and all the ships at sea,' or Gabriel Heater's, 'There's good news tonight.' *Charleston, Charleston, da da da-da dum dum ...* followed by, 'Hello, America, this is Mollie Pride.'

There was only one time she didn't use it. 'Scrub the music today,' she told Pulansky when they prepared for her broadcast on the afternoon of 15 November.

He knew why, knew what she was feeling. 'They might not like it in New York,' he warned her.

'Screw 'em,' Mollie told him succinctly. 'No music. I just can't do it.'

So she went on in dead silence, only her voice, slightly choked because of the tears lingering in the back of her throat. 'Hello America, this is Mollie Pride. Last night for nearly eleven solid hours bombs fell on a city in the English Midlands. The Nazi propaganda experts tell you they're aiming at military targets. If you've been tempted to believe it, think about this. In that peaceful city a cathedral where God has been worshipped since the Middle Ages was completely destroyed. More than five hundred civilians, most of them women and children, were killed. Military targets? No, I don't think so. Hitler thinks he can terrify the British into surrender. Fellow Americans, don't believe that either. The ancient city of Coventry has been mortally wounded, but let no one within sound of my voice doubt it: Coventry, and its cathedral, will rise again.'

A few weeks later, another Friday 13, December this time, a land mine carrying a ton of high explosives went off in the road between the NBC offices and Broadcasting House. In the chaos Fred Bate was found wandering around clutching a script, asking dazedly where he could go to broadcast, apparently unaware that one of his ears had been ripped off and both his legs were cut and burned.

A few days later, on 17 December, Roosevelt called a news conference. 'I don't think there is any particular news, except possibly one thing,' the president said. 'Suppose my neighbour's house catches fire, and I have a length of garden hose. Now I don't say to him you have to pay me fifteen dollars for it, all I want is my garden hose back after the fire is over.'

F.D.R. had introduced the idea of lend-lease. The intention was to provide aid for which the beneficiaries did not have to pay in cash, they could pay with other goods and services. 'I want to eliminate the foolish dollar sign,' the president told the nation and the Congress.

The battle in the senate was long and bitter. Borah of Idaho and Wheeler of Montana led the fight against a policy they claimed would ultimately murder every fourth American boy. But the tide was running against them, the mood in the country was beginning to shift. Sometimes Mollie dared to think she was in some small way responsible for that change.

Until January of 1941, when she had no time to congratulate herself on achieving political influence, because her world blew apart in a way that had little to do with the Blitz.

Cadging enough petrol to do outside broadcasts had become a way of life, one more battle to be fought and won. Pulansky was a master at it. The second week of the new year he got them out to location twice. Monday he managed to transport the two of them and all the necessary equipment to the elaborate air-raid shelter for the wealthy in the Dorchester Hotel. On Thursday he came up with enough gas to go some fifteen miles south of the city centre to Mitcham, where Mollie wanted to talk to three 'land girls', young women who had joined the Land Army and been sent to work on farms.

These days going even that short distance seemed like a long excursion, an adventure. Mollie thought hard about what to wear, she even consulted Sandra. 'No hat,' Phil's proper English wife decreed. 'Not even Mrs Churchill's wearing a hat these days.'

'No, it looks ridiculous, doesn't it? Some fancy gew-gaw on your head while you're strolling among the bomb sites.' Mollie untied the black and white silk scarf she happened to be wearing around her neck and wrapped it around her head turban fashion. That was the style Clementine Churchill had adopted; it was lifted straight from the working-class women who protected their hair with bandannas, but the Prime Minister's gracious lady had made it fashionable. 'How do I look?' Mollie asked.

'Fabulous.' Sandra cocked her head and studied the effect. 'Suits you. Better make it a wool scarf on the day, though. It will be cold out there in the farmyard. Tell you what, take my fur jacket.'

Mollie hesitated. 'A fur? Doesn't that seem a bit much?'

'Not this one,' Sandra assured her. 'It's nothing but coney, rabbit to you, and it's ten years old and looks it. All the same, it's warm.'

So she went to Mitcham in slacks and the rabbit jacket with a plaid wool scarf tied round her head, and interviewed a trio of enthusiastic youngsters whose contribution to the war effort was cleaning out stables and rabbit hutches. The relay went through without a hitch and they wrapped up the broadcast a little after four. 'Have to step on it if we're going to get back to town before dark.' Pulansky said while he was rapidly coiling his lines and stowing his equipment in the back of the NBC van.

'Aye aye, skipper.' Mollie felt quite gay. There hadn't been an air-raid in thirty-six hours, she'd done a good show, the sun was shining ... Okay, there was a war on, but life wasn't so terrible, not today. She climbed into the single passenger seat and rolled down the window and let the fresh air blow through the van. 'Home, James.'

'You ever think about that?' Pulansky asked as he pulled out into the two-lane road leading back to London. 'Going home, I mean.'

'To New York? Sometimes. But so much of my life is here now. And leaving at a time like this, it would be sort of like deserting.'

'Yeah, I suppose it would. Oh-oh, looks like we're gonna have company.'

She thought he meant the *Luftwaffe* and stuck her head out of the window and looked up. The sky was clear.

'Not bombs,' the engineer said. 'Hitchhikers dead ahead.'

Public transport had practically come to a halt during the blitz. The authorities struggled to keep the buses and trains on the road, but service was severely curtailed. If you were lucky enough to be driving and a stranger was going in your direction, you picked them up.

Pulansky pulled over to the side of the road and slid to a stop. The two young women with their thumbs raised had been left a few feet behind, now they ran toward the van. 'There's no room up front, you'll have to ride in the back,' he called out to them. 'Hang on and I'll come round and open up.'

Pulansky got out and headed for the rear, Mollie opened her door and jumped to the road. The hitchhikers were just pulling level with them. 'Hi, I'm Mollie Pride and this is ...' Her voice died away, the words of introduction stuck in her throat.

Both women were about her age, both wore the black berets and arm bands of the WVS, the Women's Volunteer Services who staffed canteens and emergency relief shelters. One was a chubby brunette she'd never seen before. The other one, the blonde, was Lois Lane.

They stared at each other for a few seconds. It was Lois Lane who spoke first. 'Hello, Mollie.'

'What are you doing here?'

'My friend and I had the day off, we decided to come out to the country.' A quiet, lady-like voice, the only betrayal of shock was the stiff way she held herself.

'I don't mean that.' Mollie delivered the words as if they were weapons, stones she was hurling at the blonde head of the other woman. 'What are you doing in England?'

Lois Lane got even stiffer. She was half a head taller than Mollie and she seemed to be looking down on her in an exaggerated manner, almost as if she were standing on her toes. 'I might ask you the same thing.'

'No, you might not. I work for NBC, I have a reason to be

here. My husband,' she emphasized the word, repeated it, 'my husband is here.'

'I know.'

The reply was barely more than a whisper, but to Mollie it was completely audible. And it said everything, explained everything. She felt faint, nauseous, dizzy. She staggered to the side of the road and leaned against a sapling tree, wrapped both arms around it and hung her head over the ditch that ran along side. Pulansky came over. 'Mollie, you okay?'

'Yeah, I'm fine.'

'You don't look fine. You gonna pass out or what?'

'How should I know ... I'm sorry, Bob. It's not your fault, I didn't mean to bite your head off.' She turned back. Lois Lane and the woman with her were watching them, whispering urgently between themselves. 'Fucking bitch,' Mollie cursed under her breath.

Pulansky followed her glance. 'I don't suppose you want to tell me what's going on?'

Mollie shook her head.

'Okay, I ain't asking. Only we gotta get back to town before it gets dark. What do I do about the broads? Leave 'em here? The blonde one's American I think.'

'Yes, she is. And as far as I'm concerned she can swim to the States. C'mon, let's get out of here.'

The engineer followed her back to the van, helped her get into it, then turned and looked ruefully at the two ladies in the black berets. 'Sorry, girls. I think maybe you better get a ride with somebody else.'

Forty minutes later he dropped her off in front of the apartment on Foley Street. 'Mollie, you gonna be okay?'

'Yes, fine. Thanks, Bob.' They were the first words she'd spoken since the encounter on the road. 'See you tomorrow,' she added as she walked up the steps.

The one-room flat was freezing. She tried to light the gas heater, but her fingers were trembling so badly she couldn't strike the match. After a few seconds she gave up and went and sat on the sofa which became her bed by night, huddled against the wall, still wearing the plaid bandanna and Sandra's fur coat. Lois Lane is a member of the WVS. That's

368

what kept running through Mollie's mind. Steve's mistress had been in England long enough to join the war effort.

He was due back around dinner time. She'd seen him at Broadcasting House just before she left for Mitcham, they'd talked about having a quick meal and maybe going to the movies. A little before six she heard his key in the lock.

'Hi, sweetheart, you beat me home. How did it go?' Steve took off his tweed overcoat and dropped it on a chair. 'It's cold in here. What's the matter, heater not working?'

She didn't answer.

'Mollie, what's wrong? Are you sick?' He covered the distance to the windows in three quick strides and pulled down the black-out shades while he spoke. 'Hang on a minute and I'll try and get the heater going and get you into bed. What is it? Have you seen a doctor?' Mollie still made no reply, she just kept watching him.

Steve switched on a lamp, then squatted in front of the gas fire and got it going. 'There, that will help.' He crossed to where she still sat on the sofa. 'Do you have a fever?' The last asked while he pressed a hand to her forehead.

Mollie jerked away from him. 'Don't touch me, you bastard.'

He froze, hand still extended towards her. They held the pose for a long moment; staring at each other, blue eyes and brown speaking the words neither of them could say. 'How did it happen?' he asked finally. His tone said he already knew what had happened.

'You mean how did I find out?' The words came out in a hoarse whisper, she almost didn't recognize her own voice. 'One of life's little coincidences. We stopped to pick up some hitchhikers on the way back from Mitcham, and one of them turned out to be Lois Lane.'

He sat down on the sofa opposite hers, the one which had been his bed for the nearly six months they'd lived together here. Six celibate months, except for that one night after Dunkirk. He buried his face in his hands and the lamplight shone on his red hair. That was all she could see of him, just the top of his head, everything else was in shadow. His voice was muffled, she had to strain to hear him. 'Half of me figured you'd find out sooner or later,' he murmured. 'The

369

other half said London's a big city, so maybe you wouldn't.'

'When?' she demanded. 'When did she come over here? When did it start?' The same question she'd asked him almost two years ago, when she first found out about his infidelity. How long had it gone on, how long had he duped her.

'I don't think start's the right word for it,' Steve said softly. 'Not the way you mean. It never stopped.'

'Oh Jesus ... Oh my God ...' This was a new blow, a new attack on the centre of her being, her perceptions of her life. She'd imagined that Lois Lane followed him to England, forced herself on him, forced the resumption of the affair. He was admitting something else, something far worse. He'd separated from her for ten months, April of 1939 until February of 1940, but he'd never left his mistress. 'She's been here right along,' Mollie whispered. 'She came that same April you did.'

'Not exactly. It was August before she came.'

She tried to remember back to that distant August. Was it then that she'd noticed the plants gone from the window of the brownstone on Fifty-eighth Street? She couldn't be sure, but it didn't matter a great deal. 'You asked her to come, didn't you? You suggested it.'

'Maybe, I'm not sure. Maybe it was her idea. It's been a long time, I can't remember.'

'You were in touch. All those months when I longed for a letter but you didn't write to me, when I didn't even know your address, you were writing to her.'

He didn't answer aloud, merely nodded his head.

'When I came that September, was she living at the Cobblers' Guild Hotel with you?' Why this need to interrogate, to measure with exactitude each tiny detail of his faithlessness? She didn't know, but she couldn't stop. 'Answer me, damn you! Was she in the next room? Down the hall somewhere waiting for me to go?'

'Jesus, no. It wasn't like that, Mollie. When I came back from Poland and found you here, I didn't see her. I thought maybe you and I ...'

'Where was she living?' she interrupted. 'I want to know where you saw her. Where does she live now?'

'On Fulham Road, over near Chelsea.' Like a small boy

370

purging himself of a secret he wants to be rid of, like a child who needed to confess and be forgiven. 'She's been there right along. A small flat, smaller than this.'

Mollie had grown hot, maybe it was the rage pouring through her veins, the despair, or perhaps just the gas fire and her fur coat. She neither knew nor cared. She stood up and took off Sandra's jacket then ripped off the head scarf and pulled her fingers through her tangled curls. She was pacing now, needing to move. 'Big enough for the two of you, though. Isn't it? Come on, tell me. Her place on Fulham Road's big enough for the two of you, and she's made it cosy and home-like. She does that so well, your lady from the funny papers, your Lois Lane.'

'I don't actually live with her. I mean, I never did. Not exactly. I kept the room in Holborn at first, then I moved in here.'

She thought of the paucity of personal belongings she'd found here when she moved in. 'But you slept over there lots of times, didn't you? You don't have a separate bed at her place, do you? You manage not to be impotent with Lois Lane. Isn't that right? Isn't it the truth? Tell me! We need a little truth, you and I. It's long overdue. So tell me, are you screwing her regularly? Even now? Even since I came back and we did our big reunion scene?'

Steve didn't answer, he got off the sofa and went behind the screens that shielded the makeshift kitchen. She heard the sound of the cupboard opening, then the splashing of liquid in a glass. They had a bottle of Scotch. It was difficult to get whisky now, but the week earlier Steve had done a favour for some bigwig at Broadcasting House, and got a bottle of Scotch as a thank-you. He stepped back into the room and held the drink out to her. 'Here, you need this.'

Mollie shook her head. 'I just want to know if you've still been seeing her since I came back and moved in with you.'

He looked at her a moment, then threw back his head and swallowed the liquor in one gulp. 'Yes,' he said finally. 'Yes. Not as often, but I've still been seeing her.'

'You shit.' It wasn't a particularly heartfelt curse, only a statement. All the feeling, the anger, the sense of betrayal, it was all fading away, oozing out of her, leaving her only with the sense of being something used, something dirty. Mollie sat down again, hugging herself and rocking back and forth in some primeval rhythm her body turned to for comfort.

'Don't,' he whispered.

'Don't what?'

'Look like that. Do that. It's not your fault, Mollie. I've thought about it a lot. All the while we were on that goddamn' beach in Dunkirk and I figured I was going to die, was sure I was going to die, I thought about it. You and me. The crazy way we got married, the way you grew up, the way I could never handle it.'

'I don't understand.'

'Your growing up, turning into a brainy dame, a big wheel, a celebrity. I couldn't handle that. Lois is a sweet kid, no, don't say anything. I know what you think of her, but you're wrong. She's very nice, a really good person. She loves me.' He reached back behind the screen and grabbed the bottle of Scotch and poured himself a refill. 'The only thing is, I've always loved you.'

Mollie raised her head and looked at him. 'That's what you said the last time, but I don't believe you. If you loved me, you couldn't ...'

'Yes I could,' he interrupted. 'Because with you I always felt as if I wasn't good enough, didn't measure up. I'm only an engineer, a nuts and bolts guy. I don't open my mouth and spew pearls of wisdom like you and Nick. With you I'm way out of my league, sweetheart. That's always been the problem. It's not going to go away. The night I got back from Dunkirk, I figured maybe I'd licked it. I was so desperate to see you, to hold you. And it worked. At least that once. But in the morning, looking at you sleeping, I knew it was a fluke, a one-time thing.'

'So you went to her. You went to Fulham Road and checked in with your girlfriend. That's what you did when you left me that note and disappeared for a couple of days.'

'Yeah,' he admitted. 'I owed it to her, Mollie. She was worried about me.' He walked to the chair beside the door and picked up the coat he'd dropped when he came in. 'Listen,' he said with his hand on the door knob. 'Listen ...'

She looked at him, but didn't say anything.

'Forget it,' he said softly. 'I want to say I'm sorry, but there's not much point. So just forget it.'

It was like the last time. She had to go on, no matter what she was feeling, she had to keep doing her job. She was at Broadcasting House on schedule the next morning. Pulansky looked hard at her for a moment. 'You okay?'

'Yeah, I'm fine.'

Really fine. Terrific. So goddamn fine she wanted to curl up in a corner and die. But she did her show. In the afternoon she went on the air and talked about whatever it was she was scheduled to talk about, afterwards she never could remember what it had been, and it must have been okay because nobody said it wasn't.

Phil poked his head into the studio as soon as the red light went off. 'Mollie, Nick's looking for you. He asked if you'd call him. He's at home.'

'Yeah, sure, Phil. Thanks.' She found a telephone on one of the desks in the subterranean dungeon that had become their workaday world and lifted the receiver, then realized that she didn't know the number. All her life she'd memorized almost instantly any telephone number she called more than once, but the one that connected her to the flat in Wimpole Street remained something she had to look up every time. She fished her address book out of her bag.

Nick answered. Thank God she didn't have to make polite chit-chat with Fiona. 'It's me. Phil said you wanted to talk to me.'

'Yeah, but not on the telephone.'

'Look, Nick, whatever it is, can't it wait? I'm not feeling so hot.'

'I figured as much, and no, it can't wait.'

So he knew. Steve must have told him. 'I'm not coming over there,' she said, imagining with a shudder of revulsion that Nick wanted her to go to his place.

'Okay, I'll come to you. Go on home, I'll be there in twenty minutes. Half an hour tops.'

It was a little after four-thirty when he arrived. Mollie had left the door unlocked and Nick let himself in. She was behind the screen, filling the kettle. 'I'm making some tea,' she said. 'You want some?'

'Yeah, sure.'

When she emerged he was standing beside the ornate fireplace which now housed only the gas heater. On Wimpole Street the fireplace still worked and they had real fires. 'How are you?' he asked.

'How do you think? Shitty, I guess that's the word.'

He stepped forward and took the tray from her hands and poured tea into the two chipped mugs she'd produced. 'Here, drink it. Have you eaten anything today?'

Mollie shook her head.

'That's crazy, you've got to eat.'

'Why?'

'To stay alive. Look, stop acting like a heroine in a Greek tragedy. It happens, Mollie. It's lousy when it happens to you, awful. But it does happen. You're not the first, you won't be the last.'

'Thanks for the sympathetic words.'

He ran his fingers through his thick dark hair. 'Christ, I'm sorry. I'm putting on the tough guy act because I feel guilty.'

'Guilty? You? Why the hell should you feel guilty?'

'Because I knew. Right along. I knew she'd come over here, that he was seeing her. I almost told you a dozen times, but I never did, because ...'

'Because why?' she demanded. 'How could you let me make such a fool of myself if you knew? How the hell could you do it?'

'Oh, Mollie,' he answered. 'Don't you understand?'

She shook her head. 'No. Of all the things in this whole mess I don't understand, this is maybe the biggest mystery. How could you do it to me, Nick? You of all people.'

'That's just it,' he said. 'Because it was me. Because I figured you'd think ...' He broke off. 'What difference does it make: it's done.'

Mollie stared at him, then finally she shook her head. 'I don't get it.' She was still clutching the mug of tea in both hands. She lifted it to her lips and swallowed most of the scalding liquid in one gulp, then set the mug down on the table. 'I suppose you're right. What difference does it make?'

Then she was sobbing. Until now she'd been unable to cry, but at last the tears were streaming down her cheeks and she was shaking with sobs.

Nick crossed to her, put his arms around her. 'Oh, Mollie,' he murmured, pressing her close. 'Oh, Mollie. It was doomed, you know, from the first moment. That whole crazy scene of you running away and getting married at sixteen, it was doomed.'

She pulled away from him and took the handkerchief he offered and blew her nose and wiped her eyes. 'It's hard to disagree with that now, isn't it? I suppose I've been the world's biggest jerk, I should have guessed ages ago. We didn't have a normal married life. Steve didn't ... He wasn't ... We never ...' She broke off, unable to form the words.

'No sex, you mean?' Nick said.

'Not for ages. Not in years. We've been living like brother and sister for so long I don't remember when it started. Before he left me the first time, anyway.'

'Brother and sister,' Nick whispered. He seemed to shake himself out of a reverie induced by the phrase. 'Listen, I didn't come over here only to sympathize, I've got a commission. I'm supposed to tell you something.'

'A commission from Steve?'

'Yes. I saw him a couple of hours ago. That's when he told me you'd found out. He asked me to give you a message.' She looked black and he stretched out a pleading hand. 'I couldn't refuse, Mollie. Steve and I have been through a lot together. Whatever he's done, I owe him.'

'Okay, what's the message?'

'He's joined the Army.'

Another blow, again that feeling of being deflated, of having all the breath knocked out of her. 'My God,' she moaned. 'Oh my God. Why? It's like committing suicide. Why?'

'I'm not sure,' Nick said. 'Atonement maybe. A death wish. All he said was that it was better than the life he'd been leading.'

She nodded, understanding though she didn't want to. 'The British Army?'

'No. The Canadian.'

'Oh, I see.' She sat down hard on the chair beside the fireplace. 'I suppose that makes sense.'

'Yeah, it does.'

'What are you going to do for an engineer?'

'I haven't thought about that yet. I'll get somebody out of the Mutual pool. Not as good as Steve probably, but someone.'

'He never has realized how good he is,' Mollie said. 'That's a large part of the problem. He feels inferior.'

'Yes, I think you're right.' He sat down beside her and took her hand. 'It's not hard to understand. At least it shouldn't be for us. That's how it's always been with Kate, hasn't it? Some crazy kind of insecurity and inferiority complex. Maybe some people are simply born with it, while others are born cocksure bastards like you and me.'

Mollie bit back the tears that threatened to start again. 'I haven't told you about Kate. I couldn't figure out how to, because ...'

Nick cocked his head and studied her. 'Come on,' he said after a few seconds. 'Whatever it is, tell me.'

She sighed deeply. 'Okay, but you have to accept that I can't tell you how I know.'

'How you know what?'

'That Kate's in Japan.' She filled in the details, all the stuff about Armando's art racket and his Japanese connections and Miguel escaping to Japan and taking Kate with him.

Nick listened in silence. When she was done he didn't say anything for a moment. Then, 'And you're not going to tell me how you know all this? Why you believe it's true?'

'I can't. Please, Nick, believe me. I can't. I've given my word.'

'Okay, only answer one question. Mollie, are you involved in it too in some way?'

She was startled. 'In a phoney art scam? Me?'

'In some kind of Mata Hari routine that lets you find out about things like FBI files and weapons deals.'

Mata Hari: the same comparison that had occurred to her when she sat in Bill Donovan's Wall Street office, so long ago it seemed like another life. 'I'm not Mata Hari,' she said. 'Believe me, I'm nothing like that.'

'That's not exactly an answer.'

'Nick, forgive me, I can't say any more.'

He reached out and took her hand. 'What a crazy world it's turned into. What a long way we've come from the Topsfield Fair and the East Texas Dairy Show.'

'Yes,' she agreed, clinging to him, feeling somehow more alive and more whole because he was real and beside her and they were together. 'A long, long way. The only thing is, I don't know where we're going.'

'That's simple, kid,' he said. 'We're on our way to easy street and two a day at the Palace.'

15

The almond tree was in blossom. Lustrous pink petals frosting slender ebony branches were outlined against a goose-grey March sky. Kate sat very still, contemplating her triumph. To know that there were flowers, that they were lovely, was a miracle.

Lee pushed the shoji screen back a little further, opening the tiny room wider to the outdoors. 'It's beautiful, isn't it?'

'Yes.' Kate studied the garden on the facing hillside, the large rocks, the artfully shaped evergreens, the almond tree, the tiny stream of water. 'The more I look at it, the more beautiful it seems.'

He reached out a hand and gently moved a strand of gilt hair which had fallen over her cheek, tucking it behind her ear so her profile showed more clearly. 'You're beautiful.' He said it softly, reverently. 'So beautiful, still.'

Kate put her hand over his, pressed his palm to her flesh. 'Thanks to you,' she whispered. 'It's only because of you I'm still alive.'

'Don't think about that, it's all over. You're well, this is a new life.'

She was a wraith, her skin pale and transparent, her bones brittle. She seemed a fragile bird trembling on the point of flight. But the exquisite satin kimono wrapped her in an aura of protection. The ancient style had a mannered grace; within its heavy folds Kate felt herself serene, and felt safe and anchored to the earth.

She went to the small balcony raised above the ground on bamboo stilts, moving with surprising ease in thonged rope sandals, and stared at one particular stone in the careful composition facing her. It was a large smooth boulder perfectly round, and its polished surface was flecked with some mineral which glittered in the sun.

'Lee, have you heard anything about my baby?' She asked him that every week when he came. 'Is there any news about Ricky?'

'Nothing more, I'm sorry.'

Weeks ago, when she first began to live again, to be something other than an animal screaming for release from torture, he'd told her what he knew. The house on Eighty-second Street had been empty when the police broke in. Only Armando's body had been found. There were no servants and no child. Kate turned. 'Beatriz would never leave Ricky,' she said. 'She would never have left him.'

'I know, you've told me. So she must have taken him with her when she left the house. She must have, Kate. Wherever he is, he's fine. He has to be, there's no reason to think anything else.'

'I want to go home,' she murmured. 'I want to go home and look for him. Please, Lee, I want to go home.'

He shook his head. 'I'm sorry. It's not possible. We've been all over that.'

'But I don't understand.'

'I can't tell you any more than I've told you. I have to stay, so do you. Just for a while. Some day ...' His voice trailed away. 'I want you to read something.' He reached into the wide sleeve of his black and white kimono, withdrew some papers and held them out to her.

Kate took them, but she didn't look at them, she looked into Lee's dark eyes. 'What are we doing here?' she whispered. 'How did we get so far away from Hillhaven and the fountain and the lemonade?'

'Don't.' The word was a cry that half stuck in his throat. 'Don't.' Then he was in control again, the strong, sure, powerful Lee whom she'd come to know in these long painful months. 'Read it,' he said again. 'Please, there's not a lot of time. The others will be here soon.'

She sat down on the mat, lowering herself to it in the way that she'd picked up unconsciously from Yoko, the nurse who never left her side except when Lee was with her. There were three pages and Kate read them slowly, as if the English words were some foreign tongue she had to struggle to understand. Then she went back and read them again. Finally she looked up. Lee was watching her. 'This is terrible,' she said. 'These are all lies.'

He didn't answer that. He said, 'You're going to read it on the radio.'

She shook her head. 'No, I can't do that. It's all lies. Anyway, I don't know anything about radio.'

He leaned forward suddenly and gripped her arm, his fingers making a vice around her wrist. 'Don't say that. Don't ever say it again. I told them you were a big star on radio in America. Soju and Buntamo and the others, they believed me. If we don't stick to that ...'

'What?' she said, staring at him once more. 'What if we don't ...' Her words trailed away. She did not need an answer to the question because she knew. 'Buntamo will kill me,' she said simply.

'Yes. Probably me too.'

Her only reply was one sharply-indrawn breath.

'It doesn't matter anyway.' He was trying for a light tone, a bit of the old easy-going New York Lee. 'Nobody's going to hear you except a lot of dumb women who listen to the radio during the day. They've never been to America and they'll never go. What difference does it make what you tell them?'

'It's all lies,' Kate said stubbornly. 'Besides, how will Japanese ladies understand me? I can't speak Japanese.'

He leaned forward, grabbed her arm again. 'Listen to me, don't ask questions, do exactly what I tell you. If you don't we're neither of us going to stay alive.' His lips were close to her ear, his breath brushed her cheek. 'Kate, you've got to trust me and do what I say. No matter what it looks like to you. If you don't we're both dead and you'll never see your son again.'

Before she could answer they heard the soft footsteps of Yoko approaching. The screen behind them opened with a whisper of sound and she appeared. 'Lee-sama,' she said, bowing. 'Ka-te-sama.' She pronounced Kate's name as if it were two syllables. That was all Kate understood of the other woman's speech, only names. It was enough, the communication which had developed between them was beyond words, but now Yoko spoke to Lee. 'Soju-san is coming, master. Buntame-san is with him.'

He nodded. The woman backed away and left them. He turned to Kate once more. 'Kate,' he said pleadingly. 'Kate.'

She looked again at the papers in her hand, and read the opening words. *In America no one is happy or well. There is not enough food to eat because the evil scientists of the wicked government made dust storms which covered the farmlands ...*

'It's not true,' she said again. 'It's a ridiculous story.'

'I know, but that doesn't matter. Kate?' It was a question this time.

She hesitated a moment more, then she nodded. Lee breathed a deep sigh of relief.

The second winter of the war was warmer than the first, but the news was as bad. Hitler was invincible, he and his Italian allies had conquered North Africa, and it was widely believed that soon the Nazis would attack Greece and the Balkans. Mollie hated going into Broadcasting House and hearing about the latest disaster. Still she clung to work, hung on to it as if it were a lifeline and she was drowning.

She knew nothing about Steve, where he was or how he was. She kept telling herself she didn't care, but she knew she did. The nights were the worst. If there was an air-raid her sleep was broken by having to dash to a shelter, if the bombers didn't come she'd wake anyway. Almost always, about three or four in the morning, she'd be thinking about Lois Lane, wondering if she was still in England, if Steve sent her regular letters. Or about Kate. Or about Nick. Once more she had Nick to worry about: he was in Berlin.

'No problem,' he'd said when she protested that he was crazy to stick his head back in the lion's mouth. 'I'm a neutral, an American. Lots of our guys are over there, they're not going to do a damn' thing to us, they wouldn't dare. I've got to go, I'm trying to get another interview with Hitler.'

Another coup, like Berchtesgaden. She couldn't blame him for wanting it.

There was only one bright spot, on 12 March the Lend-lease Bill was approved by Congress. It was great news for

Britain and Mollie rejoiced. Then she started wondering if the Nazis might take out their anger on the US citizens they could get their hands on, the press corps and the broadcasters.

'Get in here, quick.' Four days later on 16 March it was Bob Pulansky who stood at the doors of the station and urged her to hurry. 'They've got the president live on shortwave.'

Mollie ran after him down to the basement and wedged herself into a crowded studio. About a dozen people were huddled around a transmitter. There was a lot of static, but F.D.R.'s voice came over clearly enough for them to make out his words. 'The Nazis have seized power by force. These men and their hypnotized followers call this a new order. It is not new and it is not order.'

Mollie caught Phil's eye on the other side of the room and winked at him. He grinned back. Roosevelt was still speaking. 'The British people and their Greek allies need ships. From America they will get ships. They need planes. From America they will get planes. They will get food. This is no part-time job, it's an all-out effort. The rallying cry of the dictators, their boasting about a master-race will prove to be nonsense. There never will be any race of people on earth fit to serve as masters of their fellow men. Never have Americans faced a task so well worthwhile. May it be said of us in the days to come that our children and our children's children rise up and call us blessed.'

'Well, shit,' Pulansky murmured in Mollie's ear. 'That's sort of telling 'em, isn't it?'

'Yeah,' she agreed, 'that's telling them.'

The BBC repeated Roosevelt's speech on the Home Service, and sent it around the world by shortwave in thirty-four languages. The next day Sandra arrived at Mollie's desk with a sheaf of papers. 'Want to know what people are saying about your fearless leader?'

'I'm not sure.' Sandra looked at her oddly. Mollie didn't explain that she felt as if she'd given hostages to fortune — Nick in Germany, Kate in Japan. Least of all that; she'd never mentioned Kate to Sandra. 'Go ahead, tell me what they're saying,' she said.

'I like Goebbels's comment best,' Sandra said. 'He's such a moderate, reasonable man.' She shuffled through her papers. 'I quote. "A blustering, shameless speech. Roosevelt's a lackey of the Jews." How do you like them apples, as my husband would say.'

'What else have you got?' Mollie asked weakly.

'Well, the Italians are calling him Franklin Barnum Roosevelt. A reference to the circus I suppose. Meaning he's a clown. Oh, here's another German one. A headline from some newspaper with an unpronounceable name. "Blood-guilt of Jewish Anglo-Saxon Capitalism." What do you suppose that means?'

'I don't know, but it's not meant to be flattering, is it? Anything from Tokyo?' She didn't look at Sandra when she asked. Mollie busied herself searching for a pencil in her desk drawer.

'Yes, Tokyo coming up. Here it is, a quote from the *Japan Times.* "America is a wealthy, inflated dragon headed for war." Lord,' she added, 'I certainly hope so.'

Mollie banged the drawer shut. 'Do you? Aren't the supplies and the weapons enough? Do we have to declare war too?'

The outburst was so startling, so out of character, that Sandra simply stared at her. 'What did you eat for break-fast?' she asked finally. 'Nails?'

Mollie put her head in her hands. 'Oh Jesus, Sandra, I'm sorry. You know what I think. I'm worried about Nick. He's there in Berlin.'

'I know. Listen, I wasn't going to tell you, but I think it's better if you hear it from me. Word's circulating that the Nazis have arrested one of the United Press reporters, a guy who's been working in Germany since 1938.'

'Yeah,' a voice a few feet away said. 'Dick Hottelet. There's a lot of diplomatic activity going on, we think Washington will get him out.'

Mollie looked up. 'Nick! You're back. Why didn't you tell me?' She flew into his arms, which wrapped her in the customary bear hug.

'I am telling you. That's what I came down here for. There wasn't any point in staying in Germany, no chance of getting an interview out of Herr Stinkenführer. So I came back. Now I'm going home to take a bath. What about dinner tonight?'

'Come to my place,' she said. 'I'll make something.'

'God save me,' Nick said with an exaggerated sigh. 'But okay, anything will be better than wurst and sauerkraut.'

She had half an hour before her broadcast and she ran out into the street and around the corner to a small grocery on Langham Place. The woman behind the counter knew her. 'Afternoon, Miss Pride, how are you keeping?'

'Just fine, Mrs Owens. Listen, could you do me a favour?' She rummaged in her bag while she spoke, and drew out her ration cards. 'Use whatever you need of these, but could you make me one of your pigeon pies? For this evening?'

'Sorry, love, no pigeons to be had, with or without ration cards. Not the season for them. How about steak and kidney then? I've got two small kidneys, so I can just about manage, if you don't mind the steak being rabbit and more gravy than meat.'

'Yes, that will be fine. I'll pick it up about six. Thanks,' she called as she flew out of the shop and back to the station.

A few hours later she served it to Nick with a straight face. 'Steak and kidney, I couldn't remember whether you liked it, but I figured you probably did.'

The crust was golden and flaked apart at the touch of a fork, the filling smelled wonderful. Nick stared at the food on his plate. 'I don't believe it. Where did you learn to cook like this?'

'Oh, I've been practising,' she said airily. 'Try it, tell me what you think.'

He took a mouthful. 'It's wonderful. Mollie, are you pulling my leg?'

'Me? Why would I do anything like that?'

'Because you're a born devil.' He ate a bit more. 'It's really terrific. Fiona's cook doesn't make it as well as this.'

'What?' She spoke with exaggerated shock. 'Fiona the perfect, Fiona the wise, Fiona the all-knowing? Her cook can't make a steak and kidney pie as well as I can? For shame! How fares the realm? How will it survive if ...'

He stopped her oration by reaching behind him and picking a pillow off the sofa and flinging it at her. It sailed over her head, he'd meant it to, the table was laden with food and crockery. 'Methinks the lady doth protest too much. You're a liar. Where did you get the pie?'

'Mrs Owens, the lady who runs the shop on Langham Place. She cooks things for me once in a while.'

'That's better. You had me worried, I was beginning to think you'd changed.' He stopped speaking a moment, then lifted the glass of wine she'd produced from a bottle she'd been saving for a special occasion. 'Don't ever change, Mollie darling. You're perfect just the way you are.'

Mollie waved her hand at the shabby apartment, the mismatched china on the table. 'C'mon, you're the guy who likes antique furniture and fancy paperweights for your desk.' She had never forgotten the unpolished amethyst he'd bought with the first extra money he ever earned. 'I'm not your idea of perfect. Fiona is.'

'No.' Nick shook his head. 'I'm me. Fiona's Fiona, and you're you. That's okay. As far as I'm concerned it's fine.'

She looked at him for a long moment. 'I want you to think so,' she whispered finally. 'That's the only thing I've ever really wanted, for you to approve of me.'

'I do. I always have.'

The sirens prevented his saying more.

'Moaning Minnie,' Mollie sighed. 'I was hoping we'd be lucky tonight.'

Nick switched off the light, then went to the window and lifted the blackout curtain. 'They're over to the west of us,' he said. 'Around Notting Hill.'

Mollie came up behind him and spotted the first orange fingers of flame shredding the distant horizon. 'What do you say we stay right here and take our chances?'

'Fine.' He let the curtain drop and went back to the table, putting the light back on as he passed.

'Is the pie cold, should I warm it up?'

'No, it's okay.'

But the fun had gone out of their meal. As they listened to the bombs falling, felt the shuddering earth as the anti-aircraft guns boomed back, and knew people were losing their homes, maybe their lives, it was hard to be festive. 'The other day,' Nick said, 'I heard somebody say something prophetic: "They have sown the wind".'

Mollie shook her head. 'I don't get it.'

'It's from the Bible. "They have sown the wind and they shall reap the whirlwind." In the beginning the idea of bombing civilian populations was abhorrent to the Brits. Now, well, when the new planes start coming from home, I wouldn't promise anything.'

'They've been bombing. It's been going on for some time. What about Munich?'

'Only love pats compared to the heap of rubble the Nazis have made out there.' He jerked his head to the window and the shattered ruin of London which lay beyond. 'Scarce resources. That's why there haven't been any poison gas attacks. Germany's short of rubber, they can't make masks for everyone and they're afraid of reprisals, so no gas. So far, with bombs it didn't matter. They have more than the Brits do. But with lend-lease ... If I were a German in Hamburg or Dusseldorf or Dresden, or even Berlin, I don't think I'd sleep too well.'

'Who can sleep well these days?' she asked quietly. 'Nick, did you ever meet her?'

'Who?'

'Lois Lane.'

'Oh. No. I never met her. Steve wasn't that crude. We didn't go out on double dates.' He took a sip of his wine, poured more for himself and for her. The all-clear sounded.

'That didn't last long,' Mollie said. 'Apparently we're not the main event tonight. They must be concentrating on the north. Liverpool again.'

'Or Glasgow. They've had it in for the Scots lately. Mollie, have you heard from him?'

They'd always been able to do that, jump from one topic to the other with neither of them losing the thread of the conversation. She knew he meant Steve. 'No, not a word. Have you?'

He shook his head. 'I expected to, but there hasn't been a peep out of him. He's dropped into the great khaki swamp. I think he prefers it that way.'

'I bet she's heard from him.'

'Lois Lane? Maybe. Mollie, will you hate me if I suggest

that it's your pride that hurts more than your heart?'

'The pride of Mollie Pride, it sounds like a soap opera.'

'Am I right?' he pressed.

'Maybe. A little bit around the edges.' She needed to change the subject so she said the first thing that popped into her head. 'How's Fiona?'

'Okay I guess. I haven't seen her.'

She'd felt guilty about not asking him to bring Fiona tonight, about the fact that he didn't suggest it because he knew how she felt about his girlfriend. Now she was startled. 'You haven't? She wasn't waiting to welcome the hero home from the wars?'

'Nope. She's up in the north, the Lake District. At her family's place. Mollie, Fiona and I aren't ...'

She waited but he didn't finish the sentence. 'You're not what?' she prompted.

'We're not a romantic couple. It's not Romeo and Juliet.'

'What is it then?'

He shrugged. 'Pleasant, comfortable, fun. I could find a few more adjectives, but you get the idea.'

She was toying with her wine glass, twisting it round and round, watching the dark red liquid swirl. 'I didn't realize.'

'You never gave yourself the opportunity to realize. You decided you hated her and that was that.'

'I didn't hate her. I don't. I'm ...'

'Jealous,' he supplied.

She had the grace to blush. 'I suppose so. That's pretty awful, isn't it?'

'Nope. I understand perfectly. I was jealous as hell of Steve for years.'

'You were?'

'Of course.'

She waited a moment, thinking he would say more, but he changed the subject yet again. 'I gather there's no news of Kate. If there was you'd have told me by now.'

Mollie rose and began clearing the table. 'No news. Not a word from ...' She broke off.

'From your secret sources,' he finished for her.

'That's right.'

'Okay, what about your mother?'

'She's fine.' Mollie went behind the screen and poured ersatz coffee into her perennially chipped mugs. 'I had a letter a few days ago. She sounds cheerful. Still likes her job and gets along famously with the French ballet teacher. They bought a ouija board. Mom says it's amazing.'

He smiled. 'Zena's an original. I'll write tomorrow, see if I can get her to ask the ouija board how to keep my hair from going grey.'

Nick was barely thirty, but over the past year he'd developed silvery temples. Mollie thought they made him more handsome. 'The grey hair suits you, it makes you look distinguished.'

She felt restless and couldn't settle. She jumped up and walked to the radio. 'I can pull in Germany pretty clear. Do you want to hear what Paul Revere has to say? He's on about now. He should be in fine form tonight, considering F.D.R.'s speech.'

Nick shook his head wearily. 'It's too damned predictable. This jerk who calls himself Paul Revere, Lord Haw Haw, Ezra Pound ... All these turncoat propagandists that have crawled out of the woodwork. Where the hell did they come from?'

'God knows. They must have some private grudges, some little hate they've been nursing and looking after until it grew into a big hate, then along comes a war you can conduct on the radio. Nice and safe. Nobody can shoot at you. Bingo, they've found their vocation.'

'The Nazis have a new one,' Nick said. 'At least new to me, they call her Midge. Midge at the Mike. She claims to be an American, like Revere. Says she's in Germany because she won't go home until Roosevelt and his kike government are thrown out of office. She really said it, on the air. Roosevelt and his kike government.'

'They're an army,' Mollie said. 'A termite army, boring from inside. This must be the first time it's ever happened, the civilians able to talk at each other like this. It's nastier somehow.'

'You might call it that. It's nothing like the last war, anyway. Christmas Eve truces in the trenches, nothing like

388

that.' Nick stood up. 'Have to go, kid. I've got an early call in the morning.'

In April Hitler took Yugoslavia and Greece, and Italy annexed Bulgaria. Despite the amount of war material shipped in by the Americans, British losses were terrible. But they were used to that, they'd had a steady diet of it since 1939. Life went on. On a sunny Sunday morning in May Mollie's telephone rang. She picked it up to hear an unfamiliar English voice. 'Miss Pride, this is Reggie Bennet-Swan. I hope I'm not disturbing you.'

'No, of course not. How are you?' She was thinking fast, remembering. He was Nigel Turner's boss. She'd met him when she first came over two years ago, that time she had tea with Clementine Churchill. He was a peer, Lord somebody or other, you were supposed to address him by his title. But she couldn't bring herself to say 'your lordship', it sounded so phoney coming from her. And that wasn't important, what mattered was that he was Kate's uncle, the brother of her father.

'I'd very much like to see you,' the plummy voice said. 'Something I want to tell you about.'

'Yes, of course.' Her heart started to pound. Maybe he knew something. Maybe in some way she couldn't imagine he had news about Kate, or was in touch with her. It seemed crazy, but these days ...

'Good. May I give you dinner at my club tomorrow evening?'

'That would be very nice.'

'Wonderful. Boodle's. You know where it is, of course. Shall we say seven? They rather prefer one to dine early these days.'

The next morning she went straight to Sandra's office. 'Is there a club called Doodles or something like that?'

'Boodle's,' Sandra corrected with a smile. 'You are an ignorant little colonial, you know.'

'Yes, I suppose I am. But I'm meeting someone there for dinner tonight. I'm supposed to know where it is, but I don't. Also, what do I wear?'

'It's in St James's. And in clubland they're still dressing for dinner, war or no war. You need to be formal.'

Mollie bit her lip. 'I haven't anything like a gown.'

'I've a couple of things that might do, but I'm so much taller than you are. Who's your date, by the way? Anyone I know?'

'It's not a date, it's business. Family business,' she added. She didn't look at Sandra when she said, 'I have a sister.'

'Yes, I know. Phil told me she's gorgeous and married to a Latin society type, an art dealer.'

'Phil's information is out of date. Her husband ... died.' Mollie rushed on, afraid of being trapped into saying more. 'Actually we're half-sisters. Kate's father was English. It's her uncle I'm having dinner with.'

'Oh, I see. Well, you can always just wear a black dress and pearls. According to the lords of fashion that will pass on any occasion.'

'That's another thing. The uncle is a lord of some sort. I can't remember what lord.'

Sandra reached behind her for a thick book stamped with the word Burke's. 'Every peer is in here. Do you know his given name?'

'Reginald Bennet-Swan.'

Sandra thumbed through the pages. 'Ah yes, here he is. The Earl of Whitby. And in case you didn't know, earls are not thick on the ground, not in merry old England. You're hobnobbing with the top of the upper crust, my girl.'

'I'm impressed. Listen, do you think there's even a remote chance they might have a gown worth buying somewhere in this city?'

'Going to splash out, are we?' Sandra pursed her lips. 'Let me think a minute ... Right, I've got it. I'm going to ring someone, get back to you in quarter of an hour.'

Fifteen minutes later she was in Mollie's office. 'Get yourself to Dickens and Jones over on Regent Street. Ladies' formal wear, third floor. Ask for Miss Bundage. That's the important part. If she's not there you wait, don't let anyone else serve you.'

Mollie stared at her. 'Do I need a password?'

'Yes.'

'Come on! I don't believe it.'

'It's true. You have to say you're a friend of Lady Jane's and that you want something special.'

'Who is Lady Jane?'

'Haven't a clue, pet,' Sandra said laughing. 'I only know that's what you're supposed to say. And bring readies. Cash. Folding money, as Phil calls it. Rather a lot, I expect. Do you want to borrow some?'

Mollie grabbed her bag and extracted her purse. She had forty pounds as it happened. She'd been paid on Friday and not gone anywhere over the weekend.

'Well, that ought to do it,' Sandra said. 'But take an extra ten just to be on the safe side.' She handed two five-pound notes to Mollie. 'Imagine, squandering all your worldly wealth on a dress. I'm green with envy. Good luck, and don't forget to show me the spoils.'

Every window had been blown out at Dickens and Jones. The front of the department store was boarded over, but there were numerous signs announcing that they were open for business. Inside, the ground floor was half the size it had been previously. A land mine had ripped away a good part of the structure, and the elevators were out of service. Mollie climbed the stairs to the third floor and asked for Miss Bundage.

A stern-looking woman with iron-grey hair and rimless glasses came out of the back. 'Yes, madam, can I help you?'

'I hope so. I'm looking for a dinner dress.'

'What we have in small sizes are over here, madam.' The saleslady led her to a rack containing fewer than half a dozen items. They were all styles which had gone out of fashion years before, in poisonous shades of peach and green, colors so awful the dresses hadn't sold when they were new.

Mollie thumbed through them quickly. 'No, none of these will do. Isn't there anything else?'

'I'm sorry, madam. I realize things must be different in America, but here there's a war on.'

Her accent had given her away. Mollie saw resentment smouldering behind the woman's ultra-correct manner. 'I forgot to mention that I'm a friend of Lady Jane's,' she said. 'I'm looking for something special.' Well, she'd done it. All the way over here she'd told herself she wouldn't, that it was ridiculous. That a store was in business to sell things and that they'd sell them to whomever would buy, no matter who they might or might not claim as a friend. But she'd been wrong.

'Lady Jane, madam? I see, I didn't realize. If you'll just step this way.'

Miss Bundage's expression changed. Her whole stance seemed to soften. She led Mollie through a door marked 'Staff Only' and down a corridor into a tiny dark room. Then she snapped on a light. There was nothing to be seen at first. The walls were lined with racks and garments hung on them, but each was shrouded in a white sheet carefully pinned to cover it completely. The saleswoman cocked her head and studied Mollie. 'You did say a dinner gown, didn't you, madam?'

'Yes, that's right. Something to wear to dine at a club.'

Mollie saw a faint smile play about the narrow lips of the other woman. She had obliquely confessed her ignorance of English customs, and put herself in Miss Bundage's hands. But it was all right, everything had changed since she mentioned the mysterious Lady Jane.

'I think this one might suit you.' Miss Bundage took a hanger from one of the racks and unpinned its white covering. The sheet fell away. Mollie drew in her breath, then let it out with a sigh of deep satisfaction.

Fifteen minutes later she was hurrying out of the store with a box under her arm. She'd paid £92 in cash for what she was carrying away from Dickens and Jones, that was over $150, more than she'd ever spent on a dress in her life, but it was worth it. Nothing had buoyed her spirits so much in months.

'It's French,' she told Sandra later. 'The label's still inside. It's from Schiaparelli. And I paid her in cash and she tucked the money away in her pocket. I'm sure the store doesn't know a thing about this. It's a private operation, her own little enterprise. No sales slip and definitely no return.'

'Do you want to take it back?'

'Hell no! I don't care who Lady Jane is, or what kind of a scam is involved. Just this once I feel entitled.'

'How charming you look, my dear.' Lord Whitby bowed low over Mollie's hand when he greeted her in the lobby of

Boodle's. 'Shall we have a glass of champagne before we go into dinner?'

Mollie felt like a million dollars as she walked across the oriental carpets spread on parquet floors, among the oil portraits and the polished brass, and the mahogany tables sporting vases filled with fresh flowers. The top of the upper crust, just as Sandra had said. Reginald Bennet-Swan wore a tuxedo, and his monocle; and his accent was so ripe she sometimes had difficulty understanding him, but she knew she looked wonderful, and that made everything okay.

Her Schiaparelli original was what Miss Bundage had called a dinner suit. It was ivory moiré silk and it had a long straight skirt slit to just below the knee, and a fitted jacket with a long flared peplum-lined in coral taffeta. Sandra had lent her a beaded bag and her only jewellery was a pair of long pendant gold earrings. When she sat down on the brocade couch in the room where they were to drink their champagne, Mollie blessed Lady Jane and Miss Bundage.

'I've been intending to ring you for months,' Lord Whitby said. 'Ever since I heard you were back in London.'

'What made you finally do it?'

He seemed a bit taken aback by the frankness of her question, but he recovered. 'An impulse,' he admitted. 'And a bit of free time. That's not a ready commodity these days.'

She remembered Nigel Turner telling her his employer was one of Churchill's confidants. She had to like Lord Whitby for that, for being among that small group who'd tried to warn the country long before they wished to be warned. Even though she'd figured out that his hair was dyed. It was a solid shade of opaque brown which could not be natural. 'You're involved in the war effort somehow, aren't you?'

He smiled. 'One does one's bit. But you, my dear, you've been magnificent. That broadcast from the East End last September ...'

She understood then. It came to her in a flash. Reginald Bennet-Swan was one of those men attracted to power. He needed to be near it. Now that she was riding high again, a celebrity of sorts, now he was interested in her.

Dinner was equally instructive. 'Things aren't what they

were, but Boodle's still manages to set a decent table,' he told her.

Decent indeed. There was a delicate clear soup, and Dover sole so fresh it tasted of salt water, followed by slices of rosy roast beef carved at their table by a very old man in a high white toque, and served with a crusty egg-rich kind of popover. 'Only place in London where they know how to make proper Yorkshire pudding,' Reggie said. That's what he'd told her to call him, Reggie. They were practically family he said. Silly to stand on formality. 'I'm from Yorkshire, of course, so I should know. But I imagine your mother's told you all about Whitby Hall.'

'No, she's never mentioned it.'

'My word!' He said things like that, 'My word' and 'I say', they actually came out of his mouth. And when he was showing surprise, as now, he leaned forward and held on to his monocle with his thumb and forefinger. 'My word, I would have thought she'd have told you. It's not in Whitby, by the way, the hall's near a village called Swans Tumble. Don't ask me which Swan tumbled where or to what, we've never been able to find out. Anyway, Whitby Hall was really straight out of the storybooks in the days when Zena knew it. A huge dark monstrosity of a place; one look and you were sure it was haunted.'

'No,' Mollie said again. 'She never mentioned it. My mother didn't talk a great deal about her life before she married my father.'

Reggie motioned to the waiter and he approached and poured more champagne into their glasses. They were on their second bottle by this time. Vueve Cliquot, nothing but the best. She thought about the East End, then decided there was no profit in such thoughts, not here and now. 'Delicious,' she murmured as she took a sip.

'Yes, it is, isn't it? Can't say how long the cellar will hold out. Even at Boodle's. But we're still managing.'

'Reggie, tell me what you do if there's an air-raid.'

'Here? Not to worry, we've a quite comfortable billet fixed up in the basement.'

'Yes,' she murmured. 'I thought so.'

He leaned forward and lightly touched her hand. 'My

dear, all your American egalitarianism, I quite admire it. But this is England. We do things differently.'

'Yes,' she said again.

Reggie smiled at her. 'Shall we take coffee in the smoking lounge?'

They moved to yet another room and sat in deep leather chairs. Reggie asked her permission to light a cigar, and another very old man brought them coffee in a silver pot and left it where Mollie could pour.

'You haven't switched to waitresses, I see.'

'Not yet. Might have to, I suppose. But so far we've been able to staff the place with chaps too old to serve anywhere else, even in the Home Guard.'

That's what they were calling the Local Defence Volunteers these days. It was on the tip of her tongue to ask him if he was a member — he wasn't too old, in his late fifties she guessed — but Mollie thought better of it. She hadn't come here to prick his social conscience.

'Reggie, when you phoned yesterday, you said you wanted to discuss something with me.'

'Ah yes, so I did. It's about your sister.'

It took all her will power to keep her hand from trembling as she poured the coffee. 'What about her?'

'I ...' He broke off, looked around him. There were clusters of other people in the room and the low hum of conversation vibrated in the atmosphere like background music. 'Look, I can't really discuss it here.'

She was rigid now, trying desperately not to show it. 'Where then? Would you like to come to my place?' He was a lecher, she'd never doubted that for a moment, but it didn't matter. If he knew anything about Kate she had to find out what it was.

He thought for a moment. 'Perhaps, if I might suggest ...'

'Yes?'

'Whitby Hall?' he said with a smile. 'This coming weekend? I promise you, it's nothing like it was in your mother's day. At least the part I occupy isn't. I'm driving up Friday afternoon. Won't you come with me? I'm sure a bit of country air would do you good.'

'I'd be delighted,' Mollie said. 'How kind of you to ask me.'

'Good, that's settled. I'll send my car and driver to fetch you at three.'

So she'd come full circle in her English experience. She was back to the Rolls Royce with the chauffeur.

'And this is Sebastian, my brother, your mother's first husband.' Reggie pointed to the last picture hanging on the west wall of the long narrow portrait gallery.

Mollie stepped back and studied the painting. The gallery had tall windows at either end, but today the light was bad; it was a dull Saturday morning of lowering black clouds and rising mists which obscured the surrounding dales. Still, she could see well enough to recognize Kate's short straight nose, her high pronounced cheekbones. 'He's very ... I think the most apt word is beautiful. Kate, his daughter, she's beautiful too.'

'I seem to remember she was a pretty child,' Reggie said absently. 'Over there, behind you, that's the third earl, he lived in the time of George the First.'

She kept staring at the portrait of Sebastian, ignoring his invitation to turn around and look at yet another picture. 'How old was Sebastian when this was painted?'

'Nineteen or twenty, I imagine. It was before we went to America and he married your mother.'

'How did they meet?' she asked. 'Do you know?'

Reggie cleared his throat. 'It was arranged. By my father and Zena's, your grandfather.'

'Arranged, good God! I thought that went out in the Middle Ages.'

'Yes, well, they were originals, both father and Joe Driscoll. The last of an extinct breed, men who demanded their own way and got it.'

Mollie wandered to the long narrow window and peered out through tiny panes of leaded glass at the sodden country-side. 'Poor Zena.'

'I don't think it was that bad, actually.' Reggie joined her at the window. 'Sebastian was really very fond of her. I think they were quite happy in their way.'

His hand was touching her arm. Mollie moved away. She'd been fending him off since they left London yesterday afternoon. So far it had been easy. They'd arrived quite late last night and he'd shown her to a charming bedroom and left her alone. Men of the stripe of Reginald Bennet-Swan were accustomed to taking their time, secure in the assumption that eventually they'd get whatever they wanted. She went back to the portrait of Kate's father. 'There's something ethereal about him.'

'Yes, I guess you might call it that.'

Suddenly it hit her. She remembered what Nigel Turner had said to her mother that day on Sixtieth Street, the day they'd had the big argument. *I loved him, I tried to get him to run away with me before he had to take up that commission.*

'Sebastian was a homosexual, wasn't he?'

Reggie didn't answer. Mollie turned round and faced him. 'Well, wasn't he?'

'Yes. But I think he really was your sister's father, all the same.'

'There's no doubt about that,' Mollie said stiffly. 'You saw her, how could you doubt it? She looks just like him.'

'I never did doubt it, I thought you might.'

She shook her head. 'No. Poor Zena,' she said again. Then, 'Listen, you keep telling me you want to talk about Kate, but so far you haven't said anything. What is it? What do you want to tell me?'

He stared at her a moment, then seemed to make up his mind. 'Very well, I suppose it's best to get it out of the way, then we can enjoy what remains of our weekend. Let's go back to my rooms, shall we?'

Most of Whitby Hall was a mausoleum, an icy ruin in which it was hard to imagine any human habitation, but Reggie had refurnished the east wing. The part he called his was a spacious suite of some half-dozen rooms. They were painted in pale yellow and cream and furnished with polished woods, walnut and ebony, and with glazed chintz sofas and deep comfortable chairs. There were flowers and crackling log fires and heavy crystal ashtrays, and two elderly servants who always seemed to know what you wanted before you did.

'Sit here.' Reggie indicated one of the flowered sofas. 'Warm enough?' He poked up the fire while he spoke.

'Yes, thank you.' She was wearing a mohair sweater in that misty heather colour she often chose, and a full skirt of dark purple tweed wool. Mollie was almost too warm.

'Now, what will you drink before lunch, my dear? Sherry or gin and tonic?'

'Sherry, please.' She waited until he handed her the goblet of nut-brown wine. Sandra served sherry in glasses exactly like these: she called them schooners. 'What about Kate?' she asked again.

Reggie went to a delicate Queen Anne desk and returned with a tooled leather folder. 'It's this letter,' he said. 'It's for her.'

Mollie didn't understand immediately. 'For Kate? But how am I ...' She looked at the buff-coloured envelope he'd handed her. It was sealed, and the edges were yellow with age. The ink had faded, but she could still make out Kate's name written in an elegant spidery hand. 'It's from her father, is that it? From your brother Sebastian.'

'That's right. After he was killed we had the body brought home. His batman came with him, chap by the name of Patton, he'd been with Sebastian for years. He gave us this, gave it to my father actually. Sebastian wrote it while he was in France, some time before he died.'

'But why didn't you give it to my mother?' Her voice rose, a sense of outrage was beginning to choke her. He didn't give a damn about Kate, the only reason he was giving her the letter now was because it had been a convenient pretext to get her up here and play his big seduction scene.

'It wasn't up to me. My father kept the letter. I found it among his things when he died.'

'How long ago was that?' Mollie demanded.

Reggie had been bending over her, now he straightened and crossed to the fire and began poking it again. 'Some time ago. Ten years, maybe a bit more.'

'And all this time you've kept the damned thing? Just kept it? It didn't occur to you that to a child whose father had been killed it might be precious? Important?'

'Naturally it occurred to me. I had no idea where she was. Zena had long since taken her back to America.'

Mollie stood up and put the letter into the pocket of

her skirt. Her movement was enough to interrupt his flow of excuses. 'If you'd wanted to find her, I imagine you could have done so.' She waved her hand at the magnificence surrounding them. 'All this, you're a man of means, finding one person in America couldn't have been very daunting.'

'Have another sherry,' he said, approaching her with the decanter.

Mollie pulled her glass away. 'I don't think I will, thanks.'

'You're annoyed with me. It's really not very realistic, my dear. It has nothing to do with you or me, it was all the doing of my father and your grandfather. They had their own private war to fight. Nothing to do with us.'

'I think ...' She didn't have a chance to tell him what she thought. The door opened.

'Excuse me, milord, the telephone.'

'Thank you, Anna.' Reggie looked at Mollie and shrugged resignedly. 'Do excuse me. I'm sure it won't take long.'

Then she was alone. The elegant room was suddenly stifling hot. She was angry and confused and she felt as if she couldn't breathe. Mollie walked to the French doors and pulled them open. She stepped out into a cobbled courtyard. There were gates to the road and they stood open. She walked nearer to them. A narrow lane ran beside the house. She took a few steps, felt the weight of oppression and misery lighten a bit.

The cool damp air felt good, it soothed her flushed skin and calmed her. There was a gnarled old tree a bit further ahead. The leaves were barely unfurled, spring came late here in the north, but she decided it was oak. The trunk had contorted itself into a strangely beautiful form in its need to withstand the prevailing winds.

Mollie walked around it, trying to remember if any of the oak trees at Hillhaven had been this big. Somehow thinking about the old place, about her mother and her sister and the years they'd spent in the relative tranquillity of Red Hook, comforted her. Eventually she realized she was growing cold. And that she had to go back and deal with Reggie. She walked up the lane in the direction of the house, and waited for the gates to reappear in the mist. They didn't. Ten minutes went by before she knew she'd somehow taken a wrong turning and was lost.

Mollie heard the voices before she saw the men..

''Allo, what have we 'ere?'

It sounded like Jack from Berry Street, but it couldn't be. She wanted to turn and face the voice, but it was impossible. She was wedged between a boulder and a fallen tree trunk, at the foot of a short steep hill. She'd slipped, done something to her leg, and been here for a very long time. She couldn't see her watch, her left arm was twisted beneath her, but it had grown dark. She wanted to say something, but her exhaustion and the cold which was making her teeth chatter made the effort seem beyond her.

'Can you 'ear me?' the London voice demanded.

'Yes, but I can't move.'

She heard something else, a gasp, then, 'Mollie, sweet Christ, Mollie, is it you?'

It couldn't be Steve. She was imagining the whole thing, having delusions. A fever probably. She must have the fever and be hallucinating. She sighed and sank back into a half-conscious lethargy in which she'd lain for hours. There weren't any men, any rescuers. It was all her imagination.

'Who the bleedin' hell is she then?'

'My wife.'

'Bleedin' hell! What's she doin' 'ere?'

'I don't know. But we've got to get a doctor.'

'No doctors. Doctors ask questions. Christ, they'll never believe this back in town. We'll 'ave to get 'er out of there,' the first man said. 'Just you and me.'

Mollie felt someone tugging at her shoulders. This was a funny kind of hallucination. Remarkably real. But then she'd never had one before, maybe they always seemed real.

'Mollie, can you hear me?'

'Go away. I'm imagining you.'

'No, you're not. It's me, I'm here.'

'You can't be here. You're in the Canadian Army.'

'Yes, but I'm here.'

'C'mon, cut the chat.' The first man again. 'Just 'elp me move this 'ere tree.'

The hands left her shoulders. For a moment she felt nothing, then a sudden shaft of pain as her body rolled forward of its own accord.

'That does it. It's all right, we've got you out now.'

She felt herself being lifted into strong arms. The pain in her leg and her left arm was very bad. She looked up, forced her eyes open. Those she looked into were full of anxiety and concern. They were bright electric blue. Steve's eyes. Mollie fainted.

'Where am I? What is this place?' Mollie twisted her head to look around her at the tiny, almost bare room. She was lying on a cot of some kind, covered with a blanket. Her leg felt very peculiar, heavy and she couldn't move it. She tried to sit up. 'Where am I?'

Steve bent over her, put his hands on her shoulders and made her lie back. 'In a cabin in Yorkshire. We're miles from anywhere. Mollie, how the hell did you find me?'

'I didn't find you. I wasn't looking for you.'

'Then what are you doing up here? The nearest village is a place called Swans Tumble, it's not even on the map. How did you get here? Why?'

'I came with Reggie. He's ...' She broke off. It was all too much, she didn't have the strength to explain.

'' Ere we go, a nice cuppa tea, just what the doctor ordered.'

It was the first man again, the Londoner. Mollie looked at him. It wasn't Jack, only someone who sounded like him. This man was short and bald and fat. He had a bony head and he wore very thick glasses which made him look like an owl.

Steve took the tea and held it to her lips. She drank a couple of sips, then grasped the cup in her own hand. 'I can manage.'

'She ain't hurt bad. Told you she wasn't. It's only 'er leg wot's broke.'

Mollie realized why her leg felt so heavy: it was in a splint. 'Thank you,' she said. 'For bandaging my leg.'

'Don't mention it. Rescue damsels in distress every day, I do. Regular 'obby it is.' He glanced at his wrist. 'Little after seven, 'ave to telephone.'

'The nearest call box is at the pub in the village,' Steve explained to Mollie. Then, to the Londoner, 'All right, you go ahead. I'll stay with her.'

His doubtful expression made him look more than ever like an owl. 'I'm not supposed to leave you alone. Precious property you are, lad.' He glanced at Mollie. 'You're telling me the truth, ain't you? She's your wife?'

'Yes. Go on. It's okay. Nothing's going to happen. God knows she can't go anywhere.'

The owl hesitated a moment, then nodded. Mollie heard a door open and close. A few seconds later there was the sound of a car. Then silence.

The tea revived her. She began to think, to register the incongruity of this whole scene. 'I still don't believe it's you.'

'It's me.'

'But what are you doing here? Why are you dressed like that?' She'd expected him to be in uniform, but he wore a suit that looked strangely foreign, something about the cut of the jacket, the way it was nipped at the waist and buttoned high on his chest. And his hair was combed differently. 'How come you're not in uniform?'

Steve didn't reply. He got up and went to the table and shook a cigarette loose from a pack that was lying there and lit it.

'What's that funny smell?' she asked. Everything was so strange, so disorientating.

'My cigarette. It's French. A Gauloise.'

'You're smoking again,' she murmured. 'I thought you'd given it up.'

'Yeah, Lois was always at me to stop, so I did for a while. But I've started again.'

She heard the name of his mistress without the usual surge of anger. It was too late for anger, and she was too weak and tired for indignation. The only thing she said was, 'Oh.'

'Mollie, I still don't know what you're doing up here.'

'I told you. I came with Reggie. Reginald Bennet-Swan. He's Kate's uncle. He gave me a letter ... Oh!'

'What is it?'

'The letter ...' She struggled to reach into her pocket. 'No, it's all right, I still have it.' She withdrew it and held it out to him. 'Look.'

He took the envelope, studied it, then gave it back to her. 'Okay. How come you were wandering around on the moors by yourself?'

'Why were you?' she countered.

'We've been here a couple of days, we went out to get a breath of fresh air.'

'Yes, well so did I. I went out for a walk, and got lost. Then I fell.'

He frowned, drawing his brows together. 'This Bennet-Swan guy, Kate's uncle, he'll be looking for you, won't he?'

'I suppose so.'

'Damn!'

'Steve, I don't understand. Tell me what's going on.'

Before he could answer they heard the approach of a car. Steve went to the window and peeped out through the drawn curtains. 'It's okay, it's Will.'

Will must be the name of the Londoner, she realized. He came in stamping his feet and clapping his gloved hands. 'No way, not for a few hours at least. Fog's too thick. Bleedin' moors. I don't know why they use this place.' He jerked his head in Mollie's direction. 'And we've got a problem. All of bleedin' Yorkshire's out lookin' for 'er.'

'Are they likely to come this way?'

Will shrugged. 'Who's to say? The moors are a big place. Go on for bleedin' ever, they do.'

Mollie struggled to sit up again, and this time she managed to prop herself on her right elbow. 'Tell me what's going on.'

Steve looked at her, then at the other man. 'I have to tell her.'

'No you don't,' Will said softly. 'You don't 'ave to tell 'er nothin'. You can't.'

'Yes, I have to.'

She was thinking clearly now, putting two and two together. 'Wait a minute. This is some kind of spy operation, right? You're doing some kind of spying?'

'Don't be daft,' Will said. 'Read too many stories you do, miss. Ain't no spies in England.'

'Yes there are.' She looked at Steve. He was staring at her, but he hadn't denied her words. Only the other man had done that. 'The Baker Street Irregulars,' she said. 'That kind of spying.'

'Where did you hear about . . .' Steve began.

Will crossed to her in one step, stood over her menacingly. 'What do you know about any of that?'

Mollie faced him down. 'I'm one of them.'

'I don't bloody believe you, lady. And when people lie to me I get very nervous.'

'Call Jack, ask him.'

'Jack who?'

'I don't know his last name. But he lives in Islington. On Berry Street.'

Will looked at her a moment more, then turned to Steve. 'You said she was your wife. Is any of this true?'

'She's my wife, but I don't know.'

'We're separated,' Mollie said quickly. 'We've been separated for months.'

The eyes behind the thick glasses narrowed, flickered from her to Steve, then back again. 'I'll go and make a call, check this out,' he said.

'Yeah, you do that.' Steve stood where he was and watched the other man leave again, then he turned to Mollie. 'Were you telling him the truth? Or is this scuttlebutt you picked up in your travels?'

'It's the truth.'

He started to laugh.

'What's so funny?'

'You. Me. Us. Here I am doing this noble hero routine, and like always, Mollie got there first.'

'I'm not a hero. I only keep my eyes open and write a few letters.'

'How come you never told me?'

'I swore not to tell anyone. I probably shouldn't have said anything now. Only your friend looked as if he planned to murder me. What did he mean about there being no chance for hours. No chance for what?'

'The plane to come in.'

Suddenly the entire business wasn't half funny and half insane. It was frighteningly serious. She felt a knot of ice form in her belly. 'What plane?' He didn't say anything, but he didn't have to. Mollie answered her own question. 'The plane that's going to take you to France,' she whispered. 'The one that will drop you behind the enemy lines. That's why you're dressed like that. Why you're smoking French cigarettes.'

Steve picked up the packet from the table and lit another one. 'It's not very dramatic. Just a quick errand.'

'What kind of an errand?' she demanded.

'I'm a radio engineer. There are people over there using secret radios. Sometimes they go wrong. I fix them.'

Mollie fell back, exhausted with the physical strain and the emotion. 'I should have figured it out long ago,' she murmured. 'It's a natural, isn't it? You not only have the skills, you're a native French speaker.'

Steve shrugged. 'That's what occurred to a few other people as well.'

'And to you,' she murmured.

'Yeah, and to me.'

They heard the car again. Seconds later Will came in. 'I had to ring three different people, but it's okay, she was telling the truth. They'll make a few calls from London, tell the local coppers she was picked up and taken back there. Say she came to and said who she was. It will put an end to the hunt.'

'What do we do with her in the meantime?' Steve asked.

As if she were a bundle he didn't know how to dispose of, something he could take to the post office maybe.

'They're going to see if they can get someone to come and pick her up. Otherwise I drive her back with me.'

'That could take days.' Steve's exasperation showed. 'She needs a doctor.'

'Nothing else for it,' Will said.

'I'm fine,' Mollie said. 'Don't worry about me.'

Will was shaking a pill from a bottle. 'Got something what'll 'elp you a bit. Make you sleep.'

'Where did you get that?' Steve demanded.

Will smiled. 'Relax, it's a sleeping pill, that's all. Carry 'em regular. Some of my tourists get nervous, what with the waiting and all.' He glanced towards the window. 'Always 'ave to wait. Bleedin' weather.'

He got a glass of water and carried it and the pill to Mollie, she hesitated a moment, but the pain was getting very bad. What the hell. She took it. A few seconds later, before drowsiness overtook her, she thought of something else. 'Lord Whitby, Reggie Bennet-Swan, the man I was staying with, somebody better call him.'

'All taken care of, love,' Will assured her. 'You go to sleep and don't worry about a thing.'

Hours later she was dragged out of a sweaty black pit of unknowing by whispered voices and funny scuffling sounds, and a sense of danger that roused some primeval defence mechanism stronger than the drug she'd been given. It felt as if she'd slept for hours, but it was still pitch dark.

There was a single small lamp lit in the middle of the room, and three or four men. She couldn't be sure how many because she couldn't get them in focus. Her eyes searched for Steve and located him. He was standing a few feet from the cot she lay on, back to her, arms outstretched. Another man, the owl she thought, was patting him down.

'It's all right, not a telltale trace of nothin' what shouldn't be there. Clean as a baby you are.'

'A French baby,' someone said. There were a few chuckles.

'On your bike, lads.' The owl again. He was obviously in charge. 'Get going. Best of British luck to you.'

She saw Steve turn towards her and for some reason she didn't understand, Mollie closed her eyes and pretended to still be asleep. The next thing she knew he was kissing her forehead lightly. 'You awake?' he murmured.

Mollie opened her eyes.

'I thought so. Goodbye. Take care of yourself.' She started to say something, but her tongue was too thick and dry and her lips too parched to let any words form. 'Don't try and talk,' he whispered. 'I want to tell you something. You should dump me. Legally.'

Her eyes pleaded with him. She opened her mouth, but she still couldn't speak.

'Come on,' someone urged.

Steve twisted his head. 'Just a minute.' He turned back to

her. 'I mean it. You and Nick, you belong together. Figure out some way to make that work. Forget about all the old taboos.'

'Come on.' The same voice as before, more urgently this time.

Steve laid his hand beside her cheek, and kissed her forehead again. Then he was gone from her line of vision and she hadn't the strength to turn her head and follow him. Another man approached, whom she didn't recognize. He was filling a hypodermic needle from a small glass vial.

'I'm a doctor, Miss Pride. This is a sedative so you'll sleep on the way back to London. It will make the journey a lot more comfortable for you. Please, don't be frightened. You're going to be fine.'

It wasn't herself she was frightened for, but Mollie couldn't tell him that. She felt the needle jab her flesh, then there was only blackness.

The next thing she knew she was in a doctor's office being attended by a white-coated physician and a starched nurse. 'Steve,' Mollie murmured. 'Where is he?'

The doctor was putting a final piece of tape on her left wrist. He ignored her question. 'There, that will do it. It's only a sprain. And your leg's not broken. You tore a few ligaments, nothing more.'

Mollie reached down with her good hand. Her leg was in plaster to the knee. 'How long did it take us to get here? What day is it?'

'Sunday evening, Miss Pride,' the nurse said, smoothing back her hair with a gesture of practised concern. 'It's Sunday evening. Doctor is keeping you in our private clinic for a few days, but you mustn't worry. We've notified Broadcasting House.'

Her room in the clinic on Harley Street was pristine and elegant, it was rather like she imagined a room to be in some idyllic country inn. There were no other patients, at least none she was aware of, but there were cheerful competent nurses, and flowers. She had a lot of flowers. From Sandra and Phil, from Bob Pulansky and from Nick. Violets from Nick. Mollie had them put right beside her bed, where she could look deep into their depths. Before he left Steve had said something about Nick, it was important, she remembered that. But not the words themselves. Try as she might, she couldn't remember exactly what he'd said. The drugs and the pain and the unreality of all of it perhaps.

Sometimes, in the dead of night, it seemed to her there was another reason she couldn't remember. Mollie sensed some turmoil deep inside herself, something she'd buried because she did not want to face it. When morning came that seemed like an absurd notion.

A week later she was back at work. 'No doing the Charleston for a while,' the doctor said when he released her. He knew about her broadcasts and her theme music, but that wasn't surprising. These days everyone did. The BBC carried them on the Home Service as well as relaying them to America.

Mollie was fairly certain he was the same doctor who'd been in Yorkshire, but it was hard to tell because she saw him now in such a different context, a setting light-years away from spies and foreign-cut suits and Gauloises cigarettes. Still, he was her only link, so she kept asking him if he'd heard anything about Steve.

Usually he ignored her, but once, four or five weeks after the accident when she went back for one of her regular check-ups and asked about Steve yet again, the doctor looked at her with blank eyes. 'I'm sorry, I don't think I have a patient of that name.'

'My husband,' she murmured. 'The man who was in Yorkshire, who was going ...'

He stood up from behind his desk, spoke quickly with that artificial bonhomie that was called bedside manner. 'Fine, fine, Miss Pride. Glad you're doing so well. We'll have you out of that cast before the summer's over.' He handed her the crutches she used to walk. 'That's all, is it? Nothing else you wanted to ask? Nothing medical I mean.'

Mollie stared at him, then she shook her head. 'No, nothing.'

That day, 22 June, she was in a rage by the time she got back to the station. It wasn't only the doctor who was refusing to tell her anything. She kept adding questions to her weekly letter to Donovan, but they were never answered. He was treating her as if she were a child, or worse, a puppet. That's what she'd warned him about when he got her into this thing. I'm not a puppet you can jerk around on a string, she'd told him. Very well, she'd stop acting like one. Bill Donovan wouldn't answer her, so she'd try Harry Hopkins.

'What are my chances of getting a call through to Washington?' she asked the switchboard operator at Broadcasting House. 'DC, not the state.'

'I wouldn't fancy them, love,' the woman said. 'Not today.'

'Why not?'

'I guess you haven't heard.' The operator grinned at her. 'We've had a bit of luck. The Nazis have attacked Russia.' She nodded towards the panel of equipment in front of her. Every light was on, every line in use. 'Things are a bit busy.'

Mollie didn't want to be distracted from her private quest, but she couldn't help herself. She'd been too deeply immersed in all this for too long. She saw the implications instantly. At last it would happen, the thing she'd told listeners about years ago on *Mornings With Mollie*. The huge Red Army would now make common cause with Britain.

That evening Mollie, Phil and Sandra went to a pub on New Cavendish Street when they left Broadcasting House. Like everyone else, they had an enormous need to talk about what had happened, to speculate on the consequences. These days you could only really talk to people you knew intimately, trusted beyond doubt. *Loose Lips Sink Ships*, that's what all the posters said.

'Wouldn't you love it if they'd tell Uncle Joe to go fuck himself, that it was too late?' Phil asked.

'Yes,' Mollie said. 'But they can't do it.'

'No,' Sandra agreed. 'They can't. From this moment on they'll be our gallant Russian allies.'

Mollie sat on the outside edge of the table, her plastered leg resting on a cushion the publican had thoughtfully provided because he knew her. 'One good thing,' she said. 'At least we'll know better than to really trust the Russians.'

'Maybe,' Phil said. 'Maybe not. You can never tell with politicians. But I can think of another good thing,' he added.

'At least the *Luftwaffe* should be too busy to visit us so often.'

He proved a prophet of sorts. The blitz ended, at least for the time being.

The summer of 1941 was cool and wet, the kind that gave Britain its reputation for terrible weather. Mollie told Jack she couldn't meet him outdoors until she had the cast off. It was too difficult trying to walk with crutches on pavements slippery with rain. He suggested Lyon's Tearoom in Piccadilly Circus, Fridays at five.

It was a big place full of people absorbed by their own concerns. No one paid any attention to them when they met at a table in a back corner. Mollie always arrived first and ordered a pot of tea for two. Jack joined her minutes later. Usually he drank his tea in one gulp and she passed him her letter, her silly little letter with its sordid, probably meaningless, gossip, under the table, then he left. Mollie always paid.

'Wait a minute,' she said the second week in August. 'Don't run away. I want to ask you something.'

'Yeah, what?'

She swallowed, moistened her lips, didn't look at him. 'I want to know about my husband, if he's all right.'

There was a second's pause. 'How the bloody hell should I know anything about your husband?' Jack asked finally.

'Stop it,' she said through clenched teeth. 'Stop treating me as if I'm a moron. Why won't anybody talk about it?'

'Nothing to talk about. Talking's dangerous.'

She leaned forward, her hands gripped together so tightly the knuckles were white. 'Not to me. That's what I'm paid to do. Talk.'

Jack cocked his head. 'Is that some sort of threat?'

'Take it however you want.'

'No,' he said softly. 'You take it. Straight from me. You keep your pretty little mouth shut and you do what you're supposed to do. Like all the rest of us.'

'Why?' she demanded.

'Because there isn't any bloody choice, that's why. It's us or them, simple as that. You want to do your bit to help them win, you go right on making a nuisance of yourself until somebody has to take time from more important things to deal with you. If you're on the same side as me, same side as him over there, you keep your mouth shut and figure whatever you have to know, you'll know it soon enough.'

It was a long speech for him, more than he'd ever said to her at any one time. When it was over he suddenly switched back to being casual and unconcerned. Jack stood up, put on his cap, and waved a hand in farewell. 'Take care, love,' he said gaily. 'See you next week.'

16

The flat on Foley Street smelled of pine. Mollie had found a Christmas tree in the rubble of a nearby bombed site. She'd been taking a shortcut through an ugly gap between buildings in Tottenham Court Road, and there it was; a little fir tree about three feet tall, lying on its side, connected to the earth only by one sinewy root. God alone knew how the tree got there, but it couldn't survive. She picked it up and tugged it free and carried it home and planted it in a tin pail. She intended to decorate it for the holidays, but it was only 7 December, still a little early for that.

It had been a long, quiet Sunday, she'd spent most of it organizing her broadcasts for the week. Now Mollie figured she'd earned a treat. She had a fresh egg for supper, courtesy of Mrs Owens in the grocery on Langham Place. 'Only have five of 'em, ducky. Me sister brought 'em back from the country. One for you, cause you've been looking a bit peaky lately.'

Mollie didn't turn on the radio until she'd boiled the egg exactly three and a half minutes. She didn't want to be distracted and spoil it. Then, when it was sitting in the yellow egg cup waiting for her, and the toast was done and she'd spread it with the scant half-teaspoon of butter which was all she had left of last week's two-ounce ration, she switched on the Home Service. It was six o'clock. She heard the pips, then Al Lidell's familiar voice.

'Here is the news. Japan's long-threatened aggression in the Far East began today with air attacks on United States bases in the Pacific. Fresh reports are coming in every minute. The latest facts are these. Messages from Tokyo say that Japan has made a formal declaration of war on both the United States and Britain. Japanese air raids were made on

he Hawaiian Islands and the Philippines. Observers say that
n American battleship has been hit and that a number of
apanese bombers have been shot down. A naval action is in
rogress off Honolulu ...'

Jesus! Mollie ignored the food on the table, pulled a coat
ver her slacks and sweater, grabbed her bag and headed for
he door. Before she switched off the light and the radio she
eard Lidell say that Roosevelt had told the Army and Navy
o act on their secret orders.

The news room at Broadcasting House was a mad scene.
People running everywhere, teletype machines chattering.
Mollie stood and watched, feeling somehow out of it, a
foreigner, as if she didn't belong. She looked for Nick, but
didn't see him. She hadn't seen him for over a week, had no
idea where he was. There was no sign of Phil or Sandra
either. It was, after all, Sunday.

'Mollie,' somebody shouted. 'Over here.'

She turned and saw a BBC engineer she knew waving her
down the hall to the tiny studio where they sometimes played
back the shortwave broadcasts. When Mollie entered there
were only four other people. Everybody else was busy doing
their job, they didn't have time to listen to the radio.

'They're picking up Lee Warner in Washington,' the
engineer whispered. Mollie nodded her thanks and bent her
head towards the receiver.

'There are crowds all over this city,' the American voice
said. 'In front of the White House and the State Department
and the Japanese Embassy. They are quiet crowds, as if
nobody can quite believe what's happened ...'

Somebody rapped on the studio window. Mollie turned
and saw Phil motioning to her. She went outside.

'Figured you'd be here,' Phil said.

'It seemed the only place to be.' He was clutching a fistful
of teletype reports, and she nodded towards them. 'Anything
more than Al had at six?' she asked.

'A little more. It's worse than we thought.'

It was some hours before they knew how much worse. The
fleet at Pearl harbour had been all but destroyed. Eight
American battleships were dead or dying, and nearly two
hundred American planes which had been grouped together

413

in airfields, sitting ducks, were beyond repair. Some twent
five hundred people had been killed. Latest estimates put t
number of Japanese planes shot down at fewer than thirty.

It was Monday morning by then, but they knew it on
because the clocks said so. In the underground warren fro
which they operated, no shaft of moon or sun could ente
The yellow electric light made them all look wan and tire
Mollie was as exhausted as she appeared. Around seve
when they were still poring over the teletype print-outs, sl
leaned her head for a moment on Phil's shoulder. 'I alwa
thought I'd cheer when America finally got into this wa
Right now I don't feel like cheering.'

'No,' he agreed, 'neither do I.'

Kate missed the little house in the country and its garde
Nine months ago, when she began her radio broadcasts, Le
had moved her and Yoko to an apartment in a moder
building in Tokyo. It had a balcony looking out on a stre
that was often crowded. Kate seldom went onto the balcon
because it was shallow and seemed to her flimsy and in
substantial; besides, she always felt she must hide fror
Japanese crowds. Four times a week when she made he
broadcasts, Yoko took her to the radio station in a close
and curtained car; she led Kate into the building by a rea
door, and the little room with the table and the chair and th
microphone was always empty, except for Kate and Yok
and one armed guard.

They had become something she did without thinking
those broadcasts. Lee gave her the scripts when he came o
Sunday afternoons. Four of them, enough for the week. The
were written in his careful hand, with directions that h
enclosed in parenthesis. (Laugh here.) (Smile when you sa
this, so the smile can be heard in your voice.) Kate did no
want to smile when she read the ugly words, but she under
stood now that she was helping Lee, and herself, and in
way, Ricky. Because she did what he told her she must do
the day would come when they could all go home. But tha
day had not yet arrived. Today she sat on a mat in the larges
of the two rooms of the apartment and watched Lee.

He was on the balcony, his back to her. It was high noon

and the sun shone on Tokyo. It illuminated the street filled with people, a few automobiles and many wheeled carts. It bathed Lee in a halo of golden light, and made his black kimono with the broad white border gleam. Beneath the silky cotton cloth his broad muscular shoulders rippled as he raised his arms repeatedly and shouted, '*Bansai!*'

He kept doing it, over and over. On the street below men were marching with great brass gongs that they beat with sticks while they called out words Kate could not understand. Each time they paused the crowd, including Lee, would raise its arms and cry that other word she didn't understand although she recognized it. '*Bansai! Bansai!*'

She sat very still — legs crossed, arms folded within the wide sleeves of a kimono made of pale-blue satin, in the manner she'd learned from Yoko — and watched and listened.

Eventually it ended. The men with the gongs moved into other streets, their voices dimmed to a faint echo. Most of the crowd followed them. She saw Lee drop his arms a last time, stand for a moment, then step backwards into the apartment.

He drew the shoji screen closed and the room became shadowy. Kate relaxed. She preferred it like this, the reality of Japan and Tokyo closed away, the two of them alone in a half-light which seemed protective. 'What was all that about?' she asked.

Lee didn't answer. Instead he crossed to a small table. Before she went out Yoko had prepared a lacquer jug of warmed sake. He poured the fermented rice liquor into a tiny cup. Kate started to rise. 'That must be cold by now. I'll warm it for you. I know how to do it, Yoko showed me.'

He stopped her with a gesture. 'No, it's all right.'

She waited until he'd drunk three of the cups, emptying the jug, then crossed to where she sat. 'What's happened?' Kate asked again.

He sat down before he answered, folded his tall body gracefully and sat cross-legged opposite her. His kimono opened slightly and she could see his powerful chest. The pectorals, so well developed by his long years of musician-ship, bulged. 'Do you understand the word *samurai*?' he asked. Kate shook her head. 'It means warrior. In ancient times the *samurai* were all-powerful in Japan, the leaders of the country were chosen from among them. To be a member of a *samurai* family is still very important. I am *samurai*.'

'Through your father?'

'Yes, of course.'

They never talked about his mother. Once or twice Kate had mentioned Grace, but his look of pain had been so intense that she knew it was an impossible subject and she didn't raise it again. She was sorry now that she'd brought Grace into the conversation, even by inference. Kate groped for something else to say which would banish the ghost of his Chinese mother. 'Is that why Yoko calls you Lee-sama and not Lee-san, because you're *samurai*? I've always meant to ask.'

'Partly that, and because I'm a leader. Yoko is *samurai* as well. All the members of our group are.'

Kate didn't understand about the group. She knew it existed, that Lee was part of some clique or coalition and that they were in a struggle for power with other groups, but it was all too much for her. Besides, they were getting off the point. 'What happened out there?' she asked again. 'What were those men shouting about?'

This time for answer he drew a dagger from the folds of his kimono. Kate gasped.

Lee ignored her and lay the dagger on the low ebony table between them. Its point faced him. 'This was my father's, and his father's before that. It's been in my family for generations.'

He wasn't talking to her now. His voice came from somewhere far away, from deep within herself. 'The right to die an honourable death, to commit suicide, is a privilege of the *samurai*. It is called *seppuku*. A warrior who has failed in his duty or brought shame on his lord chooses to kill himself. He plunges the dagger into his belly and cuts up until he reaches the heart. If he is lucky he has a second, a friend who stands behind him and cuts off his head with a sword if the pain becomes too much or the *samurai's* courage fails him. I was told that my great-grandfather committed *seppuku* with this dagger.'

416

His hand snaked toward the gleaming knife. Kate screamed and lunged toward him. 'No! Lee, you mustn't.'

He flung off her restraining arm, perhaps more strongly than he meant to. She lost her balance and sprawled on the mat.

'"I cannot live with this shame,"' he said. 'Those are the ritual words with which a *samurai* announces his intention to perform *seppuku*.'

The phrase hung in the air between them. Lee's hand hovered over the dagger. Kate lay on the floor, supporting herself on her arms, and watched him and held her breath. It was very quiet. The shouting men and the crowds had all gone elsewhere. The silence was profound, it was as if they were once more in the little house in the pine forest.

Seconds went by. Then he turned to her. 'I'm sorry,' he said gently. 'I didn't mean to hurt you.' He extended his arm and helped her to sit up. 'Are you all right?'

She nodded, still so frightened by the threat of the dagger that she did not trust herself to speak.

The knife remained where it was on the table, but Lee did not touch it. 'This morning at dawn Japan attacked Pearl Harbour in Hawaii.'

Kate's long delicate hands fluttered in the air, as if she could catch hold of his words and make them comprehensible. 'But Hawaii belongs to America.'

'Yes. They bombed the US fleet. That's what the men with the gongs were announcing. Japan has won a great victory. That's what *bansai* means. Victory. They sank a great many ships. *Bansai*! And destroyed all the planes. *Bansai*! And killed thousands of people. *Bansai*! Japan has declared war on America. *Bansai*!'

'No. Oh, God, no ...'

'Yes.'

'You were out there with the rest of them. You were screaming *bansai* too.' She whispered the accusation, but it was as if she had shouted the words. 'You're an American.'

'Yes. And I'm also Japanese. And I ...' His voice broke. 'I cannot live with this shame.'

Kate waited. This time she did not try to stop him. She knew she couldn't anyway. She was no match for his strength, neither physically nor mentally. Only Lee could decide.

'If I do not live with it,' he said finally, 'that will be a greater shame.' He turned to her, laid a hand beside her cheek. 'And you, my beautiful Kate, what would happen to you?'

'I would die without you,' she said simply.

He drew in his breath, but did not respond. After a few seconds he took his hand away. 'I wish Yoko were here and we could have some tea.'

'I can make it. Yoko showed me how.' Kate stood up and went behind one of the shoji screens and returned in a few minutes carrying a tray with a round stoneware teapot and two cups without handles.

The dagger was gone, Lee must have put it away. She set the tray on the ebony table and kneeling beside it, removed the lid of the pot and stirred the tea with a bamboo whisk. Just so many times, with just the smooth even rhythm which Yoko had taught her. Then she put the whisk carefully on the tray in its proper place, replaced the cover of the pot and lifted it and poured the tea in one fluid motion, without spilling a drop. When she was done she even bowed her head to him in the Japanese manner, and Lee smiled and returned her bow, and lifted his cup. She lifted hers and they toasted each other with their eyes, and drank the bitter green liquid.

'It is very good,' he said. 'Exactly like Yoko's.'

'Thank you.'

When they had finished the tea Kate carried the tray from the room. When she returned he was standing beside a woven straw chest in one corner, his flute in his hands. 'I didn't know that was here,' she exclaimed in surprise.

'I brought it here when you first moved in. It's safe. Western music is frowned on these days. But ...' He lifted the instrument to his lips and blew softly, merely one or two hesitant notes at first, then a long ripple of notes, followed by many more.

She stood entranced by the sound, by the sight of him, eyes closed, fingers flying, body moving in concert with the beauty he created. After a few minutes he stopped. 'Mozart,' he said. 'The Flute Concerto No. 1 in G.'

'Play some more, please.'

Lee hesitated. Then, 'Yes, why not? Mozart should be acceptable. An Austrian like Hitler, our noble ally.' He lifted the instrument to his lips and the music began again, slower this time, sadder. 'That was a bit of the second movement,' he told her when he finished. 'The Adagio. But played very badly, I'm terribly out of practice.'

Kate shook her head. 'No, it was wonderful. I like the calmness of it.'

Lee wiped the instrument carefully before putting it in its case and returning it to the depths of the straw chest. When he turned back to her she was standing with both her hands outstretched. He took a step closer and clasped them in his, their fingers intertwined. 'We'll go home,' he whispered. 'Some day this will be over and we'll go home. I promise you.'

'Yes. And you will play with a great orchestra again. And I'll be sitting in the audience listening to you.'

'Some day,' he repeated.

Kate's body moved of its own accord, without her thinking about it. Her feet in the white tabi socks and the thonged rope sandals stepped forward and she freed her hands from his and put her arms around his neck. They were almost the same height, Lee only a little taller, and he barely had to bend his head to make his lips touch hers.

Yoko had left Kate's bed prepared in the next room, the tatami mat was spread on the floor with one futon, a quilt filled with down, open for her to lie upon, and another folded beside it to cover her. Lee carried her there and lay her down on the futon. Kate untied the sash of her kimono and let it fall open. He removed his and lay beside her, then paused a moment and reached for the second futon and spread it over their bodies. Beneath the covering they were alone in a world utterly removed from war.

Later, when the room was in deep rose shadow because it was the time of sunset and the shoji covered window faced west, she murmured his name. 'Lee.'

'Yes?'

'Nothing. I only want to say it. Lee.'

'Kate,' he replied.

'It's never been like that for me,' she told him simply. 'Never before. I never felt such ... such joy.'

'Because you were meant for me,' he said gravely. 'Always, since we were children, you were fated to be mine. I knew it, but you didn't realize.' He leaned over and kissed her lightly before he stood up. 'Yoko will be back soon. I have to go.'

'I know.' She was not reluctant to let him leave. There was a rhythm to this time, a tide of being and becoming and beginning and ending which was like his music, it had laws of its own and they combined in beauty. But she had one question. 'You said that Yoko calls you Lee-sama because you are samurai. Why does she call me Ka-te-sama?'

'Because you are my woman. Yoko is very wise, she's always known that. You're mine, so in her eyes you're *samurai* too.'

At Broadcasting House late in the afternoon on 8 December they heard Roosevelt ask Congress to declare war on Japan, and three hours later the news came through that Congress had done as the President requested.

Mollie was hanging on to a telephone which linked her with New York, her ear pressed tight to the receiver, trying to get as much information as she could in the brief minutes available to her on the open cue line. 'I'm doing a special for the Home Service,' she explained. 'I want to talk about whether the country will be united in the war effort. What about Borah and Wheeler? How did they vote?'

The faceless voice on the other end of the wire laughed. 'Complete about-face. What the hell do you expect, the goddamn Japs bombed us, for Christ's sake. You can tell the Brits it's full speed ahead. Wheeler had the last word. He said....'

'What? I didn't hear you. Too much static. Give it to me again,' Mollie shouted into the telephone. 'What did Wheeler say?'

'He said, "The only thing to do now is whip the hell out of 'em."'

Three days later Germany and Italy also declared war on the United States.

Nick showed up just when Mollie was digesting that piece of information. She was sitting at her desk, staring at a copy of the bulletin Al Lidell would be reading over the domestic news in a matter of minutes. Suddenly a voice spoke into her ear from just a few inches behind her.

'Cry havoc and let slip the dogs of war.'

'Jesus! Nick, where have you been? You scared the hell out of me. What does that mean?'

'I'm not sure what it means. Sounds great, though. It's from Shakespeare, *Julius Caesar.* I've been busy.'

'Doing what? You look terrible.'

He was unshaven, his eyes were red-rimmed with fatigue, his shirt was filthy and he wasn't wearing a tie. 'I was on my way to Moscow when the word came. I hadn't got very far, so I turned back.'

'Moscow!'

'Yeah, where else? I'm a war correspondent. The war's happening in Russia. At least, it was.' He shrugged. 'Now the ante's been raised. I figured it was time to come back and get some new chips. Heard your broadcast last night, by the way. The panel discussion on historic women warriors, it was ...'

'Great stuff,' she interrupted.

'How do you know that's what I was going to say?'

'Because that's what you always say. Besides, that's what it was. Great stuff. The history professor from Cambridge talking about Queen Boadicea leading a revolt against the Romans in Norfolk, hell, every woman in England must be figuring out how to make her pots into a breastplate by now.'

He perched on the corner of her desk and shook a cigarette from a pack, holding it unlit between his teeth. 'Nope, the women in England are too goddamned exhausted to play games. Besides, they've given Beaverbrook all their pots to turn into aeroplanes. Did you know that won't work, by the way?'

'Yes, I know. There's not enough aluminium in pots and pans to be worth anything. So they've got all these useless piles of junk and nobody knows what to do about them. I'm not going to put it on the air though.'

'I didn't think you were. We're all propagandists these days. Don't say anything that might lower morale.' Nick lit the cigarette, holding the match and watching it burn down until it almost singed his fingers.

'That's an over-simplification. But you don't want an argument, do you? You sound depressed. What's the matter? Are you sorry about Moscow?'

'Not really. I can't get very enthusiastic about the Russians as allies. I keep remembering what I saw in Finland. I'm not depressed, only a little jaded. I've agreed to do my duty, but I'm not excited by it.'

'What duty?'

'A desk job for Mutual. More administrative responsibilities, less broadcasting from the front lines. It's going to get pretty complicated here. London's going to be full of Americans.'

She felt a surge of relief at the thought of him safely in London, threatened by nothing more than the blitz, which seemed to be over anyway. Mollie was too smart to let him know what she was thinking. 'Yes, well that may be exciting after all. And it has to be done.'

'I guess so.' He stood up. 'Anyway, it's not the same, going out in the field without Steve.'

She didn't say anything. Nick started to go, then turned back. 'Mollie, you haven't heard anything from him, have you?'

'Not a word.' She didn't look at him when she said it. It was true as far as it went, and she'd never told him about the cottage on the Yorkshire moors.

'Nothing to worry about,' he said easily. 'Steve's too smart to get into trouble. Probably got himself a nice cushy job back in Montreal.'

At last Hitler had what he'd spoiled for from the first, total war. Through the winter and the spring and the summer of 1942 the world burned. In Russia, almost the only part of continental Europe not already theirs, the Nazis advanced to just short of Moscow and laid siege to Stalingrad, and the deaths ran into the countless millions. Whole populations were wiped out by disease, starvation, shells and bombs, and direct and pre-planned execution by the Germans. The Japanese took the Philippines, Malaya, Burma, Thailand and

Singapore — all of Southeast Asia — and were poised to attack India.

In that bleak and desperate autumn of 1942, Mollie went home. She travelled by MATS, the Military Air Transport Service which flew the brass around. All the arrangements were made by her bosses at NBC, who had summoned her for reasons not entirely clear, but which she did not oppose or question. She was soul-sick and waging a constant battle against despair, and she hungered for the sight of America and all she'd left behind. In the purple November dawn, when they circled the Statue of Liberty before landing, Mollie sobbed like an infant and felt no need to apologize.

'You're doing a bang-up job, kid,' they told her, the well-fed men in the suits and ties, who seemed to her so removed from the front line, so protected, though that was probably not fair. 'Terrific work. We're going to add a Sunday night edition of the *Mollie Pride Report.*'

'That's it?' Mollie asked. 'That's why you wanted me to come home? To tell me you're adding a Sunday night slot?'

'Sure,' the guy sitting opposite her in the sunlit office atop Manhattan said. 'Have to do some schedule planning, clue you in to the kind of topics we'll want. Besides,' he added. 'People around here figure you were due for a bit of R and R.'

'R and R?'

'Army talk. Rest and recuperation.'

'Oh, I see.'

But she didn't, not really. Still, she was too exhausted to argue or try and figure it out.

Zena, on the other hand, was a revelation. Mollie found her mother twenty pounds lighter, spry, lively, immaculately coiffed and made up. When they spoke of Kate Zena's eyes darkened with worry and pain, but clearly this was a sorrow she had assimilated as she'd assimilated so many others. Once more Zena exhibited the steel beneath her softness and vagueness, her instincts as a survivor.

'When the war's over,' she said. 'I'm sure we'll hear from Kate when the war's over. Meanwhile you're here and I can actually do something about you. You've got to eat, darling.

You're much too thin. It's difficult these days, what with rationing and all, but Simone and I will manage to feed you up.'

'Who's Simone?'

'Madame Chirault. It seemed a little silly to go on calling her that, so I use her Christian name now.'

'Her Christian name, I see. Mom, you and Simone, you still get along?'

'Famously. She's such a good friend, Mollie.' Zena's blue eyes grew moist and her smile tremulous. 'Do you know, this is the first time in my life I've ever really had a lady friend. Except for Grace of course. And that was different.'

'Why?' Mollie demanded. Hearing her mother's use of the past tense, not wanting to hear it.

'Well, because she's different for one thing. Chinese. And for another, I haven't seen her in years.'

'But why not? Haven't you called her, gone down to Mulberry Street? Mom, Grace is an American, like you and me. The fact that she's Chinese is totally irrelevant ...'

'Do hush, darling. Naturally I'd see her if she were in New York. She's not. She went to California soon after you left.' Zena shook her head. 'Poor thing, she never stopped looking for Lee.'

'Has she found him?'

'I don't know. I doubt it. Somehow I think I'd have heard from her if she'd found him.'

That's what finally propelled Mollie to seek out Bill Donovan. Not a summons from him, though she half expected one, or any concern about the work she was supposedly doing for him in Britain. It was the thought of Kate and of Grace which jarred her out of her lethargy and caused her to call the number of his pre-war Wall Street office.

They told her he wasn't there. She hadn't expected him to be: Donovan was head of some official government agency now, something called the Office of Strategic Services, which Mollie figured was a euphemism for a lot of spying. She had no idea how she'd reach him through a maze of Washington bureaucrats. 'I realize that,' she told the woman on the other end of the line. 'But presumably you know where to get hold of him.' There was no reply. 'Well, don't you?'

'I can perhaps get a message through,' the voice said tentatively.

'You do that,' Mollie replied through clenched teeth. 'Tell him Mollie Pride's in town, and that I have to see him. I'll be going back to London at the end of the week, so there isn't a lot of time.'

Two days later she got a telephone call from a nameless man who told her to be at an office in Rockefeller Center at noon. 'Who wants to see me?' Mollie demanded. It was a bit perverse, because she was pretty certain she knew who wanted to see her.

'Just be there, Miss Pride,' the voice said before the connection was broken.

She went to Rockefeller Center. There was nothing written on the glass door of the room she'd been told to go to, only its number — 552. She went in to find a single desk with an eldery woman sitting behind it.

'Good afternoon, I'm Mollie Pride. I was told to come here.'

'Yes, Miss Pride, you're expected. Please sit down.'

Mollie sat. The woman behind the desk went on typing something. Telephones rang somewhere in the distance, behind closed doors which never opened to allow any glimpse of what went on behind them. Half an hour passed. Mollie was getting ready to remind the grey-haired typist of her existence when there was a strange screeching noise, followed by a whooshing sound. Bomb, Mollie thought instantly. She dived beneath the sofa.

The woman opened her eyes wide in astonishment. 'Miss Pride, is something wrong?'

Mollie realized instantly that she'd made an ass of herself. This was New York, there were no bombs falling here. She crawled out from beneath the couch and stood up, dusting off the skirt of her new black wool suit. It came from Altmans. Zena had insisted that she buy it. Mollie was astounded at the hemline which barely covered her knees, but the saleslady had assured her that everyone was wearing their clothes this length now. There was, after all, a shortage of fabric. 'I'm sorry,' she murmured. 'I've been in London for two years. I heard a peculiar noise, I thought it was a bomb.'

425

'Oh, yes, of course. I see.' The woman held up a small brass cylinder. 'It was just this. Our offices are connected by pneumatic tubes. This will be a message about you, I expect.' She twisted open the cartridge. 'Yes, it is. You're to go to room 911. Right away. They're waiting for you.'

Mollie nodded, then while she gathered up her bag and her coat and prepared to leave, 'What is this place called, anyway?'

'British Security Coordination,' the woman said. She had a flat mid-western accent.

'You're not British.'

'No, of course not. I'm a typist, that's all. Lots of people working here aren't British. They seem to come from all over. Really amazing the accents you hear.'

'I see, thanks.'

In the hall she looked for a door marked 'stairs', then remembered that in Rockefeller Center the elevators still worked, and pressed a button to summon one. Minutes later she got off at the ninth floor.

Another characterless room and another receptionist. This one was a stunning brunette with her hair in a smart chignon and a wide mouth painted a fiery crimson. 'Miss Pride? Right through there, please. You're expected.'

Mollie opened the door the brunette indicated and stepped into a large office looking down on the empty skating rink and the flags. Bill Donovan sat behind the desk. 'Mollie, how wonderful to see you. You're looking fine.' He stood up and extended his hand, and she shook it.

'Thank you. I'm going back to London the day after tomorrow, Mr Donovan. I wanted to see you before I left.'

'I fully intended to see you before you returned. Your call anticipated mine by about three hours.'

'I see.' She wasn't sure she believed him, but it didn't matter much.

'This office belongs to friends of mine. It seemed a better place to meet, no reason to drag you down to Washington. Please, sit down. Tell me how you are, how you've been. And about your cousin Nick and your mother.'

'We're all surviving. My mother is doing very well, better than I'd expected. She and Simone Chirault are the best of friends. Their store is thriving.'

Donovan smiled and nodded. 'One of our more successful efforts.'

Suddenly she had a terrible thought, a fear that gripped her in the belly and took her breath away. 'You don't use my mother for any of your ... activities? You wouldn't. She couldn't possibly ...'

'The book store is perfectly legitimate,' he assured her. 'No reason for it not to be.'

She wouldn't get any more out of him than that, she realized. Maybe his OSS or this British Security Coordination used the place somehow, but if they did it was probably without Zena's knowledge. And it was hard to imagine that anything these men did was actually physically dangerous, not in New York. 'Okay,' she said. 'Look, I came to ask about my sister. And I'd appreciate it if you could check on a friend of mine, she went to California two years ago and we haven't heard from her since. She's Chinese, her name's Grace Mitsuno.'

Was it her imagination, or did something flicker behind his eyes? She couldn't be sure. Donovan took a pencil and asked her how to spell the name and wrote it on a piece of paper. 'Any reason you'd expect me to know anything about her?' he asked mildly. 'Anything you know about her?'

'No. I just had a hunch you might. Mostly I figured that with your connections perhaps you could find something out.'

'Right. We'll see what we can do.' He got up and walked to a thick pipe running along the wall. He put the paper he'd written on into one of the brass cylinders and inserted it into the pneumatic tube. The system activated itself at once and the cylinder disappeared with the same sound which had so startled Mollie in the office downstairs.

'I heard that a few minutes ago and thought it was a bomb,' she said. 'I dived for cover. Scared the wits out of the receptionist.'

Donovan looked at her with something new in his deceptively open face, something she'd never seen before. 'No one here really knows what it's been like to live through the blitz. You and the rest of the radio people, you've done wonders in

427

explaining it all, but Americans can't really imagine it.'

Mollie realized what his expression was. Pity. 'About Kate,' she said.

'Yes. Mollie, come with me, please.'

He led her through a series of doors and down a flight of stairs until at last they came to a small room with two pairs of earphones and a turntable. 'I'll be the engineer today,' Donovan said. 'Make yourself comfortable.'

Mollie eyed the set-up, then turned to him. 'What does any of this have to do with my sister?'

'Please, trust me. Put on the earphones, please.'

She sat down and did as he asked. There was a record already on the turntable, Donovan lifted the playing arm, but before he put it down he said, 'I'm going to play a series of recorded broadcasts. There's a paper and pencil in front of you. Will you please make a note of any of the voices you recognize.'

Mollie nodded and picked up her pencil and waited.

It took twenty minutes for him to play for her all the sounds of hate gathered in the grooves of black acetate. She knew many of them, some by their real names, others only by the titles they'd taken for their propoganda personnas. *William Joyce alias Lord Haw-Haw*, Mollie scribbled on her sheet. *Paul Revere/?Ezra Pound. P.G. Wodehouse. Midge somebody, calls herself Midge at the Mike.* Then a particularly poisonous one she'd learned about only recently from the BBC monitors who listened round the clock to everything that went over the airwaves. 'Axis Sally?' she asked Donovan aloud.

He nodded.

Mollie listened to the saccharine-sweet voice telling allied servicemen fighting in North Africa how their wives and girl friends were all betraying them with men too smart to risk their lives fighting the invincible Third Reich. 'God, she's the worst,' Mollie murmured. Donovan didn't reply. The broadcast came to an end with the singing of *Lili Marlene* in German. There was a moment's pause, then another voice, this one had an accent Mollie couldn't at first identify.

'Here I am, you poor dear things,' the woman was saying. 'Going to play you all your favourite records, the ones that remind you of home. But first, let me tell you about Private Kimberly. He's a prisoner of war in Malaya, and he's very sick. Dying quite slowly is Private Kimberly. Don't you think it's a shame that an American boy should go so far away from home to die for no good reason? I do. Now here's the music I promised you ...'

Donovan flicked a switch and stopped the playback. 'Recognize her?'

'No. I've never heard her before, thank God. Who is she?'

'The troops call her Tokyo Rose. Actually there seem to be a number of ladies broadcasting for the Japs. The GI's call them all Tokyo Rose.'

'That's what her accent was, slightly Oriental. I couldn't place it at first.'

'According to our linguistics people most of the Tokyo Roses are Japanese, at least in origin. But there's one who isn't. Listen to this, Mollie.'

He started the turntable again and she pressed the earphones to her ear to hear more clearly. 'Things are going from bad to worse in the States these days. It's never going to improve until Roosevelt and the terrible people around him are thrown out of office and Americans get a government willing to recognize that it is Japan's destiny to control Southeast Asia and make peace ...'

She sat there, absolutely frozen, unable to move. The words went on. When they ended, Donovan picked up the playing arm and set the needle back a few grooves and she heard it a second time. She still didn't believe it. Finally he turned it off. 'Mollie?' Very softly, gently in fact. Only her name. 'Mollie?'

Slowly Mollie removed the headphones and laid them on the table. 'Yes,' she said, her voice flat and without expression. 'Who was that? I've never heard her before.'

'That was Kate, Mollie. You and I both know it was Kate.'

She shook her head, unable to form a denial with her lips, but determined to refute the terrible accusation nonetheless.

'Yes,' he insisted. 'It was. You recognized your sister's voice, didn't you?'

'No.' Mollie spat out the word. 'That's not my sister. Whatever gave you an idea like that? Why should my sister

429

be a traitor to her country?'

Donovan stood up. 'Thank you. I wasn't sure and I had to be. Come, my dear, we'll go back upstairs and have a cup of coffee.'

In fact he gave her something stronger than coffee, a shot of straight bourbon. Mollie drank it gratefully, feeling the heat of the liquor melt some of the ice in her stomach. For a long time neither of them said anything. Then Mollie broke the silence.

'What is happening here?' she asked finally. 'What kind of nightmare are you creating? We're supposed to be fighting because Nazism is evil, the Japanese are evil. But the things you're doing, all this Machiavellian carrying on ... My sordid little reports on people who think I'm their friend. Steve dropping into some kind of behind-the-lines hell pretending to be a Frenchman. Kate ...' She broke off, knowing that she'd negated all the refutations she'd made earlier. 'We're as bad as they are.' She was crying now, unable to staunch the flow of tears. 'We're just as rotten.'

'No,' Donovan said softly. 'I promise you, we are nothing like as rotten and foul and depraved as they are. There are things no one yet knows, Mollie. Some day they will. Some day the whole world will know what this thing is really about, and then they'll understand that we had to do anything that was necessary, anything, in order to stop it.'

It wasn't until she was half-way to London, after they'd landed and refuelled at the airforce base in the Azores, that Mollie realized it was Bill Donovan who'd been behind the summons to New York. He'd needed her to identify Kate's voice, so he'd brought her over. She was enraged at first, then grateful. He could have used Zena for the purpose. It would have been much simpler for him. But he hadn't, he'd gone to extra trouble to use her instead. For that Mollie would be thankful to Bill Donovan for the rest of her life.

This time she could not keep what she knew from Nick. It was too much to live with by herself.

'I have to tell you something,' Mollie said.

They were in his flat on Wimpole Street. Fiona was off on one of her sorties to the Lake District, visiting what Nick called 'the family castle'. Mollie sat in the elegant living room beside a glowing fire, in a deep down-filled chair upholstered in dull gold brocade. She'd kicked off her shoes and her legs were drawn up beneath her, and she was nursing a tot of brandy Nick had poured into an enormous snifter.

'Where did you get this delicious stuff?' she asked.

'A Christmas present from she whose name I will not speak in your presence.'

'Yeah, it would be, wouldn't it?' The brandy did not taste any less glorious because it had come from Fiona. 'Dabbles in the black market, does she?'

'Don't be catty. And as a matter of fact, she doesn't. Fiona's very patriotic. The bottle came from her father's cellar, up there at the castle. Real French cognac, pre-war. You've got the last of it, so shut up and enjoy it.'

'The last of it? Christmas was only a week ago.'

'I've been thirsty. What do you have to tell me?'

She didn't answer right away.

'Stop chewing on your lip. Spit it out.'

'I don't want to spit it out, I want to drink it.'

'Mollie.'

'I'm sorry. But it's so goddamn awful.' She pressed her forehead to the glass and wouldn't meet his eyes. 'It's so terrible, Nick. That's why I waited until after the holiday to tell you.'

He sat quite composed on the sofa opposite her, legs stretched out toward the fire, hands folded loosely in his lap. 'C'mon, kid. This is me, your old reliable Nick. Whatever it is, it's okay.'

'No, it's awful.' He didn't say anything, she had to go on. 'It's not about me, it's about Kate.'

His body jerked once. 'She's not ...'

'Mollie read his mind. 'She's not dead; as far as I know she's physically okay. She sounded bright and chipper enough.'

'Sounded? You've talked to Kate?'

'No. I heard her. A recording. In New York.'

'What kind of recording? Who made it?'

'Radio monitors. Maybe British, maybe American, I don't know.' She took a long swallow of her cognac, waited for the spirit to warm her, give her courage. 'Have you ever heard of Tokyo Rose?' she asked finally.

Nick exhaled with a loud painful sound that was half sigh, half moan. 'I know who she is. Are you trying to tell me that Kate's Tokyo Rose?'

'Not exactly. Apparently there are quite a few of them. Lots of ladies going on the air to cheer up the troops. In a manner of speaking.'

'And Kate's one of them?'

She nodded.

Nick stood up, poked at the fire, scooped a few more coals from the mahogany and brass scuttle and threw them on the flames. 'Shit,' he murmured finally. 'Shit.' He turned to her. 'Mollie, for God's sake, look at me.' Then, when her brown eyes were raised to his, 'Are you sure?' Absolutely dead certain positive sure?'

'Yes. I wish I could say there was some question, but there isn't. It was Kate. I recognized her voice the instant I heard it. There's no doubt whatsoever.'

He rubbed the back of his neck for a moment. Mollie held out the snifter and he took it and tossed back what remained of the brandy. 'She's being forced,' he said finally. 'Somebody's making her do it. It's the only explanation. That goddamn Armando maybe.'

'Armando's dead,' Mollie reminded him.

'Yeah, I don't mean him, the other one.'

'Miguel. I thought of that too.'

'It's the only explanation,' Nick insisted. 'Maybe they've got the little boy too, Kate's son. They've got Ricky and she has to do whatever they tell her or they'll kill him.'

'It's a pretty good plot,' Mollie said softly. 'I've been writing more or less the same scenario in my head. I figure it's either that or drugs.'

'It's the truth. Or something close to the truth. It has to be. Kate's no traitor. She's a little flaky sometimes, naive as hell, but treason ... never.' He poked savagely at the fire. The coals sputtered into flame, then died back to glowing red. 'Mollie, I'm almost afraid to ask, but does your mother know?'

She was so glad to be able to give him at least this much

comfort. 'No. She has no idea.'

'Thank God.' He sat down again, and leaned his head on the back of the sofa. 'Okay, tell me the rest of it.'

'What rest? I don't know anything more.'

'You've left out a key piece of information. How did you find out? Who gave you the record?'

'It wasn't given to me, only played for me. And I can't tell you who.'

'Cut the crap.'

'It's not crap.'

'Yeah, it is. Mollie, we've played this game long enough. I went along with it. But this is different, this is right down in the guts of it.'

'The guts of what?'

'What we are,' he said. 'Who we are. You, me, Kate, Zena. We're connected, Mollie. Not the way an ordinary family is. We've never been an ordinary family. We're tied up in a knot that's stronger than that. I want to know what you've got yourself into.'

'Because of how we lived,' she said. 'Is that what you mean?'

'That's part of it. But there's more. We got thrown together by a lot of crazy circumstances, Fate for want of a better word. We ...' He hesitated. 'It's as if we *chose* each other. Whatever happens to any one of us, the others are involved. So tell me what you're doing and with whom. Because if it's happening to you, then it's happening to me too.'

It was the truth, Mollie knew that. It was a loyalty higher than any promise she'd made to anyone else. 'Ever hear of Bill Donovan?' she asked softly.

'Wild Bill Donovan? The OSS?'

She nodded.

'Of course. And I've been stupid, I should have guessed it would be something as simple as spying. How long have you been working for him?'

Mollie was astounded. 'What do you mean simple? And why do you sound relieved?'

He sat forward and reached across and took her hand. 'Because I imagined you doing secret deals with all kinds of

433

shady people. Mollie the daredevil. I've been terrified since you first mentioned your "secret sources". Spying for our side, that I understand.'

She couldn't help herself, she started to laugh. The laughter went on and on, became mixed with sobs, bordered on hysteria. He pulled her to him, held her on his lap, soothed her. At last she stopped. 'Good girl,' Nick murmured. 'Such a good girl.' He kissed the top of her head, then suddenly he thrust her away and stood up. 'I'll make some tea.'

A few minutes later he'd returned with two cups. They were delicate china and they weren't chipped. 'Thanks,' Mollie murmured as she took one. 'I've become as addicted to tea as any Englishman.'

'You didn't answer my last question. How long have you worked for Donovan?'

'Since early in 1940. I don't do much, I'm supposed to keep my eyes open. Tell him if I see anything that looks like the makings of a fifth column.'

He ruffled her hair. 'Good girl,' he said again.

Because of that evening of confession it was easier to tell him what she learned in March. 'I know where Grace is.'

Nick looked at her. 'You don't look happy about it.'

'I'm not. It's terrible. She's in California.'

'That doesn't sound so bad. Zena said she went out there to look for Lee. Grace is from California.' He paused. 'I'm missing something, aren't I? What is it, Mollie?'

'She was picked up last year when they arrested all the Japanese Americans on the west coast.'

'Wait a minute, that doesn't make any sense.' Nick was incredulous. 'Grace isn't Japanese.'

'She has a Japanese last name. Apparently she was living in San Francisco, in Little Tokyo, the Japanese neighbourhood. Besides,' Mollie added bitterly. 'All Orientals look alike, don't they? Little yellow people with slanty eyes. That's what Grace herself told me years ago. Sometimes I wonder what the hell we're fighting about. Maybe we're as bad as they are.'

'You're over-reacting,' Nick said quietly. 'For one thing,

we're not as bad as they are. For another, it's not impossible to understand. The Japs have swallowed up just about everything between Honolulu and Melbourne. If you're in San Francisco or LA it must feel as if you're next. And there you are with about a hundred thousand resident spies.'

'Horseshit,' Mollie said.

'Yeah, it is. I was only playing devil's advocate.'

They were in St James's Park, sitting on a bench on a day that seemed remarkably like spring. The sun shone, the birds were singing, it was easy to ignore the air-raid shelter which had been erected a few yards away, and the fact that by nightfall it would doubtless be winter again. 'Where in California?' Nick asked.

'In Santa Anita, the race track. That's where they put them. Some of them anyway. The government's taken over some inland sites, made relocation camps, but not too many. None of the other states want any part of them.'

'I suppose Wild Bill told you all this,' Nick said.

'Yes. Indirectly. When I was home in November I asked him to see if he could locate Grace, because mom said she hadn't heard from her in ages. I got this cheery news yesterday.'

'I think about that sometimes,' he said softly.

'What?'

'That you must have connections with these people. Secret ways of sending and getting messages. What is it, do you leave notes in a hollow tree trunk somewhere?'

'Don't be an ass. I meet a guy, we talk, that's all.'

He didn't reply. A bird sang, a sweeter song than the others, one you had to notice. 'Is that a nightingale, do you think?'

'I don't know, I've no idea what a nightingale sounds like.'

'... and a nightingale sang in Berkeley Square,' Nick sang softly.

She smiled despite her black mood. 'How long since you've played the piano?' she asked suddenly.

'I don't know, since I was a kid. No, wait, it was early in 1940, before France fell. Steve and I were in Calais. We went into a bar and there was a piano, and for some reason I sat down and played. I think I was drunk out of my skull. Every-

435

body started singing, I remember that.'

Mollie thought about France and about Steve. 'Is it going to come this year do you think, the second front?' That's how everyone referred to an allied invasion of Europe, as a second front. It was talked about constantly, particularly now that the Americans were in the war, but it never seemed to happen.

'I don't know,' he said. 'Somehow I don't think so. But things are looking up a bit, so maybe it will.'

Looking up because the Red Army was pressing on with a counter-offensive and the siege of Stalingrad had been lifted; because the US Navy had won the Battle of Midway and the Marines had landed at Guadalcanal; and because last November the British had retaken El Alamein and turned the tide in North Africa. 'Maybe the second front *will* come soon,' Nick said again.

'I hope so.' Mollie spoke in a small voice. 'I'm so damned tired of war.'

'Aren't we all.' Nick reached for her hand, holding it in his, each conscious of the other's flesh through the gloves they wore. 'Chin up, kid. We've had all the bad news. There's got to be some good stuff on the way.'

He was wrong.

High summer of 1943, an overcast humid day with the smell of thunder in the air. Late afternoon on a Friday. Time to meet Jack. Today Mollie felt good about that. She'd received a letter from Zena that morning: her mother wrote that everything was fine, and she had one really good piece of news.

'Grace Mitsuno's come back from California. She was mistaken for a Jap and put in one of those awful camps, but finally someone started to pay attention to her case and she was set free. Isn't that grand? Now if we only had Kate back and Grace could find Lee, everything would be perfect.'

Mollie was pretty sure she knew who it was who had provoked an interest in Grace's case. She was grateful, and meant to tell Jack so, and ask him to pass the message on.

They had given up the Lyons Tearoom as soon as Mollie's leg healed. Jack much preferred the open air. She left Broadcasting House and hurried towards lower Regent Street. American enlisted men were everywhere. New York on the Thames, Sandra called it. Mollie grinned when she thought of that. A tall freckled-face sailor thought she was giving him the come on. 'Hi, doll. I've got five of your English pounds in my pocket and I'm dying to spend it on some nice little London lady.'

'Then youse is gonna' have to keep lookin', sailor,' Mollie told him in a broad imitation of stage Brooklynese.

The sailor looked startled at first, then his face broke into a wide smile. She'd kept walking, now he turned and ran after her. 'Hey, lady! Wait a minute. I know who you are. I recognized your voice. You're Mollie Pride, aren't you? C'mon, I know you're Mollie Pride. I've been listening to you for years.'

He caught up with her and she stopped. How young he looked, how vulnerable. 'Yes, I'm Mollie Pride. How long have you been here? Where are you from?'

'From Wyoming. And I've been here about three days. Imagine me running into Mollie Pride in London.' He shook his head in wonderment. 'Nobody at home's going to believe me.'

Wyoming. How come people who'd never even seen the ocean all seemed to wind up in the Navy? Mollie smiled at him and reached into her bag for a pencil and a piece of paper. 'What's your name, Wyoming?'

'Larry, ma'am. Larry Whiterock.'

To Larry Whiterock, she wrote, *good luck and best regards.* Mollie signed her name with a flourish. 'There, now they'll believe you.'

'Yeah, they sure will.' He frowned. 'I wish it was a picture though. Nobody will believe you're so pretty, and so young. How can you be so young when I've been hearing you since I was a kid?'

'I started early, when I was six. And I'm sorry, I don't have a picture. Don't carry them around. In fact, that's the first autograph I've ever given in my whole life.'

'Really? How come?'

'Nobody's ever asked me before.'

Larry Whiterock grinned at her. 'I don't suppose you'd

437

like to come and have a beer with me?' he asked shyly. 'Or maybe just a cup of coffee.'

'I'm sorry, I can't. Tell you what though, there's a club for US servicemen around the corner there on Oxford Street. I hear the best-looking girls in London are waiting, and they like sailors best of all. Give it a try.'

He said he would, and loped off down the street, turning once to wave at her. Mollie waved back and watched him a moment. He was a baby, a little boy. What was he doing over here wearing a uniform when he ought to be a cowboy somewhere on the western plains? Making war, as they all were. It wasn't until she got to Oxford Circus where Jack was waiting for her that it occurred to Mollie that the sailor from Wyoming might well be her age. She'd turned twenty-three last month. A lot of people would say she was a baby too.

She walked up to Jack and nodded a greeting. He doffed his cap the way he always did, then put it back and started walking. Mollie fell into step beside him. They headed west towards Marble Arch. After a few moments Mollie held out her customary envelope. Jack didn't take it. 'Hang on a bit.' His voice sounded gruff.

In about ten minutes they came to Hyde Park. Jack led her into the park itself, skirting an air-raid shelter and making for an empty bench under a sycamore tree. 'You're not in a hurry, are you?' he asked.

'No, I'm in no hurry.' Mollie was more puzzled by the question than anything else. Jack always gave orders; when he said 'jump' he expected her to ask how high. Today he sounded apologetic, deferential. It was out of character. 'What's the matter?' she asked him. Without realizing it she'd clenched her fists and she was gritting her back teeth together. The organism preparing itself for fight or flight. 'What's happened? Is it something to do with my sister Kate?'

Jack shook his head. 'I don't know anything about your sister, sorry.'

What Mollie noted was that he hadn't denied that something was the matter. 'What is it then? Please, tell me and get it over with.'

438

'Don't want to forget your letter,' he said softly, holding out his hand.

Mollie gave it to him. 'There's practically nothing in it. I don't have anything to report these days.'

'That's okay. We know you're keeping your eyes open.'

Another conciliatory remark. 'Please,' she repeated.

'Jesus,' he murmured. 'I hate this. Why the bloody hell does it have to be me?'

Mollie didn't look at him. 'Steve,' she whispered. 'If it's not Kate it has to be Steve.'

Jack's sigh had about it a slight air of relief, as if by guessing she'd made it a little easier on him. 'Yeah. I'm sorry as hell. Ain't nothin' more I can say, is there?'

She needed to know for sure, to hear him say it. 'Is he dead?'

He didn't say it, simply nodded his head.

'Where did it happen? How?'

'France. We went over again last month. He was supposed to be back in a week, but he didn't come.'

'You can't be sure about it then,' she said eagerly. 'He may only be in hiding. Maybe something went wrong.'

'We're sure. I'm sorry. We know for certain.'

'How can you?' Mollie demanded.

'Don't ask,' Jack said softly. 'I don't think you want to know.'

'Yes.' She hissed the word at him. 'Yes, I do. I have to know.'

He stared up at the leaves of the tree, which hung limply in the heat. 'Very efficient the Gestapo. When they're done they take a picture of the corpse. We've got people who manage to copy them and get the pictures back to us. So we know.'

The nausea came in uncontrollable wave, it rolled through her. Mollie gagged and learned forward. Jack put his arm around her shoulders. 'Take it easy,' he murmured. 'Breathe through your mouth. Ah, go ahead. Puke if you want to, why the hell shouldn't you?'

She didn't actually throw up, she had the dry heaves for a couple of moments, then they subsided. 'I'm all right,' she murmured.

'Sure you are.' Jack patted her shoulder. 'Tough as bloody nails, like the rest of us. Anyway, tougher than them. They'll find that out in the end.'

She wanted to cry, but no tears came. 'You're sure of that, aren't you? We're right and they're wrong, and it doesn't matter what it costs to defeat them?'

'I'm sure. You are too. You're only having doubts today because you've had bad news. C'mon, I'll walk you home.'

Mollie shook her head. 'No, you go ahead. Leave me here. I'm okay. Really.'

He protested for a while, but she insisted. Eventually he got up and walked away and left her alone.

It was nine in the evening when Mollie found herself on the Fulham Road. She'd been walking for hours. There was a pub on the corner of Beaufort Street. The blackout curtains were drawn and no light showed, but she could hear the sounds of Friday night bonhomie. She pushed open the door and went in, and stood by the bar.

'Looking for someone, miss?' Ladies didn't go alone to pubs, the bartender's assumption was natural.

'Yes, not here exactly. I mean I don't know ...'

He stared at her. 'You okay? St Stephen's Hospital is right across the road. You want someone to take you over there?'

'No, no, I'm fine. I'm looking for a friend who lives on Fulham Road. I don't know the address. A woman about my age, her name's Lois Lane. She's in the WVS, an American like me.'

He thought for a moment, pouring a small sherry while he did so. 'Here, drink this. You look like you could use it.'

'Thank you. Lois Lane,' Mollie said again.

'Yeah, wait a minute, I do know. Superman's girl friend. Like in the funny papers. Hang on a minute, I think my missus knows her.'

He disappeared into the back, calling out to a woman at the other end of the bar that he'd be right back. He returned in five minutes. 'Number 26, about thirty yards up the road on the other side. My missus knows her, like I thought.'

'Thank you. What do I owe you for the drink?'

'On the house, love. Take care of yourself. You're looking a bit done in.'

Mollie thanked him again as she left.

Number 26 was a red brick building with a newsagent's shop on the ground floor, and a pair of windows above which might well belong to a flat, though with the blackout you couldn't be sure. Mollie climbed the narrow stairs and listened at the door. She heard the sounds of the radio. The light music programme on the Home Service. She took a deep breath, then knocked.

'Yes?' Lois Lane opened the door and stared into the darkened hall.

'It's me, Mollie Pride.'

'Oh.'

'Please, may I come in?'

The other woman stepped aside without saying anything. Mollie walked into a small living room. Cosy, comfortable. Exactly the way she'd expect Lois Lane's home to look. 'I'm sorry,' she said. 'I don't mean to make it worse. But it seems as if you have to know. I don't think anyone will tell you if I don't.'

The blonde sucked in her breath. 'How did it happen?' she whispered. 'When?'

More or less the same questions Mollie had asked. And like Mollie she'd known without having to hear the actual words. 'Some time in the last month. He was captured behind enemy lines in France.'

'Then he could be a prisoner ...'

She had said that too. Mollie shook her head. 'No. I'm sorry, but no.' She saw the other woman's stricken face, almost stretched out her hand in comfort, then snatched it back. 'He'd have wanted you to know, not go on hoping and waiting and never being sure. I didn't come out of spite, please believe me.'

'I know.'

'I came because you're the real widow,' Mollie said before she left. 'And to tell you I'm sorry. I mean it, I am. For everything.'

In the shadowy room Kate could hear the summer rain thrumming on the shoji screen. All the while she felt the soft futon beneath her, held him close, traced his beloved face with her fingertips, sensed herself unfolding like a flower until that ineffably sweet moment when together they burst into glorious bloom — throughout that exquisite time the staccato sound of the raindrops provided a counterpoint.

'I like it when we love in the rain,' she whispered when it was over and he lay beside her, his head pillowed on her breast in gentle rest. 'It's like music.'

Lee lifted his head and smiled at her. 'In Japanese that's what it's called, the best part at the end, it's called "the clouds and the rain". Same thing in Chinese.'

'The clouds and the rain. That's nice.' Kate laughed softly. 'What's it called in English? I don't know, do you?'

'Orgasm.'

'No!'

'Yes,' he insisted. 'Why are you looking so astounded?'

'It's such an ugly word for something so beautiful.' She rolled over, putting one leg across him because touching every part of him with every part of her was blissful. 'I prefer the clouds and the rain.'

'I have to admit it's more poetic.'

'No,' Kate said. 'Not only that. It's truer.'

He kissed her. 'You're true, the truest thing in my world. Now get up, my love. I have to talk to you, I can't do it when you're lying here being so beautiful and so tempting.'

They rose and tied themselves into the kimonos they'd discarded an hour earlier and went into the next room and sat on the mat. Lee leaned forward and took both Kate's hands in his. 'It't time,' he said.

'Time for what?'

'To go home.'

She drew in one long breath, started to say something, excitement and joy evident in her voice. 'No,' he interrupted. 'Don't talk, just listen to me. It's going to be very hard. Sometimes I think it will be impossible ...' His words trailed away, then he gathered his strength and continued. 'But I'm sure it's going to work. It has to.'

'Of course it will work!' She put her hands on his shoulders. 'You'll make it work. You can do anything, my darling.'

Lee took her hands in his again, kissed both palms. 'I'm

going to try my damndest, there's not much choice. Kate, you have to understand something, but you mustn't repeat it. Not to anyone, not even Yoko.'

'I can't say anything to anyone, especially not Yoko. Nobody here understands English except you.'

He smiled. 'That's true. But later ... Never mind, that part isn't important now. What you have to know now is that Japan is going to lose this war. The Americans and the Australians are getting stronger every day. They're taking back the Pacific islands, one at a time and it's slow going, but they're taking them back. Sooner or later they'll get to these islands, to Japan itself. I think it's going to be sooner.'

Lee, does that make you happy? Do you want Japan to win?' Her words were barely audible, a whisper so small that if he wanted to he could pretend he hadn't heard.

He didn't do that, instead he took her face in his hands. 'Right now the only thing that matters is to get you out of here alive. Do you understand? The *only* thing. Kate, if it gets bad, when it gets bad, when we're under direct attack here, nothing I could say or do would save you. Soju and Buntamo and the others, they'd take out their feelings on you.'

In his eyes she read the full horror of that future, the things he didn't say. 'I understand.'

'Good. So you are going to do exactly what I tell you, right? You're not going to argue or question me?'

'I love you,' she said. As if that were the answer to everything.

'I love you,' Lee echoed. 'I love you and I'm going to get you out.'

17

Towards the end of September Mollie received a letter from the Governor General of Canada telling her that her husband had died defending his country and the Commonwealth. At this time it was not possible for the Governor General to discuss the circumstances of Corporal Rogers's death, but he had displayed valour above and beyond the call of duty and his name was being put forward for a posthumous Victoria Cross.

My darling hero, Mollie thought, holding the official letter in limp hands. My crazy darling hero. A Victoria Cross, he'd have loved that. His eyes got all misty whenever they played 'God Save the King'. Once she'd jokingly accused him of being a closet Englishman and he'd said, 'Yeah, I guess I am. Must be the Saskatchewan side of me. Nobody better find out how soppy I really am ...'

'Well, they'll know eventually,' Mollie whispered aloud, folding the letter and putting it carefully in a drawer. 'Someday they'll know how much you loved them, how much you were willing to risk.'

Love. She thought about that a lot these days. She *had* loved Steve, really and truly loved him. But as a husband? Hard to say. What did she mean when she asked herself that question? What had their stormy, fraught, nearly seven years together proved? What had it actually been?

Mollie thought about the happiest married couple she knew, Phil and Sandra. Against all the odds, that unlikely alliance had resulted in two people who glowed whenever they were in the same room, who found excuses to touch each other's hands, to smile secret smiles, to laugh at private jokes — it hadn't ever been like that with her and Steve. Doomed from the first crazy minute, that's what Nick had said about her marriage. He was probably right. Nick ...

He was the one person she could tell about the medal, and he was unavailable. Nick had persuaded Mutual to let him go back out in the field. He'd wanted to go with the Allied troops to Salerno after Italy surrendered on 8 September. They'd talked him out of that. Then it became apparent that the Nazis were going to fight for every inch of Italian territory and there was no holding him back. This wasn't the second front, but it was the closest thing to it yet to occur, and Nick Frane was going to be there.

Thinking, as she so often did, about Nick and Steve, Mollie gave the Governor General's letter a last look, then closed the drawer and picked up her bag and left for work.

She entered the street as a vast number of planes appeared overhead. Mollie heard their drone and paused to look up. Nothing to be frightened of this time. These were ours. American most likely, since it was daylight. The RAF flew by night, the USAF by day. Both carried out the same mission. Bomb Germany. Bomb and bomb and bomb. In the newspapers there were discussions about military targets and the interruption of war production. To most Londoners the incessant raids meant only one thing. 'Pay 'em back,' people said.

It was as Nick had predicted. The Nazis were reaping what they had sown, full measure pressed down and running over. The stories of the firestorms over Hamburg and Berlin were horrifying, but the seedbed was right here in the rubble of London. Mollie looked at the blackened crater across the road; the little pink wild flower called London Pride had colonized it, softening the raw and painful edges. The planes of vengeance darkened the sky as she walked on.

'Miss Pride, there's someone asking for you. He's in reception.'

Mollie smiled at the young secretary poking her head around the temporary partitions which created what Mollie called her black hole. 'Thanks. Where's "reception" these days?'

'Upstairs on the ground floor. They've finally cleared away enough of the debris to use part of it.'

Mollie finished checking the programme schedule she'd been working on — a series of talks with women from many different social strata, who had in common only that they were married to soldiers fighting in Italy this cold, wet March of 1944 — initialled it, and put it in her 'out' box. Then she pulled her fingers through her hair, checked her stocking seams with a backward glance, and ran up the stairs.

An elderly lady with a telephone pressed to her ear sat behind a battered desk just inside the front door. To her left were half a dozen mismatched chairs and a table. Only one person was sitting in this makeshift waiting area, a child. Mollie approached the receptionist. She wasn't speaking, she seemed to be waiting for someone on the other end of the line. 'Excuse me,' Mollie said, 'did someone ask for me?'

The woman took the receiver from her ear and held it to her breast. 'Yes. He wanted Nick Frane first. When I told him Mr Frane wasn't in London, he asked for you.' She nodded in the direction of the little boy. Mollie raised her eyebrows, then went over to him.

'Hello, I'm Mollie Pride. Did you want to see me?'

The youngster jumped up. But he wasn't a youngster, she could see that now that she was standing next to him. Her visitor was a tiny Oriental man. His head barely reached her chin and he looked as if a stiff breeze would knock him over, but he didn't have a young face and on the seat beside him was a furled umbrella, a folded overcoat, and a bowler hat. Older than her, quite possibly.

'I am Kenneth Wu,' he announced. He had a high-pitched sing-song voice. 'You are Mollie Pride?'

'Yes, that's right. What can I do for you?'

'First, please to tell me, Mr Nicholas Frane is not here?'

'No, Nick's in Italy. He's covering the campaign.'

The man looked unhappy at this information. 'Yes,' he murmured, more to himself than to her. 'Very bad waste of time. Italians cannot decide what side they are on. Not worth fighting over.'

'They did decide,' Mollie explained. 'But the Germans didn't approve of their decision. Now, what did you want to see me about?'

The dark Oriental eyes studied her, looked her up and

446

down. 'Campaign in Italy may take a long time.' He was still murmuring to himself. 'Mr Frane may be delayed, yes. I must talk to you.'

Suddenly it dawned on her that this funny little man was not a joke. Someone asking for Nick or for her must be aware of the connection between them. So whatever he wanted, it had to be something personal. *Kate*. The name sounded in the back of Mollie's mind like a trumpet fanfare, a blaring warning of momentous news to follow. *Kate*. What's this about?' she demanded.

'Please, what is the name of your mother?'

'My mother?' It couldn't be anything to do with her mother. Her mother was safe in New York. 'My mother?' she repeated.

'Yes. Please, tell me her name.'

'Zena Driscoll, but what does she ...'

'Thank you, that is correct answer. And what is the name of the village in which you lived when little girl?'

'Red Hook. Look, why are you interrogating me?'

'Please, two more questions only.' He was still whispering, still speaking in a rapid breathless way that lent a sense of urgency to each word. 'Tell me please how you call the house of your mother.'

Mollie had to bite her lip to keep from screaming in frustration. 'Hillhaven.'

'Yes, thank you, very good answer. And when you were small girl you were on radio programme, acting to be a very bad child. Please tell me how you are called when you pretend to be that child.'

'Little Brat,' but this is ridiculous. There are dozens of people right here in this building who can tell you that I'm Mollie Pride.'

Kenneth Wu nodded solemnly. 'They can tell me that you are the lady they think is Mollie Pride. I must be sure you have been Mollie Pride always.'

'Well I have. I guarantee it. Now, why do you care?'

The Oriental inclined his head toward the receptionist. She had finished with the telephone and was watching them with frank curiosity. 'Please, we cannot speak here.'

Mollie looked around the lobby. There were ropes and

sandbags everywhere, delineating areas till considered unsafe, but a path had been cleared between them and she could see a few doors open at the far end of the corridor. 'Come with me, maybe we can find something.'

A number of offices had been put back in use, one more was obviously being prepared for occupancy, but it was still empty. 'In here,' Mollie led the way into the small space which contained a desk but no chairs. 'Now, what's this all about?' she asked again. 'How did you know all those deep dark secrets of my past?'

He paused in the doorway, surveyed the corridor, then closed the door. He walked around the desk and peered out the grimy window. Finally he seemed satisfied. 'We are safe,' he pronounced.

'I'm glad to hear it.'

She studied him and waited. He wore a three-piece pinstripe suit, but despite that, and despite the furled umbrella and bowler hat he carried, he did not look like an Englishman. This disparity was not because he was an Oriental, it was something in the cut of his clothes, the way he wore them. This tiny man looked as if he'd disguised himself as an Englishman.

The man knew she was examining him. He waited for her to finish, then he bowed solemnly. 'I am Kenneth Wu,' he said again. 'Lee sent me.'

Mollie looked blank.

'Lee,' the little man insisted. 'Your old friend, Lee.'

Mollie's eyes opened wide and she drew a sharp breath. 'Do you mean Lee Mitsuno?'

'Yes. He gave me something for you.'

'But is Lee in England? Where did you see him?'

Kenneth Wu was carefully unscrewing the handle of his umbrella. 'Lee is not in England, no. It does not matter where I saw him.' He had the umbrella in two pieces now and he reached into the shaft of the larger portion and withdrew a tube of very thin paper. 'This is for you.'

Mollie took it. She looked at him a moment, then she unrolled the paper. It contained only two sentences. The first said, *Marseilles-les-Aubigny, 10/3/33, after dark.* The second was yet more terse, merely three words: *Come for K.*

Mollie stared at the message, read it twice. Finally she raised her head. 'Where did you get this?' she whispered. 'How?'

'Lee gave it to me,' Kenneth Wu repeated.

She was tingling with sudden fear, with caution and doubt, and with a rising sense of elation she knew she had to suppress until she was sure. 'Where did he give it to you? Where did you see him? Why should I believe any of this?'

'"Where" and "how" have no meaning today,' Kenneth Wu said softly. 'I must know only if you understand. You will be there? It is very urgent I am told this.'

Mollie looked at the message again. She had no idea where the place mentioned was; in France, obviously, but where was a mystery. That didn't matter now, the only important thing was whether the summons and the promise were genuine. 'I can't answer that unless and until I know you're telling the truth,' she said.

'Yes, it is the truth.'

'So you say.'

Kenneth Wu reached again into the shaft of his umbrella. This time he withdrew a small square of red silk. 'I am told to give you this, so you will know I am genuine messenger.' He held out the silk, it was folded into a packet which fitted in the palm of his hand. Please, unwrap it.'

Mollie took it and did as he asked. Within the folds of what looked like a handkerchief was a clump of ash blonde hair. There was no mistaking the colour, she would swear it was Kate's hair. 'Oh no,' she moaned, clutching her stomach and bending forward. 'Oh, God, no ...'

'Please, Miss Pride, please. What is wrong?'

'That's my sister's hair. What have you done to her?'

Kenneth Wu was so agitated he was rising and falling on the balls of his feet, almost dancing on the bare wood of the office floor. 'No, no. You do not understand. Nothing has been done. The lady is missing only some hair. It is not important, it will not hurt her.'

'She's alive?' Mollie demanded. 'You swear she's alive?'

'On the souls of my ancestors,' the man said. 'I swear to you that when I was given the message she was alive.'

'What ancestors might those be, Mr Wu?' Her voice

449

became a low growl. 'What goddamn ancestors am I supposed to trust? Are you Japanese?'

He stopped dancing and stood quite still. 'Ancestors are not damned by God, I assure you. And I am not Japanese.' Wu all but spat out the word. 'If I were Japanese I would kill myself. I am half Chinese, half English.'

Mollie wrapped her arms around her torso to try and stop trembling. 'I'm sorry, I didn't mean to offend you. Like most westerners, I can't tell the difference. I'm sorry,' she said again.

'Nothing to be sorry for, you are brave lady I am told. Very big enemy of the God-cursed Japanese and the God-cursed Germans. I too am their enemy. It is good *joss* that we meet. Good luck you say in English, but luck is not the same as *joss*, no, no. *Joss* is much better than luck.'

Mollie was still shaking. 'I can't figure this. How did you get here? How did you get these things?'

Kenneth Wu sighed. 'You are one very American lady, always asks questions. Lee gave me the things.'

'But how? Has he seen Kate? Where is Lee?'

'He is where he must be.'

'That's no answer.'

'It is the only answer I can give you, Miss Mollie Pride. Perhaps ...' He hesitated, seemed to make up his mind. 'Perhaps if I remind you that I am enchantingly small, small enough to fit in rice sack, say ... Will that help?'

'You came to England in a rice sack?'

The Chinese broke into a broad grin. 'No, to come here is much easier than that. I told you, I am half English. English half has British passport. Very good passport entirely legitimate. Gives me the right to return to the mother country.'

It took Mollie only a few hours to make up her mind what to do. By six in the evening she was knocking on the door of 29 Berry Street in Islington. Nobody answered. She knocked again. Still no answer. The third time, she banged her fist on the wood and shouted.

'Hold your bloody horses, I'm coming.'

Mollie heard Jack's voice before he opened the door. 'You,' he said looking at her in obvious surprise. Then he reached out, pulled her inside, closed the door and locked it. 'What are you doing here? What's wrong?'

'I have to talk to you.'

He was unshaven, his shirt hung out of his trousers, and his feet were bare. She must have wakened him, at six in the evening. Apropos of nothing it occurred to her that this was the first time she'd seen him without his cap. 'I'm sorry,' she said. 'It's urgent.'

'Yeah, well hang on a second, I'll get ...'

'Jack,' a woman's voice interrupted. 'Who is it?'

Mollie glanced up. The woman she'd seen twice before was standing at the top of the stairs, peering down into the gloom of the hall. This time she wasn't in a housedress and a bandanna, she wore an old chenille bathrobe and she was clutching it to her in such a way that it was obvious she was naked beneath. Mollie realized what it was she'd interrupted. 'I'm sorry,' she murmured again.

'Not to worry.' Jack turned to the woman at the top of the stairs. 'It's for me, love. One of my admirers couldn't stay away. Get us some tea, will you? That's a good girl.' He took Mollie's arm and led her into the small sitting room. It was the same room in which almost three years earlier she'd met with Bill Donovan and he'd told her that Kate was in Japan.

Jack found a pack of Players lying on a table and held the cigarettes out to her. Mollie shook her head.

'Forgot you didn't smoke.' He lit one for himself. 'Sit down,' he said, the cigarette dangling between his lips. 'Tell me what's so bloody urgent it couldn't wait until Friday.'

'I have to go to France.'

Jack grinned. 'Do you now? Well, I think the Cook tours have stopped. For the duration, like.'

'Don't joke, this is serious. I have to go. Some of your people know how to get me behind the enemy lines. I want you to contact them. Arrange it.'

'What people would that be?' He didn't look at her when he spoke. He was blowing smoke rings and studying them.

'The Baker Street Irregulars. A guy named Will. A bald man. He wears thick glasses.'

The door opened before Jack could answer. The woman came in. She still wore the bathrobe and she was carrying a tray with two thick mugs. 'It's hot,' she said. 'But I can't say nothin' else for it. Stewed. We're out of tea, I had to warm up what was in the pot.'

'That'll do fine, love,' Jack said gently. 'Go on back upstairs. I'll come soon as I can.'

Without her bandanna and the shapeless housedress the woman was really quite pretty in a tired, washed-out sort of way. She must have been very pretty once, Mollie thought. Before the war. 'Thank you,' she murmured as she took the mug of tea.

'Don't mention it.'

The woman left the room. Jack sipped his tea and studied Mollie and didn't say anything.

'Will,' she reminded him. 'He's a Londoner. You must know him.'

'Yeah, maybe I do.'

'Fine. That makes it simple. Get in touch with him, tell him I have to go to France. He can arrange it.'

'Just like that.'

'Yes,' she said. 'Just like that.'

'It's not a bloody travel agency,' Jack said. But there was no malice in his words, not even real scorn. Mollie felt a surge of hope. He stirred his tea, still didn't look at her. 'It's not easy to do, you know. So you better tell me why you want to go.'

She'd already decided about this part. It was an entirely predictable question, and she saw no point in lying. In this instance the truth was the most persuasive weapon she possessed. 'My sister has been a prisoner for four years. If I go to France I can get her out.'

Jack's eyes narrowed. 'Well, well. Your sister? You're sure?'

'I'm sure.'

'Well, well.'

'You already said that. What does it mean? Will you help me?'

He shrugged. 'Not up to me, love. All I can do is pass the message on. I'll do that. Let you know next Friday.'

'That's not fast enough. I have to be someplace called Marseilles-les-Aubigny on 10 March. That's next Tuesday.

There are only eight days to set it up.'

Jack took a pencil and a piece of paper from the table near his chair. 'Spell the name of that place.'

Mollie did, and she repeated the date and told him she was to be there after dark.

'That's all?' he said, looking up. 'No other instructions?'

'None.'

'Any idea where this place is?'

'I looked it up in an atlas at Broadcasting House. It's a tiny little town near the Loire. That's all I know.'

'Okay.' He folded the paper and tucked it in his shirt pocket. 'Now tell me how you heard about this. Who told you your sister would be in this Marseilles whatever on the tenth?'

Mollie shook her head. 'No, I'm not going to tell you that. Put me in touch with Will, I'll tell him.'

'You tell me, or I won't bother passing on the message.'

'No,' she repeated stubbornly. 'I'm not telling anybody but Will.' She'd decided this before as well. It was a small gift she could make to Kenneth Wu. If he wanted to put his enchantingly small self beyond the reach of these people she would give him a brief period of grace in which to do it. Maybe he could find a sack of rice somewhere in London. 'That's final,' she added.

'Final, is it?' Jack was silent a moment, then he chuckled. 'Okay. It doesn't matter to me. Go on home, love. Sit tight. If Will wants to see you he'll be in touch.'

The summons came soon after midnight; in the early hours of Wednesday morning they gave her a small serving of hope.

The room where they spoke was airless, and blue with cigarette smoke which was making Mollie's eyes water. Will had escorted her down to the basement twenty minutes previously when she'd arrived at the house on Baker Street. That had astounded her, she'd thought they called themselves the Baker Street Irregulars only because of Sherlock Holmes. It hadn't occurred to her that the spies really did operate out of Baker Street.

'Not likely to occur to anyone else either,' Will had said

453

when she commented on it. 'Bloody good disguise that is sometimes, doing the obvious.'

Now he wasn't talking, just staring at the maps he had spread on the table. He was leaning over them and squinting at the tiny print from behind his glasses, with a cigarette dangling from his lips raising yet more clouds of smoke.

'Could I open that door a bit?' Mollie asked. 'I'm choking.'

'What? Oh, yeah, sure.' The answer was offhand and he didn't look up when he spoke. Mollie went to the door and opened it. The hall beyond was cold and smelled stale, but at least some of the smoke could get out. 'Has to be the canal,' Will said.

'What canal? I don't understand.' She went back and stood beside him.

Will's thick finger traced a line on the map. 'This here's the Canal Lateral de la Loire. That place you're supposed to go, Marseilles-les-Aubigny, it's on the canal. That's its only bleedin' claim to fame. So it has to be the reason they picked it.'

'I see. But ...' She had to stop speaking to cough.

Will looked up. 'Sorry,' he murmured. He stubbed out the cigarette. 'Now tell me again what he said. The little chink.'

'I've told you five times.' Mollie didn't try and keep the frustration from her voice. 'What good does it do to tell you again? Are you going to help me or not?'

'Listen, ducky, you're edgy, nervous. I understand, but it won't help. They tell me you're real good at your job. Well believe me, I'm real good at mine. So you just do what I tell you and everything will be fine. I want to hear it all again. From the first minute you met the little chink at Broadcasting House.'

She was offended by his characterization of Kenneth Wu, but there was nothing to be gained by saying so. She told the story again.

'Bleedin' remarkable,' Will murmured when she was through. 'It musta' been his mother was English. Bleedin' remarkable.'

Mollie had no more patience. 'Please, can you help me get there? Will you?'

'Maybe we can. Give me some time to check it out. If we can, we will.'

'Tomorrow's Thursday, I'm supposed to be there Tuesday night. There's so little time.'

'I know. That's part of the problem. But no point in rushing things, ducky. Not things like this. Have to let them get ripe, then they fall off the tree into your hand.' He began folding up the maps. 'One more thing,' he added. 'How good is your French?'

'What French?'

'The French you speak.' He stopped what he was doing and looked at her. 'You speak French, don't you? You bleedin' well wouldn't have considered this caper if you didn't speak French, would you?'

Mollie shook her head. 'Not a word.'

'Bleedin' hell!' Will shoved the maps in a drawer and slammed it. 'That's it then. Can't be done. Go home, ducky. Sorry, we can't help.'

'You have to!' Mollie grabbed his arm. 'Listen, you owe me. You sent my husband into France and he's dead. You owe me!'

Will didn't try to pull away. 'That's how you figure it, is it? We owe you?'

Mollie let him go. 'No,' she whispered. 'That's crazy, I know it is. Steve didn't do it because you told him to. He went because he wanted to, because he believed it was the right thing to do. It's not your fault he's dead, and you don't owe me a damn thing. But you're my only hope,' she added, raising her eyes to his. 'If you won't help me I'll try to get there on my own somehow. But I won't make it. I know that.'

'But you'll try anyway?'

She nodded.

'What do you have in mind? Swimming the Channel maybe?'

'I don't know. I haven't thought about it.'

'Bleedin' martyrs,' he said. 'That's what my job is, playin' nannie to a lot of bleedin' martyrs. Come on, time to go.'

They climbed the stairs in silence, then, when they were at the front door, Mollie asked him again. 'Are you going to help me?'

'We'll have a think about it. I'll talk to a couple of people. Let you know. Goodbye, ducky.'

'Goodbye.'

The call came at seven-thirty on Thursday morning. Mollie was drinking her first cup of tea of the day, looking out of the window and trying to decide what she'd do if she hadn't heard from Will before the day ended. When the telephone rang she dived for it.

'It's me. Okay, you're on.'

'Thank you. Oh, thank you! I'm so grateful. What …'

'Be quiet and listen,' Will said. 'We have to move fast. Ring your boss, say your sick, you'll have to be off work for a few days. Then come 'ere. Same place as the other night. Be expecting you by nine. You got that?'

'Yes, yes I have. I'll be there. What should I pack?'

'Nothing. You come the way you are, ducky. We'll do the rest.'

In none of her imaginings after Yorkshire, none of the sleepless hours she'd spent after she learned what Steve was involved in, had she dreamed the extent of their preparations.

'Nothin' left to chance, ducky,' Will told her. 'Not a bleedin' thing.' It was not an exaggeration.

Will was assisted by two women. They were chatty types, ordinary ladies she would never have noticed if she sat beside them in a bus. What made them all the more remarkable was that they performed their arcane magic as if it were no more extraordinary than cooking or washing and ironing, the sort of things that had doubtless occupied them completely before the war.

'You can call us Fannie and Flo,' they told her in the first ten minutes. Mollie guessed those weren't their real names. It was the least extraordinary of the things that were happening to her. They gave her French ration books and an identity card.

To Mollie the documents looked entirely authentic. 'Where do you get these things? Are they stolen?'

Flo shook her head. 'No, too much of a nuisance that

would be. We have 'em made in Canada.'

'Here's your outfit, ducky.' Fannie called her ducky, the way Will did. 'Not very pretty, but it's French down to the thread and the buttons.'

Mollie took the heavy wool trousers and the black sweater and jacket. They were coarse and they looked well worn, but they were clean.

'Clothes are specially made too,' Flo confided. 'Jewish tailors in Canada, refugees, same as the lot what makes the documents. Doin' their bit, they are. A pretty big bit at that.'

Will came in just then. 'Keep your bleedin' mouth shut,' he growled. 'The less she knows the better it is for her, and for us.'

Flo and Fannie looked properly chastened. They didn't say anything when they handed Mollie a pile of underwear. It was knitted of coarse unbleached cotton, an undershirt and a pair of pants and long black stockings with garters. No bra. She'd never seen such underwear. 'This is what French women wear?' she asked incredulously.

'It's what you'll need to wear,' Will said. 'Don't ask questions, it wastes time. Go in the next room and get changed. Take a shower first. There's carbolic soap in there. Use it. Wash your hair with it as well. Where you're goin' you don't want to be smellin' of fancy shampoo and perfume. And scrub under your fingernails, we don't want no telltale English fluff.'

Mollie emerged half an hour later. There was no mirror so she couldn't see what she looked like. 'Will I do?' she asked.

Fanny looked at her and nodded. 'Give us your things, ducky. I'll do 'em up meself. Have 'em all nicely washed and ironed and waitin' here for you when you get back.'

It sounded rather like a promise made to a child, the kind that the grown-ups knew couldn't be kept. The tooth fairy will put a dime under your pillow.

'Come over here,' Will said.

Mollie went and stood beside him. He was studying a map once more. This one looked even more finely detailed than the one he'd had last night. It was French, Mollie noted. A Michelin road map. Steve and Nick had used identical maps to plan their journeys in the life that had existed before

France fell. The life that seemed like a dream to her now.

'Here's where you're going.' Will put his finger on a tiny dot more or less in the centre of the page. 'Like I told you, it's on the Canal Lateral de la Loire. Bleedin' marvellous, the continental canals. Inland waterways they call 'em. Take you from Holland to the Mediterranean and never have to see the sea once. Built centuries ago. Still good as new. Bleedin' marvellous.'

'Will she come by canal boat?' Mollie didn't want to use Kate's name. She hadn't mentioned it once in this room. It had become a kind of fetish with her, a charm to ward off evil spirits. Like not stepping on the cracks in the sidewalk.

'We think so,' Will said. 'We're counting on it. Anyway, you will. It's the only thing that gives you a tinker's prayer. You couldn't travel through France by bus or train. Not without speaking French. But on a barge ... Well, that's a half-arsed kind of chance.' He spoke quite matter-of-factly; unlike Fanny and Flo, Will made no effort to hide the fact that he thought it unlikely she would get back to Baker Street alive.

Before they left the house he remembered something else. 'Open your mouth,' he commanded.

'My mouth? Why?'

'Look, you have to stop doin' that. Askin' questions. Follow orders, it's the only way. Now, open your mouth.'

Mollie opened her mouth. Will leaned forward and peered at her, steadying his glasses with one hand. 'Okay,' he said after a few seconds. 'No tea stains on your teeth. Lucky, that. French people don't drink much tea.'

The hard-packed sand of the beach was wet and cold. Now that she'd squirmed out of her wet suit and buried it, the dampness easily penetrated even the thick wool of the clothes from Canada. It was blowing hard, and Mollie tasted salt spray in her mouth. She lay on her belly, waiting for the man beside her to touch her arm and signal that they should move.

She could barely see him. In the black moonless night he was nothing more than a hump, a shadow. Once he turned to her, but even then she could see only the whites of his eyes.

458

His face, like hers, had been blackened with cork before they left the small fishing boat which ferried them across the Channel. He didn't say anything, but his eyes asked if she was all right. Mollie briefly inclined her head. He turned away and resumed his study of the line of fortifications dead ahead.

She didn't know where they were. The only thing she could be sure of was that they were on a beach somewhere in France. Some thirty yards inland was a high stone wall. From where she lay Mollie could make out four guard towers rising from the wall. A sentry paced between them, but he wasn't the most frightening thing. What had her so utterly terrified were the searchlights mounted in the towers and playing intermittently over the sand. She kept waiting for the beam of light to fall on them, but it never did. After a few minutes Mollie understood why.

Every once in a while the man beside her signalled that they should roll to the right or the left. The lights worked in a pattern. He knew what it was. Because of the small evasive actions he commanded, the lights never picked them up.

It seemed to Mollie that nothing happened for hours. The lights continued to move across the beach at regular intervals. They rolled to the right or the left. Then finally the man touched her shoulder and pointed straight ahead.

Mollie crawled forward, following him, using her knees and her elbows as he did. She was conscious of the need to drag her feet, the way they'd shown her on the boat. As long as she did that the sweeping contraption attached to the toes of her shoes would rub out the trail her body made in the sand. A crazy rubber broom didn't seem like much protection. Any second she expected the lights to turn towards them. Then there would be the shout. *Achtung!* That's what they said in the movies. *Achtung!*

She felt pressure on her shoulder, her guide signalling her to stop. Mollie froze. On the wall that was now only a few feet away, the sentry had paused to light a cigarette. The red glow of the match lit up his helmet, then died away. A few seconds more, then he resumed his pacing and they crawled forward a few more feet.

The wall got lower at the extreme left. It dwindled away at

the base of a cliff. There were steps. Mollie and the man stopped at the bottom of the flight. She did as he did, released the gear attached to her shoes. He took hers from her and folded the apparatus and slipped it inside his jacket.

There was some activity at the far end of the wall. The sentry was being relieved, chatting a moment to his replacement. In the few seconds of safety created by that distraction Mollie and the man hunched over and ran up the stairs.

She expected another sentry at the top, barbed wire, at least a gate. There was nothing like that. One minute they'd been forcing their way inside an armed camp, the next they'd washed their faces clean with wet handkerchiefs he'd provided and were strolling down the street of a little French town, acting as if they belonged and knew exactly where they were going.

Her companion did know. The streets were dark and unmarked, but he walked on with no hesitation, neither too slow nor too fast. Normal. That had been almost Will's last instruction. 'Do everything you're told without hesitatin' a bleedin' second. Act normal. That's the key. Act bleedin' normal.'

They rounded a corner and came to a series of wharves. Wherever this place was, it was a bargees' town. What looked like dozens of the big, low-slung, flat-bottomed black boats were moored the length of the dock. And there was a guard. Her heart stopped. It actually stopped, Mollie was sure of it. Somehow she kept walking because her guide did. He walked directly to the guard.

The man was in a uniform of some sort, but he didn't look like a soldier. Nonetheless he raised his hand in the Nazi salute. '*Heil Hitler!*'

They'd told her about this before she left London. Mollie knew what she was supposed to do. She couldn't do it. Her arm was frozen to her side. It had nothing to do with morality or defiance. It was purely and simply terror.

The man beside Mollie returned the salute. '*Heil Hitler!*'

Mollie sensed him waiting for her to follow suit. Finally she managed to make her arm move. But she couldn't say anything. She knew her life probably depended on it, but she could not open her mouth.

The guard looked at her a moment, raised his eyebrows, then turned back to her companion. '*La carte d'identité*,' he demanded loudly, holding out his hand.

The man reached into his jacket and pulled something out of his pocket. With his other arm he elbowed Mollie. She put her hand in her pocket, searching for the identity card they'd given her in London, the one that looked like the document her guide had produced. When she'd located it she held it out. Her hand was shaking. Oh sweet God, it was shaking and she couldn't stop it. The guard would know she was an impostor. Stop! she told herself. Stop! Get hold of yourself or it's all over.

The guard didn't look at her when he took the card. He acted as if he couldn't see her trembling hand or smell her fear. But of course he could. Mollie squeezed her eyes shut, waiting for the shout of accusation. Please, she prayed to that half-believed in God she called upon only in moments of desperation. Please, let me die a little bit bravely. The way Steve did. The way that would make Nick proud.

It wasn't a shout, what happened was worse. A searchlight came on and swung toward them. Mollie became aware of the brightness and opened her eyes. The spotlight picked up the three of them. She stood absolutely still. The only prayer she could think of was one Zena had taught her when she was two, before they went on the road. *Now I lay me down to sleep* ...

'*Was ist denn da unten los?*' The German voice came from somewhere above them, at the source of the searchlight.

The guard turned and called out something, held up the two identity cards he still held. The German leaned over and studied the pair of arrivals. Finally he muttered something and turned away. Seconds later the searchlight was turned off and it was dark.

Mollie's eyes hadn't adjusted to the sudden return of blackness when the most extraordinary thing of all happened. The guard laughed. It was a very soft sound, very controlled, but it was laughter. '*Cochon*,' he said under his breath.

She knew that word, she'd heard Steve use it sometimes, it meant pig.

She began to breath a little easier. She sensed the relaxation of tension in the man standing beside her. '*Bonsoir, Henri,*' he murmured. '*Comment ça va?*'

'*Comme toujours. Et vous? Je suis content que vous avez la colis.*'

Mollie's guide said something else in French to the guard. Then he touched her arm and they moved on. Her heart was still pounding. He seemed to know. 'One of ours,' he murmured under his breath. They were the first words he'd addressed to her since they left the ship. 'He said he was glad I'd brought the package. He meant you.'

Mollie's tongue was still so thick with fear she didn't trust herself to reply.

The man kept walking. She trotted beside him, doing her best to keep up. They came to the barge third from the end. He whistled softly and climbed aboard, then turned to her and offered his hand.

Mollie grasped it, grateful for the help because the gap between the barge and the dock was almost too wide for her to negotiate. The man saw the difficulty and tightened his grip, half swinging her forward. She jumped, and felt her feet hit the deck. At last she allowed herself one small sigh of relief.

Another man came out of the shadows. He and Mollie's companion murmured in French for a moment. Then the bargee held out his hand and she realized he meant her to take it. 'This way.'

The English words were spoken so quietly she wasn't at first sure she'd heard them. Then, when she realized she had, and that she was meant to follow him into the wheelhouse, she turned back. The guide who had brought her this far, whom she wanted to thank, was already gone.

The warmth of the wheelhouse was a shock after the sharp cold. So too was the way the place looked. Mollie had imagined a barge was a grimy working boat full of sweaty men and coiled ropes and winches. The cabin she stood in had lace curtains at the window and brass fittings that gleamed in the friendly glow of an oil lamp, and a windowsill lined with potted plants. She stood looking around her and blinked.

'They tell me you don't speak French,' the man said. His English was accented, but perfectly clear.

'No, I'm sorry, I don't.'

He smiled. 'I am sorry too. It makes it much more difficult. We will have to hide you, mademoiselle. We cannot pass you off as my wife's sister or cousin.'

As he spoke Mollie noticed the woman standing beside a small stove. She was about Mollie's size and she too had short curly hair. She was young and very pretty. That was the second surprise of the last five minutes. Mollie had expected a bargee's wife to look like a lady wrestler.

'This is Giselle,' the man said. 'Her English isn't very good, I'm afraid. By the way, I am Emile. They tell me you are called Mollie.'

'Yes, that's right.'

Emile smiled. He had gleaming white teeth which showed to advantage because he also had a thick black beard shot with a bit of grey. 'Welcome aboard the *Ste Vièrge*, Mademoiselle Mollie. I hope we have a good journey.'

18

'We've made a place for you down here. I'm sorry it isn't more comfortable.' Emile led Mollie across wooden planks which made a walkway on top of the coal that almost filled the hold. They had to crouch because the headroom was very limited. At the far end, directly under the wheelhouse Mollie estimated, a depression had been scooped out and lined with newspaper. It was a hollow about three feet in diameter and contained a blanket and a pillow and a large barrel.

'It's fine,' Mollie said. 'Thank you. Look, I'm terribly sorry about all the trouble I'm causing you ...'

'There is no need to be sorry, mademoiselle. These days we are all in the trouble together. It is fortunate that there is not very much coal available, if we had a full load this arrangement would not be possible. As it is ... Here, let me show you the reason for the barrel.' He hoisted her to the top of it. 'If you stand up there your eye level will be above the water line. There's a small peg, do you see it?'

Mollie ran her fingers over the interior of the wooden hull. 'Yes, I have it.'

'If you pull the peg, mademoiselle, you have a peephole. The days can be very long down here, the peephole helps.'

Mollie realized that she was not the first passenger to travel illicitly in the hold of the *Ste Vièrge*.

A quiet voice spoke from somewhere above them. Emile pointed overhead. 'There is a speaktube in the wheelhouse. If we need to, we can communicate with you. That was Giselle saying our supper is ready. It is safe for you to come up and eat with us tonight, mademoiselle. It is the days which are dangerous. On a *peniche* nothing happens at night.'

'Does *peniche* mean barge?' Mollie asked as she followed him back over the plank path.

'Yes. Very good, mademoiselle. You are learning French.'

The supper was surprisingly delicious. Thick onion soup topped with bread and stringy cheese, and a small glass of wine followed by a cup of real coffee, the first she'd tasted since she'd been in America in 1942. 'Thank you,' Mollie said as she helped Giselle clear away the dishes. 'I'm sorry to be using some of your rations.'

Giselle smiled at her, then said something in French to her husband. He turned to Mollie and translated. 'Giselle wants me to say you are not a trouble to us.'

'You are not the trouble,' the woman repeated in halting English. Her accent was very bad, but Mollie understood the words. Tears stung her eyes and she busied herself with drying the soup bowls and hoped the other woman wouldn't notice.

Emile beckoned to her. 'Come here, I will try and explain what we're going to do.'

Mollie joined him at the bare table. 'Is that a map of where we are?'

'On a boat it's called a chart, not a map,' he said with a smile. '*Alors*, you came ashore here, at St-Valéry. And we are here,' his finger traced a route for her, 'on the Canal de la Somme. We have come along the cost from Holland where we picked up that coal you saw below.' He turned to her, grinning broadly. 'As luck would have it, mademoiselle, the coal is to be delivered at Nevers, twenty kilometers south of Marseilles-les-Aubigny.'

Mollie tried to put all her gratitude into her smile. Emile nodded and returned his attention to the chart.

'We will follow the Canal de la Somme as far as Péronne. Then we pick up the Canal du Nord which leads us to the river Oise and then the Seine and Paris.' He paused. 'Paris will be the most dangerous, mademoiselle. The Boche themselves man the locks on the Seine.'

'I see. Does that mean that the other lockkeepers are French, not German?'

'For the most part yes, but they are not all to be trusted because of that. In England and America you have, I think, a romantic idea. You tell yourselves all the French are Resistance fighters waiting for liberation. It is not so.'

Mollie could not reply to that, his voice made it apparent what Emile thought of the Boche, the Resistance, and the rest. 'What is the distance between here and Paris?' she asked instead.

'A little over two hundred kilometers, but *les écluses*, the locks, are few. So we can travel after dark. We should reach Paris in two days, late Saturday.'

'And beyond that, to Marseilles-les-Aubigny?'

'Less distance, but three different canals and many more locks. If we are lucky, perhaps by Tuesday evening.'

'Perhaps? But I have to ...'

'I know,' Emile interrupted. 'I will do what I can, I promise you. A *peniche* is not very fast, mademoiselle, and the locks are not open at night. Not even the Boche can make the lockkeepers work overtime. Giselle and I will do our best; that's all I can promise. The rest is in the hands of *le bon Dieu.*'

Kate had died in January of 1944. Not physically, her body still moved and she breathed, but when she realized that Lee was not leaving Japan with her, the real Kate ceased to be alive. All her life had been desertions and betrayals, one after another, beginning with her father and Miss Dalgliesh. Here was the ultimate desertion. She had been born again in his arms, the woman she should have been had come into belated existence; now she died. Only the shell remained.

'It has to be like this,' Lee said. His eyes pleaded with her to understand. 'I cannot go, you must.'

Kate did not argue. She could find no words to explain to him that he was killing her. If he didn't know that without being told, then everything she'd believed to be true between them was nothing but sham. Her grey eyes darkened and their light went out.

'Don't,' Lee murmured. 'Don't look like that. I can't bear it.'

He touched her hair. It was very short now, and Yoko had dyed it black. Kate wore a workman's faded grey tunic and trousers. Her nails were cut short and roughened with dirt. They'd rubbed dirt into her face as well. It was not a disguise which would survive close scrutiny, but from a distance she would blend with her surroundings in a way she could not do as a tall, exquisitely beautiful blonde woman in a satin kimono.

Lee turned to Yoko and murmured something in Japanese. She answered him. He turned back to Kate. 'It's almost time, they'll come for you in a few minutes. I have to go. My darling,' he added. Only that. 'My darling.'

Yoko bowed and left them alone. Kate watched her leave. Yoko was dressed more or less as she was. Kate did not know if that meant Yoko was going with her. She didn't care. She felt Lee's arms around her, but she could not respond. It was too late, he had killed her.

'Kate,' he murmured. 'I love you, you know that. I wouldn't let us be separated if there was any other way.' And when she still didn't answer, 'Some day we'll be together again. The way we talked about. Don't forget that. It's a promise.'

Then he was gone.

Kate stood alone in the middle of the small room. Yoko returned. She murmured some words. She always spoke to Kate, even though she knew the American woman understood no Japanese. Yoko spoke, and demonstrated what she meant by her tone and her gestures. This time she was asking a question, and holding something in outstretched hands.

Kate took her eyes from the spot where she'd last seen Lee and looked at Yoko. She was offering a pillow. On the pillow was a dagger. Kate stared at it and understood. Yoko was asking her if she wished to exercise the option of a *samurai* woman. Did she want to commit suicide rather than leave Japan without Lee?

The dagger was very beautiful. The blade gleamed and the handle was carved ivory. It must be Yoko's own dagger. Kate remembered Lee telling her that Yoko was *samurai*. Her hand trembled, almost reached out of its own accord, then she drew back. 'No, I have a son.' She shook her head so that Yoko would know her decision. The Japanese woman bowed and withdrew.

Ten minutes later they were leaving Tokyo in a cart filled with corncobs; the two women crouched in the back, straw hats shading their faces, heads bent forward as if they slept. It was the first stage in a journey which would take two months and cross half the world.

Much of it Kate would make alone. Yoko left her after a junk brought them to Shanghai. The two women embraced before they parted. Now Kate was the only female among many men. At first she was afraid, but soon she realized that she was, for some reason she did not understand, a sacred trust. They did the best they could for her, no matter how difficult the route.

The faces of her guardians and guides changed frequently, but for weeks they remained Oriental faces. None of the men could speak her language. Kate was not really aware of where she was during the weeks when she was led across the heart of China. Then the faces changed again.

'Do you speak English?' Kate asked the first Caucasian man she'd seen in four years. He shook his head, but the next day he brought her someone else.

'I speak a little the English,' the man said. He was small and dark and he wore a turban and loose trousers and a tunic. At this point Kate herself was dressed in a strange black garment that covered her from head to toe, and her face was veiled.

'Where am I?' she asked the man.

'In Iran.'

'Iran, I see. When will I be in America?'

The man looked at her strangely. 'I know nothing about America. Only to bring you through Syria to the sea.'

She tried to think what sea bordered Syria, but if she'd ever known she'd forgotten. The man recognized her confusion. 'In English it is called the Mediterranean,' he explained.

Kate nodded. 'Yes, thank you. I understand. Is there war here in Iran?'

'Not now. But there are British soldiers. We must be very careful.'

So he was on the other side, on Lee's side. She nodded again.

The boat that crossed the Mediterranean was very dirty. Kate hated being cooped up below deck with the smell of fish choking her and the constant nausea caused by the rocking motion. At least on the junk she'd been able to smell the ocean and see the sky.

Eventually that part of the trek ended and she was turned over to someone else and brought to a small farmhouse in a countryside she did not recognize. The man who'd collected her spoke no English and she couldn't ask him where she was or where she would go next, but the next day there was a woman. 'Come,' the woman said. 'We must hurry.'

Kate felt a surge of joy at being addressed in her own tongue. 'Where are we going?' she asked eagerly. 'Who are you?'

'We go to the *peniche*.' The woman's voice was gruff. She was the first of the guides who did not speak with gentleness. 'Don't talk now. Later.'

Kate followed her through an early morning mist which did not quite obscure rolling green farmland and trees that reminded her of home. Eventually they came to a canal and the woman led Kate on to a barge and pried up some floorboards and indicated that Kate must climb into the small dark hole she'd revealed. There was room to lie down or to sit, but she could not stand. At first she thought she would suffocate, then she realized that there were airholes cut into the floor above her and she could breathe. They were not, however, big enough to admit light.

The only means she had of measuring the passage of time were the visits of a small girl who brought her food. The child spoke not a word and Kate decided she didn't understand English. She estimated that two days passed before she saw the woman again. 'Please,' Kate pleaded. 'You have to tell me when I'll be in America.'

'America? I do not know anything about that. Only that we can take you as far as Marseilles-les-Aubigny, a little town here in France, then we must turn around. We'll be there in two weeks. I sent the message as soon as you came aboard. So if we're lucky there will be someone to meet you at Marseilles-les-Aubigny. If not ...' She shrugged and went away.

Emile had not got it quite right. The worst was not Paris. Mollie stayed in her hiding place in the hold while they navigated the large locks of the Seine. She didn't even remove the peg and look out of her peephole, just stayed huddled in the coal and prayed. *Now I lay me down to sleep...*

God, that strange half-acknowledged God who was more a creation of her need than any theological reality, seemed to hear. He was listening until Monday afternoon, when they came to the lock at Montargis on the Canal de Briare. Montargis was the final *écluse* before they entered the Canal Lateral de la Loire which would take them to Marseilles-les-Aubigny.

'Mademoiselle, you can come up.' Emile's soft voice came through the speaktube as they left *écluse* thirty-five in the tiny hamlet of Langlée. 'The next lockkeeper is a friend.'

Mollie scurried across the plank path which brought her to the hatch leading to the deck. She pushed it open slowly, as she'd learned to do, and looked. It was a cloudy, overcast day. In the silvery mist she could see that they'd left the small stone houses of Langlée behind, here the canal banks were lined with tall reeds and a few willows. Mollie swept the vista with her eyes. No, there were no fishermen to see her. She opened the hatch the rest of the way and clambered on to the deck, then hurried past the huge coiled lines and into the wheelhouse.

'Good afternoon.' Emile kept his grip on the wheel and looked straight ahead. 'A little fresh air and daylight will do you good.'

Giselle was at the sink, peeling potatoes. Mollie found a knife and began to help her. The Frenchwoman smiled her thanks. 'We make the time good,' she said in her laboured English. 'By tomorrow night, yes.'

'She means we've a good chance to make your rendezvous on time,' Emile said.

'I know. I think her English is perfectly beautiful.' Mollie spoke the words with feeling. 'I think you are both the most beautiful people I've ever met.'

Emile smiled at her. 'Do not glamorize us, Mademoiselle Mollie, we do what needs to be done. That's all.'

'It's not all. Some day, when the war's over, I want you both to come on the radio. I want to tell everyone in

America what you've done.'

Emile chuckled and spoke to his wife in rapid French, obviously repeating Mollie's words. Giselle shook her head and said something. 'She says that bargees don't go on the radio.' Emile translated. 'They are happy only on a barge.'

Mollie had already learned that both Giselle and Emile had been born and raised on the canals. Their families had lived and worked on the *peniches* for as long as either of them could remember. It was a whole world, Mollie had realized, a sub-culture about which most people knew nothing. A fiercely independent world. That was doubtless what made it such a fertile ground for men like Bill Donovan to plough. She was sure that Emile and Giselle were not the only Resistance workers among the bargees. The regimented existence of life under the Third Reich would never appeal to people such as these.

'I think,' Mollie began. She stopped speaking because Emile had said something to Giselle. Straight ahead of them were the gates of *écluse* thirty-four, the first of the two in the village of Montargis. The gates were open. The lock was prepared to receive them.

'I lost my concentration talking to you,' Emile said with a laugh. 'I didn't realize we were so close. It's all right, stay where you are. There's no one around, and as I said, this lockkeeper is one of us.'

Mollie had noted before that the couple alternated the jobs involved in navigating the locks. This time it was Giselle who hurried on to the deck and began preparing the lines. Emile remained at the wheel.

The *écluse* at Montargis was one which descended if you were travelling south. When they entered the lock it was full, after they were safely within its confines the massive iron doors would be shut behind them and the sluice gates at the front opened. The water level would thus be lowered, and the barge with it. Mollie had never before understood how a lock worked. In the three and a half days she'd been aboard the *Ste Vièrge* she had learned a great deal.

She was standing at the sink as the barge glided into position, the window through which she looked at the outside world was a little above the level of the bank. She saw the

471

door of the lockkeeper's cottage open. She saw the German soldiers come out. 'Emile ...'

Her tone alerted him. The bargee jerked his head to the right and saw the Nazis. '*Sacré coeur*,' he cursed softly. 'The Boche.'

One of the soldiers was alongside by this time. He was staring into the wheelhouse, looking straight at Mollie. She returned his gaze because she had no choice. His eyes were blue. Cold eyes. She was close enough to see that.

Emile darted a quick glance to his left, in the direction Giselle had gone. She was not there. A half uncoiled hawser lay abandoned on the deck of the *peniche*. 'She's seen them,' he murmured to Mollie, still keeping his eyes straight ahead and tending the wheel. 'Giselle's hidden herself. You must pretend to be her.'

'But I ...'

'Get out on deck,' he whispered urgently. 'Handle the lines. Don't speak. You don't need to.'

Mollie was still holding the knife she'd been using to peel the potatoes. She glanced at it. Maybe ... Don't be an ass, she told herself. Just do what Emile says. She dropped the knife and hurried out the door of the wheelhouse and picked up the thick line Giselle had been working with.

For a moment she just stood there and held it. What was she supposed to do? How could she convince these soldiers she was a bargee? Do it! Just goddamn do it! There's no other hope.

The *peniche* was snugly fitted into position by this time. The lock was small. On either side its cement sides were a handsbreadth away from the barge. Mollie felt the throbbing of the motor below her feet change as Emile eased back on the throttle and held the craft steady by putting it in reverse. Two of the soldiers had gone up ahead and were starting to turn the wheels that opened the sluice gates. Mollie was still standing frozen on the deck, holding the line. The blue-eyed Nazi was leaning on his rifle, watching her.

She took a step to her right. She had a vague idea what she was supposed to do next as she'd seen both Emile and Giselle do it when she'd been watching them through her peephole. She lifted the end of the line and leaned over to loop it around the bollard.

The Nazi tried to take it out of her hand. '*Fräulein, darf ich Ihnen helfen?*'

She had only the vaguest idea of what he wanted. Mollie stared at him blankly. He asked another question, in French this time. She didn't understand that either. Act normal. That's what Will had told her. Your best bet is always to act as normal as you can. She managed a small smile and relinquished her hold on the line. The soldier looped it over the bollard and handed the free end back to her. Mollie nodded again.

The water level in the lock began to go down. Emile was still at the wheel, watching her. Mollie let the line play through her fingers, using the bollard to keep the *peniche* steady as it descended. The Nazi stayed where he was, staring down at her. He said something else in French. Judging from the tone of his voice, this time it was a comment not a question, but once more she had no idea what the words meant.

Mollie opened her mouth. *Oui.* She could say *oui.* But what if yes was a totally inane response? And what if her accent betrayed her, even in one word? She said nothing, only closed her mouth and managed a weak smile. The blue eyes grew colder. Mollie could smell the doubt being born behind them. And perhaps he could smell her terror. *Now I lay me down to sleep . . .*

The throbbing below her feet died away. The engine of the barge had been shut off. The sudden lack of sound was like the silence of a grave.

Suddenly Emile was there beside her, scurrying up the slimy ladder revealed as the lock emptied. He was chattering to the soldier above them. The soldier replied. Emile said something else.

My shoe, Mollie was thinking. The L pill is in the heel of my shoe. That was the absolutely last thing Will had said. Just before she boarded the boat at Newhaven he told her about the L pill. 'If there's no other way, or if you get in a bad spot and can't take any more, it'll be over quick if you manage to get the pill out and bite it. Swallowing it won't do a damn thing. But if you bite it . . .' He'd snapped his fingers.

473

'Bob's your uncle. It's over in seconds.'

If the Gestapo caught her she would take the L pill. Mollie had decided on that from the first. Stories about the Gestapo were everywhere, what they did and how they did it was not a secret. Mollie knew she couldn't stand up to torture. If they got her she would bite the L pill.

Emile was still talking to the Nazi, attempting to distract him. At the same time he was walking forward to help the other two soldiers open the gates. The one standing beside the barge answered Emile and followed him with his eyes, but he kept glancing back at Mollie. There was a death's head above the peak of his cap. SS.

Mollie took a deep breath. It had to be now. Once they took her they'd strip her and her chance at a quick death would be gone. It would be slow and painful and she knew she'd break. She'd tell them everything, about Baker Street and Jack and Will and Flo and Fanny. She'd tell them about the Jewish tailors in Canada. Oh God, I can't, I mustn't. But I know I will. And afterwards they'll take a picture of my corpse and someone will smuggle it to London ...

She bent down as if she were going to scratch her ankle. The hollow heel of the shoe worked on a swivel action. Her fingers touched it, released the spring. In seconds she could have the pill in her mouth, as long as he didn't know what she was doing.

Suddenly the blue-eyed Nazi moved from the position he'd held so long. He swivelled his body so that he was staring straight at her. Mollie froze, her hand still on her shoe. She couldn't do it with him watching. He would guess and take the pill away. She tugged at the back of her stocking, as if adjusting it, then straightened. The Nazi watched her a moment more, then he glanced down the lock to Emile. A minute later he'd turned and walked back into the lockkeeper's cottage.

Mollie's knees began to shake. The reaction was coming swiftly now, but it was too soon. The pair of soldiers working the gates could still see her. She made herself remain where she was. Finally Emile came back, freeing the line from the bollard as he passed it, and climbing down the ladder with it draped casually over his arm.

As she moved past her he dropped the hawser on the
[d]eck. Mollie picked it up and began coiling it as she'd seen
[G]iselle do. Emile returned to the wheelhouse. In a few
[s]econds they were underway.

[I]t was entirely my fault, mademoiselle. I nearly killed all of
[u]s with my over-confidence.'

'No, Emile,' Mollie protested. 'No. You mustn't say that.
[It] was only because I'm so stupid and never learned French.'

'I had no business allowing you to remain above deck
[w]hile we entered a lock. It was madness, I have been doing
[th]is too long.' Emile's voice betrayed his tiredness. 'I have
[b]ecome careless. My friend in Montargis, he must have been
[c]areless too.'

There was nothing more to be said about the absent lock-
[k]eeper, his fate was all too obvious. Giselle sat at the table in
[th]e wheelhouse. For once her busy hands were still, she used
[th]em only to hold up her head. She murmured something in
[F]rench.

'Giselle wants to know about the second front,' Emile
[sa]id. 'Will it come soon?'

'I don't know,' Mollie had to admit. 'I hope so, but I don't
[k]now.'

'I hope so too. We are all very tired, mademoiselle.
[P]erhaps too tired. I'm not sure we can go on much longer.'

There was nothing for Mollie to say. Another lock loomed
[a]head of them. She started to go below. Giselle put out a
[h]and to stop her, speaking rapidly to Emile at the same time.

'She wants to change clothes with you. In case the Boche
[b]ack there telephoned our descriptions. Quickly, mad-
[e]moiselle. I will go as slowly as I dare.'

Mollie stripped off her trousers and sweater and put on
[G]iselle's. Then, just before she dashed for the hold, Giselle
[t]ouched Mollie's hair and her own and smiled. They looked
[s]omething alike; what had been an amusing coincidence
[th]ree days ago had become a source of salvation, a matter of
[li]fe and death.

Life, Mollie thought as she huddled in the coal, I choose
[li]fe. She was conscious of the L pill still in her shoe. It
[s]eemed to be burning its message into her skin.

'Kate? Is it you?' Mollie took a tentative step forward. T
woman standing in front of her wore black fisherman's oi
skins. Her hair was entirely covered by the brimmed hat.
shadowed her face. 'Kate?'

'Mollie? I don't believe it ... Mollie?'

'Yes, oh yes, darling, it's me.'

They fell into each other's arms, clung together for
moment. hen the door of the canalbank shed was opene
and a man appeared. 'It's time. Come. *Vite!*'

The two women followed him into the dark night.

Marseilles-les-Aubigny was the tiniest of tiny village
Nothing was happening. It was past midnight, there was n
one around. But somehow a barge which hadn't been ther
when Emile dropped Mollie a couple of hours ago was ther
now. 'Someone else will take you back to the rendezvo
point.' Emile had explained. 'We can't turn around. We'r
scheduled to pick up cargo at Nevers and go on soutl
Bonne chance, Mademoiselle Mollie.'

'*Bonne chance*, Emile.'

Mollie was hoping against hope that they would hav
some of that good luck now. So far so good. The *penicl*
they boarded was immaculately clean and well tended, lik
the *Ste Vièrge*, but the bargees looked nothing like Emile an
Giselle. They were elderly, for one thing, for another the
were Dutch, quieter and less friendly. But just as brave. The
said very little as they displayed two hiding places. One wa
in a false cupboard in the wheelhouse, the other in the hol
There would be little opportunity for Kate and Mollie to tal
on the return journey. So be it. Time enough to talk whe
they were in England and safe.

The man spoke a little English. 'Six days, *mevrouw*,' h
told Mollie. 'We will be at St-Valéry in six days. It is the be:
we can do; we must stop to load and unload along the way.

Mollie nodded. 'I understand. Has anyone in Englan
been told that we're coming?'

The Dutchman nodded. 'That is all arranged.'

A journey without incident, its worst problem the physic:
discomfort of being cramped and cold. And not seeing Kat

The bargees brought their passengers out of hiding separately. 'It is safer, *mevrouw*,' the man said. Mollie made no attempt to argue with him. Like Emile and Giselle, this couple were putting their lives at risk, it wasn't her place to tell them how to do their job.

Finally, on what Mollie calculated to be 17 March, they reached St-Valéry. St Patrick's day, a good omen perhaps. Or was it? She'd first found out about Lois Lane on St Patrick's day. The hell with that. This time would be different.

It was. Some of the luck of the Irish rubbed off. The guard at the canal wharf was the Frenchman she'd seen that first night. He passed them through without comment, but once Mollie thought he winked at her.

'Go right,' the Dutchman had told her. 'Past the gate. You'll be met.'

They'd no sooner made the turn as instructed when a man fell into step behind them. It was the man who had brought Mollie here some two weeks ago. He got them back to the beach and the sea with the same silent efficiency he'd displayed before.

They sat in a cabin on the deck of a small wooden boat. Always small and always wooden for journeys like this, that had been explained to Mollie earlier. Little inshore craft could ignore the minefields, they just skimmed over the top of them. Now, sitting with Kate, both of them holding mugs of strong tea, smiling at each other for no reason except pure joy, Mollie was the first to speak. 'Let me look at you, Kate, oh Kate ...'

Kate put a self-conscious hand to her head.

'What happened to your hair?' Mollie asked softly.

'It was cut before I left Tokyo.' Kate ran her fingers through it. It had grown quite a bit, her hair came almost to her chin now. 'It must be two colours,' she said. 'Is it?'

'Yes. Half blonde, half black. You'll set a new style.'

Kate dropped her hand and leaned forward. 'Mollie, do you know anything about my son? Where is Ricky?'

'I'm sorry.' She whispered the words because it hurt her so to have to say them. 'I'm sorry, I don't know anything. He disappeared the same time you did. We hoped he was wit[h] you in Japan.'

'No, not with me. With Beatriz,' Kate said. 'He must be[.]' She was silent for a moment. 'How is mother?' she aske[d] finally. 'And Nick?'

'Fine. They're both very well. Nick was in Italy coverin[g] the campaign there the last I heard. Mom's living in the cit[y] in my old place. She works in a bookstore. Loves it.' Moll[ie] stopped speaking. Her sister's eyes had gone dull. She didn[t] seem to have heard anything beyond the fact that both Zen[o] and Nick were alive and well.

'Listen,' Mollie said. 'You don't have to explain it all ye[t,] how you got out of Tokyo and to France. But there's on[e] thing ... How did you meet Lee Mitsuno? What does h[e] have to do with any of this?'

'Lee? I see,' Kate said slowly. 'You know about Lee.'

'No, that's just it. I don't know. He disappeared years ag[o.] That was the last I heard, until some little Chinese gu[y] appeared in London and told me he had a message from Le[e] Mitsuno and that I could meet you in France. Wha[t] happened in between, Katykins? Where is Lee? Is he okay?'

'Lee,' Kate said again. She used his name as if it were [a] statement of fact. 'Lee is ... He is Lee.'

Mollie started to remonstrate with her, but she couldn'[t.] Something in Kate's face precluded any argument. God, sh[e] was so desperately thin. As beautiful as ever, but she'd age[d.] It was a different kind of beauty now; Kate had suffered an[d] it showed.

'Listen,' Mollie said with as much enthusiasm as she coul[d] muster. 'I forgot one thing, it's important. I have a letter f[or] you. From your father. Your real father, Sebastian Benne[tt] Swan. He wrote to you before he died and I've got the lette[r.] I'll give it to you as soon as we get to my place.'

Mollie watched for any response in Kate's eyes, any liftin[g] of the veil of infinite sadness that covered her face. Ther[e] was nothing.

'Landfall in five minutes, ladies,' a man said, poking hi[s] head around the door of the cabin. 'She's all right,' he sai[d,] nodding his head toward Kate's oilskins, 'but you better ge[t] this raingear on. Blowin' a bloody gale it is.'

Mollie pulled on the waterproof trousers and jacket he
ssed her. In a few minutes another member of the crew
ppeared and led them on deck.

The boat was in the process of tying up at the far end of a
ock, no other craft were nearby and nobody was around. It
as dawn. Mollie stared at the empty landscape and
ondered if she could simply bring Kate quietly back to
oley Street. Maybe Will had arranged for there to be no
rmalities, considering the circumstances. Yes, that must be
. So the real problem was finding a taxi to get them to a
ain station and the money to pay for it. Jesus, Will must
ave remembered she had no English money. He had to
ave arranged someone to meet her and give them some.

The ship was made fast now. One of the crew dropped a
lank into position. It gave them access to the wharf and
ate and Mollie scrambled over it. 'Mind how you go,' the
ewman said. 'Best of luck to you.'

Mollie turned to say thank you and to ask him about
oney, but she was distracted by two men who suddenly
ppeared from behind the nearby storage sheds. They wore
haki uniforms and white helmets and white arm bands, and
ey carried nightsticks. They also had pistols strapped to
eir hips. 'Mollie Pride?' one of them demanded as the pair
ot closer.

'Yes, that's me. Who are you? Who sent you?'

'United States Military Police, ma'am.' He turned to Kate.
Are you Kate Bennet Cuentas?'

'De Cuentas,' she corrected. 'Yes, I am.'

The MP stepped forward and took her arm. 'It is my duty
 inform you that you are under arrest.'

'Wait a minute!' Mollie shouted. 'What are you talking
out? What's going on here?'

'Sorry ma'am, my orders are quite clear. Mrs Cuentas
mes with us. You're free to go.'

'But I don't understand. Who gave you these orders? Why
e you arresting her? What's the charge?'

'Charge is treason, ma'am. High treason against the
nited States of America.'

was night by the time Mollie got back to London, almost

eleven. She caught a bus from Victoria Station to Oxfo[rd]
Circus and didn't wait for another to take her up Rege[nt]
Street, just ran through the darkened streets all the wa[y]
home. She was gasping for breath and sobbing by the tim[e]
she turned into Foley Street.

A man was leaving her building. 'Mollie, thank Go[d]
Where have you been? I've been looking everywhere f[or]
you.'

'Nick, oh, Nick, it's you, isn't it?' She fell into his arm[s]
sobbing against his chest. 'Nick, I'm so glad you're here. I d[id]
everything I could, I couldn't stop them.'

'Stop who? Where have you been? No, don't answer th[at]
yet. Come inside.' He half-carried her up the short flight [of]
steps. 'Give me your key,' he said when they stood befo[re]
Mollie's front door.

'I haven't got it. They took all my personal stuff before [I]
left.'

He didn't bother asking her what she meant. 'We'll go [to]
my place then. Stay here, I'll try and find a cab.'

'No, wait. I just remembered. There's a spare key. We hi[d]
one years ago.' She reached up to a ledge and produced [a]
key from a crevice behind a wall light that hadn't seen a bul[b]
since the blackout began. Nick took it and unlocked th[e]
door.

'I got back four days ago,' he explained. 'They told me yo[u]
were sick, only you didn't answer the phone and there wa[s]
no one here when I came looking. I've been frantic, but I wa[s]
afraid to notify anyone official in case you were doing som[e]
spy thing. Were you?' They were inside now. He'd made he[r]
sit on the sofa which doubled as a bed, and was opening a[ll]
the cabinets, looking for something to drink. 'Is that wh[at]
you were doing?'

Mollie stared at him. 'Spying,' she said softly. 'I suppos[e]
you could call it that. Nick, they took Kate. I couldn't sto[p]
them.'

'Kate? What does any of this have to do with her? Wh[o]
took her? Mollie, where in the name of Christ have yo[u]
been?'

'There's a bottle of Scotch in the kitchen,' she told him b[y]
way of answer. 'Behind the frying pans under the stove.'

Her voice had gone flat, lifeless. Nick looked at her, worry ining his face, then he went and found the whisky and rought it back with two glasses. 'Here, drink some of this. Then we'll talk.'

Beneath his black topcoat and white silk scarf she could ee a black tuxedo and a black bow tie. 'Where have you een? Somewhere formal?'

'A dinner party at Whitehall. I couldn't get out of it. Churchill and a lot of the big-time operators doing their duty y the working press. Broadcasters included for once.'

'How was Italy?'

'Savage. There's not much left of Monte Cassino. Mollie, top this. How come you're dressed like a fugitive from a B movie? Where were you? What happened?'

She told him. Everything. Beginning with Kenneth Wu nd including Jack and Will and the fishing boat, and rawling up the beach on her belly while the Nazi search-ights played over the sand, and the bargees, and the L pill in he heel of her shoe. Everything.

'Jesus Christ,' he whispered when she stopped speaking. Jesus Christ, you could have ... I'd like to get my hands on hose guys,' he added hoarsely. 'What'd you call them, Jack nd Will? I'd like to take that pair of lunatics apart with my are hands.'

The hands he mentioned were shaking with rage. He oured another shot of Scotch for both of them. Mollie only tared at hers, but Nick tossed his back in one gulp. 'Kate?' e asked finally. 'Where is she now?'

'I don't know. The MPs took her. I couldn't stop them. After we'd been through all that, they marched her off. I ried telephoning Jack and Will, they're the only two people I ctually know, but I couldn't reach either of them. So finally got a train for London. Had to borrow a pound from a voman in the station to buy a ticket.'

Mollie put a hand in the pocket of the heavy trousers and ame up with a slip of paper. 'Yes, here's her name and ddress. I'm glad I didn't lose it. I have to send the money ack.'

'Mollie,' Nick said softly. 'Oh, Mollie.'

She looked at him for a long moment, then she began to

cry again. This time she wasn't sobbing, the tears simpl
rolled down her face.

'They used me,' she whispered. 'Jack and Will an
Donovan and all the rest. They used me. They wanted Kat
because of her broadcasts, she's been on Donovan's list fo
years. I knew that, I just didn't think of it. Where was I goin
to go if not to Baker Street? How else could I do what Le
wanted? But when I told them about the message they mus
have laughed themselves sick. I was playing right into thei
hands. Delivering her on a plate. I suppose they figured the
might as well send me to get her out. It wasn't importan
enough to send a trained agent, but since I was right ther
and willing to go ... They don't miss a trick, those guys
never ignore a chance to stick it to the enemy.'

She reached for the whisky and took a sip. 'Only tell m
how I got to be the enemy?' she asked when she put the glas
down. 'How did that happen, Nick? I've been such a goo
girl. You said so yourself. I did all the sordid little things the
wanted me to do, whatever they said. Then they paid m
back by using me to get my own sister.'

He sat down beside her, stroking her back while sh
choked with sobs. 'Forget all that,' he said after a fev
moments. 'They're bastards. So what? It doesn't matter. Yo
got her out, that's what counts. You got Kate out and she'
safe.'

She turned her tear-stained face to him. 'Safe? How ca
you say that? They've charged her with treason.' Molli
began to scream. 'Treason! Jesus, don't you know what tha
means? Treason is a capital crime. They kill you for treason
Nick. Remember your history. They put you up before
firing squad and you're dead. Bang!' she shouted. 'Bang
Bang! Bang! Then Kate is dead. And I did it. I stood her u
against that wall. Me. Mollie Pride. Little Miss goddam
Magic Mollie Pride.'

He slapped her once across the face. Hard. Then again
'Shut up! Stop being hysterical and feeling sorry for yourself
It's Kate we have to worry about.'

Mollie stopped screaming and stared at him. She wante
to cry again, but there were no more tears. She had cried
river and all the tears were gone. She fell back against th

pillows and closed her eyes in a greater weariness than she'd ever known.

Nick waited for some minutes. Finally he touched her, simply pushed her hair off her face at first, then stroked her cheek with the back of his hand. Eventually he pulled her into his arms, cradling her against his chest, rocking her back and forth as if she were a child.

'Right now Kate's safer than she's been for years,' he said quietly. 'Nobody's going to do anything without due process of law, Mollie. We'll get her the best lawyers around. We know Kate's not a traitor. We'll make her tell what really happened. Meanwhile she's safe,' he said again. 'And so are you, thank God. I could have lost you. Oh, Mollie, I could have lost you.'

Mollie reached up and put her arms around his neck, pressing herself against him. It was as if all the terror of the past week suddenly burst apart inside her and shattered her into tiny fragments. If she did not hang on to Nick she would cease to be. Outside the circle of his embrace was death, within it was life.

As always, he knew what she was feeling. That mysterious communication which united them was a pulsing current of electricity, welding them into one being with one purpose, life. They clung together in a testament to being alive. 'Nick,' Mollie whispered. 'I ...'

'Don't talk,' he said softly. 'Just be. For now just be. We'll talk later.'

Then he kissed her.

It was as natural as breathing. As pure and as right and as true as sunrise or spring rain. It was the end of a long journey, safe harbour after years of struggle. It was, in a word, right.

The coupling was slow, gentle, infinitely tender. It was a statement by their bodies of what their minds had always known, but never allowed to be said. Mollie and Nick, Nick and Mollie. They were not brother and sister. They were not made one by any accident of family or genetic heritage. They were one because so it had been ordained from the moment of creation. Finally they were in reality what they had always been in spirit. Lovers. Mollie and Nick. Nick and Mollie. An entity at last made whole.

Later, naked in his arms, her head on his chest, his fingers tangled in her curls, Mollie said, 'I remember what Steve told me. I saw him before he left on a mission to France and he told me that I ought to divorce him so you and I could be together. "Just do it," he said. "You and Nick belong together. Forget about the old taboos." I'd blocked it out until now.'

'You never told me you saw Steve after he joined the army.'

'I did once. It doesn't matter how it happened. I'll tell you some day. Not now.'

'Okay. Mollie, listen, about those taboos, they don't exist.'

'Yes, they do. We're first cousins. I don't care any more. Too much has happened.'

'We're not.'

She sat up. 'Not what? What are you talking about?'

'We're not cousins. We're not related at all. Phoebe, your father's sister, she wasn't really my mother. I was her husband's kid. She never told me, just took me on and brought me up. When she knew she was going to die she fixed it so her brother Harry would take over. She must have known him pretty well. She figured she could rely on him to do what she asked, and she was right.'

Mollie stared at him in wonder. 'Are you sure of all this? How do you know?'

'Zena told me. She had a letter Phoebe wrote to your dad. The one she gave me to bring to New York from Ohio when I was nine. It explained everything. Zena showed me the letter when I moved out of Hillhaven. Said I was a grown-up, so I ought to know.'

'Why didn't you ever tell me? Why did you wait so long?'

'I planned to tell you. I always knew I wanted to marry you. I was waiting for you to grow up, that's all. But you jumped the gun and ran off and married Steve. So there didn't seem any point.' He leaned forward and pulled her back into his arms and kissed the top of her head. 'I guess the truth is I didn't want to tell you after that. I didn't want to give up as much claim on you as I could have. I didn't want you to know we weren't even related.'

'And after Steve and I slit up?'

'There was the war, and you were still married to him. Then you were a new widow. There never seemed a right time. I tried to say something once or twice, but I never managed to get it out. Until now,' he added.

'Now,' she repeated, as if the word summed up everything that had been and would be. 'Now. That's one thing the war has taught us. Only now really matters. Oh, Nick, I love you so much. I always have.'

'I know. Almost as much as I love you.'

She started to protest and he silenced her by kissing her again. 'We finally got here,' he murmured against her cheek. 'Here we are, my darling Mollie, on easy street at last.'

19

'Kate's in the Army prison at the US base in Richmond,' Nick said three days later. 'So far that's all I've managed to find out. You have any better luck?'

Mollie shook her head. 'No luck at all. Jack won't talk to me and I can't find Will. I went to the house on Baker Street, but there was nobody there. At least, no one answered the door.'

'What about Washington?'

'Nothing. I've managed to get through a couple of times, but I can't locate Donovan.'

'I suppose that's not surprising.' Nick sat down beside her on the sofa and took her hand. 'He's got a few things on his mind besides us.'

'The bastard,' Mollie said through clenched teeth. 'The bloody bastard. I hope the Gestapo get him.'

'No you don't,' Nick said softly. 'Mollie, listen, from their point of view, they've done the right thing. Total war. No holds barred. Remember what Churchill said when he took over as PM? Nothing less than victory. Whatever we have to do, we'll do it.'

'But Kate ...'

'She's going to be okay. She's in a US prison, darling, not some Japanese POW hellhole, and not a concentration camp. She'll be fed and clothed and given any medical care she needs. And it's not as if she's been tossed in with a bunch of hardened criminals. Military prisons aren't like that.' He put his hand in his pocket and pulled out a piece of paper. 'This is an official permission for her to have one visitor Saturday afternoon. Do you want to go or shall I?'

'I'll go,' Mollie said instantly. 'I want to.'

'Okay, but I'm going down there with you.'

'I'll talk to Pulansky, see if he can wangle a car and some petrol.'

'Do that,' Nick said. He lifted her hand to his lips and kissed her palm. 'And stop whipping yourself, you did the right thing, darling, the only thing.'

'Kate, this is the letter I told you about.'

'Letter?'

'Yes, the one from your father. The one Sebastian Bennet-Swan wrote before he was killed.'

Kate took it and stared at her name written on the envelope in the elegant old-fashioned hand. Mollie watched her. The two-coloured hair was pulled back and held with bobbie pins, and she was wearing a shapeless grey cardigan over a dress that looked as if it were made of mattress ticking. 'I brought you some clothes,' Mollie said. 'They said you could have them. There's almost nothing to be had in the stores, I borrowed these from Sandra Rosenberg. She's Phil's wife. Sandra's about your size.'

'Thank you.'

'Kate, don't you want to read the letter?'

'I will, later.'

'Okay. Listen, we're finding a lawyer for you. Nick's got a call in to the Judge Advocate's office in Washington.' Her voice broke. Mollie could not sustain the tone of cheerful encouragement. 'Oh, Katykins, I'm so sorry. I had no idea … I never meant to … Oh God, what else could I have done?'

Kate reached out a hand and laid it on her sister's shoulder. 'Nothing. You did what you had to do. So did I. Don't blame yourself, Mollie. None of it's your fault.'

'It is. It started being my fault years ago. I should have got you out of that house, away from Armando. Only I couldn't believe that he —

'I know,' Kate interrupted. 'I know. Anyway, it wasn't Armando. Not really. It was Miguel. Armando did whatever Miguel told him to, it was only from the outside that it looked as if it were the other way around.'

Mollie leaned forward. 'Was it because of Miguel that you made the broadcasts? Did he force you to do them, Katykins?'

487

'Miguel? No, Miguel's dead. He's been dead for years.'

'Then why ...'

'I did whatever Lee told me to do,' Kate said simply. 'I thought he loved me.'

'Loved you? Do you mean that you and Lee ...?'

Kate didn't answer, but the look on her face told Mollie a great deal.

'It was Lee Mitsuno who got her into it,' Mollie told Nick later. 'He and Kate had an affair.'

'So that's where Lee's been all these years, in Japan.'

Mollie nodded. 'It looks that way. Lee a traitor. It's hard to imagine.'

Nick was way ahead of her. 'We can't let that come out, Lee can't be Kate's defence.'

'Why not?'

'Because acting for love does not excuse you from criminal activity. And there's the question of prejudice, if it should be a jury trial ...' He let the thought trail away.

'Oh sweet Jesus,' Mollie breathed. 'What a stinking mess. You'd have to know all about Kate to understand it, wouldn't you? Nobody ever will, except you and me and maybe mom.'

'What are we going to tell Zena?' Nick asked. 'I've been thinking about that.'

'The truth. We have to, we can't keep this from her.'

'No,' Nick agreed. 'I suppose we can't. Poor Zena.'

They had two letters from Washington in late May. One was official notice from the Judge Advocate's office that a Captain Stuart Miller had been assigned to act as defence counsel for Kate de Cuentas, the second was from Miller himself.

'Under the circumstances,' he wrote 'not much can be done until I can see my client. Since it's impossible for me to leave Washington at this time, the case is being postponed. Mrs de Cuentas will continue to be held in Richmond until it is possible to bring her to the United States. A trial date will be set at that time.'

'What the hell are they waiting for?' Mollie demanded

'Isn't there something in the Constitution about a swift and speedy trial?'

'Yeah,' Nick agreed, 'there is. But I don't think Thomas Jefferson and company were figuring on a world at war.' He frowned. 'Mollie, I'm not sure, but I get the feeling there's something going on here. Something we're not aware of, behind the scenes.'

'Like what?'

'I don't know. Donovan maybe.'

'Terrific,' she said bitterly. 'Just what we need, more of Donovan's machinations.'

Ten days later events swept them up and she could only devote part of her mind to Kate.

This is Nick Frane reporting from Normandy. I'm tempted to say, at last ... 6 June 1944 has turned out to be the day and the hour we've all waited for. The second front, the invasion of Europe, has begun, and I'm here with the US First Infantry Division on a beach codenamed Omaha, but I have to tell you that Nebraska was never like this. German defences are very heavy here and the noise being picked up by my mike is only a fraction of the terrible fighting taking place ...

Hello America, this is Mollie Pride. At sunrise yesterday morning, 13 June, the Nazis unleashed a new terror on London. Explosive missiles, a kind of flying bomb. But you can trust the sense of humour of the British. The missiles already have a nickname. Everyone here is calling them doodlebugs. A doodlebug fell on Grove Street in Bow, the heart of the Cockney district. Here with me today is Mrs Ethyl Chaney, who actually saw the blast. Mrs Chaney can you tell our listeners ...

This is Nick Frane reporting to you from France on this miraculous and wonderful day, 23 August, 1944, a day the world will never forget. Paris is liberated, the city of light is free. Forgive my bad French, but Vive la France. *Long live freedom ...*

*

'Nick! Oh, my darling, darling, darling, I've been so scared.'

He wrapped her in a bearhug and picked her up and swung her around. 'Silly kid,' he murmured against her ear. 'Did you think I wasn't coming back when I finally had everything I wanted to come back to?'

'Wait till you see the apartment,' Mollie told him in the car that took them through the September sunshine to home. 'I transformed Foley Street in your honour.'

Nick loved what she'd done. 'New sofa covers, flowers, a new rug ... Have you been dabbling in the black market, Mollie my girl?'

'Never. I only did that once since the war began.'

'When?' he demanded sternly.

'A crazy scam to buy an evening dress. I'll explain about it some day, not now. There isn't time. I've so much to tell you, Nick.'

He'd walked to the table and was studying a cut glass decanter full of something that had to be wine and two crystal glasses. 'If not the blackmarket, where did you get all this stuff?'

'Connections. Pulansky found somebody who used to be rich, but was down on her uppers now. Never mind about all that. I'm torn between wanting to tell you my news and ... And other things,' she added, suddenly shy.

'Other things first,' he said, crossing to her and taking her in his arms. 'News later.'

It was two n the morning before she got out of bed and found the letter and brought it to him. 'This came five days ago, 17 September. It's from mom.'

Nick took the letter but didn't read it. 'I can't take my eyes off you. Just tell me what it says.'

'They've found Ricky.'

'Kate's son?'

'Yes. He's living on East 125th Street, Spanish Harlem. I know that doesn't sound so marvellous, but he's with his old nurse, Beatriz, and mom's seen him. She says he's doing fine. A nice bright six-year-old, speaks fluent Spanish and English.'

'He's alive,' Nick said. 'By itself that's marvellous. I never was sure once we knew he wasn't with Kate. How is she? Have you told her about Ricky?'

'Of course,' Mollie hesitated. 'I see Kate at least once every couple of weeks, and when I told her about Rick it was the first time I saw her cry.' She paused a moment, then shook her head and went on. 'Listen, Ricky isn't all of Zena's news. They found Maria and Tonio too. They were the servants in Kate's house on Eighty-second Street. Do you remember them?'

'Vaguely.'

'I never had any opinion about Tonio, but I always thought Maria genuinely cared for Kate. Anyway, they've been found. They were hiding because neither of them had legal immigration papers. Beatriz didn't either, for that matter. Tonio and Maria have told the police what happened the night Armando was killed. There was some Jap there, somebody Armando was doing business with. They had an argument and the Jap shot him. Then Miguel and the Jap ran away and took Kate with them. Tonio tried to stop them, and the Jap shot him too.'

'But you said Tonio had been found?'

'Yes, he wasn't killed, only wounded. That was another reason they went into hiding. Gunshot wounds and illegal immigration are not a good combination. Not in a house where there's been a murder.'

'I see. Is there a bottom line to this balance sheet?'

Mollie hugged herself with pleasure. 'There sure is. The police have closed the case. The NYPD is no longer interested in Kate de Cuentas.'

'Terrific!' Nick's smile faded and was replaced by a frown. 'Mollie, how the hell did Zena manage all this? You always say she can do whatever she has to, but this . . .'

'I know. All the while I was reading the letter I kept thinking, how? how? how? I was afraid mom was going to be her usual vague self and not explain that part, but in the end she did.'

'And?' he asked.

'And it was Bill Donovan who did it all,' Mollie said softly. 'He called mom one day and sent someone to take her to Spanish Harlem and explain everything. Mom says he even got immigrant visas for Beatriz and Tonio and Maria.'

Nick didn't answer right away. He rolled over and extended his arm to the table near the sofabed and poured himself a glass of wine. 'But Kate's still in the stockade in Richmond,' he said before he drank. 'Is that it?'

'That's it.'

Nick sipped thoughtfully. 'Donovan's up to something,' he said finally. 'I don't know what, but he is.'

'Is it something good?' Mollie asked. 'That's the part I can't decide about. He might just have felt sorry for my mother and Ricky and the three servants who really weren't to blame for any of it. I'm not sure that says anything about what he thinks of Kate.'

This is the BBC Home Service. Here is the news for today, 22 December 1944. On the Western Front the Nazi forces who launched a counter-offensive in the Ardennes last week sent a message to the American general, McAuliffe, demanding surrender. The general sent back a one-word reply, "Nuts." Meanwhile Allied forces have continued successful bombing raids in the Pacific . . .

Hello America, this is Mollie Pride. Merry Christmas. Do you know, for the first time in nearly five years I feel I can say that and mean it. We know the war will soon be over, and we can begin to forget the scourge of Nazism. So perhaps I can be forgiven for being sentimental today, for saying how proud I am to have been a small part of the effort to make that happen. And how proud I am of you, the people at home, who with your strength and courage and fortitude make it possible to endure and prevail. One more thing, I don't think it's out of place to tell all of you, whom I consider my personal friends, that today is also my wedding day. Many of you will have heard Nick Frane's broadcasts from the battle-front. Well, today he's safe here in London, and it is, as it happens, his birthday. And Nick and I are getting married at three o'clock this afternoon . . .

They had five days of honeymoon in Yorkshire, in a small country inn near Swans Tumble. In the surprisingly warm and bright winter weather they went for a couple of long walks, and Mollie looked for the cottage where she'd last seen Steve, but couldn't find it. Nonetheless, it gave her the chance to tell Nick the story.

'That's what gave you the idea,' he said when she'd finished. 'That's how you knew this guy Will could get you into occupied France.'

'Yes, that's how.'

He put his arm around her and drew her close. They were sitting by the fire in a pub, drinking pints of warm British beer, staring at the smouldering coals. 'You were so brave,' he murmured. 'So very, very brave. I'll never get over it.'

'What good did it do?' Mollie said wearily. 'In the end what good did it do? I keep wondering why Lee didn't just keep her in Japan with him.'

'I've thought of that too. I can't figure it out, but he must have had some reason. And she's still safe. Everything I've said before goes double. She's safe. If she were in Japan, well, it's pretty doubtful.'

Mollie nodded. 'I know that. I had a letter from Miller, by the way.'

'What did he say?'

'Same thing he's said before. Delay is in her best interest. They probably won't bring her home and try her until the war's over. It won't be possible to get at the facts until then.'

'Okay,' Nick said. 'For now let's accept that. It's the best we can do, so it's okay.'

Mollie put her head on his shoulder. 'Nick, haven't we both been brave enough?'

'Meaning?'

'Meaning can't you stay in London now? Until it's over. Mutual would be delighted to have you running things from here.'

'No can do,' he said softly. 'I came over here six years ago to report a war, darling. The job's not done yet.'

Hello America, this is Mollie Pride. I've told you before that the BBC monitors all German broadcasting. I thought you'd be interested in what Hitler said on the radio a couple of days ago, on 30 January. He told his people, 'German workers,

493

work! German soldiers, fight! German women, be as fanatical as ever! No nation can do more.' Sounds like he knows we're going to beat him once and for all in this year of 1945, doesn't it?

This is the BBC Home Service. Here is the news. Yesterday, 23 February, US Marines took the island of Iwo Jima in the Pacific and planted the American flag on top of Mt Suribachi . . .

This is Nick Frane reporting from deep inside Germany. Yesterday is a day and a date I'll never forget: 11 April 1945 is branded in my memory. I believe it will be seared on the pages of history. I went with a number of broadcasters, reporters and American officers to a comfortable prosperous town where farmers ploughed green fields and housewives stood outside the shops hoping their ration coupons would stretch to a bit extra for supper . . . And there in that normal-seeming place we were led into hell. We were taken into a concentration camp called Buchenwald. There are no words to tell you, yet I must find words . . .

Hello America, this is Mollie Pride. I've got a little sideline on history to tell you about today, the sort of meaningful details there simply isn't time for in the news bulletins. Yesterday the Stars and Stripes was raised over the rostrum of the stadium in Nuremberg, scene of the Nazi rallies. Old Glory waved there in the April breeze and when I heard about it I knew I had to share it with you, and share something somebody said to me years ago about this terrible war. 'They will reap what they have sown . . .' Yet maybe when this is all over the nation which sowed death and destruction will reap democracy. It almost seems too much to hope for, but these days hope seems possible . . .

Hello America, this is Mollie Pride. I've been thinking about how to tell you what it was like here in London yesterday, 7 May, the day we'll all always remember as VE-Day. The thing that stands out most in my mind is light. On the evening of the day we declared victory in Europe, after six years of

494

literal and figurative darkness, the lights came on. They shone in Trafalgar Square and Leicester Square, in Piccadilly Circus and Regent Street, in Oxford Street and Shaftesbury Avenue. There were bright lights in the little gardens and the narrow mews, as well as the broad avenues. Lights in the parks and on the bridges that vault the ageless river Thames, blazing blessed light everywhere in this great city which held out against all the odds, which symbolized the glow of freedom when so much else was plunged into the darkness of captivity. The lights came on and I thought of all of you, my countrymen at home, and how fate had put me in the position of being one of the links between two great peoples. So when next you hear those songs that have meant so much to us during these long dark years — 'There'll always be an England' and 'The white cliffs of Dover' — take it from me, they're not silly and sentimental. The songs are true ...

This is Nick Frane in London. News of the atomic bomb dropped on Hiroshima reached this city today, Monday, 6 August 1945 ...

Hello America, this is Mollie Pride. You know it, but I have to say it. The war is over. I'm coming home. We're all coming home. God bless Britain. God bless a world at peace. And above all, from this American, a heartfelt prayer, God bless the USA ...

'You have to understand about treason in US law,' the lawyer said. 'It's crucial to following your sister's case, Mrs Frane.'

Mollie nodded. 'Okay, I accept that. But what is it you don't think we understand?' She kept her hand in Nick's while she spoke.

Captain Stuart Miller, United States Army, was tall and so thin Mollie thought of him as gaunt, with dark hair and dark eyes and a nose much too large for his face. 'First of all,' he said. 'Our law is different from British law.'

Neither Nick nor Mollie commented on that. They knew why Miller had made the remark. The ghost of William Joyce, Lord Haw Haw, was in the room with them. He'd been executed in London two months earlier, on 3 January 1946, for the treasonous act of making seditious radio broadcasts which served to aid and abet the enemy. The parallel with Kate's case was chilling.

'It's hard to be certain, but under our system,' Miller said, 'I don't think Joyce would have been convicted.'

'But everybody heard his programmes,' Nick said. 'He didn't deny he'd made them.'

'Exactly, that's my point.' The army man leaned forward. 'The evidence was based on what people heard. When the constitution was written the idea of defining treason was very much in the mind of the framers. In the England they came from a lot of so-called enemies of the state had been conveniently got out of the way by charging them with treason. So they made it watertight over here.'

Miller reached into a drawer and brought out a sheaf of papers. 'Let me quote: "Treason against the United States shall consist only in levying war against them, or adhering to their enemies, giving them aid and comfort."' Miller cleared his throat and looked up. 'This next is the important bit. "No person shall be convicted of treason unless on the testimony of two witnesses to the same overt act." Do you understand? The prosecution has to produce at least a couple of people who actually saw Mrs de Cuentas make a broadcast.'

'Do they have such witnesses?' Mollie asked, her voice a whisper edged with strain.

'Not so far. That's why this case is still in the Army's bailiwick, Mrs Frane. If there were witnesses and it looked like a sure conviction the Justice Department would long ago have assumed jurisdiction. You can bet on it. There's nothing they'd like better than a real live Tokyo Rose and the most public trial possible. If they were fairly sure of a conviction. It would satisfy the public hunger for blood.'

Mollie winced. 'Kate isn't a traitor,' she said.

Miller pursed his lips. 'I keep wondering if she knew what she was doing? Why she did it? She's rather ... Forgive me, she's rather a difficult person to get any information from.'

'She's always been like that,' Nick said. 'Since she was a kid. Kate's in a dreamworld most of the time. She didn't know what she was doing.'

'The psychiatrists tell us she's perfectly normal,' Miller said with a shrug. 'There's no point in going down that road.'

'Of course she's not crazy!' Mollie couldn't contain her frustration. It wasn't Miller who made her feel like this, it was Kate. The fact that Kate was her own worst enemy would explain nothing. 'She was drugged by that miserable Miguel. I've told you all that.'

'So you have,' the lawyer agreed. 'But your sister says he's dead. And we've looked for Miguel de Cuentas or any record of him and come up empty. It's not surprising, Mrs Frane, Japan's pretty chaotic right now.'

'What about Lee Mitsuno?' Nick demanded.

'Nothing,' Miller admitted. 'Can't find anyone who ever heard of him.'

Mollie leaned her head on her hand. 'What happens now?'

'As little as possible. I've told you what my tactic has been, what it still is. Delay as long as possible in hopes we can come up with something that will exonerate your sister, explain the duress she was under.'

'That gives the prosecution time to find their two witnesses, too, doesn't it?' Nick asked.

'Yes,' Miller agreed. 'Nothing we can do about that. It's a risk we have to take.'

But finally the law allowed no more delay. Three military judges heard the evidence in June. Miller made a great deal of the fact that the prosecution had not produced witnesses who actually saw Kate broadcasting, but it was hard to say if the judges were impressed. There were, after all, a stream of GI's who testified to hearing her.

'I can't put Mrs de Cuentas in the witness box,' Miller told Nick and Mollie. 'She'd do herself more harm than good.'

'So we have nothing to offer,' Nick said. 'No defence of any sort.'

'Not much of a one,' Miller admitted. 'She was terrified that if she didn't do what they said, the Japanese who were holding her, she'd be killed. That's all.'

'Will it be enough?' Mollie demanded. She needed to know.

'I'm not sure.' That's all Miller would say. 'I'm not sure, I can't be.'

497

'What about Lee Mitsuno?' Mollie again, leaning over the lawyer's desk, trying to convince him with her own certitudes. 'If you could bring him in here, prosecute him for what he did, wouldn't that help Kate?'

'It might. But we can't find him, Mrs Frane. Believe me, we've tried. This Lee Mitsuno you speak of may never have existed as far as the Army authorities in Tokyo are concerned.'

So they came to the end. To the rainy July day after the holiday weekend of the Fourth. To the moment of the verdict. Kate was brought to Washington from the prison where she was being held, and put in the grey featureless room in the Pentagon that was used for such things, and told to await the decision of the court. It was Miller who secured permission for Nick and Mollie to wait with her. A small concession to a woman who was almost certainly facing a sentence of death.

Music, Mollie thought. Oh Jesus God, there ought to be music. You didn't have to go out silent did you? Who decreed you had to march down the corridor to oblivion in stoic quiet? Why the hell shouldn't there be music?

The tune played in her head, that song the three of them knew so well, a kind of theme to their lives. '*Charleston! Charleston! da da da-da dum dum . . .*'

Jerking spasms, born of memory and love and pain and terror, twisted themselves into patterns of dance and Mollie's body moved almost of its own volition. Her feet flew, her arms stood out at her sides, her hands made circles in the are. '*Charleston! Charleston! . . .*'

Kate sucked in one long, audible breath. 'Don't,' she murmured. 'Please, don't.'

Nick sprang out of his chair and reached Mollie in two strides. He grabbed her, pinning her arms to her sides, pressing her body to his. 'Mollie, stop. That's not going to help. Please stop.' For a moment she clung to him, to the beloved, familiar, warm, safe feel of his chunky muscular body beneath the correct and impeccably-tailored suit. Nick would never change, thank God.

Her next thought was the same as his, unspoken but

shared. Mustn't shut Kate out. They turned and opened their arms to her.

She hesitated.

'Kate,' Mollie whispered. 'Katykins, come on ...'

She stood up and moved towards them, glided almost; she was ethereal in her pale loveliness. Together Mollie and Nick drew her into the circle of their arms.

'It's still the three of us against all of them, isn't it?' Kate asked.

'Yup,' Nick said. 'The same as always.'

'The same,' Mollie repeated. 'The three of us. For always and always and always.' She realized what a short time that might be and searched desperately for a new subject. Something to talk about, to pass this terrible time. 'Kate, you never told us about the letter from your father.'

Kate moved out of their embrace and returned to the chair she'd been sitting in. She looked elegant again, despite everything. Mollie had bought her a navy linen two piece dress with a red, white and blue scarf. The patriotic choice of colours had not been an accident. 'My father,' Kate said. 'Yes, I meant to tell you. It was a nice letter.'

'What did he say?' Nick asked.

'That he loved me, that he was sorry he might not see me grow up. That he very much regretted having to desert me.' Kate stopped speaking, the mask came down over her face again.

'Everybody loves you,' Mollie said.

Kate shook her head. 'No, just you and Nick. You two have never deserted me. I always knew you wouldn't.'

'Not mom either,' Mollie insisted. 'I know you didn't want her here today, but ...'

'I don't blame mother for anything,' Kate said. 'I didn't think she should have to go through this, that's all.'

Both Nick and Mollie nodded.

The door opened. Two MPs came in. 'The judges are waiting for you, ma'am.'

Mollie looked around for Stuart Miller. He wasn't there. One of the judges, the one she'd realized was the most senior, cleared his throat. 'Where is the defendant's attorney?'

A clerk approached the table behind which the three officers sat and murmured something. There were questions and whispered replies. Finally the judge spoke again. 'I'm afraid there is some delay. We cannot give our verdict without the presence of defending counsel and he ...'

'Sir, my apologies to the court, sir.'

The voice was that of Stuart Miller. He was coming in from the rear.

'I apologize,' he said again. 'But the defence has a new witness. I realize how irregular this is, but in a matter of such gravity ...'

Mollie didn't turn to look at him, she couldn't take her eyes from her sister. The first indication she had that something extraordinary had happened was Kate's audible intake of breath. Mollie swivelled her head to look at the lawyer. He was not alone. 'My God!' she gasped in Nick's ear. 'It's Lee.'

'No, it can't be ... Jesus, you're right. I almost didn't recognize him.'

Lee looked at least sixty. His hair was more grey than black and his face was deeply lined. But his body was still a young man's body, and he stood tall and very still in front of the three presiding officers.

'If it please the court,' Miller said. 'This is Lee Mitsuno, an American citizen of mixed Japanese and Chinese ancestry. He has information with direct bearing on my client's case. May I be permitted to introduce his testimony before you give your verdict?'

The judges conferred. Minutes passed. Finally the senior officer nodded at the lawyer. 'It's irregular, as you said, Captain, but these are difficult times and treason is a grave charge. We'll hear your witness.'

Miller turned to Kate. He included Mollie and Nick in his glance. He smiled.

'It began in 1938,' Lee said. 'I had not seen my father since I was six. In the summer of 1938, when I was twenty-two, he came to New York and got in touch with me.'

'Your father is Japanese, Mr Mitsuno?'

'Yes, he was Japanese. He's dead.'

'I see. Please continue.'

'He, that is my father, made certain representations to me. They were ... They sounded very strange.'

'Strange in what way?'

'They were all about how I wasn't really an American, I was Japanese. Japan had a great destiny, it was my duty to work in the interests of Japan.'

'I see, and what was your reply to all this?'

'I told him I had to think about it.'

'Then what?'

'Then I went to the FBI.'

There was a sharp sound in the silent room, the indrawn breath of the dozen or so people present. Mollie shot a quick glance at Kate, but all she could see was her sister's profile. Kate was staring at Lee, with no readable expression on her face.

'Will you tell us what happened then, Mr Mitsuno?'

'Eventually I was put in contact with William Donovan and he suggested I go along with my father's wishes ...'

'Excuse me,' Miller interrupted. 'Are you saying that Donovan advised you to betray the United States?'

'No, he asked me if I'd be willing to go into what he called deep cover. At first it meant leaving my job with a major symphony orchestra because otherwise I wouldn't have enough time to devote to my father's activities. Later it meant going to Japan.'

'Yes, we understand. Thank you.' Miller paused, then continued. 'But we have already heard how Mrs de Cuentas was taken to Japan. Are we to understand that you were somehow instrumental in that?'

'No, I knew nothing about it until after she'd been there for some time. The man who brought her, not Miguel de Cuentas, the Japanese, he was part of a different group, a different faction, from the one to which I belonged. We were rivals.'

'But eventually you learned of her presence in the country.'

'I learned that there was an American woman secretly being held a prisoner. I made it my business to bribe one of her guards and get in. When I saw her, I knew it was Kate Bennet de Cuentas, whom I had, as it happened, known all my life.'

Miller paused again, adjusted the cuff of his jacket, let his eyes roam around the room before returning to the witness, then he asked, 'And in what condition did you find the defendant, Mr Mitsuno?'

'She'd been heavily drugged, apparently for some time. She was addicted to whatever they were giving her. Kate was half-dead, she was like a vegetable, and ...' His voice trailed away.

'And?' Miller prompted.

Lee spoke in a whisper. 'And she'd been sexually abused. Judging from the marks on her body, in horrific ways.'

Mollie pressed a hand to her mouth and stole a look at Kate. Her sister was smiling. She wasn't even hearing what Lee was saying, at least not registering his voice. Kate was aglow only because Lee was there in the same room with her. Mollie forced herself to listen to the testimony.

Miller was speaking. 'And what did you do then?'

'I arranged for the men who were holding her to be ... dealt with. And I hid Mrs de Cuentas in a house in the country.'

'How long did she remain there?'

'As long as I dared to keep her there. About a year I think. Long enough to get her detoxified and off dependency on drugs. After that I had to prove to my faction that she was of some use.'

'I see. If you hadn't done that, Mr Mitsuno, what would have been the result?'

'Very simple. They'd have killed her. Probably quite slowly.' Lee's voice became entirely matter-of-fact. 'They went in for that sort of thing.'

'So if she had no value to the Japanese war effort, Mrs de Cuentas faced torture and death?'

'Yes, that's right. I had to think of something. I guess the radio seemed like a natural to me because of Mollie and Nick. I mean Miss Pride and Mr Frane.'

'Of course.' The lawyer paused again. He'd had no time to prepare this testimony, obviously he was having to think on his feet, to see if they were leaving any gaps in the information being given the court. 'There's one thing I still don't understand, Mr Mitsuno. Why did the people who abducted

Mrs de Cuentas bring her to Japan in the first place? Can you tell us anything about that?'

'I've thought about it a lot,' Lee said. 'I don't know for sure, but it has to have been some kind of propaganda motive. Unless it was simply because she's so beautiful.'

The lawyer smiled. And so, Mollie noted, did at least one of the judges. 'So,' Miller said, ignoring the comment about Kate's looks, 'whatever happened, the defendant was going to be forced to do what her captors told her to do.'

'Of course,' Lee agreed. 'It was so much better if it could be me. I wrote her scripts, you see. At first they were simply broadcast to Hong Kong and Shanghai, places like that. Aimed at British women in the colonies. Then, after Pearl Harbor, it was different. Then we had to slant them toward the GIs. I know they sounded pretty horrible, but they were as innocuous as I dared to make them.'

Miller nodded. He'd been pacing, now he stopped and stood quite still at the hub of a circle which included Lee in the witness box, Kate at the table where she sat, and the three judges. He looked from one to the other for some seconds. Finally he spoke. 'Let me be quite sure I understand you, Mr Mitsuno, that we all understand you. You were a secret agent for the United States. Mrs de Cuentas was aiding you in your work, and if she had refused to do as you decided she must do, not only would her life have been forfeit, but your cover story would have been threatened. Is that what you're telling this court?'

'That's exactly what I'm telling you,' Lee said quietly. 'And everything I say can and will be corroborated by William Donovan.'

Mollie's heart sang.

The rain had stopped, and the Lincoln Memorial gleamed white in the late afternoon sun. Mollie squeezed Nick's hand. 'I think the old boy must be proud of this day's activities.' She nodded her head toward the statue of the sixteenth president of the United States.

'I guess it was about preserving the union,' Nick agreed. 'Sort of. In the end it doesn't matter if the danger comes from within or without.'

'No, I don't think so,' Mollie said. 'Look at them.' She was watching Lee and Kate strolling a short distance away, talking quietly. 'I've never seen her so radiant.'

'Lee looks pretty happy too. Not everyone approves, though. That old lady in the blue dress has been watching them. She looks like she'd like to murder them both.'

'Yes, an Oriental man and a white woman. It's not going to be easy.'

Nick said as much when the four of them joined up a few minutes later. 'After everything you two have been through I feel rotten saying this, but it's going to be tough on you.'

Neither Lee nor Kate required an explanation. 'There's little Rick to consider as well,' Lee said. 'Kate and I have just been talking about him.'

'We have to keep Beatriz with him,' Kate said. 'I don't want Ricky's life to be one desertion after another.'

'Maybe South America or maybe Europe.' Lee smiled at Kate. 'It doesn't matter as long as we're together. There are places where people are more tolerant. As long as a musician can find a job, it'll be okay.'

'After everything you've done, are you going to let them drive you away?' Mollie demanded.

'It's not like that,' Lee explained. 'We don't feel that way. It's just ...' he hesitated. 'Easier,' he said finally.

Mollie frowned. 'Leave that a minute, something else is bothering me. All the while Kate's trial was going on, why didn't Donovan just get word of the facts to the court?'

'He would have if I hadn't turned up. It was only that while they were looking for me, after I went into hiding, he was afraid to prejudice my chances of getting out of Japan alive.'

'Even now that the war's over?'

'Even now,' Lee insisted. 'The kind of people I was involved with have long memories. Do you know there are still Japanese soldiers hiding out in various Asian jungles? It's true. Everybody in Japan knows it. There are people who just don't believe it's over, that their country has surrendered. God knows if they ever will believe it.'

The thought was chilling. It cast a pall on the four of them. 'Enough serious talk,' Nick said. 'C'mon, I saw a guy selling hot dogs across the street. Let's get something to eat.'

So they stood in the sun and munched hot dogs and drank cokes and remembered how it had been when they were kids. And gave thanks because it could still be, in some small way, the same.

'You know what I want to do?' Mollie asked as dusk approached. 'I want to go dancing. There must be somewhere in Washington where you can dance.'

'Bound to be,' Nick agreed. 'We'll find it. The Fabulous Pride Family is going on the road. Plus one,' he added, putting an arm over the other man's shoulders.

Mollie turned to Lee. 'I just thought of something I never asked you. Can you Charleston?'

'Not me.' Lee shook his head.

'Well don't worry, it's easy. We'll teach you. *Charleston*,' she hummed. '*Charleston, da da da-da dum dum ...*'